GREATEST SHORT STORIES

GREATEST SHORT STORIES

RUPA

Published by
Rupa Publications India Pvt. Ltd 2020
7/16, Ansari Road, Daryaganj
New Delhi 110002

Sales Centres:
Allahabad Bengaluru Chennai
Hyderabad Jaipur Kathmandu
Kolkata Mumbai

ISBN: 978-93-90260-29-4

Eighth impression 2022

10 9 8

Printed in India

CONTENTS

THE HAPPY PRINCE

Oscar Wilde

High above the city, on a tall column, stood the statue of the Happy Prince. He was gilded all over with thin leaves of fine gold, for eyes he had two bright sapphires, and a large red ruby glowed on his sword-hilt.

He was very much admired indeed. 'He is as beautiful as a weathercock,' remarked one of the Town Councillors who wished to gain a reputation for having artistic tastes; 'only not quite so useful,' he added, fearing lest people should think him unpractical, which he really was not.

'Why can't you be like the Happy Prince?' asked a sensible mother of her little boy who was crying for the moon. 'The Happy Prince never dreams of crying for anything.'

'I am glad there is someone in the world who is quite happy,' muttered a disappointed man as he gazed at the wonderful statue.

'He looks just like an angel,' said the Charity Children as they came out of the cathedral in their bright scarlet cloaks and their clean white pinafores.

'How do you know?' said the Mathematical Master, 'you have never seen one.'

'Ah! but we have, in our dreams,' answered the children; and the Mathematical Master frowned and looked very severe, for he did not approve of children dreaming.

One night there flew over the city a little Swallow. His friends had gone away to Egypt six weeks before, but he had stayed behind, for he was in love with the most beautiful Reed. He had met her early in the spring as he was flying down the river after a big yellow moth, and had been so attracted by her slender waist that he had stopped to talk to her.

'Shall I love you?' said the Swallow, who liked to come to the point at once, and the Reed made him a low bow. So he flew round and round her, touching the water with his wings, and making silver ripples. This was his courtship, and it lasted all through the summer.

'It is a ridiculous attachment,' twittered the other Swallows; 'she has no money, and far too many relations'; and indeed the river was quite full of Reeds. Then, when the autumn came they all flew away.

After they had gone he felt lonely, and began to tire of his lady-love. 'She has no conversation,' he said, 'and I am afraid that she is a coquette, for she is always flirting with the wind.' And certainly, whenever the wind blew, the Reed made the most graceful curtseys. 'I admit that she is domestic,' he continued, 'but I love travelling, and my wife, consequently, should love travelling also.'

'Will you come away with me?' he said finally to her; but the Reed shook her head, she was so attached to her home.

'You have been trifling with me,' he cried. 'I am off to the Pyramids. Good-bye!' and he flew away.

All day long he flew, and at night-time he arrived at the city. 'Where shall I put up?' he said; 'I hope the town has made preparations.'

Then he saw the statue on the tall column.

'I will put up there,' he cried; 'it is a fine position, with plenty of fresh air.' So he alighted just between the feet of the Happy Prince.

'I have a golden bedroom,' he said softly to himself as he looked round, and he prepared to go to sleep; but just as he was putting his head under his wing a large drop of water fell on him. 'What a curious thing!' he cried; 'there is not a single cloud in the sky, the stars are quite clear and bright, and yet it is raining. The climate in the north of Europe is really dreadful. The Reed used to like the rain, but that was merely her selfishness.'

Then another drop fell.

'What is the use of a statue if it cannot keep the rain off?' he said; 'I must look for a good chimney-pot,' and he determined to fly away.

But before he had opened his wings, a third drop fell, and he looked up, and saw—Ah! what did he see?

The eyes of the Happy Prince were filled with tears, and tears were running down his golden cheeks. His face was so beautiful in the moonlight that the little Swallow was filled with pity.

'Who are you?' he said.

'I am the Happy Prince.'

'Why are you weeping then?' asked the Swallow; 'you have quite drenched me.'

'When I was alive and had a human heart,' answered the statue, 'I did not know what tears were, for I lived in the Palace of Sans-Souci, where sorrow is not allowed to enter. In the daytime I played with my companions in the garden, and in the evening I led the dance in the Great Hall. Round the garden ran a very lofty wall, but I never cared to ask what lay beyond it, everything about me was so beautiful. My courtiers called me the Happy Prince, and happy indeed I was, if pleasure be happiness. So I lived, and so I died. And now that I am dead they have set me up here so high that I can see all the ugliness and all the misery of my city, and though my heart is made of lead yet I cannot choose but weep.'

'What! Is he not solid gold?' said the Swallow to himself. He was too polite to make any personal remarks out loud.

'Far away,' continued the statue in a low musical voice, 'far away in a little street there is a poor house. One of the windows is open, and through it I can see a woman seated at a table. Her face is thin and worn, and she has coarse, red hands, all pricked by the needle, for she is a seamstress. She is embroidering passion-flowers on a satin gown for the loveliest of the Queen's maids-of-honour to wear at the next Court-ball. In a bed in the corner of the room her little boy is lying ill. He has a fever, and is asking for oranges. His mother has nothing to give him but river water, so he is crying. Swallow, Swallow, little Swallow, will you not bring her the ruby out of my sword-hilt? My feet are fastened to this pedestal and I cannot move.'

'I am waited for in Egypt,' said the Swallow. 'My friends are flying up and down the Nile, and talking to the large lotus-flowers. Soon they will go to sleep in the tomb of the great King. The King is there himself in his painted coffin. He is wrapped in yellow linen, and embalmed with spices. Round his neck is a chain of pale green jade, and his hands are like withered leaves.'

'Swallow, Swallow, little Swallow,' said the Prince, 'will you not stay with me for one night, and be my messenger? The boy is so thirsty, and the mother so sad.'

'I don't think I like boys,' answered the Swallow. 'Last summer, when I was staying on the river, there were two rude boys, the miller's sons, who were always throwing stones at me. They never hit me, of course; we swallows fly far too well for that, and besides, I come of a family famous for its agility; but still, it was a mark of disrespect.'

But the Happy Prince looked so sad that the little Swallow was sorry. 'It is very cold here,' he said; 'but I will stay with you for one night, and be your messenger.'

'Thank you, little Swallow,' said the Prince.

So the Swallow picked out the great ruby from the Prince's sword, and flew away with it in his beak over the roofs of the town.

He passed by the cathedral tower, where the white marble angels were sculptured. He passed by the palace and heard the sound of dancing. A beautiful girl came out on the balcony with her lover. 'How wonderful the stars are,' he said to her, 'and how wonderful is the power of love!'

'I hope my dress will be ready in time for the State-ball,' she answered, 'I have ordered passion-flowers to be embroidered on it; but the seamstresses are so lazy.'

He passed over the river, and saw the lanterns hanging to the masts of the ships. He passed over the Ghetto, and saw the old Jews bargaining with each other, and weighing out money in copper scales. At last he came to the poor house and looked in. The boy was tossing feverishly on his bed, and the mother had fallen asleep, she was so tired. In he hopped, and laid the great ruby on the table beside the woman's thimble. Then he flew gently round the bed, fanning the boy's forehead with his wings. 'How cool I feel!' said the boy, 'I must be getting better'; and he sank into a delicious slumber.

Then the Swallow flew back to the Happy Prince, and told him what he had done. 'It is curious,' he remarked, 'but I feel quite warm now, although it is so cold.'

'That is because you have done a good action,' said the Prince. And the little Swallow began to think, and then he fell asleep. Thinking always made him sleepy.

When day broke he flew down to the river and had a bath. 'What a remarkable phenomenon,' said the Professor of Ornithology as he was passing over the bridge. 'A swallow in winter!' And he wrote a long letter about it to the local newspaper. Every one quoted it, it was full of so many words that they could not understand.

'To-night I go to Egypt,' said the Swallow, and he was in high spirits at the prospect. He visited all the public monuments, and sat a long time on top of the church steeple. Wherever he went the Sparrows chirruped, and said to each other, 'What a distinguished stranger!' so he enjoyed himself very much.

When the moon rose he flew back to the Happy Prince. 'Have you any commissions for Egypt?' he cried, 'I am just starting.'

'Swallow, Swallow, little Swallow,' said the Prince, 'will you not stay with me one night longer?'

'I am waited for in Egypt,' answered the Swallow. 'To-morrow my friends will fly up to the Second Cataract. The river-horse couches there among the bulrushes, and on a great granite throne sits the God Memnon. All night long he watches the stars, and when the morning star shines he utters one cry of joy, and then he is silent. At noon the yellow lions come down to the water's edge to drink. They have eyes like green beryls, and their roar is louder than the roar of the cataract.'

'Swallow, Swallow, little Swallow,' said the Prince, 'far away across the city I see a young man in a garret. He is leaning over a desk covered with papers, and in a tumbler by his side there is a bunch of withered violets. His hair is brown and crisp, and his lips are red as a pomegranate, and he has large and dreamy eyes. He is trying to finish a play for the Director of the Theatre, but he is too cold to write any more. There is no fire in the grate, and hunger has made him faint.'

'I will wait with you one night longer,' said the Swallow, who really had a good heart. 'Shall I take him another ruby?'

'Alas! I have no ruby now,' said the Prince. 'My eyes are all that I have left. They are made of rare sapphires, which were brought out of India a thousand years ago. Pluck out one of them and take it to him. He will sell it to the jeweller, and buy food and firewood, and finish his play.'

'Dear Prince,' said the Swallow, 'I cannot do that', and he began to weep.

'Swallow, Swallow, little Swallow,' said the Prince, 'do as I command you.'

So the Swallow plucked out the Prince's eye, and flew away to the student's garret. It was easy enough to get in, as there was a hole in the roof. Through this he darted, and came into the room. The young man had his head buried in his hands, so he did not hear the flutter of the bird's wings, and when he looked up he found the beautiful sapphire lying on the withered violets.

'I am beginning to be appreciated,' he cried. 'This is from some great admirer. Now I can finish my play,' and he looked quite happy.

The next day the Swallow flew down to the harbour. He sat on the mast of a large vessel and watched the sailors hauling big chests out of the hold with ropes. 'Heave a-hoy!' they shouted as each chest came up. 'I am going to Egypt!' cried the Swallow, but nobody minded, and when the moon rose he flew back to the Happy Prince.

'I am come to bid you good-bye,' he cried.

'Swallow, Swallow, little Swallow,' said the Prince, 'will you not stay with me one night longer?'

'It is winter,' answered the Swallow, 'and the chill snow will soon be here. In Egypt the sun is warm on the green palm-trees, and the crocodiles lie in the mud and look lazily about them. My companions are building a nest in the Temple of Baalbek, and the pink and white doves are watching them, and cooing to each other. Dear Prince, I must leave you, but I will never forget you, and next spring I will bring you back two beautiful jewels in place of those you have given away. The ruby shall be redder than a red rose, and the sapphire shall be as blue as the great sea.'

'In the square below,' said the Happy Prince, 'there stands a little match-girl. She has let her matches fall in the gutter, and they are all spoiled. Her father will beat her if she does not bring home some money, and she is crying. She has no shoes or stockings, and her little head is bare. Pluck out my other eye and give it to her, and her father will not beat her.'

'I will stay with you one night longer,' said the Swallow, 'but I cannot pluck out your eye. You would be quite blind then.'

'Swallow, Swallow, little Swallow,' said the Prince, 'do as I command you.'

So he plucked out the Prince's other eye, and darted down with it. He swooped past the match-girl, and slipped the jewel into the palm of her hand. 'What a lovely bit of glass!' cried the little girl; and she ran home, laughing.

Then the Swallow came back to the Prince. 'You are blind now,' he said, 'so I will stay with you always.'

'No, little Swallow,' said the poor Prince, 'you must go away to Egypt.'

'I will stay with you always,' said the Swallow, and he slept at the Prince's feet.

All the next day he sat on the Prince's shoulder, and told him stories of what he had seen in strange lands. He told him of the red ibises, who stand in long rows on the banks of the Nile, and catch gold-fish in their beaks; of the Sphinx, who is as old as the world itself, and lives in the desert, and knows everything; of the merchants, who walk slowly by the side of their camels and carry amber beads in their hands; of the King of the Mountains of the Moon, who is as black as ebony, and worships a large crystal; of the great green snake that sleeps in a palm tree, and has twenty priests to feed it with honey-cakes; and of the pygmies who sail over a big lake on large flat leaves, and are always at war with the butterflies.

'Dear little Swallow,' said the Prince, 'you tell me of marvellous things, but more marvellous than anything is the suffering of men and of women. There is no Mystery so great as Misery. Fly over my city, little Swallow, and tell me what you see there.'

So the Swallow flew over the great city, and saw the rich making merry in their beautiful houses, while the beggars were sitting at the gates. He flew into dark lanes, and saw the white faces of starving children looking out listlessly at the black streets. Under the archway of a bridge two little boys were lying in one another's arms to try and keep themselves warm. 'How hungry we are!' they said. 'You must not lie here,' shouted the Watchman, and they wandered out into the rain.

Then he flew back and told the Prince what he had seen.

'I am covered with fine gold,' said the Prince, 'you must take it off, leaf by leaf, and give it to my poor; the living always think that gold can make them happy.'

Leaf after leaf of the fine gold the Swallow picked off, till the Happy Prince looked quite dull and grey. Leaf after leaf of the fine gold he brought to the poor, and the children's faces grew rosier, and they laughed and played games in the street. 'We have bread now!' they cried.

Then the snow came, and after the snow came the frost. The streets looked as if they were made of silver, they were so bright and glistening; long icicles like crystal daggers hung down from the eaves of the houses, everybody went about in furs, and the little boys wore scarlet caps and skated on the ice.

The poor little Swallow grew colder and colder, but he would not leave the Prince, he loved him too well. He picked up crumbs outside the baker's door when the baker was not looking, and tried to keep himself warm by flapping his wings.

But at last he knew that he was going to die. He had just strength to fly up to the Prince's shoulder once more. 'Good-bye, dear Prince!' he murmured, 'will you let me kiss your hand?'

'I am glad that you are going to Egypt at last, little Swallow,' said the Prince, 'you have stayed too long here; but you must kiss me on the lips, for I love you.'

'It is not to Egypt that I am going,' said the Swallow. 'I am going to the House of Death. Death is the brother of Sleep, is he not?'

And he kissed the Happy Prince on the lips, and fell down dead at his feet.

At that moment a curious crack sounded inside the statue, as if something had broken. The fact is that the leaden heart had snapped right in two. It certainly was a dreadfully hard frost.

Early the next morning the Mayor was walking in the square below in company with the Town Councillors. As they passed the column he looked up at the statue, 'Dear me! How shabby the Happy Prince looks!' he said.

'How shabby, indeed!' cried the Town Councillors, who always agreed with the Mayor; and they went up to look at it.

'The ruby has fallen out of his sword, his eyes are gone, and he is golden no longer,' said the Mayor. 'In fact, he is little better than a beggar!'

'Little better than a beggar,' said the Town Councillors.

'And here is actually a dead bird at his feet!' continued the Mayor. 'We must really issue a proclamation that birds are not to be allowed to die here.' And the Town Clerk made a note of the suggestion.

So they pulled down the statue of the Happy Prince. 'As he is no longer beautiful he is no longer useful,' said the Art Professor at the University.

Then they melted the statue in a furnace, and the Mayor held a meeting of the Corporation to decide what was to be done with the metal. 'We must have another statue, of course,' he said, 'and it shall be a statue of myself.'

'Of myself,' said each of the Town Councillors, and they quarrelled. When I last heard of them they were quarrelling still.

'What a strange thing!' said the overseer of the workmen at the foundry. 'This broken lead heart will not melt in the furnace. We must throw it away.' So they threw it on a dust-heap where the dead Swallow was also lying.

'Bring me the two most precious things in the city,' said God to one of His Angels; and the Angel brought Him the leaden heart and the dead bird.

'You have rightly chosen,' said God, 'for in my garden of Paradise this little bird shall sing for evermore, and in my city of gold the Happy Prince shall praise me.'

THE SELFISH GIANT

Oscar Wilde

Every afternoon, as they were coming from school, the children used to go and play in the Giant's garden.

It was a large lovely garden, with soft green grass. Here and there over the grass stood beautiful flowers like stars, and there were twelve peach-trees that in the spring-time broke out into delicate blossoms of pink and pearl, and in the autumn bore rich fruit. The birds sat on the trees and sang so sweetly that the children used to stop their games in order to listen to them. 'How happy we are here!' they cried to each other.

One day the Giant came back. He had been to visit his friend the Cornish ogre, and had stayed with him for seven years. After the seven years were over he had said all that he had to say, for his conversation was limited, and he determined to return to his own castle. When he arrived he saw the children playing in the garden.

'What are you doing here?' he cried in a very gruff voice, and the children ran away.

'My own garden is my own garden,' said the Giant; 'anyone can understand that, and I will allow nobody to play in it but myself.'

So he built a high wall all round it, and put up a notice-board.

TRESPASSERS WILL BE PROSECUTED

He was a very selfish Giant.

The poor children had now nowhere to play. They tried to play on the road, but the road was very dusty and full of hard stones, and they did not like it. They used to wander round the high wall when their lessons were over, and talk about the beautiful garden inside. 'How happy we were there!' they said to each other.

Then the Spring came, and all over the country there were little blossoms and little birds. Only in the garden of the Selfish Giant it was still winter. The birds did not care to sing in it as there were no children, and the trees forgot to blossom. Once a beautiful flower put its head out from the grass, but when it saw the notice-board it was so sorry for the children that it slipped back into the ground again, and went off to sleep. The only people who were pleased were the Snow and the Frost. 'Spring has forgotten this garden,' they cried, 'so we will live here all the year round.' The Snow covered up the grass with her great white cloak, and the Frost painted all the trees silver. Then they invited the North Wind to stay with them, and he came. He was wrapped in furs, and he roared all day about the garden, and blew the chimney-pots down. 'This is a delightful spot,' he said, 'we must ask the Hail on a visit.' So the Hail came. Every day for three hours he rattled on the roof of the castle till he broke most of the slates, and then he ran round and round the garden as fast as he could go. He was dressed in grey, and his breath was like ice.

'I cannot understand why the Spring is so late in coming,' said the Selfish Giant, as he sat at the window and looked out at his cold white garden; 'I hope there will be a change in the weather.'

But the Spring never came, nor the Summer. The Autumn gave golden fruit to every garden, but to the Giant's garden she gave none. 'He is too selfish,' she said. So it was always Winter there, and the North Wind and the Hail, and the Frost, and the Snow danced about through the trees.

One morning the Giant was lying awake in bed when he heard some lovely music. It sounded so sweet to his ears that he thought it must be the King's musicians passing by. It was really only a little linnet singing outside his window, but it was so long since he had heard a bird sing in his garden that it seemed to him to be the most beautiful music in the world. Then the Hail stopped dancing over his head, and the North Wind ceased roaring, and a delicious perfume came to him through the open casement. 'I believe the Spring has come at last,' said the Giant; and he jumped out of bed and looked out.

What did he see?

He saw a most wonderful sight. Through a little hole in the wall the children had crept in, and they were sitting in the branches of the trees. In every tree that he could see there was a little child. And the trees were so glad to have the children back again that they had covered themselves with blossoms, and were waving their arms gently above the children's heads. The birds were flying about and twittering with delight, and the flowers were looking up through the green grass and laughing. It was a lovely scene, only in one corner it was still winter.

It was the farthest corner of the garden, and in it was standing a little boy.

He was so small that he could not reach up to the branches of the tree, and he was wandering all round it, crying bitterly. The poor tree was still quite covered with frost and snow, and the North Wind was blowing and roaring above it. 'Climb up! little boy,' said the Tree, and it bent its branches down as low as it could; but the boy was too tiny.

And the Giant's heart melted as he looked out. 'How selfish I have been!' he said; 'now I know why the Spring would not come here. I will put that poor little boy on the top of the tree, and then I will knock down the wall, and my garden shall be the children's playground for ever and ever.' He was really very sorry for what he had done.

So he crept downstairs and opened the front door quite softly, and went out into the garden. But when the children saw him they were so frightened that they all ran away, and the garden became winter again. Only the little boy did not run, for his eyes were so full of tears that he did not see the Giant coming. And the Giant stole up behind him and took him gently in his hand, and put him up into the tree. And the tree broke at once into blossom, and the birds came and sang on it, and the little boy stretched out his two arms and flung them round the Giant's neck, and kissed him. And the other children, when they saw that the Giant was not wicked any longer, came running back, and with them came the Spring. 'It is your garden now, little children,' said the Giant, and he took a great axe and knocked down the wall. And when the people were going to market at twelve o'clock they found the Giant playing with the children in the most beautiful garden they had ever seen.

All day long they played, and in the evening they came to the Giant to bid him good-bye.

'But where is your little companion?' he said, 'The boy I put into the tree.' The Giant loved him the best because he had kissed him.

'We don't know,' answered the children; 'he has gone away.'

'You must tell him to be sure and come here to-morrow,' said the Giant. But the children said that they did not know where he lived, and had never seen him before; and the Giant felt very sad.

Every afternoon, when school was over, the children came and played with the Giant. But the little boy whom the Giant loved was never seen again. The Giant was very kind to all the children, yet he longed for his first little friend, and often spoke of him. 'How I would like to see him!' he used to say.

Years went over, and the Giant grew very old and feeble. He could not play about any more, so he sat in a huge armchair, and watched the children at their games, and admired his garden. 'I have many beautiful flowers,' he said, 'but the children are the most beautiful flowers of all.'

One winter morning he looked out of his window as he was dressing. He did not hate the winter now, for he knew that it was merely the Spring asleep, and that the flowers were resting.

Suddenly he rubbed his eyes in wonder and looked and looked. It certainly was a marvellous sight. In the farthest corner of the garden was a tree quite covered with lovely white blossoms. Its branches were all golden, and silver fruit hung down from them, and underneath it stood the little boy he had loved.

Downstairs ran the Giant in great joy, and out into the garden. He hastened across the grass, and came near to the child. And when he came quite close his face grew red with anger, and he said, 'Who hath dared to wound thee?' For on the palms of the child's hands were the prints of two nails, and the prints of two nails were on the little feet.

'Who hath dared to wound thee?' cried the Giant; 'tell me, that I might take my big sword and slay him.'

'Nay!' answered the child; 'but these are the wounds of Love.'

'Who art thou?' said the Giant, and a strange awe fell on him, and he knelt before the little child.

And the child smiled on the Giant, and said to him, 'You let me play once in your garden, to-day you shall come with me to my garden, which is Paradise.'

And when the children ran in that afternoon, they found the Giant lying dead under the tree, all covered with white blossoms.

THE CHRISTMAS TREE AND THE WEDDING

Fyodor M. Dostoyevsky

The other day I saw a wedding... But no! I would rather tell you about a Christmas tree. The wedding was superb. I liked it immensely. But the other incident was still finer. I don't know why it is that the sight of the wedding reminded me of the Christmas tree. This is the way it happened:

Exactly five years ago, on New Year's Eve, I was invited to a children's ball by a man high up in the business world, who had his connections, his circle of acquaintances, and his intrigues. So it seemed as though the children's ball was merely a pretext for the parents to come together and discuss matters of interest to themselves, quite innocently and casually.

I was an outsider, and, as I had no special matters to air, I was able to spend the evening independently of the others. There was another gentleman present who like myself had just stumbled upon this affair of domestic bliss. He was the first to attract my attention. His appearance was not that of a man of birth or high family. He was tall, rather thin, very serious, and well dressed. Apparently he had no heart for the family festivities. The instant he went off into a corner by himself the smile disappeared from his face, and his thick dark brows knitted into a frown. He knew no one except the host and showed every sign of being bored to death, though bravely sustaining the role of thorough enjoyment to the end. Later I learned that he was a provincial, had come to the capital on some important, brain-racking business, had brought a letter of recommendation to our host, and our host had taken him under his protection, not at all *con amore*. It was merely out of politeness that he had invited him to the children's ball.

They did not play cards with him, they did not offer him cigars. No one entered into conversation with him. Possibly they recognized the bird by its feathers from a distance. Thus, my gentleman, not knowing what to do with his hands, was compelled to spend the evening stroking his whiskers. His whiskers were really fine, but he stroked them so assiduously that one got the feeling that the whiskers had come into the world first and afterwards the man in order to stroke them.

There was another guest who interested me. But he was of quite a different order. He was a personage. They called him Julian Mastakovich. At first glance one could tell he was an honoured guest and stood in the same relation to the host as the host to the gentleman of the whiskers. The host and hostess said no end of amiable things to him, were most attentive, wining him, hovering over him, bringing guests up to be introduced, but never leading him to any one else. I noticed tears glisten in our host's eyes when Julian Mastakovich remarked that he had rarely spent such a pleasant evening. Somehow I began to feel uncomfortable in this personage's presence. So, after amusing myself with the children, five of whom, remarkably well-fed young persons, were our host's, I went into a little sitting-room, entirely unoccupied, and seated myself at the end that was a conservatory and took up almost half the room.

The children were charming. They absolutely refused to resemble their elders, notwithstanding the efforts of mothers and governesses. In a jiffy they had denuded the Christmas tree down to the very last sweet and had already succeeded in breaking half of their playthings before they even found out which belonged to whom.

One of them was a particularly handsome little lad, dark-eyed, curly-haired, who stubbornly persisted in aiming at me with his wooden gun. But the child that attracted the greatest attention was his sister, a girl of about eleven, lovely as a Cupid. She was quiet and thoughtful, with large, full, dreamy eyes. The children had somehow offended her, and she left them and walked into the same room that I had withdrawn into. There she seated herself with her doll in a corner.

'Her father is an immensely wealthy business man,' the guests informed each other in tones of awe. 'Three hundred thousand rubles set aside for her dowry already.'

As I turned to look at the group from which I heard this news item issuing, my glance met Julian Mastakovich's. He stood listening to the insipid chatter in an attitude of concentrated attention, with his hands behind his back and his head inclined to one side.

All the while I was quite lost in admiration of the shrewdness our host displayed in the dispensing of the gifts. The little maid of the many-rubied dowry received the handsomest doll, and the rest of the gifts were graded in value according to the diminishing scale of the parents' stations in life. The last child, a tiny chap of ten, thin, red-haired, freckled, came into possession of a small book of nature stories without illustrations or even head and tail pieces. He was the governess's child. She was a poor widow, and her little boy, clad in a sorry-looking little nankeen jacket, looked thoroughly crushed and intimidated. He took the book of nature stories and circled slowly about the children's toys. He would have given anything to play with them. But he did not dare to. You could tell he already knew his place.

I like to observe children. It is fascinating to watch the individuality in them struggling for self-assertion. I could see that the other children's things had tremendous charm for the red-haired boy, especially a toy theatre, in which he was so anxious to take a part that he resolved to fawn upon the other children. He smiled and began to play with them. His one and only apple he handed over to a puffy urchin whose pockets were already crammed with sweets, and he even carried another youngster pickaback—all simply that he might be allowed to stay with the theatre.

But in a few moments an impudent young person fell on him and gave him a pummelling. He did not dare even to cry. The governess came and told him to leave off interfering with the other children's games, and he crept away to the same room the little girl and I were in. She let him sit down beside her, and the two set themselves busily dressing the expensive doll.

Almost half an hour passed, and I was nearly dozing off, as I sat there in the conservatory half listening to the chatter of the red-haired boy and the dowered beauty, when Julian Mastakovich entered suddenly. He had slipped out of the drawing-room under cover of a noisy scene among the children. From my secluded corner it had not escaped my notice that a few moments before he had been eagerly conversing with the rich girl's father, to whom he had only just been introduced.

He stood still for a while reflecting and mumbling to himself, as if counting something on his fingers.

'Three hundred…three hundred', he was whispering. 'Eleven…

twelve…thirteen', and so on. 'Sixteen—in five years! Let's say four per cent…five times twelve…sixty, and on these sixty… Let us assume that in five years it will amount to—well, four hundred. Hm—hm! But the shrewd old fox isn't likely to be satisfied with four per cent. He gets eight or even ten, perhaps. Let's suppose five hundred, five hundred thousand, at least, that's sure. Anything above that for pocket money…hm…'

He blew his nose and was about to leave the room when he spied the girl and stood still. I, behind the plants, escaped his notice. He seemed to me to be quivering with excitement. It must have been his calculations that upset him so. He rubbed his hands and danced from place to place, and kept getting more and more excited. Finally, however, he conquered his emotions and came to a standstill. He cast a determined look at the future bride and wanted to move toward her, but glanced about first. Then, as if with a guilty conscience, he stepped over to the child on tip-toe, smiling, and bent down and kissed her head.

His coming was so unexpected that she uttered a shriek of alarm.

'What are you doing here, dear child?' he whispered, looking around and pinching her cheek.

'We're playing.'

'What, with him?' said Julian Mastakovich with a look askance at the governess's child. 'You should go into the drawing-room, my lad,' he said to him.

The boy remained silent and looked up at the man with wide-open eyes. Julian Mastakovich glanced round again cautiously and bent down over the girl.

'What have you got, a doll, my dear?'

'Yes, sir.' The child quailed a little, and her brow wrinkled.

'A doll? And do you know, my dear, what dolls are made of?'

'No, sir,' she said weakly, and lowered her head.

'Out of rags, my dear. You, boy, you go back to the drawing-room, to the children,' said Julian Mastakovich looking at the boy sternly.

The two children frowned. They caught hold of each other and would not part.

'And do you know why they gave you the doll?' asked Julian Mastakovich, dropping his voice lower and lower.

'No.'

'Because you were a good, very good little girl the whole week.'

Saying which, Julian Mastakovich was seized with a paroxysm of agitation. He looked round and said in a tone faint, almost inaudible with excitement and impatience.

'If I come to visit your parents will you love me, my dear?'

He tried to kiss the sweet little creature, but the red-haired boy saw that she was on the verge of tears, and he caught her hand and sobbed out loud in sympathy. That enraged the man.

'Go away! Go away! Go back to the other room, to your playmates.'

'I don't want him to. I don't want him to! You go away!' cried the girl. 'Let him alone! Let him alone!' She was almost weeping.

There was a sound of footsteps in the doorway. Julian Mastakovich started and straightened up his respectable body. The red-haired boy was even more alarmed. He let go the girl's hand, sidled along the wall, and escaped through the drawing-room into the dining-room.

Not to attract attention, Julian Mastakovich also made for the dining-room. He was red as a lobster. The sight of himself in a mirror seemed to embarrass him. Presumably he was annoyed at his own ardour and impatience. Without due respect to his importance and dignity, his calculations had lured and pricked him to the greedy eagerness of a boy, who makes straight for his object—though this was not as yet an object; it only would be so in five years' time. I followed the worthy man into the dining-room, where I witnessed a remarkable play.

Julian Mastakovich, all flushed with vexation, venom in his look, began to threaten the red-haired boy. The red-haired boy retreated farther and farther until there was no place left for him to retreat to, and he did not know where to turn in his fright.

'Get out of here! What are you doing here? Get out, I say, you good-for-nothing! Stealing fruit, are you? Oh, so, stealing fruit! Get out, you freckle face, go to your likes!'

The frightened child, as a last desperate resort, crawled quickly under the table. His persecutor, completely infuriated, pulled out his large linen handkerchief and used it as a lash to drive the boy out of his position.

Here I must remark that Julian Mastakovich was a somewhat

corpulent man, heavy, well-fed, puffy-cheeked, with a paunch and ankles as round as nuts. He perspired and puffed and panted. So strong was his dislike (or was it jealousy?) of the child that he actually began to carry on like a madman.

I laughed heartily. Julian Mastakovich turned. He was utterly confused and for a moment, apparently, quite oblivious of his immense importance. At that moment our host appeared in the doorway opposite. The boy crawled out from under the table and wiped his knees and elbows. Julian Mastakovich hastened to carry his handkerchief, which he had been dangling by the corner, to his nose. Our host looked at the three of us rather suspiciously. But, like a man who knows the world and can readily adjust himself, he seized upon the opportunity to lay hold of his very valuable guest and get what he wanted out of him.

'Here's the boy I was talking to you about,' he said, indicating the red-haired child. 'I took the liberty of presuming on your goodness in his behalf.'

'Oh,' replied Julian Mastakovich, still not quite master of himself.

'He's my governess's son,' our host continued in a beseeching tone. 'She's a poor creature, the widow of an honest official. That's why, if it were possible for you—'

'Impossible, impossible!' Julian Mastakovich cried hastily. 'You must excuse me, Philip Alexeyevich, I really cannot. I've made inquiries. There are no vacancies, and there is a waiting list of ten who have a greater right—I'm sorry.'

'Too bad,' said our host. 'He's a quiet, unobtrusive child.'

'A very naughty little rascal, I should say,' said Julian Mastakovich, wryly. 'Go away, boy. Why are you here still? Be off with you to the other children.'

Unable to control himself, he gave me a sidelong glance. Nor could I control myself. I laughed straight in his face. He turned away and asked our host, in tones quite audible to me, who that odd young fellow was. They whispered to each other and left the room, disregarding me.

I shook with laughter. Then I, too, went to the drawing-room. There the great man, already surrounded by the fathers and mothers and the host and the hostess, had begun to talk eagerly with a lady to whom he had just been introduced. The lady held the rich little girl's hand.

Julian Mastakovich went into fulsome praise of her. He waxed ecstatic over the dear child's beauty, her talents, her grace, her excellent breeding, plainly laying himself out to flatter the mother, who listened scarcely able to restrain tears of joy, while the father showed his delight by a gratified smile.

The joy was contagious. Everybody shared in it. Even the children were obliged to stop playing so as not to disturb the conversation. The atmosphere was surcharged with awe. I heard the mother of the important little girl, touched to her profoundest depths, ask Julian Mastakovich in the choicest language of courtesy, whether he would honour them by coming to see them. I heard Julian Mastakovich accept the invitation with unfeigned enthusiasm. Then the guests scattered decorously to different parts of the room, and I heard them, with veneration in their tones, extol the business man, the business man's wife, the business man's daughter, and, especially, Julian Mastakovich.

'Is he married?' I asked out loud of an acquaintance of mine standing beside Julian Mastakovich.

Julian Mastakovich gave me a venomous look.

'No,' answered my acquaintance, profoundly shocked by my—intentional—indiscretion.

∞

Not long ago I passed the Church of—I was struck by the concourse of people gathered there to witness a wedding. It was a dreary day. A drizzling rain was beginning to come down. I made my way through the throng into the church. The bridegroom was a round, well-fed, pot-bellied little man, very much dressed up. He ran and fussed about and gave orders and arranged things. Finally word was passed that the bride was coming. I pushed through the crowd, and I beheld a marvellous beauty whose first spring was scarcely commencing. But the beauty was pale and sad. She looked distracted. It seemed to me even that her eyes were red from recent weeping. The classic severity of every line of her face imparted a peculiar significance and solemnity to her beauty. But through that severity and solemnity, through the sadness, shone the innocence of a child. There was something inexpressibly naïve, unsettled and young in her features, which, without words, seemed to plead for mercy.

They said she was just sixteen years old. I looked at the bridegroom carefully. Suddenly I recognized Julian Mastakovich, whom I had not seen again in all those five years. Then I looked at the bride again—Good God! I made my way, as quickly as I could, out of the church. I heard gossiping in the crowd about the bride's wealth—about her dowry of five hundred thousand rubles—so and so much for pocket money.

'Then his calculations were correct,' I thought, as I pressed out into the street.

THE GIFT OF THE MAGI

O. Henry

One dollar and eighty-seven cents. That was all. And sixty cents of it was in pennies. Pennies saved one and two at a time by bulldozing the grocer and the vegetable man and the butcher until one's cheeks burned with the silent imputation of parsimony that such close dealing implied. Three times Della counted it. One dollar and eighty-seven cents. And the next day would be Christmas.

There was clearly nothing to do but flop down on the shabby little couch and howl. So Della did it. Which instigates the moral reflection that life is made up of sobs, sniffles, and smiles, with sniffles predominating.

While the mistress of the home is gradually subsiding from the first stage to the second, take a look at the home. A furnished flat at $8 per week. It did not exactly beggar description, but it certainly had that word on the lookout for the mendicancy squad.

In the vestibule below was a letter-box into which no letter would go, and an electric button from which no mortal finger could coax a ring. Also appertaining thereunto was a card bearing the name 'Mr James Dillingham Young.'

The 'Dillingham' had been flung to the breeze during a former period of prosperity when its possessor was being paid $30 per week. Now, when the income was shrunk to $20, though, they were thinking seriously of contracting to a modest and unassuming D. But whenever Mr James Dillingham Young came home and reached his flat above he was called 'Jim' and greatly hugged by Mrs James Dillingham Young, already introduced to you as Della. Which is all very good.

Della finished her cry and attended to her cheeks with the powder rag. She stood by the window and looked out dully at a grey cat walking a grey fence in a grey backyard. Tomorrow would be Christmas Day, and she had only $1.87 with which to buy Jim a present. She had been saving every penny she could for months, with this result. Twenty dollars a week doesn't go far. Expenses had been greater than she had calculated. They always are. Only $1.87 to buy a present for Jim. Her Jim. Many a happy hour she had spent planning for something nice for him. Something fine and rare and sterling—something just a little bit near to being worthy of the honour of being owned by Jim.

There was a pier-glass between the windows of the room. Perhaps you have seen a pier glass in an $8 flat. A very thin and very agile person may, by observing his reflection in a rapid sequence of longitudinal strips, obtain a fairly accurate conception of his looks. Della, being slender, had mastered the art.

Suddenly she whirled from the window and stood before the glass. Her eyes were shining brilliantly, but her face had lost its colour within twenty seconds. Rapidly she pulled down her hair and let it fall to its full length.

Now, there were two possessions of the James Dillingham Youngs in which they both took a mighty pride. One was Jim's gold watch that had been his father's and his grandfather's. The other was Della's hair. Had the queen of Sheba lived in the flat across the airshaft, Della would have let her hair hang out the window someday to dry just to depreciate Her Majesty's jewels and gifts. Had King Solomon been the janitor, with all his treasures piled up in the basement, Jim would have pulled out his watch every time he passed, just to see him pluck at his beard from envy.

So now Della's beautiful hair fell about her rippling and shining like a cascade of brown waters. It reached below her knee and made itself almost a garment for her. And then she did it up again nervously and quickly. Once she faltered for a minute and stood still while a tear or two splashed on the worn red carpet.

On went her old brown jacket; on went her old brown hat. With a whirl of skirts and with the brilliant sparkle still in her eyes, she fluttered out the door and down the stairs to the street.

Where she stopped the sign read: 'Mme. Sofronie. Hair Goods of All Kinds.' One flight up Della ran, and collected herself, panting. Madame, large, too white, chilly, hardly looked the 'Sofronie.'

'Will you buy my hair?' asked Della.

'I buy hair,' said Madame. 'Take yer hat off and let's have a sight at the looks of it.'

Down rippled the brown cascade.

'Twenty dollars,' said Madame, lifting the mass with a practised hand.

'Give it to me quick,' said Della.

Oh, and the next two hours tripped by on rosy wings. Forget the hashed metaphor. She was ransacking the stores for Jim's present.

She found it at last. It surely had been made for Jim and no one else. There was no other like it in any of the stores, and she had turned all of them inside out. It was a platinum fob chain simple and chaste in design, properly proclaiming its value by substance alone and not by meretricious ornamentation—as all good things should do. It was even worthy of The Watch. As soon as she saw it she knew that it must be Jim's. It was like him. Quietness and value—the description applied to both. Twenty-one dollars they took from her for it, and she hurried home with the 87 cents. With that chain on his watch Jim might be properly anxious about the time in any company. Grand as the watch was, he sometimes looked at it on the sly on account of the old leather strap that he used in place of a chain.

When Della reached home her intoxication gave way a little to prudence and reason. She got out her curling irons and lighted the gas and went to work repairing the ravages made by generosity added to love. Which is always a tremendous task, dear friends—a mammoth task.

Within forty minutes her head was covered with tiny, close-lying curls that made her look wonderfully like a truant schoolboy. She looked at her reflection in the mirror long, carefully, and critically.

'If Jim doesn't kill me,' she said to herself, 'before he takes a second look at me, he'll say I look like a Coney Island chorus girl. But what could I do—oh! what could I do with a dollar and eighty-seven cents?'

At 7 o'clock the coffee was made and the frying-pan was on the back of the stove hot and ready to cook the chops.

Jim was never late. Della doubled the fob chain in her hand and sat on the corner of the table near the door that he always entered. Then she heard his step on the stair away down on the first flight, and she turned white for just a moment. She had a habit of saying a little silent prayer about the simplest everyday things, and now she whispered:

'Please God, make him think I am still pretty.'

The door opened and Jim stepped in and closed it. He looked thin and very serious. Poor fellow, he was only twenty-two—and to be burdened with a family! He needed a new overcoat and he was without gloves.

Jim stopped inside the door, as immovable as a setter at the scent of quail. His eyes were fixed upon Della, and there was an expression in them that she could not read, and it terrified her. It was not anger, nor surprise, nor disapproval, nor horror, nor any of the sentiments that she had been prepared for. He simply stared at her fixedly with that peculiar expression on his face.

Della wriggled off the table and went for him.

'Jim, darling,' she cried, 'don't look at me that way. I had my hair cut off and sold because I couldn't have lived through Christmas without giving you a present. It'll grow out again—you won't mind, will you? I just had to do it. My hair grows awfully fast. Say "Merry Christmas!" Jim, and let's be happy. You don't know what a nice—what a beautiful, nice gift I've got for you.'

'You've cut off your hair?' asked Jim, laboriously, as if he had not arrived at that patent fact yet even after the hardest mental labour.

'Cut it off and sold it,' said Della. 'Don't you like me just as well, anyhow? I'm me without my hair, ain't I?'

Jim looked about the room curiously.

'You say your hair is gone?' he said, with an air almost of idiocy.

'You needn't look for it,' said Della. 'It's sold, I tell you—sold and gone, too. It's Christmas Eve, boy. Be good to me, for it went for you. Maybe the hairs of my head were numbered,' she went on with sudden serious sweetness, 'but nobody could ever count my love for you. Shall I put the chops on, Jim?'

Out of his trance Jim seemed quickly to wake. He enfolded his Della. For ten seconds let us regard with discreet scrutiny some inconsequential object in the other direction. Eight dollars a week or a million a year—what is the difference? A mathematician or a wit would give you the wrong answer. The magi brought valuable gifts, but that was not among them. This dark assertion will be illuminated later on.

Jim drew a package from his overcoat pocket and threw it upon the table.

'Don't make any mistake, Dell,' he said, 'about me. I don't think there's anything in the way of a haircut or a shave or a shampoo that could make me like my girl any less. But if you'll unwrap that package you may see why you had me going a while at first.'

White fingers and nimble tore at the string and paper. And then an ecstatic scream of joy; and then, alas! a quick feminine change to hysterical tears and wails, necessitating the immediate employment of all the comforting powers of the lord of the flat.

For there lay The Combs—the set of combs, side and back, that Della had worshipped long in a Broadway window. Beautiful combs, pure tortoise shell, with jewelled rims—just the shade to wear in the beautiful vanished hair. They were expensive combs, she knew, and her heart had simply craved and yearned over them without the least hope of possession. And now, they were hers, but the tresses that should have adorned the coveted adornments were gone.

But she hugged them to her bosom, and at length she was able to look up with dim eyes and a smile and say: 'My hair grows so fast, Jim!'

And then Della leaped up like a little singed cat and cried, 'Oh, oh!'

Jim had not yet seen his beautiful present. She held it out to him eagerly upon her open palm. The dull precious metal seemed to flash with a reflection of her bright and ardent spirit.

'Isn't it a dandy, Jim? I hunted all over town to find it. You'll have to look at the time a hundred times a day now. Give me your watch. I want to see how it looks on it.'

Instead of obeying, Jim tumbled down on the couch and put his hands under the back of his head and smiled.

'Dell,' said he, 'let's put our Christmas presents away and keep 'em a while. They're too nice to use just at present. I sold the watch to get the money to buy your combs. And now suppose you put the chops on.'

The magi, as you know, were wise men—wonderfully wise men—who brought gifts to the Babe in the manger. They invented the art of giving Christmas presents. Being wise, their gifts were no doubt wise ones, possibly bearing the privilege of exchange in case of duplication.

And here I have lamely related to you the uneventful chronicle of two foolish children in a flat who most unwisely sacrificed for each other the greatest treasures of their house. But in a last word to the wise of these days let it be said that of all who give gifts these two were the wisest. Of all who give and receive gifts, such as they are wisest. Everywhere they are wisest. They are the magi.

THE GIRL AND THE HABIT

O. Henry

HABIT—a tendency or aptitude acquired by custom or frequent repetition.

The critics have assailed every source of inspiration save one. To that one we are driven for our moral theme. When we levied upon the masters of old they gleefully dug up the parallels to our columns. When we strove to set forth real life they reproached us for trying to imitate Henry George, George Washington, Washington Irving, and Irving Bacheller. We wrote of the West and the East, and they accused us of both Jesse and Henry James. We wrote from our heart—and they said something about a disordered liver. We took a text from Matthew or—er—yes, Deuteronomy, but the preachers were hammering away at the inspiration idea before we could get into type. So, driven to the wall, we go for our subject-matter to the reliable, old, moral, unassailable vade mecum—the unabridged dictionary.

Miss Merriam was cashier at Hinkle's. Hinkle's is one of the big downtown restaurants. It is in what the papers call the 'financial district'. Each day from 12 o'clock to 2 Hinkle's was full of hungry customers—messenger boys, stenographers, brokers, owners of mining stock, promoters, inventors with patents pending—and also people with money.

The cashiership at Hinkle's was no sinecure. Hinkle egged and toasted and griddle-caked and coffeed a good many customers; and he lunched (as good a word as 'dined') many more. It might be said that Hinkle's breakfast crowd was a contingent, but his luncheon patronage amounted to a horde.

Miss Merriam sat on a stool at a desk enclosed on three sides by a strong, high fencing of woven brass wire. Through an arched opening at the bottom you thrust your waiter's check and the money, while your heart went pit-a-pat.

For Miss Merriam was lovely and capable. She could take 45 cents out of a $2 bill and refuse an offer of marriage before you could—Next!—lost your chance—please don't shove. She could keep cool and collected while she collected your check, give you the correct change, win your heart, indicate the toothpick stand, and rate you to a quarter of a cent better than Bradstreet could to a thousand in less time than it takes to pepper an egg with one of Hinkle's casters.

There is an old and dignified allusion to the 'fierce light that beats upon a throne'. The light that beats upon the young lady cashier's cage is also something fierce. The other fellow is responsible for the slang.

Every male patron of Hinkle's, from the A.D.T. boys up to the curb stone brokers, adored Miss Merriam. When they paid their checks they wooed her with every wile known to Cupid's art. Between the meshes of the brass railing went smiles, winks, compliments, tender vows, invitations to dinner, sighs, languishing looks and merry banter that was wafted pointedly back by the gifted Miss Merriam.

There is no coign of vantage more effective than the position of young lady cashier. She sits there, easily queen of the court of commerce; she is duchess of dollars and devoirs, countess of compliments and coin, leading lady of love and luncheon. You take from her a smile and a Canadian dime, and you go your way uncomplaining. You count the cheery word or two that she tosses you as misers count their treasures; and you pocket the change for a five uncomputed. Perhaps the brass-bound inaccessibility multiplies her charms—anyhow, she is a shirt-waisted angel, immaculate, trim, manicured, seductive, bright-eyed, ready, alert—Psyche, Circe, and Ate in one, separating you from your circulating medium after your sirloin medium.

The young men who broke bread at Hinkle's never settled with the cashier without an exchange of badinage and open compliment. Many of them went to greater lengths and dropped promissory hints of theatre tickets and chocolates. The older men spoke plainly of orange blossoms, generally withering the tentative petals by after-allusions to Harlem flats. One broker, who had been squeezed by copper proposed to Miss Merriam more regularly than he ate.

During a brisk luncheon hour Miss Merriam's conversation, while she took money for checks, would run something like this:

'Good morning, Mr Haskins—sir?—it's natural, thank you—don't be quite so fresh… Hello, Johnny—ten, fifteen, twenty—chase along now or they'll take the letters off your cap … Beg pardon—count it again, please—Oh, don't mention it… Vaudeville?—thanks; not on your moving picture—I was to see Carter in Hedda Gabler on Wednesday night with Mr Simmons… 'Scuse me, I thought that was a quarter… Twenty-five and seventy-five's a dollar—got that ham-and-cabbage habit yet. I see, Billy… Who are you addressing?—say—you'll get all that's coming to you in a minute… Oh, fudge! Mr Bassett—you're always fooling—no—? Well, maybe I'll marry you some day—three, four and sixty-five is five… Kindly keep them remarks to yourself, if you please… Ten cents?—'Scuse me; the check calls for seventy—well, maybe it is a one instead of a seven… Oh, do you like it that way, Mr Saunders?—some prefer a pomp; but they say this Cleo de Merody does suit refined features…and ten is fifty… Hike along there, buddy; don't take this for a Coney Island ticket booth… Huh?—why, Macy's—don't it fit nice? Oh, no, it isn't too cool—these light-weight fabrics is all the go this season… Come again, please—that's the third time you've tried to—what?—forget it—that lead quarter is an old friend of mine… Sixty-five?—must have had your salary raised, Mr Wilson… I seen you on Sixth Avenue Tuesday afternoon, Mr De Forest—swell?—oh, my!—who is she? … What's the matter with it?—why, it ain't money—what?—Columbian half?—well, this ain't South America … Yes, I like the mixed best—Friday?—awfully sorry, but I take my jiu-jitsu lesson on Friday—Thursday, then … Thanks—that's sixteen times I've been told that this morning—I guess I must be beautiful … Cut that out, please—who do you think I am? … Why, Mr Westbrook—do you really think so?—the idea!—one—eighty and twenty's a dollar—thank you ever so much, but I don't ever go automobile riding with gentlemen—your aunt?—well, that's different—perhaps… Please don't get fresh—your check was fifteen cents, I believe—kindly step aside and let… Hello, Ben—coming around Thursday evening?—there's a gentleman going to send around a box of chocolates, and…forty and sixty is a dollar, and one is two…'

About the middle of one afternoon the dizzy goddess Vertigo—whose other name is Fortune—suddenly smote an old, wealthy and eccentric banker while he was walking past Hinkle's, on his way to a street car. A wealthy and eccentric banker who rides in street cars is—move up, please; there are others.

A Samaritan, a Pharisee, a man and a policeman who were first on the spot lifted Banker McRamsey and carried him into Hinkle's restaurant. When the aged but indestructible banker opened his eyes he saw a beautiful vision bending over him with a pitiful, tender smile, bathing his forehead with beef tea and chafing his hands with something frappé out of a chafing-dish. Mr McRamsey sighed, lost a vest button, gazed with deep gratitude upon his fair preserveress, and then recovered consciousness.

To the Seaside Library all who are anticipating a romance! Banker McRamsey had an aged and respected wife, and his sentiments toward Miss Merriam were fatherly. He talked to her for half an hour with interest—not the kind that went with his talks during business hours. The next day he brought Mrs McRamsey down to see her. The old couple were childless—they had only a married daughter living in Brooklyn.

To make a short story shorter, the beautiful cashier won the hearts of the good old couple. They came to Hinkle's again and again; they invited her to their old-fashioned but splendid home in one of the East Seventies. Miss Merriam's winning loveliness, her sweet frankness and impulsive heart took them by storm. They said a hundred times that Miss Merriam reminded them so much of their lost daughter. The Brooklyn matron, née Ramsey, had the figure of Buddha and a face like the ideal of an art photographer. Miss Merriam was a combination of curves, smiles, rose leaves, pearls, satin and hair-tonic posters. Enough of the fatuity of parents.

A month after the worthy couple became acquainted with Miss Merriam, she stood before Hinkle one afternoon and resigned her cashiership.

'They're going to adopt me,' she told the bereft restaurateur. 'They're funny old people, but regular dears. And the swell home they have got! Say, Hinkle, there isn't any use of talking—I'm on the à la carte to wear brown duds and goggles in a whiz wagon, or marry a duke at least.

Still, I somehow hate to break out of the old cage. I've been cashiering so long I feel funny doing anything else. I'll miss joshing the fellows awfully when they line up to pay for the buckwheat. But I can't let this chance slide. And they're awfully good, Hinkle; I know I'll have a swell time. You owe me nine-sixty-two and a half for the week. Cut out the half if it hurts you, Hinkle.'

And they did. Miss Merriam became Miss Rosa McRamsey. And she graced the transition. Beauty is only skin-deep, but the nerves lie very near to the skin. Nerve—but just here will you oblige by perusing again the quotation with which this story begins?

The McRamseys poured out money like domestic champagne to polish their adopted one. Milliners, dancing masters and private tutors got it. Miss—er—McRamsey was grateful, loving, and tried to forget Hinkle's. To give ample credit to the adaptability of the American girl, Hinkle's did fade from her memory and speech most of the time.

Not everyone will remember when the Earl of Hitesbury came to East Seventy—Street, America. He was only a fair-to-medium earl, without debts, and he created little excitement. But you will surely remember the evening when the Daughters of Benevolence held their bazaar in the W——f-A——a Hotel. For you were there, and you wrote a note to Fannie on the hotel paper, and mailed it, just to show her that—you did not?

Very well; that was the evening the baby was sick, of course.

At the bazaar the McRamseys were prominent. Miss Mer…er… McRamsey was exquisitely beautiful. The Earl of Hitesbury had been very attentive to her since he dropped in to have a look at America. At the charity bazaar the affair was supposed to be going to be pulled off to a finish. An earl is as good as a duke. Better. His standing may be lower, but his outstanding accounts are also lower.

Our ex-young-lady-cashier was assigned to a booth. She was expected to sell worthless articles to nobs and snobs at exorbitant prices. The proceeds of the bazaar were to be used for giving the poor children of the slums a Christmas din—Say! Did you ever wonder where they get the other 364?

Miss McRamsey—beautiful, palpitating, excited, charming, radiant—

fluttered about in her booth. An imitation brass network, with a little arched opening, fenced her in.

Along came the Earl, assured, delicate, accurate, admiring—admiring greatly, and faced the open wicket.

'You look chawming, you know—'pon my word you do—my deah,' he said, beguilingly.

Miss McRamsey whirled around.

'Cut that joshing out,' she said, coolly and briskly. 'Who do you think you are talking to? Your check, please. Oh, Lordy—!'

Patrons of the bazaar became aware of a commotion and pressed around a certain booth. The Earl of Hitesbury stood nearby pulling a pale blond and puzzled whisker.

'Miss McRamsey has fainted,' someone explained.

THE CACTUS

O. Henry

'The garments of his soul must have appeared sorry and threadbare. Vanity and conceit? These were the joints in his armour. And how free from either she had always been—But why—'

The most notable thing about Time is that it is so purely relative. A large amount of reminiscence is, by common consent, conceded to the drowning man; and it is not past belief that one may review an entire courtship while removing one's gloves.

That is what Trysdale was doing, standing by a table in his bachelor apartments. On the table stood a singular-looking green plant in a red earthen jar. The plant was one of the species of cacti, and was provided with long, tentacular leaves that perpetually swayed with the slightest breeze with a peculiar beckoning motion.

Trysdale's friend, the brother of the bride, stood at a sideboard complaining at being allowed to drink alone. Both men were in evening dress. White favours like stars upon their coats shone through the gloom of the apartment.

As he slowly unbuttoned his gloves, there passed through Trysdale's mind a swift, scarifying retrospect of the last few hours. It seemed that in his nostrils was still the scent of the flowers that had been banked in odorous masses about the church, and in his ears the low-pitched hum of a thousand well-bred voices, the rustle of crisp garments, and, most insistently recurring, the drawling words of the minister irrevocably binding her to another.

From this last hopeless point of view he still strove, as if it had become a habit of his mind, to reach some conjecture as to why and how he had lost her. Shaken rudely by the uncompromising fact, he had suddenly found himself confronted by a thing he had never before faced—his own innermost, unmitigated, arid unbedecked self. He saw all the garbs of pretence and egoism that he had worn now turn to rags of folly. He shuddered at the thought that to others, before now, the garments of his soul must have appeared sorry and threadbare. Vanity and conceit? These were the joints in his armour. And how free from either she had always been—But why?

As she had slowly moved up the aisle toward the altar he had felt an unworthy, sullen exultation that had served to support him. He had told himself that her paleness was from thoughts of another than the man to whom she was about to give herself. But even that poor consolation had been wrenched from him. For, when he saw that swift, limpid, upward look that she gave the man when he took her hand, he knew himself to be forgotten. Once that same look had been raised to him, and he had gauged its meaning. Indeed, his conceit had crumbled; its last prop was gone. Why had it ended thus? There had been no quarrel between them, nothing.

For the thousandth time he remarshalled in his mind the events of those last few days before the tide had so suddenly turned.

She had always insisted upon placing him upon a pedestal, and he had accepted her homage with royal grandeur. It had been a very sweet incense that she had burned before him; so modest (he told himself); so childlike and worshipful, and (he would once have sworn) so sincere. She had invested him with an almost supernatural number of high attributes and excellencies and talents, and he had absorbed the oblation as a desert drinks the rain that can coax from it no promise of blossom or fruit.

As Trysdale grimly wrenched apart the seam of his last glove, the crowning instance of his fatuous and tardily mourned egoism came vividly back to him. The scene was the night when he had asked her to come up on his pedestal with him and share his greatness. He could not, now, for the pain of it, allow his mind to dwell upon the memory of her convincing beauty that night—the careless wave of her hair, the tenderness and virginal charm of her looks and words. But they had been enough, and they had brought him to speak. During their conversation she had said, 'And Captain Carruthers tells me that you speak the Spanish language like a native. Why have you hidden this accomplishment from me? Is there anything you do not know?'

Now, Carruthers was an idiot. No doubt he (Trysdale) had been guilty (he sometimes did such things) of airing at the club some old, canting Castilian proverb dug from the hotchpotch at the back of dictionaries. Carruthers, who was one of his incontinent admirers, was the very man to have magnified this exhibition of doubtful erudition.

But, alas! The incense of her admiration had been so sweet and flattering. He allowed the imputation to pass without denial. Without protest, he allowed her to twine about his brow this spurious bay of Spanish scholarship. He let it grace his conquering head, and, among its soft convolutions, he did not feel the prick of the thorn that was to pierce him later.

How glad, how shy, how tremulous she was! How she fluttered like a snared bird when he laid his mightiness at her feet! He could have sworn, and he could swear now, that unmistakable consent was in her eyes, but, coyly, she would give him no direct answer. 'I will send you my answer to-morrow,' she said; and he, the indulgent, confident victor, smilingly granted the delay. The next day he waited, impatient, in his rooms for the word. At noon her groom came to the door and left the strange cactus in the red earthen jar. There was no note, no message, merely a tag upon the plant bearing a barbarous foreign or botanical name. He waited until night, but her answer did not come. His large pride and hurt vanity kept him from seeking her. Two evenings later they met at a dinner. Their greetings were conventional, but she looked at him, breathless, wondering, eager. He was courteous, adamant, waiting her explanation. With womanly swiftness she took her cue from his manner, and turned to snow and ice. Thus, and wider from this on, they had drifted apart. Where was his fault? Who had been to blame? Humbled now, he sought the answer amid the ruins of his self-conceit. If...

The voice of the other man in the room, querulously intruding upon his thoughts, aroused him.

'I say, Trysdale, what the deuce is the matter with you? You look unhappy as if you yourself had been married instead of having acted merely as an accomplice. Look at me, another accessory, come two thousand miles on a garlicky, cockroachy banana steamer all the way from South America to connive at the sacrifice—please to observe how lightly my guilt rests upon my shoulders. Only little sister I had, too, and now she's gone. Come now! Take something to ease your conscience.'

'I don't drink just now, thanks,' said Trysdale.

'Your brandy,' resumed the other, coming over and joining him, 'is abominable. Run down to see me some time at Punta Redonda, and try some of our stuff that old Garcia smuggles in. It's worth the, trip. Hallo! Here's an old acquaintance. Wherever did you rake up this cactus, Trysdale?'

'A present,' said Trysdale, 'from a friend. Know the species?'

'Very well. It's a tropical concern. See hundreds of 'em around Punta every day. Here's the name on this tag tied to it. Know any Spanish, Trysdale?'

'No,' said Trysdale, with the bitter wraith of a smile—'Is it Spanish?'

'Yes. The natives imagine the leaves are reaching out and beckoning to you. They call it by this name—Ventomarme. Name means in English, 'Come and take me.'

THE LAST LEAF

O. Henry

In a little district west of Washington Square the streets have run crazy and broken themselves into small strips called 'places'. These 'places' make strange angles and curves. One street crosses itself a time or two. An artist once discovered a valuable possibility in this street. Suppose a collector with a bill for paints, paper and canvas should, in traversing this route, suddenly meet himself coming back, without a cent having been paid on account!

So, to quaint old Greenwich Village the art people soon came prowling, hunting for north windows and eighteenth-century gables and Dutch attics and low rents. Then they imported some pewter mugs and a chafing dish or two from Sixth avenue, and became a 'colony'.

At the top of a squatty, three-story brick Sue and Johnsy had their studio. 'Johnsy' was familiar for Joanna. One was from Maine; the other from California. They had met at the *table d'hote* of an Eighth street 'Delmonico's', and found their tastes in art, chicory salad and bishop sleeves so congenial that the joint studio resulted.

That was in May. In November a cold, unseen stranger, whom the doctors called Pneumonia, stalked about the colony, touching one here and there with his icy fingers. Over on the east side this ravager strode boldly, smiting his victims by scores, but his feet trod slowly through the maze of the narrow and moss-grown 'places.'

Mr Pneumonia was not what you would call a chivalric old gentleman. A mite of a little woman with blood thinned by California zephyrs was hardly fair game for the red-fisted, short-breathed old duffer. But Johnsy he smote; and she lay, scarcely moving, on her painted iron bedstead, looking through the small Dutch window-panes at the blank side of the next brick house.

One morning the busy doctor invited Sue into the hallway with a shaggy, grey eyebrow.

'She has one chance in—let us say, ten,' he said, as he shook down the mercury in his clinical thermometer. 'And that chance is for her to want to live. This way people have of lining-up on the side of the undertaker makes the entire pharmacopeia look silly. Your little lady has made up her mind that she's not going to get well. Has she anything on her mind?'

'She—she wanted to paint the Bay of Naples someday,' said Sue.

'Paint?—bosh! Has she anything on her mind worth thinking about twice—a man, for instance?'

'A man?' said Sue, with a jew's-harp twang in her voice. 'Is a man worth—but, no, doctor; there is nothing of the kind.'

'Well, it is the weakness, then,' said the doctor. 'I will do all that science, so far as it may filter through my efforts, can accomplish. But whenever my patient begins to count the carriages in her funeral procession I subtract 50 per cent from the curative power of medicines. If you will get her to ask one question about the new winter styles in cloak sleeves I will promise you a one-in-five chance for her, instead of one in ten.'

After the doctor had gone Sue went into the workroom and cried a Japanese napkin to a pulp. Then she swaggered into Johnsy's room with her drawing board, whistling ragtime.

Johnsy lay, scarcely making a ripple under the bedclothes, with her face toward the window. Sue stopped whistling, thinking she was asleep.

She arranged her board and began a pen-and-ink drawing to illustrate a magazine story. Young artists must pave their way to Art by drawing pictures for magazine stories that young authors write to pave their way to Literature.

As Sue was sketching a pair of elegant horseshow riding trousers and a monocle on the figure of the hero, an Idaho cowboy, she heard a low sound, several times repeated. She went quickly to the bedside.

Johnsy's eyes were open wide. She was looking out the window and counting—counting backward.

'Twelve,' she said, and a little later 'eleven'; and then 'ten' and 'nine'; and then 'eight' and 'seven', almost together.

Sue looked solicitously out the window. What was there to count? There was only a bare, dreary yard to be seen, and the blank side of the brick house twenty feet away. An old, old ivy vine, gnarled and decayed at the roots, climbed half way up the brick wall. The cold breath of autumn had stricken its leaves from the vine until its skeleton branches clung, almost bare, to the crumbling bricks.

'What is it, dear?' asked Sue.

'Six,' said Johnsy, in almost a whisper. 'They're falling faster now. Three days ago there were almost a hundred. It made my head ache to count them. But now it's easy. There goes another one. There are only five left now.'

'Five what, dear. Tell your Sudie.'

'Leaves. On the ivy vine. When the last one falls I must go, too. I've known that for three days. Didn't the doctor tell you?'

'Oh, I never heard of such nonsense,' complained Sue, with magnificent scorn. 'What have old ivy leaves to do with your getting well? And you used to love that vine so, you naughty girl. Don't be a goosey. Why, the doctor told me this morning that your chances for getting well real soon were—let's see exactly what he said—he said the chances were ten to one! Why, that's almost as good a chance as we have in New York when we ride on the street cars or walk past a new building. Try to take some broth now, and let Sudie go back to her drawing, so she can sell the editor man with it, and buy port wine for her sick child, and pork chops for her greedy self.'

'You needn't get any more wine,' said Johnsy, keeping her eyes fixed out the window. 'There goes another. No, I don't want any broth. That leaves just four. I want to see the last one fall before it gets dark. Then I'll go, too.'

'Johnsy, dear,' said Sue, bending over her, 'will you promise me to keep your eyes closed, and not look out the window until I am done working? I must hand those drawings in by to-morrow. I need the light, or I would draw the shade down.'

'Couldn't you draw in the other room?' asked Johnsy, coldly.

'I'd rather be here by you,' said Sue. 'Besides I don't want you to keep looking at those silly ivy leaves.'

'Tell me as soon as you have finished,' said Johnsy, closing her eyes, and lying white and still as a fallen statue, 'because I want to see the last one fall. I'm tired of waiting. I'm tired of thinking. I want to turn loose my hold on everything, and go sailing down, down, just like one of those poor, tired leaves.'

'Try to sleep,' said Sue. 'I must call Behrman up to be my model for the old hermit miner. I'll not be gone a minute. Don't try to move 'till I come back.'

Old Behrman was a painter who lived on the ground floor beneath them. He was past sixty and had a Michael Angelo's Moses beard curling down from the head of a satyr along the body of an imp. Behrman was a failure in art. Forty years he had wielded the brush without getting near enough to touch the hem of his Mistress's robe. He had been always about to paint a masterpiece, but had never yet begun it. For several years he had painted nothing except now and then a daub in the line of commerce or advertising. He earned a little by serving as a model to those young artists in the colony who could not pay the price of a professional. He drank gin to excess, and still talked of his coming masterpiece. For the rest he was a fierce little old man, who scoffed terribly at softness in any one, and who regarded himself as especial mastiff-in-waiting to protect the two young artists in the studio above.

Sue found Behrman smelling strongly of juniper berries in his dimly lighted den below. In one corner was a blank canvas on an easel that had been waiting there for twenty-five years to receive the first line of the masterpiece. She told him of Johnsy's fancy, and how she feared she would, indeed, light and fragile as a leaf herself, float away when her slight hold upon the world grew weaker.

Old Behrman, with his red eyes, plainly streaming, shouted his contempt and derision for such idiotic imaginings.

'Vass!' he cried. 'Is dere people in de world mit der foolishness to die because leafs dey drop off from a confounded vine? I haf not heard of such a thing. No, I will not bose as a model for your fool hermit-dunderhead. Vy do you allow dot silly pusiness to come in der prain of her? Ach, dot poor lettle Miss Johnsy.'

'She is very ill and weak,' said Sue, 'and the fever has left her mind morbid and full of strange fancies. Very well, Mr Behrman, if you do not care to pose for me, you needn't. But I think you are a horrid old—old flibbertigibbet.'

'You are just like a woman!' yelled Behrman. 'Who said I will not bose? Go on. I come mit you. For half an hour I haf peen trying to say dot I am ready to bose. Gott! dis is not any blace in which one so goot as Miss Yohnsy shall lie sick. Someday I vill baint a masterpiece, and ve shall all go away. Gott! yes.'

Johnsy was sleeping when they went upstairs. Sue pulled the shade down to the window-sill, and motioned Behrman into the other room. In there they peered out the window fearfully at the ivy vine. Then they looked at each other for a moment without speaking. A persistent, cold rain was falling, mingled with snow. Behrman, in his old blue shirt, took his seat as the hermit-miner on an upturned kettle for a rock.

When Sue awoke from an hour's sleep the next morning she found Johnsy with dull, wide-open eyes staring at the drawn green shade.

'Pull it up; I want to see,' she ordered, in a whisper.

Wearily Sue obeyed.

But, lo! after the beating rain and fierce gusts of wind that had endured through the livelong night, there yet stood out against the brick wall one ivy leaf. It was the last on the vine. Still dark green near its stem, but with its serrated edges tinted with the yellow of dissolution and decay, it hung bravely from a branch some twenty feet above the ground.

'It is the last one,' said Johnsy. 'I thought it would surely fall during the night. I heard the wind. It will fall to-day, and I shall die at the same time.'

'Dear, dear!' said Sue, leaning her worn face down to the pillow, 'think of me, if you won't think of yourself. What would I do?'

But Johnsy did not answer. The lonesomest thing in all the world is a soul when it is making ready to go on its mysterious, far journey. The fancy seemed to possess her more strongly as one by one the ties that bound her to friendship and to earth were loosed.

The day wore away, and even through the twilight they could see the lone ivy leaf clinging to its stem against the wall. And then, with the coming of the night the north wind was again loosed, while the rain still beat against the windows and pattered down from the low Dutch eaves.

When it was light enough Johnsy, the merciless, commanded that the shade be raised.

The ivy leaf was still there.

Johnsy lay for a long time looking at it. And then she called to Sue, who was stirring her chicken broth over the gas stove.

'I've been a bad girl, Sudie,' said Johnsy. 'Something has made that last leaf stay there to show me how wicked I was. It is a sin to want to die. You may bring me a little broth now, and some milk with a little port in it, and—no; bring me a hand-mirror first, and then pack some pillows about me, and I will sit up and watch you cook.'

An hour later she said.

'Sudie, someday I hope to paint the Bay of Naples.'

The doctor came in the afternoon, and Sue had an excuse to go into the hallway as he left.

'Even chances,' said the doctor, taking Sue's thin, shaking hand in his. 'With good nursing you'll win. And now I must see another case I have downstairs. Behrman, his name is—some kind of an artist, I believe. Pneumonia, too. He is an old, weak man, and the attack is acute. There is no hope for him; but he goes to the hospital to-day to be made more comfortable.'

The next day the doctor said to Sue, 'She's out of danger. You've won. Nutrition and care now—that's all.'

And that afternoon Sue came to the bed where Johnsy lay, contentedly knitting a very blue and very useless woollen shoulder scarf, and put one arm around her, pillows and all.

'I have something to tell you, white mouse,' she said. 'Mr Behrman died of pneumonia to-day in the hospital. He was ill only two days. The janitor found him on the morning of the first day in his room downstairs helpless with pain. His shoes and clothing were wet through and icy cold. They couldn't imagine where he had been on such a dreadful night. And then they found a lantern, still lighted, and a ladder that had been dragged from its place, and some scattered brushes, and a palette with green and yellow colours mixed on it, and—look out the window, dear, at the last ivy leaf on the wall. Didn't you wonder why it never fluttered or moved when the wind blew? Ah, darling, it's Behrman's masterpiece—he painted it there the night that the last leaf fell.'

A FABLE

Mark Twain

Once upon a time an artist who had painted a small and very beautiful picture placed it so that he could see it in the mirror. He said, 'This doubles the distance and softens it, and it is twice as lovely as it was before.'

The animals out in the woods heard of this through the housecat, who was greatly admired by them because he was so learned, and so refined and civilized, and so polite and high-bred, and could tell them so much which they didn't know before, and were not certain about afterward.

They were much excited about this new piece of gossip, and they asked questions, so as to get at a full understanding of it. They asked what a picture was, and the cat explained.

'It is a flat thing,' he said. 'Wonderfully flat, marvellously flat, enchantingly flat and elegant. And, oh, so beautiful!'

That excited them almost to a frenzy, and they said they would give the world to see it. Then the bear asked, 'What is it that makes it so beautiful?'

'It is the looks of it,' said the cat.

This filled them with admiration and uncertainty, and they were more excited than ever. Then the cow asked, 'What is a mirror?'

'It is a hole in the wall,' said the cat. 'You look in it, and there you see the picture, and it is so dainty and charming and ethereal and inspiring in its unimaginable beauty that your head turns round and round, and you almost swoon with ecstasy.'

The ass had not said anything as yet; he now began to throw doubts. He said there had never been anything as beautiful as this before, and probably wasn't now. He said that when it took a whole basketful of sesquipedalian adjectives to whoop up a thing of beauty, it was time for suspicion.

It was easy to see that these doubts were having an effect upon the animals, so the cat went off offended. The subject was dropped for a couple of days, but in the meantime curiosity was taking a fresh start, and there was a revival of interest perceptible. Then the animals assailed the ass for spoiling what could possibly have been a pleasure to them, on a mere suspicion that the picture was not beautiful, without any evidence that such was the case. The ass was not troubled; he was calm, and said there was one way to find out who was in the right, himself or the cat: he would go and look in that hole, and come back and tell what he found there. The animals felt relieved and grateful, and asked him to go at once—which he did.

But he did not know where he ought to stand; and so, through error, he stood between the picture and the mirror. The result was that the picture had no chance, and didn't show up. He returned home and said, 'The cat lied. There was nothing in that hole but an ass. There wasn't a sign of a flat thing visible. It was a handsome ass, and friendly, but just an ass, and nothing more.'

The elephant asked, 'Did you see it good and clear? Were you close to it?'

'I saw it good and clear, O Hathi, King of Beasts. I was so close that I touched noses with it.'

'This is very strange,' said the elephant; 'the cat was always truthful before—as far as we could make out. Let another witness try. Go, Baloo, look in the hole, and come and report.'

So the bear went. When he came back, he said, 'Both the cat and the ass have lied; there was nothing in the hole but a bear.'

Great was the surprise and puzzlement of the animals. Each was now anxious to make the test himself and get at the straight truth. The elephant sent them one at a time.

First, the cow. She found nothing in the hole but a cow.

The tiger found nothing in it but a tiger.

The lion found nothing in it but a lion.

The leopard found nothing in it but a leopard.

The camel found a camel, and nothing more.

Then Hathi was wroth, and said he would have the truth, if he had to go and fetch it himself. When he returned, he abused his whole subjectry for liars, and was in an unappeasable fury with the moral and mental blindness of the cat. He said that anybody but a near-sighted fool could see that there was nothing in the hole but an elephant.

MORAL, BY THE CAT

You can find in a text whatever you bring, if you will stand between it and the mirror of your imagination. You may not see your ears, but they will be there.

HUNTING THE DECEITFUL TURKEY

Mark Twain

When I was a boy my uncle and his big boys hunted with the rifle, the youngest boy Fred and I with a shotgun—a small single-barrelled shotgun which was properly suited to our size and strength; it was not much heavier than a broom. We carried it turnabout, half an hour at a time.

I was not able to hit anything with it, but I liked to try. Fred and I hunted feathered small game, the others hunted deer, squirrels, wild turkeys, and such things. My uncle and the big boys were good shots. They killed hawks and wild geese and such like on the wing; and they didn't wound or kill squirrels, they stunned them. When the dogs treed a squirrel, the squirrel would scamper aloft and run out on a limb and flatten himself along it, hoping to make himself invisible in that way—and not quite succeeding. You could see his wee little ears sticking up. You couldn't see his nose, but you knew where it was. Then the hunter, despising a 'rest' for his rifle, stood up and took offhand aim at the limb and sent a bullet into it immediately under the squirrel's nose, and down tumbled the animal, unwounded, but unconscious; the dogs gave him a shake and he was dead. Sometimes when the distance was great and the wind not accurately allowed for, the bullet would hit the squirrel's head; the dogs could do as they pleased with that one—the hunter's pride was hurt, and he wouldn't allow it to go into the game bag.

In the first faint grey of the dawn the stately wild turkeys would be stalking around in great flocks, and ready to be sociable and answer invitations to come and converse with other excursionists of their kind. The hunter concealed himself and imitated the turkey-call by sucking the air through the leg-bone of a turkey which had previously answered a call like that and lived only just long enough to regret it. There is nothing that furnishes a perfect turkey-call except that bone. Another of Nature's treacheries, you see. She is full of them; half the time she doesn't know which she likes best—to betray her child or protect it. In the case of the turkey she is badly mixed: she gives it a bone to be used in getting it into trouble, and she also furnishes it with a trick for getting itself out of the trouble again. When a mamma-turkey answers an invitation and finds she has made a mistake in accepting it, she does as the mamma-partridge does—remembers a previous engagement—and goes limping and scrambling away, pretending to be very lame; and at the same time she is saying to her not-visible children, 'Lie low, keep still, don't expose yourselves; I shall be back as soon as I have beguiled this shabby swindler out of the country.'

When a person is ignorant and confiding, this immoral device can have tiresome results. I followed an ostensibly lame turkey over a considerable part of the United States one morning, because I believed in her and could not think she would deceive a mere boy, and one who was trusting her and considering her honest. I had the single-barrelled shotgun, but my idea was to catch her alive. I often got within rushing distance of her, and then made my rush; but always, just as I made my final plunge and put my hand down where her back had been, it wasn't there; it was only two or three inches from there and I brushed the tail-feathers as I landed on my stomach—a very close call, but still not quite close enough; that is, not close enough for success, but just close enough to convince me that I could do it next time. She always waited for me, a little piece away, and let on to be resting and greatly fatigued; which was a lie, but I believed it, for I still thought her honest long after I ought to have begun to doubt her, suspecting that this was no way for a high-minded bird to be acting. I followed, and followed, and followed, making my periodical rushes, and getting up and brushing the dust off, and resuming the voyage with patient confidence; indeed, with a confidence which grew, for I could see by the change of climate and vegetation that we were getting up into the high latitudes, and as she always looked a little tireder and a little more discouraged after each rush, I judged that I was safe to win, in the end, the competition being purely a matter of staying power and the advantage lying with me from the start because she was lame.

Along in the afternoon I began to feel fatigued myself. Neither of us had had any rest since we first started on the excursion, which was upwards of ten hours before, though latterly we had paused awhile after rushes, I letting on to be thinking about something else; but neither of us sincere, and both of us waiting for the other to call game but in no real hurry about it, for indeed those little evanescent snatches of rest were very grateful to the feelings of us both; it would naturally be so, skirmishing along like that ever since dawn and not a bite in the meantime; at least for me, though sometimes as she lay on her side fanning herself with a wing and praying for strength to get out of this difficulty a grasshopper happened along whose time had come, and that was well for her, and fortunate, but I had nothing—nothing the whole day.

More than once, after I was very tired, I gave up taking her alive, and was going to shoot her, but I never did it, although it was my right, for I did not believe I could hit her; and besides, she always stopped and posed, when I raised the gun, and this made me suspicious that she knew about me and my marksmanship, and so I did not care to expose myself to remarks.

I did not get her, at all. When she got tired of the game at last, she rose from almost under my hand and flew aloft with the rush and whir of a shell and lit on the highest limb of a great tree and sat down and crossed her legs and smiled down at me, and seemed gratified to see me so astonished.

I was ashamed, and also lost; and it was while wandering the woods hunting for myself that I found a deserted log cabin and had one of the best meals there that in my life-days I have eaten. The weed-grown garden was full of ripe tomatoes, and I ate them ravenously, though I had never liked them before. Not more than two or three times since have I tasted anything that was so delicious as those tomatoes. I surfeited myself with them, and did not taste another one until I was in middle life. I can eat them now, but I do not like the look of them. I suppose we have all experienced a surfeit at one time or another. Once, in stress of circumstances, I ate part of a barrel of sardines, there being nothing else at hand, but since then I have always been able to get along without sardines.

THE MCWILLIAMSES AND THE BURGLAR ALARM

Mark Twain

The conversation drifted smoothly and pleasantly along from weather to crops, from crops to literature, from literature to scandal, from scandal to religion; then took a random jump, and landed on the subject of burglar alarms. And now for the first time Mr McWilliams showed feeling. Whenever I perceive this sign on this man's dial, I comprehend it, and lapse into silence, and give him opportunity to unload his heart. Said he, with but ill-controlled emotion—

'I do not go one single cent on burglar alarms, Mr Twain—not a single cent—and I will tell you why. When we were finishing our house, we found we had a little cash left over, on account of the plumber not knowing it. I was for enlightening the heathen with it, for I was always unaccountably down on the heathen somehow; but Mrs McWilliams said no, let's have a burglar alarm. I agreed to this compromise. I will explain that whenever I want a thing, and Mrs McWilliams wants another thing, and we decide upon the thing that Mrs McWilliams wants—as we always do—she calls that a compromise. Very well, the man came up from New York and put in the alarm, and charged three hundred and twenty-five dollars for it, and said we could sleep without uneasiness now. So we did for a while—say a month. Then one night we smelled smoke, and I was advised to get up and see what the matter was. I lit a candle, and started toward the stairs, and met a burglar coming out of a room with a basket of tin ware, which he had mistaken for solid silver in the dark. He was smoking a pipe. I said, "My friend, we do not allow smoking in this room." He said he was a stranger, and could not be expected to know the rules of the house, said he had been in many houses just as good as this one, and it had never been objected to before. He added that as far as his experience went, such rules had never been considered to apply to burglars, anyway.

I said, 'Smoke along, then, if it is the custom, though I think that the conceding of a privilege to a burglar which is denied to a bishop is a conspicuous sign of the looseness of the times. But waiving all that, what business have you to be entering this house in this furtive and clandestine way, without ringing the burglar alarm?'

He looked confused and ashamed, and said, with embarrassment, 'I beg a thousand pardons. I did not know you had a burglar alarm, else I would have rung it. I beg you will not mention it where my parents may hear of it, for they are old and feeble, and such a seemingly wanton breach of the hallowed conventionalities of our Christian civilization might all too rudely sunder the frail bridge which hangs darkling between the pale and evanescent present and the solemn great deeps of the eternities. May I trouble you for a match?'

I said, 'Your sentiments do you honour, but if you will allow me to say it, metaphor is not your best hold. Spare your thigh; this kind light only on the box, and seldom there, in fact, if my experience may be trusted. But to return to business: how did you get in here?'

'Through a second-story window.'

It was even so. I redeemed the tin ware at pawnbroker's rates, less cost of advertising, bade the burglar good-night, closed the window after him, and retired to headquarters to report. Next morning we sent for the burglar-alarm man, and he came up and explained that the reason the alarm did not 'go off' was that no part of the house but the first floor was attached to the alarm. This was simply idiotic; one might as well have no armour on at all in battle as to have it only on his legs. The expert now put the whole second story on the alarm, charged three hundred dollars for it, and went his way. By and by, one night, I found a burglar in the third story, about to start down a ladder with a lot of miscellaneous property. My first impulse was to crack his head with a billiard cue; but my second was to refrain from this attention, because he was between me and the cue rack. The second impulse was plainly the soundest, so I refrained, and proceeded to compromise. I redeemed the property at former rates, after deducting ten per cent. for use of ladder, it being my ladder, and, next day we sent down for the expert once more, and had the third story attached to the alarm, for three hundred dollars.

By this time the 'annunciator' had grown to formidable dimensions.

It had forty-seven tags on it, marked with the names of the various rooms and chimneys, and it occupied the space of an ordinary wardrobe. The gong was the size of a wash-bowl, and was placed above the head of our bed. There was a wire from the house to the coachman's quarters in the stable, and a noble gong alongside his pillow.

We should have been comfortable now but for one defect. Every morning at five the cook opened the kitchen door, in the way of business, and rip went that gong! The first time this happened I thought the last day was come sure. I didn't think it in bed—no, but out of it—for the first effect of that frightful gong is to hurl you across the house, and slam you against the wall, and then curl you up, and squirm you like a spider on a stove lid, till somebody shuts the kitchen door. In solid fact, there is no clamour that is even remotely comparable to the dire clamour which that gong makes. Well, this catastrophe happened every morning regularly at five o'clock, and lost us three hours sleep; for, mind you, when that thing wakes you, it doesn't merely wake you in spots; it wakes you all over, conscience and all, and you are good for eighteen hours of wide-awakeness subsequently—eighteen hours of the very most inconceivable wide-awakeness that you ever experienced in your life. A stranger died on our hands one time, and we vacated and left him in our room overnight. Did that stranger wait for the general judgment? No, sir; he got up at five the next morning in the most prompt and unostentatious way. I knew he would; I knew it mighty well. He collected his life-insurance, and lived happy ever after, for there was plenty of proof as to the perfect squareness of his death.

Well, we were gradually fading toward a better land, on account of the daily loss of sleep; so we finally had the expert up again, and he ran a wire to the outside of the door, and placed a switch there, whereby Thomas, the butler, always made one little mistake—he switched the alarm off at night when he went to bed, and switched it on again at daybreak in the morning, just in time for the cook to open the kitchen door, and enable that gong to slam us across the house, sometimes breaking a window with one or the other of us. At the end of a week we recognized that this switch business was a delusion and a snare. We also discovered that a band of burglars had been lodging in the house the whole time—not exactly to steal, for there wasn't much left now, but to hide from the police, for they were hot pressed, and they shrewdly judged that the detectives would never think of a tribe of burglars taking sanctuary in a house notoriously protected by the most imposing and elaborate burglar alarm in America.

Sent down for the expert again, and this time he struck a most dazzling idea—he fixed the thing so that opening the kitchen door would take off the alarm. It was a noble idea, and he charged accordingly. But you already foresee the result. I switched on the alarm every night at bed-time, no longer trusting on Thomas's frail memory; and as soon as the lights were out the burglars walked in at the kitchen door, thus taking the alarm off without waiting for the cook to do it in the morning. You see how aggravatingly we were situated. For months we couldn't have any company. Not a spare bed in the house; all occupied by burglars.

Finally, I got up a cure of my own. The expert answered the call, and ran another ground wire to the stable, and established a switch there, so that the coachman could put on and take off the alarm. That worked first rate, and a season of peace ensued, during which we got to inviting company once more and enjoying life.

But by and by the irrepressible alarm invented a new kink. One winter's night we were flung out of bed by the sudden music of that awful gong, and when we hobbled to the annunciator, turned up the gas, and saw the word 'Nursery' exposed, Mrs McWilliams fainted dead away, and I came precious near doing the same thing myself. I seized my shotgun, and stood timing the coachman whilst that appalling buzzing went on. I knew that his gong had flung him out, too, and that he would be along with his gun as soon as he could jump into his clothes. When I judged that the time was ripe, I crept to the room next the nursery, glanced through the window, and saw the dim outline of the coachman in the yard below, standing at present-arms and waiting for a chance. Then I hopped into the nursery and fired, and in the same instant the coachman fired at the red flash of my gun. Both of us were successful; I crippled a nurse, and he shot off all my back hair. We turned up the gas, and telephoned for a surgeon. There was not a sign of a burglar, and no window had been raised. One glass was absent, but that was where the coachman's charge had come through. Here was a fine mystery—a burglar alarm 'going off' at midnight of its own accord, and not a burglar in the neighbourhood!

The expert answered the usual call, and explained that it was a 'False alarm.' Said it was easily fixed. So he overhauled the nursery window, charged a remunerative figure for it, and departed.

What we suffered from false alarms for the next three years no stylographic pen can describe. During the next three months I always flew with my gun to the room indicated, and the coachman always sallied forth with his battery to support me. But there was never anything to shoot at—windows all tight and secure. We always sent down for the expert next day, and he fixed those particular windows so they would keep quiet a week or so, and always remembered to send us a bill about like this:

Wire	$2.15
Nipple	$0.75
Two hours' labour	$1.50
Wax	$0.47
Tape	$0.34
Screws	$0.15
Recharging battery	$0.98
Three hours' labour	$2.25
String	$0.02
Lard	$0.66
Pond's Extract	$1.25
Springs at 50	$2.00
Railroad fares	$7.25

At length a perfectly natural thing came about—after we had answered three or four hundred false alarms—to wit, we stopped answering them. Yes, I simply rose up calmly, when slammed across the house by the alarm, calmly inspected the annunciator, took note of the room indicated; and then calmly disconnected that room from the alarm, and went back to bed as if nothing had happened. Moreover, I left that room off permanently, and did not send for the expert. Well, it goes without saying that in the course of time all the rooms were taken off, and the entire machine was out of service.

It was at this unprotected time that the heaviest calamity of all happened. The burglars walked in one night and carried off the burglar alarm! Yes, sir, every hide and hair of it—ripped it out, tooth and nail; springs, bells, gongs, battery, and all; they took a hundred and fifty miles of copper wire; they just cleaned her out, bag and baggage, and never left us a vestige of her to swear at—swear by, I mean.

We had a time of it to get her back; but we accomplished it finally, for money. The alarm firm said that what we needed now was to have her put in right—with their new patent springs in the windows to make false alarms impossible, and their new patent clock attached to take off and put on the alarm morning and night without human assistance. That seemed a good scheme. They promised to have the whole thing finished in ten days. They began work, and we left for the summer. They worked a couple of days; then they left for the summer. After which the burglars moved in, and began their summer vacation. When we returned in the fall, the house was as empty as a beer closet in premises where painters have been at work. We refurnished, and then sent down to hurry up the expert. He came up and finished the job, and said, 'Now this clock is set to put on the alarm every night at 10, and take it off every morning at 5:45. All you've got to do is to wind her up every week, and then leave her alone—she will take care of the alarm herself.'

After that we had a most tranquil season during three months. The bill was prodigious, of course, and I had said I would not pay it until the new machinery had proved itself to be flawless. The time stipulated was three months. So I paid the bill, and the very next day the alarm went to buzzing like ten thousand bee swarms at ten o'clock in the morning. I turned the hands around twelve hours, according to instructions, and this took off the alarm; but there was another hitch at night, and I had to set her ahead twelve hours once more to get her to put the alarm on again. That sort of nonsense went on a week or two, then the expert came up and put in a new clock. He came up every three months during the next three years, and put in a new clock. But it was always a failure. His clocks all had the same perverse defect—they would put the alarm on in the daytime, and they would not put it on at night; and if you forced it on yourself, they would take it off again the minute your back was turned.

Now there is the history of that burglar alarm—everything just as it happened; nothing extenuated, and naught set down in malice. Yes, sir,—and when I had slept nine years with burglars, and maintained an expensive burglar alarm the whole time, for their protection, not mine, and at my sole cost—for not a d—d cent could I ever get THEM to contribute—I just said to Mrs McWilliams that I had had enough of that kind of pie; so with her full consent I took the whole thing out and traded it off for a dog, and shot the dog. I don't know what you think about it, Mr Twain; but I think those things are made solely in the interest of the burglars. Yes, sir, a burglar alarm combines in its person all that is objectionable about a fire, a riot, and a harem, and at the same time had none of the compensating advantages, of one sort or another, that customarily belong with that combination. Good-by, I get off here.

WIT INSPIRATIONS OF THE 'TWO-YEAR-OLDS'

Mark Twain

All infants appear to have an impertinent and disagreeable fashion nowadays of saying 'smart' things on most occasions that offer, and especially on occasions when they ought not to be saying anything at all. Judging by the average published specimens of smart sayings, the rising generation of children are little better than idiots. And the parents must surely be but little better than the children, for in most cases they are the publishers of the sunbursts of infantile imbecility which dazzle us from the pages of our periodicals. I may seem to speak with some heat, not to say a suspicion of personal spite; and I do admit that it nettles me to hear about so many gifted infants in these days, and remember that I seldom said anything smart when I was a child. I tried it once or twice, but it was not popular. The family was not expecting brilliant remarks from me, and so they snubbed me sometimes and spanked me the rest. But it makes my flesh creep and my blood run cold to think what might have happened to me if I had dared to utter some of the smart things of this generation's 'four-year-olds' where my father could hear me. To have simply skinned me alive and considered his duty at an end would have seemed to him criminal leniency toward one so sinning. He was a stern, unsmiling man, and hated all forms of precocity. If I had said some of the things I have referred to, and said them in his hearing, he would have destroyed me. He would, indeed. He would, provided the opportunity remained with him. But it would not, for I would have had judgment enough to take some strychnine first and say my smart thing afterward. The fair record of my life has been tarnished by just one pun. My father overheard that, and he hunted me over four or five townships seeking to take my life. If I had been full-grown, of course he would have been right; but, child as I was, I could not know how wicked a thing I had done.

I made one of those remarks ordinarily called 'smart things' before that, but it was not a pun. Still, it came near causing a serious rupture between my father and myself. My father and mother, my uncle Ephraim and his wife, and one or two others were present, and the conversation turned on a name for me. I was lying there trying some India-rubber rings of various patterns, and endeavouring to make a selection, for I was tired of trying to cut my teeth on people's fingers, and wanted to get hold of something that would enable me to hurry the thing through and get something else. Did you ever notice what a nuisance it was cutting your teeth on your nurse's finger, or how back-breaking and tiresome it was trying to cut them on your big toe? And did you never get out of patience and wish your teeth were in Jerico long before you got them half cut? To me it seems as if these things happened yesterday. And they did, to some children. But I digress. I was lying there trying the India-rubber rings. I remember looking at the clock and noticing that in an hour and twenty-five minutes I would be two weeks old, and thinking how little I had done to merit the blessings that were so unsparingly lavished upon me.

My father said, 'Abraham is a good name. My grandfather was named Abraham.'

My mother said, 'Abraham is a good name. Very well. Let us have Abraham for one of his names.'

I said, 'Abraham suits the subscriber.'

My father frowned, my mother looked pleased; my aunt said, 'What a little darling it is!'

My father said, 'Isaac is a good name, and Jacob is a good name.'

My mother assented, and said, 'No names are better. Let us add Isaac and Jacob to his names.'

I said, 'All right. Isaac and Jacob are good enough for yours truly. Pass me that rattle, if you please. I can't chew India-rubber rings all day.'

Not a soul made a memorandum of these sayings of mine, for publication. I saw that, and did it myself, else they would have been utterly lost. So far from meeting with a generous encouragement like other children when developing intellectually, I was now furiously scowled upon by my father; my mother looked grieved and anxious, and even my aunt had about her an expression of seeming to think that maybe I had gone too far. I took a vicious bite out of an India-rubber ring, and covertly broke the rattle over the kitten's head, but said nothing.

Presently my father said, 'Samuel is a very excellent name.'

I saw that trouble was coming. Nothing could prevent it. I laid down my rattle; over the side of the cradle I dropped my uncle's silver watch, the clothes-brush, the toy dog, my tin soldier, the nutmeg-grater, and other matters which I was accustomed to examine, and meditate upon and make pleasant noises with, and bang and batter and break when I needed wholesome entertainment. Then I put on my little frock and my little bonnet, and took my pygmy shoes in one hand and my liquorice in the other, and climbed out on the floor. I said to myself, Now, if the worse comes to worst, I am ready.

Then I said aloud, in a firm voice, 'Father, I cannot, cannot wear the name of Samuel.'

'My son!'

'Father, I mean it. I cannot.'

'Why?'

'Father, I have an invincible antipathy to that name.'

'My son, this is unreasonable. Many great and good men have been named Samuel.'

'Sir, I have yet to hear of the first instance.'

'What! There was Samuel the prophet. Was not he great and good?'

'Not so very.'

'My son! With His own voice the Lord called him.'

'Yes, sir, and had to call him a couple times before he could come!'

And then I sallied forth, and that stern old man sallied forth after me. He overtook me at noon the following day, and when the interview was over I had acquired the name of Samuel, and a thrashing, and other useful information; and by means of this compromise my father's wrath was appeased and a misunderstanding bridged over which might have become a permanent rupture if I had chosen to be unreasonable. But just judging by this episode, what would my father have done to me if I had ever uttered in his hearing one of the flat, sickly things these 'two-years-olds' say in print nowadays? In my opinion there would have been a case of infanticide in our family.

THE LUMBER ROOM

H.H. Munro (SAKI)

The children were to be driven, as a special treat, to the sands at Jagborough. Nicholas was not to be of the party; he was in disgrace. Only that morning he had refused to eat his wholesome bread-and-milk on the seemingly frivolous ground that there was a frog in it. Older and wiser and better people had told him that there could not possibly be a frog in his bread-and-milk and that he was not to talk nonsense; he continued, nevertheless, to talk what seemed the veriest nonsense, and described with much detail the colouration and markings of the alleged frog. The dramatic part of the incident was that there really was a frog in Nicholas' basin of bread-and-milk; he had put it there himself, so he felt entitled to know something about it. The sin of taking a frog from the garden and putting it into a bowl of wholesome bread-and-milk was enlarged on at great length, but the fact that stood out clearest in the whole affair, as it presented itself to the mind of Nicholas, was that the older, wiser, and better people had been proved to be profoundly in error in matters about which they had expressed the utmost assurance.

'You said there couldn't possibly be a frog in my bread-and-milk; there *was* a frog in my bread-and-milk,' he repeated, with the insistence of a skilled tactician who does not intend to shift from favourable ground.

So his boy-cousin and girl-cousin and his quite uninteresting younger brother were to be taken to Jagborough sands that afternoon and he was to stay at home. His cousins' aunt, who insisted, by an unwarranted stretch of imagination, in styling herself his aunt also, had hastily invented the Jagborough expedition in order to impress on Nicholas the delights that he had justly forfeited by his disgraceful conduct at the breakfast-table. It was her habit, whenever one of the children fell from grace, to improvise something of a festival nature from which the offender would be rigorously debarred; if all the children sinned collectively they were suddenly informed of a circus in a neighbouring town, a circus of unrivalled merit and uncounted elephants, to which, but for their depravity, they would have been taken that very day.

A few decent tears were looked for on the part of Nicholas when the moment for the departure of the expedition arrived. As a matter of fact, however, all the crying was done by his girl-cousin, who scraped her knee rather painfully against the step of the carriage as she was scrambling in.

'How she did howl,' said Nicholas cheerfully, as the party drove off without any of the elation of high spirits that should have characterised it.

'She'll soon get over that,' said the *soi-disant* aunt. 'It will be a glorious afternoon for racing about over those beautiful sands. How they will enjoy themselves!'

'Bobby won't enjoy himself much, and he won't race much either,' said Nicholas with a grim chuckle; his boots are hurting him. They're too tight.'

'Why didn't he tell me they were hurting?' asked the aunt with some asperity.

'He told you twice, but you weren't listening. You often don't listen when we tell you important things.'

'You are not to go into the gooseberry garden,' said the aunt, changing the subject.

'Why not?' demanded Nicholas.

'Because you are in disgrace,' said the aunt loftily.

Nicholas did not admit the flawlessness of the reasoning; he felt perfectly capable of being in disgrace and in a gooseberry garden at the same moment. His face took on an expression of considerable obstinacy. It was clear to his aunt that he was determined to get into the gooseberry garden, 'only', as she remarked to herself, 'because I have told him he is not to.'

Now the gooseberry garden had two doors by which it might be entered, and once a small person like Nicholas could slip in there he could effectually disappear from view amid the masking growth of artichokes, raspberry canes, and fruit bushes. The aunt had many other things to do that afternoon, but she spent an hour or two in trivial gardening operations among flower beds and shrubberies, whence she could keep a watchful eye on the two doors that led to the forbidden paradise.

She was a woman of few ideas, with immense powers of concentration.

Nicholas made one or two sorties into the front garden, wriggling his way with obvious stealth of purpose towards one or other of the doors, but never able for a moment to evade the aunt's watchful eye. As a matter of fact, he had no intention of trying to get into the gooseberry garden, but it was extremely convenient for him that his aunt should believe that he had; it was a belief that would keep her on self-imposed sentry-duty for the greater part of the afternoon. Having thoroughly confirmed and fortified her suspicions Nicholas slipped back into the house and rapidly put into execution a plan of action that had long germinated in his brain. By standing on a chair in the library one could reach a shelf on which reposed a fat, important-looking key. The key was as important as it looked; it was the instrument which kept the mysteries of the lumber-room secure from unauthorized intrusion, which opened a way only for aunts and such-like privileged persons. Nicholas had not had much experience of the art of fitting keys into keyholes and turning locks, but for some days past he had practised with the key of the schoolroom door; he did not believe in trusting too much to luck and accident. The key turned stiffly in the lock, but it turned. The door opened, and Nicholas was in an unknown land, compared with which the gooseberry garden was a stale delight, a mere material pleasure.

Often and often Nicholas had pictured to himself what the lumber-room might be like, that region that was so carefully sealed from youthful eyes and concerning which no questions were ever answered. It came up to his expectations. In the first place it was large and dimly lit, one high window opening on to the forbidden garden being its only source of illumination. In the second place it was a storehouse of unimagined treasures. The aunt-by-assertion was one of those people who think that things spoil by use and consign them to dust and damp by way of preserving them. Such parts of the house as Nicholas knew best were rather bare and cheerless, but here there were wonderful things for the eye to feast on. First and foremost there was a piece of framed tapestry that was evidently meant to be a fire-screen. To Nicholas it was a living, breathing story; he sat down on a roll of Indian hangings, glowing in wonderful colours beneath a layer of dust, and took in all the details of the tapestry picture. A man, dressed in the hunting costume of some remote period, had just transfixed a stag with an arrow; it could not have been a difficult shot because the stag was only one or two paces away from him; in the thickly-growing vegetation that the picture suggested it would not have been difficult to creep up to a feeding stag, and the two spotted dogs that were springing forward to join in the chase had evidently been trained to keep to heel till the arrow was discharged. That part of the picture was simple, if interesting, but did the huntsman see, what Nicholas saw, that four galloping wolves were coming in his direction through the wood? There might be more than four of them hidden behind the trees, and in any case would the man and his dogs be able to cope with the four wolves if they made an attack? The man had only two arrows left in his quiver, and he might miss with one or both of them; all one knew about his skill in shooting was that he could hit a large stag at a ridiculously short range. Nicholas sat for many golden minutes revolving the possibilities of the scene; he was inclined to think that there were more than four wolves and that the man and his dogs were in a tight corner.

But there were other objects of delight and interest claiming his instant attention. There were quaint twisted candlesticks in the shape of snakes, and a teapot fashioned like a china duck, out of whose open beak the tea was supposed to come. How dull and shapeless the nursery teapot seemed in comparison! And there was a carved sandal-wood box packed tight with aromatic cotton wool, and between the layers of cotton wool were little brass figures, hump-necked bulls, and peacocks and goblins, delightful to see and to handle. Less promising in appearance was a large square book with plain black covers; Nicholas peeped into it, and, behold, it was full of coloured pictures of birds. And such birds! In the garden, and in the lanes when he went for a walk, Nicholas came across a few birds, of which the largest were an occasional magpie or wood-pigeon; here were herons and bustards, kites, toucans, tiger-bitterns, brush turkeys, ibises, golden pheasants, a whole portrait gallery of undreamed-of creatures. And as he was admiring the colouring of the mandarin duck and assigning a life-history to it, the voice of his aunt in shrill vociferation of his name came from the gooseberry garden without. She had grown suspicious at his long disappearance, and had leapt to the conclusion that he had climbed over the wall behind the sheltering screen of the lilac bushes; she was now engaged in energetic and rather hopeless search for him among the artichokes and raspberry canes.

'Nicholas, Nicholas!' she screamed, 'you are to come out of this at once. It's no use trying to hide there; I can see you all the time.'

It was probably the first time for twenty years that anyone had smiled in that lumber-room.

Presently the angry repetitions of Nicholas' name gave way to a shriek, and a cry for somebody to come quickly. Nicholas shut the book, restored it carefully to its place in a corner, and shook some dust from a neighbouring pile of newspapers over it. Then he crept from the room, locked the door, and replaced the key exactly where he had found it. His aunt was still calling his name when he sauntered into the front garden.

'Who's calling?' he asked.

'Me,' came the answer from the other side of the wall; 'didn't you hear me? I've been looking for you in the gooseberry garden, and I've slipped into the rain-water tank. Luckily there's no water in it, but the sides are slippery and I can't get out. Fetch the little ladder from under the cherry tree…'

'I was told I wasn't to go into the gooseberry garden,' said Nicholas promptly.

'I told you not to, and now I tell you that you may,' came the voice from the rain-water tank, rather impatiently.

'Your voice doesn't sound like aunt's,' objected Nicholas. 'You may be the Evil One tempting me to be disobedient. Aunt often tells me that the Evil One tempts me and that I always yield. This time I'm not going to yield.'

'Don't talk nonsense,' said the prisoner in the tank. 'Go and fetch the ladder.'

'Will there be strawberry jam for tea?' asked Nicholas innocently.

'Certainly there will be,' said the aunt, privately resolving that

Nicholas should have none of it.

'Now I know that you are the Evil One and not aunt,' shouted Nicholas gleefully. 'When we asked aunt for strawberry jam yesterday she said there wasn't any. I know there are four jars of it in the store cupboard, because I looked, and of course you know it's there, but she doesn't, because she said there wasn't any. Oh, Devil, you *have* sold yourself!'

There was an unusual sense of luxury in being able to talk to an aunt as though one was talking to the Evil One, but Nicholas knew, with childish discernment, that such luxuries were not to be over-indulged in. He walked noisily away, and it was a kitchen maid, in search of parsley, who eventually rescued the aunt from the rain-water tank.

Tea that evening was partaken of in a fearsome silence. The tide had been at its highest when the children had arrived at Jagborough Cove, so there had been no sands to play on—a circumstance that the aunt had overlooked in the haste of organising her punitive expedition. The tightness of Bobby's boots had had disastrous effect on his temper the whole of the afternoon, and altogether the children could not have been said to have enjoyed themselves. The aunt maintained the frozen muteness of one who has suffered undignified and unmerited detention in a rain-water tank for thirty-five minutes. As for Nicholas, he, too, was silent, in the absorption of one who has much to think about; it was just possible, he considered, that the huntsman would escape with his hounds while the wolves feasted on the stricken stag.

THE OPEN WINDOW

H.H. Munro (SAKI)

'Out through that window, three years ago to a day, her husband and her two young brothers went off for their day's shooting. They never came back.'

'My aunt will be down presently, Mr Nuttel,' said a very self-possessed young lady of fifteen. 'In the meantime you must try and put up with me.'

Framton Nuttel endeavoured to say the correct something which should duly flatter the niece of the moment without unduly discounting the aunt that was to come. Privately he doubted more than ever whether these formal visits on a succession of total strangers would do much towards helping the nerve cure which he was supposed to be undergoing

'I know how it will be,' his sister had said when he was preparing to migrate to this rural retreat; 'you will bury yourself down there and not speak to a living soul, and your nerves will be worse than ever from moping. I shall just give you letters of introduction to all the people I know there. Some of them, as far as I can remember, were quite nice.'

Framton wondered whether Mrs Sappleton, the lady to whom he was presenting one of the letters of introduction came into the nice division.

'Do you know many of the people round here?' asked the niece, when she judged that they had had sufficient silent communion.

'Hardly a soul,' said Framton. 'My sister was staying here, at the rectory, you know, some four years ago, and she gave me letters of introduction to some of the people here.'

He made the last statement in a tone of distinct regret.

'Then you know practically nothing about my aunt?' pursued the self-possessed young lady.

'Only her name and address,' admitted the caller. He was wondering whether Mrs Sappleton was in the married or widowed state. An undefinable something about the room seemed to suggest masculine habitation.

'Her great tragedy happened just three years ago,' said the child. 'That would be since your sister's time.'

'Her tragedy?' asked Framton; somehow in this restful country spot tragedies seemed out of place.

'You may wonder why we keep that window wide open on an October afternoon,' said the niece, indicating a large French window that opened on to a lawn.

'It is quite warm for the time of the year,' said Framton. 'But has that window got anything to do with the tragedy?'

'Out through that window, three years ago to a day, her husband and her two young brothers went off for their day's shooting. They never came back. In crossing the moor to their favourite snipe-shooting ground they were all three engulfed in a treacherous piece of bog. It had been that dreadful wet summer, you know, and places that were safe in other years gave way suddenly without warning. Their bodies were never recovered. That was the dreadful part of it.' Here the child's voice lost its self-possessed note and became falteringly human. 'Poor aunt always thinks that they will come back someday, they and the little brown spaniel that was lost with them, and walk in at that window just as they used to do. That is why the window is kept open every evening till it is quite dusk. Poor dear aunt, she has often told me how they went out, her husband with his white waterproof coat over his arm, and Ronnie, her youngest brother, singing "Bertie, why do you bound?" as he always did to tease her, because she said it got on her nerves. Do you know, sometimes on still, quiet evenings like this, I almost get a creepy feeling that they will all walk in through that window—'

She broke off with a little shudder. It was a relief to Framton when the aunt bustled into the room with a whirl of apologies for being late in making her appearance.

'I hope Vera has been amusing you?' she said.

'She has been very interesting,' said Framton.

'I hope you don't mind the open window,' said Mrs Sappleton briskly. 'My husband and brothers will be home directly from shooting, and they always come in this way. They've been out for snipe in the marshes today, so they'll make a fine mess over my poor carpets. So like you menfolk, isn't it?'

She rattled on cheerfully about the shooting and the scarcity of birds, and the prospects for duck in the winter. To Framton it was all purely horrible. He made a desperate but only partially successful effort to turn the talk on to a less ghastly topic, he was conscious that his hostess was giving him only a fragment of her attention, and her eyes were constantly straying past him to the open window and the lawn beyond. It was certainly an unfortunate coincidence that he should have paid his visit on this tragic anniversary.

'The doctors agree in ordering me complete rest, an absence of mental excitement, and avoidance of anything in the nature of violent physical exercise,' announced Framton, who laboured under the tolerably widespread delusion that total strangers and chance acquaintances are hungry for the least detail of one's ailments and infirmities, their cause and cure. 'On the matter of diet they are not so much in agreement,' he continued.

'No?' said Mrs Sappleton, in a voice which only replaced a yawn at the last moment. Then she suddenly brightened into alert attention—but not to what Framton was saying.

'Here they are at last!' she cried. 'Just in time for tea, and don't they look as if they were muddy up to the eyes!'

Framton shivered slightly and turned towards the niece with a look intended to convey sympathetic comprehension. The child was staring out through the open window with a dazed horror in her eyes. In a chill shock of nameless fear Framton swung round in his seat and looked in the same direction.

In the deepening twilight three figures were walking across the lawn towards the window, they all carried guns under their arms, and one of them was additionally burdened with a white coat hung over his shoulders. A tired brown spaniel kept close at their heels. Noiselessly they neared the house, and then a hoarse young voice chanted out of the dusk: 'I said, Bertie, why do you bound?'

Framton grabbed wildly at his stick and hat; the hall door, the gravel drive, and the front gate were dimly noted stages in his headlong retreat. A cyclist coming along the road had to run into the hedge to avoid imminent collision.

'Here we are, my dear,' said the bearer of the white mackintosh, coming in through the window, 'fairly muddy, but most of it's dry. Who was that who bolted out as we came up?'

'A most extraordinary man, a Mr Nuttel,' said Mrs Sappleton. 'Could only talk about his illnesses, and dashed off without a word of goodbye or apology when you arrived. One would think he had seen a ghost.'

'I expect it was the spaniel,' said the niece calmly. 'He told me he had a horror of dogs. He was once hunted into a cemetery somewhere on the banks of the Ganges by a pack of pariah dogs, and had to spend the night in a newly dug grave with the creatures snarling and grinning and foaming just above him. Enough to make anyone lose their nerve.'

Romance at short notice was her speciality.

THE PHANTOM LUNCHEON

H.H. Munro (SAKI)

'The Smithly-Dubbs are in Town,' said Sir James. 'I wish you would show them some attention. Ask them to lunch with you at the Ritz or somewhere.'

'From the little I've seen of the Smithly-Dubbs I don't thing I want to cultivate their acquaintance,' said Lady Drakmanton.

'They always work for us at election times,' said her husband. 'I don't suppose they influence very many votes, but they have an uncle who is on one of my ward committees, and another uncle speaks sometimes at some of our less important meetings. Those sort of people expect some return in the shape of hospitality.'

'Expect it!' exclaimed Lady Drakmanton. 'The Misses Smithly-Dubb do more than that; they almost demand it. They belong to my club, and hang about the lobby just about lunch-time, all three of them, with their tongues hanging out of their mouths and the six-course look in their eyes. If I were to breathe the word "lunch" they would hustle me into a taxi and scream "Ritz" or "Dieudonne's" to the driver before I knew what was happening.'

'All the same, I think you ought to ask them to a meal of some sort,' persisted Sir James.

'I consider that showing hospitality to the Smithly-Dubbs is carrying Free Food principles to a regrettable extreme,' said Lady Drakmanton. 'I've entertained the Joneses and the Browns and the Snapheimers and the Lubrikoffs, and heaps of others whose names I forget, but I don't see why I should inflict the society of the Misses Smithly-Dubb on myself for a solid hour. Imagine it, sixty minutes, more or less, of unrelenting gobble and gabble. Why can't you take them on, Milly?' she asked, turning hopefully to her sister.

'I don't know them,' said Milly hastily.

'All the better; you can pass yourself off as me. People say that we are so alike that they can hardly tell us apart, and I've only spoken to these tiresome young women about twice in my life, at committee-rooms, and bowed to them in the club. Any of the club page-boys will point them out to you; they're always to be found lolling about the hall just before lunch-time.'

'My dear Betty, don't be absurd,' protested Milly. 'I've got some people lunching with me at the Carlton to-morrow, and I'm leaving Town the day afterwards.'

'What time is your lunch to-morrow?' asked Lady Drakmanton reflectively.

'Two o'clock,' said Milly.

'Good,' said her sister. 'The Smithly-Dubbs shall lunch with me to-morrow. It shall be rather an amusing lunch-party. At least, I shall be amused.'

The last two remarks she made to herself. Other people did not always appreciate her ideas of humour. Sir James never did.

The next day Lady Drakmanton made some marked variations in her usual toilet effects. She dressed her hair in an unaccustomed manner, and put on a hat that added to the transformation of her appearance. When she had made one or two minor alterations she was sufficiently unlike her usual smart self to produce some hesitation in the greeting which the Misses Smithly-Dubb bestowed on her in the club-lobby. She responded, however, with a readiness which set their doubts at rest.

'What is the Carlton like for lunching in?' she asked breezily.

The restaurant received an enthusiastic recommendation from the three sisters.

'Let's go and lunch there, shall we?' she suggested, and in a few minutes' time the Smithly-Dubb mind was contemplating at close quarters a happy vista of baked meats and approved vintage.

'Are you going to start with caviar? I am,' confided Lady Drakmanton, and the Smithly-Dubbs started with caviar. The subsequent dishes were chosen in the same ambitious spirit, and by the time they had arrived at the wild duck course it was beginning to be a rather expensive lunch.

The conversation hardly kept pace with the brilliancy of the menu. Repeated references on the part of the guests to the local political conditions and prospects in Sir James's constituency were met with vague 'ahs' and 'indeeds' from Lady Drakmanton, who might have been expected to be specially interested.

'I think when the Insurance Act is a little better understood it will lose some of its present unpopularity,' hazarded Cecilia Smithly-Dubb.

'Will it? I dare say. I'm afraid politics don't interest me very much,' said Lady Drakmanton.

The three Miss Smithly-Dubbs put down their cups of Turkish coffee and stared. Then they broke into protesting giggles.

'Of course, you're joking,' they said.

'Not me,' was the disconcerting answer; 'I can't make head or tail of these bothering old politics. Never could, and never want to. I've quite enough to do to manage my own affairs, and that's a fact.'

'But,' exclaimed Amanda Smithly-Dubb, with a squeal of bewilderment breaking into her voice, 'I was told you spoke so informingly about the Insurance Act at one of our social evenings.'

It was Lady Drakmanton who stared now. 'Do you know,' she said, with a scared look around her, 'rather a dreadful thing is happening. I'm suffering from a complete loss of memory. I can't even think who I am. I remember meeting you somewhere, and I remember you asking me to come and lunch with you here, and that I accepted your kind invitation. Beyond that my mind is a positive blank.'

The scared look was transferred with intensified poignancy to the faces of her companions.

'You asked us to lunch,' they exclaimed hurriedly. That seemed a more immediately important point to clear up than the question of identity.

'Oh, no,' said the vanishing hostess, 'that I do remember about. You insisted on my coming here because the feeding was so good, and I must say it comes up to all you said about it. A very nice lunch it's been. What I'm worrying about is who on earth am I? I haven't the faintest notion?'

'You are Lady Drakmanton,' exclaimed the three sisters in chorus.

'Now, don't make fun of me,' she replied, crossly, 'I happen to know her quite well by sight, and she isn't a bit like me. And it's an odd thing you should have mentioned her, for it so happens she's just come into the room. That lady in black, with the yellow plume in her hat, there over by the door.'

The Smithly-Dubbs looked in the indicated direction, and the uneasiness in their eyes deepened into horror. In outward appearance the lady who had just entered the room certainly came rather nearer to their recollection of their Member's wife than the individual who was sitting at table with them.

'Who are you, then, if that is Lady Drakmanton?' they asked in panic-stricken bewilderment.

'That is just what I don't know,' was the answer; 'and you don't seem to know much better than I do.'

'You came up to us in the club—'

'In what club?'

'The New Didactic, in Calais Street.'

'The New Didactic!' exclaimed Lady Drakmanton with an air of returning illumination. 'Thank you so much. Of course, I remember now who I am. I'm Ellen Niggle, of the Ladies' Brasspolishing Guild. The Club employs me to come now and then and see to the polishing of the brass fittings. That's how I came to know Lady Drakmanton by sight; she's very often in the Club. And you are the ladies who so kindly asked me out to lunch. Funny how it should all have slipped my memory, all of a sudden. The unaccustomed good food and wine must have been too much for me; for the moment I really couldn't call to mind who I was. Good gracious,' she broke off suddenly, 'it's ten past two; I should be at a polishing job in Whitehall. I must scuttle off like a giddy rabbit. Thanking you ever so.'

She left the room with a scuttle sufficiently suggestive of the animal she had mentioned, but the giddiness was all on the side of her involuntary hostesses. The restaurant seemed to be spinning round them; and the bill when it appeared did nothing to restore their composure. They were as nearly in tears as it is permissible to be during the luncheon hour in a really good restaurant. Financially speaking, they were well able to afford the luxury of an elaborate lunch, but their ideas on the subject of entertaining differed very sharply, according to the circumstances of whether they were dispensing or receiving hospitality. To have fed themselves liberally at their own expense was, perhaps, an extravagance to be deplored, but, at any rate, they had had something for their money; to have drawn an unknown and socially unremunerative Ellen Niggle into the net of their hospitality was a catastrophe that they could not contemplate with any degree of calmness.

The Smithly-Dubbs never quite recovered from their unnerving experience. They have given up politics and taken to doing good.

DUSK

H.H. Munro (SAKI)

Norman Gortsby sat on a bench in the Park, with his back to a strip of bush-planted sward, fenced by the park railings, and the Row fronting him across a wide stretch of carriage drive. Hyde Park Corner, with its rattle and hoot of traffic, lay immediately to his right. It was some thirty minutes past six on an early March evening, and dusk had fallen heavily over the scene, dusk mitigated by some faint moonlight and many street lamps. There was a wide emptiness over road and sidewalk, and yet there were many unconsidered figures moving silently through the half-light, or dotted unobtrusively on bench and chair, scarcely to be distinguished from the shadowed gloom in which they sat.

The scene pleased Gortsby and harmonised with his present mood. Dusk, to his mind, was the hour of the defeated. Men and women, who had fought and lost, who hid their fallen fortunes and dead hopes as far as possible from the scrutiny of the curious, came forth in this hour of gloaming, when their shabby clothes and bowed shoulders and unhappy eyes might pass unnoticed, or, at any rate, unrecognized.

A king that is conquered must see strange looks, So bitter a thing is the heart of man.

The wanderers in the dusk did not choose to have strange looks fasten on them, therefore they came out in this bat-fashion, taking their pleasure sadly in a pleasure-ground that had emptied of its rightful occupants. Beyond the sheltering screen of bushes and palings came a realm of brilliant lights and noisy, rushing traffic. A blazing, many-tiered stretch of windows shone through the dusk and almost dispersed it, marking the haunts of those other people, who held their own in life's struggle, or at any rate had not had to admit failure. So Gortsby's imagination pictured things as he sat on his bench in the almost deserted walk. He was in the mood to count himself among the defeated. Money troubles did not press on him; had he so wished he could have strolled into the thoroughfares of light and noise, and taken his place among the jostling ranks of those who enjoyed prosperity or struggled for it. He had failed in a more subtle ambition, and for the moment he was heart sore and disillusioned, and not disinclined to take a certain cynical pleasure in observing and labelling his fellow wanderers as they went their ways in the dark stretches between the lamp-lights.

On the bench by his side sat an elderly gentleman with a drooping air of defiance that was probably the remaining vestige of self-respect in an individual who had ceased to defy successfully anybody or anything. His clothes could scarcely be called shabby, at least they passed muster in the half-light, but one's imagination could not have pictured the wearer embarking on the purchase of a half-crown box of chocolates or laying out nine pence on a carnation buttonhole. He belonged unmistakably to that forlorn orchestra to whose piping no one dances; he was one of the world's lamenters who induce no responsive weeping. As he rose to go Gortsby imagined him returning to a home circle where he was snubbed and of no account, or to some bleak lodging where his ability to pay a weekly bill was the beginning and end of the interest he inspired. His retreating figure vanished slowly into the shadows, and his place on the bench was taken almost immediately by a young man, fairly well dressed but scarcely more cheerful of mien than his predecessor. As if to emphasize the fact that the world went badly with him the new-corner unburdened himself of an angry and very audible expletive as he flung himself into the seat.

'You don't seem in a very good temper,' said Gortsby, judging that he was expected to take due notice of the demonstration.

The young man turned to him with a look of disarming frankness which put him instantly on his guard.

'You wouldn't be in a good temper if you were in the fix I'm in,' he said; 'I've done the silliest thing I've ever done in my life.'

'Yes?' said Gortsby dispassionately.

'Came up this afternoon, meaning to stay at the Patagonian Hotel in Berkshire Square,' continued the young man; 'when I got there I found it had been pulled down some weeks ago and a cinema theatre run up on the site. The taxi driver recommended me to another hotel some way off and I went there. I just sent a letter to my people, giving them the address, and then I went out to buy some soap—I'd forgotten to pack any and I hate using hotel soap. Then I strolled about a bit, had a drink at a bar and looked at the shops, and when I came to turn my steps back to the hotel I suddenly realized that I didn't remember its name or even what street it was in. There's a nice predicament for a fellow who hasn't any friends or connections in London! Of course I can wire to my people for the address, but they won't have got my letter till to-morrow; meantime I'm without any money, came out with about a shilling on me, which went in buying the soap and getting the drink, and here I am, wandering about with two pence in my pocket and nowhere to go for the night.'

There was an eloquent pause after the story had been told. 'I suppose you think I've spun you rather an impossible yarn,' said the young man presently, with a suggestion of resentment in his voice.

'Not at all impossible,' said Gortsby judicially; 'I remember doing exactly the same thing once in a foreign capital, and on that occasion there were two of us, which made it more remarkable. Luckily we remembered that the hotel was on a sort of canal, and when we struck the canal we were able to find our way back to the hotel.'

The youth brightened at the reminiscence. 'In a foreign city I wouldn't mind so much,' he said; 'one could go to one's Consul and get the requisite help from him. Here in one's own land one is far more derelict if one gets into a fix. Unless I can find some decent chap to swallow my story and lend me some money I seem likely to spend the night on the Embankment. I'm glad, anyhow, that you don't think the story outrageously improbable.'

He threw a good deal of warmth into the last remark, as though perhaps to indicate his hope that Gortsby did not fall far short of the requisite decency.

'Of course,' said Gortsby slowly, 'the weak point of your story is that you can't produce the soap.'

The young man sat forward hurriedly, felt rapidly in the pockets of his overcoat, and then jumped to his feet.

'I must have lost it,' he muttered angrily.

'To lose an hotel and a cake of soap on one afternoon suggests wilful carelessness,' said Gortsby, but the young man scarcely waited to hear the end of the remark. He flitted away down the path, his head held high, with an air of somewhat jaded jauntiness.

'It was a pity,' mused Gortsby. 'The going out to get one's own soap was the one convincing touch in the whole story, and yet it was just that little detail that brought him to grief. If he had had the brilliant forethought to provide himself with a cake of soap, wrapped and sealed with all the solicitude of the chemist's counter, he would have been a genius in his particular line. In his particular line genius certainly consists of an infinite capacity for taking precautions.'

With that reflection Gortsby rose to go; as he did so an exclamation of concern escaped him. Lying on the ground by the side of the bench was a small oval packet, wrapped and sealed with the solicitude of a chemist's counter. It could be nothing else but a cake of soap, and it had evidently fallen out of the youth's overcoat pocket when he flung himself down on the seat. In another moment Gortsby was scudding along the dusk-shrouded path in anxious quest for a youthful figure in a light overcoat. He had nearly given up the search when he caught sight of the object of his pursuit standing irresolutely on the border of the carriage drive, evidently uncertain whether to strike across the Park or make for the bustling pavements of Knightsbridge. He turned round sharply with an air of defensive hostility when he found Gortsby hailing him.

'The important witness to the genuineness of your story has turned up,' said Gortsby, holding out the cake of soap. 'It must have slid out of your overcoat pocket when you sat down on the seat. I saw it on the ground after you left. You must excuse my disbelief, but appearances were really rather against you, and now, as I appealed to the testimony of the soap I think I ought to abide by its verdict. If the loan of a sovereign is any good to you...'

The young man hastily removed all doubt on the subject by pocketing the coin.

'Here is my card with my address,' continued Gortsby. 'Any day this week will do for returning the money, and here is the soap—don't lose it again it's been a good friend to you.'

'Lucky thing your finding it,' said the youth, and then, with a catch in his voice, he blurted out a word or two of thanks and fled headlong in the direction of Knightsbridge.

'Poor boy, he as nearly as possible broke down,' said Gortsby to himself. 'I don't wonder either; the relief from his quandary must have been acute. It's a lesson to me not to be too clever in judging by circumstances.'

As Gortsby retraced his steps past the seat where the little drama had taken place he saw an elderly gentleman poking and peering beneath it and on all sides of it, and recognized his earlier fellow occupant.

'Have you lost anything, sir?' he asked.

'Yes, sir, a cake of soap.'

THE NECKLACE

Guy de Maupassant

The girl was one of those pretty and charming young creatures who sometimes are born, as if by a slip of fate, into a family of clerks. She had no dowry, no expectations, no way of being known, understood, loved, married by any rich and distinguished man; so she let herself be married to a little clerk of the Ministry of Public Instruction.

She dressed plainly because she could not dress well, but she was unhappy as if she had really fallen from a higher station; since with women there is neither caste nor rank, for beauty, grace and charm take the place of family and birth. Natural ingenuity, instinct for what is elegant, a supple mind are their sole hierarchy, and often make of women of the people the equals of the very greatest ladies.

Mathilde suffered ceaselessly, feeling herself born to enjoy all delicacies and all luxuries. She was distressed at the poverty of her dwelling, at the bareness of the walls, at the shabby chairs, the ugliness of the curtains. All those things, of which another woman of her rank would never even have been conscious, tortured her and made her angry. The sight of the little Breton peasant who did her humble housework aroused in her despairing regrets and bewildering dreams. She thought of silent antechambers hung with Oriental tapestry, illumined by tall bronze candelabra, and of two great footmen in knee breeches who sleep in the big armchairs, made drowsy by the oppressive heat of the stove. She thought of long reception halls hung with ancient silk, of the dainty cabinets containing priceless curiosities and of the little coquettish perfumed reception rooms made for chatting at five o'clock with intimate friends, with men famous and sought after, whom all women envy and whose attention they all desire.

When she sat down to dinner, before the round table covered with a tablecloth in use three days, opposite her husband, who uncovered the soup tureen and declared with a delighted air, 'Ah, the good soup! I don't know anything better than that,' she thought of dainty dinners, of shining silverware, of tapestry that peopled the walls with ancient personages and with strange birds flying in the midst of a fairy forest; and she thought of delicious dishes served on marvellous plates and of the whispered gallantries to which you listen with a sphinx-like smile while you are eating the pink meat of a trout or the wings of a quail.

She had no gowns, no jewels, nothing. And she loved nothing but that. She felt made for that. She would have liked so much to please, to be envied, to be charming, to be sought after.

She had a friend, a former schoolmate at the convent, who was rich, and whom she did not like to go to see any more because she felt so sad when she came home.

But one evening her husband reached home with a triumphant air and holding a large envelope in his hand.

'There,' said he, 'there is something for you.'

She tore the paper quickly and drew out a printed card which bore these words:

The Minister of Public Instruction and Madame Georges Ramponneau request the honour of M. and Madame Loisel's company at the palace of the Ministry on Monday evening, January 18th.

Instead of being delighted, as her husband had hoped, she threw the invitation on the table crossly, muttering, 'What do you wish me to do with that?'

'Why, my dear, I thought you would be glad. You never go out, and this is such a fine opportunity. I had great trouble to get it. Everyone wants to go; it is very select, and they are not giving many invitations to clerks. The whole official world will be there.'

She looked at him with an irritated glance and said impatiently, 'And what do you wish me to put on my back?'

He had not thought of that. He stammered, 'Why, the gown you go to the theatre in. It looks very well to me.'

He stopped, distracted, seeing that his wife was weeping. Two great tears ran slowly from the corners of her eyes toward the corners of her mouth.

'What's the matter? What's the matter?' he answered.

By a violent effort she conquered her grief and replied in a calm voice, while she wiped her wet cheeks, 'Nothing. Only I have no gown, and, therefore, I can't go to this ball. Give your card to some colleague whose wife is better equipped than I am.'

He was in despair. He resumed, 'Come, let us see, Mathilde. How much would it cost, a suitable gown, which you could use on other occasions—something very simple?'

She reflected several seconds, making her calculations and wondering also what sum she could ask without drawing on herself an immediate refusal and a frightened exclamation from the economical clerk.

Finally she replied hesitating, 'I don't know exactly, but I think I could manage it with four hundred francs.'

He grew a little pale, because he was laying aside just that amount to buy a gun and treat himself to a little shooting next summer on the plain of Nanterre, with several friends who went to shoot larks there of a Sunday.

But he said, 'Very well. I will give you four hundred francs. And try to have a pretty gown.'

The day of the ball drew near and Madame Loisel seemed sad, uneasy, anxious. Her frock was ready, however. Her husband said to her one evening, 'What is the matter? Come, you have seemed very queer these last three days.'

And she answered, 'It annoys me not to have a single piece of jewellery, not a single ornament, nothing to put on. I shall look poverty-stricken. I would almost rather not go at all.'

'You might wear natural flowers,' said her husband. 'They're very stylish at this time of year. For ten francs you can get two or three magnificent roses.'

She was not convinced.

'No; there's nothing more humiliating than to look poor among other women who are rich.'

'How stupid you are!' her husband cried. 'Go look up your friend, Madame Forestier, and ask her to lend you some jewels. You're intimate enough with her to do that.'

She uttered a cry of joy, 'True! I never thought of it.'

The next day she went to her friend and told her of her distress.

Madame Forestier went to a wardrobe with a mirror, took out a large jewel box, brought it back, opened it and said to Madame Loisel, 'Choose, my dear.'

She saw first some bracelets, then a pearl necklace, then a Venetian gold cross set with precious stones, of admirable workmanship. She tried on the ornaments before the mirror, hesitated and could not make up her mind to part with them, to give them back. She kept asking, 'Haven't you anymore?'

'Why, yes. Look further; I don't know what you like.'

Suddenly she discovered, in a black satin box, a superb diamond necklace, and her heart throbbed with an immoderate desire. Her hands trembled as she took it. She fastened it round her throat, outside her high-necked waist, and was lost in ecstasy at her reflection in the mirror.

Then she asked, hesitating, filled with anxious doubt, 'Will you lend me this, only this?'

'Why, yes, certainly.'

She threw her arms round her friend's neck, kissed her passionately, then fled with her treasure.

The night of the ball arrived. Madame Loisel was a great success. She was prettier than any other woman present, elegant, graceful, smiling and wild with joy. All the men looked at her, asked her name, sought to be introduced. All the attaches of the Cabinet wished to waltz with her. She was remarked by the minister himself.

She danced with rapture, with passion, intoxicated by pleasure, forgetting all in the triumph of her beauty, in the glory of her success, in a sort of cloud of happiness comprised of all this homage, admiration, these awakened desires and of that sense of triumph which is so sweet to woman's heart.

She left the ball about four o'clock in the morning. Her husband had been sleeping since midnight in a little deserted anteroom with three other gentlemen whose wives were enjoying the ball.

He threw over her shoulders the wraps he had brought, the modest wraps of common life, the poverty of which contrasted with the elegance of the ball dress. She felt this and wished to escape so as not to be remarked by the other women, who were enveloping themselves in costly furs.

Loisel held her back, saying, 'Wait a bit. You will catch cold outside. I will call a cab.'

But she did not listen to him and rapidly descended the stairs. When they reached the street they could not find a carriage and began to look for one, shouting after the cabmen passing at a distance.

They went toward the Seine in despair, shivering with cold. At last they found on the quay one of those ancient night cabs which, as though they were ashamed to show their shabbiness during the day, are never seen round Paris until after dark.

It took them to their dwelling in the Rue des Martyrs, and sadly they mounted the stairs to their flat. All was ended for her. As to him, he reflected that he must be at the ministry at ten o'clock that morning.

She removed her wraps before the glass so as to see herself once more in all her glory. But suddenly she uttered a cry. She no longer had the necklace around her neck!

'What is the matter with you?' demanded her husband, already half undressed.

She turned distractedly toward him.

'I have—I have—I've lost Madame Forestier's necklace,' she cried.

He stood up, bewildered.

'What!—how? Impossible!'

They looked among the folds of her skirt, of her cloak, in her pockets, everywhere, but did not find it.

'You're sure you had it on when you left the ball?' he asked.

'Yes, I felt it in the vestibule of the minister's house.'

'But if you had lost it in the street we should have heard it fall. It must be in the cab.'

'Yes, probably. Did you take his number?'

'No. And you—didn't you notice it?'

'No.'

They looked, thunderstruck, at each other. At last Loisel put on his clothes.

'I shall go back on foot,' said he, 'over the whole route, to see whether I can find it.'

He went out. She sat waiting on a chair in her ball dress, without strength to go to bed, overwhelmed, without any fire, without a thought.

Her husband returned about seven o'clock. He had found nothing.

He went to police headquarters, to the newspaper offices to offer a reward; he went to the cab companies—everywhere, in fact, whither he was urged by the least spark of hope.

She waited all day, in the same condition of mad fear before this terrible calamity.

Loisel returned at night with a hollow, pale face. He had discovered nothing.

'You must write to your friend,' said he, 'that you have broken the clasp of her necklace and that you are having it mended. That will give us time to turn round.'

She wrote at his dictation.

At the end of a week they had lost all hope. Loisel, who had aged five years, declared, 'We must consider how to replace that ornament.'

The next day they took the box that had contained it and went to the jeweller whose name was found within. He consulted his books.

'It was not I, Madame, who sold that necklace; I must simply have furnished the case.'

Then they went from jeweller to jeweller, searching for a necklace like the other, trying to recall it, both sick with chagrin and grief.

They found, in a shop at the Palais Royal, a string of diamonds that seemed to them exactly like the one they had lost. It was worth forty thousand francs. They could have it for thirty-six.

So they begged the jeweller not to sell it for three days yet. And they made a bargain that he should buy it back for thirty-four thousand francs, in case they should find the lost necklace before the end of February.

Loisel possessed eighteen thousand francs which his father had left him. He would borrow the rest.

He did borrow, asking a thousand francs of one, five hundred of another, five louis here, three louis there. He gave notes, took up ruinous obligations, dealt with usurers and all the race of lenders. He compromised all the rest of his life, risked signing a note without even knowing whether he could meet it; and, frightened by the trouble yet to come, by the black misery that was about to fall upon him, by the prospect of all the physical privations and moral tortures that he was to suffer, he went to get the new necklace, laying upon the jeweller's counter thirty-six thousand francs.

When Madame Loisel took back the necklace Madame Forestier said to her with a chilly manner, 'You should have returned it sooner; I might have needed it.'

She did not open the case, as her friend had so much feared. If she had detected the substitution, what would she have thought, what would she have said? Would she not have taken Madame Loisel for a thief?

Thereafter Madame Loisel knew the horrible existence of the needy. She bore her part, however, with sudden heroism. That dreadful debt must be paid. She would pay it. They dismissed their servant; they changed their lodgings; they rented a garret under the roof.

She came to know what heavy housework meant and the odious cares of the kitchen. She washed the dishes, using her dainty fingers and rosy nails on greasy pots and pans. She washed the soiled linen, the shirts and the dishcloths, which she dried upon a line; she carried the slops down to the street every morning and carried up the water, stopping for breath at every landing. And dressed like a woman of the people, she went to the fruiterer, the grocer, the butcher, a basket on her arm, bargaining, meeting with impertinence, defending her miserable money, sou by sou.

Every month they had to meet some notes, renew others, obtain more time.

Her husband worked evenings, making up a tradesman's accounts, and late at night he often copied manuscript for five sous a page.

This life lasted ten years.

At the end of ten years they had paid everything, everything, with the rates of usury and the accumulations of the compound interest.

Madame Loisel looked old now. She had become the woman of impoverished households—strong and hard and rough. With frowsy hair, skirts askew and red hands, she talked loud while washing the floor with great swishes of water. But sometimes, when her husband was at the office, she sat down near the window and she thought of that gay evening of long ago, of that ball where she had been so beautiful and so admired.

What would have happened if she had not lost that necklace? Who knows? who knows? How strange and changeful is life! How small a thing is needed to make or ruin us!

But one Sunday, having gone to take a walk in the Champs Elysees to refresh herself after the labours of the week, she suddenly perceived a woman who was leading a child. It was Madame Forestier, still young, still beautiful, still charming.

Madame Loisel felt moved. Should she speak to her? Yes, certainly. And now that she had paid, she would tell her all about it. Why not?

She went up.

'Good-day, Jeanne.'

The other, astonished to be familiarly addressed by this plain goodwife, did not recognize her at all and stammered, 'But… Madame! … I do not know… You must have mistaken.'

'No. I am Mathilde Loisel.'

Her friend uttered a cry.

'Oh, my poor Mathilde! How you are changed!'

'Yes, I have had a pretty hard life, since I last saw you, and great poverty—and that because of you!'

'Of me! How so?'

'Do you remember that diamond necklace you lent me to wear at the ministerial ball?'

'Yes. Well?'

'Well, I lost it.'

'What do you mean? You brought it back.'

'I brought you back another exactly like it. And it has taken us ten years to pay for it. You can understand that it was not easy for us, for us who had nothing. At last it is ended, and I am very glad.'

Madame Forestier had stopped.

'You say that you bought a necklace of diamonds to replace mine?'

'Yes. You never noticed it, then! They were very similar.'

And she smiled with a joy that was at once proud and ingenuous.

Madame Forestier, deeply moved, took her hands.

'Oh, my poor Mathilde! Why, my necklace was paste! It was worth at most only five hundred francs!'

THE CHILD

Guy de Maupassant

Lemonnier had remained a widower with one child. He had loved his wife devotedly, with a tender and exalted love, without a slip, during their entire married life. He was a good, honest man, perfectly simple, sincere, without suspicion or malice.

He fell in love with a poor neighbour, proposed and was accepted. He was making a very comfortable living out of the wholesale cloth business, and he did not for a minute suspect that the young girl might have accepted him for anything else but himself.

She made him happy. She was everything to him; he only thought of her, looked at her continually, with worshiping eyes. During meals he would make any number of blunders, in order not to have to take his eyes from the beloved face; he would pour the wine in his plate and the water in the salt-cellar, then he would laugh like a child, repeating, 'You see, I love you too much; that makes me crazy.'

She would smile with a calm and resigned look; then she would look away, as though embarrassed by the adoration of her husband, and try to make him talk about something else; but he would take her hand under the table and he would hold it in his, whispering, 'My little Jeanne, my darling little Jeanne!'

She sometimes lost patience and said, 'Come, come, be reasonable; eat and let me eat.'

He would sigh and break off a mouthful of bread, which he would then chew slowly.

For five years they had no children. Then suddenly she announced to him that this state of affairs would soon cease. He was wild with joy. He no longer left her for a minute, until his old nurse, who had brought him up and who often ruled the house, would push him out and close the door behind him, in order to compel him to go out in the fresh air.

He had grown very intimate with a young man who had known his wife since childhood, and who was one of the prefect's secretaries. M. Duretour would dine three times a week with the Lemonniers, bringing flowers to madame, and sometimes a box at the theatre; and often, at the end of the dinner, Lemonnier, growing tender, turning towards his wife, would explain, 'With a companion like you and a friend like him, a man is completely happy on earth.'

She died in childbirth. The shock almost killed him. But the sight of the child, a poor, moaning little creature, gave him courage.

He loved it with a passionate and sorrowful love, with a morbid love in which stuck the memory of death, but in which lived something of his worship for the dead mother. It was the flesh of his wife, her being continued, a sort of quintessence of herself. This child was her very life transferred to another body; she had disappeared that it might exist, and the father would smother it in with kisses. But also, this child had killed her; he had stolen this beloved creature, his life was at the cost of hers. And M. Lemonnier would place his son in the cradle and would sit down and watch him. He would sit this way by the hour, looking at him, dreaming of thousands of things, sweet or sad. Then, when the little one was asleep, he would bend over him and sob.

The child grew. The father could no longer spend an hour away from him; he would stay near him, take him out for walks, and himself dress him, wash him, make him eat. His friend, M. Duretour, also seemed to love the boy; he would kiss him wildly, in those frenzies of tenderness which are characteristic of parents. He would toss him in his arms, he would trot him on his knees, by the hour, and M. Lemonnier, delighted, would mutter,

'Isn't he a darling? Isn't he a darling?'

And M. Duretour would hug the child in his arms and tickle his neck with his moustache.

Celeste, the old nurse, alone, seemed to have no tenderness for the little one. She would grow angry at his pranks, and seemed impatient at the caresses of the two men. She would exclaim:

'How can you expect to bring a child up like that? You'll make a perfect monkey out of him.'

Years went by, and Jean was nine years old. He hardly knew how to read; he had been so spoiled, and only did as he saw fit. He was wilful, stubborn and quick-tempered. The father always gave in to him and let him have his own way. M. Duretour would always buy him all the toys he wished, and he fed him on cake and candies. Then Celeste would grow angry and exclaim, 'It's a shame, monsieur, a shame. You are spoiling this child. But it will have to stop; yes, sir, I tell you it will have to stop, and before long, too.'

M. Lemonnier would answer, smiling, 'What can you expect? I love him too much, I can't resist him; you must get used to it.'

Jean was delicate, rather. The doctor said that he was anaemic, prescribed iron, rare meat and broth.

But the little fellow loved only cake and refused all other nourishment; and the father, in despair, stuffed him with cream-puffs and chocolate eclairs.

One evening, as they were sitting down to supper, Celeste brought on the soup with an air of authority and an assurance which she did not usually have. She took off the cover and, dipping the ladle into the dish, she declared, 'Here is some broth such as I have never made; the young one will have to take some this time.'

M. Lemonnier, frightened, bent his head. He saw a storm brewing.

Celeste took his plate, filled it herself and placed it in front of him.

He tasted the soup and said, 'It is, indeed, excellent.'

The servant took the boy's plate and poured a spoonful of soup in it. Then she retreated a few steps and waited.

Jean smelled the food and pushed his plate away with an expression of disgust. Celeste, suddenly pale, quickly stepped forward and forcibly poured a spoonful down the child's open mouth.

He choked, coughed, sneezed, spat; howling, he seized his glass and threw it at his nurse. She received it full in the stomach. Then, exasperated, she took the young shaver's head under her arm and began pouring spoonful after spoonful of soup down his throat. He grew as red as a beet, and he would cough it up, stamping, twisting, choking, beating the air with his hands.

At first the father was so surprised that he could not move. Then, suddenly, he rushed forward, wild with rage, seized the servant by the throat and threw her up against the wall stammering, 'Out! Out! Out! you brute!'

But she shook him off, and, her hair streaming down her back, her eyes snapping, she cried out:

'What's gettin' hold of you? You're trying to thrash me because I am making this child eat soup when you are filling him with sweet stuff!'

He kept repeating, trembling from head to foot, 'Out! Get out-get out, you brute!'

Then, wild, she turned to him and, pushing her face up against his, her voice trembling, 'Ah!—you think-you think that you can treat me like that? Oh! no. And for whom?—for that brat who is not even yours. No, not yours! No, not yours—not yours! Everybody knows it, except yourself! Ask the grocer, the butcher, the baker, all of them, any one of them!'

She was growling and mumbling, choked with passion; then she stopped and looked at him.

He was motionless livid, his arms hanging by his sides. After a short pause, he murmured in a faint, shaky voice, instinct with deep feeling, 'You say? you say? What do you say?'

She remained silent, frightened by his appearance. Once more he stepped forward, repeating, 'You say—what do you say?'

Then in a calm voice, she answered, 'I say what I know, what everybody knows.'

He seized her and, with the fury of a beast, he tried to throw her down. But, although old, she was strong and nimble. She slipped under his arm, and running around the table once more furious, she screamed, 'Look at him, just look at him, fool that you are! Isn't he the living image of M. Durefour? just look at his nose and his eyes! Are yours like that? And his hair! Is it like his mother's? I tell you that everyone knows it, everyone except yourself! It's the joke of the town! Look at him!'

She went to the door, opened it, and disappeared.

Jean, frightened, sat motionless before his plate of soup.

At the end of an hour, she returned gently, to see how matters stood. The child, after doing away with all the cakes and a pitcher full of cream and one of syrup, was now emptying the jam-pot with his soup-spoon.

The father had gone out.

Celeste took the child, kissed him, and gently carried him to his room and put him to bed. She came back to the dining-room, cleared the table, put everything in place, feeling very uneasy all the time.

Not a single sound could be heard throughout the house. She put her ear against her master's door. He seemed to be perfectly still. She put her eye to the keyhole. He was writing, and seemed very calm.

Then she returned to the kitchen and sat down, ready for any emergency. She slept on a chair and awoke at daylight.

She did the rooms as she had been accustomed to every morning; she swept and dusted, and, towards eight o'clock, prepared M. Lemonnier's breakfast.

But she did not dare bring it to her master, knowing too well how she would be received; she waited for him to ring. But he did not ring. Nine o'clock, then ten o'clock went by.

Celeste, not knowing what to think, prepared her tray and started up with it, her heart beating fast.

She stopped before the door and listened. Everything was still. She knocked; no answer. Then, gathering up all her courage, she opened the door and entered. With a wild shriek, she dropped the breakfast tray which she had been holding in her hand.

In the middle of the room, M. Lemonnier was hanging by a rope from a ring in the ceiling. His tongue was sticking out horribly. His right slipper was lying on the ground, his left one still on his foot. An upturned chair had rolled over to the bed.

Celeste, dazed, ran away shrieking. All the neighbours crowded together. The physician declared that he had died at about midnight.

A letter addressed to M. Duretdur was found on the table of the suicide. It contained these words, 'I leave and entrust the child to you!'

A WIDOW

Guy de Maupassant

This story was told during the hunting season at the Chateau Baneville. The autumn had been rainy and sad. The red leaves, instead of rustling under the feet, were rotting under the heavy downfalls.

The forest was as damp as it could be. From it came an odour of must, of rain, of soaked grass and wet earth; and the sportsmen, their backs hunched under the downpour, mournful dogs, with tails between their legs and hairs sticking to their sides, and the young women, with their clothes drenched, returned every evening, tired in body and in mind.

After dinner, in the large drawing-room, everybody played lotto, without enjoyment, while the wind whistled madly around the house. Then they tried telling stories like those they read in books, but no one was able to invent anything amusing. The hunters told tales of wonderful shots and of the butchery of rabbits; and the women racked their brains for ideas without revealing the imagination of Scheherezade. They were about to give up this diversion when a young woman, who was idly caressing the hand of an old maiden aunt, noticed a little ring made of blond hair, which she had often seen, without paying any attention to it.

She fingered it gently and asked, 'Auntie, what is this ring? It looks as if it were made from the hair of a child.'

The old lady blushed, grew pale, then answered in a trembling voice, 'It is sad, so sad that I never wish to speak of it. All the unhappiness of my life comes from that. I was very young then, and the memory has remained so painful that I weep every time I think of it.'

Immediately everybody wished to know the story, but the old lady refused to tell it. Finally, after they had coaxed her for a long time, she yielded. Here is the story: 'You have often heard me speak of the Santeze family, now extinct. I knew the last three male members of this family. They all died in the same manner; this hair belongs to the last one. He was thirteen when he killed himself for me. That seems strange to you, doesn't it?

'Oh! it was a strange family—mad, if you will, but a charming madness, the madness of love. From father to son, all had violent passions which filled their whole being, which impelled them to do wild things, drove them to frantic enthusiasm, even to crime. This was born in them, just as burning devotion is in certain souls. Trappers have not the same nature as minions of the drawing-room. There was a saying, "As passionate as a Santeze." This could be noticed by looking at them. They all had wavy hair, falling over their brows, curly beards and large eyes whose glance pierced and moved one, though one could not say why.

'The grandfather of the owner of this hair, of whom it is the last souvenir, after many adventures, duels and elopements, at about sixty-five fell madly in love with his farmer's daughter. I knew them both. She was blond, pale, distinguished-looking, with a slow manner of talking, a quiet voice and a look so gentle that one might have taken her for a Madonna. The old nobleman took her to his home and was soon so captivated with her that he could not live without her for a minute. His daughter and daughter-in-law, who lived in the chateau, found this perfectly natural, love was such a tradition in the family. Nothing in regard to a passion surprised them, and if one spoke before them of parted lovers, even of vengeance after treachery, both said in the same sad tone, "Oh, how he must have suffered to come to that point!" That was all. They grew sad over tragedies of love, but never indignant, even when they were criminal.

'Now, one day a young man named Monsieur de Gradelle, who had been invited for the shooting, eloped with the young girl.

'Monsieur de Santeze remained calm as if nothing had happened, but one morning he was found hanging in the kennels, among his dogs.

'His son died in the same manner in a hotel in Paris during a journey which he made there in 1841, after being deceived by a singer from the opera.

'He left a twelve-year-old child and a widow, my mother's sister. She came to my father's house with the boy, while we were living at Bertillon. I was then seventeen.

'You have no idea how wonderful and precocious this Santeze child was. One might have thought that all the tenderness and exaltation of the whole race had been stored up in this last one. He was always dreaming and walking about alone in a great alley of elms leading from the chateau to the forest. I watched from my window this sentimental boy, who walked with thoughtful steps, his hands behind his back, his head bent, and at times stopping to raise his eyes as if he could see and understand things that were not comprehensible at his age.

'Often, after dinner on clear evenings, he would say to me: "Let us go outside and dream, cousin." And we would go outside together in the park. He would stop quickly before a clearing where the white vapour of the moon lights the woods, and he would press my hand, saying, 'Look! look! but you don't understand me; I feel it. If you understood me, we should be happy. One must love to know! I would laugh and then kiss this child, who loved me madly.

'Often, after dinner, he would sit on my mother's knees. "Come, auntie," he would say, "tell me some love-stories." And my mother, as a joke, would tell him all the old legends of the family, all the passionate adventures of his forefathers, for thousands of them were current, some true and some false. It was their reputation for love and gallantry which was the ruin of every one of these-men; they gloried in it and then thought that they had to live up to the renown of their house.

'The little fellow became exalted by these tender or terrible stories, and at times he would clap his hands, crying, "I, too, I, too, know how to love, better than all of them!"

'Then, he began to court me in a timid and tender manner, at which everyone laughed, it was, so amusing. Every morning I had some flowers picked by him, and every evening before going to his room he would kiss my hand and murmur, "I love you!"

'I was guilty, very guilty, and I grieved continually about it, and I have been doing penance all my life; I have remained an old maid—or, rather, I have lived as a widowed fiancée, his widow.

'I was amused at this childish tenderness, and I even encouraged him. I was coquettish, as charming as with a man, alternately caressing and severe. I maddened this child. It was a game for me and a joyous diversion for his mother and mine. He was twelve! think of it! Who would have taken this atom's passion seriously? I kissed him as often as he wished; I even wrote him little notes, which were read by our respective mothers; and he answered me by passionate letters, which I have kept. Judging himself as a man, he thought that our loving intimacy was secret. We had forgotten that he was a Santeze.

'This lasted for about a year. One evening in the park he fell at my feet and, as he madly kissed the hem of my dress, he kept repeating, "I love you! I love you! I love you! If ever you deceive me, if ever you leave me for another, I'll do as my father did." And he added in a hoarse voice, which gave me a shiver, "You know what he did!"

'I stood there astonished. He arose, and standing on the tips of his toes in order to reach my ear, for I was taller than he, he pronounced my first name, "Genevieve!" in such a gentle, sweet, tender tone that I trembled all over. I stammered, "Let us return! Let us return!" He said no more and followed me; but as we were going up the steps of the porch, he stopped me, saying, "You know, if ever you leave me, I'll kill myself."

'This time I understood that I had gone too far, and I became quite reserved. One day, as he was reproaching me for this, I answered, "You are now too old for jesting and too young for serious love. I'll wait."

'I thought that this would end the matter. In the autumn he was sent to a boarding-school. When he returned the following summer I was engaged to be married. He understood immediately, and for a week he became so pensive that I was quite anxious.

'On the morning of the ninth day I saw a little paper under my door as I got up. I seized it, opened it and read, "You have deserted me and you know what I said. It is death to which you have condemned me. As I do not wish to be found by another than you, come to the park just where I told you last year that I loved you and look in the air."

'I thought that I should go mad. I dressed as quickly as I could and ran wildly to the place that he had mentioned. His little cap was on the ground in the mud. It had been raining all night. I raised my eyes and saw something swinging among the leaves, for the wind was blowing a gale.

'I don't know what I did after that. I must have screamed at first, then fainted and fallen, and finally have run to the chateau. The next thing that I remember I was in bed, with my mother sitting beside me.

'I thought that I had dreamed all this in a frightful nightmare. I stammered, "And what of him, what of him, Gontran?" There was no answer. It was true!

'I did not dare see him again, but I asked for a lock of his blond hair. Here—here it is!'

And the old maid stretched out her trembling hand in a despairing gesture. Then she blew her nose several times, wiped her eyes and continued, 'I broke off my marriage—without saying why. And I—I always have remained the—the widow of this thirteen-year-old boy.' Then her head fell on her breast and she wept for a long time.

As the guests were retiring for the night a large man, whose quiet she had disturbed, whispered in his neighbour's ear, 'Isn't it unfortunate to, be so sentimental?'

SLEEPY

Anton Chekhov

Night. Varka, the little nurse, a girl of thirteen, is rocking the cradle in which the baby is lying, and humming hardly audibly:

'Hush-a-bye, my baby wee,
While I sing a song for thee.'

A little green lamp is burning before the ikon; there is a string stretched from one end of the room to the other, on which baby-clothes and a pair of big black trousers are hanging. There is a big patch of green on the ceiling from the ikon lamp, and the baby-clothes and the trousers throw long shadows on the stove, on the cradle, and on Varka. When the lamp begins to flicker, the green patch and the shadows come to life, and are set in motion, as though by the wind. It is stuffy. There is a smell of cabbage soup, and of the inside of a boot-shop.

The baby's crying. For a long while he has been hoarse and exhausted with crying; but he still goes on screaming, and there is no knowing when he will stop. And Varka is sleepy. Her eyes are glued together, her head droops, her neck aches. She cannot move her eyelids or her lips, and she feels as though her face is dried and wooden, as though her head has become as small as the head of a pin.

'Hush-a-bye, my baby wee,' she hums, 'while I cook the groats for thee…'

A cricket is chirring in the stove. Through the door in the next room the master and the apprentice Afanasy are snoring… The cradle creaks plaintively, Varka murmurs—and it all blends into that soothing music of the night to which it is so sweet to listen, when one is lying in bed. Now that music is merely irritating and oppressive, because it goads her to sleep, and she must not sleep; if Varka—God forbid!—should fall asleep, her master and mistress would beat her.

The lamp flickers. The patch of green and the shadows are set in motion, forcing themselves on Varka's fixed, half-open eyes, and in her half slumbering brain are fashioned into misty visions. She sees dark clouds chasing one another over the sky, and screaming like the baby. But then the wind blows, the clouds are gone, and Varka sees a broad high road covered with liquid mud; along the high road stretch files of wagons, while people with wallets on their backs are trudging along and shadows flit backwards and forwards; on both sides she can see forests through the cold harsh mist. All at once the people with their wallets and their shadows fall on the ground in the liquid mud. 'What is that for?' Varka asks. 'To sleep, to sleep!' they answer her. And they fall sound asleep, and sleep sweetly, while crows and magpies sit on the telegraph wires, scream like the baby, and try to wake them.

'Hush-a-bye, my baby wee, and I will sing a song to thee,' murmurs Varka, and now she sees herself in a dark stuffy hut.

Her dead father, Yefim Stepanov, is tossing from side to side on the floor. She does not see him, but she hears him moaning and rolling on the floor from pain. 'His guts have burst,' as he says, the pain is so violent that he cannot utter a single word, and can only draw in his breath and clack his teeth like the rattling of a drum:

'Boo—boo—boo—boo…'

Her mother, Pelageya, has run to the master's house to say that Yefim is dying. She has been gone a long time, and ought to be back. Varka lies awake on the stove, and hears her father's 'boo—boo—boo.' And then she hears someone has driven up to the hut. It is a young doctor from the town, who has been sent from the big house where he is staying on a visit. The doctor comes into the hut; he cannot be seen in the darkness, but he can be heard coughing and rattling the door.

'Light a candle,' he says.

'Boo—boo—boo,' answers Yefim.

Pelageya rushes to the stove and begins looking for the broken pot with the matches. A minute passes in silence. The doctor, feeling in his pocket, lights a match.

'In a minute, sir, in a minute,' says Pelageya. She rushes out of the hut, and soon afterwards comes back with a bit of candle.

Yefim's cheeks are rosy and his eyes are shining, and there is a peculiar keenness in his glance, as though he were seeing right through the hut and the doctor.

'Come, what is it? What are you thinking about?' says the doctor, bending down to him. 'Aha! have you had this long?'

'What? Dying, your honour, my hour has come… I am not to stay among the living.'

'Don't talk nonsense! We will cure you!'

'That's as you please, your honour, we humbly thank you, only we understand… Since death has come, there it is.'

The doctor spends a quarter of an hour over Yefim, then he gets up and says, 'I can do nothing. You must go into the hospital, there they will operate on you. Go at once… You must go! It's rather late, they will all be asleep in the hospital, but that doesn't matter, I will give you a note. Do you hear?'

'Kind sir, but what can he go in?' says Pelageya. 'We have no horse.'

'Never mind. I'll ask your master, he'll let you have a horse.'

The doctor goes away, the candle goes out, and again there is the sound of 'boo—boo—boo.' Half an hour later someone drives up to the hut. A cart has been sent to take Yefim to the hospital. He gets ready and goes…

But now it is a clear bright morning. Pelageya is not at home; she has gone to the hospital to find what is being done to Yefim. Somewhere there is a baby crying, and Varka hears someone singing with her own voice:

'Hush-a-bye, my baby wee,
I will sing a song to thee.'

Pelageya comes back; she crosses herself and whispers, 'They put him to rights in the night, but towards morning he gave up his soul to God… The Kingdom of Heaven be his and peace everlasting… They say he was taken too late… He ought to have gone sooner…'

Varka goes out into the road and cries there, but all at once someone hits her on the back of her head so hard that her forehead knocks against a birch tree. She raises her eyes, and sees facing her, her master, the shoemaker.

'What are you about, you scabby slut?' he says. 'The child is crying, and you are asleep!'

He gives her a sharp slap behind the ear, and she shakes her head, rocks the cradle, and murmurs her song. The green patch and the shadows from the trousers and the baby-clothes move up and down, nod to her, and soon take possession of her brain again. Again she sees the high road covered with liquid mud. The people with wallets on their backs and the shadows have lain down and are fast asleep. Looking at them, Varka has a passionate longing for sleep; she would lie down with enjoyment, but her mother Pelageya is walking beside her, hurrying her on. They are hastening together to the town to find situations.

'Give alms, for Christ's sake!' her mother begs of the people they meet. 'Show us the Divine Mercy, kind-hearted gentlefolk!'

'Give the baby here!' a familiar voice answers. 'Give the baby here!' the same voice repeats, this time harshly and angrily. 'Are you asleep, you wretched girl?'

Varka jumps up, and looking round grasps what is the matter. There is no high road, no Pelageya, no people meeting them, there is only her mistress, who has come to feed the baby, and is standing in the middle of the room. While the stout, broad-shouldered woman nurses the child and soothes it, Varka stands looking at her and waiting till she has done. And outside the windows the air is already turning blue, the shadows and the green patch on the ceiling are visibly growing pale, it will soon be morning.

'Take him,' says her mistress, buttoning up her chemise over her bosom. 'He is crying. He must be bewitched.'

Varka takes the baby, puts him in the cradle and begins rocking it again. The green patch and the shadows gradually disappear, and now there is nothing to force itself on her eyes and cloud her brain. But she is as sleepy as before, fearfully sleepy! Varka lays her head on the edge of the cradle, and rocks her whole body to overcome her sleepiness, but yet her eyes are glued together, and her head is heavy.

'Varka, heat the stove!' she hears the master's voice through the door.

So it is time to get up and set to work. Varka leaves the cradle, and runs to the shed for firewood. She is glad. When one moves and runs about, one is not so sleepy as when one is sitting down. She brings the wood, heats the stove, and feels that her wooden face is getting supple again, and that her thoughts are growing clearer.

'Varka, set the samovar!' shouts her mistress.

Varka splits a piece of wood, but has scarcely time to light the splinters and put them in the samovar, when she hears a fresh order, 'Varka, clean the master's galoshes!'

She sits down on the floor, cleans the galoshes, and thinks how nice it would be to put her head into a big deep galosh, and have a little nap in it... And all at once the galosh grows, swells, fills up the whole room. Varka drops the brush, but at once shakes her head, opens her eyes wide, and tries to look at things so that they may not grow big and move before her eyes.

'Varka, wash the steps outside; I am ashamed for the customers to see them!'

Varka washes the steps, sweeps and dusts the rooms, then heats another stove and runs to the shop. There is a great deal of work, she hasn't one minute free.

But nothing is so hard as standing in the same place at the kitchen table peeling potatoes. Her head droops over the table, the potatoes dance before her eyes, the knife tumbles out of her hand while her fat, angry mistress is moving about near her with her sleeves tucked up, talking so loud that it makes a ringing in Varka's ears. It is agonising, too, to wait at dinner, to wash, to sew, there are minutes when she longs to flop on to the floor regardless of everything, and to sleep.

The day passes. Seeing the windows getting dark, Varka presses her temples that feel as though they were made of wood, and smiles, though she does not know why. The dusk of evening caresses her eyes that will hardly keep open, and promises her sound sleep soon. In the evening visitors come.

'Varka, set the samovar!' shouts her mistress. The samovar is a little one, and before the visitors have drunk all the tea they want, she has to heat it five times. After tea Varka stands for a whole hour on the same spot, looking at the visitors, and waiting for orders.

'Varka, run and buy three bottles of beer!'

She starts off, and tries to run as quickly as she can, to drive away sleep.

'Varka, fetch some vodka! Varka, where's the corkscrew? Varka, clean a herring!'

But now, at last, the visitors have gone; the lights are put out, the master and mistress go to bed.

'Varka, rock the baby!' she hears the last order.

The cricket chirrs in the stove; the green patch on the ceiling and the shadows from the trousers and the baby-clothes force themselves on Varka's half-opened eyes again, wink at her and cloud her mind.

'Hush-a-bye, my baby wee,' she murmurs, 'and I will sing a song to thee.'

And the baby screams, and is worn out with screaming. Again Varka sees the muddy high road, the people with wallets, her mother Pelageya, her father Yefim. She understands everything, she recognizes everyone, but through her half sleep she cannot understand the force which binds her, hand and foot, weighs upon her, and prevents her from living. She looks round, searches for that force that she may escape from it, but she cannot find it. At last, tired to death, she does her very utmost, strains her eyes, looks up at the flickering green patch, and listening to the screaming, finds the foe who will not let her live.

That foe is the baby.

She laughs. It seems strange to her that she has failed to grasp such a simple thing before. The green patch, the shadows, and the cricket seem to laugh and wonder too.

The hallucination takes possession of Varka. She gets up from her stool, and with a broad smile on her face and wide unblinking eyes, she walks up and down the room. She feels pleased and tickled at the thought that she will be rid directly of the baby that binds her hand and foot… Kill the baby and then sleep, sleep, sleep…

Laughing and winking and shaking her fingers at the green patch, Varka steals up to the cradle and bends over the baby. When she has strangled him, she quickly lies down on the floor, laughs with delight that she can sleep, and in a minute is sleeping as sound as the dead.

THE MAN WHO COULD WORK MIRACLES

H.G. Wells

It is doubtful whether the gift was innate. For my own part, I think it came to him suddenly. Indeed, until he was thirty he was a sceptic, and did not believe in miraculous powers. And here, since it is the most convenient place, I must mention that he was a little man, and had eyes of a hot brown, very erect red hair, a moustache with ends that he twisted up, and freckles. His name was George McWhirter Fotheringay—not the sort of name by any means to lead to any expectation of miracles—and he was clerk at Gomshott's. He was greatly addicted to assertive argument. It was while he was asserting the impossibility of miracles that he had his first intimation of his extraordinary powers. This particular argument was being held in the bar of the Long Dragon, and Toddy Beamish was conducting the opposition by a monotonous but effective 'So you say,' that drove Mr Fotheringay to the very limit of his patience.

There were present, besides these two, a very dusty cyclist, landlord Cox, and Miss Maybridge, the perfectly respectable and rather portly barmaid of the Dragon. Miss Maybridge was standing with her back to Mr Fotheringay, washing glasses; the others were watching him, more or less amused by the present ineffectiveness of the assertive method. Goaded by the Torres Vedras tactics of Mr Beamish, Mr Fotheringay determined to make an unusual rhetorical effort. 'Looky here, Mr Beamish,' said Mr Fotheringay. 'Let us clearly understand what a miracle is. It's something contrariwise to the course of nature, done by power of will, something what couldn't happen without being specially willed.'

'So you say,' said Mr Beamish, repulsing him.

Mr Fotheringay appealed to the cyclist, who had hitherto been a silent auditor, and received his assent—given with a hesitating cough and a glance at Mr Beamish. The landlord would express no opinion, and Mr Fotheringay, returning to Mr Beamish, received the unexpected concession of a qualified assent to his definition of a miracle.

'For instance,' said Mr Fotheringay, greatly encouraged. 'Here would be a miracle. That lamp, in the natural course of nature, couldn't burn like that upsy-down, could it, Beamish?'

'You say it couldn't,' said Beamish.

'And you?' said Fotheringay. 'You don't mean to say—eh?'

'No,' said Beamish reluctantly. 'No, it couldn't.'

'Very well,' said Mr Fotheringay. 'Then here comes someone, as it might be me, along here, and stands as it might be here, and says to that lamp, as I might do, collecting all my will—Turn upsy-down without breaking, and go on burning steady, and—Hullo!'

It was enough to make anyone say 'Hullo!' The impossible, the incredible, was visible to them all. The lamp hung inverted in the air, burning quietly with its flame pointing down. It was as solid, as indisputable as ever a lamp was, the prosaic common lamp of the Long Dragon bar.

Mr Fotheringay stood with an extended forefinger and the knitted brows of one anticipating a catastrophic smash. The cyclist, who was sitting next the lamp, ducked and jumped across the bar. Everybody jumped, more or less. Miss Maybridge turned and screamed. For nearly three seconds the lamp remained still. A faint cry of mental distress came from Mr Fotheringay. 'I can't keep it up,' he said, 'any longer.' He staggered back, and the inverted lamp suddenly flared, fell against the corner of the bar, bounced aside, smashed upon the floor, and went out.

It was lucky it had a metal receiver, or the whole place would have been in a blaze. Mr Cox was the first to speak, and his remark, shorn of needless excrescences, was to the effect that Fotheringay was a fool. Fotheringay was beyond disputing even so fundamental a proposition as that! He was astonished beyond measure at the thing that had occurred. The subsequent conversation threw absolutely no light on the matter so far as Fotheringay was concerned; the general opinion not only followed Mr Cox very closely but very vehemently. Everyone accused Fotheringay of a silly trick, and presented him to himself as a foolish destroyer of comfort and security. His mind was in a tornado of perplexity, he was himself inclined to agree with them, and he made a remarkably ineffectual opposition to the proposal of his departure.

He went home flushed and heated, coat-collar crumpled, eyes

smarting, and ears red. He watched each of the ten street lamps nervously as he passed it. It was only when he found himself alone in his little bedroom in Church Row that he was able to grapple seriously with his memories of the occurrence, and ask, 'What on earth happened?'

He had removed his coat and boots, and was sitting on the bed with his hands in his pockets repeating the text of his defence for the seventeenth time, 'I didn't want the confounded thing to upset,' when it occurred to him that at the precise moment he had said the commanding words he had inadvertently willed the thing he said, and that when he had seen the lamp in the air he had felt that it depended on him to maintain it there without being clear how this was to be done. He had not a particularly complex mind, or he might have stuck for a time at that 'inadvertently willed,' embracing, as it does, the abstrusest problems of voluntary action; but as it was, the idea came to him with a quite acceptable haziness. And from that, following, as I must admit, no clear logical path, he came to the test of experiment.

He pointed resolutely to his candle and collected his mind, though he felt he did a foolish thing. 'Be raised up,' he said. But in a second that feeling vanished. The candle was raised, hung in the air one giddy moment, and as Mr Fotheringay gasped, fell with a smash on his toilet-table, leaving him in darkness save for the expiring glow of its wick.

For a time Mr Fotheringay sat in the darkness, perfectly still. 'It did happen, after all,' he said. 'And 'ow I'm to explain it I don't know.' He sighed heavily, and began feeling in his pockets for a match. He could find none, and he rose and groped about the toilet-table. 'I wish I had a match,' he said. He resorted to his coat, and there was none there, and then it dawned upon him that miracles were possible even with matches. He extended a hand and scowled at it in the dark. 'Let there be a match in that hand,' he said. He felt some light object fall across his palm and his fingers closed upon a match.

After several ineffectual attempts to light this, he discovered it was a safety match. He threw it down, and then it occurred to him that he might have willed it lit. He did, and perceived it burning in the midst of his toilet-table mat. He caught it up hastily, and it went out. His perception of possibilities enlarged, and he felt for and replaced the candle in its candlestick. 'Here! You be lit,' said Mr Fotheringay, and forthwith the candle was flaring, and he saw a little black hole in the toilet-cover, with a wisp of smoke rising from it. For a time he stared from this to the little flame and back, and then looked up and met his own gaze in the looking-glass. By this help he communed with himself in silence for a time.

'How about miracles now?' said Mr Fotheringay at last, addressing his reflection.

The subsequent meditations of Mr Fotheringay were of a severe but confused description. So far, he could see it was a case of pure willing with him. The nature of his experiences so far disinclined him for any further experiments, at least until he had reconsidered them. But he lifted a sheet of paper, and turned a glass of water pink and then green, and he created a snail, which he miraculously annihilated, and got himself a miraculous new tooth-brush. Somewhere in the small hours he had reached the fact that his will-power must be of a particularly rare and pungent quality, a fact of which he had indeed had inklings before, but no certain assurance. The scare and perplexity of his first discovery was now qualified by pride in this evidence of singularity and by vague intimations of advantage. He became aware that the church clock was striking one, and as it did not occur to him that his daily duties at Gomshott's might be miraculously dispensed with, he resumed undressing, in order to get to bed without further delay. As he struggled to get his shirt over his head, he was struck with a brilliant idea. 'Let me be in bed,' he said, and found himself so. 'Undressed,' he stipulated; and, finding the sheets cold, added hastily, 'and in my nightshirt—ho, in a nice soft woollen nightshirt. Ah!' he said with immense enjoyment. 'And now let me be comfortably asleep...'

He awoke at his usual hour and was pensive all through breakfast-time, wondering whether his over-night experience might not be a particularly vivid dream. At length his mind turned again to cautious experiments. For instance, he had three eggs for breakfast; two his landlady had supplied, good, but shoppy, and one was a delicious fresh goose-egg, laid, cooked, and served by his extraordinary will. He hurried off to Gomshott's in a state of profound but carefully concealed excitement, and only remembered the shell of the third egg when his landlady spoke of it that night. All day he could do no work because of this astonishing new self-knowledge, but this caused him no inconvenience, because he made up for it miraculously in his last ten minutes.

As the day wore on his state of mind passed from wonder to elation, albeit the circumstances of his dismissal from the Long Dragon were still disagreeable to recall, and a garbled account of the matter that had reached his colleagues led to some badinage. It was evident he must be careful how he lifted frangible articles, but in other ways his gift promised more and more as he turned it over in his mind. He intended among other things to increase his personal property by unostentatious acts of creation. He called into existence a pair of very splendid diamond studs, and hastily annihilated them again as young Gomshott came across the counting-house to his desk. He was afraid young Gomshott might wonder how he had come by them. He saw quite clearly the gift required caution and watchfulness in its exercise, but so far as he could judge the difficulties attending its mastery would be no greater than those he had already faced in the study of cycling. It was that analogy, perhaps, quite as much as the feeling that he would be unwelcome in the Long Dragon, that drove him out after supper into the lane beyond the gasworks, to rehearse a few miracles in private.

There was possibly a certain want of originality in his attempts, for, apart from his will-power, Mr Fotheringay was not a very exceptional man. The miracle of Moses' rod came to his mind, but the night was dark and unfavourable to the proper control of large miraculous snakes. Then he recollected the story of 'Tannhuser' that he had read on the back of the Philharmonic programme. That seemed to him singularly attractive and harmless. He stuck his walking-stick—a very nice Poona-Penang lawyer—into the turf that edged the footpath, and commanded the dry wood to blossom. The air was immediately full of the scent of roses, and by means of a match he saw for himself that this beautiful miracle was indeed accomplished. His satisfaction was ended by advancing footsteps. Afraid of a premature discovery of his powers, he addressed the blossoming stick hastily, 'Go back.' What he meant was

'Change back'; but of course he was confused. The stick receded at a considerable velocity, and incontinently came a cry of anger and a bad word from the approaching person. 'Who are you throwing brambles at, you fool?' cried a voice. 'That got me on the shin.'

'I'm sorry, old chap,' said Mr Fotheringay, and then, realising the awkward nature of the explanation, caught nervously at his moustache. He saw Winch, one of the three Immering constables, advancing.

'What d'yer mean by it?' asked the constable. 'Hullo! it's you, is it? The gent that broke the lamp at the Long Dragon!'

'I don't mean anything by it,' said Mr Fotheringay. 'Nothing at all.'

'What d'yer do it for then?'

'Oh, bother!' said Mr Fotheringay.

'Bother indeed! D'yer know that stick hurt? What d'yer do it for, eh?'

For the moment Mr Fotheringay could not think what he had done it for. His silence seemed to irritate Mr Winch. 'You've been assaulting the police, young man, this time. That's what you done.'

'Look here, Mr Winch,' said Mr Fotheringay, annoyed and confused, 'I'm sorry, very. The fact is...'

'Well?'

He could think of no way but the truth. 'I was working a miracle.' He tried to speak in an off-hand way, but try as he would he couldn't.

'Working a—! 'Ere, don't you talk rot. Working a miracle, indeed! Miracle! Well, that's downright funny! Why, you's the chap that don't believe in miracles... Fact is, this is another of your silly conjuring tricks—that's what this is. Now, I tell you—'

But Mr Fotheringay never heard what Mr Winch was going to tell him. He realized he had given himself away, flung his valuable secret to all the winds of heaven. A violent gust of irritation swept him to action. He turned on the constable swiftly and fiercely. 'Here,' he said, 'I've had enough of this, I have! I'll show you a silly conjuring trick, I will! Go to Hades! Go, now!'

He was alone!

Mr Fotheringay performed no more miracles that night, nor did he trouble to see what had become of his flowering stick. He returned to the town, scared and very quiet, and went to his bedroom. 'Lord!'

he said, 'it's a powerful gift—an extremely powerful gift. I didn't hardly mean as much as that. Not really... I wonder what Hades is like!'

He sat on the bed taking off his boots. Struck by a happy thought he transferred the constable to San Francisco, and without any more interference with normal causation went soberly to bed. In the night he dreamt of the anger of Winch.

The next day Mr Fotheringay heard two interesting items of news. Someone had planted a most beautiful climbing rose against the elder Mr Gomshott's private house in the Lullaborough Road, and the river as far as Rawling's Mill was to be dragged for Constable Winch.

Mr Fotheringay was abstracted and thoughtful all that day, and performed no miracles except certain provisions for Winch, and the miracle of completing his day's work with punctual perfection in spite of all the bee-swarm of thoughts that hummed through his mind. And the extraordinary abstraction and meekness of his manner was remarked by several people, and made a matter for jesting. For the most part he was thinking of Winch.

On Sunday evening he went to chapel, and oddly enough, Mr Maydig, who took a certain interest in occult matters, preached about 'things that are not lawful.' Mr Fotheringay was not a regular chapelgoer, but the system of assertive scepticism, to which I have already alluded, was now very much shaken. The tenor of the sermon threw an entirely new light on these novel gifts, and he suddenly decided to consult Mr Maydig immediately after the service. So soon as that was determined, he found himself wondering why he had not done so before.

Mr Maydig, a lean, excitable man with quite remarkably long wrists and neck, was gratified at a request for a private conversation from a young man whose carelessness in religious matters was a subject for general remark in the town. After a few necessary delays, he conducted him to the study of the manse, which was contiguous to the chapel, seated him comfortably, and, standing in front of a cheerful fire—his legs threw a Rhodian arch of shadow on the opposite wall—requested Mr Fotheringay to state his business.

At first Mr Fotheringay was a little abashed, and found some difficulty in opening the matter. 'You will scarcely believe me, Mr Maydig, I am afraid'—and so forth for some time. He tried a question at last, and asked Mr Maydig his opinion of miracles.

Mr Maydig was still saying 'Well' in an extremely judicial tone, when Mr Fotheringay interrupted again, 'You don't believe, I suppose, that some common sort of person—like myself, for instance—as it might be sitting here now, might have some sort of twist inside him that made him able to do things by his will.'

'It's possible,' said Mr Maydig. 'Something of the sort, perhaps, is possible.'

'If I might make free with something here, I think I might show you by a sort of experiment,' said Mr Fotheringay. 'Now, take that tobacco-jar on the table, for instance. What I want to know is whether what I am going to do with it is a miracle or not. Just half a minute, Mr Maydig, please.'

He knitted his brows, pointed to the tobacco-jar and said, 'Be a bowl of vi'lets.'

The tobacco-jar did as it was ordered.

Mr Maydig started violently at the change, and stood looking from the thaumaturgist to the bowl of flowers. He said nothing. Presently he ventured to lean over the table and smell the violets; they were fresh-picked and very fine ones. Then he stared at Mr Fotheringay again.

'How did you do that?' he asked.

Mr Fotheringay pulled his moustache. 'Just told it—and there you are. Is that a miracle, or is it black art, or what is it? And what do you think's the matter with me? That's what I want to ask.'

'It's a most extraordinary occurrence.'

'And this day last week I knew no more that I could do things like that than you did. It came quite sudden. It's something odd about my will, I suppose, and that's as far as I can see.'

'Is that—the only thing. Could you do other things besides that?'

'Lord, yes!' said Mr Fotheringay. 'Just anything.' He thought, and suddenly recalled a conjuring entertainment he had seen. 'Here!' he pointed, 'change into a bowl of fish—no, not that—change into a glass bowl full of water with goldfish swimming in it. That's better! You see that, Mr Maydig?'

'It's astonishing. It's incredible. You are either a most extraordinary... But no...'

'I could change it into anything,' said Mr Fotheringay. 'Just anything. Here! be a pigeon, will you?'

In another moment a blue pigeon was fluttering round the room and making Mr Maydig duck every time it came near him. 'Stop there, will you?' said Mr Fotheringay; and the pigeon hung motionless in the air. 'I could change it back to a bowl of flowers,' he said, and after replacing the pigeon on the table worked that miracle. 'I expect you will want your pipe in a bit,' he said, and restored the tobacco-jar.

Mr Maydig had followed all these later changes in a sort of ejaculatory silence. He stared at Mr Fotheringay and in a very gingerly manner picked up the tobacco-jar, examined it, replaced it on the table. 'Well!' was the only expression of his feelings.

'Now, after that it's easier to explain what I came about,' said Mr Fotheringay, and proceeded to a lengthy and involved narrative of his strange experiences, beginning with the affair of the lamp in the Long Dragon and complicated by persistent allusions to Winch. As he went on, the transient pride Mr Maydig's consternation had caused passed away; he became the very ordinary Mr Fotheringay of everyday intercourse again. Mr Maydig listened intently, the tobacco-jar in his hand, and his bearing changed also with the course of the narrative. Presently, while Mr Fotheringay was dealing with the miracle of the third egg, the minister interrupted with a fluttering, extended hand.

'It is possible,' he said. 'It is credible. It is amazing, of course, but it reconciles a number of amazing difficulties. The power to work miracles is a gift—a peculiar quality like genius or second sight; hitherto it has come very rarely and to exceptional people. But in this case...I have always wondered at the miracles of Mahomet, and at Yogi's miracles, and the miracles of Madame Blavatsky. But, of course—Yes, it is simply a gift! It carries out so beautifully the arguments of that great thinker'—Mr Maydig's voice sank—'his Grace the Duke of Argyll. Here we plumb some profounder law—deeper than the ordinary laws of nature. Yes—yes. Go on. Go on!'

Mr Fotheringay proceeded to tell of his misadventure with Winch, and Mr Maydig, no longer overawed or scared, began to jerk his limbs about and interject astonishment. 'It's this what troubled me most,' proceeded Mr Fotheringay; 'it's this I'm most mijitly in want of advice for; of course he's at San Francisco—wherever San Francisco may be—but of course it's awkward for both of us, as you'll see, Mr Maydig. I don't see how he can understand what has happened, and I daresay he's scared and exasperated something tremendous, and trying to get at me. I daresay he keeps on starting off to come here. I send him back, by a miracle, every few hours, when I think of it. And, of course, that's a thing he won't be able to understand, and it's bound to annoy him; and, of course, if he takes a ticket every time it will cost him a lot of money. I done the best I could for him, but, of course, it's difficult for him to put himself in my place. I thought afterwards that his clothes might have got scorched, you know—if Hades is all it's supposed to be—before I shifted him. In that case I suppose they'd have locked him up in San Francisco. Of course I willed him a new suit of clothes on him directly I thought of it. But, you see, I'm already in a deuce of a tangle...'

Mr Maydig looked serious. 'I see you are in a tangle. Yes, it's a difficult position. How you are to end it...' He became diffuse and inconclusive.

'However, we'll leave Winch for a little and discuss the larger question. I don't think this is a case of the black art or anything of the sort. I don't think there is any taint of criminality about it at all, Mr Fotheringay—none whatever, unless you are suppressing material facts. No, it's miracles—pure miracles—miracles, if I may say so, of the very highest class.'

He began to pace the hearthrug and gesticulate, while Mr Fotheringay sat with his arm on the table and his head on his arm, looking worried. 'I don't see how I'm to manage about Winch,' he said.

'A gift of working miracles—apparently a very powerful gift,' said Mr Maydig, 'will find a way about Winch—never fear. My dear sir, you are a most important man—a man of the most astonishing possibilities. As evidence, for example! And in other ways, the things you may do...'

'Yes, I've thought of a thing or two,' said Mr Fotheringay. 'But...

some of the things came a bit twisty. You saw that fish at first? Wrong sort of bowl and wrong sort of fish. And I thought I'd ask someone.'

'A proper course,' said Mr Maydig, 'a very proper course—altogether the proper course.' He stopped and looked at Mr Fotheringay. 'It's practically an unlimited gift. Let us test your powers, for instance. If they really are... If they really are all they seem to be.'

And so, incredible as it may seem, in the study of the little house behind the Congregational Chapel, on the evening of Sunday, Nov. 10, 1896, Mr Fotheringay, egged on and inspired by Mr Maydig, began to work miracles. The reader's attention is specially and definitely called to the date. He will object, probably has already objected, that certain points in this story are improbable, that if any things of the sort already described had indeed occurred, they would have been in all the papers at that time. The details immediately following he will find particularly hard to accept, because among other things they involve the conclusion that he or she, the reader in question, must have been killed in a violent and unprecedented manner more than a year ago. Now a miracle is nothing if not improbable, and as a matter of fact the reader was killed in a violent and unprecedented manner in 1896. In the subsequent course of this story that will become perfectly clear and credible, as every right-minded and reasonable reader will admit. But this is not the place for the end of the story, being but little beyond the hither side of the middle. And at first the miracles worked by Mr Fotheringay were timid little miracles—little things with the cups and parlour fitments, as feeble as the miracles of Theosophists, and, feeble as they were, they were received with awe by his collaborator. He would have preferred to settle the Winch business out of hand, but Mr Maydig would not let him. But after they had worked a dozen of these domestic trivialities, their sense of power grew, their imagination began to show signs of stimulation, and their ambition enlarged. Their first larger enterprise was due to hunger and the negligence of Mrs Minchin, Mr Maydig's housekeeper. The meal to which the minister conducted Mr Fotheringay was certainly ill-laid and uninviting as refreshment for two industrious miracle-workers; but they were seated, and Mr Maydig was descanting in sorrow rather than in anger upon his housekeeper's shortcomings, before it occurred to Mr Fotheringay that an opportunity lay before him. 'Don't you think, Mr Maydig,' he said, 'if it isn't a liberty, I...'

'My dear Mr Fotheringay! Of course! No—I didn't think.'

Mr Fotheringay waved his hand. 'What shall we have?' he said, in a large, inclusive spirit, and, at Mr Maydig's order, revised the supper very thoroughly. 'As for me,' he said, eyeing Mr Maydig's selection, 'I am always particularly fond of a tankard of stout and a nice Welsh rarebit, and I'll order that. I ain't much given to Burgundy,' and forthwith stout and Welsh rarebit promptly appeared at his command. They sat long at their supper, talking like equals, as Mr Fotheringay presently perceived, with a glow of surprise and gratification, of all the miracles they would presently do. 'And, by-the-by, Mr Maydig,' said Mr Fotheringay, 'I might perhaps be able to help you—in a domestic way.'

'Don't quite follow,' said Mr Maydig, pouring out a glass of miraculous old Burgundy.

Mr Fotheringay helped himself to a second Welsh rarebit out of vacancy, and took a mouthful. 'I was thinking,' he said, 'I might be able [—chum, chum—] to work [—chum, chum—] a miracle with Mrs Minchin [—chum, chum—]—make her a better woman.'

Mr Maydig put down the glass and looked doubtful.

'She's... She strongly objects to interference, you know, Mr Fotheringay. And—as a matter of fact—it's well past eleven and she's probably in bed and asleep. Do you think, on the whole...'

Mr Fotheringay considered these objections. 'I don't see that it shouldn't be done in her sleep.'

For a time Mr Maydig opposed the idea, and then he yielded. Mr Fotheringay issued his orders, and a little less at their ease, perhaps, the two gentlemen proceeded with their repast. Mr Maydig was enlarging on the changes he might expect in his housekeeper next day, with an optimism, that seemed even to Mr Fotheringay's supper senses a little forced and hectic, when a series of confused noises from upstairs began. Their eyes exchanged interrogations, and Mr Maydig left the room hastily. Mr Fotheringay heard him calling up to his housekeeper and then his footsteps going softly up to her.

In a minute or so the minister returned, his step light, his face radiant. 'Wonderful!' he said, 'and touching! Most touching!'

He began pacing the hearthrug. 'A repentance…a most touching repentance…through the crack of the door. Poor woman! A most wonderful change! She had got up. She must have got up at once. She had got up out of her sleep to smash a private bottle of brandy in her box. And to confess it too!… But this gives us—it opens—a most amazing vista of possibilities. If we can work this miraculous change in…her..'

'The thing's unlimited seemingly,' said Mr Fotheringay. 'And about Mr Winch…'

'Altogether unlimited.' And from the hearthrug Mr Maydig, waving the Winch difficulty aside, unfolded a series of wonderful proposals—proposals he invented as he went along.

Now what those proposals were does not concern the essentials of this story. Suffice it that they were designed in a spirit of infinite benevolence, the sort of benevolence that used to be called post-prandial. Suffice it, too, that the problem of Winch remained unsolved. Nor is it necessary to describe how far that series got to its fulfilment. There were astonishing changes. The small hours found Mr Maydig and Mr Fotheringay careering across the chilly market square under the still moon, in a sort of ecstasy of thaumaturgy, Mr Maydig all flap and gesture, Mr Fotheringay short and bristling, and no longer abashed at his greatness. They had reformed every drunkard in the Parliamentary division, changed all the beer and alcohol to water (Mr Maydig had overruled Mr Fotheringay on this point); they had, further, greatly improved the railway communication of the place, drained Flinder's swamp, improved the soil of One Tree Hill, and cured the vicar's wart. And they were going to see what could be done with the injured pier at South Bridge. 'The place,' gasped Mr Maydig, 'won't be the same place to-morrow. How surprised and thankful everyone will be!' And just at that moment the church clock struck three.

'I say,' said Mr Fotheringay, 'that's three o'clock! I must be getting back. I've got to be at business by eight. And besides, Mrs Wimms—'

'We're only beginning,' said Mr Maydig, full of the sweetness of unlimited power. 'We're only beginning. Think of all the good we're doing. When people wake—'

'But…,' said Mr Fotheringay.

Mr Maydig gripped his arm suddenly. His eyes were bright and wild. 'My dear chap,' he said, 'there's no hurry. Look'—he pointed to the moon at the zenith—'Joshua!'

'Joshua?' said Mr Fotheringay.

'Joshua,' said Mr Maydig. 'Why not? Stop it.'

Mr Fotheringay looked at the moon.

'That's a bit tall,' he said, after a pause.

'Why not?' said Mr Maydig. 'Of course it doesn't stop. You stop the rotation of the earth, you know. Time stops. It isn't as if we were doing harm.'

'H'm!' said Mr Fotheringay. 'Well,' he sighed, 'I'll try. Here!'

He buttoned up his jacket and addressed himself to the habitable globe, with as good an assumption of confidence as lay in his power. 'Jest stop rotating, will you?' said Mr Fotheringay.

Incontinently he was flying head over heels through the air at the rate of dozens of miles a minute. In spite of the innumerable circles he was describing per second, he thought; for thought is wonderful—sometimes as sluggish as flowing pitch, sometimes as instantaneous as light. He thought in a second, and willed. 'Let me come down safe and sound. Whatever else happens, let me down safe and sound.'

He willed it only just in time, for his clothes, heated by his rapid flight through the air, were already beginning to singe. He came down with a forcible, but by no means injurious, bump in what appeared to be a mound of fresh-turned earth. A large mass of metal and masonry, extraordinarily like the clock-tower in the middle of the market square, hit the earth near him, ricocheted over him, and flew into stonework, bricks, and cement, like a bursting bomb. A hurtling cow hit one of the larger blocks and smashed like an egg. There was a crash that made all the most violent crashes of his past life seem like the sound of falling dust, and this was followed by a descending series of lesser crashes. A vast wind roared throughout earth and heaven, so that he could scarcely lift his head to look. For a while he was too breathless and astonished even to see where he was or what had happened. And his first movement was to feel his head and reassure himself that his streaming hair was still his own.

'Lord!' gasped Mr Fotheringay, scarce able to speak for the gale, 'I've had a squeak! What's gone wrong? Storms and thunder. And only a minute ago a fine night. It's Maydig set me on to this sort of thing. What a wind! If I go on fooling in this way I'm bound to have a thundering accident! Where's Maydig?

'What a confounded mess everything's in!'

He looked about him so far as his flapping jacket would permit. The appearance of things was really extremely strange. 'The sky's all right anyhow,' said Mr Fotheringay. 'And that's about all that is all right. And even there it looks like a terrific gale coming up. But there's the moon overhead. Just as it was just now. Bright as midday. But as for the rest… Where's the village? Where's—where's anything? And what on earth set this wind a-blowing? I didn't order no wind.'

Mr Fotheringay struggled to get to his feet in vain, and after one failure, remained on all fours, holding on. He surveyed the moonlit world to leeward, with the tails of his jacket streaming over his head. 'There's something seriously wrong,' said Mr Fotheringay. 'And what it is…goodness knows.'

Far and wide nothing was visible in the white glare through the haze of dust that drove before a screaming gale but tumbled masses of earth and heaps of inchoate ruins, no trees, no houses, no familiar shapes, only a wilderness of disorder, vanishing at last into the darkness beneath the whirling columns and streamers, the lightning and thundering of a swiftly rising storm. Near him in the livid glare was something that might once have been an elm-tree, a smashed mass of splinters, shivered from boughs to base, and further a twisted mass of iron girders—only too evidently the viaduct—rose out of the piled confusion.

You see, when Mr Fotheringay had arrested the rotation of the solid globe, he had made no stipulation concerning the trifling movables upon its surface. And the earth spins so fast that the surface at its equator is travelling at rather more than a thousand miles an hour, and in these latitudes at more than half that pace. So that the village, and Mr Maydig, and Mr Fotheringay, and everybody and everything had been jerked violently forward at about nine miles per second—that is to say, much more violently than if they had been fired out of a cannon. And every human being, every living creature, every house, and every tree—all the world as we know it—had been so jerked and smashed and utterly destroyed. That was all.

These things Mr Fotheringay did not, of course, fully appreciate. But he perceived that his miracle had miscarried, and with that a great disgust of miracles came upon him. He was in darkness now, for the clouds had swept together and blotted out his momentary glimpse of the moon, and the air was full of fitful struggling tortured wraiths of hail. A great roaring of wind and waters filled earth and sky, and peering under his hand through the dust and sleet to windward, he saw by the play of the lightning a vast wall of water pouring towards him.

'Maydig!' screamed Mr Fotheringay's feeble voice amid the elemental uproar. 'Here!—Maydig!'

'Stop!' cried Mr Fotheringay to the advancing water. 'Oh, for goodness' sake, stop!'

'Just a moment,' said Mr Fotheringay to the lightning and thunder. 'Stop jest a moment while I collect my thoughts... And now what shall I do?' he said. 'What shall I do? Lord! I wish Maydig was about.'

'I know,' said Mr Fotheringay. 'And for goodness' sake let's have it right this time.'

He remained on all fours, leaning against the wind, very intent to have everything right.

'Ah!' he said. 'Let nothing what I'm going to order happen until I say 'Off!'...Lord! I wish I'd thought of that before!'

He lifted his little voice against the whirlwind, shouting louder and louder in the vain desire to hear himself speak. 'Now then!—here goes! Mind about that what I said just now. In the first place, when all I've got to say is done, let me lose my miraculous power, let my will become just like anybody else's will, and all these dangerous miracles be stopped. I don't like them. I'd rather I didn't work 'em. Ever so much. That's the first thing. And the second is—let me be back just before the miracles begin; let everything be just as it was before that blessed lamp turned up. It's a big job, but it's the last. Have you got it? No more miracles, everything as it was—me back in the Long Dragon just before I drank my half-pint. That's it! Yes.'

He dug his fingers into the mould, closed his eyes, and said 'Off!'

Everything became perfectly still. He perceived that he was standing erect.

'So you say,' said a voice.

He opened his eyes. He was in the bar of the Long Dragon, arguing about miracles with Toddy Beamish. He had a vague sense of some great thing forgotten that instantaneously passed. You see that, except for the loss of his miraculous powers, everything was back as it had been, his mind and memory therefore were now just as they had been at the time when this story began. So that he knew absolutely nothing of all that is told here…knows nothing of all that is told here to this day. And among other things, of course, he still did not believe in miracles.

'I tell you that miracles, properly speaking, can't possibly happen,' he said, 'whatever you like to hold. And I'm prepared to prove it up to the hilt.'

'That's what you think,' said Toddy Beamish, and 'Prove it if you can.'

'Looky here, Mr Beamish,' said Mr Fotheringay. 'Let us clearly understand what a miracle is. It's something contrariwise to the course of nature done by power of Will...'

A NOSE FOR THE KING

Jack London

In the morning calm of Korea, when its peace and tranquillity truly merited its ancient name, 'Cho-sen,' there lived a politician by name Yi Chin Ho. He was a man of parts, and—who shall say?—perhaps in no wise worse than politicians the world over. But, unlike his brethren in other lands, Yi Chin Ho was in jail. Not that he had inadvertently diverted to himself public moneys, but that he had inadvertently diverted too much. Excess is to be deplored in all things, even in grafting, and Yi Chin Ho's excess had brought him to most deplorable straits.

Ten thousand strings of cash he owed the Government, and he lay in prison under sentence of death. There was one advantage to the situation—he had plenty of time in which to think. And he thought well. Then called he the jailer to him.

'Most worthy man, you see before you one most wretched,' he began. 'Yet all will be well with me if you will but let me go free for one short hour this night. And all will be well with you, for I shall see to your advancement through the years, and you shall come at length to the directorship of all the prisons of Cho-sen.'

'How now?' demanded the jailer. 'What foolishness is this? One short hour, and you but waiting for your head to be chopped off! And I, with an aged and much-to-be-respected mother, not to say anything of a wife and several children of tender years! Out upon you for the scoundrel that you are!'

'From the Sacred City to the ends of all the Eight Coasts there is no place for me to hide,' Yi Chin Ho made reply. 'I am a man of wisdom, but of what worth my wisdom here in prison? Were I free, well I know I could seek out and obtain the money wherewith to repay the Government. I know of a nose that will save me from all my difficulties.'

'A nose!' cried the jailer.

'A nose,' said Yi Chin Ho. 'A remarkable nose, if I may say so, a most remarkable nose.'

The jailer threw up his hands despairingly. 'Ah, what a wag you are, what a wag,' he laughed. 'To think that that very admirable wit of yours must go the way of the chopping-block!'

And so saying, he turned and went away. But in the end, being a man soft of head and heart, when the night was well along he permitted Yi Chin Ho to go.

Straight he went to the Governor, catching him alone and arousing him from his sleep.

'Yi Chin Ho, or I'm no Governor!' cried the Governor. 'What do you here who should be in prison waiting on the chopping-block?'

'I pray Your Excellency to listen to me,' said Yi Chin Ho, squatting on his hams by the bedside and lighting his pipe from the fire-box. 'A dead man is without value. It is true, I am as a dead man, without value to the Government, to Your Excellency, or to myself. But if, so to say, Your Excellency were to give me my freedom—'

'Impossible!' cried the Governor. 'Beside, you are condemned to death.'

'Your Excellency well knows that if I can repay the ten thousand strings of cash, the Government will pardon me,' Yi Chin Ho went on. 'So, as I say, if Your Excellency were to give me my freedom for a few days, being a man of understanding, I should then repay the Government and be in position to be of service to Your Excellency. I should be in position to be of very great service to Your Excellency.'

'Have you a plan whereby you hope to obtain this money?' asked the Governor.

'I have,' said Yi Chin Ho.

'Then come with it to me to-morrow night; I would now sleep,' said the Governor, taking up his snore where it had been interrupted.

On the following night, having again obtained leave of absence from the jailer, Yi Chin Ho presented himself at the Governor's bedside.

'Is it you, Yi Chin Ho?' asked the Governor. 'And have you the plan?'

'It is I, Your Excellency,' answered Yi Chin Ho, 'and the plan is here.'

'Speak,' commanded the Governor.

'The plan is here,' repeated Yi Chin Ho, 'here in my hand.'

The Governor sat up and opened his eyes. Yi Chin Ho proffered in his hand a sheet of paper. The Governor held it to the light.

'Nothing but a nose,' said he.

'A bit pinched, so, and so, Your Excellency,' said Yi Chin Ho.

'Yes, a bit pinched here and there, as you say,' said the Governor.

'Withal it is an exceeding corpulent nose, thus, and so, all in one place, at the end,' proceeded Yi Chin Ho. 'Your Excellency would seek far and wide and many a day for that nose and find it not!'

'An unusual nose,' admitted the Governor.

'There is a wart upon it,' said Yi Chin Ho.

'A most unusual nose,' said the Governor. 'Never have I seen the like. But what do you with this nose, Yi Chin Ho?'

'I seek it whereby to repay the money to the Government,' said Yi Chin Ho. 'I seek it to be of service to Your Excellency, and I seek it to save my own worthless head. Further, I seek Your Excellency's seal upon this picture of the nose.'

And the Governor laughed and affixed the seal of State, and Yi Chin Ho departed. For a month and a day he travelled the King's Road which leads to the shore of the Eastern Sea; and there, one night, at the gate of the largest mansion of a wealthy city he knocked loudly for admittance.

'None other than the master of the house will I see,' said he fiercely to the frightened servants. 'I travel upon the King's business.'

Straightway was he led to an inner room, where the master of the house was roused from his sleep and brought blinking before him.

'You are Pak Chung Chang, head man of this city,' said Yi Chin Ho in tones that were all-accusing. 'I am upon the King's business.'

Pak Chung Chang trembled. Well he knew the King's business was ever a terrible business. His knees smote together, and he near fell to the floor.

'The hour is late,' he quavered. 'Were it not well to—'

'The King's business never waits!' thundered Yi Chin Ho. 'Come apart with me, and swiftly. I have an affair of moment to discuss with you.

'It is the King's affair,' he added with even greater fierceness; so that Pak Chung Chang's silver pipe dropped from his nerveless fingers and clattered on the floor.

'Know then,' said Yi Chin Ho, when they had gone apart, 'that the King is troubled with an affliction, a very terrible affliction. In that he failed to cure, the Court physician has had nothing else than his head chopped off. From all the Eight Provinces have the physicians come to wait upon the King. Wise consultation have they held, and they have decided that for a remedy for the King's affliction nothing else is required than a nose, a certain kind of nose, a very peculiar certain kind of nose.

'Then by none other was I summoned than His Excellency the Prime Minister himself. He put a paper into my hand. Upon this paper was the very peculiar kind of nose drawn by the physicians of the Eight Provinces, with the seal of State upon it.

'Go,' said His Excellency the Prime Minister. 'Seek out this nose, for the King's affliction is sore. And wheresoever you find this nose upon the face of a man, strike it off forthright and bring it in all haste to the Court, for the King must be cured. Go, and come not back until your search is rewarded.'

'And so I departed upon my quest,' said Yi Chin Ho. 'I have sought out the remotest corners of the kingdom; I have travelled the Eight Highways, searched the Eight Provinces, and sailed the seas of the Eight Coasts. And here I am.'

With a great flourish he drew a paper from his girdle, unrolled it with many snappings and cracklings, and thrust it before the face of Pak Chung Chang. Upon the paper was the picture of the nose.

Pak Chung Chang stared upon it with bulging eyes.

'Never have I beheld such a nose,' he began.

'There is a wart upon it,' said Yi Chin Ho.

'Never have I beheld—' Pak Chung Chang began again.

'Bring your father before me,' Yi Chin Ho interrupted sternly.

'My ancient and very-much-to-be-respected ancestor sleeps,' said Pak Chung Chang.

'Why dissemble?' demanded Yi Chin Ho. 'You know it is your father's nose. Bring him before me that I may strike it off and be gone. Hurry, lest I make bad report of you.'

'Mercy!' cried Pak Chung Chang, falling on his knees. 'It is impossible! It is impossible! You cannot strike off my father's nose.

He cannot go down without his nose to the grave. He will become a laughter and a byword, and all my days and nights will be filled with woe. O reflect! Report that you have seen no such nose in your travels. You, too, have a father.'

Pak Chung Chang clasped Yi Chin Ho's knees and fell to weeping on his sandals.

'My heart softens strangely at your tears,' said Yi Chin Ho. 'I, too, know filial piety and regard. But—' He hesitated, then added, as though thinking aloud, 'It is as much as my head is worth.'

'How much is your head worth?' asked Pak Chung Chang in a thin, small voice.

'A not remarkable head,' said Yi Chin Ho. 'An absurdly unremarkable head; but, such is my great foolishness, I value it at nothing less than one hundred thousand strings of cash.'

'So be it,' said Pak Chung Chang, rising to his feet.

'I shall need horses to carry the treasure,' said Yi Chin Ho, 'and men to guard it well as I journey through the mountains. There are robbers abroad in the land.'

'There are robbers abroad in the land,' said Pak Chung Chang, sadly. 'But it shall be as you wish, so long as my ancient and very-much-to-be-respected ancestor's nose abide in its appointed place.'

'Say nothing to any man of this occurrence,' said Yi Chin Ho, 'else will other and more loyal servants than I be sent to strike off your father's nose.'

And so Yi Chin Ho departed on his way through the mountains, blithe of heart and gay of song as he listened to the jingling bells of his treasure-laden ponies.

There is little more to tell. Yi Chin Ho prospered through the years. By his efforts the jailer attained at length to the directorship of all the prisons of Cho-sen; the Governor ultimately betook himself to the Sacred City to be Prime Minister to the King, while Yi Chin Ho became the King's boon companion and sat at table with him to the end of a round, fat life. But Pak Chung Chang fell into a melancholy, and ever after he shook his head sadly, with tears in his eyes, whenever he regarded the expensive nose of his ancient and very-much-to-be-respected ancestor.

A WICKED WOMAN

Jack London

It was because she had broken with Billy that Loretta had come visiting to Santa Clara. Billy could not understand. His sister had reported that he had walked the floor and cried all night. Loretta had not slept all night either, while she had wept most of the night. Daisy knew this, because it was in her arms that the weeping had been done. And Daisy's husband, Captain Kitt, knew, too. The tears of Loretta, and the comforting by Daisy, had lost him some sleep.

Now Captain Kitt did not like to lose sleep. Neither did he want Loretta to marry Billy—nor anybody else. It was Captain Kitt's belief that Daisy needed the help of her younger sister in the household. But he did not say this aloud. Instead, he always insisted that Loretta was too young to think of marriage. So it was Captain Kitt's idea that Loretta should be packed off on a visit to Mrs Hemingway. There wouldn't be any Billy there.

Before Loretta had been at Santa Clara a week, she was convinced that Captain Kitt's idea was a good one. In the first place, though Billy wouldn't believe it, she did not want to marry Billy. And in the second place, though Captain Kitt wouldn't believe it, she did not want to leave Daisy. By the time Loretta had been at Santa Clara two weeks, she was absolutely certain that she did not want to marry Billy. But she was not so sure about not wanting to leave Daisy. Not that she loved Daisy less, but that she—had doubts.

The day of Loretta's arrival, a nebulous plan began shaping itself in Mrs Hemingway's brain. The second day she remarked to Jack Hemingway, her husband, that Loretta was so innocent a young thing that were it not for her sweet guilelessness she would be positively stupid. In proof of which, Mrs Hemingway told her husband several things that made him chuckle. By the third day Mrs Hemingway's plan had taken recognizable form. Then it was that she composed a letter. On the envelope she wrote, 'Mr Edward Bashford, Athenian Club, San Francisco.'

'Dear Ned,' the letter began. She had once been violently loved by him for three weeks in her pre-marital days. But she had covenanted herself to Jack Hemingway, who had prior claims, and her heart as well; and Ned Bashford had philosophically not broken his heart over it. He merely added the experience to a large fund of similarly collected data out of which he manufactured philosophy. Artistically and temperamentally he was a Greek...a tired Greek. He was fond of quoting from Nietzsche, in token that he, too, had passed through the long sickness that follows upon the ardent search for truth; that he too had emerged, too experienced, too shrewd, too profound, ever again to be afflicted by the madness of youths in their love of truth. 'To worship appearance,' he often quoted; 'to believe in forms, in tones, in words, in the whole Olympus of appearance!' This particular excerpt he always concluded with, 'Those Greeks were superficial—OUT OF PROFUNDITY!'

He was a fairly young Greek, jaded and worn. Women were faithless and unveracious, he held—at such times that he had relapses and descended to pessimism from his wonted high philosophical calm. He did not believe in the truth of women; but, faithful to his German master, he did not strip from them the airy gauzes that veiled their untruth. He was content to accept them as appearances and to make the best of it. He was superficial—OUT OF PROFUNDITY.

'Jack says to be sure to say to you, "good swimming,"' Mrs Hemingway wrote in her letter; 'and also "to bring your fishing duds along."' Mrs Hemingway wrote other things in the letter. She told him that at last she was prepared to exhibit to him an absolutely true, unsullied, and innocent woman. 'A more guileless, immaculate bud of womanhood never blushed on the planet,' was one of the several ways in which she phrased the inducement. And to her husband she said triumphantly, 'If I don't marry Ned off this time—' leaving unstated the terrible alternative that she lacked either vocabulary to express or imagination to conceive.

Contrary to all her forebodings, Loretta found that she was not unhappy at Santa Clara. Truly, Billy wrote to her every day, but his letters were less distressing than his presence. Also, the ordeal of being away from Daisy was not so severe as she had expected. For the first time in her life she was not lost in eclipse in the blaze of Daisy's brilliant and mature personality. Under such favourable circumstances Loretta came rapidly to the front, while Mrs Hemingway modestly and shamelessly retreated into the background.

Loretta began to discover that she was not a pale orb shining by reflection. Quite unconsciously she became a small centre of things. When she was at the piano, there was someone to turn the pages for her and to express preferences for certain songs. When she dropped her handkerchief, there was someone to pick it up. And there was someone to accompany her in ramblings and flower gatherings. Also, she learned to cast flies in still pools and below savage riffles, and how not to entangle silk lines and gut-leaders with the shrubbery.

Jack Hemingway did not care to teach beginners, and fished much by himself, or not at all, thus giving Ned Bashford ample time in which to consider Loretta as an appearance. As such, she was all that his philosophy demanded. Her blue eyes had the direct gaze of a boy, and out of his profundity he delighted in them and forbore to shudder at the duplicity his philosophy bade him to believe lurked in their depths. She had the grace of a slender flower, the fragility of colour and line of fine china, in all of which he pleasured greatly, without thought of the Life Force palpitating beneath and in spite of Bernard Shaw—in whom he believed.

Loretta burgeoned. She swiftly developed personality. She discovered a will of her own and wishes of her own that were not everlastingly entwined with the will and the wishes of Daisy. She was petted by Jack Hemingway, spoiled by Alice Hemingway, and devotedly attended by Ned Bashford. They encouraged her whims and laughed at her follies, while she developed the pretty little tyrannies that are latent in all pretty and delicate women. Her environment acted as a soporific upon her ancient desire always to live with Daisy. This desire no longer prodded her as in the days of her companionship with Billy. The more she saw of Billy, the more certain she had been that she could not live away from Daisy. The more she saw of Ned Bashford, the more she forgot her pressing need of Daisy.

Ned Bashford likewise did some forgetting. He confused superficiality with profundity, and entangled appearance with reality until he accounted them one. Loretta was different from other women. There was no masquerade about her. She was real. He said as much to Mrs Hemingway, and more, who agreed with him and at the same time caught her husband's eyelid drooping down for the moment in an unmistakable wink.

It was at this time that Loretta received a letter from Billy that was somewhat different from his others. In the main, like all his letters, it was pathological. It was a long recital of symptoms and sufferings, his nervousness, his sleeplessness, and the state of his heart. Then followed reproaches, such as he had never made before. They were sharp enough to make her weep, and true enough to put tragedy into her face. This tragedy she carried down to the breakfast table. It made Jack and Mrs Hemingway speculative, and it worried Ned. They glanced to him for explanation, but he shook his head.

'I'll find out to-night,' Mrs Hemingway said to her husband.

But Ned caught Loretta in the afternoon in the big living-room. She tried to turn away. He caught her hands, and she faced him with wet lashes and trembling lips. He looked at her, silently and kindly. The lashes grew wetter.

'There, there, don't cry, little one,' he said soothingly.

He put his arm protectingly around her shoulder. And to his shoulder, like a tired child, she turned her face. He thrilled in ways unusual for a Greek who has recovered from the long sickness.

'Oh, Ned,' she sobbed on his shoulder, 'if you only knew how wicked I am!'

He smiled indulgently, and breathed in a great breath freighted with the fragrance of her hair. He thought of his world-experience of women, and drew another long breath. There seemed to emanate from her the perfect sweetness of a child—'the aura of a white soul,' was the way he phrased it to himself.

Then he noticed that her sobs were increasing.

'What's the matter, little one?' he asked pettingly and almost paternally. 'Has Jack been bullying you? Or has your dearly beloved sister failed to write?'

She did not answer, and he felt that he really must kiss her hair, that he could not be responsible if the situation continued much longer.

'Tell me,' he said gently, 'and we'll see what I can do.'

'I can't. You will despise me.—Oh, Ned, I am so ashamed!'

He laughed incredulously, and lightly touched her hair with his lips—so lightly that she did not know.

'Dear little one, let us forget all about it, whatever it is. I want to tell you how I love—'

She uttered a sharp cry that was all delight, and then moaned—

'Too late!'

'Too late?' he echoed in surprise.

'Oh, why did I? Why did I?' she was moaning.

He was aware of a swift chill at his heart.

'What?' he asked.

'Oh, I…he…Billy.'

'I am such a wicked woman, Ned. I know you will never speak to me again.'

'This—er—this Billy,' he began haltingly. 'He is your brother?'

'No…he…I didn't know. I was so young. I could not help it. Oh, I shall go mad! I shall go mad!'

It was then that Loretta felt his shoulder and the encircling arm become limp. He drew away from her gently, and gently he deposited her in a big chair, where she buried her face and sobbed afresh. He twisted his moustache fiercely, then drew up another chair and sat down.

'I—I do not understand,' he said.

'I am so unhappy,' she wailed.

'Why unhappy?'

'Because…he…he wants me to marry him.'

His face cleared on the instant, and he placed a hand soothingly on hers.

'That should not make any girl unhappy,' he remarked sagely. 'Because you don't love him is no reason—of course, you don't love him?'

Loretta shook her head and shoulders in a vigorous negative.

'What?'

Bashford wanted to make sure.

'No,' she asserted explosively. 'I don't love Billy! I don't want to love Billy!'

'Because you don't love him,' Bashford resumed with confidence, 'is no reason that you should be unhappy just because he has proposed to you.'

She sobbed again, and from the midst of her sobs she cried—

'That's the trouble. I wish I did love him. Oh, I wish I were dead!'

'Now, my dear child, you are worrying yourself over trifles.' His other hand crossed over after its mate and rested on hers. 'Women do it every day. Because you have changed your mind or did not know your mind, because you have—to use an unnecessarily harsh word—jilted a man—'

'Jilted!' She had raised her head and was looking at him with tear-dimmed eyes. 'Oh, Ned, if that were all!'

'All?' he asked in a hollow voice, while his hands slowly retreated from hers. He was about to speak further, then remained silent.

'But I don't want to marry him,' Loretta broke forth protestingly.

'Then I shouldn't,' he counselled.

'But I ought to marry him.'

'OUGHT to marry him?'

She nodded.

'That is a strong word.'

'I know it is,' she acquiesced, while she strove to control her trembling lips. Then she spoke more calmly. 'I am a wicked woman, a terribly wicked woman. No one knows how wicked I am—except Billy.'

There was a pause. Ned Bashford's face was grave, and he looked queerly at Loretta.

'He—Billy knows?' he asked finally.

A reluctant nod and flaming cheeks was the reply.

He debated with himself for a while, seeming, like a diver, to be preparing himself for the plunge.

'Tell me about it.' He spoke very firmly. 'You must tell me all of it.'

'And will you—ever—forgive me?' she asked in a faint, small voice.

He hesitated, drew a long breath, and made the plunge.

'Yes,' he said desperately. 'I'll forgive you. Go ahead.'

'There was no one to tell me,' she began. 'We were with each other so much. I did not know anything of the world—then.'

She paused to meditate. Bashford was biting his lip impatiently.

'If I had only known—'

She paused again.

'Yes, go on,' he urged.

'We were together almost every evening.'

'Billy?' he demanded, with a savageness that startled her.

'Yes, of course, Billy. We were with each other so much… If I had only known… There was no one to tell me… I was so young—'

Her lips parted as though to speak further, and she regarded him anxiously.

'The scoundrel!'

With the explosion Ned Bashford was on his feet, no longer a tired Greek, but a violently angry young man.

'Billy is not a scoundrel; he is a good man,' Loretta defended, with a firmness that surprised Bashford.

'I suppose you'll be telling me next that it was all your fault,' he said sarcastically.

She nodded.

'What?' he shouted.

'It was all my fault,' she said steadily. 'I should never have let him. I was to blame.'

Bashford ceased from his pacing up and down, and when he spoke, his voice was resigned.

'All right,' he said. 'I don't blame you in the least, Loretta. And you have been very honest. But Billy is right, and you are wrong. You must get married.'

'To Billy?' she asked, in a dim, far-away voice.

'Yes, to Billy. I'll see to it. Where does he live? I'll make him.'

'But I don't want to marry Billy!' she cried out in alarm. 'Oh, Ned, you won't do that?'

'I shall,' he answered sternly. 'You must. And Billy must. Do you understand?'

Loretta buried her face in the cushioned chair back, and broke into a passionate storm of sobs.

All that Bashford could make out at first, as he listened, was, 'But I don't want to leave Daisy! I don't want to leave Daisy!'

He paced grimly back and forth, then stopped curiously to listen.

'How was I to know?—Boo—hoo,' Loretta was crying. 'He didn't tell me. Nobody else ever kissed me. I never dreamed a kiss could be so terrible…until, boo-hoo…until he wrote to me. I only got the letter this morning.'

His face brightened. It seemed as though light was dawning on him.

'Is that what you're crying about?'

'N—no.'

His heart sank.

'Then what are you crying about?' he asked in a hopeless voice.

'Because you said I had to marry Billy. And I don't want to marry Billy. I don't want to leave Daisy. I don't know what I want. I wish I were dead.'

He nerved himself for another effort.

'Now look here, Loretta, be sensible. What is this about kisses. You haven't told me everything?'

'I—I don't want to tell you everything.'

She looked at him beseechingly in the silence that fell.

'Must I?' she quavered finally.

'You must,' he said imperatively. 'You must tell me everything.'

'Well, then…must I?'

'You must.'

'He…I…we…' she began flounderingly. Then blurted out, 'I let him, and he kissed me.'

'Go on,' Bashford commanded desperately.

'That's all,' she answered.

'All?' There was a vast incredulity in his voice.

'All?' In her voice was an interrogation no less vast.

'I mean—er—nothing worse?' He was overwhelmingly aware of his own awkwardness.

'Worse?' She was frankly puzzled. 'As though there could be! Billy said...'

'When did he say it?' Bashford demanded abruptly.

'In his letter I got this morning. Billy said that my...our...our kisses were terrible if we didn't get married.'

Bashford's head was swimming.

'What else did Billy say?' he asked.

'He said that when a woman allowed a man to kiss her, she always married him—that it was terrible if she didn't. It was the custom, he said; and I say it is a bad, wicked custom, and I don't like it. I know I'm terrible,' she added defiantly, 'but I can't help it.'

Bashford absent-mindedly brought out a cigarette.

'Do you mind if I smoke?' he asked, as he struck a match.

Then he came to himself.

'I beg your pardon,' he cried, flinging away match and cigarette. 'I don't want to smoke. I didn't mean that at all. What I mean is—'

He bent over Loretta, caught her hands in his, then sat on the arm of the chair and softly put one arm around her.

'Loretta, I am a fool. I mean it. And I mean something more. I want you to be my wife.'

He waited anxiously in the pause that followed.

'You might answer me,' he urged.

'I will...if—'

'Yes, go on. If what?'

'If I don't have to marry Billy.'

'You can't marry both of us,' he almost shouted.

'And it isn't the custom...what...what Billy said?'

'No, it isn't the custom. Now, Loretta, will you marry me?'

'Don't be angry with me,' she pouted demurely.

He gathered her into his arms and kissed her.

'I wish it were the custom,' she said in a faint voice, from the midst of the embrace, 'because then I'd have to marry you, Ned dear... wouldn't I?'

HUNTED DOWN

Charles Dickens

I

Most of us see some romances in life. In my capacity as Chief Manager of a Life Assurance Office, I think I have within the last thirty years seen more romances than the generality of men, however unpromising the opportunity may, at first sight, seem.

As I have retired, and live at my ease, I possess the means that I used to want, of considering what I have seen, at leisure. My experiences have a more remarkable aspect, so reviewed, than they had when they were in progress. I have come home from the Play now, and can recall the scenes of the Drama upon which the curtain has fallen, free from the glare, bewilderment, and bustle of the Theatre.

Let me recall one of these Romances of the real world.

There is nothing truer than physiognomy, taken in connection with manner. The art of reading that book of which Eternal Wisdom obliges every human creature to present his or her own page with the individual character written on it, is a difficult one, perhaps, and is little studied. It may require some natural aptitude, and it must require (for everything does) some patience and some pains. That these are not usually given to it,—that numbers of people accept a few stock commonplace expressions of the face as the whole list of characteristics, and neither seek nor know the refinements that are truest,—that You, for instance, give a great deal of time and attention to the reading of music, Greek, Latin, French, Italian, Hebrew, if you please, and do not qualify yourself to read the face of the master or mistress looking over your shoulder teaching it to you,—I assume to be five hundred times more probable than improbable. Perhaps a little self-sufficiency may be at the bottom of this; facial expression requires no study from you, you think; it comes by nature to you to know enough about it, and you are not to be taken in.

I confess, for my part, that I have been taken in, over and over again. I have been taken in by acquaintances, and I have been taken in (of course) by friends; far oftener by friends than by any other class of persons. How come I to be so deceived? Had I quite misread their faces?

No. Believe me, my first impression of those people, founded on face and manner alone, was invariably true. My mistake was in suffering them to come nearer to me and explain themselves away.

II

The partition which separated my own office from our general outer office in the City was of thick plate-glass. I could see through it what passed in the outer office, without hearing a word. I had it put up in place of a wall that had been there for years,—ever since the house was built. It is no matter whether I did or did not make the change in order that I might derive my first impression of strangers, who came to us on business, from their faces alone, without being influenced by anything they said. Enough to mention that I turned my glass partition to that account, and that a Life Assurance Office is at all times exposed to be practised upon by the most crafty and cruel of the human race.

It was through my glass partition that I first saw the gentleman whose story I am going to tell.

He had come in without my observing it, and had put his hat and umbrella on the broad counter, and was bending over it to take some papers from one of the clerks. He was about forty or so, dark, exceedingly well dressed in black,—being in mourning,—and the hand he extended with a polite air, had a particularly well-fitting black-kid glove upon it. His hair, which was elaborately brushed and oiled, was parted straight up the middle; and he presented this parting to the clerk, exactly (to my thinking) as if he had said, in so many words: 'You must take me, if you please, my friend, just as I show myself. Come straight up here, follow the gravel path, keep off the grass, I allow no trespassing.'

I conceived a very great aversion to that man the moment I thus saw him.

He had asked for some of our printed forms, and the clerk was giving them to him and explaining them. An obliged and agreeable smile was on his face, and his eyes met those of the clerk with a sprightly look. (I have known a vast quantity of nonsense talked about bad men not looking you in the face. Don't trust that conventional idea. Dishonesty will stare honesty out of countenance, any day in the week, if there is anything to be got by it.)

I saw, in the corner of his eyelash, that he became aware of my looking at him. Immediately he turned the parting in his hair toward the glass partition, as if he said to me with a sweet smile, 'Straight up here, if you please. Off the grass!'

In a few moments he had put on his hat and taken up his umbrella, and was gone.

I beckoned the clerk into my room, and asked, 'Who was that?'

He had the gentleman's card in his hand. 'Mr Julius Slinkton, Middle Temple.'

'A barrister, Mr Adams?'

'I think not, sir.'

'I should have thought him a clergyman, but for his having no Reverend here,' said I.

'Probably, from his appearance,' Mr Adams replied, 'he is reading for orders.'

I should mention that he wore a dainty white cravat, and dainty linen altogether.

'What did he want, Mr Adams?'

'Merely a form of proposal, sir, and form of reference.'

'Recommended here? Did he say?'

'Yes, he said he was recommended here by a friend of yours. He noticed you, but said that as he had not the pleasure of your personal acquaintance he would not trouble you.'

'Did he know my name?'

'O yes, sir! He said, 'There is Mr Sampson, I see!'

'A well-spoken gentleman, apparently?'

'Remarkably so, sir.'

'Insinuating manners, apparently?'

'Very much so, indeed, sir.'

'Hah!' said I. 'I want nothing at present, Mr Adams.'

Within a fortnight of that day I went to dine with a friend of mine, a merchant, a man of taste, who buys pictures and books, and the first man I saw among the company was Mr Julius Slinkton. There he was, standing before the fire, with good large eyes and an open expression of face; but still (I thought) requiring everybody to come at him by the prepared way he offered, and by no other.

I noticed him ask my friend to introduce him to Mr Sampson, and my friend did so. Mr Slinkton was very happy to see me. Not too happy; there was no over-doing of the matter; happy in a thoroughly well-bred, perfectly unmeaning way.

'I thought you had met,' our host observed.

'No,' said Mr Slinkton. 'I did look in at Mr Sampson's office, on your recommendation; but I really did not feel justified in troubling Mr Sampson himself, on a point in the everyday routine of an ordinary clerk.'

I said I should have been glad to show him any attention on our friend's introduction.

'I am sure of that,' said he, 'and am much obliged. At another time, perhaps, I may be less delicate. Only, however, if I have real business; for I know, Mr Sampson, how precious business time is, and what a vast number of impertinent people there are in the world.'

I acknowledged his consideration with a slight bow. 'You were thinking,' said I, 'of effecting a policy on your life.'

'O dear no! I am afraid I am not so prudent as you pay me the compliment of supposing me to be, Mr Sampson. I merely inquired for a friend. But you know what friends are in such matters. Nothing may ever come of it. I have the greatest reluctance to trouble men of business with inquiries for friends, knowing the probabilities to be a thousand to one that the friends will never follow them up. People are so fickle, so selfish, so inconsiderate. Don't you, in your business, find them so every day, Mr Sampson?'

I was going to give a qualified answer; but he turned his smooth, white parting on me with its 'Straight up here, if you please!' and I answered 'Yes.'

'I hear, Mr Sampson,' he resumed presently, for our friend had a new cook, and dinner was not so punctual as usual, 'that your profession has recently suffered a great loss.'

'In money?' said I.

He laughed at my ready association of loss with money, and replied, 'No, in talent and vigour.'

Not at once following out his allusion, I considered for a moment. 'Has it sustained a loss of that kind?' said I. 'I was not aware of it.'

'Understand me, Mr Sampson. I don't imagine that you have retired. It is not so bad as that. But Mr Meltham—'

'O, to be sure!' said I. 'Yes! Mr Meltham, the young actuary of the "Inestimable".'

'Just so,' he returned in a consoling way.

'He is a great loss. He was at once the most profound, the most original, and the most energetic man I have ever known connected with Life Assurance.'

I spoke strongly; for I had a high esteem and admiration for Meltham; and my gentleman had indefinitely conveyed to me some suspicion that he wanted to sneer at him. He recalled me to my guard by presenting that trim pathway up his head, with its internal 'Not on the grass, if you please—the gravel.'

'You knew him, Mr Slinkton.'

'Only by reputation. To have known him as an acquaintance or as a friend, is an honour I should have sought if he had remained in society, though I might never have had the good fortune to attain it, being a man of far inferior mark. He was scarcely above thirty, I suppose?'

'About thirty.'

'Ah!' he sighed in his former consoling way. 'What creatures we are! To break up, Mr Sampson, and become incapable of business at that time of life!—Any reason assigned for the melancholy fact?'

('Humph!' thought I, as I looked at him. 'But I WON'T go up the track, and I WILL go on the grass.')

'What reason have you heard assigned, Mr Slinkton?' I asked, point-blank.

'Most likely a false one. You know what Rumour is, Mr Sampson. I never repeat what I hear; it is the only way of paring the nails and shaving the head of Rumour. But when you ask me what reason I have heard assigned for Mr Meltham's passing away from among men, it is another thing. I am not gratifying idle gossip then. I was told, Mr Sampson, that Mr Meltham had relinquished all his avocations and all his prospects, because he was, in fact, broken-hearted. A disappointed attachment I heard,—though it hardly seems probable, in the case of a man so distinguished and so attractive.'

'Attractions and distinctions are no armour against death,' said I.

'O, she died? Pray pardon me. I did not hear that. That, indeed, makes it very, very sad. Poor Mr Meltham! She died? Ah, dear me! Lamentable, lamentable!'

I still thought his pity was not quite genuine, and I still suspected an unaccountable sneer under all this, until he said, as we were parted, like the other knots of talkers, by the announcement of dinner:

'Mr Sampson, you are surprised to see me so moved on behalf of a man whom I have never known. I am not so disinterested as you may suppose. I have suffered, and recently too, from death myself. I have lost one of two charming nieces, who were my constant companions. She died young—barely three-and-twenty; and even her remaining sister is far from strong. The world is a grave!'

He said this with deep feeling, and I felt reproached for the coldness of my manner. Coldness and distrust had been engendered in me, I knew, by my bad experiences; they were not natural to me; and I often thought how much I had lost in life, losing trustfulness, and how little I had gained, gaining hard caution. This state of mind being habitual to me, I troubled myself more about this conversation than I might have troubled myself about a greater matter. I listened to his talk at dinner, and observed how readily other men responded to it, and with what a graceful instinct he adapted his subjects to the knowledge and habits of those he talked with. As, in talking with me, he had easily started the subject I might be supposed to understand best, and to be the most interested in, so, in talking with others, he guided himself by the same rule. The company was of a varied character; but he was not at fault, that I could discover, with any member of it. He knew just as much of each man's pursuit as made him agreeable to that man in reference to it, and just as little as made it natural in him to seek modestly for information when the theme was broached.

As he talked and talked—but really not too much, for the rest of us seemed to force it upon him—I became quite angry with myself. I took his face to pieces in my mind, like a watch, and examined it in detail. I could not say much against any of his features separately; I could say even less against them when they were put together. 'Then is it not monstrous,' I asked myself, 'that because a man happens to part his hair straight up the middle of his head, I should permit myself to suspect, and even to detest him?'

(I may stop to remark that this was no proof of my sense. An observer of men who finds himself steadily repelled by some apparently trifling thing in a stranger is right to give it great weight. It may be the clue to the whole mystery. A hair or two will show where a lion is hidden. A very little key will open a very heavy door.)

I took my part in the conversation with him after a time, and we got on remarkably well. In the drawing-room I asked the host how long he had known Mr Slinkton. He answered, not many months; he had met him at the house of a celebrated painter then present, who had known him well when he was travelling with his nieces in Italy for their health. His plans in life being broken by the death of one of them, he was reading with the intention of going back to college as a matter of form, taking his degree, and going into orders. I could not but argue with myself that here was the true explanation of his interest in poor Meltham, and that I had been almost brutal in my distrust on that simple head.

III

On the very next day but one I was sitting behind my glass partition, as before, when he came into the outer office, as before. The moment I saw him again without hearing him, I hated him worse than ever.

It was only for a moment that I had this opportunity; for he waved his tight-fitting black glove the instant I looked at him, and came straight in.

'Mr Sampson, good-day! I presume, you see, upon your kind permission to intrude upon you. I don't keep my word in being justified by business, for my business here—if I may so abuse the word—is of the slightest nature.'

I asked, was it anything I could assist him in?

'I thank you, no. I merely called to inquire outside whether my dilatory friend had been so false to himself as to be practical and sensible. But, of course, he has done nothing. I gave him your papers with my own hand, and he was hot upon the intention, but of course he has done nothing. Apart from the general human disinclination to do anything that ought to be done, I dare say there is a specialty about assuring one's life. You find it like will-making. People are so superstitious, and take it for granted they will die soon afterwards.'

'Up here, if you please; straight up here, Mr Sampson. Neither to the right nor to the left.' I almost fancied I could hear him breathe the words as he sat smiling at me, with that intolerable parting exactly opposite the bridge of my nose.

'There is such a feeling sometimes, no doubt,' I replied; 'but I don't think it obtains to any great extent.'

'Well,' said he, with a shrug and a smile, 'I wish some good angel would influence my friend in the right direction. I rashly promised his mother and sister in Norfolk to see it done, and he promised them that he would do it. But I suppose he never will.'

He spoke for a minute or two on indifferent topics, and went away.

I had scarcely unlocked the drawers of my writing-table next morning, when he reappeared. I noticed that he came straight to the door in the glass partition, and did not pause a single moment outside.

'Can you spare me two minutes, my dear Mr Sampson?'

'By all means.'

'Much obliged,' laying his hat and umbrella on the table; 'I came early, not to interrupt you. The fact is, I am taken by surprise in reference to this proposal my friend has made.'

'Has he made one?' said I.

'Ye-es,' he answered, deliberately looking at me; and then a bright idea seemed to strike him—'or he only tells me he has. Perhaps that may be a new way of evading the matter. By Jupiter, I never thought of that!'

Mr Adams was opening the morning's letters in the outer office.

'What is the name, Mr Slinkton?' I asked.

'Beckwith.'

I looked out at the door and requested Mr Adams, if there were a proposal in that name, to bring it in. He had already laid it out of his hand on the counter. It was easily selected from the rest, and he gave it me. Alfred Beckwith. Proposal to effect a policy with us for two thousand pounds. Dated yesterday.

'From the Middle Temple, I see, Mr Slinkton.'

'Yes. He lives on the same staircase with me; his door is opposite. I never thought he would make me his reference though.'

'It seems natural enough that he should.'

'Quite so, Mr Sampson; but I never thought of it. Let me see.' He took the printed paper from his pocket. 'How am I to answer all these questions?'

'According to the truth, of course,' said I.

'O, of course!' he answered, looking up from the paper with a smile; 'I meant they were so many. But you do right to be particular. It stands to reason that you must be particular. Will you allow me to use your pen and ink?'

'Certainly.'

'And your desk?'

'Certainly.'

He had been hovering about between his hat and his umbrella for a place to write on. He now sat down in my chair, at my blotting-paper and inkstand, with the long walk up his head in accurate perspective before me, as I stood with my back to the fire.

Before answering each question he ran over it aloud, and discussed it. How long had he known Mr Alfred Beckwith? That he had to calculate by years upon his fingers. What were his habits? No difficulty about them; temperate in the last degree, and took a little too much exercise, if anything. All the answers were satisfactory. When he had written them all, he looked them over, and finally signed them in a very pretty hand. He supposed he had now done with the business. I told him he was not likely to be troubled any farther. Should he leave the papers there? If he pleased. Much obliged. Good-morning.

I had had one other visitor before him; not at the office, but at my own house. That visitor had come to my bedside when it was not yet daylight, and had been seen by no one else but by my faithful confidential servant.

A second reference paper (for we required always two) was sent down into Norfolk, and was duly received back by post. This, likewise, was satisfactorily answered in every respect. Our forms were all complied with; we accepted the proposal, and the premium for one year was paid.

IV

For six or seven months I saw no more of Mr Slinkton. He called once at my house, but I was not at home; and he once asked me to dine with him in the Temple, but I was engaged. His friend's assurance was effected in March. Late in September or early in October I was down at Scarborough for a breath of sea-air, where I met him on the beach. It was a hot evening; he came toward me with his hat in his hand; and there was the walk I had felt so strongly disinclined to take in perfect order again, exactly in front of the bridge of my nose.

He was not alone, but had a young lady on his arm.

She was dressed in mourning, and I looked at her with great interest. She had the appearance of being extremely delicate, and her face was remarkably pale and melancholy; but she was very pretty. He introduced her as his niece, Miss Niner.

'Are you strolling, Mr Sampson? Is it possible you can be idle?'

It was possible, and I was strolling.

'Shall we stroll together?'

'With pleasure.'

The young lady walked between us, and we walked on the cool sea sand, in the direction of Filey.

'There have been wheels here,' said Mr Slinkton. 'And now I look again, the wheels of a hand-carriage! Margaret, my love, your shadow without doubt!'

'Miss Niner's shadow?' I repeated, looking down at it on the sand.

'Not that one,' Mr Slinkton returned, laughing. 'Margaret, my dear, tell Mr Sampson.'

'Indeed,' said the young lady, turning to me, 'there is nothing to tell—except that I constantly see the same invalid old gentleman at all times, wherever I go. I have mentioned it to my uncle, and he calls the gentleman my shadow.'

'Does he live in Scarborough?' I asked.

'He is staying here.'

'Do you live in Scarborough?'

'No, I am staying here. My uncle has placed me with a family here, for my health.'

'And your shadow?' said I, smiling.

'My shadow,' she answered, smiling too, 'is—like myself—not very robust, I fear; for I lose my shadow sometimes, as my shadow loses me at other times. We both seem liable to confinement to the house. I have not seen my shadow for days and days; but it does oddly happen, occasionally, that wherever I go, for many days together, this gentleman goes. We have come together in the most unfrequented nooks on this shore.'

'Is this he?' said I, pointing before us.

The wheels had swept down to the water's edge, and described a great loop on the sand in turning. Bringing the loop back towards us, and spinning it out as it came, was a hand-carriage, drawn by a man.

'Yes,' said Miss Niner, 'this really is my shadow, uncle.'

As the carriage approached us and we approached the carriage, I saw within it an old man, whose head was sunk on his breast, and who was enveloped in a variety of wrappers. He was drawn by a very quiet but very keen-looking man, with iron-grey hair, who was slightly lame. They had passed us, when the carriage stopped, and the old gentleman within, putting out his arm, called to me by my name. I went back, and was absent from Mr Slinkton and his niece for about five minutes.

When I re-joined them, Mr Slinkton was the first to speak. Indeed, he said to me in a raised voice before I came up with him, 'It is well you have not been longer, or my niece might have died of curiosity to know who her shadow is, Mr Sampson.'

'An old East India Director,' said I. 'An intimate friend of our friend's, at whose house I first had the pleasure of meeting you. A certain Major Banks. You have heard of him?'

'Never.'

'Very rich, Miss Niner; but very old, and very crippled. An amiable man, sensible—much interested in you. He has just been expatiating on the affection that he has observed to exist between you and your uncle.'

Mr Slinkton was holding his hat again, and he passed his hand up the straight walk, as if he himself went up it serenely, after me.

'Mr Sampson,' he said, tenderly pressing his niece's arm in his, 'our affection was always a strong one, for we have had but few near ties. We have still fewer now. We have associations to bring us together, that are not of this world, Margaret.'

'Dear uncle!' murmured the young lady, and turned her face aside to hide her tears.

'My niece and I have such remembrances and regrets in common, Mr Sampson,' he feelingly pursued, 'that it would be strange indeed if the relations between us were cold or indifferent. If I remember a conversation we once had together, you will understand the reference I make. Cheer up, dear Margaret. Don't droop, don't droop. My Margaret! I cannot bear to see you droop!'

The poor young lady was very much affected, but controlled herself. His feelings, too, were very acute. In a word, he found himself under such great need of a restorative, that he presently went away, to take a bath of sea-water, leaving the young lady and me sitting by a point of rock, and probably presuming—but that you will say was a pardonable indulgence in a luxury—that she would praise him with all her heart.

She did, poor thing! With all her confiding heart, she praised him to me, for his care of her dead sister, and for his untiring devotion in her last illness. The sister had wasted away very slowly, and wild and terrible fantasies had come over her toward the end, but he had never been impatient with her, or at a loss; had always been gentle, watchful, and self-possessed. The sister had known him, as she had known him, to be the best of men, the kindest of men, and yet a man of such admirable strength of character, as to be a very tower for the support of their weak natures while their poor lives endured.

'I shall leave him, Mr Sampson, very soon,' said the young lady;

'I know my life is drawing to an end; and when I am gone, I hope he will marry and be happy. I am sure he has lived single so long, only for my sake, and for my poor, poor sister's.'

The little hand-carriage had made another great loop on the damp sand, and was coming back again, gradually spinning out a slim figure of eight, half a mile long.

'Young lady,' said I, looking around, laying my hand upon her arm, and speaking in a low voice, 'time presses. You hear the gentle murmur of that sea?'

'Young Lady,' said I, laying my Hand upon her Arm.. 'Time presses'

She looked at me with the utmost wonder and alarm, saying, 'Yes!'

'And you know what a voice is in it when the storm comes?'

'Yes!'

'You see how quiet and peaceful it lies before us, and you know what an awful sight of power without pity it might be, this very night!'

'Yes!'

'But if you had never heard or seen it, or heard of it in its cruelty, could you believe that it beats every inanimate thing in its way to pieces, without mercy, and destroys life without remorse?'

'You terrify me, sir, by these questions!'

'To save you, young lady, to save you! For God's sake, collect your strength and collect your firmness! If you were here alone, and hemmed in by the rising tide on the flow to fifty feet above your head, you could not be in greater danger than the danger you are now to be saved from.'

The figure on the sand was spun out, and straggled off into a crooked little jerk that ended at the cliff very near us.

'As I am, before Heaven and the Judge of all mankind, your friend, and your dead sister's friend, I solemnly entreat you, Miss Niner, without one moment's loss of time, to come to this gentleman with me!'

If the little carriage had been less near to us, I doubt if I could have got her away; but it was so near that we were there before she had recovered the hurry of being urged from the rock. I did not remain there with her two minutes. Certainly within five, I had the inexpressible satisfaction of seeing her—from the point we had sat on, and to which I had returned—half supported and half carried up some rude steps notched in the cliff, by the figure of an active man. With that figure beside her, I knew she was safe anywhere.

I sat alone on the rock, awaiting Mr Slinkton's return. The twilight was deepening and the shadows were heavy, when he came round the point, with his hat hanging at his button-hole, smoothing his wet hair with one of his hands, and picking out the old path with the other and a pocket-comb.

'My niece not here, Mr Sampson?' he said, looking about.

'Miss Niner seemed to feel a chill in the air after the sun was down, and has gone home.'

He looked surprised, as though she were not accustomed to do anything without him; even to originate so slight a proceeding.

'I persuaded Miss Niner,' I explained.

'Ah!' said he. 'She is easily persuaded—for her good. Thank you, Mr Sampson; she is better within doors. The bathing-place was farther than I thought, to say the truth.'

'Miss Niner is very delicate,' I observed.

He shook his head and drew a deep sigh. 'Very, very, very. You may recollect my saying so. The time that has since intervened has not strengthened her. The gloomy shadow that fell upon her sister so early in life seems, in my anxious eyes, to gather over her, ever darker, ever darker. Dear Margaret, dear Margaret! But we must hope.'

The hand-carriage was spinning away before us at a most indecorous pace for an invalid vehicle, and was making most irregular curves upon the sand. Mr Slinkton, noticing it after he had put his handkerchief to his eyes, said, 'If I may judge from appearances, your friend will be upset, Mr Sampson.'

'It looks probable, certainly,' said I.

'The servant must be drunk.'

'The servants of old gentlemen will get drunk sometimes,' said I.

'The major draws very light, Mr Sampson.'

'The major does draw light,' said I.

By this time the carriage, much to my relief, was lost in the darkness. We walked on for a little, side by side over the sand, in silence. After a short while he said, in a voice still affected by the emotion that his niece's state of health had awakened in him,

'Do you stay here long, Mr Sampson?'

'Why, no. I am going away to-night.'

'So soon? But business always holds you in request. Men like Mr Sampson are too important to others, to be spared to their own need of relaxation and enjoyment.'

'I don't know about that,' said I. 'However, I am going back.'

'To London?'

'To London.'

'I shall be there too, soon after you.'

I knew that as well as he did. But I did not tell him so. Any more than I told him what defensive weapon my right hand rested on in my pocket, as I walked by his side. Any more than I told him why I did not walk on the sea side of him with the night closing in.

We left the beach, and our ways diverged. We exchanged good-night, and had parted indeed, when he said, returning,

'Mr Sampson, may I ask? Poor Meltham, whom we spoke of,—dead yet?'

'Not when I last heard of him; but too broken a man to live long, and hopelessly lost to his old calling.'

'Dear, dear, dear!' said he, with great feeling. 'Sad, sad, sad! The world is a grave!' And so went his way.

It was not his fault if the world were not a grave; but I did not call that observation after him, any more than I had mentioned those other things just now enumerated. He went his way, and I went mine with all expedition. This happened, as I have said, either at the end of September or beginning of October. The next time I saw him, and the last time, was late in November.

V

I had a very particular engagement to breakfast in the Temple. It was a bitter north-easterly morning, and the sleet and slush lay inches deep in the streets. I could get no conveyance, and was soon wet to the knees; but I should have been true to that appointment, though I had to wade to it up to my neck in the same impediments.

The appointment took me to some chambers in the Temple. They were at the top of a lonely corner house overlooking the river. The name, Mr Alfred Beckwith, was painted on the outer door. On the door opposite, on the same landing, the name Mr Julius Slinkton. The doors of both sets of chambers stood open, so that anything said aloud in one set could be heard in the other.

I had never been in those chambers before. They were dismal, close, unwholesome, and oppressive; the furniture, originally good, and not yet old, was faded and dirty,—the rooms were in great disorder; there was a strong prevailing smell of opium, brandy, and tobacco; the grate and fire-irons were splashed all over with unsightly blotches of rust; and on a sofa by the fire, in the room where breakfast had been prepared, lay the host, Mr Beckwith, a man with all the appearances of the worst kind of drunkard, very far advanced upon his shameful way to death.

'Slinkton is not come yet,' said this creature, staggering up when I went in; 'I'll call him.—Halloa! Julius Cæsar! Come and drink!' As he hoarsely roared this out, he beat the poker and tongs together in a mad way, as if that were his usual manner of summoning his associate.

The voice of Mr Slinkton was heard through the clatter from the opposite side of the staircase, and he came in. He had not expected the pleasure of meeting me. I have seen several artful men brought to a stand, but I never saw a man so aghast as he was when his eyes rested on mine.

'Julius Cæsar,' cried Beckwith, staggering between us, 'Mist' Sampson! Mist' Sampson, Julius Cæsar! Julius, Mist' Sampson, is the friend of my soul. Julius keeps me plied with liquor, morning, noon, and night. Julius is a real benefactor. Julius threw the tea and coffee out of window when I used to have any. Julius empties all the water-jugs of their contents, and fills 'em with spirits. Julius winds me up and keeps me going.—Boil the brandy, Julius!'

There was a rusty and furred saucepan in the ashes,—the ashes looked like the accumulation of weeks,—and Beckwith, rolling and staggering between us as if he were going to plunge headlong into the fire, got the saucepan out, and tried to force it into Slinkton's hand.

'Boil the brandy, Julius Cæsar! Come! Do your usual office. Boil the brandy!'

He became so fierce in his gesticulations with the saucepan, that I expected to see him lay open Slinkton's head with it. I therefore put out my hand to check him. He reeled back to the sofa, and sat there panting, shaking, and red-eyed, in his rags of dressing-gown, looking at us both. I noticed then that there was nothing to drink on the table but brandy, and nothing to eat but salted herrings, and a hot, sickly, highly-peppered stew.

'At all events, Mr Sampson,' said Slinkton, offering me the smooth gravel path for the last time, 'I thank you for interfering between me and this unfortunate man's violence. However you came here, Mr Sampson, or with whatever motive you came here, at least I thank you for that.'

'Boil the brandy,' muttered Beckwith.

Without gratifying his desire to know how I came there, I said, quietly, 'How is your niece, Mr Slinkton?'

He looked hard at me, and I looked hard at him.

'I am sorry to say, Mr Sampson, that my niece has proved treacherous and ungrateful to her best friend. She left me without a word of notice or explanation. She was misled, no doubt, by some designing rascal. Perhaps you may have heard of it.'

'I did hear that she was misled by a designing rascal. In fact, I have proof of it.'

'Are you sure of that?' said he.

'Quite.'

'Boil the brandy,' muttered Beckwith. 'Company to breakfast, Julius Cæsar. Do your usual office,—provide the usual breakfast, dinner, tea, and supper. Boil the brandy!'

The eyes of Slinkton looked from him to me, and he said, after a moment's consideration,

'Mr Sampson, you are a man of the world, and so am I. I will be plain with you.'

'O no, you won't,' said I, shaking my head.

'I tell you, sir, I will be plain with you.'

'And I tell you you will not,' said I. 'I know all about you. You plain with any one? Nonsense, nonsense!'

'I plainly tell you, Mr Sampson,' he went on, with a manner almost composed, 'that I understand your object. You want to save your funds, and escape from your liabilities; these are old tricks of trade with you Office-gentlemen. But you will not do it, sir; you will not succeed. You have not an easy adversary to play against, when you play against me. We shall have to inquire, in due time, when and how Mr Beckwith fell into his present habits. With that remark, sir, I put this poor creature, and his incoherent wanderings of speech, aside, and wish you a good morning and a better case next time.'

While he was saying this, Beckwith had filled a half-pint glass with brandy. At this moment, he threw the brandy at his face, and threw the glass after it. Slinkton put his hands up, half blinded with the spirit, and cut with the glass across the forehead. At the sound of the breakage, a fourth person came into the room, closed the door, and stood at it; he was a very quiet but very keen-looking man, with iron-grey hair, and slightly lame.

Slinkton pulled out his handkerchief, assuaged the pain in his smarting eyes, and dabbled the blood on his forehead. He was a long time about it, and I saw that in the doing of it, a tremendous change came over him, occasioned by the change in Beckwith,—who ceased to pant and tremble, sat upright, and never took his eyes off him. I never in my life saw a face in which abhorrence and determination were so forcibly painted as in Beckwith's then.

'Look at me, you villain,' said Beckwith, 'and see me as I really am. I took these rooms, to make them a trap for you. I came into them as a drunkard, to bait the trap for you. You fell into the trap, and you will never leave it alive. On the morning when you last went to Mr Sampson's office, I had seen him first. Your plot has been known to both of us, all along, and you have been counter-plotted all along. What? Having been cajoled into putting that prize of two thousand pounds in your power, I was to be done to death with brandy, and, brandy not proving quick enough, with something quicker? Have I never seen you, when you thought my senses gone, pouring from your little bottle into my glass? Why, you Murderer and Forger, alone here with you in the dead of night, as I have so often been, I have had my hand upon the trigger of a pistol, twenty times, to blow your brains out!'

This sudden starting up of the thing that he had supposed to be his imbecile victim into a determined man, with a settled resolution to hunt him down and be the death of him, mercilessly expressed from head to foot, was, in the first shock, too much for him. Without any figure of speech, he staggered under it. But there is no greater mistake than to suppose that a man who is a calculating criminal, is, in any phase of his guilt, otherwise than true to himself, and perfectly consistent with his whole character. Such a man commits murder, and murder is the natural culmination of his course; such a man has to outface murder, and will do it with hardihood and effrontery. It is a sort of fashion to express surprise that any notorious criminal, having such crime upon his conscience, can so brave it out. Do you think that if he had it on his conscience at all, or had a conscience to have it upon, he would ever have committed the crime?

Perfectly consistent with himself, as I believe all such monsters to be, this Slinkton recovered himself, and showed a defiance that was sufficiently cold and quiet. He was white, he was haggard, he was changed; but only as a sharper who had played for a great stake and had been outwitted and had lost the game.

'Listen to me, you villain,' said Beckwith, 'and let every word you hear me say be a stab in your wicked heart. When I took these rooms, to throw myself in your way and lead you on to the scheme that I knew my appearance and supposed character and habits would suggest to such a devil, how did I know that? Because you were no stranger to me. I knew you well. And I knew you to be the cruel wretch who, for so much money, had killed one innocent girl while she trusted him implicitly, and who was by inches killing another.'

Slinkton took out a snuff-box, took a pinch of snuff, and laughed.

'But see here,' said Beckwith, never looking away, never raising his voice, never relaxing his face, never unclenching his hand. 'See what a dull wolf you have been, after all! The infatuated drunkard who never drank a fiftieth part of the liquor you plied him with, but poured it away, here, there, everywhere—almost before your eyes; who bought over the fellow you set to watch him and to ply him, by outbidding you in his bribe, before he had been at his work three days—with whom you have observed no caution, yet who was so bent on ridding the earth of you as a wild beast, that he would have defeated you if you had been ever so prudent—that drunkard whom you have, many a time, left on the floor of this room, and who has even let you go out of it, alive and undeceived, when you have turned him over with your foot—has, almost as often, on the same night, within an hour, within a few minutes, watched you awake, had his hand at your pillow when you were asleep, turned over your papers, taken samples from your bottles and packets of powder, changed their contents, rifled every secret of your life!'

He had had another pinch of snuff in his hand, but had gradually let it drop from between his fingers to the floor; where he now smoothed it out with his foot, looking down at it the while.

He had another pinch of snuff in his hand, but gradually let it drop from between his fingers

'That drunkard,' said Beckwith, 'who had free access to your rooms at all times, that he might drink the strong drinks that you left in his way and be the sooner ended, holding no more terms with you than he would hold with a tiger, has had his master-key for all your locks, his test for all your poisons, his clue to your cipher-writing. He can tell you, as well as you can tell him, how long it took to complete that deed, what doses there were, what intervals, what signs of gradual decay upon mind and body; what distempered fancies were produced, what observable changes, what physical pain. He can tell you, as well as you can tell him, that all this was recorded day by day, as a lesson of experience for future service. He can tell you, better than you can tell him, where that journal is at this moment.'

Slinkton stopped the action of his foot, and looked at Beckwith.

'No,' said the latter, as if answering a question from him. 'Not in the drawer of the writing-desk that opens with a spring; it is not there, and it never will be there again.'

'Then you are a thief!' said Slinkton.

Without any change whatever in the inflexible purpose, which it was quite terrific even to me to contemplate, and from the power of which I had always felt convinced it was impossible for this wretch to escape, Beckwith returned,

'And I am your niece's shadow, too.'

With an imprecation Slinkton put his hand to his head, tore out some hair, and flung it to the ground. It was the end of the smooth walk; he destroyed it in the action, and it will soon be seen that his use for it was past.

Beckwith went on, 'Whenever you left here, I left here. Although I understood that you found it necessary to pause in the completion of that purpose, to avert suspicion, still I watched you close, with the poor confiding girl. When I had the diary, and could read it word by word,—it was only about the night before your last visit to Scarborough,—you remember the night? you slept with a small flat vial tied to your wrist,—I sent to Mr Sampson, who was kept out of view. This is Mr Sampson's trusty servant standing by the door. We three saved your niece among us.'

Slinkton looked at us all, took an uncertain step or two from the place where he had stood, returned to it, and glanced about him in a very curious way,—as one of the meaner reptiles might, looking for a hole to hide in. I noticed at the same time, that a singular change took place in the figure of the man,—as if it collapsed within his clothes, and they consequently became ill-shapen and ill-fitting.

'You shall know,' said Beckwith, 'for I hope the knowledge will be bitter and terrible to you, why you have been pursued by one man, and why, when the whole interest that Mr Sampson represents would have expended any money in hunting you down, you have been tracked to death at a single individual's charge. I hear you have had the name of Meltham on your lips sometimes?'

I saw, in addition to those other changes, a sudden stoppage come upon his breathing.

'When you sent the sweet girl whom you murdered (you know with what artfully made-out surroundings and probabilities you sent her) to Meltham's office, before taking her abroad to originate the transaction that doomed her to the grave, it fell to Meltham's lot to see her and to speak with her. It did not fall to his lot to save her, though I know he would freely give his own life to have done it. He admired her;—I would say he loved her deeply, if I thought it possible that you could understand the word. When she was sacrificed, he was thoroughly assured of your guilt. Having lost her, he had but one object left in life, and that was to avenge her and destroy you.'

I saw the villain's nostrils rise and fall convulsively; but I saw no moving at his mouth.

'That man Meltham,' Beckwith steadily pursued, 'was as absolutely certain that you could never elude him in this world, if he devoted himself to your destruction with his utmost fidelity and earnestness, and if he divided the sacred duty with no other duty in life, as he was certain that in achieving it he would be a poor instrument in the hands of Providence, and would do well before Heaven in striking you out from among living men. I am that man, and I thank God that I have done my work!'

If Slinkton had been running for his life from swift-footed savages, a dozen miles, he could not have shown more emphatic signs of being oppressed at heart and labouring for breath, than he showed now, when he looked at the pursuer who had so relentlessly hunted him down.

'You never saw me under my right name before; you see me under my right name now. You shall see me once again in the body, when you are tried for your life. You shall see me once again in the spirit, when the cord is round your neck, and the crowd are crying against you!'

When Meltham had spoken these last words, the miscreant suddenly turned away his face, and seemed to strike his mouth with his open hand. At the same instant, the room was filled with a new and powerful odour, and, almost at the same instant, he broke into a crooked run, leap, start,—I have no name for the spasm,—and fell, with a dull weight that shook the heavy old doors and windows in their frames.

That was the fitting end of him.

When we saw that he was dead, we drew away from the room, and Meltham, giving me his hand, said, with a weary air,

'I have no more work on earth, my friend. But I shall see her again elsewhere.'

It was in vain that I tried to rally him. He might have saved her, he said; he had not saved her, and he reproached himself; he had lost her, and he was broken-hearted.

'The purpose that sustained me is over, Sampson, and there is nothing now to hold me to life. I am not fit for life; I am weak and spiritless; I have no hope and no object; my day is done.'

In truth, I could hardly have believed that the broken man who then spoke to me was the man who had so strongly and so differently impressed me when his purpose was before him. I used such entreaties with him, as I could; but he still said, and always said, in a patient, undemonstrative way—nothing could avail him—he was broken-hearted.

He died early in the next spring. He was buried by the side of the poor young lady for whom he had cherished those tender and unhappy regrets; and he left all he had to her sister. She lived to be a happy wife and mother; she married my sister's son, who succeeded poor Meltham; she is living now, and her children ride about the garden on my walking-stick when I go to see her.

LYING AWAKE

Charles Dickens

'My uncle lay with his eyes half closed, and his nightcap drawn almost down to his nose. His fancy was already wandering, and began to mingle up the present scene with the crater of Vesuvius, the French Opera, the Coliseum at Rome, Dolly's Chop-house in London, and all the farrago of noted places with which the brain of a traveller is crammed; in a word, he was just falling asleep.'

Thus, that delightful writer, Washington Irving, in his *Tales of a Traveller*. But, it happened to me the other night to be lying—not with my eyes half closed, but with my eyes wide open; not with my nightcap drawn almost down to my nose, for on sanitary principles I never wear a nightcap—but with my hair pitchforked and tousled all over the pillow; not just falling asleep by any means, but glaringly, persistently, and obstinately, broad awake. Perhaps, with no scientific intention or invention, I was illustrating the theory of the Duality of the Brain; perhaps one part of my brain, being wakeful, sat up to watch the other part which was sleepy. Be that as it may, something in me was as desirous to go to sleep as it possibly could be, but something else in me would not go to sleep, and was as obstinate as George the Third.

Thinking of George the Third—for I devote this paper to my train of thoughts as I lay awake. Most people lying awake sometimes, and having some interest in the subject—put me in mind of Benjamin Franklin, and so Benjamin Franklin's paper on the art of procuring pleasant dreams, which would seem necessarily to include the art of going to sleep, came into my head. Now, as I often used to read that paper when I was a very small boy, and as I recollect everything I read then as perfectly as I forget everything I read now, I quoted 'Get out of bed, beat up and turn your pillow, shake the bed-clothes well with at least twenty shakes, then throw the bed open and leave it to cool; in the meanwhile, continuing undress, walk about your chamber. When you begin to feel the cold air unpleasant, then return to your bed, and you will soon fall asleep, and your sleep will be sweet and pleasant.' Not a bit of it! I performed the whole ceremony, and if it were possible for me to be more saucer-eyed than I was before, that was the only result that came of it.

Except Niagara. The two quotations from Washington Irving and Benjamin Franklin may have put it in my head by an American association of ideas; but there I was, and the Horse-shoe Fall was thundering and tumbling in my eyes and ears, and the very rainbows that I left upon the spray when I really did last look upon it, were beautiful to see. The night-light being quite as plain, however, and sleep seeming to be many thousand miles further off than Niagara, I made up my mind to think a little about Sleep; which I no sooner did than I whirled off in spite of myself to Drury Lane Theatre, and there saw a great actor and dear friend of mine (whom I had been thinking of in the day) playing Macbeth, and heard him apostrophising 'the death of each day's life,' as I have heard him many a time, in the days that are gone.

But, Sleep. I will think about Sleep. I am determined to think (this is the way I went on) about Sleep. I must hold the word Sleep, tight and fast, or I shall be off at a tangent in half a second. I feel myself unaccountably straying, already, into Clare Market. Sleep. It would be curious, as illustrating the equality of sleep, to inquire how many of its phenomena are common to all classes, to all degrees of wealth and poverty, to every grade of education and ignorance. Here, for example, is her Majesty Queen Victoria in her palace, this present blessed night, and here is Winking Charley, a sturdy vagrant, in one of her Majesty's jails. Her Majesty has fallen, many thousands of times, from that same Tower, which I claim a right to tumble off now and then. So has Winking Charley. Her Majesty in her sleep has opened or prorogued Parliament, or has held a Drawing Room, attired in some very scanty dress, the deficiencies and improprieties of which have caused her great uneasiness. I, in my degree, have suffered unspeakable agitation of mind from taking the chair at a public dinner at the London Tavern in my night-clothes, which not all the courtesy of my kind friend and host Mr Bathe could persuade me were quite adapted to the occasion. Winking Charley has been repeatedly tried in a worse condition. Her Majesty is no stranger to a vault or firmament, of a sort of floor cloth, with an indistinct pattern distantly resembling eyes, which occasionally obtrudes itself on her repose. Neither am I. Neither is Winking Charley. It is quite common to all three of us to skim along with airy strides a little above the ground; also to hold, with the deepest interest, dialogues with various people, all represented by ourselves; and to be at our wit's end to know what they are going to tell us; and to be indescribably astonished by the secrets they disclose. It is probable that we have all three committed murders and hidden bodies. It is pretty certain that we have all desperately wanted to cry out, and have had no voice; that we have all gone to the play and not been able to get in; that we have all dreamed much more of our youth than of our later lives; that—I have lost it! The thread's broken.

And up I go. I, lying here with the night-light before me, up I go, for no reason on earth that I can find out, and drawn by no links that are visible to me, up the Great Saint Bernard! I have lived in Switzerland, and rambled among the mountains; but, why I should go there now, and why up the Great Saint Bernard in preference to any other mountain, I have no idea. As I lie here broad awake, and with every sense so sharpened that I can distinctly hear distant noises inaudible to me at another time, I make that journey, as I really did, on the same summer day, with the same happy party—ah! two since dead, I grieve to think—and there is the same track, with the same black wooden arms to point the way, and there are the same storm-refuges here and there; and there is the same snow falling at the top, and there are the same frosty mists, and there is the same intensely cold convent with its menagerie smell, and the same breed of dogs fast dying out, and the same breed of jolly young monks whom I mourn to know as humbugs, and the same convent parlour with its piano and the sitting round the fire, and the same supper, and the same lone night in a cell, and the same bright fresh morning when going out into the highly rarefied air was like a plunge into an icy bath. Now, see here what comes along; and why does this thing stalk into my mind on the top of a Swiss mountain!

It is a figure that I once saw, just after dark, chalked upon a door in a little back lane near a country church—my first church. How young a child I may have been at the time I don't know, but it horrified me so intensely—in connexion with the churchyard, I suppose, for it smokes a pipe, and has a big hat with each of its ears sticking out in a horizontal line under the brim, and is not in itself more oppressive than a mouth from ear to ear, a pair of goggle eyes, and hands like two bunches of carrots, five in each, can make it—that it is still vaguely alarming to me to recall (as I have often done before, lying awake) the running home, the looking behind, the horror, of its following me; though whether disconnected from the door, or door and all, I can't say, and perhaps never could. It lays a disagreeable train. I must resolve to think of something on the voluntary principle.

The balloon ascents of this last season. They will do to think about, while I lie awake, as well as anything else. I must hold them tight though, for I feel them sliding away, and in their stead are the Mannings, husband and wife, hanging on the top of Horse-monger Lane Jail. In connexion with which dismal spectacle, I recall this curious fantasy of the mind. That, having beheld that execution, and having left those two forms dangling on the top of the entrance gateway—the man's, a limp, loose suit of clothes as if the man had gone out of them; the woman's, a fine shape, so elaborately corseted and artfully dressed, that it was quite unchanged in its trim appearance as it slowly swung from side to side—I never could, by my uttermost efforts, for some weeks, present the outside of that prison to myself (which the terrible impression I had received continually obliged me to do) without presenting it with the two figures still hanging in the morning air. Until, strolling past the gloomy place one night, when the street was deserted and quiet, and actually seeing that the bodies were not there, my fancy was persuaded, as it were, to take them down and bury them within the precincts of the jail, where they have lain ever since.

The balloon ascents of last season. Let me reckon them up. There were the horse, the bull, the parachute—and the tumbler hanging on—chiefly by his toes, I believe—below the car. Very wrong, indeed, and decidedly to be stopped. But, in connexion with these and similar dangerous exhibitions, it strikes me that that portion of the public whom they entertain, is unjustly reproached. Their pleasure is in the difficulty overcome. They are a public of great faith, and are quite confident that the gentleman will not fall off the horse, or the lady off the bull or out of the parachute, and that the tumbler has a firm hold with his toes. They do not go to see the adventurer vanquished, but triumphant. There is no parallel in public combats between men and beasts, because nobody can answer for the particular beast—unless it were always the same beast, in which case it would be a mere stage-show, which the same public would go in the same state of mind to see, entirely believing in the brute being beforehand safely subdued by the man. That they are not accustomed to calculate hazards and dangers with any nicety, we may know from their rash exposure of themselves in overcrowded steamboats, and unsafe conveyances and places of all kinds. And I cannot help thinking that instead of railing, and attributing savage motives to a people naturally well-disposed and humane, it is better to teach them, and lead them argumentatively and reasonably—for they are very reasonable, if you will discuss a matter with them—to more considerate and wise conclusions.

This is a disagreeable intrusion! Here is a man with his throat cut, dashing towards me as I lie awake! A recollection of an old story of a kinsman of mine, who, going home one foggy winter night to Hampstead, when London was much smaller and the road lonesome, suddenly encountered such a figure rushing past him, and presently two keepers from a madhouse in pursuit. A very unpleasant creature indeed, to come into my mind unbidden, as I lie awake.

The balloon ascents of last season. I must return to the balloons. Why did the bleeding man start out of them? Never mind; if I inquire, he will be back again. The balloons. This particular public have inherently a great pleasure in the contemplation of physical difficulties overcome; mainly, as I take it, because the lives of a large majority of them are exceedingly monotonous and real, and further, are a struggle against continual difficulties, and further still, because anything in the form of accidental injury, or any kind of illness or disability is so very serious in their own sphere. I will explain this seeming paradox of mine. Take the case of a Christmas Pantomime. Surely nobody supposes that the young mother in the pit who falls into fits of laughter when the baby is boiled or sat upon, would be at all diverted by such an occurrence off the stage. Nor is the decent workman in the gallery, who is transported beyond the ignorant present by the delight with which he sees a stout gentleman pushed out of a two pair of stairs window, to be slandered by the suspicion that he would be in the least entertained by such a spectacle in any street in London, Paris, or New York. It always appears to me that the secret of this enjoyment lies in the temporary superiority to the common hazards and mischances of life; in seeing casualties, attended when they really occur with bodily and mental suffering, tears, and poverty, happen through a very rough sort of poetry without the least harm being done to any one—the pretence of distress in a pantomime being so broadly humorous as to be no pretence at all. Much as in the comic fiction I can understand the mother with a very vulnerable baby at home, greatly relishing the invulnerable baby on the stage, so in the Cremorne reality I can understand the mason who is always liable to fall off a scaffold in his working jacket and to be carried to the hospital, having an infinite admiration of the radiant personage in spangles who goes into the clouds upon a bull, or upside down, and who, he takes it for granted—not reflecting upon the thing—has, by uncommon skill and dexterity, conquered such mischances as those to which he and his acquaintance are continually exposed.

I wish the Morgue in Paris would not come here as I lie awake, with its ghastly beds, and the swollen saturated clothes hanging up, and the water dripping, dripping all day long, upon that other swollen saturated something in the corner, like a heap of crushed over-ripe figs that I have seen in Italy! And this detestable Morgue comes back again at the head of a procession of forgotten ghost stories. This will never do. I must think of something else as I lie awake; or, like that sagacious animal in the United States who recognized the colonel who was such a dead shot, I am a gone 'Coon. What shall I think of? The late brutal assaults. Very good subject. The late brutal assaults.

(Though whether, supposing I should see, here before me as I lie awake, the awful phantom described in one of those ghost stories, who, with a head-dress of shroud, was always seen looking in through a certain glass door at a certain dead hour—whether, in such a case it would be the least consolation to me to know on philosophical grounds that it was merely my imagination, is a question I can't help asking myself by the way.)

The late brutal assaults. I strongly question the expediency of advocating the revival of whipping for those crimes. It is a natural and generous impulse to be indignant at the perpetration of inconceivable brutality, but I doubt the whipping panacea gravely. Not in the least regard or pity for the criminal, whom I hold in far lower estimation than a mad wolf, but in consideration for the general tone and feeling, which is very much improved since the whipping times. It is bad for a people to be familiarized with such punishments. When the whip went out of Bridewell, and ceased to be flourished at the carts tail and at the whipping-post, it began to fade out of madhouses, and workhouses, and schools and families, and to give place to a better system everywhere, than cruel driving. It would be hasty, because a few brutes may be inadequately punished, to revive, in any aspect, what, in so many aspects, society is hardly yet happily rid of. The whip is a very contagious kind of thing, and difficult to confine within one set of bounds. Utterly abolish punishment by fine—a barbarous device, quite as much out of date as wager by battle, but particularly connected in the vulgar mind with this class of offence—at least quadruple the term of imprisonment for aggravated assaults—and above all let us, in such cases, have no Pet Prisoning, vain glorifying, strong soup, and roasted meats, but hard work, and one unchanging and uncompromising dietary of bread and water, well or ill; and we shall do much better than by going down into the dark to grope for the whip among the rusty fragments of the rack, and the branding iron, and the chains and gibbet from the public roads, and the weights that pressed men to death in the cells of Newgate.

I had proceeded thus far, when I found I had been lying awake so long that the very dead began to wake too, and to crowd into my thoughts most sorrowfully. Therefore, I resolved to lie awake no more, but to get up and go out for a night walk—which resolution was an acceptable relief to me, as I dare say it may prove now to a great many more.

THE ROCKING-HORSE WINNER

D.H. Lawrence

'Now!' he would silently command the snorting steed. 'Now take me to where there is luck! Now take me!'

He knew the horse could take him to where there was luck, if only he forced it.'

There was a woman who was beautiful, who started with all the advantages, yet she had no luck. She married for love, and the love turned to dust. She had boney children, yet she felt they had been thrust upon her, and she could not love them. They looked at her coldly, as if they were finding fault with her. And hurriedly she felt she must cover up some fault in herself. Yet what it was that she must cover up she never knew. Nevertheless, when her children were present, she always felt the centre of her heart go hard. This troubled her, and in her manner she was all the more gentle and anxious for her children, as if she loved them very much. Only she herself knew that at the centre of her heart was a hard little place that could not feel love, no, not for anybody. Everybody else said of her: 'She is such a good mother. She adores her children.' Only she herself, and her children themselves, knew it was not so. They read it in each other's eyes.

There were a boy and two little girls. They lived in a pleasant house, with a garden, and they had discreet servants, and felt themselves superior to anyone in the neighbourhood.

Although they lived in style, they felt always an anxiety in the house. There was never enough money. The mother had a small income, and the father had a small income, but not nearly enough for the social position which they had to keep up. The father went into town to some office. But though he had good prospects, these prospects never materialized. There was always the grinding sense of the shortage of money, though the style was always kept up.

At last the mother said, 'I will see if I can't make something.' But she did not know where to begin. She racked her brains, and tried this thing and the other, but could not find anything successful. The failure made deep lines come into her face. Her children were growing up, they would have to go to school. There must be more money, there must be more money. The father, who was always very handsome and expensive in his tastes, seemed as if he never would be able to do anything worth doing. And the mother, who had a great belief in herself, did not succeed any better, and her tastes were just as expensive.

And so the house came to be haunted by the unspoken phrase: There must be more money! There must be more money! The children could hear it all the time though nobody said it aloud. They heard it at Christmas, when the expensive and splendid toys filled the nursery. Behind the shining modern rocking-horse, behind the smart doll's house, a voice would start whispering, 'There must be more money! There must be more money!' And the children would stop playing, to listen for a moment. They would look into each other's eyes, to see if they had all heard. And each one saw in the eyes of the other two that they too had heard. 'There must be more money! There must be more money!'

It came whispering from the springs of the still-swaying rocking-horse, and even the horse, bending his wooden, champing head, heard it. The big doll, sitting so pink and smirking in her new pram, could hear it quite plainly, and seemed to be smirking all the more self-consciously because of it. The foolish puppy, too, that took the place of the teddy-bear, he was looking so extraordinarily foolish for no other reason but that he heard the secret whisper all over the house: 'There must be more money!'

Yet nobody ever said it aloud. The whisper was everywhere, and therefore no one spoke it. Just as no one ever says, 'We are breathing!' in spite of the fact that breath is coming and going all the time.

'Mother,' said the boy Paul one day, 'why don't we keep a car of our own? Why do we always use uncle's, or else a taxi?'

'Because we're the poor members of the family,' said the mother.

'But why are we, mother?'

'Well, I suppose,' she said slowly and bitterly, 'it's because your father has no luck.'

The boy was silent for some time.

'Is luck money, mother?' he asked, rather timidly.

'No, Paul. Not quite. It's what causes you to have money.'

'Oh!' said Paul vaguely. 'I thought when Uncle Oscar said filthy lucker, it meant money.'

'Filthy lucre does mean money,' said the mother. 'But it's lucre, not luck.'

'Oh!' said the boy. 'Then what is luck, mother?'

'It's what causes you to have money. If you're lucky you have money. That's why it's better to be born lucky than rich. If you're rich, you may lose your money. But if you're lucky, you will always get more money.'

'Oh! Will you? And is father not lucky?'

'Very unlucky, I should say,' she said bitterly.

The boy watched her with unsure eyes.

'Why?' he asked.

'I don't know. Nobody ever knows why one person is lucky and another unlucky.'

'Don't they? Nobody at all? Does nobody know?'

'Perhaps God. But He never tells.'

'He ought to, then. And aren't you lucky either, mother?'

'I can't be, if I married an unlucky husband.'

'But by yourself, aren't you?'

'I used to think I was, before I married. Now I think I am very unlucky indeed.'

'Why?'

'Well, never mind! Perhaps I'm not really,' she said.

The child looked at her to see if she meant it. But he saw, by the lines of her mouth, that she was only trying to hide something from him.

'Well, anyhow,' he said stoutly, 'I'm a lucky person.'

'Why?' said his mother, with a sudden laugh.

He stared at her. He didn't even know why he had said it.

'God told me,' he asserted, brazening it out.

'I hope He did, dear!', she said, again with a laugh, but rather bitter.

'He did, mother!'

'Excellent!' said the mother, using one of her husband's exclamations.

The boy saw she did not believe him; or rather, that she paid no attention to his assertion. This angered him somewhere, and made him want to compel her attention.

He went off by himself, vaguely, in a childish way, seeking for the clue to 'luck'. Absorbed, taking no heed of other people, he went about with a sort of stealth, seeking inwardly for luck. He wanted luck, he wanted it, he wanted it. When the two girls were playing dolls in the nursery, he would sit on his big rocking-horse, charging madly into space, with a frenzy that made the little girls peer at him uneasily. Wildly the horse careered, the waving dark hair of the boy tossed, his eyes had a strange glare in them. The little girls dared not speak to him.

When he had ridden to the end of his mad little journey, he climbed down and stood in front of his rocking-horse, staring fixedly into its lowered face. Its red mouth was slightly open, its big eye was wide and glassy-bright.

'Now!' he would silently command the snorting steed. 'Now take me to where there is luck! Now take me!'

And he would slash the horse on the neck with the little whip he had asked Uncle Oscar for. He knew the horse could take him to where there was luck, if only he forced it. So he would mount again and start on his furious ride, hoping at last to get there.

'You'll break your horse, Paul!' said the nurse.

'He's always riding like that! I wish he'd leave off!' said his elder sister Joan.

But he only glared down on them in silence. Nurse gave him up. She could make nothing of him. Anyhow, he was growing beyond her.

One day his mother and his Uncle Oscar came in when he was on one of his furious rides. He did not speak to them.

'Hallo, you young jockey! Riding a winner?' said his uncle.

'Aren't you growing too big for a rocking-horse? You're not a very little boy any longer, you know,' said his mother.

But Paul only gave a blue glare from his big, rather close-set eyes. He would speak to nobody when he was in full tilt. His mother watched him with an anxious expression on her face.

At last he suddenly stopped forcing his horse into the mechanical gallop and slid down.

'Well, I got there!' he announced fiercely, his blue eyes still flaring, and his sturdy long legs straddling apart.

'Where did you get to?' asked his mother.

'Where I wanted to go,' he flared back at her.

'That's right, son!' said Uncle Oscar. 'Don't you stop till you get there. What's the horse's name?'

'He doesn't have a name,' said the boy.

'Get's on without all right?' asked the uncle.

'Well, he has different names. He was called Sansovino last week.'

'Sansovino, eh? Won the Ascot. How did you know this name?'

'He always talks about horse-races with Bassett,' said Joan.

The uncle was delighted to find that his small nephew was posted with all the racing news. Bassett, the young gardener, who had been wounded in the left foot in the war and had got his present job through Oscar Cresswell, whose batman he had been, was a perfect blade of the 'turf'. He lived in the racing events, and the small boy lived with him.

Oscar Cresswell got it all from Bassett.

'Master Paul comes and asks me, so I can't do more than tell him, sir,' said Bassett, his face terribly serious, as if he were speaking of religious matters.

'And does he ever put anything on a horse he fancies?'

'Well, I don't want to give him away—he's a young sport, a fine sport, sir. Would you mind asking him himself? He sort of takes a pleasure in it, and perhaps he'd feel I was giving him away, sir, if you don't mind.

Bassett was serious as a church.

The uncle went back to his nephew and took him off for a ride in the car.

'Say, Paul, old man, do you ever put anything on a horse?' the uncle asked.

The boy watched the handsome man closely.

'Why, do you think I oughtn't to?' he parried.

'Not a bit of it! I thought perhaps you might give me a tip for the Lincoln.'

The car sped on into the country, going down to Uncle Oscar's place in Hampshire.

'Honour bright?' said the nephew.

'Honour bright, son!' said the uncle.

'Well, then, Daffodil.'

'Daffodil! I doubt it, sonny. What about Mirza?'

'I only know the winner,' said the boy. 'That's Daffodil.'

'Daffodil, eh?'

There was a pause. Daffodil was an obscure horse comparatively.

'Uncle!'

'Yes, son?'

'You won't let it go any further, will you? I promised Bassett.'

'Bassett be damned, old man! What's he got to do with it?'

'We're partners. We've been partners from the first. Uncle, he lent me my first five shillings, which I lost. I promised him, honour bright, it was only between me and him; only you gave me that ten-shilling note I started winning with, so I thought you were lucky. You won't let it go any further, will you?'

The boy gazed at his uncle from those big, hot, blue eyes, set rather close together. The uncle stirred and laughed uneasily.

'Right you are, son! I'll keep your tip private. How much are you putting on him?'

'All except twenty pounds,' said the boy. 'I keep that in reserve.'

The uncle thought it a good joke.

'You keep twenty pounds in reserve, do you, you young romancer? What are you betting, then?'

'I'm betting three hundred,' said the boy gravely. 'But it's between you and me, Uncle Oscar! Honour bright?'

'It's between you and me all right, you young Nat Gould,' he said, laughing. 'But where's your three hundred?'

'Bassett keeps it for me. We're partner's.'

'You are, are you! And what is Bassett putting on Daffodil?'

'He won't go quite as high as I do, I expect. Perhaps he'll go a hundred and fifty.'

'What, pennies?' laughed the uncle.

'Pounds,' said the child, with a surprised look at his uncle. 'Bassett keeps a bigger reserve than I do.'

Between wonder and amusement Uncle Oscar was silent. He pursued the matter no further, but he determined to take his nephew with him to the Lincoln races.

'Now, son,' he said, 'I'm putting twenty on Mirza, and I'll put five on for you on any horse you fancy. What's your pick?'

'Daffodil, uncle.'

'No, not the fiver on Daffodil!'

'I should if it was my own fiver,' said the child.

'Good! Good! Right you are! A fiver for me and a fiver for you on Daffodil.'

The child had never been to a race-meeting before, and his eyes were blue fire. He pursed his mouth tight and watched. A Frenchman just in front had put his money on Lancelot. Wild with excitement, he flayed his arms up and down, yelling 'Lancelot!, Lancelot!' in his French accent.

Daffodil came in first, Lancelot second, Mirza third. The child, flushed and with eyes blazing, was curiously serene. His uncle brought him four five-pound notes, four to one.

'What am I to do with these?' he cried, waving them before the boys eyes.

'I suppose we'll talk to Bassett,' said the boy. 'I expect I have fifteen hundred now; and twenty in reserve; and this twenty.'

His uncle studied him for some moments.

'Look here, son!' he said. 'You're not serious about Bassett and that fifteen hundred, are you?'

'Yes, I am. But it's between you and me, uncle. Honour bright?'

'Honour bright all right, son! But I must talk to Bassett.'

'If you'd like to be a partner, uncle, with Bassett and me, we could all be partners. Only, you'd have to promise, honour bright, uncle, not to let it go beyond us three. Bassett and I are lucky, and you must be lucky, because it was your ten shillings I started winning with ...'

Uncle Oscar took both Bassett and Paul into Richmond Park for an afternoon, and there they talked.

'It's like this, you see, sir,' Bassett said. 'Master Paul would get me talking about racing events, spinning yarns, you know, sir. And he was always keen on knowing if I'd made or if I'd lost. It's about a year since, now, that I put five shillings on Blush of Dawn for him: and we lost. Then the luck turned, with that ten shillings he had from you: that we put on Singhalese. And since that time, it's been pretty steady, all things considering. What do you say, Master Paul?'

'We're all right when we're sure,' said Paul. 'It's when we're not quite sure that we go down.'

'Oh, but we're careful then,' said Bassett.

'But when are you sure?' smiled Uncle Oscar.

'It's Master Paul, sir,' said Bassett in a secret, religious voice. 'It's as if he had it from heaven. Like Daffodil, now, for the Lincoln. That was as sure as eggs.'

'Did you put anything on Daffodil?' asked Oscar Cresswell.

'Yes, sir, I made my bit.'

'And my nephew?'

Bassett was obstinately silent, looking at Paul.

'I made twelve hundred, didn't I, Bassett? I told uncle I was putting three hundred on Daffodil.'

'That's right,' said Bassett, nodding.

'But where's the money?' asked the uncle.

'I keep it safe locked up, sir. Master Paul he can have it any minute he likes to ask for it.'

'What, fifteen hundred pounds?'

'And twenty! And forty, that is, with the twenty he made on the course.'

'It's amazing!' said the uncle.

'If Master Paul offers you to be partners, sir, I would, if I were you: if you'll excuse me,' said Bassett.

Oscar Cresswell thought about it.

'I'll see the money,' he said.

They drove home again, and, sure enough, Bassett came round to the garden-house with fifteen hundred pounds in notes. The twenty pounds reserve was left with Joe Glee, in the Turf Commission deposit.

'You see, it's all right, uncle, when I'm sure! Then we go strong, for all we're worth, don't we, Bassett?'

'We do that, Master Paul.'

'And when are you sure?' said the uncle, laughing.

'Oh, well, sometimes I'm absolutely sure, like about Daffodil,' said the boy; 'and sometimes I have an idea; and sometimes I haven't even an idea, have I, Bassett? Then we're careful, because we mostly go down.'

'You do, do you! And when you're sure, like about Daffodil, what makes you sure, sonny?'

'Oh, well, I don't know,' said the boy uneasily. 'I'm sure, you know, uncle; that's all.'

'It's as if he had it from heaven, sir,' Bassett reiterated.

'I should say so!' said the uncle.

But he became a partner. And when the Leger was coming on Paul was 'sure' about Lively Spark, which was a quite inconsiderable horse. The boy insisted on putting a thousand on the horse, Bassett went for five hundred, and Oscar Cresswell two hundred. Lively Spark came in first, and the betting had been ten to one against him. Paul had made ten thousand.

'You see,' he said. 'I was absolutely sure of him.'

Even Oscar Cresswell had cleared two thousand.

'Look here, son,' he said, 'this sort of thing makes me nervous.'

'It needn't, uncle! Perhaps I shan't be sure again for a long time.'

'But what are you going to do with your money?' asked the uncle.

'Of course,' said the boy, 'I started it for mother. She said she had no luck, because father is unlucky, so I thought if I was lucky, it might stop whispering.'

'What might stop whispering?'

'Our house. I hate our house for whispering.'

'What does it whisper?'

'Why—why'—the boy fidgeted—'why, I don't know. But it's always short of money, you know, uncle.'

'I know it, son, I know it.'

'You know people send mother writs, don't you, uncle?'

'I'm afraid I do,' said the uncle.

'And then the house whispers, like people laughing at you behind your back. It's awful, that is! I thought if I was lucky—'

'You might stop it,' added the uncle.

The boy watched him with big blue eyes, that had an uncanny cold fire in them, and he said never a word.

'Well, then!' said the uncle. 'What are we doing?'

'I shouldn't like mother to know I was lucky,' said the boy.

'Why not, son?'

'She'd stop me.'

'I don't think she would.'

'Oh!'—and the boy writhed in an odd way—'I don't want her to know, uncle.'

'All right, son! We'll manage it without her knowing.'

They managed it very easily. Paul, at the other's suggestion, handed over five thousand pounds to his uncle, who deposited it with the family lawyer, who was then to inform Paul's mother that a relative had put five thousand pounds into his hands, which sum was to be paid out a thousand pounds at a time, on the mother's birthday, for the next five years.

'So she'll have a birthday present of a thousand pounds for five successive years,' said Uncle Oscar. 'I hope it won't make it all the harder for her later.'

Paul's mother had her birthday in November. The house had been 'whispering' worse than ever lately, and, even in spite of his luck, Paul could not bear up against it. He was very anxious to see the effect of the birthday letter, telling his mother about the thousand pounds.

When there were no visitors, Paul now took his meals with his parents, as he was beyond the nursery control. His mother went into town nearly every day. She had discovered that she had an odd knack of sketching furs and dress materials, so she worked secretly in the studio of a friend who was the chief 'artist' for the leading drapers. She drew the figures of ladies in furs and ladies in silk and sequins for the newspaper advertisements. This young woman artist earned several thousand pounds a year, but Paul's mother only made several hundreds, and she was again dissatisfied. She so wanted to be first in something, and she did not succeed, even in making sketches for drapery advertisements.

She was down to breakfast on the morning of her birthday. Paul watched her face as she read her letters. He knew the lawyer's letter. As his mother read it, her face hardened and became more expressionless. Then a cold, determined look came on her mouth. She hid the letter under the pile of others, and said not a word about it.

'Didn't you have anything nice in the post for your birthday, mother?' said Paul.

'Quite moderately nice,' she said, her voice cold and hard and absent.

She went away to town without saying more.

But in the afternoon Uncle Oscar appeared. He said Paul's mother had had a long interview with the lawyer, asking if the whole five thousand could not be advanced at once, as she was in debt.

'What do you think, uncle?' said the boy.

'I leave it to you, son.'

'Oh, let her have it, then! We can get some more with the other,' said the boy.

'A bird in the hand is worth two in the bush, laddie!' said Uncle Oscar.

'But I'm sure to know for the Grand National; or the Lincolnshire; or else the Derby. I'm sure to know for one of them,' said Paul.

So Uncle Oscar signed the agreement, and Paul's mother touched the whole five thousand. Then something very curious happened. The voices in the house suddenly went mad, like a chorus of frogs on a spring evening. There were certain new furnishings, and Paul had a tutor. He was really going to Eton, his father's school, in the following autumn. There were flowers in the winter, and a blossoming of the luxury Paul's mother had been used to. And yet the voices in the house, behind the sprays of mimosa and almond-blossom, and from under the piles of iridescent cushions, simply trilled and screamed in a sort of ecstasy, 'There must be more money! Oh-h-h; there must be more money. Oh, now, now-w! Now-w-w - there must be more money!—more than ever! More than ever!'

It frightened Paul terribly. He studied away at his Latin and Greek with his tutor. But his intense hours were spent with Bassett. The Grand

National had gone by—he had not 'known', and had lost a hundred pounds. Summer was at hand. He was in agony for the Lincoln. But even for the Lincoln he didn't 'know', and he lost fifty pounds. He became wild-eyed and strange, as if something were going to explode in him.

'Let it alone, son! Don't you bother about it!' urged Uncle Oscar. But it was as if the boy couldn't really hear what his uncle was saying.

'I've got to know for the Derby! I've got to know for the Derby!' the child reiterated, his big blue eyes blazing with a sort of madness.

His mother noticed how overwrought he was.

'You'd better go to the seaside. Wouldn't you like to go now to the seaside, instead of waiting? I think you'd better,' she said, looking down at him anxiously, her heart curiously heavy because of him.

But the child lifted his uncanny blue eyes.

'I couldn't possibly go before the Derby, mother!' he said. 'I couldn't possibly!'

'Why not?' she said, her voice becoming heavy when she was opposed. 'Why not? You can still go from the seaside to see the Derby with your Uncle Oscar, if that that's what you wish. No need for you to wait here. Besides, I think you care too much about these races. It's a bad sign. My family has been a gambling family, and you won't know till you grow up how much damage it has done. But it has done damage. I shall have to send Bassett away, and ask Uncle Oscar not to talk racing to you, unless you promise to be reasonable about it—go away to the seaside and forget it. You're all nerves!'

'I'll do what you like, mother, so long as you don't send me away till after the Derby,' the boy said.

'Send you away from where? Just from this house?'

'Yes,' he said, gazing at her.

'Why, you curious child, what makes you care about this house so much, suddenly? I never knew you loved it.'

He gazed at her without speaking. He had a secret within a secret, something he had not divulged, even to Bassett or to his Uncle Oscar.

But his mother, after standing undecided and a little bit sullen for some moments, said, 'Very well, then! Don't go to the seaside till after the Derby, if you don't wish it. But promise me you won't think so much about horse-racing and events as you call them!'

'Oh no,' said the boy casually. 'I won't think much about them, mother. You needn't worry. I wouldn't worry, mother, if I were you.'

'If you were me and I were you,' said his mother, 'I wonder what we should do!'

'But you know you needn't worry, mother, don't you?' the boy repeated.

'I should be awfully glad to know it,' she said wearily.

'Oh, well, you can, you know. I mean, you ought to know you needn't worry,' he insisted.

'Ought I? Then I'll see about it,' she said.

Paul's secret of secrets was his wooden horse, that which had no name. Since he was emancipated from a nurse and a nursery-governess, he had had his rocking-horse removed to his own bedroom at the top of the house.

'Surely you're too big for a rocking-horse!' his mother had remonstrated.

'Well, you see, mother, till I can have a real horse, I like to have some sort of animal about,' had been his quaint answer.

'Do you feel he keeps you company?' she laughed.

'Oh yes! He's very good, he always keeps me company, when I'm there,' said Paul.

So the horse, rather shabby, stood in an arrested prance in the boy's bedroom.

The Derby was drawing near, and the boy grew more and more tense. He hardly heard what was spoken to him, he was very frail, and his eyes were really uncanny. His mother had sudden strange seizures of uneasiness about him. Sometimes, for half an hour, she would feel a sudden anxiety about him that was almost anguish. She wanted to rush to him at once, and know he was safe.

Two nights before the Derby, she was at a big party in town, when one of her rushes of anxiety about her boy, her first-born, gripped her heart till she could hardly speak. She fought with the feeling, might and main, for she believed in common sense. But it was too strong. She had to leave the dance and go downstairs to telephone to the country.

The children's nursery-governess was terribly surprised and startled at being rung up in the night.

'Are the children all right, Miss Wilmot?'

'Oh yes, they are quite all right.'

'Master Paul? Is he all right?'

'He went to bed as right as a trivet. Shall I run up and look at him?'

'No,' said Paul's mother reluctantly. 'No! Don't trouble. It's all right. Don't sit up. We shall be home fairly soon.' She did not want her son's privacy intruded upon.

'Very good,' said the governess.

It was about one o'clock when Paul's mother and father drove up to their house. All was still. Paul's mother went to her room and slipped off her white fur cloak. She had told her maid not to wait up for her. She heard her husband downstairs, mixing a whisky and soda.

And then, because of the strange anxiety at her heart, she stole upstairs to her son's room. Noiselessly she went along the upper corridor. Was there a faint noise? What was it?

She stood, with arrested muscles, outside his door, listening. There was a strange, heavy, and yet not loud noise. Her heart stood still. It was a soundless noise, yet rushing and powerful. Something huge, in violent, hushed motion. What was it? What in God's name was it? She ought to know. She felt that she knew the noise. She knew what it was.

Yet she could not place it. She couldn't say what it was. And on and on it went, like a madness.

Softly, frozen with anxiety and fear, she turned the door-handle.

The room was dark. Yet in the space near the window, she heard and saw something plunging to and fro. She gazed in fear and amazement.

Then suddenly she switched on the light, and saw her son, in his green pyjamas, madly surging on the rocking-horse. The blaze of light suddenly lit him up, as he urged the wooden horse, and lit her up, as she stood, blonde, in her dress of pale green and crystal, in the doorway.

'Paul!' she cried. 'Whatever are you doing?'

'It's Malabar!' he screamed in a powerful, strange voice. 'It's Malabar!'

His eyes blazed at her for one strange and senseless second, as he ceased urging his wooden horse. Then he fell with a crash to the ground, and she, all her tormented motherhood flooding upon her, rushed to gather him up.

But he was unconscious, and unconscious he remained, with some brain-fever. He talked and tossed, and his mother sat stonily by his side.

'Malabar! It's Malabar! Bassett, Bassett, I know! It's Malabar!'

So the child cried, trying to get up and urge the rocking-horse that gave him his inspiration.

'What does he mean by Malabar?' asked the heart-frozen mother.

'I don't know,' said the father stonily.

'What does he mean by Malabar?' she asked her brother Oscar.

'It's one of the horses running for the Derby,' was the answer.

And, in spite of himself, Oscar Cresswell spoke to Bassett, and himself put a thousand on Malabar: at fourteen to one.

The third day of the illness was critical: they were waiting for a change. The boy, with his rather long, curly hair, was tossing ceaselessly on the pillow. He neither slept nor regained consciousness, and his eyes were like blue stones. His mother sat, feeling her heart had gone, turned actually into a stone.

In the evening Oscar Cresswell did not come, but Bassett sent a message, saying could he come up for one moment, just one moment? Paul's mother was very angry at the intrusion, but on second thoughts she agreed. The boy was the same. Perhaps Bassett might bring him to consciousness.

The gardener, a shortish fellow with a little brown moustache and sharp little brown eyes, tiptoed into the room, touched his imaginary cap to Paul's mother, and stole to the bedside, staring with glittering, smallish eyes at the tossing, dying child.

'Master Paul!' he whispered. 'Master Paul! Malabar came in first all right, a clean win. I did as you told me. You've made over seventy thousand pounds, you have; you've got over eighty thousand. Malabar came in all right, Master Paul.'

'Malabar! Malabar! Did I say Malabar, mother? Did I say Malabar? Do you think I'm lucky, mother? I knew Malabar, didn't I? Over eighty thousand pounds! I call that lucky, don't you, mother? Over eighty thousand pounds! I knew, didn't I know I knew? Malabar came in all right. If I ride my horse till I'm sure, then I tell you, Bassett, you can go as high as you like. Did you go for all you were worth, Bassett?'

'I went a thousand on it, Master Paul.'

'I never told you, mother, that if I can ride my horse, and get there, then I'm absolutely sure—oh, absolutely! Mother, did I ever tell you? I am lucky!'

'No, you never did,' said his mother.

But the boy died in the night.

And even as he lay dead, his mother heard her brother's voice saying to her, 'My God, Hester, you're eighty-odd thousand to the good, and a poor devil of a son to the bad. But, poor devil, poor devil, he's best gone out of a life where he rides his rocking-horse to find a winner.'

SECOND BEST

D.H. Lawrence

'Oh, I'm tired!' Frances exclaimed petulantly, and in the same instant she dropped down on the turf, near the hedge-bottom.

Anne stood a moment surprised, then, accustomed to the vagaries of her beloved Frances, said, 'Well, and aren't you always likely to be tired, after travelling that blessed long way from Liverpool yesterday?' and she plumped down beside her sister. Anne was a wise young body of fourteen, very buxom, brimming with common sense. Frances was much older, about twenty-three, and whimsical, spasmodic. She was the beauty and the clever child of the family. She plucked the goose-grass buttons from her dress in a nervous, desperate fashion. Her beautiful profile, looped above with black hair, warm with the dusky-and-scarlet complexion of a pear, was calm as a mask, her thin brown hand plucked nervously.

'It's not the journey,' she said, objecting to Anne's obtuseness. Anne looked inquiringly at her darling. The young girl, in her self-confident, practical way, proceeded to reckon up this whimsical creature. But suddenly she found herself full in the eyes of Frances; felt two dark, hectic eyes flaring challenge at her, and she shrank away. Frances was peculiar for these great, exposed looks, which disconcerted people by their violence and their suddenness.

'What's a matter, poor old duck?' asked Anne, as she folded the slight, wilful form of her sister in her arms. Frances laughed shakily, and nestled down for comfort on the budding breasts of the strong girl.

'Oh, I'm only a bit tired,' she murmured, on the point of tears.

'Well, of course you are, what do you expect?' soothed Anne. It was a joke to Frances that Anne should play elder, almost mother to her. But then, Anne was in her unvexed teens; men were like big dogs to her: while Frances, at twenty-three, suffered a good deal.

The country was intensely morning-still. On the common everything shone beside its shadow, and the hillside gave off heat in silence. The brown turf seemed in a low state of combustion, the leaves of the oaks were scorched brown. Among the blackish foliage in the distance shone the small red and orange of the village.

The willows in the brook-course at the foot of the common suddenly shook with a dazzling effect like diamonds. It was a puff of wind. Anne resumed her normal position. She spread her knees, and put in her lap a handful of hazel nuts, white-green leafy things, whose one cheek was tanned between brown and pink. These she began to crack and eat. Frances, with bowed head, mused bitterly.

'Eh, you know Tom Smedley?' began the young girl, as she pulled a tight kernel out of its shell.

'I suppose so,' replied Frances sarcastically.

'Well, he gave me a wild rabbit what he'd caught, to keep with my tame one—and it's living.'

'That's a good thing,' said Frances, very detached and ironic.

'Well, it is! He reckoned he'd take me to Ollerton Feast, but he never did. Look here, he took a servant from the rectory; I saw him.'

'So he ought,' said Frances.

'No, he oughtn't! and I told him so. And I told him I should tell you—an' I have done.'

Click and snap went a nut between her teeth. She sorted out the kernel, and chewed complacently.

'It doesn't make much difference,' said Frances.

'Well, 'appen it doesn't; but I was mad with him all the same.'

'Why?'

'Because I was; he's no right to go with a servant.'

'He's a perfect right,' persisted Frances, very just and cold.

'No, he hasn't, when he'd said he'd take me.'

Frances burst into a laugh of amusement and relief.

'Oh, no; I'd forgot that,' she said, adding, 'And what did he say when you promised to tell me?'

'He laughed and said, 'he won't fret her fat over that.'

'And she won't,' sniffed Frances.

There was silence. The common, with its sere, blonde-headed thistles, its heaps of silent bramble, its brown-husked gorse in the glare of sunshine, seemed visionary. Across the brook began the immense pattern of agriculture, white chequering of barley stubble, brown squares of wheat, khaki patches of pasture, red stripes of fallow, with the woodland and the tiny village dark like ornaments, leading away to the distance, right to the hills, where the check-pattern grew smaller and smaller, till, in the blackish haze of heat, far off, only the tiny white squares of barley stubble showed distinct.

'Eh, I say, here's a rabbit hole!' cried Anne suddenly. 'Should we watch if one comes out? You won't have to fidget, you know.'

The two girls sat perfectly still. Frances watched certain objects in her surroundings: they had a peculiar, unfriendly look about them: the weight of greenish elderberries on their purpling stalks; the twinkling of the yellowing crab-apples that clustered high up in the hedge, against the sky: the exhausted, limp leaves of the primroses lying flat in the hedge-bottom: all looked strange to her. Then her eyes caught a movement. A mole was moving silently over the warm, red soil, nosing, shuffling hither and thither, flat, and dark as a shadow, shifting about, and as suddenly brisk, and as silent, like a very ghost of joie de vivre. Frances started, from habit was about to call on Anne to kill the little pest. But, to-day, her lethargy of unhappiness was too much for her. She watched the little brute paddling, snuffing, touching things to discover them, running in blindness, delighted to ecstasy by the sunlight and the hot, strange things that caressed its belly and its nose. She felt a keen pity for the little creature.

'Eh, our Fran, look there! It's a mole.'

Anne was on her feet, standing watching the dark, unconscious beast. Frances frowned with anxiety.

'It doesn't run off, does it?' said the young girl softly. Then she stealthily approached the creature. The mole paddled fumblingly away. In an instant Anne put her foot upon it, not too heavily. Frances could see the struggling, swimming movement of the little pink hands of the brute, the twisting and twitching of its pointed nose, as it wrestled under the sole of the boot.

'It does wriggle!' said the bonny girl, knitting her brows in a frown at the eerie sensation. Then she bent down to look at her trap. Frances could now see, beyond the edge of the boot-sole, the heaving of the velvet shoulders, the pitiful turning of the sightless face, the frantic rowing of the flat, pink hands.

'Kill the thing,' she said, turning away her face.

'Oh—I'm not,' laughed Anne, shrinking. 'You can, if you like.'

'I don't like,' said Frances, with quiet intensity.

After several dabbling attempts, Anne succeeded in picking up the little animal by the scruff of its neck. It threw back its head, flung its long blind snout from side to side, the mouth open in a peculiar oblong, with tiny pinkish teeth at the edge. The blind, frantic mouth gaped and writhed. The body, heavy and clumsy, hung scarcely moving.

'Isn't it a snappy little thing,' observed Anne twisting to avoid the teeth.

'What are you going to do with it?' asked Frances sharply.

'It's got to be killed—look at the damage they do. I s'll take it home and let dadda or somebody kill it. I'm not going to let it go.'

She swaddled the creature clumsily in her pocket-handkerchief and sat down beside her sister. There was an interval of silence, during which Anne combated the efforts of the mole.

'You've not had much to say about Jimmy this time. Did you see him often in Liverpool?' Anne asked suddenly.

'Once or twice,' replied Frances, giving no sign of how the question troubled her.

'And aren't you sweet on him anymore, then?'

'I should think I'm not, seeing that he's engaged.'

'Engaged? Jimmy Barrass! Well, of all things! I never thought he'd get engaged.'

'Why not, he's as much right as anybody else?' snapped Frances.

Anne was fumbling with the mole.

"Appen so,' she said at length; 'but I never thought Jimmy would, though.'

'Why not?' snapped Frances.

'I don't know—this blessed mole, it'll not keep still!—who's he got engaged to?'

'How should I know?'

'I thought you'd ask him; you've known him long enough. I s'd think he thought he'd get engaged now he's a Doctor of Chemistry.'

Frances laughed in spite of herself.

'What's that got to do with it?' she asked.

'I'm sure it's got a lot. He'll want to feel somebody now, so he's got engaged. Hey, stop it; go in!'

But at this juncture the mole almost succeeded in wriggling clear. It wrestled and twisted frantically, waved its pointed blind head, its mouth standing open like a little shaft, its big, wrinkled hands spread out.

'Go in with you!' urged Anne, poking the little creature with her forefinger, trying to get it back into the handkerchief. Suddenly the mouth turned like a spark on her finger.

'Oh!' she cried, 'he's bit me.'

She dropped him to the floor. Dazed, the blind creature fumbled round. Frances felt like shrieking. She expected him to dart away in a flash, like a mouse, and there he remained groping; she wanted to cry to him to be gone. Anne, in a sudden decision of wrath, caught up her sister's walking-cane. With one blow the mole was dead. Frances was startled and shocked. One moment the little wretch was fussing in the heat, and the next it lay like a little bag, inert and black—not a struggle, scarce a quiver.

'It is dead!' Frances said breathlessly.

Anne took her finger from her mouth, looked at the tiny pinpricks, and said, 'Yes, he is, and I'm glad. They're vicious little nuisances, moles are.'

With which her wrath vanished. She picked up the dead animal.

'Hasn't it got a beautiful skin,' she mused, stroking the fur with her forefinger, then with her cheek.

'Mind,' said Frances sharply. 'You'll have the blood on your skirt!'

One ruby drop of blood hung on the small snout, ready to fall. Anne shook it off on to some harebells. Frances suddenly became calm; in that moment, grown-up.

'I suppose they have to be killed,' she said, and a certain rather dreary indifference succeeded to her grief. The twinkling crab-apples, the glitter of brilliant willows now seemed to her trifling, scarcely worth the notice. Something had died in her, so that things lost their poignancy. She was calm, indifference overlying her quiet sadness. Rising, she walked down to the brook course.

'Here, wait for me,' cried Anne, coming tumbling after.

Frances stood on the bridge, looking at the red mud trodden into pockets by the feet of cattle. There was not a drain of water left, but everything smelled green, succulent. Why did she care so little for Anne, who was so fond of her? she asked herself. Why did she care so little for anyone? She did not know, but she felt a rather stubborn pride in her isolation and indifference.

They entered a field where stooks of barley stood in rows, the straight, blonde tresses of the corn streaming on to the ground. The stubble was bleached by the intense summer, so that the expanse glared white. The next field was sweet and soft with a second crop of seeds; thin, straggling clover whose little pink knobs rested prettily in the dark green. The scent was faint and sickly. The girls came up in single file, Frances leading.

Near the gate a young man was mowing with the scythe some fodder for the afternoon feed of the cattle. As he saw the girls he left off working and waited in an aimless kind of way. Frances was dressed in white muslin, and she walked with dignity, detached and forgetful. Her lack of agitation, her simple, unheeding advance made him nervous. She had loved the far-off Jimmy for five years, having had in return his half-measures. This man only affected her slightly.

Tom was of medium stature, energetic in build. His smooth, fair-skinned face was burned red, not brown, by the sun, and this ruddiness enhanced his appearance of good humour and easiness. Being a year older than Frances, he would have courted her long ago had she been so inclined. As it was, he had gone his uneventful way amiably, chatting with many a girl, but remaining unattached, free of trouble for the most part. Only he knew he wanted a woman. He hitched his trousers just a trifle self-consciously as the girls approached. Frances was a rare, delicate kind of being, whom he realized with a queer and delicious stimulation in his veins. She gave him a slight sense of suffocation. Somehow, this morning, she affected him more than usual. She was dressed in white.

He, however, being matter-of-fact in his mind, did not realize. His feeling had never become conscious, purposive.

Frances knew what she was about. Tom was ready to love her as soon as she would show him. Now that she could not have Jimmy, she did not poignantly care. Still, she would have something. If she could not have the best—Jimmy, whom she knew to be something of a snob—she would have the second best, Tom. She advanced rather indifferently.

'You are back, then!' said Tom. She marked the touch of uncertainty in his voice.

'No,' she laughed, 'I'm still in Liverpool,' and the undertone of intimacy made him burn.

'This isn't you, then?' he asked.

Her heart leapt up in approval. She looked in his eyes, and for a second was with him.

'Why, what do you think?' she laughed.

He lifted his hat from his head with a distracted little gesture. She liked him, his quaint ways, his humour, his ignorance, and his slow masculinity.

'Here, look here, Tom Smedley,' broke in Anne.

'A moudiwarp! Did you find it dead?' he asked.

'No, it bit me,' said Anne.

'Oh, aye! An' that got your rag out, did it?'

'No, it didn't!' Anne scolded sharply. 'Such language!'

'Oh, what's up wi' it?'

'I can't bear you to talk broad.'

'Can't you?'

He glanced at Frances.

'It isn't nice,' Frances said. She did not care, really. The vulgar speech jarred on her as a rule; Jimmy was a gentleman. But Tom's manner of speech did not matter to her.

'I like you to talk nicely,' she added.

'Do you,' he replied, tilting his hat, stirred.

'And generally you do, you know,' she smiled.

'I s'll have to have a try,' he said, rather tensely gallant.

'What?' she asked brightly.

'To talk nice to you,' he said. Frances coloured furiously, bent her head for a moment, then laughed gaily, as if she liked this clumsy hint.

'Eh now, you mind what you're saying,' cried Anne, giving the young man an admonitory pat.

'You wouldn't have to give yon mole many knocks like that,' he teased, relieved to get on safe ground, rubbing his arm.

'No indeed, it died in one blow,' said Frances, with a flippancy that was hateful to her.

'You're not so good at knockin' 'em?' he said, turning to her.

'I don't know, if I'm cross,' she said decisively.

'No?' he replied, with alert attentiveness.

'I could,' she added, harder, 'if it was necessary.'

He was slow to feel her difference.

'And don't you consider it is necessary?' he asked, with misgiving.

'W—ell—is it?' she said, looking at him steadily, coldly.

'I reckon it is,' he replied, looking away, but standing stubborn.

She laughed quickly.

'But it isn't necessary for me,' she said, with slight contempt.

'Yes, that's quite true,' he answered.

She laughed in a shaky fashion.

'I know it is,' she said; and there was an awkward pause.

'Why, would you like me to kill moles then?' she asked tentatively, after a while.

'They do us a lot of damage,' he said, standing firm on his own ground, angered.

'Well, I'll see the next time I come across one,' she promised, defiantly. Their eyes met, and she sank before him, her pride troubled. He felt uneasy and triumphant and baffled, as if fate had gripped him. She smiled as she departed.

'Well,' said Anne, as the sisters went through the wheat stubble; 'I don't know what you two's been jawing about, I'm sure.'

'Don't you?' laughed Frances significantly.

'No, I don't. But, at any rate, Tom Smedley's a good deal better to my thinking than Jimmy, so there—and nicer.'

'Perhaps he is,' said Frances coldly.

And the next day, after a secret, persistent hunt, she found another mole playing in the heat. She killed it, and in the evening, when Tom came to the gate to smoke his pipe after supper, she took him the dead creature.

'Here you are then!' she said.

'Did you catch it?' he replied, taking the velvet corpse into his fingers and examining it minutely. This was to hide his trepidation.

'Did you think I couldn't?' she asked, her face very near his.

'Nay, I didn't know.'

She laughed in his face, a strange little laugh that caught her breath, all agitation, and tears, and recklessness of desire. He looked frightened and upset. She put her hand to his arm.

'Shall you go out wi' me?' he asked, in a difficult, troubled tone.

She turned her face away, with a shaky laugh. The blood came up in him, strong, overmastering. He resisted it. But it drove him down, and he was carried away. Seeing the winsome, frail nape of her neck, fierce love came upon him for her, and tenderness.

'We s'll 'ave to tell your mother,' he said. And he stood, suffering, resisting his passion for her.

'Yes,' she replied, in a dead voice. But there was a thrill of pleasure in this death.

THE CANDLE

Leo Tolstoy

'Ye have heard that it hath been said, an eye for an eye and a tooth for a tooth: but I say unto you, That ye resist not evil.'
—St Matthew V. 38, 39

It was in the time of serfdom—many years before Alexander II's liberation of the sixty million serfs in 1862. In those days the people were ruled by different kinds of lords. There were not a few who, remembering God, treated their slaves in a humane manner, and not as beasts of burden, while there were others who were seldom known to perform a kind or generous action; but the most barbarous and tyrannical of all were those former serfs who arose from the dirt and became princes.

It was this latter class who made life literally a burden to those who were unfortunate enough to come under their rule. Many of them had arisen from the ranks of the peasantry to become superintendents of noblemen's estates.

The peasants were obliged to work for their master a certain number of days each week. There was plenty of land and water and the soil was rich and fertile, while the meadows and forests were sufficient to supply the needs of both the peasants and their lord.

There was a certain nobleman who had chosen a superintendent from the peasantry on one of his other estates. No sooner had the power to govern been vested in this newly-made official than he began to practice the most outrageous cruelties upon the poor serfs who had been placed under his control. Although this man had a wife and two married daughters, and was making so much money that he could have lived happily without transgressing in any way against either God or man, yet he was filled with envy and jealousy and deeply sunk in sin.

Michael Simeonovitch began his persecutions by compelling the peasants to perform more days of service on the estate every week than the laws obliged them to work. He established a brick-yard, in which he forced the men and women to do excessive labour, selling the bricks for his own profit.

On one occasion the overworked serfs sent a delegation to Moscow to complain of their treatment to their lord, but they obtained no satisfaction. When the poor peasants returned disconsolate from the nobleman their superintendent determined to have revenge for their boldness in going above him for redress, and their life and that of their fellow-victims became worse than before.

It happened that among the serfs there were some very treacherous people who would falsely accuse their fellows of wrong-doing and sow seeds of discord among the peasantry, whereupon Michael would become greatly enraged, while his poor subjects began to live in fear of their lives. When the superintendent passed through the village the people would run and hide themselves as from a wild beast. Seeing thus the terror which he had struck to the hearts of the moujiks, Michael's treatment of them became still more vindictive, so that from over-work and ill-usage the lot of the poor serfs was indeed a hard one.

There was a time when it was possible for the peasants, when driven to despair, to devise means whereby they could rid themselves of an inhuman monster such as Simeonovitch, and so these unfortunate people began to consider whether something could not be done to relieve THEM of their intolerable yoke. They would hold little meetings in secret places to bewail their misery and to confer with one another as to which would be the best way to act. Now and then the boldest of the gathering would rise and address his companions in this strain: 'How much longer can we tolerate such a villain to rule over us? Let us make an end of it at once, for it were better for us to perish than to suffer. It is surely not a sin to kill such a devil in human form.'

It happened once, before the Easter holidays, that one of these meetings was held in the woods, where Michael had sent the serfs to make a clearance for their master. At noon they assembled to eat their dinner and to hold a consultation. 'Why can't we leave now?' said one. 'Very soon we shall be reduced to nothing. Already we are almost worked to death—there being no rest, night or day, either for us or our poor women. If anything should be done in a way not exactly to please him he will find fault and perhaps flog some of us to death—as was the case with poor Simeon, whom he killed not long ago. Only recently Anisim was tortured in irons till he died. We certainly cannot stand this much longer.' 'Yes,' said another, 'what is the use of waiting? Let us act at once. Michael will be here this evening, and will be certain to abuse us shamefully. Let us, then, thrust him from his horse and with one blow of an axe give him what he deserves, and thus end our misery. We can then dig a big hole and bury him like a dog, and no one will know what became of him. Now let us come to an agreement—to stand together as one man and not to betray one another.'

The last speaker was Vasili Minayeff, who, if possible, had more cause to complain of Michael's cruelty than any of his fellow-serfs. The superintendent was in the habit of flogging him severely every week, and he took also Vasili's wife to serve him as cook.

Accordingly, during the evening that followed this meeting in the woods Michael arrived on the scene on horseback. He began at once to find fault with the manner in which the work had been done, and to complain because some lime-trees had been cut down.

'I told you not to cut down any lime-trees!' shouted the enraged superintendent. 'Who did this thing? Tell me at once, or I shall flog every one of you!'

On investigation, a peasant named Sidor was pointed out as the guilty one, and his face was roundly slapped. Michael also severely punished Vasili, because he had not done sufficient work, after which the master rode safely home.

In the evening the serfs again assembled, and poor Vasili said, 'Oh, what kind of people ARE we, anyway? We are only sparrows, and not men at all! We agree to stand by each other, but as soon as the time for action comes we all run and hide. Once a lot of sparrows conspired against a hawk, but no sooner did the bird of prey appear than they sneaked off in the grass. Selecting one of the choicest sparrows, the hawk took it away to eat, after which the others came out crying, 'Twee-twee!' and found that one was missing. 'Who is killed?' they asked. 'Vanka! Well, he deserved it.' You, my friends, are acting in just the same manner. When Michael attacked Sidor you should have stood by your promise. Why didn't you arise, and with one stroke put an end to him and to our misery?'

The effect of this speech was to make the peasants more firm in their determination to kill their superintendent. The latter had already given orders that they should be ready to plough during the Easter holidays, and to sow the field with oats, whereupon the serfs became stricken with grief, and gathered in Vasili's house to hold another indignation meeting. 'If he has really forgotten God,' they said, 'and shall continue to commit such crimes against us, it is truly necessary that we should kill him. If not, let us perish, for it can make no difference to us now.'

This despairing programme, however, met with considerable opposition from a peaceably-inclined man named Peter Mikhayeff. 'Brethren,' said he, 'you are contemplating a grievous sin. The taking of human life is a very serious matter. Of course it is easy to end the mortal existence of a man, but what will become of the souls of those who commit the deed? If Michael continues to act toward us unjustly God will surely punish him. But, my friends, we must have patience.'

This pacific utterance only served to intensify the anger of Vasili. Said he: 'Peter is forever repeating the same old story, 'It is a sin to kill any one.' Certainly it is sinful to murder; but we should consider the kind of man we are dealing with. We all know it is wrong to kill a good man, but even God would take away the life of such a dog as he is. It is our duty, if we have any love for mankind, to shoot a dog that is mad. It is a sin to let him live. If, therefore, we are to suffer at all, let it be in the interests of the people—and they will thank us for it. If we remain quiet any longer a flogging will be our only reward. You are talking nonsense, Mikhayeff. Why don't you think of the sin we shall be committing if we work during the Easter holidays—for you will refuse to work then yourself?'

'Well, then,' replied Peter, 'if they shall send me to plough, I will go. But I shall not be going of my own free will, and God will know whose sin it is, and shall punish the offender accordingly. Yet we must not forget him. Brethren, I am not giving you my own views only. The law of God is not to return evil for evil; indeed, if you try in this way to stamp out wickedness it will come upon you all the stronger. It is not difficult for you to kill the man, but his blood will surely stain your own soul. You may think you have killed a bad man—that you have gotten rid of evil—but you will soon find out that the seeds of still greater wickedness have been planted within you. If you yield to misfortune it will surely come to you.'

As Peter was not without sympathizers among the peasants, the poor serfs were consequently divided into two groups: the followers of Vasili and those who held the views of Mikhayeff.

On Easter Sunday no work was done. Toward the evening an elder came to the peasants from the nobleman's court and said, 'Our superintendent, Michael Simeonovitch, orders you to go to-morrow to plough the field for the oats.' Thus the official went through the village and directed the men to prepare for work the next day—some by the river and others by the roadway. The poor people were almost overcome with grief, many of them shedding tears, but none dared to disobey the orders of their master.

On the morning of Easter Monday, while the church bells were calling the inhabitants to religious services, and while everyone else was about to enjoy a holiday, the unfortunate serfs started for the field to plough. Michael arose rather late and took a walk about the farm. The domestic servants were through with their work and had dressed themselves for the day, while Michael's wife and their widowed daughter (who was visiting them, as was her custom on holidays) had been to church and returned. A steaming samovar awaited them, and they began to drink tea with Michael, who, after lighting his pipe, called the elder to him.

'Well,' said the superintendent, 'have you ordered the moujiks to plough to-day?'

'Yes, sir, I did,' was the reply.

'Have they all gone to the field?'

'Yes, sir; all of them. I directed them myself where to begin.'

'That is all very well. You gave the orders, but are they ploughing? Go at once and see, and you may tell them that I shall be there after dinner. I shall expect to find one and a half acres done for every two ploughs, and the work must be well done; otherwise they shall be severely punished, notwithstanding the holiday.'

'I hear, sir, and obey.'

The elder started to go, but Michael called him back. After hesitating for some time, as if he felt very uneasy, he said, 'By the way, listen to what those scoundrels say about me. Doubtless some of them will curse me, and I want you to report the exact words. I know what villains they are. They don't find work at all pleasant. They would rather lie down all day and do nothing. They would like to eat and drink and make merry on holidays, but they forget that if the ploughing is not done it will soon be too late. So you go and listen to what is said, and tell it to me in detail. Go at once.'

'I hear, sir, and obey.'

Turning his back and mounting his horse, the elder was soon at the field where the serfs were hard at work.

It happened that Michael's wife, a very good-hearted woman, overheard the conversation which her husband had just been holding with the elder. Approaching him, she said, 'My good friend, Mishinka [diminutive of Michael], I beg of you to consider the importance and solemnity of this holy-day. Do not sin, for Christ's sake. Let the poor moujiks go home.'

Michael laughed, but made no reply to his wife's humane request. Finally he said to her:

'You've not been whipped for a very long time, and now you have become bold enough to interfere in affairs that are not your own.'

'Mishinka,' she persisted, 'I have had a frightful dream concerning you. You had better let the moujiks go.'

'Yes,' said he; 'I perceive that you have gained so much flesh of late that you think you would not feel the whip. Lookout!'

Rudely thrusting his hot pipe against her cheek, Michael chased his wife from the room, after which he ordered his dinner. After eating a hearty meal consisting of cabbage-soup, roast pig, meat-cake, pastry with milk, jelly, sweet cakes, and vodka, he called his woman cook to him and ordered her to be seated and sing songs, Simeonovitch accompanying her on the guitar.

While the superintendent was thus enjoying himself to the fullest satisfaction in the musical society of his cook the elder returned, and, making a low bow to his superior, proceeded to give the desired information concerning the serfs.

'Well,' asked Michael, 'did they plough?'

'Yes,' replied the elder; 'they have accomplished about half the field.'

'Is there no fault to be found?'

'Not that I could discover. The work seems to be well done. They are evidently afraid of you.'

'How is the soil?'

'Very good. It appears to be quite soft.'

'Well,' said Simeonovitch, after a pause, 'what did they say about me? Cursed me, I suppose?'

As the elder hesitated somewhat, Michael commanded him to speak and tell him the whole truth. 'Tell me all,' said he; 'I want to know their exact words. If you tell me the truth I shall reward you; but if you conceal anything from me you will be punished. See here, Catherine, pour out a glass of vodka to give him courage!'

After drinking to the health of his superior, the elder said to himself: 'It is not my fault if they do not praise him. I shall tell him the truth.' Then turning suddenly to the superintendent he said, 'They complain, Michael Simeonovitch! They complain bitterly.'

'But what did they say?' demanded Michael. 'Tell me!'

'Well, one thing they said was, 'He does not believe in God.'

Michael laughed. 'Who said that?' he asked.

'It seemed to be their unanimous opinion. 'He has been overcome by the Evil One,' they said.'

'Very good,' laughed the superintendent; 'but tell me what each of them said. What did Vasili say?'

The elder did not wish to betray his people, but he had a certain grudge against Vasili, and he said, 'He cursed you more than did any of the others.'

'But what did he say?'

'It is awful to repeat it, sir. Vasili said, 'He shall die like a dog, having no chance to repent!'

'Oh, the villain!' exclaimed Michael. 'He would kill me if he were not afraid. All right, Vasili; we shall have an accounting with you. And Tishka—he called me a dog, I suppose?'

'Well,' said the elder, 'they all spoke of you in anything but complimentary terms; but it is mean in me to repeat what they said.'

'Mean or not you must tell me, I say!'

'Some of them declared that your back should be broken.'

Simeonovitch appeared to enjoy this immensely, for he laughed outright. 'We shall see whose back will be the first to be broken,' said he. 'Was that Tishka's opinion? While I did not suppose they would say anything good about me, I did not expect such curses and threats. And Peter Mikhayeff—was that fool cursing me too?'

'No; he did not curse you at all. He appeared to be the only silent one among them. Mikhayeff is a very wise moujik, and he surprises me very much. At his actions all the other peasants seemed amazed.'

'What did he do?'

'He did something remarkable. He was diligently ploughing, and as I approached him I heard someone singing very sweetly. Looking between the ploughshares, I observed a bright object shining.'

'Well, what was it? Hurry up!'

'It was a small, five-kopeck wax candle, burning brightly, and the wind was unable to blow it out. Peter, wearing a new shirt, sang beautiful hymns as he ploughed, and no matter how he handled the implement the candle continued to burn. In my presence he fixed the plough, shaking it violently, but the bright little object between the coulters remained undisturbed.'

'And what did Mikhayeff say?'

'He said nothing—except when, on seeing me, he gave me the holy-day salutation, after which he went on his way singing and ploughing as before. I did not say anything to him, but, on approaching the other moujiks, I found that they were laughing and making sport of their silent companion. 'It is a great sin to plough on Easter Monday,' they said. 'You could not get absolution from your sin if you were to pray all your life.'

'And did Mikhayeff make no reply?'

'He stood long enough to say: 'There should be peace on earth and good-will to men,' after which he resumed his ploughing and singing, the candle burning even more brightly than before.'

Simeonovitch had now ceased to ridicule, and, putting aside his guitar, his head dropped on his breast and he became lost in thought. Presently he ordered the elder and cook to depart, after which Michael went behind a screen and threw himself upon the bed. He was sighing and moaning, as if in great distress, when his wife came in and spoke kindly to him. He refused to listen to her, exclaiming:

'He has conquered me, and my end is near!'

'Mishinka,' said the woman, 'arise and go to the moujiks in the field. Let them go home, and everything will be all right. Heretofore you have run far greater risks without any fear, but now you appear to be very much alarmed.'

'He has conquered me!' he repeated. 'I am lost!'

'What do you mean?' demanded his wife, angrily. 'If you will go and do as I tell you there will be no danger. Come, Mishinka,' she added, tenderly; 'I shall have the saddle-horse brought for you at once.'

When the horse arrived the woman persuaded her husband to mount the animal, and to fulfil her request concerning the serfs. When he reached the village a woman opened the gate for him to enter, and as he did so the inhabitants, seeing the brutal superintendent whom everybody feared, ran to hide themselves in their houses, gardens, and other secluded places.

At length Michael reached the other gate, which he found closed also, and, being unable to open it himself while seated on his horse, he called loudly for assistance. As no one responded to his shouts he dismounted and opened the gate, but as he was about to remount, and had one foot in the stirrup, the horse became frightened at some pigs and sprang suddenly to one side. The superintendent fell across the fence and a very sharp picket pierced his stomach, when Michael fell unconscious to the ground.

Toward the evening, when the serfs arrived at the village gate, their horses refused to enter. On looking around, the peasants discovered the dead body of their superintendent lying face downward in a pool of blood, where he had fallen from the fence. Peter Mikhayeff alone had sufficient courage to dismount and approach the prostrate form, his companions riding around the village and entering by way of the back yards. Peter closed the dead man's eyes, after which he put the body in a wagon and took it home.

When the nobleman learned of the fatal accident which had befallen his superintendent, and of the brutal treatment which he had meted out to those under him, he freed the serfs, exacting a small rent for the use of his land and the other agricultural opportunities.

And thus the peasants clearly understood that the power of God is manifested not in evil, but in goodness.

MY DREAM

Leo Tolstoy

I

'As a daughter she no longer exists for me. Can't you understand? She simply doesn't exist. Still, I cannot possibly leave her to the charity of strangers. I will arrange things so that she can live as she pleases, but I do not wish to hear of her. Who would ever have thought…the horror of it, the horror of it.'

He shrugged his shoulders, shook his head, and raised his eyes. These words were spoken by Prince Michael Ivanovich to his brother Peter, who was governor of a province in Central Russia. Prince Peter was a man of fifty, Michael's junior by ten years.

On discovering that his daughter, who had left his house a year before, had settled here with her child, the elder brother had come from St Petersburg to the provincial town, where the above conversation took place.

Prince Michael Ivanovich was a tall, handsome, white-haired, fresh coloured man, proud and attractive in appearance and bearing. His family consisted of a vulgar, irritable wife, who wrangled with him continually over every petty detail, a son, a ne'er-do-well, spendthrift and roué—yet a 'gentleman,' according to his father's code, two daughters, of whom the elder had married well, and was living in St Petersburg; and the younger, Lisa—his favourite, who had disappeared from home a year before. Only a short while ago he had found her with her child in this provincial town.

Prince Peter wanted to ask his brother how, and under what circumstances, Lisa had left home, and who could possibly be the father of her child. But he could not make up his mind to inquire.

That very morning, when his wife had attempted to condole with her brother-in-law, Prince Peter had observed a look of pain on his brother's face. The look had at once been masked by an expression of unapproachable pride, and he had begun to question her about their flat, and the price she paid. At luncheon, before the family and guests, he had been witty and sarcastic as usual. Towards every one, excepting the children, whom he treated with almost reverent tenderness, he adopted an attitude of distant hauteur. And yet it was so natural to him that everyone somehow acknowledged his right to be haughty.

In the evening his brother arranged a game of whist. When he retired to the room which had been made ready for him, and was just beginning to take out his artificial teeth, someone tapped lightly on the door with two fingers.

'Who is that?'

'C'est moi, Michael.'

Prince Michael Ivanovich recognized the voice of his sister-in-law, frowned, replaced his teeth, and said to himself, 'What does she want?' Aloud he said, 'Entrez.'

His sister-in-law was a quiet, gentle creature, who bowed in submission to her husband's will. But to many she seemed a crank, and some did not hesitate to call her a fool. She was pretty, but her hair was always carelessly dressed, and she herself was untidy and absent-minded. She had, also, the strangest, most unaristocratic ideas, by no means fitting in the wife of a high official. These ideas she would express most unexpectedly, to everybody's astonishment, her husband's no less than her friends'.

'Fous pouvez me renvoyer, mais je ne m'en irai pas, je vous le dis d'avance,' she began, in her characteristic, indifferent way.

'Dieu preserve,' answered her brother-in-law, with his usual somewhat exaggerated politeness, and brought forward a chair for her.

'Ca ne vous derange pas?' she asked, taking out a cigarette. 'I'm not going to say anything unpleasant, Michael. I only wanted to say something about Lisochka.'

Michael Ivanovich sighed—the word pained him; but mastering himself at once, he answered with a tired smile. 'Our conversation can only be on one subject, and that is the subject you wish to discuss.' He spoke without looking at her, and avoided even naming the subject. But his plump, pretty little sister-in-law was unabashed. She continued to regard him with the same gentle, imploring look in her blue eyes, sighing even more deeply.

'Michael, mon bon ami, have pity on her. She is only human.'

'I never doubted that,' said Michael Ivanovich with a bitter smile. 'She is your daughter.'

'She was—but my dear Aline, why talk about this?'

'Michael, dear, won't you see her? I only wanted to say, that the one who is to blame—'

Prince Michael Ivanovich flushed; his face became cruel.

'For heaven's sake, let us stop. I have suffered enough. I have now but one desire, and that is to put her in such a position that she will be independent of others, and that she shall have no further need of communicating with me. Then she can live her own life, and my family and I need know nothing more about her. That is all I can do.'

'Michael, you say nothing but "I"! She, too, is "I".'

'No doubt; but, dear Aline, please let us drop the matter. I feel it too deeply.'

Alexandra Dmitrievna remained silent for a few moments, shaking her head. 'And Masha, your wife, thinks as you do?'

'Yes, quite.'

Alexandra Dmitrievna made an inarticulate sound.

'Brisons la dessus et bonne nuit,' said he. But she did not go. She stood silent a moment. Then,—'Peter tells me you intend to leave the money with the woman where she lives. Have you the address?'

'I have.'

'Don't leave it with the woman, Michael! Go yourself. Just see how she lives. If you don't want to see her, you need not. HE isn't there; there is no one there.'

Michael Ivanovich shuddered violently.

'Why do you torture me so? It's a sin against hospitality!'

Alexandra Dmitrievna rose, and almost in tears, being touched by her own pleading, said, 'She is so miserable, but she is such a dear.'

He got up, and stood waiting for her to finish. She held out her hand.

'Michael, you do wrong,' said she, and left him.

For a long while after she had gone Michael Ivanovich walked to and fro on the square of carpet. He frowned and shivered, and exclaimed, 'Oh, oh!' And then the sound of his own voice frightened him, and he was silent.

His wounded pride tortured him. His daughter—his—brought up in the house of her mother, the famous Avdotia Borisovna, whom the Empress honoured with her visits, and acquaintance with whom was an honour for all the world! His daughter—; and he had lived his life as a knight of old, knowing neither fear nor blame. The fact that he had a natural son born of a Frenchwoman, whom he had settled abroad, did not lower his own self-esteem. And now this daughter, for whom he had not only done everything that a father could and should do; this daughter to whom he had given a splendid education and every opportunity to make a match in the best Russian society…this daughter to whom he had not only given all that a girl could desire, but whom he had really LOVED; whom he had admired, been proud of—this daughter had repaid him with such disgrace, that he was ashamed and could not face the eyes of men!

He recalled the time when she was not merely his child, and a member of his family, but his darling, his joy and his pride. He saw her again, a little thing of eight or nine, bright, intelligent, lively, impetuous, graceful, with brilliant black eyes and flowing auburn hair. He remembered how she used to jump up on his knees and hug him, and tickle his neck; and how she would laugh, regardless of his protests, and continue to tickle him, and kiss his lips, his eyes, and his cheeks. He was naturally opposed to all demonstration, but this impetuous love moved him, and he often submitted to her petting. He remembered also how sweet it was to caress her. To remember all this, when that sweet child had become what she now was, a creature of whom he could not think without loathing.

He also recalled the time when she was growing into womanhood, and the curious feeling of fear and anger that he experienced when he became aware that men regarded her as a woman. He thought of his jealous love when she came coquettishly to him dressed for a ball, and knowing that she was pretty. He dreaded the passionate glances which fell upon her, that she not only did not understand but rejoiced in. 'Yes,' thought he, 'that superstition of woman's purity! Quite the contrary, they do not know shame—they lack this sense.' He remembered how, quite inexplicably to him, she had refused two very good suitors. She had become more and more fascinated by her own success in the round of gaieties she lived in.

But this success could not last long. A year passed, then two, then three. She was a familiar figure, beautiful—but her first youth had passed, and she had become somehow part of the ball-room furniture. Michael Ivanovich remembered how he had realized that she was on the road to spinsterhood, and desired but one thing for her. He must get her married off as quickly as possible, perhaps not quite so well as might have been arranged earlier, but still a respectable match.

But it seemed to him she had behaved with a pride that bordered on insolence. Remembering this, his anger rose more and more fiercely against her. To think of her refusing so many decent men, only to end in this disgrace. 'Oh, oh!' he groaned again.

Then stopping, he lit a cigarette, and tried to think of other things. He would send her money, without ever letting her see him. But memories came again. He remembered—it was not so very long ago, for she was more than twenty then—her beginning a flirtation with a boy of fourteen, a cadet of the Corps of Pages who had been staying with them in the country. She had driven the boy half crazy; he had wept in his distraction. Then how she had rebuked her father severely, coldly, and even rudely, when, to put an end to this stupid affair, he had sent the boy away. She seemed somehow to consider herself insulted. Since then father and daughter had drifted into undisguised hostility.

'I was right,' he said to himself. 'She is a wicked and shameless woman.'

And then, as a last ghastly memory, there was the letter from Moscow, in which she wrote that she could not return home; that she was a miserable, abandoned woman, asking only to be forgiven and forgotten. Then the horrid recollection of the scene with his wife came to him; their surmises and their suspicions, which became a certainty. The calamity had happened in Finland, where they had let her visit her aunt; and the culprit was an insignificant Swede, a student, an empty-headed, worthless creature—and married.

All this came back to him now as he paced backwards and forwards on the bedroom carpet, recollecting his former love for her, his pride in her. He recoiled with terror before the incomprehensible fact of her downfall, and he hated her for the agony she was causing him. He remembered the conversation with his sister-in-law, and tried to imagine how he might forgive her. But as soon as the thought of 'him' arose, there surged up in his heart horror, disgust, and wounded pride. He groaned aloud, and tried to think of something else.

'No, it is impossible; I will hand over the money to Peter to give her monthly. And as for me, I have no longer a daughter.'

And again a curious feeling overpowered him: a mixture of self-pity at the recollection of his love for her, and of fury against her for causing him this anguish.

II

During the last year Lisa had without doubt lived through more than in all the preceding twenty-five. Suddenly she had realized the emptiness of her whole life. It rose before her, base and sordid—this life at home and among the rich set in St Petersburg—this animal existence that never sounded the depths, but only touched the shallows of life.

It was well enough for a year or two, or perhaps even three. But when it went on for seven or eight years, with its parties, balls, concerts, and suppers; with its costumes and coiffures to display the charms of the body; with its adorers old and young, all alike seemingly possessed of some unaccountable right to have everything, to laugh at everything; and with its summer months spent in the same way, everything yielding but a superficial pleasure, even music and reading merely touching upon life's problems, but never solving them—all this holding out no promise of change, and losing its charm more and more—she began to despair. She had desperate moods when she longed to die.

Her friends directed her thoughts to charity. On the one hand, she saw poverty which was real and repulsive, and a sham poverty even more repulsive and pitiable; on the other, she saw the terrible indifference of the lady patronesses who came in carriages and gowns worth thousands. Life became to her more and more unbearable. She yearned for something real, for life itself—not this playing at living, not this skimming life of its cream. Of real life there was none. The best of her memories was her love for the little cadet Koko. That had been a good, honest, straight-forward impulse, and now there was nothing like it. There could not be. She grew more and more depressed, and in this gloomy mood she went to visit an aunt in Finland. The fresh scenery and surroundings, the people strangely different to her own, appealed to her at any rate as a new experience.

How and when it all began she could not clearly remember. Her aunt had another guest, a Swede. He talked of his work, his people, the latest Swedish novel. Somehow, she herself did not know how that terrible fascination of glances and smiles began, the meaning of which cannot be put into words.

These smiles and glances seemed to reveal to each, not only the soul of the other, but some vital and universal mystery. Every word they spoke was invested by these smiles with a profound and wonderful significance. Music, too, when they were listening together, or when they sang duets, became full of the same deep meaning. So, also, the words in the books they read aloud. Sometimes they would argue, but the moment their eyes met, or a smile flashed between them, the discussion remained far behind. They soared beyond it to some higher plane consecrated to themselves.

How it had come about, how and when the devil, who had seized hold of them both, first appeared behind these smiles and glances, she could not say. But, when terror first seized her, the invisible threads that bound them were already so interwoven that she had no power to tear herself free. She could only count on him and on his honour. She hoped that he would not make use of his power; yet all the while she vaguely desired it.

Her weakness was the greater, because she had nothing to support her in the struggle. She was weary of society life and she had no affection for her mother. Her father, so she thought, had cast her away from him, and she longed passionately to live and to have done with play.

Love, the perfect love of a woman for a man, held the promise of life for her. Her strong, passionate nature, too, was dragging her thither. In the tall, strong figure of this man, with his fair hair and light upturned moustache, under which shone a smile attractive and compelling, she saw the promise of that life for which she longed. And then the smiles and glances, the hope of something so incredibly beautiful, led, as they were bound to lead, to that which she feared but unconsciously awaited.

Suddenly all that was beautiful, joyous, spiritual, and full of promise for the future, became animal and sordid, sad and despairing.

She looked into his eyes and tried to smile, pretending that she feared nothing, that everything was as it should be; but deep down in her soul she knew it was all over. She understood that she had not found in him what she had sought; that which she had once known in herself and in Koko. She told him that he must write to her father asking her hand in marriage. This he promised to do; but when she met him next he said it was impossible for him to write just then. She saw something vague and furtive in his eyes, and her distrust of him grew. The following day he wrote to her, telling her that he was already married, though his wife had left him long since; that he knew she would despise him for the wrong he had done her, and implored her forgiveness. She made him come to see her. She said she loved him; that she felt herself bound to him for ever whether he was married or not, and would never leave him. The next time they met he told her that he and his parents were so poor that he could only offer her the meanest existence. She answered that she needed nothing, and was ready to go with him at once wherever he wished. He endeavoured to dissuade her, advising her to wait; and so she waited. But to live on with this secret, with occasional meetings, and merely corresponding with him, all hidden from her family, was agonising, and she insisted again that he must take her away. At first, when she returned to St Petersburg, be wrote promising to come, and then letters ceased and she knew no more of him.

She tried to lead her old life, but it was impossible. She fell ill, and the efforts of the doctors were unavailing; in her hopelessness she resolved to kill herself. But how was she to do this, so that her death might seem natural? She really desired to take her life, and imagined that she had irrevocably decided on the step. So, obtaining some poison, she poured it into a glass, and in another instant would have drunk it, had not her sister's little son of five at that very moment run in to show her a toy his grandmother had given him. She caressed the child, and, suddenly stopping short, burst into tears.

The thought overpowered her that she, too, might have been a mother had he not been married, and this vision of motherhood made her look into her own soul for the first time. She began to think not of what others would say of her, but of her own life. To kill oneself because of what the world might say was easy; but the moment she saw her own life dissociated from the world, to take that life was out of the question. She threw away the poison, and ceased to think of suicide.

Then her life within began. It was real life, and despite the torture of it, had the possibility been given her, she would not have turned back from it. She began to pray, but there was no comfort in prayer; and her suffering was less for herself than for her father, whose grief she foresaw and understood.

Thus months dragged along, and then something happened which entirely transformed her life. One day, when she was at work upon a quilt, she suddenly experienced a strange sensation. No—it seemed impossible. Motionless she sat with her work in hand. Was it possible that this was IT. Forgetting everything, his baseness and deceit, her mother's querulousness, and her father's sorrow, she smiled. She shuddered at the recollection that she was on the point of killing it, together with herself.

She now directed all her thoughts to getting away—somewhere where she could bear her child—and become a miserable, pitiful mother, but a mother withal. Somehow she planned and arranged it all, leaving her home and settling in a distant provincial town, where no one could find her, and where she thought she would be far from her people. But, unfortunately, her father's brother received an appointment there, a thing she could not possibly foresee. For four months she had been living in the house of a midwife—one Maria Ivanovna; and, on learning that her uncle had come to the town, she was preparing to fly to a still remoter hiding-place.

III

Michael Ivanovich awoke early next morning. He entered his brother's study, and handed him the cheque, filled in for a sum which he asked him to pay in monthly instalments to his daughter. He inquired when the express left for St Petersburg. The train left at seven in the evening, giving him time for an early dinner before leaving. He breakfasted with his sister-in-law, who refrained from mentioning the subject which was so painful to him, but only looked at him timidly; and after breakfast he went out for his regular morning walk.

Alexandra Dmitrievna followed him into the hall.

'Go into the public gardens, Michael—it is very charming there, and quite near to Everything,' said she, meeting his sombre looks with a pathetic glance.

Michael Ivanovich followed her advice and went to the public gardens, which were so near to Everything, and meditated with annoyance on the stupidity, the obstinacy, and heartlessness of women.

'She is not in the very least sorry for me,' he thought of his sister-in-law. 'She cannot even understand my sorrow. And what of her?' He was thinking of his daughter. 'She knows what all this means to me—the torture. What a blow in one's old age! My days will be shortened by it! But I'd rather have it over than endure this agony. And all that 'pour les beaux yeux d'un chenapan'—oh!' he moaned; and a wave of hatred and fury arose in him as he thought of what would be said in the town when everyone knew. (And no doubt everyone knew already.) Such a feeling of rage possessed him that he would have liked to beat it into her head, and make her understand what she had done. These women never understand. 'It is quite near Everything,' suddenly came to his mind, and getting out his notebook, he found her address. Vera Ivanovna Silvestrova, Kukonskaya Street, Abromov's house. She was living under this name. He left the gardens and called a cab.

'Whom do you wish to see, sir?' asked the midwife, Maria Ivanovna, when he stepped on the narrow landing of the steep, stuffy staircase.

'Does Madame Silvestrova live here?'

'Vera Ivanovna? Yes; please come in. She has gone out; she's gone to the shop round the corner. But she'll be back in a minute.'

Michael Ivanovich followed the stout figure of Maria Ivanovna into a tiny parlour, and from the next room came the screams of a baby, sounding cross and peevish, which filled him with disgust. They cut him like a knife.

Maria Ivanovna apologized, and went into the room, and he could hear her soothing the child. The child became quiet, and she returned.

'That is her baby; she'll be back in a minute. You are a friend of hers, I suppose?'

'Yes—a friend—but I think I had better come back later on,' said Michael Ivanovich, preparing to go. It was too unbearable, this preparation to meet her, and any explanation seemed impossible.

He had just turned to leave, when he heard quick, light steps on the stairs, and he recognized Lisa's voice.

'Maria Ivanovna—has he been crying while I've been gone—I was—'

Then she saw her father. The parcel she was carrying fell from her hands.

'Father!' she cried, and stopped in the doorway, white and trembling.

He remained motionless, staring at her. She had grown so thin. Her eyes were larger, her nose sharper, her hands worn and bony. He neither knew what to do, nor what to say. He forgot all his grief about his dishonour. He only felt sorrow, infinite sorrow for her; sorrow for her thinness, and for her miserable rough clothing; and most of all, for her pitiful face and imploring eyes.

'Father—forgive,' she said, moving towards him.

'Forgive—forgive me,' he murmured; and he began to sob like a child, kissing her face and hands, and wetting them with his tears.

In his pity for her he understood himself. And when he saw himself as he was, he realized how he had wronged her, how guilty he had been in his pride, in his coldness, even in his anger towards her. He was glad that it was he who was guilty, and that he had nothing to forgive, but that he himself needed forgiveness. She took him to her tiny room, and told him how she lived; but she did not show him the child, nor did she mention the past, knowing how painful it would be to him.

He told her that she must live differently.

'Yes; if I could only live in the country,' said she.

'We will talk it over,' he said. Suddenly the child began to wail and to scream. She opened her eyes very wide; and, not taking them from her father's face, remained hesitating and motionless.

'Well—I suppose you must feed him,' said Michael Ivanovich, and frowned with the obvious effort.

She got up, and suddenly the wild idea seized her to show him whom she loved so deeply the thing she now loved best of all in the world. But first she looked at her father's face. Would he be angry or not? His face revealed no anger, only suffering.

'Yes, go, go,' said he; 'God bless you. Yes. I'll come again to-morrow, and we will decide. Good-bye, my darling—good-bye.' Again he found it hard to swallow the lump in his throat.

When Michael Ivanovich returned to his brother's house, Alexandra Dmitrievna immediately rushed to him.

'Well?'

'Well? Nothing.'

'Have you seen?' she asked, guessing from his expression that something had happened.

'Yes,' he answered shortly, and began to cry. 'I'm getting old and stupid,' said he, mastering his emotion.

'No; you are growing wise—very wise.'

.007

Rudyard Kipling

A locomotive is, next to a marine engine, the most sensitive thing man ever made; and No. .007, besides being sensitive, was new. The red paint was hardly dry on his spotless bumper-bar, his headlight shone like a fireman's helmet, and his cab might have been a hard-wood-finish parlour. They had run him into the round-house after his trial—he had said good-bye to his best friend in the shops, the overhead travelling-crane—the big world was just outside; and the other locos were taking stock of him. He looked at the semicircle of bold, unwinking headlights, heard the low purr and mutter of the steam mounting in the gauges—scornful hisses of contempt as a slack valve lifted a little—and would have given a month's oil for leave to crawl through his own driving-wheels into the brick ash-pit beneath him. .007 was an eight-wheeled 'American' loco, slightly different from others of his type, and as he stood he was worth ten thousand dollars on the Company's books. But if you had bought him at his own valuation, after half an hour's waiting in the darkish, echoing round-house, you would have saved exactly nine thousand nine hundred and ninety-nine dollars and ninety-eight cents.

A heavy Mogul freight, with a short cow-catcher and a fire-box that came down within three inches of the rail, began the impolite game, speaking to a Pittsburgh Consolidation, who was visiting.

'Where did this thing blow in from?' he asked, with a dreamy puff of light steam.

'It's all I can do to keep track of our makes,' was the answer, 'without lookin' after your back-numbers. Guess it's something Peter Cooper left over when he died.'

.007 quivered; his steam was getting up, but he held his tongue. Even a hand-car knows what sort of locomotive it was that Peter Cooper experimented upon in the far-away Thirties. It carried its coal and water in two apple-barrels, and was not much bigger than a bicycle.

Then up and spoke a small, newish switching-engine, with a little step in front of his bumper-timber, and his wheels so close together that he looked like a broncho getting ready to buck.

'Something's wrong with the road when a Pennsylvania gravel pusher tells us anything about our stock, I think. That kid's all right. Eustis designed him, and Eustis designed me. Ain't that good enough?'

.007 could have carried the switching-loco round the yard in his tender, but he felt grateful for even this little word of consolation.

'We don't use hand-cars on the Pennsylvania,' said the Consolidation. 'That-er-peanut-stand is old enough and ugly enough to speak for himself.'

'He hasn't bin spoken to yet. He's bin spoke at. Hain't ye any manners on the Pennsylvania?' said the switching-loco.

'You ought to be in the yard, Poney,' said the Mogul, severely. 'We're all long-haulers here.'

'That's what you think,' the little fellow replied. 'You'll know more 'fore the night's out. I've bin down to Track 17, and the freight there—oh, Christmas!'

'I've trouble enough in my own division,' said a lean, light suburban loco with very shiny brake-shoes. 'My commuters wouldn't rest till they got a parlour car. They've hitched it back of all, and it hauls worsen a snow-plough. I'll snap her off someday sure, and then they'll blame everyone except their foolselves. They'll be askin' me to haul a vestibuled next!'

'They made you in New Jersey, didn't they?' said Poney. 'Thought so. Commuters and truck-wagons ain't any sweet haulin', but I tell you they're a heap better 'n cuttin' out refrigerator-cars or oil-tanks. Why, I've hauled—'

'Haul! You?' said the Mogul, contemptuously. 'It's all you can do to bunt a cold-storage car up the yard. Now, I—' he paused a little to let the words sink in—'I handle the Flying Freight-e-leven cars worth just anything you please to mention. On the stroke of eleven I pull out; and I'm timed for thirty-five an hour. Costly-perishable-fragile-immediate—that's me! Suburban traffic's only but one degree better than switching. Express freight's what pays.'

'Well, I ain't given to blowing, as a rule,' began the Pittsburgh Consolidation.

'No? You was sent in here because you grunted on the grade,' Poney interrupted.

'Where I grunt, you'd lie down, Poney: but, as I was saying, I don't blow much. Notwithstandin', if you want to see freight that is freight moved lively, you should see me warbling through the Alleghanies with thirty-seven ore-cars behind me, and my brakemen fightin' tramps so's they can't attend to my tooter. I have to do all the holdin' back then, and, though I say it, I've never had a load get away from me yet. No, sir. Haulin's's one thing, but judgment and discretion's another. You want judgment in my business.'

'Ah! But—but are you not paralysed by a sense of your overwhelming responsibilities?' said a curious, husky voice from a corner.

'Who's that?' .007 whispered to the Jersey commuter.

'Compound-experiment-N.G. She's bin switchin' in the B. & A. yards for six months, when she wasn't in the shops. She's economical (I call it mean) in her coal, but she takes it out in repairs. Ahem! I presume you found Boston somewhat isolated, madam, after your New York season?'

'I am never so well occupied as when I am alone.' The Compound seemed to be talking from half-way up her smoke-stack.

'Sure,' said the irreverent Poney, under his breath. 'They don't hanker after her any in the yard.'

'But, with my constitution and temperament—my work lies in Boston—I find your outrecuidance—'

'Outer which?' said the Mogul freight. 'Simple cylinders are good enough for me.'

'Perhaps I should have said faroucherie,' hissed the Compound.

'I don't hold with any make of papier-mache wheel,' the Mogul insisted.

The Compound sighed pityingly, and said no more.

'Git 'em all shapes in this world, don't ye?' said Poney. 'that's Mass'chusetts all over. They half start, an' then they stick on a dead-centre, an' blame it all on other folk's ways o' treatin' them. Talkin' o'

Boston, Comanche told me, last night, he had a hot-box just beyond the Newtons, Friday. That was why, he says, the Accommodation was held up. Made out no end of a tale, Comanche did.'

'If I'd heard that in the shops, with my boiler out for repairs, I'd know 't was one o' Comanche's lies,' the New Jersey commuter snapped. 'Hot-box! Him! What happened was they'd put an extra car on, and he just lay down on the grade and squealed. They had to send 127 to help him through. Made it out a hotbox, did he? Time before that he said he was ditched! Looked me square in the headlight and told me that as cool as as a water-tank in a cold wave. Hot-box! You ask 127 about Comanche's hot-box. Why, Comanche he was side-tracked, and 127 (he was just about as mad as they make 'em on account o' being called out at ten o'clock at night) took hold and snapped her into Boston in seventeen minutes. Hot-box! Hot fraud! that's what Comanche is.'

Then .007 put both drivers and his pilot into it, as the saying is, for he asked what sort of thing a hot-box might be?

'Paint my bell sky-blue!' said Poney, the switcher. 'Make me a surface-railroad loco with a hard-wood skirtin'-board round my wheels. Break me up and cast me into five-cent sidewalk-fakirs' mechanical toys! Here's an eight-wheel coupled 'American' don't know what a hot-box is! Never heard of an emergency-stop either, did ye? Don't know what ye carry jack-screws for? You're too innocent to be left alone with your own tender. Oh, you—you flatcar!'

There was a roar of escaping steam before anyone could answer, and .007 nearly blistered his paint off with pure mortification.

'A hot-box,' began the Compound, picking and choosing her words as though they were coal, 'a hotbox is the penalty exacted from inexperience by haste. Ahem!'

'Hot-box!' said the Jersey Suburban. 'It's the price you pay for going on the tear. It's years since I've had one. It's a disease that don't attack short haulers, as a rule.'

'We never have hot-boxes on the Pennsylvania,' said the Consolidation. 'They get 'em in New York—same as nervous prostration.'

'Ah, go home on a ferry-boat,' said the Mogul. 'You think because you use worse grades than our road 'u'd allow, you're a kind of Alleghany angel. Now, I'll tell you what you ... Here's my folk. Well, I can't stop. See you later, perhaps.'

He rolled forward majestically to the turn-table, and swung like a man-of-war in a tideway, till he picked up his track. 'But as for you, you pea-green swivelling' coffee-pot (this to .007'), you go out and learn something before you associate with those who've made more mileage in a week than you'll roll up in a year. Costly-perishable-fragile-immediate-that's me! S' long.'

'Split my tubes if that's actin' polite to a new member o' the Brotherhood,' said Poney. 'There wasn't any call to trample on ye like that. But manners was left out when Moguls was made. Keep up your fire, kid, an' burn your own smoke. 'Guess we'll all be wanted in a minute.'

Men were talking rather excitedly in the roundhouse. One man, in a dingy jersey, said that he hadn't any locomotives to waste on the yard. Another man, with a piece of crumpled paper in his hand, said that the yard-master said that he was to say that if the other man said anything, he (the other man) was to shut his head. Then the other man waved his arms, and wanted to know if he was expected to keep locomotives in his hip-pocket. Then a man in a black Prince Albert, without a collar, came up dripping, for it was a hot August night, and said that what he said went; and between the three of them the locomotives began to go, too—first the Compound; then the Consolidation; then .007.

Now, deep down in his fire-box, .007 had cherished a hope that as soon as his trial was done, he would be led forth with songs and shoutings, and attached to a green-and-chocolate vestibuled flyer, under charge of a bold and noble engineer, who would pat him on his back, and weep over him, and call him his Arab steed. (The boys in the shops where he was built used to read wonderful stories of railroad life, and .007 expected things to happen as he had heard.) But there did not seem to be many vestibuled fliers in the roaring, rumbling, electric-lighted yards, and his engineer only said, 'Now, what sort of a fool-sort of an injector has Eustis loaded on to this rig this time?' And he put the lever over with an angry snap, crying: 'Am I supposed to switch with this thing, hey?'

The collarless man mopped his head, and replied that, in the present state of the yard and freight and a few other things, the engineer would switch and keep on switching till the cows came home. .007 pushed out gingerly, his heart in his headlight, so nervous that the clang of his own bell almost made him jump the track. Lanterns waved, or danced up and down, before and behind him; and on every side, six tracks deep, sliding backward and forward, with clashings of couplers and squeals of hand-brakes, were cars—more cars than .007 had dreamed of. There were oil-cars, and hay-cars, and stock-cars full of lowing beasts, and ore-cars, and potato-cars with stovepipe-ends sticking out in the middle; cold-storage and refrigerator cars dripping ice water on the tracks; ventilated fruit and milk cars; flatcars with truck-wagons full of market-stuff; flat-cars loaded with reapers and binders, all red and green and gilt under the sizzling electric lights; flat-cars piled high with strong-scented hides, pleasant hemlock-plank, or bundles of shingles; flat-cars creaking to the weight of thirty-ton castings, angle-irons, and rivet-boxes for some new bridge; and hundreds and hundreds and hundreds of box-cars loaded, locked, and chalked. Men—hot and angry—crawled among and between and under the thousand wheels; men took flying jumps through his cab, when he halted for a moment; men sat on his pilot as he went forward, and on his tender as he returned; and regiments of men ran along the tops of the box-cars beside him, screwing down brakes, waving their arms, and crying curious things.

He was pushed forward a foot at a time; whirled backward, his rear drivers clinking and clanking, a quarter of a mile; jerked into a switch (yard-switches are very stubby and unaccommodating), bunted into a Red D, or Merchant's Transport car, and, with no hint or knowledge of the weight behind him, started up anew. When his load was fairly on the move, three or four cars would be cut off, and .007 would bound forward, only to be held hiccupping on the brake. Then he would wait a few minutes, watching the whirled lanterns, deafened with the clang of the bells, giddy with the vision of the sliding cars, his brake-pump panting forty to the minute, his front coupler lying sideways on his cow-catcher, like a tired dog's tongue in his mouth, and the whole of him covered with half-burnt coal-dust.

'T isn't so easy switching with a straight-backed tender,' said his little friend of the round-house, bustling by at a trot. 'But you're comin' on pretty fair. 'Ever seen a flyin' switch? No? Then watch me.'

Poney was in charge of a dozen heavy flat-cars. Suddenly he shot away from them with a sharp 'Whutt!' A switch opened in the shadows ahead; he turned up it like a rabbit as it snapped behind him, and the long line of twelve-foot-high lumber jolted on into the arms of a full-sized road-loco, who acknowledged receipt with a dry howl.

'My man's reckoned the smartest in the yard at that trick,' he said, returning. 'Gives me cold shivers when another fool tries it, though. That's where my short wheel-base comes in. Like as not you'd have your tender scraped off if you tried it.'

.007 had no ambitions that way, and said so.

'No? Of course this ain't your regular business, but say, don't you think it's interestin'? Have you seen the yard-master? Well, he's the greatest man on earth, an' don't you forget it. When are we through? Why, kid, it's always like this, day an' night—Sundays an' week-days. See that thirty-car freight slidin' in four, no, five tracks off? She's all mixed freight, sent here to be sorted out into straight trains. That's why we're cuttin' out the cars one by one.' He gave a vigorous push to a west-bound car as he spoke, and started back with a little snort of surprise, for the car was an old friend—an M.T.K. box-car.

'Jack my drivers, but it's Homeless Kate! Why, Kate, ain't there no gettin' you back to your friends? There's forty chasers out for you from your road, if there's one. Who's holdin' you now?'

'Wish I knew,' whimpered Homeless Kate. 'I belong in Topeka, but I've bin to Cedar Rapids; I've bin to Winnipeg; I've bin to Newport News; I've bin all down the old Atlanta and West Point; an' I've bin to Buffalo. Maybe I'll fetch up at Haverstraw. I've only bin out ten months, but I'm homesick—I'm just achin' homesick.'

'Try Chicago, Katie,' said the switching-loco; and the battered old car lumbered down the track, jolting: 'I want to be in Kansas when the sunflowers bloom.'

'Yard's full o' Homeless Kates an' Wanderin' Willies,' he explained to .007. 'I knew an old Fitchburg flat-car out seventeen months; an' one of ours was gone fifteen 'fore ever we got track of her. Dunno quite how our men fix it. 'Swap around, I guess. Anyway, I've done my duty. She's on her way to Kansas, via Chicago; but I'll lay my next boilerful she'll be held there to wait consignee's convenience, and sent back to us with wheat in the fall.'

Just then the Pittsburgh Consolidation passed, at the head of a dozen cars.

'I'm goin' home,' he said proudly.

'Can't get all them twelve on to the flat. Break 'em in half, Dutchy!' cried Poney. But it was .007 who was backed down to the last six cars, and he nearly blew up with surprise when he found himself pushing them on to a huge ferry-boat. He had never seen deep water before, and shivered as the flat drew away and left his bogies within six inches of the black, shiny tide.

After this he was hurried to the freight-house, where he saw the yard-master, a smallish, white-faced man in shirt, trousers, and slippers, looking down upon a sea of trucks, a mob of bawling truckmen, and squadrons of backing, turning, sweating, spark-striking horses.

'That's shippers' carts loadin' on to the receivin' trucks,' said the small engine, reverently. 'But he don't care. He lets 'em cuss. He's the Czar-King-Boss! He says 'Please,' and then they kneel down an' pray. There's three or four strings o' today's freight to be pulled before he can attend to them. When he waves his hand that way, things happen.'

A string of loaded cars slid out down the track, and a string of empties took their place. Bales, crates, boxes, jars, carboys, frails, cases, and packages flew into them from the freight-house as though the cars had been magnets and they iron filings.

'Ki-yah!' shrieked little Poney. 'Ain't it great?'

A purple-faced truckman shouldered his way to the yard-master, and shook his fist under his nose. The yard-master never looked up from his bundle of freight receipts. He crooked his forefinger slightly, and a tall young man in a red shirt, lounging carelessly beside him, hit the truckman under the left ear, so that he dropped, quivering and clucking, on a hay-bale.

'Eleven, seven, ninety-seven, L.Y.S.; fourteen ought ought three;

nineteen thirteen; one one four; seventeen ought twenty-one M. B.; and the ten westbound. All straight except the two last. Cut 'em off at the junction. An' that's all right. Pull that string.' The yard-master, with mild blue eyes, looked out over the howling truckmen at the waters in the moonlight beyond, and hummed:

'All things bright and beautiful,
All creatures great and small,
All things wise and wonderful,
The Lawd Gawd He made all!'

.007 moved out the cars and delivered them to the regular road-engine. He had never felt quite so limp in his life before.

'Curious, ain't it?' said Poney, puffing, on the next track. 'You an' me, if we got that man under our bumpers, we'd work him into red waste an' not know what we'd done; but-up there—with the steam hummin' in his boiler that awful quiet way ... '

'I know,' said .007. 'Makes me feel as if I'd dropped my Fire an' was getting cold. He is the greatest man on earth.'

They were at the far north end of the yard now, under a switch tower, looking down on the four-track way of the main traffic. The Boston Compound was to haul .007's string to some far-away northern junction over an indifferent road-bed, and she mourned aloud for the ninety-six pound rails of the B. & A.

'You're young; you're young,' she coughed. 'You don't realize your responsibilities.'

'Yes, he does,' said Poney, sharply; 'but he don't lie down under 'em.' Then, with aside-spurt of steam, exactly like a tough spitting: 'There ain't more than fifteen thousand dollars' worth o' freight behind her anyway, and she goes on as if 't were a hundred thousand—same as the Mogul's. Excuse me, madam, but you've the track .... She's stuck on a dead-centre again—bein' specially designed not to.'

The Compound crawled across the tracks on a long slant, groaning horribly at each switch, and moving like a cow in a snow-drift. There was a little pause along the yard after her tail-lights had disappeared; switches locked crisply, and everyone seemed to be waiting.

'Now I'll show you something worth,' said Poney. 'When the Purple

Emperor ain't on time, it's about time to amend the Constitution. The first stroke of twelve is—'

'Boom!' went the clock in the big yard-tower, and far away .007 heard a full, vibrating ' Yah! Yah! Yah!' A headlight twinkled on the horizon like a star, grew an overpowering blaze, and whooped up the humming track to the roaring music of a happy giant's song:

'With a michnai - ghignai - shtingal! Yah! Yah! Yah!
Ein - zwei - drei - Mutter! Yah! Yah! Yah!
She climb upon der shteeple,
Und she frighten all der people.
Singin' michnai - ghignai - shtingal! Yah! Yah!'

The last defiant 'yah! yah!' was delivered a mile and a half beyond the passenger-depot; but .007 had caught one glimpse of the superb six-wheel-coupled racing-locomotive, who hauled the pride and glory of the road—the gilt-edged Purple Emperor, the millionaires' south-bound express, laying the miles over his shoulder as a man peels a shaving from a soft board. The rest was a blur of maroon enamel, a bar of white light from the electrics in the cars, and a flicker of nickel-plated hand-rail on the rear platform.

'Ooh!' said .007.

'Seventy-five miles an hour these five miles. Baths, I've heard; barber's shop; ticker; and a library and the, rest to match. Yes, sir; seventy-five an hour! But he'll talk to you in the round-house just as democratic as I would. And I—cuss my wheel-base!—I'd kick clean off the track at half his gait. He's the Master of our Lodge. Cleans up at our house. I'll introdooce you some day. He's worth knowin'! There ain't many can sing that song, either.'

.007 was too full of emotions to answer. He did not hear a raging of telephone-bells in the switch-tower, nor the man, as he leaned out and called to .007's engineer: 'Got any steam?'

''Nough to run her a hundred mile out o' this, if I could,' said the engineer, who belonged to the open road and hated switching.

'Then get. The Flying Freight's ditched forty mile out, with fifty rod o' track ploughed up. No; no one's hurt, but both tracks are blocked. Lucky the wreckin'-car an' derrick are this end of the yard. Crew 'll be along in a minute. Hurry! You've the track.'

'Well, I could jest kick my little sawed-off self,' said Poney, as .007 was backed, with a bang, on to a grim and grimy car like a caboose, but full of tools—a flatcar and a derrick behind it. 'Some folks are one thing, and some are another; but you're in luck, kid. They push a wrecking-car. Now, don't get rattled. Your wheel-base will keep you on the track, and there ain't any curves worth mentionin'. Oh, say! Comanche told me there's one section o' sawedged track that's liable to jounce ye a little. Fifteen an' a half out, after the grade at Jackson's crossin'. You'll know it by a farmhouse an' a windmill an' five maples in the dooryard. Windmill's west o' the maples. An' there's an eighty-foot iron bridge in the middle o' that section with no guard-rails. See you later. Luck!'

Before he knew well what had happened, .007 was flying up the track into the dumb, dark world. Then fears of the night beset him. He remembered all he had ever heard of landslides, rain-piled boulders, blown trees, and strayed cattle, all that the Boston Compound had ever said of responsibility, and a great deal more that came out of his own head. With a very quavering voice he whistled for his first grade-crossing (an event in the life of a locomotive), and his nerves were in no way restored by the sight of a frantic horse and a white-faced man in a buggy less than a yard from his right shoulder. Then he was sure he would jump the track; felt his flanges mounting the rail at every curve; knew that his first grade would make him lie down even as Comanche had done at the Newtons. He whirled down the grade to Jackson's crossing, saw the windmill west of the maples, felt the badly laid rails spring under him, and sweated big drops all over his boiler. At each jarring bump he believed an axle had smashed, and he took the eighty-foot bridge without the guard-rail like a hunted cat on the top of a fence. Then a wet leaf stuck against the glass of his headlight and threw a flying shadow on the track, so that he thought it was some little dancing animal that would feel soft if he ran over it; and anything soft underfoot frightens a locomotive as it does an elephant. But the men behind seemed quite calm. The wrecking-crew were climbing carelessly from the caboose to the tender—even jesting with the engineer, for he heard a shuffling of feet among the coal, and the snatch of a song, something like this:

'Oh, the Empire State must learn to wait,
And the Cannon-ball go hang!
When the West-bound's ditched, and the tool-car's hitched,
And it's 'way for the Breakdown Gang (Tare-ra!)
'Way for the Breakdown Gang!'

'Say! Eustis knew what he was doin' when he designed this rig. She's a hummer. New, too.'

'Snff! Phew! She is new. That ain't paint. That's—'

A burning pain shot through .007's right rear driver—a crippling, stinging pain.

'This,' said .007, as he flew, 'is a hot-box. Now I know what it means. I shall go to pieces, I guess. My first road-run, too!'

'Het a bit, ain't she?' the fireman ventured to suggest to the engineer.

'She'll hold for all we want of her. We're 'most there. Guess you chaps back had better climb into your car,' said the engineer, his hand on the brake lever. 'I've seen men snapped off—'

But the crew fled back with laughter. They had no wish to be jerked on to the track. The engineer half turned his wrist, and .007 found his drivers pinned firm.

'Now it's come!' said .007, as he yelled aloud, and slid like a sleigh. For the moment he fancied that he would jerk bodily from off his underpinning.

'That must be the emergency-stop that Poney guyed me about,' he gasped, as soon as he could think. 'Hot-box-emergency-stop. They both hurt; but now I can talk back in the round-house.'

He was halted, all hissing hot, a few feet in the rear of what doctors would call a compound-comminuted car. His engineer was kneeling down among his drivers, but he did not call .007 his 'Arab steed,' nor cry over him, as the engineers did in the newspapers. He just bad worded .007, and pulled yards of charred cotton-waste from about the axles, and hoped he might someday catch the idiot who had packed it. Nobody else attended to him, for Evans, the Mogul's engineer, a little cut about the head, but very angry, was exhibiting, by lantern-light, the mangled corpse of a slim blue pig.

'T weren't even a decent-sized hog,' he said. "T were a shote.'

'Dangerousest beasts they are,' said one of the crew. 'Get under the pilot an' sort o' twiddle ye off the track, don't they? '

'Don't they?' roared Evans, who was a red-headed Welshman. 'You talk as if I was ditched by a hog every fool-day o' the week. I ain't friends with all the cussed half-fed shotes in the State o' New York. No, indeed! Yes, this is him—an' look what he's done!'

It was not a bad night's work for one stray piglet. The Flying Freight seemed to have flown in every direction, for the Mogul had mounted the rails and run diagonally a few hundred feet from right to left, taking with him such cars as cared to follow. Some did not. They broke their couplers and lay down, while rear cars frolicked over them. In that game, they had ploughed up and removed and twisted a good deal of the left-hand track. The Mogul himself had waddled into a corn-field, and there he knelt—fantastic wreaths of green twisted round his crankpins; his pilot covered with solid clods of field, on which corn nodded drunkenly; his fire put out with dirt (Evans had done that as soon as he recovered his senses); and his broken headlight half full of half-burnt moths. His tender had thrown coal all over him, and he looked like a disreputable buffalo who had tried to wallow in a general store. For there lay scattered over the landscape, from the burst cars, type-writers, sewing-machines, bicycles in crates, a consignment of silver-plated imported harness, French dresses and gloves, a dozen finely moulded hard-wood mantels, a fifteen-foot naphtha-launch, with a solid brass bedstead crumpled around her bows, a case of telescopes and microscopes, two coffins, a case of very best candies, some gilt-edged dairy produce, butter and eggs in an omelette, a broken box of expensive toys, and a few hundred other luxuries. A camp of tramps hurried up from nowhere, and generously volunteered to help the crew. So the brakemen, armed with coupler-pins, walked up and down on one side, and the freight-conductor and the fireman patrolled the other with their hands in their hip-pockets. A long-bearded man came out of a house beyond the corn-field, and told Evans that if the accident had happened a little later in the year, all his corn would have been burned, and accused Evans of carelessness. Then he ran away, for Evans was at his heels shrieking: "T was his hog done it—his hog done it! Let me kill him! Let me kill him!' Then the wrecking-crew laughed; and the farmer put his head out of a window and said that Evans was no gentleman.

But .007 was very sober. He had never seen a wreck before, and it frightened him. The crew still laughed, but they worked at the same time; and .007 forgot horror in amazement at the way they handled the Mogul freight. They dug round him with spades; they put ties in front of his wheels, and jack-screws under him; they embraced him with the derrick-chain and tickled him with crowbars; while .007 was hitched on to wrecked cars and backed away till the knot broke or the cars rolled clear of the track. By dawn thirty or forty men were at work, replacing and ramming down the ties, gauging the rails and spiking them. By daylight all cars who could move had gone on in charge of another loco; the track was freed for traffic; and .007 had hauled the old Mogul over a small pavement of ties, inch by inch, till his flanges bit the rail once more, and he settled down with a clank. But his spirit was broken, and his nerve was gone.

"T weren't even a hog,' he repeated dolefully; "t were a shote; and you—you of all of 'em—had to help me on.'

'But how in the whole long road did it happen?' asked .007, sizzling with curiosity.

'Happen! It didn't happen! It just come! I sailed right on top of him around that last curve—thought he was a skunk. Yes; he was all as little as that. He hadn't more 'n squealed once 'fore I felt my bogies lift (he'd rolled right under the pilot), and I couldn't catch the track again to save me. Swivelled clean off, I was. Then I felt him sling himself along, all greasy, under my left leadin' driver, and, oh, Boilers! that mounted the rail. I heard my flanges zippin' along the ties, an' the next I knew I was playin' 'Sally, Sally Waters' in the corn, my tender shuckin' coal through my cab, an' old man Evans lyin' still an' bleedin' in front o' me. Shook? There ain't a stay or a bolt or a rivet in me that ain't sprung to glory somewhere,'

'Umm!' said .007. 'What d' you reckon you weigh?'

'Without these lumps o' dirt I'm all of a hundred thousand pound.'

'And the shote?'

'Eighty. Call him a hundred pound at the outside. He's worth about four 'n' a half dollars. Ain't it awful? Ain't it enough to give you nervous prostration? Ain't it paralysin'? Why, I come just around that curve—' and the Mogul told the tale again, for he was very badly shaken.

'Well, it's all in the day's run, I guess,' said .007, soothingly; 'an'—an' a corn-field's pretty soft fallin'.'

'If it had bin a sixty-foot bridge, an' I could ha' slid off into deep water an' blown up an' killed both men, same as others have done, I wouldn't ha' cared; but to be ditched by a shote—an' you to help me out—in a corn-field—an' an old hayseed in his nightgown cussin' me like as if I was a sick truck-horse! ... Oh, it's awful! Don't call me Mogul! I'm a sewin'-machine. They'll guy my sand-box off in the yard.'

And .007, his hot-box cooled and his experience vastly enlarged, hauled the Mogul freight slowly to the roundhouse.

'Hello, old man! Bin out all night, hain't ye?' said the irrepressible Poney, who had just come off duty. 'Well, I must say you look it. Costly-perishable-fragile-immediate—that's you! Go to the shops, take them vine-leaves out o' your hair, an' git 'em to play the hose on you.'

'Leave him alone, Poney,' said .007 severely, as he was swung on the turn-table, 'or I'll—'

'Didn't know the old granger was any special friend o' yours, kid. He wasn't over-civil to you last time I saw him.'

'I know it; but I've seen a wreck since then, and it has about scared the paint off me. I'm not going to guy anyone as long as I steam—not when they're new to the business an' anxious to learn. And I'm not goin' to guy the old Mogul either, though I did find him wreathed around with roastin'-ears. 'T was a little bit of a shote—not a hog—just a shote, Poney—no bigger'n a lump of anthracite—I saw it—that made all the mess. Anybody can be ditched, I guess.'

'Found that out already, have you? Well, that's a good beginnin'.' It was the Purple Emperor, with his high, tight, plate-glass cab and green velvet cushion, waiting to be cleaned for his next day's fly.

'Let me make you two gen'lemen acquainted,' said Poney. 'This is our Purple Emperor, kid, whom you were admirin' and, I may say, envyin' last night. This is a new brother, worshipful sir, with most of his mileage ahead of him, but, so far as a serving-brother can, I'll answer for him.'

'Happy to meet you,' said the Purple Emperor, with a glance round the crowded round-house. 'I guess there are enough of us here to form a full meetin'. Ahem! By virtue of the authority vested in me as Head of the Road, I hereby declare and pronounce No. .007 a full and accepted Brother of the Amalgamated Brotherhood of Locomotives, and as such entitled to all shop, switch, track, tank, and round-house privileges throughout my jurisdiction, in the Degree of Superior Flier, it bein' well-known and credibly reported to me that our Brother has covered forty-one miles in thirty-nine minutes and a half on an errand of mercy to the afflicted. At a convenient time, I myself will communicate to you the Song and Signal of this Degree whereby you may be recognized in the darkest night. Take your stall, newly entered Brother among Locomotives!'

Now, in the darkest night, even as the Purple Emperor said, if you will stand on the bridge across the freight yard, looking down upon the four-track way, at 2:30 A. M., neither before nor after, when the White Moth, that takes the overflow from the Purple Emperor, tears south with her seven vestibuled cream-white cars, you will hear, as the yard-clock makes the half-hour, a far-away sound like the bass of a violoncello, and then, a hundred feet to each word.

'With a michnai - ghignai - shtingal! Yah! Yah! Yah!
Ein - zwei - drei - Mutter! Yah! Yah! Yah!
She climb upon der shteeple,
Und she frighten all der people,
Singin' michnai - ghignai - shtingal! Yah! Yah!'

That is .007 covering his one hundred and fifty-six miles in two hundred and twenty-one minutes.

KIDNAPPED

Rudyard Kipling

There is a tide in the affairs of men,
Which, taken any way you please, is bad,
And strands them in forsaken guts and creeks
No decent soul would think of visiting.
You cannot stop the tide; but now and then,
You may arrest some rash adventurer
Who—h'm—will hardly thank you for your pains.
—Vibart's Moralities

We are a high-caste and enlightened race, and infant-marriage is very shocking and the consequences are sometimes peculiar; but, nevertheless, the Hindu notion—which is the Continental notion—which is the aboriginal notion—of arranging marriages irrespective of the personal inclinations of the married, is sound. Think for a minute, and you will see that it must be so; unless, of course, you believe in 'affinities.' In which case you had better not read this tale. How can a man who has never married; who cannot be trusted to pick up at sight a moderately sound horse; whose head is hot and upset with visions of domestic felicity, go about the choosing of a wife? He cannot see straight or think straight if he tries; and the same disadvantages exist in the case of a girl's fancies. But when mature, married and discreet people arrange a match between a boy and a girl, they do it sensibly, with a view to the future, and the young couple live happily ever afterwards. As everybody knows.

Properly speaking, Government should establish a Matrimonial Department, efficiently officered, with a Jury of Matrons, a Judge of the Chief Court, a Senior Chaplain, and an Awful Warning, in the shape of a love-match that has gone wrong, chained to the trees in the courtyard. All marriages should be made through the Department, which might be subordinate to the Educational Department, under the same penalty as that attaching to the transfer of land without a stamped document. But Government won't take suggestions. It pretends that it is too busy. However, I will put my notion on record, and explain the example that illustrates the theory.

Once upon a time there was a good young man—a first-class officer in his own Department—a man with a career before him and, possibly, a K.C.G.E. at the end of it. All his superiors spoke well of him, because he knew how to hold his tongue and his pen at the proper times. There are to-day only eleven men in India who possess this secret; and they have all, with one exception, attained great honour and enormous incomes.

This good young man was quiet and self-contained—too old for his years by far. Which always carries its own punishment. Had a Subaltern, or a Tea-Planter's Assistant, or anybody who enjoys life and has no care for to-morrow, done what he tried to do not a soul would have cared. But when Peythroppe—the estimable, virtuous, economical, quiet, hard-working, young Peythroppe—fell, there was a flutter through five Departments.

The manner of his fall was in this way. He met a Miss Castries—d'Castries it was originally, but the family dropped the d' for administrative reasons—and he fell in love with her even more energetically that he worked. Understand clearly that there was not a breath of a word to be said against Miss Castries—not a shadow of a breath. She was good and very lovely—possessed what innocent people at home call a 'Spanish' complexion, with thick blue-black hair growing low down on her forehead, into a 'widow's peak,' and big violet eyes under eyebrows as black and as straight as the borders of a Gazette Extraordinary when a big man dies. But—but—but—. Well, she was a VERY sweet girl and very pious, but for many reasons she was 'impossible.' Quite so. All good Mammas know what 'impossible' means. It was obviously absurd that Peythroppe should marry her. The little opal-tinted onyx at the base of her fingernails said this as plainly as print. Further, marriage with Miss Castries meant marriage with several other Castries—Honorary Lieutenant Castries, her Papa, Mrs Eulalie Castries, her Mamma, and all the ramifications of the Castries family, on incomes ranging from

Rs 175 to Rs 470 a month, and THEIR wives and connections again.

It would have been cheaper for Peythroppe to have assaulted a Commissioner with a dog-whip, or to have burned the records of a Deputy Commissioner's Office, than to have contracted an alliance with the Castries. It would have weighted his after-career less—even under a Government which never forgets and NEVER forgives. Everybody saw this but Peythroppe. He was going to marry Miss Castries, he was—being of age and drawing a good income—and woe betide the house that would not afterwards receive Mrs Virginie Saulez Peythroppe with the deference due to her husband's rank. That was Peythroppe's ultimatum, and any remonstrance drove him frantic.

These sudden madnesses most afflict the sanest men. There was a case once—but I will tell you of that later on. You cannot account for the mania, except under a theory directly contradicting the one about the Place wherein marriages are made. Peythroppe was burningly anxious to put a millstone round his neck at the outset of his career and argument had not the least effect on him. He was going to marry Miss Castries, and the business was his own business. He would thank you to keep your advice to yourself. With a man in this condition, mere words only fix him in his purpose. Of course he cannot see that marriage out here does not concern the individual but the Government he serves.

Do you remember Mrs Hauksbee—the most wonderful woman in India? She saved Pluffles from Mrs Reiver, won Tarrion his appointment in the Foreign Office, and was defeated in open field by Mrs Cusack-Bremmil. She heard of the lamentable condition of Peythroppe, and her brain struck out the plan that saved him. She had the wisdom of the Serpent, the logical coherence of the Man, the fearlessness of the Child, and the triple intuition of the Woman. Never—no, never—as long as a tonga buckets down the Solon dip, or the couples go a-riding at the back of Summer Hill, will there be such a genius as Mrs Hauksbee. She attended the consultation of Three Men on Peythroppe's case; and she stood up with the lash of her riding-whip between her lips and spake.

❧

Three weeks later, Peythroppe dined with the Three Men, and the Gazette of India came in. Peythroppe found to his surprise that he had been gazetted a month's leave. Don't ask me how this was managed. I believe firmly that if Mrs Hauksbee gave the order, the whole Great Indian Administration would stand on its head.

The Three Men had also a month's leave each. Peythroppe put the Gazette down and said bad words. Then there came from the compound the soft 'pad-pad' of camels—'thieves' camels,' the bikaneer breed that don't bubble and howl when they sit down and get up.

After that I don't know what happened. This much is certain. Peythroppe disappeared—vanished like smoke—and the long foot-rest chair in the house of the Three Men was broken to splinters. Also a bedstead departed from one of the bedrooms.

Mrs Hauksbee said that Mr Peythroppe was shooting in Rajputana with the Three Men; so we were compelled to believe her.

At the end of the month, Peythroppe was gazetted twenty days' extension of leave; but there was wrath and lamentation in the house of Castries. The marriage-day had been fixed, but the bridegroom never came; and the D'Silvas, Pereiras, and Ducketts lifted their voices and mocked Honorary Lieutenant Castries as one who had been basely imposed upon. Mrs Hauksbee went to the wedding, and was much astonished when Peythroppe did not appear. After seven weeks, Peythroppe and the Three Men returned from Rajputana. Peythroppe was in hard, tough condition, rather white, and more self-contained than ever.

One of the Three Men had a cut on his nose, cause by the kick of a gun. Twelve-bores kick rather curiously.

Then came Honorary Lieutenant Castries, seeking for the blood of his perfidious son-in-law to be. He said things—vulgar and 'impossible' things which showed the raw rough 'ranker' below the 'Honorary,' and I fancy Peythroppe's eyes were opened. Anyhow, he held his peace till the end; when he spoke briefly. Honorary Lieutenant Castries asked for a 'peg' before he went away to die or bring a suit for breach of promise.

Miss Castries was a very good girl. She said that she would have no breach of promise suits. She said that, if she was not a lady, she was refined enough to know that ladies kept their broken hearts to themselves; and, as she ruled her parents, nothing happened. Later on, she married a most respectable and gentlemanly person. He travelled for an enterprising firm in Calcutta, and was all that a good husband should be.

So Peythroppe came to his right mind again, and did much good work, and was honoured by all who knew him. One of these days he will marry; but he will marry a sweet pink-and-white maiden, on the Government House List, with a little money and some influential connections, as every wise man should. And he will never, all his life, tell her what happened during the seven weeks of his shooting tour in Rajputana.

But just think how much trouble and expense—for camel hire is not cheap, and those Bikaneer brutes had to be fed like humans—might have been saved by a properly conducted Matrimonial Department, under the control of the Director General of Education, but corresponding direct with the Viceroy.

MY OWN TRUE GHOST STORY

Rudyard Kipling

As I came through the Desert thus it was—
As I came through the Desert.
—The City of Dreadful Night

Somewhere in the Other World, where there are books and pictures and plays and shop windows to look at, and thousands of men who spend their lives in building up all four, lives a gentleman who writes real stories about the real insides of people; and his name is Mr Walter Besant. But he will insist upon treating his ghosts—he has published half a workshopful of them—with levity. He makes his ghost-seers talk familiarly, and, in some cases, flirt outrageously, with the phantoms. You may treat anything, from a Viceroy to a Vernacular Paper, with levity; but you must behave reverently toward a ghost, and particularly an Indian one.

There are, in this land, ghosts who take the form of fat, cold, pobby corpses, and hide in trees near the roadside till a traveller passes. Then they drop upon his neck and remain. There are also terrible ghosts of women who have died in child-bed. These wander along the pathways at dusk, or hide in the crops near a village, and call seductively. But to answer their call is death in this world and the next. Their feet are turned backward that all sober men may recognize them. There are ghosts of little children who have been thrown into wells. These haunt well curbs and the fringes of jungles, and wail under the stars, or catch women by the wrist and beg to be taken up and carried. These and the corpse ghosts, however, are only vernacular articles and do not attack Sahibs. No native ghost has yet been authentically reported to have frightened an Englishman; but many English ghosts have scared the life out of both white and black.

Nearly every other Station owns a ghost. There are said to be two at Simla, not counting the woman who blows the bellows at Syree dak-bungalow on the Old Road; Mussoorie has a house haunted of a very lively Thing; a White Lady is supposed to do night-watchman round a house in Lahore; Dalhousie says that one of her houses 'repeats' on autumn evenings all the incidents of a horrible horse-and-precipice accident; Murree has a merry ghost, and, now that she has been swept by cholera, will have room for a sorrowful one; there are Officers' Quarters in Mian Mir whose doors open without reason, and whose furniture is guaranteed to creak, not with the heat of June but with the weight of Invisibles who come to lounge in the chairs; Peshawur possesses houses that none will willingly rent; and there is something—not fever—wrong with a big bungalow in Allahabad. The older Provinces simply bristle with haunted houses, and march phantom armies along their main thoroughfares.

Some of the dak-bungalows on the Grand Trunk Road have handy little cemeteries in their compound—witnesses to the 'changes and chances of this mortal life' in the days when men drove from Calcutta to the Northwest. These bungalows are objectionable places to put up in. They are generally very old, always dirty, while the khansamah is as ancient as the bungalow. He either chatters senilely, or falls into the long trances of age. In both moods he is useless. If you get angry with him, he refers to some Sahib dead and buried these thirty years, and says that when he was in that Sahib's service not a khansamah in the Province could touch him. Then he jabbers and mows and trembles and fidgets among the dishes, and you repent of your irritation.

In these dak-bungalows, ghosts are most likely to be found, and when found, they should be made a note of. Not long ago it was my business to live in dak-bungalows. I never inhabited the same house for three nights running, and grew to be learned in the breed. I lived in Government-built ones with red brick walls and rail ceilings, an inventory of the furniture posted in every room, and an excited snake at the threshold to give welcome. I lived in 'converted' ones—old houses officiating as dak-bungalows—where nothing was in its proper place and there wasn't even a fowl for dinner. I lived in second-hand palaces where the wind blew through open-work marble tracery just as uncomfortably as through a broken pane. I lived in dak-bungalows where the last entry in the visitors' book was fifteen months old, and where they slashed off the curry-kid's head with a sword. It was my good luck to meet all sorts of men, from sober traveling missionaries and deserters flying from British Regiments, to drunken loafers who threw whisky bottles at all who passed; and my still greater good fortune just to escape a maternity case. Seeing that a fair proportion of the tragedy of our lives out here acted itself in dak-bungalows, I wondered that I had met no ghosts. A ghost that would voluntarily hang about a dak-bungalow would be mad of course; but so many men have died mad in dak-bungalows that there must be a fair percentage of lunatic ghosts.

In due time I found my ghost, or ghosts rather, for there were two of them. Up till that hour I had sympathized with Mr Besant's method of handling them, as shown in 'The Strange Case of Mr Lucraft and Other Stories.' I am now in the Opposition.

We will call the bungalow Katmal dak-bungalow. But THAT was the smallest part of the horror. A man with a sensitive hide has no right to sleep in dak-bungalows. He should marry. Katmal dak-bungalow was old and rotten and unrepaired. The floor was of worn brick, the walls were filthy, and the windows were nearly black with grime. It stood on a bypath largely used by native Sub-Deputy Assistants of all kinds, from Finance to Forests; but real Sahibs were rare. The khansamah, who was nearly bent double with old age, said so.

When I arrived, there was a fitful, undecided rain on the face of the land, accompanied by a restless wind, and every gust made a noise like the rattling of dry bones in the stiff toddy palms outside. The khansamah completely lost his head on my arrival. He had served a Sahib once. Did I know that Sahib? He gave me the name of a well-known man who has been buried for more than a quarter of a century, and showed me an ancient daguerreotype of that man in his prehistoric youth. I had seen a steel engraving of him at the head of a double volume of Memoirs a month before, and I felt ancient beyond telling.

The day shut in and the khansamah went to get me food. He did not go through the pretence of calling it 'khana'—man's victuals. He said 'ratub,' and that means, among other things, 'grub'—dog's rations. There was no insult in his choice of the term. He had forgotten the other word, I suppose.

While he was cutting up the dead bodies of animals, I settled myself down, after exploring the dak-bungalow. There were three rooms, beside my own, which was a corner kennel, each giving into the other through dingy white doors fastened with long iron bars. The bungalow was a very solid one, but the partition walls of the rooms were almost jerry-built in their flimsiness. Every step or bang of a trunk echoed from my room down the other three, and every footfall came back tremulously from the far walls. For this reason I shut the door. There were no lamps—only candles in long glass shades. An oil wick was set in the bathroom.

For bleak, unadulterated misery that dak-bungalow was the worst of the many that I had ever set foot in. There was no fireplace, and the windows would not open; so a brazier of charcoal would have been useless. The rain and the wind splashed and gurgled and moaned round the house, and the toddy palms rattled and roared. Half a dozen jackals went through the compound singing, and a hyena stood afar off and mocked them. A hyena would convince a Sadducee of the Resurrection of the Dead—the worst sort of Dead. Then came the ratub—a curious meal, half native and half English in composition—with the old khansamah babbling behind my chair about dead and gone English people, and the wind-blown candles playing shadow-bo-peep with the bed and the mosquito-curtains. It was just the sort of dinner and evening to make a man think of every single one of his past sins, and of all the others that he intended to commit if he lived.

Sleep, for several hundred reasons, was not easy. The lamp in the bath-room threw the most absurd shadows into the room, and the wind was beginning to talk nonsense.

Just when the reasons were drowsy with blood-sucking I heard the regular—'Let—us—take—and—heave—him—over' grunt of doolie-bearers in the compound. First one doolie came in, then a second, and then a third. I heard the doolies dumped on the ground, and the shutter in front of my door shook. 'That's someone trying to come in,' I said. But no one spoke, and I persuaded myself that it was the gusty wind. The shutter of the room next to mine was attacked, flung back, and the inner door opened. 'That's some Sub-Deputy Assistant,' I said, 'and he has brought his friends with him. Now they'll talk and spit and smoke for an hour.'

But there were no voices and no footsteps. No one was putting his luggage into the next room. The door shut, and I thanked Providence that I was to be left in peace. But I was curious to know where the doolies had gone. I got out of bed and looked into the darkness. There was never a sign of a doolie. Just as I was getting into bed again, I heard, in the next room, the sound that no man in his senses can possibly mistake—the whir of a billiard ball down the length of the slates when the striker is stringing for break. No other sound is like it. A minute afterwards there was another whir, and I got into bed. I was not frightened—indeed I was not. I was very curious to know what had become of the doolies. I jumped into bed for that reason.

Next minute I heard the double click of a cannon and my hair sat up. It is a mistake to say that hair stands up. The skin of the head tightens and you can feel a faint, prickly, bristling all over the scalp. That is the hair sitting up.

There was a whir and a click, and both sounds could only have been made by one thing—a billiard ball. I argued the matter out at great length with myself; and the more I argued the less probable it seemed that one bed, one table, and two chairs—all the furniture of the room next to mine—could so exactly duplicate the sounds of a game of billiards. After another cannon, a three-cushion one to judge by the whir, I argued no more. I had found my ghost and would have given worlds to have escaped from that dak-bungalow. I listened, and with each listen the game grew clearer. There was whir on whir and click on click. Sometimes there was a double click and a whir and another click. Beyond any sort of doubt, people were playing billiards in the next room. And the next room was not big enough to hold a billiard table!

Between the pauses of the wind I heard the game go forward—stroke after stroke. I tried to believe that I could not hear voices; but that attempt was a failure.

Do you know what fear is? Not ordinary fear of insult, injury or death, but abject, quivering dread of something that you cannot see—fear that dries the inside of the mouth and half of the throat—fear that makes you sweat on the palms of the hands, and gulp in order to keep the uvula at work? This is a fine Fear—a great cowardice, and must be felt to be appreciated. The very improbability of billiards in a dak-bungalow proved the reality of the thing. No man—drunk or sober—could imagine a game at billiards, or invent the spitting crack of a 'screw-cannon.'

A severe course of dak-bungalows has this disadvantage—it breeds infinite credulity. If a man said to a confirmed dak-bungalow-haunter:—'There is a corpse in the next room, and there's a mad girl in the next but one, and the woman and man on that camel have just eloped from a place sixty miles away,' the hearer would not disbelieve because he would know that nothing is too wild, grotesque, or horrible to happen in a dak-bungalow.

This credulity, unfortunately, extends to ghosts. A rational person fresh from his own house would have turned on his side and slept. I did not. So surely as I was given up as a bad carcass by the scores of things in the bed because the bulk of my blood was in my heart, so surely did I hear every stroke of a long game at billiards played in the echoing room behind the iron-barred door. My dominant fear was that the players might want a marker. It was an absurd fear; because creatures who could play in the dark would be above such superfluities. I only know that that was my terror; and it was real.

After a long, long while the game stopped, and the door banged. I slept because I was dead tired. Otherwise I should have preferred to have kept awake. Not for everything in Asia would I have dropped the door-bar and peered into the dark of the next room.

When the morning came, I considered that I had done well and wisely, and inquired for the means of departure.

'By the way, khansamah,' I said, 'what were those three doolies doing in my compound in the night?'

'There were no doolies,' said the khansamah.

I went into the next room and the daylight streamed through the open door. I was immensely brave. I would, at that hour, have played Black Pool with the owner of the big Black Pool down below.

'Has this place always been a dak-bungalow?' I asked.

'No,' said the khansamah. 'Ten or twenty years ago, I have forgotten how long, it was a billiard room.'

'A how much?'

'A billiard room for the Sahibs who built the Railway. I was khansamah then in the big house where all the Railway-Sahibs lived, and I used to come across with brandy-shrab. These three rooms were all one, and they held a big table on which the Sahibs played every evening. But the Sahibs are all dead now, and the Railway runs, you say, nearly to Kabul.'

'Do you remember anything about the Sahibs?'

'It is long ago, but I remember that one Sahib, a fat man and always angry, was playing here one night, and he said to me:—'Mangal Khan, brandy-pani do,' and I filled the glass, and he bent over the table to strike, and his head fell lower and lower till it hit the table, and his spectacles came off, and when we—the Sahibs and I myself—ran to lift him he was dead. I helped to carry him out. Aha, he was a strong Sahib! But he is dead and I, old Mangal Khan, am still living, by your favour.'

That was more than enough! I had my ghost—a first hand, authenticated article. I would write to the Society for Psychical Research—I would paralyse the Empire with the news! But I would, first of all, put eighty miles of assessed crop land between myself and that dak-bungalow before nightfall. The Society might send their regular agent to investigate later on.

I went into my own room and prepared to pack after noting down the facts of the case. As I smoked I heard the game begin again,—with a miss in balk this time, for the whir was a short one.

The door was open and I could see into the room. Click—click! That was a cannon. I entered the room without fear, for there was sunlight within and a fresh breeze without. The unseen game was going on at a tremendous rate. And well it might, when a restless little rat was running to and fro inside the dingy ceiling-cloth, and a piece of loose window-sash was making fifty breaks off the window-bolt as it shook in the breeze!

Impossible to mistake the sound of billiard balls! Impossible to mistake the whir of a ball over the slate! But I was to be excused. Even when I shut my enlightened eyes the sound was marvellously like that of a fast game.

Entered angrily the faithful partner of my sorrows, Kadir Baksh. 'This bungalow is very bad and low-caste! No wonder the Presence was disturbed and is speckled. Three sets of doolie-bearers came to the bungalow late last night when I was sleeping outside, and said that it was their custom to rest in the rooms set apart for the English people! What honour has the khansamah? They tried to enter, but I told them to go. No wonder, if these Oorias have been here, that the Presence is sorely spotted. It is shame, and the work of a dirty man!'

Kadir Baksh did not say that he had taken from each gang two annas for rent in advance, and then, beyond my earshot, had beaten them with the big green umbrella whose use I could never before divine. But Kadir Baksh has no notions of morality.

There was an interview with the khansamah, but as he promptly lost his head, wrath gave place to pity, and pity led to a long conversation, in the course of which he put the fat Engineer Sahib's tragic death in three separate stations—two of them fifty miles away. The third shift was to Calcutta, and there the Sahib died while driving a dogcart.

If I had encouraged him the khansamah would have wandered all through Bengal with his corpse.

I did not go away as soon as I intended. I stayed for the night, while the wind and the rat and the sash and the window-bolt played a ding-dong 'hundred and fifty up.' Then the wind ran out and the billiards stopped, and I felt that I had ruined my one genuine, hall-marked ghost story.

Had I only stopped at the proper time, I could have made ANYTHING out of it.

That was the bitterest thought of all!

THE PHANTOM RICKSHAW

Rudyard Kipling

May no ill dreams disturb my rest,
Nor Powers of Darkness me molest.
—Evening hymn

One of the few advantages that India has over England is a great Knowability. After five years' service a man is directly or indirectly acquainted with the two or three hundred Civilians in his Province, all the Messes of ten or twelve Regiments and Batteries, and some fifteen hundred other people of the non-official caste, in ten years his knowledge should be doubled, and at the end of twenty he knows, or knows something about, every Englishman in the Empire, and may travel anywhere and everywhere without paying hotel-bills.

Globe-trotters who expect entertainment as a right, have, even within my memory, blunted this open-heartedness, but none the less to-day, if you belong to the Inner Circle and are neither a Bear nor a Black Sheep, all houses are open to you, and our small world is very, very kind and helpful.

Rickett of Kamartha stayed with Polder of Kumaon some fifteen years ago. He meant to stay two nights, but was knocked down by rheumatic fever, and for six weeks disorganized Polder's establishment, stopped Polder's work, and nearly died in Polder's bedroom. Polder behaves as though he had been placed under eternal obligation by Rickett, and yearly sends the little Ricketts a box of presents and toys. It is the same everywhere. The men who do not take the trouble to conceal from you their opinion that you are an incompetent ass, and the women who blacken your character and misunderstand your wife's amusements, will work themselves to the bone in your behalf if you fall sick or into serious trouble,

Heatherlegh, the Doctor, kept, in addition to his regular practice, a hospital on his private account—an arrangement of loose boxes for

Incurables, his friend called it—but it was really a sort of fitting-up shed for craft that had been damaged by stress of weather. The weather in India is often sultry, and since the tale of bricks is always a fixed quantity, and the only liberty allowed is permission to work overtime and get no thanks, men occasionally break down and become as mixed as the metaphors in this sentence.

Heatherlegh is the dearest doctor that ever was, and his invariable prescription to all his patients is, 'lie low, go slow, and keep cool.' He says that more men are killed by overwork than the importance of this world justifies. He maintains that overwork slew Pansay, who died under his hands about three years ago. He has, of course, the right to speak authoritatively, and he laughs at my theory that there was a crack in Pansay's head and a little bit of the Dark World came through and pressed him to death. 'Pansay went off the handle,' says Heatherlegh, 'after the stimulus of long leave at Home. He may or he may not have behaved like a blackguard to Mrs Keith-Wessington. My notion is that the work of the Katabundi Settlement ran him off his legs, and that he took to brooding and making much of an ordinary P. & O. flirtation. He certainly was engaged to Miss Mannering, and she certainly broke off the engagement. Then he took a feverish chill and all that nonsense about ghosts developed. Overwork started his illness, kept it alight, and killed him, poor devil. Write him off to the System—one man to take the work of two and a half men.'

I do not believe this. I used to sit up with Pansay sometimes when Heatherlegh was called out to patients, and I happened to be within claim. The man would make me most unhappy by describing in a low, even voice, the procession that was always passing at the bottom of his bed. He had a sick man's command of language. When he recovered I suggested that he should write out the whole affair from beginning to end, knowing that ink might assist him to ease his mind. When little boys have learned a new bad word they are never happy till they have chalked it up on a door. And this also is Literature.

He was in a high fever while he was writing, and the blood-and-thunder Magazine diction he adopted did not calm him. Two months afterward he was reported fit for duty, but, in spite of the fact that he was urgently needed to help an undermanned Commission stagger through a deficit, he preferred to die; vowing at the last that he was hag-ridden. I got his manuscript before he died, and this is his version of the affair, dated 1885.

My doctor tells me that I need rest and change of air. It is not improbable that I shall get both ere long—rest that neither the red-coated messenger nor the midday gun can break, and change of air far beyond that which any homeward-bound steamer can give me. In the meantime I am resolved to stay where I am; and, in flat defiance of my doctor's orders, to take all the world into my confidence. You shall learn for yourselves the precise nature of my malady; and shall, too, judge for yourselves whether any man born of woman on this weary earth was ever so tormented as I.

Speaking now as a condemned criminal might speak ere the drop-bolts are drawn, my story, wild and hideously improbable as it may appear, demands at least attention. That it will ever receive credence I utterly disbelieve. Two months ago I should have scouted as mad or drunk the man who had dared tell me the like. Two months ago I was the happiest man in India. To-day, from Peshawur to the sea, there is no one more wretched. My doctor and I are the only two who know this. His explanation is, that my brain, digestion, and eyesight are all slightly affected; giving rise to my frequent and persistent 'delusions.' Delusions, indeed! I call him a fool; but he attends me still with the same unwearied smile, the same bland professional manner, the same neatly trimmed red whiskers, till I begin to suspect that I am an ungrateful, evil-tempered invalid. But you shall judge for yourselves.

Three years ago it was my fortune—my great misfortune—to sail from Gravesend to Bombay, on return from long leave, with one Agnes Keith-Wessington, wife of an officer on the Bombay side. It does not in the least concern you to know what manner of woman she was. Be content with the knowledge that, ere the voyage had ended, both she and I were desperately and unreasonably in love with one another. Heaven knows that I can make the admission now without one particle of vanity. In matters of this sort there is always one who gives and another who accepts. From the first day of our ill-omened attachment,

I was conscious that Agnes's passion was a stronger, a more dominant, and—if I may use the expression—a purer sentiment than mine. Whether she recognized the fact then, I do not know. Afterward it was bitterly plain to both of as.

Arrived at Bombay in the spring of the year, we went our respective ways, to meet no more for the next three or four months, when my leave and her love took us both to Simla. There we spent the season together; and there my fire of straw burned itself out to a pitiful end with the closing year. I attempt no excuse. I make no apology. Mrs Wessington had given up much for my sake, and was prepared to give up all. From my own lips, in August, 1882, she learned that I was sick of her presence, tired of her company, and weary of the sound of her voice. Ninety-nine women out of a hundred would have wearied of me as I wearied of them; seventy-five of that number would have promptly avenged themselves by active and obtrusive flirtation with other men. Mrs Wessington was the hundredth. On her neither my openly expressed aversion nor the cutting brutalities with which I garnished our interviews had the least effect.

'Jack, darling!' was her one eternal cuckoo cry: 'I'm sure it's all a mistake—a hideous mistake; and we'll be good friends again someday. Please forgive me, Jack, dear.'

I was the offender, and I knew it. That knowledge transformed my pity into passive endurance, and, eventually, into blind hate—the same instinct, I suppose, which prompts a man to savagely stamp on the spider he has but half killed. And with this hate in my bosom the season of 1882 came to an end.

Next year we met again at Simla—she with her monotonous face and timid attempts at reconciliation, and I with loathing of her in every fibre of my frame. Several times I could not avoid meeting her alone; and on each occasion her words were identically the same. Still the unreasoning wail that it was all a 'mistake'; and still the hope of eventually 'making friends.' I might have seen had I cared to look, that that hope only was keeping her alive. She grew more wan and thin month by month. You will agree with me, at least, that such conduct would have driven any one to despair. It was uncalled for; childish; unwomanly.

I maintain that she was much to blame. And again, sometimes, in the black, fever-stricken night-watches, I have begun to think that I might have been a little kinder to her. But that really is a 'delusion.' I could not have continued pretending to love her when I didn't, could I? It would have been unfair to us both.

Last year we met again—on the same terms as before. The same weary appeals, and the same curt answers from my lips. At least I would make her see how wholly wrong and hopeless were her attempts at resuming the old relationship. As the season wore on, we fell apart—that is to say, she found it difficult to meet me, for I had other and more absorbing interests to attend to. When I think it over quietly in my sick-room, the season of 1884 seems a confused nightmare wherein light and shade were fantastically intermingled—my courtship of little Kitty Mannering; my hopes, doubts, and fears; our long rides together; my trembling avowal of attachment; her reply; and now and again a vision of a white face flitting by in the 'rickshaw with the black and white liveries I once watched for so earnestly; the wave of Mrs Wessington's gloved hand; and, when she met me alone, which was but seldom, the irksome monotony of her appeal. I loved Kitty Mannering; honestly, heartily loved her, and with my love for her grew my hatred for Agnes. In August Kitty and I were engaged. The next day I met those accursed 'magpie' jhampanies at the back of Jakko, and, moved by some passing sentiment of pity, stopped to tell Mrs Wessington everything. She knew it already.

'So I hear you're engaged, Jack dear.' Then, without a moment's pause:—'I'm sure it's all a mistake—a hideous mistake. We shall be as good friends someday, Jack, as we ever were.'

My answer might have made even a man wince. It cut the dying woman before me like the blow of a whip. 'Please forgive me, Jack; I didn't mean to make you angry; but it's true, it's true!'

And Mrs Wessington broke down completely. I turned away and left her to finish her journey in peace, feeling, but only for a moment or two, that I had been an unutterably mean hound. I looked back, and saw that she had turned her 'rickshaw with the idea, I suppose, of overtaking me.

The scene and its surroundings were photographed on my memory. The rain-swept sky (we were at the end of the wet weather), the sodden, dingy pines, the muddy road, and the black powder-riven cliffs formed a gloomy background against which the black and white liveries of the jhampanies, the yellow-panelled 'rickshaw and Mrs Wessington's down-bowed golden head stood out clearly. She was holding her handkerchief in her left hand and was leaning back exhausted against the 'rickshaw cushions. I turned my horse up a bypath near the Sanjowlie Reservoir and literally ran away. Once I fancied I heard a faint call of 'Jack!' This may have been imagination. I never stopped to verify it. Ten minutes later I came across Kitty on horseback; and, in the delight of a long ride with her, forgot all about the interview.

A week later Mrs Wessington died, and the inexpressible burden of her existence was removed from my life. I went Plainsward perfectly happy. Before three months were over I had forgotten all about her, except that at times the discovery of some of her old letters reminded me unpleasantly of our bygone relationship. By January I had disinterred what was left of our correspondence from among my scattered belongings and had burned it. At the beginning of April of this year, 1885, I was at Simla—semi-deserted Simla—once more, and was deep in lover's talks and walks with Kitty. It was decided that we should be married at the end of June. You will understand, therefore, that, loving Kitty as I did, I am not saying too much when I pronounce myself to have been, at that time, the happiest man in India.

Fourteen delightful days passed almost before I noticed their flight. Then, aroused to the sense of what was proper among mortals circumstanced as we were, I pointed out to Kitty that an engagement ring was the outward and visible sign of her dignity as an engaged girl; and that she must forthwith come to Hamilton's to be measured for one. Up to that moment, I give you my word, we had completely forgotten so trivial a matter. To Hamilton's we accordingly went on the 15th of April, 1885. Remember that—whatever my doctor may say to the contrary—I was then in perfect health, enjoying a well-balanced mind and an absolutely tranquil spirit. Kitty and I entered Hamilton's shop together, and there, regardless of the order of affairs, I measured

Kitty for the ring in the presence of the amused assistant. The ring was a sapphire with two diamonds. We then rode out down the slope that leads to the Combermere Bridge and Peliti's shop.

While my Waler was cautiously feeling his way over the loose shale, and Kitty was laughing and chattering at my side—while all Simla, that is to say as much of it as had then come from the Plains, was grouped round the Reading-room and Peliti's veranda,—I was aware that someone, apparently at a vast distance, was calling me by my Christian name. It struck me that I had heard the voice before, but when and where I could not at once determine. In the short space it took to cover the road between the path from Hamilton's shop and the first plank of the Combermere Bridge I had thought over half a dozen people who might have committed such a solecism, and had eventually decided that it must have been singing in my ears. Immediately opposite Peliti's shop my eye was arrested by the sight of four jhampanies in 'magpie' livery, pulling a yellow-panelled, cheap, bazar 'rickshaw. In a moment my mind flew back to the previous season and Mrs Wessington with a sense of irritation and disgust. Was it not enough that the woman was dead and done with, without her black and white servitors reappearing to spoil the day's happiness? Whoever employed them now I thought I would call upon, and ask as a personal favour to change her jhampanies' livery. I would hire the men myself, and, if necessary, buy their coats from off their backs. It is impossible to say here what a flood of undesirable memories their presence evoked.

'Kitty,' I cried, 'there are poor Mrs Wessington's jhampanies turned up again! I wonder who has them now?'

Kitty had known Mrs Wessington slightly last season, and had always been interested in the sickly woman.

'What? Where?' she asked. 'I can't see them anywhere.'

Even as she spoke, her horse, swerving from a laden mule, threw himself directly in front of the advancing 'rickshaw. I had scarcely time to utter a word of warning when, to my unutterable horror, horse and rider passed through men and carriage as if they had been thin air.

'What's the matter?' cried Kitty; 'what made you call out so foolishly, Jack? If I am engaged I don't want all creation to know about it. There was lots of space between the mule and the veranda; and, if you think I can't ride—There!'

Whereupon wilful Kitty set off, her dainty little head in the air, at a hand-gallop in the direction of the Band-stand; fully expecting, as she herself afterward told me, that I should follow her. What was the matter? Nothing indeed. Either that I was mad or drunk, or that Simla was haunted with devils. I reined in my impatient cob, and turned round. The 'rickshaw had turned too, and now stood immediately facing me, near the left railing of the Combermere Bridge.

'Jack! Jack, darling!' (There was no mistake about the words this time: they rang through my brain as if they had been shouted in my ear.) 'It's some hideous mistake, I'm sure. Please forgive me, Jack, and let's be friends again.'

The 'rickshaw-hood had fallen back, and inside, as I hope and pray daily for the death I dread by night, sat Mrs Keith-Wessington, handkerchief in hand, and golden head bowed on her breast,

How long I stared motionless I do not know. Finally, I was aroused by my syce taking the Waler's bridle and asking whether I was ill. From the horrible to the commonplace is but a step. I tumbled off my horse and dashed, half fainting, into Peliti's for a glass of cherry-brandy. There two or three couples were gathered round the coffee-tables discussing the gossip of the day. Their trivialities were more comforting to me just then than the consolations of religion could have been. I plunged into the midst of the conversation at once; chatted, laughed, and jested with a face (when I caught a glimpse of it in a mirror) as white and drawn as that of a corpse. Three or four men noticed my condition; and, evidently setting it down to the results of over-many pegs, charitably endeavoured to draw me apart from the rest of the loungers. But I refused to be led away, I wanted the company of my kind—as a child rushes into the midst of the dinner-party after a fright in the dark. I must have talked for about ten minutes or so, though it seemed an eternity to me, when I heard Kitty's clear voice outside inquiring for me. In another minute she had entered the shop, prepared to roundly upbraid me for failing so signally in my duties. Something in my face stopped her.

'Why, Jack,' she cried, 'what have you been doing? What has

happened? Are you ill?' Thus driven into a direct lie, I said that the sun had been a little too much for me. It was close upon five o'clock of a cloudy April afternoon, and the sun had been hidden all day. I saw my mistake as soon as the words were out of my mouth: attempted to recover it; blundered hopelessly and followed Kitty in a regal rage, out of doors, amid the smiles of my acquaintances. I made some excuse (I have forgotten what) on the score of my feeling faint; and cantered away to my hotel, leaving Kitty to finish the ride by herself.

In my room I sat down and tried calmly to reason out the matter. Here was I, Theobald Jack Pansay, a well-educated Bengal Civilian in the year of grace 1885, presumably sane, certainly healthy, driven in terror from my sweetheart's side by the apparition of a woman who had been dead and buried eight months ago. These were facts that I could not blink. Nothing was further from my thought than any memory of Mrs Wessington when Kitty and I left Hamilton's shop. Nothing was more utterly commonplace than the stretch of wall opposite Peliti's. It was broad daylight. The road was full of people; and yet here, look you, in defiance of every law of probability, in direct outrage of Nature's ordinance, there had appeared to me a face from the grave.

Kitty's Arab had gone through the 'rickshaw: so that my first hope that some woman marvellously like Mrs Wessington had hired the carriage and the coolies with their old livery was lost. Again and again I went round this treadmill of thought; and again and again gave up baffled and in despair. The voice was as inexplicable as the apparition, I had originally some wild notion of confiding it all to Kitty; of begging her to marry me at once; and in her arms defying the ghostly occupant of the 'rickshaw. 'After all,' I argued, 'the presence of the 'rickshaw is in itself enough to prove the existence of a spectral illusion. One may see ghosts of men and women, but surely never of coolies and carriages. The whole thing is absurd. Fancy the ghost of a hillman!'

Next morning I sent a penitent note to Kitty, imploring her to overlook my strange conduct of the previous afternoon. My Divinity was still very wroth, and a personal apology was necessary. I explained, with a fluency born of nightlong pondering over a falsehood, that I had been attacked with a sudden palpitation of the heart—the result of indigestion. This eminently practical solution had its effect; and Kitty and I rode out that afternoon with the shadow of my first lie dividing us.

Nothing would please her save a canter round Jakko. With my nerves still unstrung from the previous night I feebly protested against the notion, suggesting Observatory Hill, Jutogh, the Boileaugunge road—anything rather than the Jakko round. Kitty was angry and a little hurt: so I yielded from fear of provoking further misunderstanding, and we set out together toward Chota Simla. We walked a greater part of the way, and, according to our custom, cantered from a mile or so below the Convent to the stretch of level road by the Sanjowlie Reservoir. The wretched horses appeared to fly, and my heart beat quicker and quicker as we neared the crest of the ascent. My mind had been full of Mrs Wessington all the afternoon; and every inch of the Jakko road bore witness to our old-time walks and talks. The bowlders were full of it; the pines sang it aloud overhead; the rain-fed torrents giggled and chuckled unseen over the shameful story; and the wind in my ears chanted the iniquity aloud.

As a fitting climax, in the middle of the level men call the Ladies' Mile the Horror was awaiting me. No other 'rickshaw was in sight—only the four black and white jhampanies, the yellow-panelled carriage, and the golden head of the woman within—all apparently just as I had left them eight months and one fortnight ago! For an instant I fancied that Kitty must see what I saw—we were so marvellously sympathetic in all things. Her next words undeceived me—'Not a soul in sight! Come along, Jack, and I'll race you to the Reservoir buildings!' Her wiry little Arab was off like a bird, my Waler following close behind, and in this order we dashed under the cliffs. Half a minute brought us within fifty yards of the 'rickshaw, I pulled my Waler and fell back a little. The 'rickshaw was directly in the middle of the road; and once more the Arab passed through it, my horse following. 'Jack! Jack dear! Please forgive me,' rang with a wail in my ears, and, after an interval:—'It's all a mistake, a hideous mistake!'

I spurred my horse like a man possessed. When I turned my head at the Reservoir works, the black and white liveries were still waiting—

patiently waiting—under the grey hillside, and the wind brought me a mocking echo of the words I had just heard. Kitty bantered me a good deal on my silence throughout the remainder of the ride, I had been talking up till then wildly and at random. To save my life I could not speak afterward naturally, and from Sanjowlie to the Church wisely held my tongue.

I was to dine with the Mannerings that night, and had barely time to canter home to dress. On the road to Elysium Hill I overheard two men talking together in the dusk. 'It's a curious thing,' said one, 'how completely all trace of it disappeared. You know my wife was insanely fond of the woman ('never could see anything in her myself), and wanted me to pick up her old 'rickshaw and coolies if they were to be got for love or money. Morbid sort of fancy I call it; but I've got to do what the Memsahib tells me. Would you believe that the man she hired it from tells me that all four of the men—they were brothers—died of cholera on the way to Hard-war, poor devils; and the 'rickshaw has been broken up by the man himself. 'Told me he never used a dead Memsahib's 'rickshaw. 'Spoiled his luck. Queer notion, wasn't it? Fancy poor little Mrs Wessington spoiling any one's luck except her own!' I laughed aloud at this point; and my laugh jarred on me as I uttered it. So there were ghosts of 'rickshaws after all, and ghostly employments in the other world! How much did Mrs Wessington give her men? What were their hours? Where did they go?

And for visible answer to my last question I saw the infernal Thing blocking my path in the twilight. The dead travel fast, and by short cuts unknown to ordinary coolies. I laughed aloud a second time and checked my laughter suddenly, for I was afraid I was going mad. Mad to a certain extent I must have been, for I recollect that I reined in my horse at the head of the 'rickshaw, and politely wished Mrs Wessington 'Good-evening,' Her answer was one I knew only too well. I listened to the end; and replied that I had heard it all before, but should be delighted if she had anything further to say. Some malignant devil stronger than I must have entered into me that evening, for I have a dim recollection of talking the commonplaces of the day for five minutes to the Thing in front of me.

'Mad as a hatter, poor devil—or drunk. Max, try and get him to come home.'

Surely that was not Mrs Wessington's voice! The two men had overheard me speaking to the empty air, and had returned to look after me. They were very kind and considerate, and from their words evidently gathered that I was extremely drunk, I thanked them confusedly and cantered away to my hotel, there changed, and arrived at the Mannerings' ten minutes late. I pleaded the darkness of the night as an excuse; was rebuked by Kitty for my unlover-like tardiness; and sat down.

The conversation had already become general; and under cover of it, I was addressing some tender small talk to my sweetheart when I was aware that at the further end of the table a short red-whiskered man was describing, with much embroidery, his encounter with a mad unknown that evening.

A few sentences convinced me that he was repeating the incident of half an hour ago. In the middle of the story he looked round for applause, as professional story-tellers do, caught my eye, and straightway collapsed. There was a moment's awkward silence, and the red-whiskered man muttered something to the effect that he had 'forgotten the rest,' thereby sacrificing a reputation as a good story-teller which he had built up for six seasons past. I blessed him from the bottom of my heart, and—went on with my fish.

In the fullness of time that dinner came to an end; and with genuine regret I tore myself away from Kitty—as certain as I was of my own existence that It would be waiting for me outside the door. The red-whiskered man, who had been introduced to me as Doctor Heatherlegh of Simla, volunteered to bear me company as far as our roads lay together. I accepted his offer with gratitude.

My instinct had not deceived me. It lay in readiness in the Mall, and, in what seemed devilish mockery of our ways, with a lighted headlamp. The red-whiskered man went to the point at once, in a manner that showed he had been thinking over it all dinner time.

'I say, Pansay, what the deuce was the matter with you this evening on the Elysium road?' The suddenness of the question wrenched an answer from me before I was aware.

'That!' said I, pointing to it.

'That may be either D.T. or Eyes for aught I know. Now you don't liquor. I saw as much at dinner, so it can't be D.T. There's nothing whatever where you're pointing, though you're sweating and trembling with fright like a scared pony. Therefore, I conclude that it's Eyes. And I ought to understand all about them. Come along home with me. I'm on the Blessington lower road.'

To my intense delight the 'rickshaw instead of waiting for us kept about twenty yards ahead—and this, too, whether we walked, trotted, or cantered. In the course of that long night ride I had told my companion almost as much as I have told you here.

'Well, you've spoiled one of the best tales I've ever laid tongue to,' said he, 'but I'll forgive you for the sake of what you've gone through. Now come home and do what I tell you; and when I've cured you, young man, let this be a lesson to you to steer clear of women and indigestible food till the day of your death.'

The 'rickshaw kept steady in front; and my red-whiskered friend seemed to derive great pleasure from my account of its exact whereabouts.

'Eyes, Pansay—all Eyes, Brain, and Stomach. And the greatest of these three is Stomach. You've too much conceited Brain, too little Stomach, and thoroughly unhealthy Eyes. Get your Stomach straight and the rest follows. And all that's French for a liver pill. I'll take sole medical charge of you from this hour! for you're too interesting a phenomenon to be passed over.'

By this time we were deep in the shadow of the Blessington lower road and the 'rickshaw came to a dead stop under a pine-clad, overhanging shale cliff. Instinctively I halted too, giving my reason. Heatherlegh rapped out an oath.

'Now, if you think I'm going to spend a cold night on the hillside for the sake of a Stomach-cum-Brain-cum-Eye illusion ... Lord, ha' mercy! What's that?'

There was a muffled report, a blinding smother of dust just in front of us, a crack, the noise of rent boughs, and about ten yards of the cliff-side—pines, undergrowth, and all—slid down into the road below, completely blocking it up. The uprooted trees swayed and tottered for a moment like drunken giants in the gloom, and then fell prone among their fellows with a thunderous crash. Our two horses stood motionless and sweating with fear. As soon as the rattle of falling earth and stone had subsided, my companion muttered:—'Man, if we'd gone forward we should have been ten feet deep in our graves by now. 'There are more things in heaven and earth.' ... Come home, Pansay, and thank God. I want a peg badly.'

We retraced our way over the Church Ridge, and I arrived at Dr. Heatherlegh's house shortly after midnight.

His attempts toward my cure commenced almost immediately, and for a week I never left his sight. Many a time in the course of that week did I bless the good-fortune which had thrown me in contact with Simla's best and kindest doctor. Day by day my spirits grew lighter and more equable. Day by day, too, I became more and more inclined to fall in with Heatherlegh's 'spectral illusion' theory, implicating eyes, brain, and stomach. I wrote to Kitty, telling her that a slight sprain caused by a fall from my horse kept me indoors for a few days; and that I should be recovered before she had time to regret my absence.

Heatherlegh's treatment was simple to a degree. It consisted of liver pills, cold-water baths, and strong exercise, taken in the dusk or at early dawn—for, as he sagely observed:—'A man with a sprained ankle doesn't walk a dozen miles a day, and your young woman might be wondering if she saw you.'

At the end of the week, after much examination of pupil and pulse, and strict injunctions as to diet and pedestrianism, Heatherlegh dismissed me as brusquely as he had taken charge of me. Here is his parting benediction:—'Man, I certify to your mental cure, and that's as much as to say I've cured most of your bodily ailments. Now, get your traps out of this as soon as you can; and be off to make love to Miss Kitty.'

I was endeavouring to express my thanks for his kindness. He cut me short.

'Don't think I did this because I like you. I gather that you've behaved like a blackguard all through. But, all the same, you're a phenomenon, and as queer a phenomenon as you are a blackguard. No! '—checking me a second time—'not a rupee please. Go out and see if you can find the eyes-brain-and-stomach business again. I'll give you a lakh for each time you see it.'

Half an hour later I was in the Mannerings' drawing-room with Kitty—drunk with the intoxication of present happiness and the foreknowledge that I should never more be troubled with Its hideous presence. Strong in the sense of my new-found security, I proposed a ride at once; and, by preference, a canter round Jakko.

Never had I felt so well, so overladen with vitality and mere animal spirits, as I did on the afternoon of the 30th of April. Kitty was delighted at the change in my appearance, and complimented me on it in her delightfully frank and outspoken manner. We left the Mannerings' house together, laughing and talking, and cantered along the Chota Simla road as of old.

I was in haste to reach the Sanjowlie Reservoir and there make my assurance doubly sure. The horses did their best, but seemed all too slow to my impatient mind, Kitty was astonished at my boisterousness. 'Why, Jack!' she cried at last, 'you are behaving like a child, What are you doing?'

We were just below the Convent, and from sheer wantonness I was making my Waler plunge and curvet across the road as I tickled it with the loop of my riding-whip.

'Doing?' I answered; 'nothing, dear. That's just it. If you'd been doing nothing for a week except lie up, you'd be as riotous as I.

'Singing and murmuring in your feastful mirth,
Joying to feel yourself alive;
Lord over Nature, Lord of the visible Earth,
Lord of the senses five.'

My quotation was hardly out of my lips before we had rounded the corner above the Convent; and a few yards further on could see across to Sanjowlie. In the centre of the level road stood the black and white liveries, the yellow-panelled 'rickshaw, and Mrs Keith-Wessington. I pulled up, looked, rubbed my eyes, and, I believe, must have said something. The next thing I knew was that I was lying face downward on the road, with Kitty kneeling above me in tears.

'Has it gone, child!' I gasped. Kitty only wept more bitterly.

'Has what gone, Jack dear? what does it all mean? There must be a mistake somewhere, Jack. A hideous mistake.' Her last words brought me to my feet—mad—raving for the time being.

'Yes, there is a mistake somewhere,' I repeated, 'a hideous mistake. Come and look at It.'

I have an indistinct idea that I dragged Kitty by the wrist along the road up to where It stood, and implored her for pity's sake to speak to It; to tell It that we were betrothed; that neither Death nor Hell could break the tie between us: and Kitty only knows how much more to the same effect. Now and again I appealed passionately to the Terror in the 'rickshaw to bear witness to all I had said, and to release me from a torture that was killing me. As I talked I suppose I must have told Kitty of my old relations with Mrs Wessington, for I saw her listen intently with white face and blazing eyes.

'Thank you, Mr Pansay,' she said, 'that's quite enough. Syce ghora lao.'

The syces, impassive as Orientals always are, had come up with the recaptured horses; and as Kitty sprang into her saddle I caught hold of the bridle, entreating her to hear me out and forgive. My answer was the cut of her riding-whip across my face from mouth to eye, and a word or two of farewell that even now I cannot write down. So I judged, and judged rightly, that Kitty knew all; and I staggered back to the side of the 'rickshaw. My face was cut and bleeding, and the blow of the riding-whip had raised a livid blue wheal on it. I had no self-respect. Just then, Heatherlegh, who must have been following Kitty and me at a distance, cantered up.

'Doctor,' I said, pointing to my face, 'here's Miss Mannering's signature to my order of dismissal and ... I'll thank you for that lakh as soon as convenient.'

Heatherlegh's face, even in my abject misery, moved me to laughter. 'I'll stake my professional reputation'—he began. 'Don't be a fool,' I whispered. 'I've lost my life's happiness and you'd better take me home.'

As I spoke the 'rickshaw was gone. Then I lost all knowledge of what was passing. The crest of Jakko seemed to heave and roll like the crest of a cloud and fall in upon me.

Seven days later (on the 7th of May, that is to say) I was aware that

I was lying in Heatherlegh's room as weak as a little child. Heatherlegh was watching me intently from behind the papers on his writing-table. His first words were not encouraging; but I was too far spent to be much moved by them.

'Here's Miss Kitty has sent back your letters. You corresponded a good deal, you young people. Here's a packet that looks like a ring, and a cheerful sort of a note from Mannering Papa, which I've taken the liberty of reading and burning. The old gentleman's not pleased with you.'

'And Kitty?' I asked, dully.

'Rather more drawn than her father from what she says. By the same token you must have been letting out any number of queer reminiscences just before I met you. 'Says that a man who would have behaved to a woman as you did to Mrs Wessington ought to kill himself out of sheer pity for his kind. She's a hot headed little virago, your mash. 'Will have it too that you were suffering from D. T. when that row on the Jakko road turned up, 'Says she'll die before she ever speaks to you again.'

I groaned and turned over on the other side.

'Now you've got your choice, my friend. This engagement has to be broken off; and the Mannerings don't want to be too hard on you. Was it broken through D, T. or epileptic fits? Sorry I can't offer you a better exchange unless you'd prefer hereditary insanity. Say the word and I'll tell 'em it's fits. All Simla knows about that scene on the Ladies' Mile. Come! I'll give you five minutes to think over it.'

During those five minutes I believe that I explored thoroughly the lowest circles of the Inferno which it is permitted man to tread on earth. And at the same time I myself was watching myself faltering through the dark labyrinths of doubt, misery, and utter despair. I wondered, as Heatherlegh in his chair might have wondered, which dreadful alternative I should adopt. Presently I heard myself answering in a voice that I hardly recognized, 'They're confoundedly particular about morality in these parts. Give 'em fits, Heatherlegh, and my love. Now let me sleep a bit longer.'

Then my two selves joined, and it was only I (half crazed, devil-driven I) that tossed in my bed, tracing step by step the history of the past month.

'But I am in Simla,' I kept repeating to myself. 'I, Jack Pansay, am in Simla, and there are no ghosts here. It's unreasonable of that woman to pretend there are. Why couldn't Agnes have left me alone? I never did her any harm. It might just as well have been me as Agnes. Only I'd never have come back on purpose to kill her. Why can't I be left alone—left alone and happy?'

It was high noon when I first awoke: and the sun was low in the sky before I slept—slept as the tortured criminal sleeps on his rack, too worn to feel further pain.

Next day I could not leave my bed. Heatherlegh told me in the morning that he had received an answer from Mr Mannering, and that, thanks to his (Heatherlegh's) friendly offices, the story of my affliction had travelled through the length and breadth of Simla, where I was on all sides much pitied.

'And that's rather more than you deserve,' he concluded, pleasantly, 'though the Lord knows you've been going through a pretty severe mill. Never mind; we'll cure you yet, you perverse phenomenon.'

I declined firmly to be cured, 'You've been much too good to me already, old man,' said I; 'but I don't think I need trouble you further.'

In my heart I knew that nothing Heatherlegh could do would lighten the burden that had been laid upon me.

With that knowledge came also a sense of hopeless, impotent rebellion against the unreasonableness of it all. There were scores of men no better than I whose punishments had at least been reserved for another world; and I felt that it was bitterly, cruelly unfair that I alone should have been singled out for so hideous a fate. This mood would in time give place to another where it seemed that the 'rickshaw and I were the only realities in a world of shadows; that Kitty was a ghost; that Mannering, Heatherlegh, and all the other men and women I knew were all ghosts; and the great, grey hills themselves but vain shadows devised to torture me. From mood to mood I tossed backward and forward for seven weary days; my body growing daily stronger and stronger, until the bedroom looking-glass told me that I had returned to everyday life, and was as other men once more. Curiously enough my face showed no signs of the struggle I had gone through. It was pale indeed, but as expressionless and commonplace as ever. I had expected some permanent alteration—visible evidence of the disease that was eating me away. I found nothing.

On the 15th of May I left Heatherlegh's house at eleven o'clock in the morning; and the instinct of the bachelor drove me to the Club. There I found that every man knew my story as told by Heatherlegh, and was, in clumsy fashion, abnormally kind and attentive. Nevertheless I recognized that for the rest of my natural life I should be among but not of my fellows; and I envied very bitterly indeed the laughing coolies on the Mall below. I lunched at the Club, and at four o'clock wandered aimlessly down the Mall in the vague hope of meeting Kitty. Close to the Band-stand the black and white liveries joined me; and I heard Mrs Wessington's old appeal at my side. I had been expecting this ever since I came out; and was only surprised at her delay. The phantom 'rickshaw and I went side by side along the Chota Simla road in silence. Close to the bazar, Kitty and a man on horseback overtook and passed us. For any sign she gave I might have been a dog in the road. She did not even pay me the compliment of quickening her pace; though the rainy afternoon had served for an excuse.

So Kitty and her companion, and I and my ghostly Light-o'-Love, crept round Jakko in couples. The road was streaming with water; the pines dripped like roof-pipes on the rocks below, and the air was full of fine, driving rain. Two or three times I found myself saying to myself almost aloud: 'I'm Jack Pansay on leave at Simla—at Simla! Everyday, ordinary Simla. I mustn't forget that—I mustn't forget that.' Then I would try to recollect some of the gossip I had heard at the Club: the prices of So-and-So's horses—anything, in fact, that related to the workaday Anglo-Indian world I knew so well. I even repeated the multiplication-table rapidly to myself, to make quite sure that I was not taking leave of my senses. It gave me much comfort; and must have prevented my hearing Mrs Wessington for a time.

Once more I wearily climbed the Convent slope and entered the level road. Here Kitty and the man started off at a canter, and I was left alone with Mrs Wessington. 'Agnes,' said I, 'will you put back your hood and tell me what it all means?' The hood dropped noiselessly, and

I was face to face with my dead and buried mistress. She was wearing the dress in which I had last seen her alive; carried the same tiny handkerchief in her right hand; and the same card case in her left. (A woman eight months dead with a card case!) I had to pin myself down to the multiplication-table, and to set both hands on the stone parapet of the road, to assure myself that that at least was real.

'Agnes,' I repeated, 'for pity's sake tell me what it all means.' Mrs Wessington leaned forward, with that odd, quick turn of the head I used to know so well, and spoke.

If my story had not already so madly overleaped the bounds of all human belief I should apologize to you now. As I know that no one—no, not even Kitty, for whom it is written as some sort of justification of my conduct—will believe me, I will go on. Mrs Wessington spoke and I walked with her from the Sanjowlie road to the turning below the Commander-in-Chief's house as I might walk by the side of any living woman's 'rickshaw, deep in conversation. The second and most tormenting of my moods of sickness had suddenly laid hold upon me, and like the Prince in Tennyson's poem, 'I seemed to move amid a world of ghosts.' There had been a garden-party at the Commander-in-Chief's, and we two joined the crowd of homeward-bound folk. As I saw them then it seemed that they were the shadows—impalpable, fantastic shadows—that divided for Mrs Wessington's 'rickshaw to pass through. What we said during the course of that weird interview I cannot—indeed, I dare not—tell. Heatherlegh's comment would have been a short laugh and a remark that I had been 'mashing a brain-eye-and-stomach chimera.' It was a ghastly and yet in some indefinable way a marvellously dear experience. Could it be possible, I wondered, that I was in this life to woo a second time the woman I had killed by my own neglect and cruelty?

I met Kitty on the homeward road—a shadow among shadows.

If I were to describe all the incidents of the next fortnight in their order, my story would never come to an end; and your patience would be exhausted. Morning after morning and evening after evening the ghostly 'rickshaw and I used to wander through Simla together. Wherever I went there the four black and white liveries followed me and bore me company to and from my hotel. At the Theatre I found them amid the crowd of yelling jhampanies; outside the Club veranda, after a long evening of whist; at the Birthday Ball, waiting patiently for my reappearance; and in broad daylight when I went calling. Save that it cast no shadow, the 'rickshaw was in every respect as real to look upon as one of wood and iron. More than once, indeed, I have had to check myself from warning some hard-riding friend against cantering over it. More than once I have walked down the Mall deep in conversation with Mrs Wessington to the unspeakable amazement of the passers-by.

Before I had been out and about a week I learned that the 'fit' theory had been discarded in favour of insanity. However, I made no change in my mode of life. I called, rode, and dined out as freely as ever. I had a passion for the society of my kind which I had never felt before; I hungered to be among the realities of life; and at the same time I felt vaguely unhappy when I had been separated too long from my ghostly companion. It would be almost impossible to describe my varying moods from the 15th of May up to to-day.

The presence of the 'rickshaw filled me by turns with horror, blind fear, a dim sort of pleasure, and utter despair. I dared not leave Simla; and I knew that my stay there was killing me. I knew, moreover, that it was my destiny to die slowly and a little every day. My only anxiety was to get the penance over as quietly as might be. Alternately I hungered for a sight of Kitty and watched her outrageous flirtations with my successor—to speak more accurately, my successors—with amused interest. She was as much out of my life as I was out of hers. By day I wandered with Mrs Wessington almost content. By night I implored Heaven to let me return to the world as I used to know it. Above all these varying moods lay the sensation of dull, numbing wonder that the Seen and the Unseen should mingle so strangely on this earth to hound one poor soul to its grave.

❧

August 27—Heatherlegh has been indefatigable in his attendance on me; and only yesterday told me that I ought to send in an application for sick leave. An application to escape the company of a phantom! A request that the Government would graciously permit me to get rid of five ghosts and an airy 'rickshaw by going to England! Heatherlegh's proposition moved me to almost hysterical laughter. I told him that I should await the end quietly at Simla; and I am sure that the end is not far off. Believe me that I dread its advent more than any word can say; and I torture myself nightly with a thousand speculations as to the manner of my death.

Shall I die in my bed decently and as an English gentleman should die; or, in one last walk on the Mall, will my soul be wrenched from me to take its place forever and ever by the side of that ghastly phantasm? Shall I return to my old lost allegiance in the next world, or shall I meet Agnes loathing her and bound to her side through all eternity? Shall we two hover over the scene of our lives till the end of Time? As the day of my death draws nearer, the intense horror that all living flesh feels toward escaped spirits from beyond the grave grows more and more powerful. It is an awful thing to go down quick among the dead with scarcely one-half of your life completed. It is a thousand times more awful to wait as I do in your midst, for I know not what unimaginable terror. Pity me, at least on the score of my 'delusion,' for I know you will never believe what I have written here. Yet as surely as ever a man was done to death by the Powers of Darkness I am that man.

In justice, too, pity her. For as surely as ever woman was killed by man, I killed Mrs Wessington. And the last portion of my punishment is even now upon me.

A LOST MASTERPIECE

A.A. Milne

The short essay on 'The Improbability of the Infinite' which I was planning for you yesterday will now never be written. Last night my brain was crammed with lofty thoughts on the subject—and for that matter, on every other subject. My mind was never so fertile. Ten thousand words on any theme from Tin-tacks to Tomatoes would have been easy to me. That was last night. This morning I have only one word in my brain, and I cannot get rid of it. The word is 'Teralbay.'

Teralbay is not a word which one uses much in ordinary life. Rearrange the letters, however, and it becomes such a word. A friend—no, I can call him a friend no longer—a person gave me this collection of letters as I was going to bed and challenged me to make a proper word of it. He added that Lord Melbourne—this, he alleged, is a well-known historical fact—Lord Melbourne had given this word to Queen Victoria once, and it had kept her awake the whole night. After this, one could not be so disloyal as to solve it at once. For two hours or so, therefore, I merely toyed with it. Whenever I seemed to be getting warm I hurriedly thought of something else. This quixotic loyalty has been the undoing of me; my chances of a solution have slipped by, and I am beginning to fear that they will never return. While this is the case, the only word I can write about is Teralbay.

Teralbay—what does it make? There are two ways of solving a problem of this sort. The first is to waggle your eyes and see what you get. If you do this, words like 'alterably' and 'laboratory' emerge, which a little thought shows you to be wrong. You may then waggle your eyes again, look at it upside down or sideways, or stalk it carefully from the southwest and plunge upon it suddenly when it is not ready for you. In this way it may be surprised into giving up its secret. But if you find that it cannot be captured by strategy or assault, then there is only one way of taking it. It must be starved into surrender. This will take a long time, but victory is certain.

There are eight letters in Teralbay and two of them are the same, so that there must be 181,440 ways of writing the letters out. This may not be obvious to you at once; you may have thought that it was only 181,439; but you may take my word for it that I am right. (Wait a moment while I work it out again.... Yes, that's it.) Well, now suppose that you put down a new order of letters—such as 'raytable'—every six seconds, which is very easy going, and suppose that you can spare an hour a day for it; then by the 303rd day—a year hence, if you rest on Sundays—you are bound to have reached a solution.

But perhaps this is not playing the game. This, I am sure, is not what Queen Victoria did. And now I think of it, history does not tell us what she did do, beyond that she passed a sleepless night. (And that she still liked Melbourne afterwards—which is surprising.) Did she ever guess it? Or did Lord Melbourne have to tell her in the morning, and did she say, 'Why, of course!' I expect so. Or did Lord Melbourne say, 'I'm awfully sorry, madam, but I find I put a 'y' in too many?' But no—history could not have remained silent over such a tragedy as that. Besides, she went on liking him.

When I die 'Teralbay' will be written on my heart. While I live it shall be my telegraphic address. I shall patent a breakfast food called 'Teralbay'; I shall say 'Teralbay!' when I miss a 2-ft. putt; the Teralbay carnation will catch your eye at the Temple show. I shall write anonymous letters over the name. 'Fly at once; all is discovered—Teralbay.' Yes, that would look rather well.

I wish I knew more about Lord Melbourne. What sort of words did he think of? The thing couldn't he 'aeroplane' or 'telephone' or 'googly,' because these weren't invented in his time. That gives us three words less. Nor, probably, would it be anything to eat; a Prime Minister would hardly discuss such subjects with his Sovereign. I have no doubt that after hours of immense labour you will triumphantly suggest 'rateably.' I suggested that myself, but it is wrong. There is no such word in the dictionary. The same objection applies to 'bat-early'—it ought to mean something, but it doesn't.

So I hand the word over to you. Please do not send the solution to me, for by the time you read this I shall either have found it out or else I shall be in a nursing home. In either case it will be of no use to me. Send it to the Postmaster-General or one of the Geddeses or Mary Pickford. You will want to get it off your mind.

As for myself I shall write to my fr——, to the person who first said 'Teralbay' to me, and ask him to make something of 'sabet' and 'donureb.' When he has worked out the corrections—which, in case he gets the wrong ones, I may tell him here are 'beast' and 'bounder'—I shall search the dictionary for some long word like 'intellectual.' I shall alter the order of the letters and throw in a couple of 'g's' and a 'k'. And then I shall tell them to keep a spare bed for him in my nursing home.

Well, I have got 'Teralbay' a little off my mind. I feel better able now to think of other things. Indeed, I might almost begin my famous essay on 'The Improbability of the Infinite.' It would be a pity for the country to lose such a masterpiece—she has had quite enough trouble already what with one thing and another. For my view of the Infinite is this: that although beyond the Finite, or, as one might say, the Commensurate, there may or may not be a—

Just a moment. I think I have it now. T—R—A——No....

THE DOG

Banjo Paterson

The dog is a member of society who likes to have his day's work, and who does it more conscientiously than most human beings. A dog always looks as if he ought to have a pipe in his mouth and a black bag for his lunch, and then he would go quite happily to office every day.

A dog without work is like a man without work, a nuisance to himself and everybody else. People who live about town, and keep a dog to give the children hydatids and to keep the neighbours awake at night, imagine that the animal is fulfilling his destiny. All town dogs, fancy dogs, show dogs, lap-dogs, and other dogs with no work to do, should be abolished; it is only in the country that a dog has any justification for his existence.

The old theory that animals have only instinct, not reason, to guide them, is knocked endways by the dog. A dog can reason as well as a human being on some subjects, and better on others, and the best reasoning dog of all is the sheep-dog. The sheep-dog is a professional artist with a pride in his business. Watch any drover's dogs bringing sheep into the yards. How thoroughly they feel their responsibility, and how very annoyed they get if a stray dog with no occupation wants them to stop and fool about! They snap at him and hurry off, as much as to say: 'You go about your idleness. Don't you see this is my busy day?'

Sheep-dogs are followers of Thomas Carlyle. They hold that the only happiness for a dog in this life is to find his work and to do it. The idle, `dilettante', non-working, aristocratic dog they have no use for.

The training of a sheep-dog for his profession begins at a very early age. The first thing is to take him out with his mother and let him see her working. He blunders light-heartedly, frisking along in front of the horse, and his owner tries to ride over him, and generally succeeds. It is amusing to see how that knocks all the gas out of a puppy, and with what a humble air he falls to the rear and glues himself to the horse's heels, scarcely daring to look to the right or to the left, for fear of committing some other breach of etiquette.

He has had his first lesson—to keep behind the horse until he is wanted. Then he watches the old slut work, and is allowed to go with her round the sheep; and if he shows any disposition to get out of hand and frolic about, the old lady will bite him sharply to prevent his interfering with her work.

By degrees, slowly, like any other professional, he learns his business. He learns to bring sheep after a horse simply at a wave of the hand; to force the mob up to a gate where they can be counted or drafted; to follow the scent of lost sheep, and to drive sheep through a town without any master, one dog going on ahead to block the sheep from turning off into by-streets while the other drives them on from the rear.

How do they learn all these things? Dogs for show work are taught painstakingly by men who are skilled in handling them; but, after all, they teach themselves more than the men teach them. It looks as if the acquired knowledge of generations were transmitted from dog to dog. The puppy, descended from a race of sheep-dogs, starts with all his faculties directed towards the working of sheep; he is half-educated as soon as he is born. He can no more help working sheep than a born musician can help being musical, or a Hebrew can help gathering in shekels. It is bred in him. If he can't get sheep to work, he will work a fowl; often and often one can see a collie pup painstakingly and carefully driving a bewildered old hen into a stable, or a stock-yard, or any other enclosed space on which he has fixed his mind. How does he learn to do that? He didn't learn it at all. The knowledge was born with him.

When the dog has been educated, or has educated himself, he enjoys his work; but very few dogs like work 'in the yards'. The sun is hot, the dust rises in clouds, and there is nothing to do but bark, bark, bark—which is all very well for learners and amateurs, but is beneath the dignity of the true professional sheep-dog. When they are hoarse with barking and nearly choked with dust, the men lose their tempers and swear at them, and throw clods of earth at them, and sing out to them 'Speak up, blast you!'

Then the dogs suddenly decide that they have done enough for the day. Watching their opportunity, they silently steal over the fence, and hide in any cool place they can find. After a while the men notice that hardly any are left, and operations are suspended while a great hunt is made into outlying pieces of cover, where the dogs are sure to be found lying low and looking as guilty as so many thieves. A clutch at the scruff of the neck, a kick in the ribs, and they are hauled out of hiding-places; and accompany their masters to the yard frolicking about and pretending that they are quite delighted to be going back, and only hid in those bushes out of sheer thoughtlessness. He is a champion hypocrite, is the dog.

Dogs, like horses, have very keen intuition. They know when the men around them are frightened, though they may not know the cause. In a great Queensland strike, when the shearers attacked and burnt Dagworth shed, some rifle-volleys were exchanged. The air was full of human electricity, each man giving out waves of fear and excitement. Mark now the effect it had on the dogs. They were not in the fighting; nobody fired at them, and nobody spoke to them; but every dog left his master, left the sheep, and went away to the homestead, about six miles off. There wasn't a dog about the shed next day after the fight. The noise of the rifles had not frightened them, because they were well-accustomed to that.

The same thing happened constantly with horses in the South African War. A loose horse would feed contentedly while our men were firing, but when our troops were being fired at the horses became uneasy, and the loose ones would trot away. The excitement of the men communicated itself to them.

Dogs have an amazing sense of responsibility. Sometimes, when there are sheep to be worked, an old slut who has young puppies may be greatly exercised in her mind whether she should go out or not. On the one hand, she does not care about leaving the puppies, on the other, she feels that she really ought to go rather than allow the sheep to be knocked about by those learners. Hesitatingly, with many a look behind her, she trots out after the horses and the other dogs. An impassioned appeal from the head boundary rider, 'Go back home, will yer!' is treated with the contempt it deserves. She goes out to the yards, works, perhaps half the day, and then slips quietly under the fences and trots off home, contented.

THE WHISTLE

Benjamin Franklin

Franklin reminiscences when he was a small boy and paid too much for a whistle. He sure did learn how to strike a bargain, though.

To Madame Brillon,

I received my dear friend's two letters, one for Wednesday and one for Saturday. This is again Wednesday. I do not deserve one for to-day, because I have not answered the former. But, indolent as I am, and averse to writing, the fear of having no more of your pleasing epistles, if I do not contribute to the correspondence, obliges me to take up my pen; and as Mr B. has kindly sent me word that he sets out to-morrow to see you, instead of spending this Wednesday evening, as I have done its namesakes, in your delightful company, I sit down to spend it in thinking of you, in writing to you, and in reading over and over again your letters.

I am charmed with your description of Paradise, and with your plan of living there; and I approve much of your conclusion, that, in the meantime, we should draw all the good we can from this world. In my opinion we might all draw more good from it than we do, and suffer less evil, if we would take care not to give too much for whistles. For to me it seems that most of the unhappy people we meet with are become so by neglect of that caution. You ask what I mean? You love stories, and will excuse my telling one of myself.

When I was a child of seven years old, my friends, on a holiday, filled my pocket with coppers. I went directly to a shop where they sold toys for children; and being charmed with the sound of a whistle, that I met by the way in the hands of another boy, I voluntarily offered and gave all my money for one. I then came home, and went whistling all over the house, much pleased with my whistle, but disturbing all the family. My brothers, and sisters, and cousins, understanding the bargain I had made, told me I had given four times as much for it as it was worth; put me in mind what good things I might have bought with the rest of the money; and laughed at me so much for my folly, that I cried with vexation; and the reflection gave me more chagrin than the whistle gave me pleasure.

This, however, was afterwards of use to me, the impression continuing on my mind; so that often, when I was tempted to buy some unnecessary thing, I said to myself, Don't give too much for the whistle; and I saved my money.

As I grew up, came into the world, and observed the actions of men, I thought I met with many, very many, who gave too much for the whistle. When I saw one too ambitious of court favour, sacrificing his time in attendance on levees, his repose, his liberty, his virtue, and perhaps his friends, to attain it, I have said to myself, This man gives too much for his whistle.

When I saw another fond of popularity, constantly employing himself in political bustles, neglecting his own affairs, and ruining them by that neglect, He pays, indeed, said I, too much for his whistle.

If I knew a miser, who gave up every kind of comfortable living, all the pleasure of doing good to others, all the esteem of his fellow-citizens, and the joys of benevolent friendship, for the sake of accumulating wealth, Poor man, said I, you pay too much for your whistle. When I met with a man of pleasure, sacrificing every laudable improvement of the mind, or of his fortune, to mere corporeal sensations, and ruining his health in their pursuit, Mistaken man, said I, you are providing pain for yourself, instead of pleasure; you give too much for your whistle. If I see one fond of appearance, or fine clothes, fine houses, fine furniture, fine equipages, all above his fortune, for which he contracts debts, and ends his career in a prison, Alas! say I, he has paid dear, very dear, for his whistle.

When I see a beautiful sweet-tempered girl married to an ill-natured brute of a husband, What a pity, say I, that she should pay so much for a whistle! In short, I conceive that great part of the miseries of mankind are brought upon them by the false estimates they have made of the value of things, and by their giving too much for their whistles.

Yet I ought to have charity for these unhappy people, when I consider that, with all this wisdom of which I am boasting, there are certain things in the world so tempting, for example, the apples of King John, which happily are not to be bought; for if they were put to sale by auction, I might very easily be led to ruin myself in the purchase, and find that I had once more given too much for the whistle. Adieu, my dear friend, and believe me ever yours very sincerely and with unalterable affection.

THE STORY OF AN HOUR*

Kate Chopin

Knowing that Mrs Mallard was afflicted with a heart trouble, great care was taken to break to her as gently as possible the news of her husband's death.

It was her sister Josephine who told her, in broken sentences; veiled hints that revealed in half concealing. Her husband's friend Richards was there, too, near her. It was he who had been in the newspaper office when intelligence of the railroad disaster was received, with Brently Mallard's name leading the list of 'killed.' He had only taken the time to assure himself of its truth by a second telegram, and had hastened to forestall any less careful, less tender friend in bearing the sad message.

She did not hear the story as many women have heard the same, with a paralysed inability to accept its significance. She wept at once, with sudden, wild abandonment, in her sister's arms. When the storm of grief had spent itself she went away to her room alone. She would have no one follow her.

There stood, facing the open window, a comfortable, roomy armchair. Into this she sank, pressed down by a physical exhaustion that haunted her body and seemed to reach into her soul.

She could see in the open square before her house the tops of trees that were all aquiver with the new spring life. The delicious breath of rain was in the air. In the street below a peddler was crying his wares. The notes of a distant song which someone was singing reached her faintly, and countless sparrows were twittering in the eaves.

There were patches of blue sky showing here and there through the clouds that had met and piled one above the other in the west facing her window.

She sat with her head thrown back upon the cushion of the chair,

---

*This story was first published in 1894 as *The Dream of an Hour* before being republished under this title in 1895.

quite motionless, except when a sob came up into her throat and shook her, as a child who has cried itself to sleep continues to sob in its dreams.

She was young, with a fair, calm face, whose lines bespoke repression and even a certain strength. But now there was a dull stare in her eyes, whose gaze was fixed away off yonder on one of those patches of blue sky. It was not a glance of reflection, but rather indicated a suspension of intelligent thought.

There was something coming to her and she was waiting for it, fearfully. What was it? She did not know; it was too subtle and elusive to name. But she felt it, creeping out of the sky, reaching toward her through the sounds, the scents, the colour that filled the air.

Now her bosom rose and fell tumultuously. She was beginning to recognize this thing that was approaching to possess her, and she was striving to beat it back with her will—as powerless as her two white slender hands would have been. When she abandoned herself a little whispered word escaped her slightly parted lips. She said it over and over under the breath: 'free, free, free!' The vacant stare and the look of terror that had followed it went from her eyes. They stayed keen and bright. Her pulses beat fast, and the coursing blood warmed and relaxed every inch of her body.

She did not stop to ask if it were or were not a monstrous joy that held her. A clear and exalted perception enabled her to dismiss the suggestion as trivial. She knew that she would weep again when she saw the kind, tender hands folded in death; the face that had never looked save with love upon her, fixed and grey and dead. But she saw beyond that bitter moment a long procession of years to come that would belong to her absolutely. And she opened and spread her arms out to them in welcome.

There would be no one to live for during those coming years; she would live for herself. There would be no powerful will bending hers in that blind persistence with which men and women believe they have a right to impose a private will upon a fellow-creature. A kind intention or a cruel intention made the act seem no less a crime as she looked upon it in that brief moment of illumination.

And yet she had loved him—sometimes. Often she had not. What did it matter! What could love, the unsolved mystery, count for in the face of this possession of self-assertion which she suddenly recognized as the strongest impulse of her being!

'Free! Body and soul free!' she kept whispering.

Josephine was kneeling before the closed door with her lips to the keyhole, imploring for admission. 'Louise, open the door! I beg; open the door—you will make yourself ill. What are you doing, Louise? For heaven's sake open the door.'

'Go away. I am not making myself ill.' No; she was drinking in a very elixir of life through that open window.

Her fancy was running riot along those days ahead of her. Spring days, and summer days, and all sorts of days that would be her own. She breathed a quick prayer that life might be long. It was only yesterday she had thought with a shudder that life might be long.

She arose at length and opened the door to her sister's importunities. There was a feverish triumph in her eyes, and she carried herself unwittingly like a goddess of Victory. She clasped her sister's waist, and together they descended the stairs. Richards stood waiting for them at the bottom.

Someone was opening the front door with a latchkey. It was Brently Mallard who entered, a little travel-stained, composedly carrying his grip-sack and umbrella. He had been far from the scene of the accident, and did not even know there had been one. He stood amazed at Josephine's piercing cry; at Richards' quick motion to screen him from the view of his wife.

When the doctors came they said she had died of heart disease—of the joy that kills.

THE BRAVE TIN SOLDIER*

Hans Christian Andersen

There were once five-and-twenty tin soldiers, who were all brothers, for they had been made out of the same old tin spoon. They shouldered arms and looked straight before them, and wore a splendid uniform, red and blue. The first thing in the world they ever heard were the words, 'Tin soldiers!' uttered by a little boy, who clapped his hands with delight when the lid of the box, in which they lay, was taken off. They were given him for a birthday present, and he stood at the table to set them up. The soldiers were all exactly alike, excepting one, who had only one leg; he had been left to the last, and then there was not enough of the melted tin to finish him, so they made him to stand firmly on one leg, and this caused him to be very remarkable.

The table on which the tin soldiers stood, was covered with other playthings, but the most attractive to the eye was a pretty little paper castle. Through the small windows the rooms could be seen. In front of the castle a number of little trees surrounded a piece of looking-glass, which was intended to represent a transparent lake. Swans, made of wax, swam on the lake, and were reflected in it. All this was very pretty, but the prettiest of all was a tiny little lady, who stood at the open door of the castle; she, also, was made of paper, and she wore a dress of clear muslin, with a narrow blue ribbon over her shoulders just like a scarf. In front of these was fixed a glittering tinsel rose, as large as her whole face. The little lady was a dancer, and she stretched out both her arms, and raised one of her legs so high, that the tin soldier could not see it at all, and he thought that she, like himself, had only one leg. 'That is the wife for me,' he thought; 'but she is too grand, and lives in a castle, while I have only a box to live in, five-and-twenty of us altogether, that is no place for her. Still I must try and make her

---

*This lesser-known Hans Christian Andersen story is also known as 'The Steadfast Tin Soldier'.

acquaintance.' Then he laid himself at full length on the table behind a snuff-box that stood upon it, so that he could peep at the little delicate lady, who continued to stand on one leg without losing her balance. When evening came, the other tin soldiers were all placed in the box, and the people of the house went to bed. Then the playthings began to have their own games together, to pay visits, to have sham fights, and to give balls. The tin soldiers rattled in their box; they wanted to get out and join the amusements, but they could not open the lid. The nut-crackers played at leap-frog, and the pencil jumped about the table. There was such a noise that the canary woke up and began to talk, and in poetry too. Only the tin soldier and the dancer remained in their places. She stood on tiptoe, with her legs stretched out, as firmly as he did on his one leg. He never took his eyes from her for even a moment. The clock struck twelve, and, with a bounce, up sprang the lid of the snuff-box; but, instead of snuff, there jumped up a little black goblin; for the snuff-box was a toy puzzle.

'Tin soldier,' said the goblin, 'don't wish for what does not belong to you.'

But the tin soldier pretended not to hear.

'Very well; wait till to-morrow, then,' said the goblin.

When the children came in the next morning, they placed the tin soldier in the window. Now, whether it was the goblin who did it, or the draught, is not known, but the window flew open, and out fell the tin soldier, heels overhead, from the third story, into the street beneath. It was a terrible fall; for he came head downwards, his helmet and his bayonet stuck in between the flagstones, and his one leg up in the air. The servant maid and the little boy went down stairs directly to look for him; but he was nowhere to be seen, although once they nearly trod upon him. If he had called out, 'Here I am,' it would have been all right, but he was too proud to cry out for help while he wore a uniform.

Presently it began to rain, and the drops fell faster and faster, till there was a heavy shower. When it was over, two boys happened to pass by, and one of them said, 'Look, there is a tin soldier. He ought to have a boat to sail in.'

So they made a boat out of a newspaper, and placed the tin soldier in it, and sent him sailing down the gutter, while the two boys ran by the side of it, and clapped their hands. Good gracious, what large waves arose in that gutter! and how fast the stream rolled on! for the rain had been very heavy. The paper boat rocked up and down, and turned itself round sometimes so quickly that the tin soldier trembled; yet he remained firm; his countenance did not change; he looked straight before him, and shouldered his musket. Suddenly the boat shot under a bridge which formed a part of a drain, and then it was as dark as the tin soldier's box.

'Where am I going now?' thought he. 'This is the black goblin's fault, I am sure. Ah, well, if the little lady were only here with me in the boat, I should not care for any darkness.'

Suddenly there appeared a great water-rat, who lived in the drain.

'Have you a passport?' asked the rat, 'give it to me at once.' But the tin soldier remained silent and held his musket tighter than ever. The boat sailed on and the rat followed it. How he did gnash his teeth and cry out to the bits of wood and straw, 'Stop him, stop him; he has not paid toll, and has not shown his pass.' But the stream rushed on stronger and stronger. The tin soldier could already see daylight shining where the arch ended. Then he heard a roaring sound quite terrible enough to frighten the bravest man. At the end of the tunnel the drain fell into a large canal over a steep place, which made it as dangerous for him as a waterfall would be to us. He was too close to it to stop, so the boat rushed on, and the poor tin soldier could only hold himself as stiffly as possible, without moving an eyelid, to show that he was not afraid. The boat whirled round three or four times, and then filled with water to the very edge; nothing could save it from sinking. He now stood up to his neck in water, while deeper and deeper sank the boat, and the paper became soft and loose with the wet, till at last the water closed over the soldier's head. He thought of the elegant little dancer whom he should never see again, and the words of the song sounded in his ears:

'Farewell, warrior! ever brave,

Drifting onward to thy grave.'

Then the paper boat fell to pieces, and the soldier sank into the water and immediately afterwards was swallowed up by a great fish. Oh how dark it was inside the fish! A great deal darker than in the tunnel, and narrower too, but the tin soldier continued firm, and lay at full length shouldering his musket. The fish swam to and fro, making the most wonderful movements, but at last he became quite still. After a while, a flash of lightning seemed to pass through him, and then the daylight approached, and a voice cried out, 'I declare here is the tin soldier.' The fish had been caught, taken to the market and sold to the cook, who took him into the kitchen and cut him open with a large knife. She picked up the soldier and held him by the waist between her finger and thumb, and carried him into the room. They were all anxious to see this wonderful soldier who had travelled about inside a fish; but he was not at all proud. They placed him on the table, and—how many curious things do happen in the world!—there he was in the very same room from the window of which he had fallen, there were the same children, the same playthings, standing on the table, and the pretty castle with the elegant little dancer at the door; she still balanced herself on one leg, and held up the other, so she was as firm as himself. It touched the tin soldier so much to see her that he almost wept tin tears, but he kept them back. He only looked at her and they both remained silent. Presently one of the little boys took up the tin soldier, and threw him into the stove. He had no reason for doing so, therefore it must have been the fault of the black goblin who lived in the snuff-box. The flames lighted up the tin soldier, as he stood, the heat was very terrible, but whether it proceeded from the real fire or from the fire of love he could not tell. Then he could see that the bright colours were faded from his uniform, but whether they had been washed off during his journey or from the effects of his sorrow, no one could say. He looked at the little lady, and she looked at him. He felt himself melting away, but he still remained firm with his gun on his shoulder. Suddenly the door of the room flew open and the draught of air caught up the little dancer, she fluttered like a sylph right into the stove by the side of the tin soldier, and was instantly in flames and was gone. The tin soldier melted down into a lump, and the next morning, when the maid servant took the ashes out of the stove, she found him in the shape of a little tin heart. But of the little dancer nothing remained but the tinsel rose, which was burnt black as a cinder.

THE NIGHT CAME SLOWLY

Kate Chopin

I am losing my interest in human beings; in the significance of their lives and their actions. Someone has said it is better to study one man than ten books. I want neither books nor men; they make me suffer. Can one of them talk to me like the night – the Summer night? Like the stars or the caressing wind?

The night came slowly, softly, as I lay out there under the maple tree. It came creeping, creeping stealthily out of the valley, thinking I did not notice. And the outlines of trees and foliage nearby blended in one black mass and the night came stealing out from them, too, and from the east and west, until the only light was in the sky, filtering through the maple leaves and a star looking down through every cranny.

The night is solemn and it means mystery.

Human shapes flitted by like intangible things. Some stole up like little mice to peep at me. I did not mind. My whole being was abandoned to the soothing and penetrating charm of the night.

The katydids began their slumber song: they are at it yet. How wise they are. They do not chatter like people. They tell me only: 'sleep, sleep, sleep.' The wind rippled the maple leaves like little warm love thrills.

Why do fools cumber the Earth! It was a man's voice that broke the necromancer's spell. A man came to-day with his 'Bible Class.' He is detestable with his red cheeks and bold eyes and coarse manner and speech. What does he know of Christ? Shall I ask a young fool who was born yesterday and will die tomorrow to tell me things of Christ? I would rather ask the stars: they have seen him.

AN IDLE FELLOW

Kate Chopin

I am tired. At the end of these years I am very tired. I have been studying in books the languages of the living and those we call dead. Early in the fresh morning I have studied in books, and throughout the day when the sun was shining; and at night when there were stars, I have lighted my oil-lamp and studied in books. Now my brain is weary and I want rest.

I shall sit here on the door-step beside my friend Paul. He is an idle fellow with folded hands. He laughs when I upbraid him, and bids me, with a motion, hold my peace. He is listening to a thrush's song that comes from the blur of yonder apple-tree. He tells me the thrush is singing a complaint. She wants her mate that was with her last blossom-time and builded a nest with her. She will have no other mate. She will call for him till she hears the notes of her beloved-one's song coming swiftly towards her across forest and field.

Paul is a strange fellow. He gazed idly at a billowy white cloud that rolls lazily over and over along the edge of the blue sky.

He turns away from me and the words with which I would instruct him, to drink deep the scent of the clover-field and the thick perfume from the rose-hedge.

We rise from the door-step and walk together down the gentle slope of the hill; past the apple-tree, and the rose-hedge; and along the border of the field where wheat is growing. We walk down to the foot of the gentle slope where women and men and children are living.

Paul is a strange fellow. He looks into the faces of people who pass us by. He tells me that in their eyes he reads the story of their souls. He knows men and women and the little children, and why they look this way and that way. He knows the reasons that turn them to and fro and cause them to go and come. I think I shall walk a space through the world with my friend Paul. He is very wise, he knows the language of God which I have not learned.

THE HAUNTED MIND

Nathaniel Hawthorne

'In the depths of every heart there is a tomb and a dungeon, though the lights, the music and revelry, above may cause us to forget their existence and the buried ones or prisoners whom they hide. But sometimes, and oftenest at midnight, those dark receptacles are flung wide open.'

What a singular moment is the first one, when you have hardly begun to recollect yourself, after starting from midnight slumber! By unclosing your eyes so suddenly you seem to have surprised the personages of your dream in full convocation round your bed, and catch one broad glance at them before they can flit into obscurity. Or, to vary the metaphor, you find yourself for a single instant wide awake in that realm of illusions whither sleep has been the passport, and behold its ghostly inhabitants and wondrous scenery with a perception of their strangeness such as you never attain while the dream is undisturbed. The distant sound of a church-clock is borne faintly on the wind. You question with yourself, half seriously, whether it has stolen to your waking ear from some grey tower that stood within the precincts of your dream. While yet in suspense another clock flings its heavy clang over the slumbering town with so full and distinct a sound, and such a long murmur in the neighbouring air, that you are certain it must proceed from the steeple at the nearest corner; You count the strokes—one, two; and there they cease with a booming sound like the gathering of a third stroke within the bell.

If you could choose an hour of wakefulness out of the whole night, it would be this. Since your sober bedtime, at eleven, you have had rest enough to take off the pressure of yesterday's fatigue, while before you, till the sun comes from 'Far Cathay' to brighten your window, there is almost the space of a summer night—one hour to be spent in thought with the mind's eye half shut, and two in pleasant dreams, and two in that strangest of enjoyments the forgetfulness alike of joy and woe. The moment of rising belongs to another period of time, and appears so distant that the plunge out of a warm bed into the frosty air cannot yet be anticipated with dismay. Yesterday has already vanished among the shadows of the past; to-morrow has not yet emerged from the future. You have found an intermediate space where the business of life does not intrude, where the passing moment lingers and becomes truly the present; a spot where Father Time, when he thinks nobody is watching him, sits down by the wayside to take breath. Oh that he would fall asleep and let mortals live on without growing older!

Hitherto you have lain perfectly still, because the slightest motion would dissipate the fragments of your slumber. Now, being irrevocably awake, you peep through the half-drawn window-curtain, and observe that the glass is ornamented with fanciful devices in frost-work, and that each pane presents something like a frozen dream. There will be time enough to trace out the analogy while waiting the summons to breakfast. Seen through the clear portion of the glass where the silvery mountain-peaks of the frost-scenery do not ascend, the most conspicuous object is the steeple, the white spire of which directs you to the wintry lustre of the firmament. You may almost distinguish the figures on the clock that has just told the hour. Such a frosty sky and the snow-covered roofs and the long vista of the frozen street, all white, and the distant water hardened into rock, might make you shiver even under four blankets and a woollen comforter. Yet look at that one glorious star! Its beams are distinguishable from all the rest, and actually cast the shadow of the casement on the bed with a radiance of deeper hue than moonlight, though not so accurate an outline.

You sink down and muffle your head in the clothes, shivering all the while, but less from bodily chill than the bare idea of a polar atmosphere. It is too cold even for the thoughts to venture abroad. You speculate on the luxury of wearing out a whole existence in bed like an oyster in its shell, content with the sluggish ecstasy of inaction, and drowsily conscious of nothing but delicious warmth such as you now feel again. Ah! that idea has brought a hideous one in its train. You think how the dead are lying in their cold shrouds and narrow coffins through the drear winter of the grave, and cannot persuade your fancy that they neither shrink nor shiver when the snow is drifting over their little hillocks and the bitter blast howls against the door of the tomb. That gloomy thought will collect a gloomy multitude and throw its complexion over your wakeful hour.

In the depths of every heart there is a tomb and a dungeon, though the lights, the music and revelry, above may cause us to forget their existence and the buried ones or prisoners whom they hide. But sometimes, and oftenest at midnight, those dark receptacles are flung wide open. In an hour like this, when the mind has a passive sensibility, but no active strength—when the imagination is a mirror imparting vividness to all ideas without the power of selecting or controlling them—then pray that your griefs may slumber and the brotherhood of remorse not break their chain. It is too late. A funeral train comes gliding by your bed in which passion and feeling assume bodily shape and things of the mind become dim spectres to the eye. There is your earliest sorrow, a pale young mourner wearing a sister's likeness to first love, sadly beautiful, with a hallowed sweetness in her melancholy features and grace in the flow of her sable robe. Next appears a shade of ruined loveliness with dust among her golden hair and her bright garments all faded and defaced, stealing from your glance with drooping head, as fearful of reproach: she was your fondest hope, but a delusive one; so call her Disappointment now. A sterner form succeeds, with a brow of wrinkles, a look and gesture of iron authority; there is no name for him unless it be Fatality—an emblem of the evil influence that rules your fortunes, a demon to whom you subjected yourself by some error at the outset of life, and were bound his slave for ever by once obeying him. See those fiendish lineaments graven on the darkness, the writhed lip of scorn, the mockery of that living eye, the pointed finger touching the sore place in your heart! Do you remember any act of enormous folly at which you would blush even in the remotest cavern of the earth? Then recognize your shame.

Pass, wretched band! Well for the wakeful one if, riotously miserable, a fiercer tribe do not surround him—the devils of a guilty heart that holds its hell within itself. What if Remorse should assume the features of an injured friend? What if the fiend should come in woman's garments with a pale beauty amid sin and desolation, and lie down by your side? What if he should stand at your bed's foot in the likeness of a corpse with a bloody stain upon the shroud? Sufficient without such guilt is this nightmare of the soul, this heavy, heavy sinking of the spirits, this wintry gloom about the heart, this indistinct horror of the mind blending itself with the darkness of the chamber.

By a desperate effort you start upright, breaking from a sort of conscious sleep and gazing wildly round the bed, as if the fiends were anywhere but in your haunted mind. At the same moment the slumbering embers on the hearth send forth a gleam which palely illuminates the whole outer room and flickers through the door of the bedchamber, but cannot quite dispel its obscurity. Your eye searches for whatever may remind you of the living world. With eager minuteness you take note of the table near the fireplace, the book with an ivory knife between its leaves, the unfolded letter, the hat and the fallen glove. Soon the flame vanishes, and with it the whole scene is gone, though its image remains an instant in your mind's eye when darkness has swallowed the reality. Throughout the chamber there is the same obscurity as before, but not the same gloom within your breast.

As your head falls back upon the pillow you think—in a whisper be it spoken—how pleasant in these night solitudes would be the rise and fall of a softer breathing than your own, the slight pressure of a tenderer bosom, the quiet throb of a purer heart, imparting its peacefulness to your troubled one, as if the fond sleeper were involving you in her dream. Her influence is over you, though she have no existence but in that momentary image. You sink down in a flowery spot on the borders of sleep and wakefulness, while your thoughts rise before you in pictures, all disconnected, yet all assimilated by a pervading gladsomeness and beauty. The wheeling of gorgeous squadrons that glitter in the sun is succeeded by the merriment of children round the door of a schoolhouse beneath the glimmering shadow of old trees at the corner of a rustic lane. You stand in the sunny rain of a summer shower, and wander among the sunny trees of an autumnal wood, and look upward at the brightest of all rainbows overarching the unbroken sheet of snow on the American side of Niagara. Your mind struggles pleasantly between the dancing radiance round the hearth of a young man and his recent bride and the twittering flight of birds in spring about their new-made nest. You feel the merry bounding of a ship before the breeze, and watch the tuneful feet of rosy girls as they twine their last and merriest dance in a splendid ball-room, and find yourself in the brilliant circle of a crowded theatre as the curtain falls over a light and airy scene.

With an involuntary start you seize hold on consciousness, and prove yourself but half-awake by running a doubtful parallel between human life and the hour which has now elapsed. In both you emerge from mystery, pass through a vicissitude that you can but imperfectly control, and are borne onward to another mystery. Now comes the peal of the distant clock with fainter and fainter strokes as you plunge farther into the wilderness of sleep. It is the knell of a temporary death. Your spirit has departed, and strays like a free citizen among the people of a shadowy world, beholding strange sights, yet without wonder or dismay. So calm, perhaps, will be the final change—so undisturbed, as if among familiar things, the entrance of the soul to its eternal home.

AN ANGEL IN DISGUISE*

T.S. Arthur

Idleness, vice, and intemperance had done their miserable work, and the dead mother lay cold and still amid her wretched children. She had fallen upon the threshold of her own door in a drunken fit, and died in the presence of her frightened little ones.

Death touches the spring of our common humanity. This woman had been despised, scoffed at, and angrily denounced by nearly every man, woman, and child in the village; but now, as the fact of her death was passed from lip to lip, in subdued tones, pity took the place of anger, and sorrow of denunciation. Neighbours went hastily to the old tumble-down hut, in which she had secured little more than a place of shelter from summer heats and winter cold: some with grave-clothes for a decent interment of the body; and some with food for the half-starving children, three in number. Of these, John, the oldest, a boy of twelve, was a stout lad, able to earn his living with any farmer. Kate, between ten and eleven, was bright, active girl, out of whom something clever might be made, if in good hands; but poor little Maggie, the youngest, was hopelessly diseased. Two years before a fall from a window had injured her spine, and she had not been able to leave her bed since, except when lifted in the arms of her mother.

'What is to be done with the children?' That was the chief question now. The dead mother would go underground, and be forever beyond all care or concern of the villagers. But the children must not be left to starve. After considering the matter, and talking it over with his wife, farmer Jones said that he would take John, and do well by him, now that his mother was out of the way; and Mrs Ellis, who had been looking out for a bound girl, concluded that it would be charitable in

---

*'An Angel in Disguise' (1851) was featured in Arthur's collection, *After a Shadow and Other Stories.* 'The sweetness of that sick child, looking ever to her in love, patience, and gratitude, was as honey to her soul, and she carried her in her heart as well as in her arms, a precious burden.'

her to make choice of Katy, even though she was too young to be of much use for several years.

'I could do much better, I know,' said Mrs Ellis; 'but as no one seems inclined to take her, I must act from a sense of duty expect to have trouble with the child; for she's an undisciplined thing—used to having her own way.'

But no one said 'I'll take Maggie.' Pitying glances were cast on her wan and wasted form and thoughts were troubled on her account. Mothers brought cast-off garments and, removing her soiled and ragged clothes, dressed her in clean attire. The sad eyes and patient face of the little one touched many hearts, and even knocked at them for entrance. But none opened to take her in. Who wanted a bed-ridden child?

'Take her to the poorhouse,' said a rough man, of whom the question 'What's to be done with Maggie?' was asked. 'Nobody's going to be bothered with her.'

'The poorhouse is a sad place for a sick and helpless child,' answered one.

'For your child or mine,' said the other, lightly speaking; 'but for tis brat it will prove a blessed change, she will be kept clean, have healthy food, and be doctored, which is more than can be said of her past condition.'

There was reason in that, but still it didn't satisfy. The day following the day of death was made the day of burial. A few neighbours were at the miserable hovel, but none followed dead cart as it bore the unhonoured remains to its pauper grave. Farmer Jones, after the coffin was taken out, placed John in his wagon and drove away, satisfied that he had done his part. Mrs Ellis spoke to Kate with a hurried air, 'Bid your sister good bye,' and drew the tearful children apart ere scarcely their lips had touched in a sobbing farewell. Hastily others went out, some glancing at Maggie, and some resolutely refraining from a look, until all had gone. She was alone! Just beyond the threshold Joe Thompson, the wheelwright, paused, and said to the blacksmith's wife, who was hastening off with the rest.

'It's a cruel thing to leave her so.'

'Then take her to the poorhouse: she'll have to go there,' answered the blacksmith's wife, springing away, and leaving Joe behind.

For a little while the man stood with a puzzled air; then he turned back, and went into the hovel again. Maggie with painful effort, had raised herself to an upright position and was sitting on the bed, straining her eyes upon the door out of which all had just departed, A vague terror had come into her thin white face.

'O, Mr Thompson!' she cried out, catching her suspended breath, 'don't leave me here all alone!'

Though rough in exterior, Joe Thompson, the wheelwright, had a heart, and it was very tender in some places. He liked children, and was pleased to have them come to his shop, where sleds and wagons were made or mended for the village lads without a draft on their hoarded sixpences.

'No, dear,' he answered, in a kind voice, going to the bed, and stooping down over the child, 'You sha'n't be left here alone.' Then he wrapped her with the gentleness almost of a woman, in the clean bedclothes which some neighbour had brought; and, lifting her in his strong arms, bore her out into the air and across the field that lay between the hovel and his home.

Now, Joe Thompson's wife, who happened to be childless, was not a woman of saintly temper, nor much given to self-denial for others' good, and Joe had well-grounded doubts touching the manner of greeting he should receive on his arrival. Mrs Thompson saw him approaching from the window, and with ruffling feathers met him a few paces from the door, as he opened the garden gate, and came in. He bore a precious burden, and he felt it to be so. As his arms held the sick child to his breast, a sphere of tenderness went out from her, and penetrated his feelings. A bond had already corded itself around them both, and love was springing into life.

'What have you there?' sharply questioned Mrs Thompson.

Joe, felt the child start and shrink against him. He did not reply, except by a look that was pleading and cautionary, that said, 'Wait a moment for explanations, and be gentle'; and, passing in, carried Maggie to the small chamber on the first floor, and laid her on a bed. Then, stepping back, he shut the door, and stood face to face with his vinegar-tempered wife in the passage-way outside.

'You haven't brought home that sick brat!' Anger and astonishment were in the tones of Mrs Joe Thompson; her face was in a flame.

'I think women's hearts are sometimes very hard,' said Joe. Usually Joe Thompson got out of his wife's way, or kept rigidly silent and non-combative when she fired up on any subject; it was with some surprise, therefore, that she now encountered a firmly-set countenance and a resolute pair of eyes.

'Women's hearts are not half so hard as men's!'

Joe saw, by a quick intuition, that his resolute bearing had impressed his wife and he answered quickly, and with real indignation, 'Be that as it may, every woman at the funeral turned her eyes steadily from the sick child's face, and when the cart went off with her dead mother, hurried away, and left her alone in that old hut, with the sun not an hour in the sky.'

'Where were John and Kate?' asked Mrs Thompson.

'Farmer Jones tossed John into his wagon, and drove off. Katie went home with Mrs Ellis; but nobody wanted the poor sick one. 'Send her to the poorhouse,' was the cry.'

'Why didn't you let her go, then. What did you bring her here for?'

'She can't walk to the poorhouse,' said Joe; 'somebody's arms must carry her, and mine are strong enough for that task.'

'Then why didn't you keep on? Why did you stop here?' demanded the wife.

'Because I'm not apt to go on fools' errands. The Guardians must first be seen, and a permit obtained.'

There was no gainsaying this.

'When will you see the Guardians?' was asked, with irrepressible impatience.

'To-morrow.'

'Why put it off till to-morrow? Go at once for the permit, and get the whole thing off of your hands to-night.'

'Jane,' said the wheelwright, with an impressiveness of tone that greatly subdued his wife, 'I read in the Bible sometimes, and find much said about little children. How the Savior rebuked the disciples who would not receive them; how he took them up in his arms, and blessed them; and how he said that 'whosoever gave them even a cup of cold water should not go unrewarded.' Now, it is a small thing for us to keep this poor motherless little one for a single night; to be kind to her for a single night; to make her life comfortable for a single night.'

The voice of the strong, rough man shook, and he turned his head away, so that the moisture in his eyes might not be seen. Mrs Thompson did not answer, but a soft feeling crept into her heart.

'Look at her kindly, Jane; speak to her kindly,' said Joe. 'Think of her dead mother, and the loneliness, the pain, the sorrow that must be on all her coming life.' The softness of his heart gave unwonted eloquence to his lips.

Mrs Thompson did not reply, but presently turned towards the little chamber where her husband had deposited Maggie; and, pushing open the door, went quietly in. Joe did not follow; he saw that, her state had changed, and felt that it would be best to leave her alone with the child. So he went to his shop, which stood near the house, and worked until dusky evening released him from labour. A light shining through the little chamber windows was the first object that attracted Joe's attention on turning towards the house: it was a good omen. The path led him by this windows and, when opposite, he could not help pausing to look in. It was now dark enough outside to screen him from observation. Maggie lay, a little raised on the pillow with the lamp shining full upon her face. Mrs Thompson was sitting by the bed, talking to the child; but her back was towards the window, so that her countenance was not seen. From Maggie's face, therefore, Joe must read the character of their intercourse. He saw that her eyes were intently fixed upon his wife; that now and then a few words came, as if in answers from her lips; that her expression was sad and tender; but he saw nothing of bitterness or pain. A deep-drawn breath was followed by one of relief, as a weight lifted itself from his heart.

On entering, Joe did not go immediately to the little chamber. His heavy tread about the kitchen brought his wife somewhat hurriedly from the room where she had been with Maggie. Joe thought it best not to refer to the child, nor to manifest any concern in regard to her.

'How soon will supper be ready?' he asked.

'Right soon,' answered Mrs Thompson, beginning to bustle about. There was no asperity in her voice.

After washing from his hands and face the dust and soil of work, Joe left the kitchen, and went to the little bedroom. A pair of large bright eyes looked up at him from the snowy bed; looked at him tenderly, gratefully, pleadingly. How his heart swelled in his bosom! With what a quicker motion came the heart-beats! Joe sat down, and now, for the first time, examining the thin frame carefully under the lamp light, saw that it was an attractive face, and full of a childish sweetness which suffering had not been able to obliterate.

'Your name is Maggie?' he said, as he sat down and took her soft little hand in his.

'Yes, sir.' Her voice struck a chord that quivered in a low strain of music.

'Have you been sick long?'

'Yes, sir.' What a sweet patience was in her tone!

'Has the doctor been to see you?'

'He used to come.'

'But not lately?'

'No, sir.'

'Have you any pain?'

'Sometimes, but not now.'

'When had you pain?'

'This morning my side ached, and my back hurt when you carried me.'

'It hurts you to be lifted or moved about?'

'Yes, sir.'

'Your side doesn't ache now?'

'No, sir.'

'Does it ache a great deal?'

'Yes, sir; but it hasn't ached any since I've been on this soft bed.'

'The soft bed feels good.'

'O, yes, sir—so good!' What a satisfaction, mingled with gratitude, was in her voice!

'Supper is ready,' said Mrs Thompson, looking into the room a little while afterwards.

Joe glanced from his wife's face to that of Maggie; she understood him, and answered—

'She can wait until we are done; then I will bring her somethings to eat.' There was an effort at indifference on the part of Mrs Thompson, but her husband had seen her through the window, and understood that the coldness was assumed. Joe waited, after sitting down to the table, for his wife to introduce the subject uppermost in both of their thoughts; but she kept silent on that theme, for many minutes, and he maintained a like reserve. At last she said, abruptly—

'What are you going to do with that child?'

'I thought you understood me that she was to go to the poorhouse,' replied Joe, as if surprised at her question.

Mrs Thompson looked rather strangely at her husband for sonic moments, and then dropped her eyes. The subject was not again referred to during the meal. At its close, Mrs Thompson toasted a slice of bread, and softened, it with milk and butter; adding to this a cup of tea, she took them into Maggie, and held the small waiter, on which she had placed them, while the hungry child ate with every sign of pleasure.

'Is it good?' asked Mrs Thompson, seeing with what a keen relish the food was taken.

The child paused with the cup in her hand, and answered with a look of gratitude that awoke to new life old human feelings which had been slumbering in her heart for half a score of years.

'We'll keep her a day or two longer; she is so weak and helpless,' said Mrs Joe Thompson, in answer to her husband's remark, at breakfast-time on the next morning, that he must step down and see the Guardians of the Poor about Maggie.

'She'll be so much in your way,' said Joe.

'I sha'n't mind that for a day or two. Poor thing!'

Joe did not see the Guardians of the Poor on that day, on the next, nor on the day following. In fact, he never saw them at all on Maggie's account, for in less than a week Mrs Joe Thompson would as soon leave thought of taking up her own abode in the alms-house as sending Maggie there.

What light and blessing did that sick and helpless child bring to the home of Joe Thompson, the poor wheelwright! It had been dark, and cold, and miserable there for a long time just because his wife had nothing to love and care for out of herself, and so became sore, irritable, ill-tempered, and self-afflicting in the desolation of her woman's nature. Now the sweetness of that sick child, looking ever to her in love, patience, and gratitude, was as honey to her soul, and she carried her in her heart as well as in her arms, a precious burden. As for Joe Thompson, there was not a man in all the neighbourhood who drank daily of a more precious wine of life than he. An angel had come into his house, disguised as a sick, helpless, and miserable child, and filled all its dreary chambers with the sunshine of love.

A FIGHT WITH A CANNON

Victor Hugo

One of the carronades of the battery, a twenty-four pound cannon, had become loose.

La vieuville was suddenly cut short by a cry of despair, and a the same time a noise was heard wholly unlike any other sound. The cry and sounds came from within the vessel.

The captain and lieutenant rushed toward the gun-deck but could not get down. All the gunners were pouring up in dismay.

Something terrible had just happened.

One of the carronades of the battery, a twenty-four pounder, had broken loose.

This is the most dangerous accident that can possibly take place on shipboard. Nothing more terrible can happen to a sloop of was in open sea and under full sail.

A cannon that breaks its moorings suddenly becomes some strange, supernatural beast. It is a machine transformed into a monster. That short mass on wheels moves like a billiard-ball, rolls with the rolling of the ship, plunges with the pitching goes, comes, stops, seems to meditate, starts on its course again, shoots like an arrow from one end of the vessel to the other, whirls around, slips away, dodges, rears, bangs, crashes, kills, exterminates. It is a battering ram capriciously assaulting a wall. Add to this the fact that the ram is of metal, the wall of wood.

It is matter set free; one might say, this eternal slave was avenging itself; it seems as if the total depravity concealed in what we call inanimate things has escaped, and burst forth all of a sudden; it appears to lose patience, and to take a strange mysterious revenge; nothing more relentless than this wrath of the inanimate. This enraged lump leaps like a panther, it has the clumsiness of an elephant, the nimbleness of a mouse, the obstinacy of an ox, the uncertainty of the billows, the zigzag of the lightning, the deafness of the grave. It weighs ten thousand pounds, and it rebounds like a child's ball. It spins and then abruptly darts off at right angles.

And what is to be done? How put an end to it? A tempest ceases, a cyclone passes over, a wind dies down, a broken mast can be replaced, a leak can be stopped, a fire extinguished, but what will become of this enormous brute of bronze. How can it be captured? You can reason with a bulldog, astonish a bull, fascinate a boa, frighten a tiger, tame a lion; but you have no resource against this monster, a loose cannon. You cannot kill it, it is dead; and at the same time it lives. It lives with a sinister life which comes to it from the infinite. The deck beneath it gives it full swing. It is moved by the ship, which is moved by the sea, which is moved by the wind. This destroyer is a toy. The ship, the waves, the winds, all play with it, hence its frightful animation. What is to be done with this apparatus? How fetter this stupendous engine of destruction? How anticipate its comings and goings, its returns, its stops, its shocks? Any one of its blows on the side of the ship may stave it in. How foretell its frightful meanderings? It is dealing with a projectile, which alters its mind, which seems to have ideas, and changes its direction every instant. How check the course of what must be avoided? The horrible cannon struggles, advances, backs, strikes right, strikes left, retreats, passes by, disconcerts expectation, grinds up obstacles, crushes men like flies. All the terror of the situation is in the fluctuations of the flooring. How fight an inclined plane subject to caprices? The ship has, so to speak, in its belly, an imprisoned thunderstorm, striving to escape; something like a thunderbolt rumbling above an earthquake.

In an instant the whole crew was on foot. It was the fault of the gun captain, who had neglected to fasten the screw-nut of the mooring-chain, and had insecurely clogged the four wheels of the gun carriage; this gave play to the sole and the framework, separated the two platforms, and the breeching. The tackle had given way, so that the cannon was no longer firm on its carriage. The stationary breeching, which prevents recoil, was not in use at this time. A heavy sea struck the port, the carronade, insecurely fastened, had recoiled and broken its chain, and began its terrible course over the deck.

To form an idea of this strange sliding, let one imagine a drop of water running over a glass.

At the moment when the fastenings gave way, the gunners were in the battery, some in groups, others scattered about, busied with the customary work among sailors getting ready for a signal for action. The carronade, hurled forward by the pitching of the vessel, made a gap in this crowd of men and crushed four at the first blow; then sliding back and shot out again as the ship rolled, it cut in two a fifth unfortunate, and knocked a piece of the battery against the larboard side with such force as to unship it. This caused the cry of distress just heard. All the men rushed to the companion-way. The gun-deck was vacated in a twinkling.

The enormous gun was left alone. It was given up to itself. It was its own master and master of the ship. It could do what it pleased. This whole crew, accustomed to laugh in time of battle, now trembled. To describe the terror is impossible.

Captain Boisberthelot and Lieutenant la Vieuville, although both dauntless men, stopped at the head of the companion-way and, dumb, pale, and hesitating, looked down on the deck below. Someone elbowed past and went down.

It was their passenger, the peasant, the man of whom they had just been speaking a moment before.

Reaching the foot of the companion-way, he stopped.

The cannon was rushing back and forth on the deck. One might have supposed it to be the living chariot of the Apocalypse. The marine lantern swinging overhead added a dizzy shifting of light and shade to the picture. The form of the cannon disappeared in the violence of its course, and it looked now black in the light, now mysteriously white in the darkness.

It went on in its destructive work. It had already shattered four other guns and made two gaps in the side of the ship, fortunately above the water-line, but where the water would come in, in case of heavy weather. It rushed frantically against the framework; the strong timbers withstood the shock; the curved shape of the wood gave them great power of resistance; but they creaked beneath the blows of this huge club, beating on all sides at once, with a strange sort of ubiquity. The percussions of a grain of shot shaken in a bottle are not swifter or more senseless. The four wheels passed back and forth over the dead men, cutting them, carving them, slashing them, till the five corpses were a score of stumps rolling across the deck; the heads of the dead men seemed to cry out; streams of blood curled over the deck with the rolling of the vessel; the planks, damaged in several places, began to gape open. The whole ship was filled with the horrid noise and confusion.

The captain promptly recovered his presence of mind and ordered everything that could check and impede the cannon's mad course to be thrown through the hatchway down on the gun-deck—mattresses, hammocks, spare sails, rolls of cordage, bags belonging to the crew, and bales of counterfeit assignats, of which the corvette carried a large quantity—a characteristic piece of English villainy regarded as legitimate warfare.

But what could these rags do? As nobody dared to go below to dispose of them properly, they were reduced to lint in a few minutes.

There was just sea enough to make the accident as bad as possible. A tempest would have been desirable, for it might have upset the cannon, and with its four wheels once in the air there would be some hope of getting it under control. Meanwhile, the havoc increased.

There were splits and fractures in the masts, which are set into the framework of the keel and rise above the decks of ships like great, round pillars. The convulsive blows of the cannon had cracked the mizzenmast, and had cut into the mainmast.

The battery was being ruined. Ten pieces out of thirty were disabled; the breaches in the side of the vessel were increasing, and the corvette was beginning to leak.

The old passenger having gone down to the gun-deck, stood like a man of stone at the foot of the steps. He cast a stern glance over this scene of devastation. He did not move. It seemed impossible to take a step forward. Every movement of the loose carronade threatened the ship's destruction. A few moments more and shipwreck would be inevitable.

They must perish or put a speedy end to the disaster; some course must be decided on; but what? What an opponent was this carronade! Something must be done to stop this terrible madness—to capture this lightning—to overthrow this thunderbolt.

Boisberthelot said to La Vieuville:

'Do you believe in God, chevalier?'

La Vieuville replied:

'Yes—no. Sometimes.'

'During a tempest?'

'Yes, and in moments like this.'

'God alone can save us from this,' said Boisberthelot.

Everybody was silent, letting the carronade continue its horrible din.

Outside, the waves beating against the ship responded with their blows to the shocks of the cannon. It was like two hammers alternating.

Suddenly, in the midst of this inaccessible ring, where the escaped cannon was leaping, a man was seen to appear, with an iron bar in his hand. He was the author of the catastrophe, the captain of the gun, guilty of criminal carelessness, and the cause of the accident, the master of the carronade. Having done the mischief, he was anxious to repair it. He had seized the iron bar in one hand, a tiller-rope with a slip-noose in the other, and jumped, down the hatchway to the gun-deck.

Then began an awful sight; a Titanic scene; the contest between gun and gunner; the battle of matter and intelligence; the duel between man and the inanimate.

The man stationed himself in a corner, and, with bar and rope in his two hands, he leaned against one of the riders, braced himself on his legs, which seemed two steel posts; and livid, calm, tragic, as if rooted to the deck, he waited.

He waited for the cannon to pass by him.

The gunner knew his gun, and it seemed to him as if the gun ought to know him. He had lived long with it. How many times he had thrust his hand into its mouth! It was his own familiar monster. He began to speak to it as if it were his dog.

'Come!' he said. Perhaps he loved it.

He seemed to wish it to come to him.

But to come to him was to come upon him. And then he would be lost. How could he avoid being crushed? That was the question. All looked on in terror.

Not a breast breathed freely, unless perhaps that of the old man, who was alone in the battery with the two contestants, a stern witness.

He might be crushed himself by the cannon. He did not stir.

Beneath them the sea blindly directed the contest.

At the moment when the gunner, accepting this frightful hand-to-hand conflict, challenged the cannon, some chance rocking of the sea caused the carronade to remain for an instant motionless and as if stupefied. 'Come, now!' said the man.

It seemed to listen.

Suddenly it leaped toward him. The man dodged the blow.

The battle began. Battle unprecedented. Frailty struggling against the invulnerable. The gladiator of flesh attacking the beast of brass. On one side, brute force; on the other, a human soul.

All this was taking place in semi-darkness. It was like the shadowy vision of a miracle.

A soul—strange to say, one would have thought the cannon also had a soul; but a soul full of hatred and rage. This sightless thing seemed to have eyes. The monster appeared to lie in wait for the man. One would have at least believed that there was craft in this mass. It also chose its time. It was a strange, gigantic insect of metal, having or seeming to have the will of a demon. For a moment this colossal locust would beat against the low ceiling overhead, then it would come down on its four wheels like a tiger on its four paws, and begin to run at the man. He, supple, nimble, expert, writhed away like an adder from all these lightning movements. He avoided a collision, but the blows which he parried fell against the, vessel, and continued their work of destruction.

An end of broken chain was left hanging to the carronade. This chain had in some strange way become twisted about the screw of the cascabel. One end of the chain was fastened to the gun-carriage. The other, left loose, whirled desperately about the cannon, making all its blows more dangerous.

The screw held it in a firm grip, adding a thong to a battering-ram, making a terrible whirlwind around the cannon, an iron lash in a brazen hand. This chain complicated the contest.

However, the man went on fighting. Occasionally, it was the man who attacked the cannon; he would creep along the side of the vessel, bar and rope in hand; and the cannon, as if it understood, and as though suspecting some snare, would flee away. The man, bent on victory, pursued it.

Such things cannot long continue. The cannon seemed to say to itself, all of a sudden, 'Come, now! Make an end of it!' and it stopped. One felt that the crisis was at hand. The cannon, as if in suspense, seemed to have, or really had—for to all it was a living being—a ferocious malice prepense. It made a sudden, quick dash at the gunner. The gunner sprang out of the way, let it pass by, and cried out to it with a laugh, 'Try it again!' The cannon, as if enraged, smashed a carronade on the port side; then, again seized by the invisible sling which controlled it, it was hurled to the starboard side at the man, who made his escape. Three carronades gave way under the blows of the cannon; then, as if blind and not knowing what more to do, it turned its back on the man, rolled from stern to bow, injured the stern and made a breach in the planking of the prow. The man took refuge at the foot of the steps, not far from the old man who was looking on. The gunner held his iron bar in rest. The cannon seemed to notice it, and without taking the trouble to turn around, slid back on the man, swift as the blow of an axe. The man, driven against the side of the ship, was lost. The whole crew cried out with horror.

But the old passenger, till this moment motionless, darted forth more quickly than any of this wildly swift rapidity. He seized a package of counterfeit assignats, and, at the risk of being crushed, succeeded in throwing it between the wheels of the carronade. This decisive and perilous movement could not have been made with more exactness and precision by a man trained in all the exercises described in Durosel's 'Manual of Gun Practice at Sea.'

The package had the effect of a clog. A pebble may stop a log, the branch of a tree turn aside an avalanche. The carronade stumbled. The gunner, taking advantage of this critical opportunity, plunged his iron bar between the spokes of one of the hind wheels. The cannon stopped. It leaned forward. The man, using the bar as a lever, held it in equilibrium. The heavy mass was overthrown, with the crash of a falling bell, and the man, rushing with all his might, dripping with perspiration, passed the slip noose around the bronze neck of the subdued monster.

It was ended. The man had conquered. The ant had control over the mastodon; the pygmy had taken the thunderbolt prisoner.

The mariners and sailors clapped their hands.

The whole crew rushed forward with cables and chains, and in an instant the cannon was secured.

The gunner saluted the passenger.

'Sir,' he said, 'you have saved my life.'

The old man had resumed his impassive attitude, and made no reply.

The man had conquered, but the cannon might be said to have conquered as well. Immediate shipwreck had been avoided, but the corvette was not saved. The damage to the vessel seemed beyond repair. There were five breaches in her sides, one, very large, in the bow; twenty of the thirty carronades lay useless in their frames. The one which had just been captured and chained again was disabled; the screw of the cascabel was sprung, and consequently levelling the gun made impossible. The battery was reduced to nine pieces. The ship was leaking. It was necessary to repair the damages at once, and to work the pumps.

The gun-deck, now that one could look over it, was frightful to behold. The inside of an infuriated elephant's cage would not be more completely demolished.

However great might be the necessity of escaping observation, the necessity of immediate safety was still more imperative to the corvette. They had been obliged to light up the deck with lanterns hung here and there on the sides.

However, all the while this tragic play was going on, the crew were absorbed by a question of life and death, and they were wholly ignorant of what was taking place outside the vessel. The fog had grown thicker; the weather had changed; the wind had worked its pleasure with the ship; they were out of their course, with Jersey and Guernsey close at hand, further to the south than they ought to have been, and in the midst of a heavy sea. Great billows kissed the gaping wounds of the vessel—kisses full of danger. The rocking of the sea threatened destruction. The breeze had become a gale. A squall, a tempest, perhaps, was brewing. It was impossible to see four waves ahead.

While the crew were hastily repairing the damages to the gun-deck, stopping the leaks, and putting in place the guns which had been uninjured in the disaster, the old passenger had gone on deck again.

He stood with his back against the mainmast.

He had not noticed a proceeding which had taken place on the vessel. The Chevalier de la Vieuville had drawn up the marines in line on both sides of the mainmast, and at the sound of the boatswain's whistle the sailors formed in line, standing on the yards.

The Count de Boisberthelot approached the passenger.

Behind the captain walked a man, haggard, out of breath, his dress disordered, but still with a look of satisfaction on his face.

It was the gunner who had just shown himself so skilful in subduing monsters, and who had gained the mastery over the cannon.

The count gave the military salute to the old man in peasant's dress, and said to him:

'General, there is the man.'

The gunner remained standing, with downcast eyes, in military attitude.

The Count de Boisberthelot continued:

'General, in consideration of what this man has done, do you not think there is something due him from his commander?'

'I think so,' said the old man.

'Please give your orders,' replied Boisberthelot.

'It is for you to give them, you are the captain.'

'But you are the general,' replied Boisberthelot.

The old man looked at the gunner.

'Come forward,' he said.

The gunner approached.

The old man turned toward the Count de Boisberthelot, took off the cross of Saint-Louis from the captain's coat and fastened it on the gunner's jacket.

'Hurrah!' cried the sailors.

The mariners presented arms.

And the old passenger, pointing to the dazzled gunner, added:

'Now, have this man shot.'

Dismay succeeded the cheering.

Then in the midst of the death-like stillness, the old man raised his voice and said, 'Carelessness has compromised this vessel. At this very hour it is perhaps lost. To be at sea is to be in front of the enemy. A ship making a voyage is an army waging war. The tempest is concealed, but it is at hand. The whole sea is an ambuscade. Death is the penalty of any misdemeanour committed in the face of the enemy. No fault is reparable. Courage should be rewarded, and negligence punished.'

These words fell one after another, slowly, solemnly, in a sort of inexorable metre, like the blows of an axe upon an oak.

And the man, looking at the soldiers, added:

'Let it be done.'

The man on whose jacket hung the shining cross of Saint-Louis bowed his head.

At a signal from Count de Boisberthelot, two sailors went below and came back bringing the hammock-shroud; the chaplain, who since they sailed had been at prayer in the officers' quarters, accompanied the two sailors; a sergeant detached twelve marines from the line and arranged them in two files, six by six; the gunner, without uttering a word, placed himself between the two files. The chaplain, crucifix in hand, advanced and stood beside him. 'March,' said the sergeant. The platoon marched with slow steps to the bow of the vessel. The two sailors, carrying the shroud, followed. A gloomy silence fell over the vessel. A hurricane howled in the distance.

A few moments later, a light flashed, a report sounded through the darkness, then all was still, and the sound of a body falling into the sea was heard.

The old passenger, still leaning against the mainmast, had crossed his arms, and was buried in thought.

Boisberthelot pointed to him with the forefinger of his left hand, and said to La Vieuville in a low voice:

'La Vendée has a head.'

COUSIN TRIBULATION'S STORY

Louisa May Alcott

Dear Merrys,

As a subject appropriate to the season, I want to tell you about a New Year's breakfast which I had when I was a little girl. What do you think it was? A slice of dry bread and an apple. This is how it happened, and it is a true story, every word.

As we came down to breakfast that morning, with very shiny faces and spandy clean aprons, we found father alone in the dining-room.

'Happy New Year, papa! Where is mother?' we cried.

'A little boy came begging and said they were starving at home, so your mother went to see and—ah, here she is.'

As papa spoke, in came mamma, looking very cold, rather sad, and very much excited.

'Children, don't begin till you hear what I have to say,' she cried; and we sat staring at her, with the breakfast untouched before us.

'Not far away from here, lies a poor woman with a little new-born baby. Six children are huddled into one bed to keep from freezing, for they have no fire. There is nothing to eat over there; and the oldest boy came here to tell me they were starving this bitter cold day. My little girls, will you give them your breakfast, as a New Year's gift?'

We sat silent a minute, and looked at the nice, hot porridge, creamy milk, and good bread and butter; for we were brought up like English children, and never drank tea or coffee, or ate anything but porridge for our breakfast.

'I wish we'd eaten it up,' thought I, for I was rather a selfish child, and very hungry.

'I'm so glad you come before we began,' said Nan, cheerfully.

'May I go and help carry it to the poor, little children?' asked Beth, who had the tenderest heart that ever beat under a pinafore.

'I can carry the lassy pot,' said little May, proudly giving the thing she loved best.

'And I shall take all the porridge,' I burst in, heartily ashamed of my first feeling.

'You shall put on your things and help me, and when we come back, we'll get something to eat,' said mother, beginning to pile the bread and butter into a big basket.

We were soon ready, and the procession set out. First, papa, with a basket of wood on one arm and coal on the other; mamma next, with a bundle of warm things and the teapot; Nan and I carried a pail of hot porridge between us, and each a pitcher of milk; Beth brought some cold meat, May the 'lassy pot,' and her old hood and boots; and Betsey, the girl, brought up the rear with a bag of potatoes and some meal.

Fortunately it was early, and we went along back streets, so few people saw us, and no one laughed at the funny party.

What a poor, bare, miserable place it was, to be sure,—broken windows, no fire, ragged clothes, wailing baby, sick mother, and a pile of pale, hungry children cuddled under one quilt, trying to keep warm. How the big eyes stared and the blue lips smiled as we came in!

'Ah, mein Gott! it is the good angels that come to us!' cried the poor woman, with tears of joy.

'Funny angels, in woollen hoods and red mittens,' said I; and they all laughed.

Then we fell to work, and in fifteen minutes, it really did seem as if fairies had been at work there. Papa made a splendid fire in the old fireplace and stopped up the broken window with his own hat and coat. Mamma set the shivering children round the fire, and wrapped the poor woman in warm things. Betsey and the rest of us spread the table, and fed the starving little ones.

'Das ist gute!' 'Oh, nice!' 'Der angel—Kinder!' cried the poor things as they ate and smiled and basked in the warm blaze. We had never been called 'angel-children' before, and we thought it very charming, especially I who had often been told I was 'a regular Sancho.' What fun it was! Papa, with a towel for an apron, fed the smallest child; mamma dressed the poor little new-born baby as tenderly as if it had been her own. Betsey gave the mother gruel and tea, and comforted her with assurance of better days for all. Nan, Lu, Beth, and May flew about among the seven children, talking and laughing and trying to understand their funny, broken English. It was a very happy breakfast, though we didn't get any of it; and when we came away, leaving them all so comfortable, and promising to bring clothes and food by and by, I think there were not in all the hungry little girls who gave away their breakfast, and contented themselves with a bit of bread and an apple of New Year's day.

ARABY*

James Joyce

North Richmond Street, being blind, was a quiet street except at the hour when the Christian Brothers' School set the boys free. An uninhabited house of two storeys stood at the blind end, detached from its neighbours in a square ground. The other houses of the street, conscious of decent lives within them, gazed at one another with brown imperturbable faces.

The former tenant of our house, a priest, had died in the back drawing-room. Air, musty from having been long enclosed, hung in all the rooms, and the waste room behind the kitchen was littered with old useless papers. Among these I found a few paper-covered books, the pages of which were curled and damp: *The Abbot*, by Walter Scott, *The Devout Communicant*, and *The Memoirs of Vidocq*. I liked the last best because its leaves were yellow. The wild garden behind the house contained a central apple-tree and a few straggling bushes, under one of which I found the late tenant's rusty bicycle-pump. He had been a very charitable priest; in his will he had left all his money to institutions and the furniture of his house to his sister.

When the short days of winter came, dusk fell before we had well eaten our dinners. When we met in the street the houses had grown sombre. The space of sky above us was the colour of ever-changing violet and towards it the lamps of the street lifted their feeble lanterns. The cold air stung us and we played till our bodies glowed. Our shouts echoed in the silent street. The career of our play brought us through the dark muddy lanes behind the houses, where we ran the gauntlet of the rough tribes from the cottages, to the back doors of the dark dripping gardens where odours arose from the ash pits, to the dark odorous stables where a coachman smoothed and combed the horse

---

*'Araby' was published in James Joyce's short story collection *Dubliners* in 1914. It is widely considered to be his finest short story, featured in our collection, *Short Stories for High School.*

or shook music from the buckled harness. When we returned to the street, light from the kitchen windows had filled the areas. If my uncle was seen turning the corner, we hid in the shadow until we had seen him safely housed. Or if Mangan's sister came out on the doorstep to call her brother in to his tea, we watched her from our shadow peer up and down the street. We waited to see whether she would remain or go in and, if she remained, we left our shadow and walked up to Mangan's steps resignedly. She was waiting for us, her figure defined by the light from the half-opened door. Her brother always teased her before he obeyed, and I stood by the railings looking at her. Her dress swung as she moved her body, and the soft rope of her hair tossed from side to side.

Every morning I lay on the floor in the front parlour watching her door. The blind was pulled down to within an inch of the sash so that I could not be seen. When she came out on the doorstep my heart leaped. I ran to the hall, seized my books and followed her. I kept her brown figure always in my eye and, when we came near the point at which our ways diverged, I quickened my pace and passed her. This happened morning after morning. I had never spoken to her, except for a few casual words, and yet her name was like a summons to all my foolish blood.

Her image accompanied me even in places the most hostile to romance. On Saturday evenings when my aunt went marketing I had to go to carry some of the parcels. We walked through the flaring streets, jostled by drunken men and bargaining women, amid the curses of labourers, the shrill litanies of shop-boys who stood on guard by the barrels of pigs' cheeks, the nasal chanting of street-singers, who sang a come-all-you about O'Donovan Rossa, or a ballad about the troubles in our native land. These noises converged in a single sensation of life for me: I imagined that I bore my chalice safely through a throng of foes. Her name sprang to my lips at moments in strange prayers and praises which I myself did not understand. My eyes were often full of tears (I could not tell why) and at times a flood from my heart seemed to pour itself out into my bosom. I thought little of the future. I did not know whether I would ever speak to her or not or, if I spoke to her, how I could tell her of my confused adoration. But my body was like a harp and her words and gestures were like fingers running upon the wires.

One evening I went into the back drawing-room in which the priest had died. It was a dark rainy evening and there was no sound in the house. Through one of the broken panes I heard the rain impinge upon the earth, the fine incessant needles of water playing in the sodden beds. Some distant lamp or lighted window gleamed below me. I was thankful that I could see so little. All my senses seemed to desire to veil themselves and, feeling that I was about to slip from them, I pressed the palms of my hands together until they trembled, murmuring: 'O love! O love!' many times.

At last she spoke to me. When she addressed the first words to me I was so confused that I did not know what to answer. She asked me was I going to Araby. I forgot whether I answered yes or no. It would be a splendid bazaar; she said she would love to go.

'And why can't you?' I asked.

While she spoke she turned a silver bracelet round and round her wrist. She could not go, she said, because there would be a retreat that week in her convent. Her brother and two other boys were fighting for their caps, and I was alone at the railings. She held one of the spikes, bowing her head towards me. The light from the lamp opposite our door caught the white curve of her neck, lit up her hair that rested there and, falling, lit up the hand upon the railing. It fell over one side of her dress and caught the white border of a petticoat, just visible as she stood at ease.

'It's well for you,' she said.

'If I go,' I said, 'I will bring you something.'

What innumerable follies laid waste my waking and sleeping thoughts after that evening! I wished to annihilate the tedious intervening days. I chafed against the work of school. At night in my bedroom and by day in the classroom her image came between me and the page I strove to read. The syllables of the word Araby were called to me through the silence in which my soul luxuriated and cast an Eastern enchantment over me. I asked for leave to go to the bazaar on Saturday night. My aunt was surprised, and hoped it was not some Freemason affair. I answered few questions in class. I watched my master's face pass from amiability to sternness; he hoped I was not beginning to idle. I could not call my wandering thoughts together. I had hardly any patience with the serious work of life which, now that it stood between me and my desire, seemed to me child's play, ugly monotonous child's play.

On Saturday morning I reminded my uncle that I wished to go to the bazaar in the evening. He was fussing at the hallstand, looking for the hat-brush, and answered me curtly:

'Yes, boy, I know.'

As he was in the hall I could not go into the front parlour and lie at the window. I left the house in bad humour and walked slowly towards the school. The air was pitilessly raw and already my heart misgave me.

When I came home to dinner my uncle had not yet been home. Still it was early. I sat staring at the clock for some time and, when its ticking began to irritate me, I left the room. I mounted the staircase and gained the upper part of the house. The high, cold, empty, gloomy rooms liberated me and I went from room to room singing. From the front window I saw my companions playing below in the street. Their cries reached me weakened and indistinct and, leaning my forehead against the cool glass, I looked over at the dark house where she lived. I may have stood there for an hour, seeing nothing but the brown-clad figure cast by my imagination, touched discreetly by the lamplight at the curved neck, at the hand upon the railings and at the border below the dress.

When I came downstairs again I found Mrs Mercer sitting at the fire. She was an old, garrulous woman, a pawnbroker's widow, who collected used stamps for some pious purpose. I had to endure the gossip of the tea-table. The meal was prolonged beyond an hour and still my uncle did not come. Mrs Mercer stood up to go: she was sorry she couldn't wait any longer, but it was after eight o'clock and she did not like to be out late, as the night air was bad for her. When she had gone I began to walk up and down the room, clenching my fists.

My aunt said, 'I'm afraid you may put off your bazaar for this night of Our Lord.'

At nine o'clock I heard my uncle's latchkey in the hall door. I heard him talking to himself and heard the hallstand rocking when it had received the weight of his overcoat. I could interpret these signs. When he was midway through his dinner I asked him to give me the money to go to the bazaar. He had forgotten.

'The people are in bed and after their first sleep now,' he said.

I did not smile. My aunt said to him energetically:

'Can't you give him the money and let him go? You've kept him late enough as it is.'

My uncle said he was very sorry he had forgotten. He said he believed in the old saying: 'All work and no play makes Jack a dull boy.' He asked me where I was going and, when I told him a second time, he asked me did I know *The Arab's Farewell to His Steed*. When I left the kitchen he was about to recite the opening lines of the piece to my aunt.

I held a florin tightly in my hand as I strode down Buckingham Street towards the station. The sight of the streets thronged with buyers and glaring with gas recalled to me the purpose of my journey. I took my seat in a third-class carriage of a deserted train. After an intolerable delay the train moved out of the station slowly. It crept onward among ruinous houses and over the twinkling river. At Westland Row Station a crowd of people pressed to the carriage doors; but the porters moved them back, saying that it was a special train for the bazaar. I remained alone in the bare carriage. In a few minutes the train drew up beside an improvised wooden platform. I passed out on to the road and saw by the lighted dial of a clock that it was ten minutes to ten. In front of me was a large building which displayed the magical name.

I could not find any sixpenny entrance and, fearing that the bazaar would be closed, I passed in quickly through a turnstile, handing a shilling to a weary-looking man. I found myself in a big hall girded at half its height by a gallery. Nearly all the stalls were closed and the greater part of the hall was in darkness. I recognized a silence like that which pervades a church after a service. I walked into the centre of the bazaar timidly. A few people were gathered about the stalls which were still open. Before a curtain, over which the words Caf Chantant were written in coloured lamps, two men were counting money on a salver.

I listened to the fall of the coins.

Remembering with difficulty why I had come, I went over to one of the stalls and examined porcelain vases and flowered tea-sets. At the door of the stall a young lady was talking and laughing with two young gentlemen. I remarked their English accents and listened vaguely to their conversation.

'O, I never said such a thing!'

'O, but you did!'

'O, but I didn't!'

'Didn't she say that?'

'Yes. I heard her.'

'O, there's a... fib!'

Observing me, the young lady came over and asked me did I wish to buy anything. The tone of her voice was not encouraging; she seemed to have spoken to me out of a sense of duty. I looked humbly at the great jars that stood like eastern guards at either side of the dark entrance to the stall and murmured:

'No, thank you.'

The young lady changed the position of one of the vases and went back to the two young men. They began to talk of the same subject. Once or twice the young lady glanced at me over her shoulder.

I lingered before her stall, though I knew my stay was useless, to make my interest in her wares seem the more real. Then I turned away slowly and walked down the middle of the bazaar. I allowed the two pennies to fall against the sixpence in my pocket. I heard a voice call from one end of the gallery that the light was out. The upper part of the hall was now completely dark.

Gazing up into the darkness I saw myself as a creature driven and derided by vanity; and my eyes burned with anguish and anger.

A DARK BROWN DOG

Stephen Crane

A child was standing on a street-corner. He leaned with one shoulder against a high board-fence and swayed the other to and fro, the while kicking carelessly at the gravel.

Sunshine beat upon the cobbles, and a lazy summer wind raised yellow dust which trailed in clouds down the avenue. Clattering trucks moved with indistinctness through it. The child stood dreamily gazing.

After a time, a little dark-brown dog came trotting with an intent air down the sidewalk. A short rope was dragging from his neck. Occasionally he trod upon the end of it and stumbled.

He stopped opposite the child, and the two regarded each other. The dog hesitated for a moment, but presently he made some little advances with his tail. The child put out his hand and called him. In an apologetic manner the dog came close, and the two had an interchange of friendly pattings and waggles. The dog became more enthusiastic with each moment of the interview, until with his gleeful caperings he threatened to overturn the child. Whereupon the child lifted his hand and struck the dog a blow upon the head.

This thing seemed to overpower and astonish the little dark-brown dog, and wounded him to the heart. He sank down in despair at the child's feet. When the blow was repeated, together with an admonition in childish sentences, he turned over upon his back, and held his paws in a peculiar manner. At the same time with his ears and his eyes he offered a small prayer to the child.

He looked so comical on his back, and holding his paws peculiarly, that the child was greatly amused and gave him little taps repeatedly, to keep him so. But the little dark-brown dog took this chastisement in the most serious way, and no doubt considered that he had committed some grave crime, for he wriggled contritely and showed his repentance in every way that was in his power. He pleaded with the child and petitioned him, and offered more prayers.

At last the child grew weary of this amusement and turned toward home. The dog was praying at the time. He lay on his back and turned his eyes upon the retreating form.

Presently he struggled to his feet and started after the child. The latter wandered in a perfunctory way toward his home, stopping at times to investigate various matters. During one of these pauses he discovered the little dark-brown dog who was following him with the air of a footpad.

The child beat his pursuer with a small stick he had found. The dog lay down and prayed until the child had finished, and resumed his journey. Then he scrambled erect and took up the pursuit again.

On the way to his home the child turned many times and beat the dog, proclaiming with childish gestures that he held him in contempt as an unimportant dog, with no value save for a moment. For being this quality of animal the dog apologized and eloquently expressed regret, but he continued stealthily to follow the child. His manner grew so very guilty that he slunk like an assassin.

When the child reached his door-step, the dog was industriously ambling a few yards in the rear. He became so agitated with shame when he again confronted the child that he forgot the dragging rope. He tripped upon it and fell forward.

The child sat down on the step and the two had another interview. During it the dog greatly exerted himself to please the child. He performed a few gambols with such abandon that the child suddenly saw him to be a valuable thing. He made a swift, avaricious charge and seized the rope.

He dragged his captive into a hall and up many long stairways in a dark tenement. The dog made willing efforts, but he could not hobble very skilfully up the stairs because he was very small and soft, and at last the pace of the engrossed child grew so energetic that the dog became panic-stricken. In his mind he was being dragged toward a grim unknown. His eyes grew wild with the terror of it. He began to wiggle his head frantically and to brace his legs.

The child redoubled his exertions. They had a battle on the stairs. The child was victorious because he was completely absorbed in his purpose, and because the dog was very small. He dragged his acquirement to the door of his home, and finally with triumph across the threshold.

No one was in. The child sat down on the floor and made overtures to the dog. These the dog instantly accepted. He beamed with affection upon his new friend. In a short time they were firm and abiding comrades.

When the child's family appeared, they made a great row. The dog was examined and commented upon and called names. Scorn was levelled at him from all eyes, so that he became much embarrassed and drooped like a scorched plant. But the child went sturdily to the centre of the floor, and, at the top of his voice, championed the dog. It happened that he was roaring protestations, with his arms clasped about the dog's neck, when the father of the family came in from work.

The parent demanded to know what the blazes they were making the kid howl for. It was explained in many words that the infernal kid wanted to introduce a disreputable dog into the family.

A family council was held. On this depended the dog's fate, but he in no way heeded, being busily engaged in chewing the end of the child's dress.

The affair was quickly ended. The father of the family, it appears, was in a particularly savage temper that evening, and when he perceived that it would amaze and anger everybody if such a dog were allowed to remain, he decided that it should be so. The child, crying softly, took his friend off to a retired part of the room to hobnob with him, while the father quelled a fierce rebellion of his wife. So it came to pass that the dog was a member of the household.

He and the child were associated together at all times save when the child slept. The child became a guardian and a friend. If the large folk kicked the dog and threw things at him, the child made loud and violent objections. Once when the child had run, protesting loudly, with tears raining down his face and his arms outstretched, to protect his friend, he had been struck in the head with a very large saucepan from the hand of his father, enraged at some seeming lack of courtesy in the dog. Ever after, the family were careful how they threw things at the dog. Moreover, the latter grew very skilful in avoiding missiles and feet. In a small room containing a stove, a table, a bureau and some chairs, he would display strategic ability of a high order, dodging, feinting and scuttling about among the furniture. He could force three or four people armed with brooms, sticks and handfuls of coal, to use all their ingenuity to get in a blow. And even when they did, it was seldom that they could do him a serious injury or leave any imprint.

But when the child was present, these scenes did not occur. It came to be recognized that if the dog was molested, the child would burst into sobs, and as the child, when started, was very riotous and practically unquenchable, the dog had therein a safeguard.

However, the child could not always be near. At night, when he was asleep, his dark-brown friend would raise from some black corner a wild, wailful cry, a song of infinite lowliness and despair, that would go shuddering and sobbing among the buildings of the block and cause people to swear. At these times the singer would often be chased all over the kitchen and hit with a great variety of articles.

Sometimes, too, the child himself used to beat the dog, although it is not known that he ever had what could be truly called a just cause. The dog always accepted these thrashings with an air of admitted guilt. He was too much of a dog to try to look to be a martyr or to plot revenge. He received the blows with deep humility, and furthermore he forgave his friend the moment the child had finished, and was ready to caress the child's hand with his little red tongue.

When misfortune came upon the child, and his troubles overwhelmed him, he would often crawl under the table and lay his small distressed head on the dog's back. The dog was ever sympathetic. It is not to be supposed that at such times he took occasion to refer to the unjust beatings his friend, when provoked, had administered to him.

He did not achieve any notable degree of intimacy with the other members of the family. He had no confidence in them, and the fear that he would express at their casual approach often exasperated them exceedingly. They used to gain a certain satisfaction in underfeeding him, but finally his friend the child grew to watch the matter with some care, and when he forgot it, the dog was often successful in secret for himself.

So the dog prospered. He developed a large bark, which came wondrously from such a small rug of a dog. He ceased to howl persistently at night. Sometimes, indeed, in his sleep, he would utter little yells, as from pain, but that occurred, no doubt, when in his dreams he encountered huge flaming dogs who threatened him direfully.

His devotion to the child grew until it was a sublime thing. He wagged at his approach; he sank down in despair at his departure. He could detect the sound of the child's step among all the noises of the neighbourhood. It was like a calling voice to him.

The scene of their companionship was a kingdom governed by this terrible potentate, the child; but neither criticism nor rebellion ever lived for an instant in the heart of the one subject. Down in the mystic, hidden fields of his little dog-soul bloomed flowers of love and fidelity and perfect faith.

The child was in the habit of going on many expeditions to observe strange things in the vicinity. On these occasions his friend usually jogged aimfully along behind. Perhaps, though, he went ahead. This necessitated his turning around every quarter-minute to make sure the child was coming. He was filled with a large idea of the importance of these journeys. He would carry himself with such an air! He was proud to be the retainer of so great a monarch.

One day, however, the father of the family got quite exceptionally drunk. He came home and held carnival with the cooking utensils, the furniture and his wife. He was in the midst of this recreation when the child, followed by the dark-brown dog, entered the room. They were returning from their voyages.

The child's practised eye instantly noted his father's state. He dived under the table, where experience had taught him was a rather safe place. The dog, lacking skill in such matters, was, of course, unaware of the true condition of affairs. He looked with interested eyes at his friend's sudden dive. He interpreted it to mean: Joyous gambol. He started to patter across the floor to join him. He was the picture of a little dark-brown dog en route to a friend.

The head of the family saw him at this moment. He gave a huge howl of joy, and knocked the dog down with a heavy coffee-pot. The dog, yelling in supreme astonishment and fear, writhed to his feet and ran for cover. The man kicked out with a ponderous foot. It caused the dog to swerve as if caught in a tide. A second blow of the coffee-pot laid him upon the floor.

Here the child, uttering loud cries, came valiantly forth like a knight. The father of the family paid no attention to these calls of the child, but advanced with glee upon the dog. Upon being knocked down twice in swift succession, the latter apparently gave up all hope of escape. He rolled over on his back and held his paws in a peculiar manner. At the same time with his eyes and his ears he offered up a small prayer.

But the father was in a mood for having fun, and it occurred to him that it would be a fine thing to throw the dog out of the window. So he reached down and grabbing the animal by a leg, lifted him, squirming, up. He swung him two or three times hilariously about his head, and then flung him with great accuracy through the window.

The soaring dog created a surprise in the block. A woman watering plants in an opposite window gave an involuntary shout and dropped a flower-pot. A man in another window leaned perilously out to watch the flight of the dog. A woman, who had been hanging out clothes in a yard, began to caper wildly. Her mouth was filled with clothes-pins, but her arms gave vent to a sort of exclamation. In appearance she was like a gagged prisoner. Children ran whooping.

The dark-brown body crashed in a heap on the roof of a shed five stories below. From thence it rolled to the pavement of an alleyway.

The child in the room far above burst into a long, dirge-like cry, and toddled hastily out of the room. It took him a long time to reach the alley, because his size compelled him to go downstairs backward, one step at a time, and holding with both hands to the step above.

When they came for him later, they found him seated by the body of his dark-brown friend.

THE CAT

Mary E. Wilkins Freeman

The snow was falling, and the Cat's fur was stiffly pointed with it, but he was imperturbable. He sat crouched, ready for the death-spring, as he had sat for hours. It was night—but that made no difference—all times were as one to the Cat when he was in wait for prey. Then, too, he was under no constraint of human will, for he was living alone that winter. Nowhere in the world was any voice calling him; on no hearth was there a waiting dish. He was quite free except for his own desires, which tyrannized over him when unsatisfied as now. The Cat was very hungry—almost famished, in fact. For days the weather had been very bitter, and all the feebler wild things which were his prey by inheritance, the born serfs to his family, had kept, for the most part, in their burrows and nests, and the Cat's long hunt had availed him nothing. But he waited with the inconceivable patience and persistency of his race; besides, he was certain. The Cat was a creature of absolute convictions, and his faith in his deductions never wavered. The rabbit had gone in there between those low-hung pine boughs. Now her little doorway had before it a shaggy curtain of snow, but in there she was. The Cat had seen her enter, so like a swift grey shadow that even his sharp and practised eyes had glanced back for the substance following, and then she was gone. So he sat down and waited, and he waited still in the white night, listening angrily to the north wind starting in the upper heights of the mountains with distant screams, then swelling into an awful crescendo of rage, and swooping down with furious white wings of snow like a flock of fierce eagles into the valleys and ravines. The Cat was on the side of a mountain, on a wooded terrace. Above him a few feet away towered the rock ascent as steep as the wall of a cathedral. The Cat had never climbed it—trees were the ladders to his heights of life. He had often looked with wonder at the rock, and miauled bitterly and resentfully as man does in the face of a forbidding Providence. At his left was the sheer precipice. Behind him, with a short stretch of woody growth between, was the frozen perpendicular wall of a mountain stream. Before him was the way to his home. When the rabbit came out she was trapped; her little cloven feet could not scale such unbroken steeps. So the Cat waited. The place in which he was looked like a maelstrom of the wood. The tangle of trees and bushes clinging to the mountain-side with a stern clutch of roots, the prostrate trunks and branches, the vines embracing everything with strong knots and coils of growth, had a curious effect, as of things which had whirled for ages in a current of raging water, only it was not water, but wind, which had disposed everything in circling lines of yielding to its fiercest points of onset. And now over all this whirl of wood and rock and dead trunks and branches and vines descended the snow. It blew down like smoke over the rock-crest above; it stood in a gyrating column like some death-wraith of nature, on the level, then it broke over the edge of the precipice, and the Cat cowered before the fierce backward set of it. It was as if ice needles pricked his skin through his beautiful thick fur, but he never faltered and never once cried. He had nothing to gain from crying, and everything to lose; the rabbit would hear him cry and know he was waiting.

It grew darker and darker, with a strange white smother, instead of the natural blackness of night. It was a night of storm and death superadded to the night of nature. The mountains were all hidden, wrapped about, overawed, and tumultuously overborne by it, but in the midst of it waited, quite unconquered, this little, unswerving, living patience and power under a little coat of grey fur.

A fiercer blast swept over the rock, spun on one mighty foot of whirlwind athwart the level, then was over the precipice.

Then the Cat saw two eyes luminous with terror, frantic with the impulse of flight, he saw a little, quivering, dilating nose, he saw two pointing ears, and he kept still, with every one of his fine nerves and muscles strained like wires. Then the rabbit was out—there was one long line of incarnate flight and terror—and the Cat had her.

Then the Cat went home, trailing his prey through the snow.

The Cat lived in the house which his master had built, as rudely as a child's block-house, but staunchly enough. The snow was heavy on the low slant of its roof, but it would not settle under it. The two windows and the door were made fast, but the Cat knew a way in. Up a pine-tree behind the house he scuttled, though it was hard work with his heavy rabbit, and was in his little window under the eaves, then down through the trap to the room below, and on his master's bed with a spring and a great cry of triumph, rabbit and all. But his master was not there; he had been gone since early fall and it was now February. He would not return until spring, for he was an old man, and the cruel cold of the mountains clutched at his vitals like a panther, and he had gone to the village to winter. The Cat had known for a long time that his master was gone, but his reasoning was always sequential and circuitous; always for him what had been would be, and the more easily for his marvellous waiting powers so he always came home expecting to find his master.

When he saw that he was still gone, he dragged the rabbit off the rude couch which was the bed to the floor, put one little paw on the carcass to keep it steady, and began gnawing with head to one side to bring his strongest teeth to bear.

It was darker in the house than it had been in the wood, and the cold was as deadly, though not so fierce. If the Cat had not received his fur coat unquestioningly of Providence, he would have been thankful that he had it. It was a mottled grey, white on the face and breast, and thick as fur could grow.

The wind drove the snow on the windows with such force that it rattled like sleet, and the house trembled a little. Then all at once the Cat heard a noise, and stopped gnawing his rabbit and listened, his shining green eyes fixed upon a window. Then he heard a hoarse shout, a halloo of despair and entreaty; but he knew it was not his master come home, and he waited, one paw still on the rabbit. Then the halloo came again, and then the Cat answered. He said all that was essential quite plainly to his own comprehension. There was in his cry of response inquiry, information, warning, terror, and finally, the offer of comradeship; but the man outside did not hear him, because of the howling of the storm.

Then there was a great battering pound at the door, then another, and another. The Cat dragged his rabbit under the bed. The blows came thicker and faster. It was a weak arm which gave them, but it was nerved by desperation. Finally the lock yielded, and the stranger came in. Then the Cat, peering from under the bed, blinked with a sudden light, and his green eyes narrowed. The stranger struck a match and looked about. The Cat saw a face wild and blue with hunger and cold, and a man who looked poorer and older than his poor old master, who was an outcast among men for his poverty and lowly mystery of antecedents; and he heard a muttered, unintelligible voicing of distress from the harsh piteous mouth. There was in it both profanity and prayer, but the Cat knew nothing of that.

The stranger braced the door which he had forced, got some wood from the stock in the corner, and kindled a fire in the old stove as quickly as his half-frozen hands would allow. He shook so pitiably as he worked that the Cat under the bed felt the tremor of it. Then the man, who was small and feeble and marked with the scars of suffering which he had pulled down upon his own head, sat down in one of the old chairs and crouched over the fire as if it were the one love and desire of his soul, holding out his yellow hands like yellow claws, and he groaned. The Cat came out from under the bed and leaped up on his lap with the rabbit. The man gave a great shout and start of terror, and sprang, and the Cat slid clawing to the floor, and the rabbit fell inertly, and the man leaned, gasping with fright, and ghastly, against the wall. The Cat grabbed the rabbit by the slack of its neck and dragged it to the man's feet. Then he raised his shrill, insistent cry, he arched his back high, his tail was a splendid waving plume. He rubbed against the man's feet, which were bursting out of their torn shoes.

The man pushed the Cat away, gently enough, and began searching about the little cabin. He even climbed painfully the ladder to the loft, lit a match, and peered up in the darkness with straining eyes. He feared lest there might be a man, since there was a cat. His experience with men had not been pleasant, and neither had the experience of men been pleasant with him. He was an old wandering Ishmael among his kind; he had stumbled upon the house of a brother, and the brother was not at home, and he was glad.

He returned to the Cat, and stooped stiffly and stroked his back, which the animal arched like the spring of a bow.

Then he took up the rabbit and looked at it eagerly by the firelight. His jaws worked. He could almost have devoured it raw. He fumbled—the Cat close at his heels—around some rude shelves and a table, and found, with a grunt of self-gratulation, a lamp with oil in it. That he lighted; then he found a frying-pan and a knife, and skinned the rabbit, and prepared it for cooking, the Cat always at his feet.

When the odour of the cooking flesh filled the cabin, both the man and the Cat looked wolfish. The man turned the rabbit with one hand and stooped to pat the Cat with the other. The Cat thought him a fine man. He loved him with all his heart, though he had known him such a short time, and though the man had a face both pitiful and sharply set at variance with the best of things.

It was a face with the grimy grizzle of age upon it, with fever hollows in the cheeks, and the memories of wrong in the dim eyes, but the Cat accepted the man unquestioningly and loved him. When the rabbit was half cooked, neither the man nor the Cat could wait any longer. The man took it from the fire, divided it exactly in halves, gave the Cat one, and took the other himself. Then they ate.

Then the man blew out the light, called the Cat to him, got on the bed, drew up the ragged coverings, and fell asleep with the Cat in his bosom.

The man was the Cat's guest all the rest of the winter, and winter is long in the mountains. The rightful owner of the little hut did not return until May. All that time the Cat toiled hard, and he grew rather thin himself, for he shared everything except mice with his guest; and sometimes game was wary, and the fruit of patience of days was very little for two. The man was ill and weak, however, and unable to eat much, which was fortunate, since he could not hunt for himself. All day long he lay on the bed, or else sat crouched over the fire. It was a good thing that fire-wood was ready at hand for the picking up, not a stone's-throw from the door, for that he had to attend to himself.

The Cat foraged tirelessly. Sometimes he was gone for days together, and at first the man used to be terrified, thinking he would never return;

then he would hear the familiar cry at the door, and stumble to his feet and let him in. Then the two would dine together, sharing equally; then the Cat would rest and purr, and finally sleep in the man's arms.

Towards spring the game grew plentiful; more wild little quarry were tempted out of their homes, in search of love as well as food. One day the Cat had luck—a rabbit, a partridge, and a mouse. He could not carry them all at once, but finally he had them together at the house door. Then he cried, but no one answered. All the mountain streams were loosened, and the air was full of the gurgle of many waters, occasionally pierced by a bird-whistle. The trees rustled with a new sound to the spring wind; there was a flush of rose and gold-green on the breasting surface of a distant mountain seen through an opening in the wood. The tips of the bushes were swollen and glistening red, and now and then there was a flower; but the Cat had nothing to do with flowers. He stood beside his booty at the house door, and cried and cried with his insistent triumph and complaint and pleading, but no one came to let him in. Then the cat left his little treasures at the door, and went around to the back of the house to the pine-tree, and was up the trunk with a wild scramble, and in through his little window, and down through the trap to the room, and the man was gone.

The Cat cried again—that cry of the animal for human companionship which is one of the sad notes of the world; he looked in all the corners; he sprang to the chair at the window and looked out; but no one came. The man was gone and he never came again.

The Cat ate his mouse out on the turf beside the house; the rabbit and the partridge he carried painfully into the house, but the man did not come to share them. Finally, in the course of a day or two, he ate them up himself; then he slept a long time on the bed, and when he waked the man was not there.

Then the Cat went forth to his hunting-grounds again, and came home at night with a plump bird, reasoning with his tireless persistency in expectancy that the man would be there; and there was a light in the window, and when he cried his old master opened the door and let him in.

His master had strong comradeship with the Cat, but not affection.

He never patted him like that gentler outcast, but he had a pride in him and an anxiety for his welfare, though he had left him alone all winter without scruple. He feared lest some misfortune might have come to the Cat, though he was so large of his kind, and a mighty hunter. Therefore, when he saw him at the door in all the glory of his glossy winter coat, his white breast and face shining like snow in the sun, his own face lit up with welcome, and the Cat embraced his feet with his sinuous body vibrant with rejoicing purrs.

The Cat had his bird to himself, for his master had his own supper already cooking on the stove. After supper the Cat's master took his pipe, and sought a small store of tobacco which he had left in his hut over winter. He had thought often of it; that and the Cat seemed something to come home to in the spring. But the tobacco was gone; not a dust left. The man swore a little in a grim monotone, which made the profanity lose its customary effect. He had been, and was, a hard drinker; he had knocked about the world until the marks of its sharp corners were on his very soul, which was thereby calloused, until his very sensibility to loss was dulled. He was a very old man.

He searched for the tobacco with a sort of dull combativeness of persistency; then he stared with stupid wonder around the room. Suddenly many features struck him as being changed. Another stove-lid was broken; an old piece of carpet was tacked up over a window to keep out the cold; his fire-wood was gone. He looked and there was no oil left in his can. He looked at the coverings on his bed; he took them up, and again he made that strange remonstrant noise in his throat. Then he looked again for his tobacco.

Finally he gave it up. He sat down beside the fire, for May in the mountains is cold; he held his empty pipe in his mouth, his rough forehead knitted, and he and the Cat looked at each other across that impassable barrier of silence which has been set between man and beast from the creation of the world.

AN OCCURRENCE AT OWL CREEK BRIDGE*

Ambrose Bierce

I

A man stood upon a railroad bridge in northern Alabama, looking down into the swift water twenty feet below. The man's hands were behind his back, the wrists bound with a cord. A rope closely encircled his neck. It was attached to a stout cross-timber above his head and the slack fell to the level of his knees. Some loose boards laid upon the sleepers supporting the metals of the railway supplied a footing for him and his executioners—two private soldiers of the Federal army, directed by a sergeant who in civil life may have been a deputy sheriff. At a short remove upon the same temporary platform was an officer in the uniform of his rank, armed. He was a captain. A sentinel at each end of the bridge stood with his rifle in the position known as 'support,' that is to say, vertical in front of the left shoulder, the hammer resting on the forearm thrown straight across the chest—a formal and unnatural position, enforcing an erect carriage of the body. It did not appear to be the duty of these two men to know what was occurring at the centre of the bridge; they merely blockaded the two ends of the foot planking that traversed it. Beyond one of the sentinels nobody was in sight; the railroad ran straight away into a forest for a hundred yards, then, curving, was lost to view. Doubtless there was an outpost farther along. The other bank of the stream was open ground—a gentle acclivity topped with a stockade of vertical tree trunks, loop-holed for rifles, with a single embrasure through which protruded the muzzle of a brass cannon commanding the bridge. Midway of the slope between the bridge and fort were the spectators—a single company of infantry in line, at 'parade rest,' the butts of the rifles on the ground, the barrels inclining

*Set during the American Civil War, 'An Occurrence at Owl Creek' is Bierce's most famous short story.

slightly backward against the right shoulder, the hands crossed upon the stock. A lieutenant stood at the right of the line, the point of his sword upon the ground, his left hand resting upon his right. Excepting the group of four at the centre of the bridge, not a man moved. The company faced the bridge, staring stonily, motionless. The sentinels, facing the banks of the stream, might have been statues to adorn the bridge. The captain stood with folded arms, silent, observing the work of his subordinates, but making no sign. Death is a dignitary who when he comes announced is to be received with formal manifestations of respect, even by those most familiar with him. In the code of military etiquette silence and fixity are forms of deference.

The man who was engaged in being hanged was apparently about thirty-five years of age. He was a civilian, if one might judge from his habit, which was that of a planter. His features were good—a straight nose, firm mouth, broad forehead, from which his long, dark hair was combed straight back, falling behind his ears to the collar of his well-fitting frock coat. He wore a moustache and pointed beard, but no whiskers; his eyes were large and dark grey, and had a kindly expression which one would hardly have expected in one whose neck was in the hemp. Evidently this was no vulgar assassin. The liberal military code makes provision for hanging many kinds of persons, and gentlemen are not excluded.

The preparations being complete, the two private soldiers stepped aside and each drew away the plank upon which he had been standing. The sergeant turned to the captain, saluted and placed himself immediately behind that officer, who in turn moved apart one pace. These movements left the condemned man and the sergeant standing on the two ends of the same plank, which spanned three of the cross-ties of the bridge. The end upon which the civilian stood almost, but not quite, reached a fourth. This plank had been held in place by the weight of the captain; it was now held by that of the sergeant. At a signal from the former the latter would step aside, the plank would tilt and the condemned man go down between two ties. The arrangement commended itself to his judgment as simple and effective. His face had not been covered nor his eyes bandaged. He looked a moment at his 'unsteadfast footing,' then let his gaze wander to the swirling water of the stream racing madly beneath his feet. A piece of dancing driftwood caught his attention and his eyes followed it down the current. How slowly it appeared to move, What a sluggish stream!

He closed his eyes in order to fix his last thoughts upon his wife and children. The water, touched to gold by the early sun, the brooding mists under the banks at some distance down the stream, the fort, the soldiers, the piece of drift—all had distracted him. And now he became conscious of a new disturbance. Striking through the thought of his dear ones was a sound which he could neither ignore nor understand, a sharp, distinct, metallic percussion like the stroke of a blacksmith's hammer upon the anvil; it had the same ringing quality. He wondered what it was, and whether immeasurably distant or nearby—it seemed both. Its recurrence was regular, but as slow as the tolling of a death knell. He awaited each stroke with impatience and—he knew not why—apprehension. The intervals of silence grew progressively longer, the delays became maddening. With their greater infrequency the sounds increased in strength and sharpness. They hurt his ear like the thrust of a knife; he feared he would shriek. What he heard was the ticking of his watch.

He unclosed his eyes and saw again the water below him. 'If I could free my hands,' he thought, 'I might throw off the noose and spring into the stream. By diving I could evade the bullets and, swimming vigorously, reach the bank, take to the woods and get away home. My home, thank God, is as yet outside their lines; my wife and little ones are still beyond the invader's farthest advance.'

As these thoughts, which have here to be set down in words, were flashed into the doomed man's brain rather than evolved from it the captain nodded to the sergeant. The sergeant stepped aside.

II

Peyton Farquhar was a well-to-do planter, of an old and highly respected Alabama family. Being a slave owner and like other slave owners a politician he was naturally an original secessionist and ardently devoted to the Southern cause. Circumstances of an imperious nature, which it is unnecessary to relate here, had prevented him from taking service with the gallant army that had fought the disastrous campaigns ending with the fall of Corinth, and he chafed under the inglorious restraint, longing for the release of his energies, the larger life of the soldier, the opportunity for distinction. That opportunity, he felt, would come, as it comes to all in war time. Meanwhile he did what he could. No service was too humble for him to perform in aid of the South, no adventure too perilous for him to undertake if consistent with the character of a civilian who was at heart a soldier, and who in good faith and without too much qualification assented to at least a part of the frankly villainous dictum that all is fair in love and war.

One evening while Farquhar and his wife were sitting on a rustic bench near the entrance to his grounds, a grey-clad soldier rode up to the gate and asked for a drink of water. Mrs Farquhar was only too happy to serve him with her own white hands. While she was fetching the water her husband approached the dusty horseman and inquired eagerly for news from the front.

'The Yanks are repairing the railroads,' said the man, 'and are getting ready for another advance. They have reached the Owl Creek bridge, put it in order and built a stockade on the north bank. The commandant has issued an order, which is posted everywhere, declaring that any civilian caught interfering with the railroad, its bridges, tunnels or trains will be summarily hanged. I saw the order.'

'How far is it to the Owl Creek bridge?' Farquhar asked.

'About thirty miles.'

'Is there no force on this side the creek?'

'Only a picket post half a mile out, on the railroad, and a single sentinel at this end of the bridge.'

'Suppose a man—a civilian and student of hanging—should elude the picket post and perhaps get the better of the sentinel,' said Farquhar, smiling, 'what could he accomplish?'

The soldier reflected. 'I was there a month ago,' he replied. 'I observed that the flood of last winter had lodged a great quantity of driftwood against the wooden pier at this end of the bridge. It is now dry and would burn like tow.'

The lady had now brought the water, which the soldier drank. He thanked her ceremoniously, bowed to her husband and rode away. An hour later, after nightfall, he repassed the plantation, going northward in the direction from which he had come. He was a Federal scout.

III

As Peyton Farquhar fell straight downward through the bridge he lost consciousness and was as one already dead. From this state he was awakened—ages later, it seemed to him—by the pain of a sharp pressure upon his throat, followed by a sense of suffocation. Keen, poignant agonies seemed to shoot from his neck downward through every fibre of his body and limbs. These pains appeared to flash along well-defined lines of ramification and to beat with an inconceivably rapid periodicity. They seemed like streams of pulsating fire heating him to an intolerable temperature. As to his head, he was conscious of nothing but a feeling of fullness—of congestion. These sensations were unaccompanied by thought. The intellectual part of his nature was already effaced; he had power only to feel, and feeling was torment. He was conscious of motion. Encompassed in a luminous cloud, of which he was now merely the fiery heart, without material substance, he swung through unthinkable arcs of oscillation, like a vast pendulum. Then all at once, with terrible suddenness, the light about him shot upward with the noise of a loud splash; a frightful roaring was in his ears, and all was cold and dark. The power of thought was restored; he knew that the rope had broken and he had fallen into the stream. There was no additional strangulation; the noose about his neck was already suffocating him and kept the water from his lungs. To die of hanging at the bottom of a river!—the idea seemed to him ludicrous. He opened his eyes in the darkness and saw above him a gleam of light, but how distant, how inaccessible! He was still sinking, for the light became fainter and fainter until it was a mere glimmer. Then it began to grow and brighten, and he knew that he was rising toward the surface—knew it with reluctance, for he was now very comfortable. 'To be hanged and drowned,' he thought? 'that is not so bad; but I do not wish to be shot. No; I will not be shot; that is not fair.'

He was not conscious of an effort, but a sharp pain in his wrist apprised him that he was trying to free his hands. He gave the struggle his attention, as an idler might observe the feat of a juggler, without interest in the outcome. What splendid effort!—what magnificent, what superhuman strength! Ah, that was a fine endeavour! Bravo! The cord fell away; his arms parted and floated upward, the hands dimly seen on each side in the growing light. He watched them with a new interest as first one and then the other pounced upon the noose at his neck. They tore it away and thrust it fiercely aside, its undulations resembling those of a water snake. 'Put it back, put it back!' He thought he shouted these words to his hands, for the undoing of the noose had been succeeded by the direst pang that he had yet experienced. His neck ached horribly; his brain was on fire; his heart, which had been fluttering faintly, gave a great leap, trying to force itself out at his mouth. His whole body was racked and wrenched with an insupportable anguish! But his disobedient hands gave no heed to the command. They beat the water vigorously with quick, downward strokes, forcing him to the surface. He felt his head emerge; his eyes were blinded by the sunlight; his chest expanded convulsively, and with a supreme and crowning agony his lungs engulfed a great draught of air, which instantly he expelled in a shriek!

He was now in full possession of his physical senses. They were, indeed, preternaturally keen and alert. Something in the awful disturbance of his organic system had so exalted and refined them that they made record of things never before perceived. He felt the ripples upon his face and heard their separate sounds as they struck. He looked at the forest on the bank of the stream, saw the individual trees, the leaves and the veining of each leaf—saw the very insects upon them: the locusts, the brilliant-bodied flies, the grey spiders stretching their webs from twig to twig. He noted the prismatic colours in all the dewdrops upon a million blades of grass. The humming of the gnats that danced above the eddies of the stream, the beating of the dragon flies' wings, the strokes of the water-spiders' legs, like oars which had lifted their boat—all these made audible music. A fish slid along beneath his eyes and he heard the rush of its body parting the water.

He had come to the surface facing down the stream; in a moment the visible world seemed to wheel slowly round, himself the pivotal point, and he saw the bridge, the fort, the soldiers upon the bridge, the captain, the sergeant, the two privates, his executioners. They were in silhouette against the blue sky. They shouted and gesticulated, pointing at him. The captain had drawn his pistol, but did not fire; the others were unarmed. Their movements were grotesque and horrible, their forms gigantic.

Suddenly he heard a sharp report and something struck the water smartly within a few inches of his head, spattering his face with spray. He heard a second report, and saw one of the sentinels with his rifle at his shoulder, a light cloud of blue smoke rising from the muzzle. The man in the water saw the eye of the man on the bridge gazing into his own through the sights of the rifle. He observed that it was a grey eye and remembered having read that grey eyes were keenest, and that all famous marksmen had them. Nevertheless, this one had missed.

A counter-swirl had caught Farquhar and turned him half round; he was again looking into the forest on the bank opposite the fort. The sound of a clear, high voice in a monotonous singsong now rang out behind him and came across the water with a distinctness that pierced and subdued all other sounds, even the beating of the ripples in his ears. Although no soldier, he had frequented camps enough to know the dread significance of that deliberate, drawling, aspirated chant; the lieutenant on shore was taking a part in the morning's work. How coldly and pitilessly—with what an even, calm intonation, presaging, and enforcing tranquillity in the men—with what accurately measured intervals fell those cruel words:

'Attention, company! … Shoulder arms! … Ready! … Aim! … Fire!'

Farquhar dived—dived as deeply as he could. The water roared in his ears like the voice of Niagara, yet he heard the dulled thunder of the volley and, rising again toward the surface, met shining bits of metal, singularly flattened, oscillating slowly downward. Some of them touched him on the face and hands, then fell away, continuing their descent. One lodged between his collar and neck; it was uncomfortably warm and he snatched it out.

As he rose to the surface, gasping for breath, he saw that he had been a long time under water; he was perceptibly farther downstream nearer to safety. The soldiers had almost finished reloading; the metal ramrods flashed all at once in the sunshine as they were drawn from the barrels, turned in the air, and thrust into their sockets. The two sentinels fired again, independently and ineffectually.

The hunted man saw all this over his shoulder; he was now swimming vigorously with the current. His brain was as energetic as his arms and legs; he thought with the rapidity of lightning.

'The officer,' he reasoned, 'will not make that martinet's error a second time. It is as easy to dodge a volley as a single shot. He has probably already given the command to fire at will. God help me, I cannot dodge them all!'

An appalling splash within two yards of him was followed by a loud, rushing sound, diminuendo, which seemed to travel back through the air to the fort and died in an explosion which stirred the very river to its deeps!

A rising sheet of water curved over him, fell down upon him, blinded him, strangled him! The cannon had taken a hand in the game. As he shook his head free from the commotion of the smitten water he heard the deflected shot humming through the air ahead, and in an instant it was cracking and smashing the branches in the forest beyond.

'They will not do that again,' he thought; 'the next time they will use a charge of grape. I must keep my eye upon the gun; the smoke will apprise me—the report arrives too late; it lags behind the missile. That is a good gun.'

Suddenly he felt himself whirled round and round—spinning like a top. The water, the banks, the forests, the now distant bridge, fort and men—all were commingled and blurred. Objects were represented by their colours only; circular horizontal streaks of colour—that was all he saw. He had been caught in a vortex and was being whirled on with a velocity of advance and gyration that made him giddy and sick. In a few moments he was flung upon the gravel at the foot of the left bank of the stream—the southern bank—and behind a projecting point which concealed him from his enemies. The sudden arrest of his motion, the abrasion of one of his hands on the gravel, restored him, and he wept with delight. He dug his fingers into the sand, threw it over himself in handfuls and audibly blessed it. It looked like diamonds, rubies, emeralds; he could think of nothing beautiful which it did not resemble. The trees upon the bank were giant garden plants; he noted a definite order in their arrangement, inhaled the fragrance of their blooms. A strange, roseate light shone through the spaces among their trunks and the wind made in their branches the music of olian harps. He had no wish to perfect his escape—was content to remain in that enchanting spot until retaken.

A whiz and rattle of grapeshot among the branches high above his head roused him from his dream. The baffled cannoneer had fired him a random farewell. He sprang to his feet, rushed up the sloping bank, and plunged into the forest.

All that day he travelled, laying his course by the rounding sun. The forest seemed interminable; nowhere did he discover a break in it, not even a woodman's road. He had not known that he lived in so wild a region. There was something uncanny in the revelation.

By nightfall he was fatigued, footsore, famishing. The thought of his wife and children urged him on. At last he found a road which led him in what he knew to be the right direction. It was as wide and straight as a city street, yet it seemed untraveled. No fields bordered it, no dwelling anywhere. Not so much as the barking of a dog suggested human habitation. The black bodies of the trees formed a straight wall on both sides, terminating on the horizon in a point, like a diagram in a lesson in perspective. Overhead, as he looked up through this rift in the wood, shone great garden stars looking unfamiliar and grouped in strange constellations. He was sure they were arranged in some order which had a secret and malign significance. The wood on either side was full of singular noises, among which—once, twice, and again—he distinctly heard whispers in an unknown tongue.

His neck was in pain and lifting his hand to it found it horribly swollen. He knew that it had a circle of black where the rope had bruised it. His eyes felt congested; he could no longer close them. His tongue was swollen with thirst; he relieved its fever by thrusting it forward from between his teeth into the cold air. How softly the turf had carpeted the untraveled avenue—he could no longer feel the roadway beneath his feet!

Doubtless, despite his suffering, he had fallen asleep while walking, for now he sees another scene—perhaps he has merely recovered from a delirium. He stands at the gate of his own home. All is as he left it, and all bright and beautiful in the morning sunshine. He must have travelled the entire night. As he pushes open the gate and passes up the wide white walk, he sees a flutter of female garments; his wife, looking fresh and cool and sweet, steps down from the veranda to meet him. At the bottom of the steps she stands waiting, with a smile of ineffable joy, an attitude of matchless grace and dignity. Ah, how beautiful she is! He springs forward with extended arms. As he is about to clasp her he feels a stunning blow upon the back of the neck; a blinding white light blazes all about him with a sound like the shock of a cannon—then all is darkness and silence!

Peyton Farquhar was dead; his body, with a broken neck, swung gently from side to side beneath the timbers of the Owl Creek bridge.

THE DISTRICT DOCTOR

Ivan S. Turgenev

One day in autumn on my way back from a remote part of the country I caught cold and fell ill. Fortunately the fever attacked me in the district town at the inn; I sent for the doctor. In half-an-hour the district doctor appeared, a thin, dark-haired man of middle height. He prescribed me the usual sudorific, ordered a mustard-plaster to be put on, very deftly slid a five-ruble note up his sleeve, coughing drily and looking away as he did so, and then was getting up to go home, but somehow fell into talk and remained. I was exhausted with feverishness; I foresaw a sleepless night, and was glad of a little chat with a pleasant companion. Tea was served. My doctor began to converse freely. He was a sensible fellow, and expressed himself with vigour and some humour. Queer things happen in the world: you may live a long while with some people, and be on friendly terms with them, and never once speak openly with them from your soul; with others you have scarcely time to get acquainted, and all at once you are pouring out to him—or he to you—all your secrets, as though you were at confession. I don't know how I gained the confidence of my new friend—anyway, with nothing to lead up to it, he told me a rather curious incident; and here I will report his tale for the information of the indulgent reader. I will try to tell it in the doctor's own words.

'You don't happen to know,' he began in a weak and quavering voice (the common result of the use of unmixed Berezov snuff); 'you don't happen to know the judge here, Mylov, Pavel Lukich?... You don't know him?... Well, it's all the same.' (He cleared his throat and rubbed his eyes.) 'Well, you see, the thing happened, to tell you exactly without mistake, in Lent, at the very time of the thaws. I was sitting at his house—our judge's, you know—playing preference. Our judge is a good fellow, and fond of playing preference. Suddenly' (the doctor made frequent use of this word, suddenly) 'they tell me, 'There's a servant asking for you.' I say, 'What does he want?' They say, He has brought a note—it must be from a patient.' 'Give me the note,' I say. So it is from a patient—well and good—you understand—it's our bread and butter... But this is how it was: a lady, a widow, writes to me; she says, 'My daughter is dying. Come, for God's sake!' she says, 'and the horses have been sent for you.'... Well, that's all right. But she was twenty miles from the town, and it was midnight out of doors, and the roads in such a state, my word! And as she was poor herself, one could not expect more than two silver rubles, and even that problematic; and perhaps it might only be a matter of a roll of linen and a sack of oatmeal in payment. However, duty, you know, before everything: a fellow-creature may be dying. I hand over my cards at once to Kalliopin, the member of the provincial commission, and return home. I look; a wretched little trap was standing at the steps, with peasant's horses, fat—too fat—and their coat as shaggy as felt; and the coachman sitting with his cap off out of respect. Well, I think to myself, 'It's clear, my friend, these patients aren't rolling in riches.'... You smile; but I tell you, a poor man like me has to take everything into consideration... If the coachman sits like a prince, and doesn't touch his cap, and even sneers at you behind his beard, and flicks his whip—then you may bet on six rubles. But this case, I saw, had a very different air. However, I think there's no help for it; duty before everything. I snatch up the most necessary drugs, and set off. Will you believe it? I only just managed to get there at all. The road was infernal: streams, snow, watercourses, and the dyke had suddenly burst there—that was the worst of it! However, I arrived at last. It was a little thatched house. There was a light in the windows; that meant they expected me. I was met by an old lady, very venerable, in a cap. 'Save her!' she says; 'she is dying.' I say, 'Pray don't distress yourself—Where is the invalid?' 'Come this way.' I see a clean little room, a lamp in the corner; on the bed a girl of twenty, unconscious. She was in a burning heat, and breathing heavily—it was fever. There were two other girls, her sisters, scared and in tears. 'Yesterday,' they tell me, 'she was perfectly well and had a good appetite; this morning she complained of her head, and this evening, suddenly, you see, like this.' I say again: 'Pray don't be uneasy.' It's a doctor's duty, you know—and I went up to her and bled her, told them to put on a mustard-plaster, and prescribed a mixture. Meantime I looked at her; I looked at her, you know—there, by God! I had never seen such a face!—she was a beauty, in a word! I felt quite shaken with pity. Such lovely features; such eyes!... But, thank God! she became easier; she fell into a perspiration, seemed to come to her senses, looked round, smiled, and passed her hand over her face... Her sisters bent over her. They ask, 'How are you?' 'All right,' she says, and turns away. I looked at her; she had fallen asleep. 'Well,' I say, 'now the patient should be left alone.' So we all went out on tiptoe; only a maid remained, in case she was wanted. In the parlour there was a samovar standing on the table, and a bottle of rum; in our profession one can't get on without it. They gave me tea; asked me to stop the night... I consented: where could I go, indeed, at that time of night? The old lady kept groaning. 'What is it?' I say; 'she will live; don't worry yourself; you had better take a little rest yourself; it is about two o'clock.' 'But will you send to wake me if anything happens?' 'Yes, yes.' The old lady went away, and the girls too went to their own room; they made up a bed for me in the parlour.

Well, I went to bed—but I could not get to sleep, for a wonder! For in reality I was very tired. I could not get my patient out of my head. At last I could not put up with it any longer; I got up suddenly; I think to myself, 'I will go and see how the patient is getting on.' Her bedroom was next to the parlour. Well, I got up, and gently opened the door—how my heart beat! I looked in: the servant was asleep, her mouth wide open, and even snoring, the wretch! but the patient lay with her face towards me and her arms flung wide apart, poor girl! I went up to her ... when suddenly she opened her eyes and stared at me! 'Who is it? who is it?' I was in confusion. 'Don't be alarmed, madam,' I say; 'I am the doctor; I have come to see how you feel.' 'You the doctor?' 'Yes, the doctor; your mother sent for me from the town; we have bled you, madam; now pray go to sleep, and in a day or two, please God! we will set you on your feet again.' 'Ah, yes, yes, doctor, don't let me die... please, please.' 'Why do you talk like that? God bless you!' She is in a fever again, I think to myself; I felt her pulse; yes, she was feverish. She looked at me, and then took me by the hand. 'I will tell you why I don't want to die: I will tell you... Now we are alone; and only, please don't you ... not to any one ... Listen...' I bent down; she moved her lips quite to my ear; she touched my cheek with her hair—I confess my head went round—and began to whisper... I could make out nothing of it... Ah, she was delirious! ... She whispered and whispered, but so quickly, and as if it were not in Russian; at last she finished, and shivering dropped her head on the pillow, and threatened me with her finger: 'Remember, doctor, to no one.' I calmed her somehow, gave her something to drink, waked the servant, and went away.'

At this point the doctor again took snuff with exasperated energy, and for a moment seemed stupefied by its effects.

'However,' he continued, 'the next day, contrary to my expectations, the patient was no better. I thought and thought, and suddenly decided to remain there, even though my other patients were expecting me... And you know one can't afford to disregard that; one's practice suffers if one does. But, in the first place, the patient was really in danger; and secondly, to tell the truth, I felt strongly drawn to her. Besides, I liked the whole family. Though they were really badly off, they were singularly, I may say, cultivated people... Their father had been a learned man, an author; he died, of course, in poverty, but he had managed before he died to give his children an excellent education; he left a lot of books too. Either because I looked after the invalid very carefully, or for some other reason; anyway, I can venture to say all the household loved me as if I were one of the family... Meantime the roads were in a worse state than ever; all communications, so to say, were cut off completely; even medicine could with difficulty be got from the town... The sick girl was not getting better... Day after day, and day after day ... but ... here...' (The doctor made a brief pause.) 'I declare I don't know how to tell you.' ... (He again took snuff, coughed, and swallowed a little tea.) 'I will tell you without beating about the bush. My patient ... how should I say?... Well she had fallen in love with me ... or, no, it was not that she was in love ... however ... really, how should one say?' (The doctor looked down and grew red.) 'No,' he went on quickly, 'in love, indeed! A man should not over-estimate himself. She was an educated girl, clever and well-read, and I had even forgotten my Latin, one may say, completely. As to appearance' (the doctor looked himself over with a smile) 'I am nothing to boast of there either. But God Almighty did not make me a fool; I don't take black for white; I know a thing or two; I could see very clearly, for instance that Aleksandra Andreyevna—that was her name—did not feel love for me, but had a friendly, so to say, inclination—a respect or something for me. Though she herself perhaps mistook this sentiment, anyway this was her attitude; you may form your own judgment of it. But,' added the doctor, who had brought out all these disconnected sentences without taking breath, and with obvious embarrassment, 'I seem to be wandering rather—you won't understand anything like this ... There, with your leave, I will relate it all in order.'

He drank off a glass of tea, and began in a calmer voice.

'Well, then. My patient kept getting worse and worse. You are not a doctor, my good sir; you cannot understand what passes in a poor fellow's heart, especially at first, when he begins to suspect that the disease is getting the upper hand of him. What becomes of his belief in himself? You suddenly grow so timid; it's indescribable. You fancy then that you have forgotten everything you knew, and that the patient has no faith in you, and that other people begin to notice how distracted you are, and tell you the symptoms with reluctance; that they are looking at you suspiciously, whispering... Ah! it's horrid! There must be a remedy, you think, for this disease, if one could find it. Isn't this it? You try—no, that's not it! You don't allow the medicine the necessary time to do good... You clutch at one thing, then at another. Sometimes you take up a book of medical prescriptions—here it is, you think! Sometimes, by Jove, you pick one out by chance, thinking to leave it to fate... But meantime a fellow-creature's dying, and another doctor would have saved him. 'We must have a consultation,' you say; 'I will not take the responsibility on myself.' And what a fool you look at such times! Well, in time you learn to bear it; it's nothing to you. A man has died—but it's not your fault; you treated him by the rules. But what's still more torture to you is to see blind faith in you, and to feel yourself that you are not able to be of use. Well, it was just this blind faith that the whole of Aleksandra Andreyevna's family had in me; they had forgotten to think that their daughter was in danger. I, too, on my side assure them that it's nothing, but meantime my heart sinks into my boots. To add to our troubles, the roads were in such a state that the coachman was gone for whole days together to get medicine. And I never left the patient's room; I could not tear myself away; I tell her amusing stories, you know, and play cards with her. I watch by her side at night. The old mother thanks me with tears in her eyes; but I think to myself, 'I don't deserve your gratitude.' Ifrankly confess to you—there is no object in concealing it now—I was in love with my patient. And Aleksandra Andreyevna had grown fond of me; she would not sometimes let anyone be in her room but me. She began to talk to me, to ask me questions; where I had studied, how I lived, who are my people, whom I go to see. I feel that she ought not to talk; but to forbid her to—to forbid her resolutely, you know—I could not. Sometimes I held my head in my hands, and asked myself, 'What are you doing, villain?'... And she would take my hand and hold it, give me a long, long look, and turn away, sigh, and say, 'How good you are!' Her hands were so feverish, her eyes so large and languid... 'Yes,' she says, 'you are a good, kind man; you are not like our neighbours... No, you are not like that... Why did I not know you till now!' 'Aleksandra Andreyevna, calm yourself,' I say... 'I feel, believe me, I don't know how I have gained ... but there, calm yourself... All will be right; you will be well again.' And meanwhile I must tell you,' continued the doctor, bending forward and raising his eyebrows, 'that they associated very little with the neighbours, because the smaller people were not on their level, and pride hindered them from being friendly with the rich. I tell you, they were an exceptionally cultivated family; so you know it was gratifying for me. She would only take her medicine from my hands ... she would lift herself up, poor girl, with my aid, take it, and gaze at me... My heart felt as if it were bursting. And meanwhile she was growing worse and worse, worse and worse, all the time; she will die, I think to myself; she must die. Believe me, I would sooner have gone to the grave myself; and here were her mother and sisters watching me, looking into my eyes ... and their faith in me was wearing away. 'Well? how is she?' 'Oh, all right, all right!' All right, indeed! My mind was failing me. Well, I was sitting one night alone again by my patient. The maid was sitting there too, and snoring away in full swing; I can't find fault with the poor girl, though; she was worn out too. Aleksandra Andreyevna had felt very unwell all the evening; she was very feverish. Until midnight she kept tossing about; at last she seemed to fall asleep; at least, she lay still without stirring. The lamp was burning in the corner before the holy image. I sat there, you know, with my head bent; I even dozed a little. Suddenly it seemed as though some one touched me in the side; I turned round... Good God! Aleksandra Andreyevna was gazing with intent eyes at me ... her lips parted, her cheeks seemed burning. 'What is it?' 'Doctor, shall I die?' 'Merciful Heavens!' 'No, doctor, no; please don't tell me I shall live ... don't say so... If you knew... Listen! for God's sake don't conceal my real position,' and her breath came so fast. 'If I can know for certain that I must die ... then I will tell you all—all!' 'Aleksandra Andreyevna, I beg!' 'Listen; I have not been asleep at all ... I have been looking at you a long while... For God's sake!... I believe in you; you are a good man, an honest man; I entreat you by all that is sacred in the world—tell me the truth! If you knew how important it is for me... Doctor, for God's sake tell me... Am I in danger?' 'What can I tell you, Aleksandra Andreyevna, pray?' 'For God's sake, I beseech you!' 'I can't disguise from you,' I say, 'Aleksandra Andreyevna; you are certainly in danger; but God is merciful.' 'I shall die, I shall die.' And it seemed as though she were pleased; her face grew so bright; I was alarmed. 'Don't be afraid, don't be afraid! I am not frightened of death at all.' She suddenly sat up and leaned on her elbow. 'Now ... yes, now I can tell you that I thank you with my whole heart ... that you are kind and good—that I love you!' I stare at her, like one possessed; it was terrible for me, you know. 'Do you hear, I love you!' 'Aleksandra Andreyevna, how have I deserved—' 'No, no, you don't—you don't understand me.'... And suddenly she stretched out her arms, and taking my head in her hands, she kissed it... Believe me, I almost screamed aloud... I threw myself on my knees, and buried my head in the pillow. She did not speak; her fingers trembled in my hair; I listen; she is weeping. I began to soothe her, to assure her... I really don't know what I did say to her. 'You will wake up the girl,' I say to her; 'Aleksandra Andreyevna, I thank you ... believe me ... calm yourself.' 'Enough, enough!' she persisted; 'never mind all of them; let them wake, then; let them come in—it does not matter; I am dying, you see... And what do you fear? why are you afraid? Lift up your head... Or, perhaps, you don't love me; perhaps I am wrong... In that case, forgive me.' 'Aleksandra Andreyevna, what are you saying!... I love you, Aleksandra Andreyevna.' She looked straight into my eyes, and opened her arms wide. 'Then take me in your arms.' I tell you frankly, I don't know how it was I did not go mad that night. I feel that my patient is killing herself; I see that she is not fully herself; I understand, too, that if she did not consider herself on the point of death, she would never have thought of me; and, indeed, say what you will, it's hard to die at twenty without having known love; this was what was torturing her; this was why, in despair, she caught at me—do you understand now? But she held me in her arms, and would not let me go. 'Have pity on me, Aleksandra Andreyevna, and have pity on yourself,' I say. 'Why,' she says; 'what is there to think of? You know I must die.' ... This she repeated incessantly ... 'If I knew that I should return to life, and be a proper young lady again, I should be ashamed ... of course, ashamed ... but why now?' 'But who has said you will die?' 'Oh, no, leave off! you will not deceive me; you don't know how to lie—look at your face.' ... 'You shall live, Aleksandra Andreyevna; I will cure you; we will ask your mother's blessing ... we will be united—we will be happy.' 'No, no, I have your word; I must die ... you have promised me ... you have told me.' ... It was cruel for me—cruel for many reasons. And see what trifling things can do sometimes; it seems nothing at all, but it's painful. It occurred to her to ask me, what is my name; not my surname, but my first name. I must needs be so unlucky as to be called Trifon. Yes, indeed; Trifon Ivanich. Everyone in the house called me doctor.However, there's no help for it. I say, 'Trifon, madam.' She frowned, shook her head, and muttered something in French—ah, something unpleasant, of course!—and then she laughed—disagreeably too. Well, I spent the whole night with her in this way. Before morning I went away, feeling as though I were mad. When I went again into her room it was daytime, after morning tea. Good God! I could scarcely recognize her; people are laid in their grave looking better than that. I swear to you, on my honour, I don't understand—I absolutely don't understand—now, how I lived through that experience. Three days and nights my patient still lingered on. And what nights! What things she said to me! And on the last night—only imagine to yourself—I was sitting near her, and kept praying to God for one thing only: 'Take her,' I said, 'quickly, and me with her.' Suddenly the old mother comes unexpectedly into the room. I had already the evening before told her—the mother—there was little hope, and it would be well to send for a priest. When the sick girl saw her mother she said, 'It's very well you have come; look at us, we love one another—we have given each other our word.' 'What does she say, doctor? what does she say?' I turned livid. 'She is wandering,' I say; 'the fever.' But she: 'Hush, hush; you told me something quite different just now, and have taken my ring. Why do you pretend? My mother is good—she will forgive—she will understand—and I am dying... I have no need to tell lies; give me your hand.' I jumped up and ran out of the room. The old lady, of course, guessed how it was.

'I will not, however, weary you any longer, and to me too, of course, it's painful to recall all this. My patient passed away the next day. God rest her soul!' the doctor added, speaking quickly and with a sigh. 'Before her death she asked her family to go out and leave me alone with her.'

'Forgive me,' she said; 'I am perhaps to blame towards you ... my illness ... but believe me, I have loved no one more than you ... do not forget me ... keep my ring.'

The doctor turned away; I took his hand.

'Ah!' he said, 'let us talk of something else, or would you care to play preference for a small stake? It is not for people like me to give way to exalted emotions. There's only one thing for me to think of; how to keep the children from crying and the wife from scolding.

Since then, you know, I have had time to enter into lawful wedlock, as they say... Oh ... I took a merchant's daughter—seven thousand for her dowry. Her name's Akulina; it goes well with Trifon. She is an ill-tempered woman, I must tell you, but luckily she's asleep all day... Well, shall it be preference?'

We sat down to preference for halfpenny points. Trifon Ivanich won tworubles and a half from me, and went home late, well pleased with his success.

A JOURNEY*

Edith Wharton

As she lay in her berth, staring at the shadows overhead, the rush of the wheels was in her brain, driving her deeper and deeper into circles of wakeful lucidity. The sleeping-car had sunk into its night-silence. Through the wet window-pane she watched the sudden lights, the long stretches of hurrying blackness. Now and then she turned her head and looked through the opening in the hangings at her husband's curtains across the aisle.

She wondered restlessly if he wanted anything and if she could hear him if he called. His voice had grown very weak within the last months and it irritated him when she did not hear. This irritability, this increasing childish petulance seemed to give expression to their imperceptible estrangement. Like two faces looking at one another through a sheet of glass they were close together, almost touching, but they could not hear or feel each other: the conductivity between them was broken. She, at least, had this sense of separation, and she fancied sometimes that she saw it reflected in the look with which he supplemented his failing words. Doubtless the fault was hers. She was too impenetrably healthy to be touched by the irrelevancies of disease. Her self-reproachful tenderness was tinged with the sense of his irrationality: she had a vague feeling that there was a purpose in his helpless tyrannies. The suddenness of the change had found her so unprepared. A year ago their pulses had beat to one robust measure; both had the same prodigal confidence in an exhaustless future. Now their energies no longer kept step: hers still bounded ahead of life, pre-empting unclaimed regions of hope and activity, while his lagged behind, vainly struggling to overtake her.

When they married, she had such arrears of living to make up: her

*'A Journey' was published in 1889, about a woman's mixed emotions as her husband's health declines rapidly on their train ride home. 'Life had a grudge against her: she was never to be allowed to spread her wings.'

days had been as bare as the whitewashed school-room where she forced innutritious facts upon reluctant children. His coming had broken in on the slumber of circumstance, widening the present till it became the encloser of remotest chances. But imperceptibly the horizon narrowed. Life had a grudge against her: she was never to be allowed to spread her wings.

At first the doctors had said that six weeks of mild air would set him right; but when he came back this assurance was explained as having of course included a winter in a dry climate. They gave up their pretty house, storing the wedding presents and new furniture, and went to Colorado. She had hated it there from the first. Nobody knew her or cared about her; there was no one to wonder at the good match she had made, or to envy her the new dresses and the visiting-cards which were still a surprise to her. And he kept growing worse. She felt herself beset with difficulties too evasive to be fought by so direct a temperament. She still loved him, of course; but he was gradually, undefinably ceasing to be himself. The man she had married had been strong, active, gently masterful: the male whose pleasure it is to clear a way through the material obstructions of life; but now it was she who was the protector, he who must be shielded from importunities and given his drops or his beef-juice though the skies were falling. The routine of the sick-room bewildered her; this punctual administering of medicine seemed as idle as some uncomprehended religious mummery.

There were moments, indeed, when warm gushes of pity swept away her instinctive resentment of his condition, when she still found his old self in his eyes as they groped for each other through the dense medium of his weakness. But these moments had grown rare. Sometimes he frightened her: his sunken expressionless face seemed that of a stranger; his voice was weak and hoarse; his thin-lipped smile a mere muscular contraction. Her hand avoided his damp soft skin, which had lost the familiar roughness of health: she caught herself furtively watching him as she might have watched a strange animal. It frightened her to feel that this was the man she loved; there were hours when to tell him what she suffered seemed the one escape from her fears. But in general she judged herself more leniently, reflecting that she had perhaps been too long alone with him, and that she would feel differently when they were at home again, surrounded by her robust and buoyant family. How she had rejoiced when the doctors at last gave their consent to his going home! She knew, of course, what the decision meant; they both knew. It meant that he was to die; but they dressed the truth in hopeful euphuisms, and at times, in the joy of preparation, she really forgot the purpose of their journey, and slipped into an eager allusion to next year's plans.

At last the day of leaving came. She had a dreadful fear that they would never get away; that somehow at the last moment he would fail her; that the doctors held one of their accustomed treacheries in reserve; but nothing happened. They drove to the station, he was installed in a seat with a rug over his knees and a cushion at his back, and she hung out of the window waving unregretful farewells to the acquaintances she had really never liked till then.

The first twenty-four hours had passed off well. He revived a little and it amused him to look out of the window and to observe the humours of the car. The second day he began to grow weary and to chafe under the dispassionate stare of the freckled child with the lump of chewing-gum. She had to explain to the child's mother that her husband was too ill to be disturbed: a statement received by that lady with a resentment visibly supported by the maternal sentiment of the whole car.

That night he slept badly and the next morning his temperature frightened her: she was sure he was growing worse. The day passed slowly, punctuated by the small irritations of travel. Watching his tired face, she traced in its contractions every rattle and jolt of the tram, till her own body vibrated with sympathetic fatigue. She felt the others observing him too, and hovered restlessly between him and the line of interrogative eyes. The freckled child hung about him like a fly; offers of candy and picture-books failed to dislodge her: she twisted one leg around the other and watched him imperturbably. The porter, as he passed, lingered with vague proffers of help, probably inspired by philanthropic passengers swelling with the sense that 'something ought to be done'; and one nervous man in a skull-cap was audibly concerned as to the possible effect on his wife's health.

The hours dragged on in a dreary inoccupation. Towards dusk she sat down beside him and he laid his hand on hers. The touch startled her. He seemed to be calling her from far off. She looked at him helplessly and his smile went through her like a physical pang.

'Are you very tired?' she asked.

'No, not very.'

'We'll be there soon now.'

'Yes, very soon.'

'This time to-morrow—'

He nodded and they sat silent. When she had put him to bed and crawled into her own berth she tried to cheer herself with the thought that in less than twenty-four hours they would be in New York. Her people would all be at the station to meet her—she pictured their round unanxious faces pressing through the crowd. She only hoped they would not tell him too loudly that he was looking splendidly and would be all right in no time: the subtler sympathies developed by long contact with suffering were making her aware of a certain coarseness of texture in the family sensibilities.

Suddenly she thought she heard him call. She parted the curtains and listened. No, it was only a man snoring at the other end of the car. His snores had a greasy sound, as though they passed through tallow. She lay down and tried to sleep... Had she not heard him move? She started up trembling... The silence frightened her more than any sound. He might not be able to make her hear—he might be calling her now... What made her think of such things? It was merely the familiar tendency of an over-tired mind to fasten itself on the most intolerable chance within the range of its forebodings.... Putting her head out, she listened; but she could not distinguish his breathing from that of the other pairs of lungs about her. She longed to get up and look at him, but she knew the impulse was a mere vent for her restlessness, and the fear of disturbing him restrained her.... The regular movement of his curtain reassured her, she knew not why; she remembered that he had wished her a cheerful good-night; and the sheer inability to endure her fears a moment longer made her put them from her with an effort of her whole sound tired body. She turned on her side and slept.

She sat up stiffly, staring out at the dawn. The train was rushing through a region of bare hillocks huddled against a lifeless sky. It looked like the first day of creation. The air of the car was close, and she pushed up her window to let in the keen wind. Then she looked at her watch: it was seven o'clock, and soon the people about her would be stirring. She slipped into her clothes, smoothed her dishevelled hair and crept to the dressing-room. When she had washed her face and adjusted her dress she felt more hopeful. It was always a struggle for her not to be cheerful in the morning. Her cheeks burned deliciously under the coarse towel and the wet hair about her temples broke into strong upward tendrils. Every inch of her was full of life and elasticity. And in ten hours they would be at home!

She stepped to her husband's berth: it was time for him to take his early glass of milk. The window-shade was down, and in the dusk of the curtained enclosure she could just see that he lay sideways, with his face away from her. She leaned over him and drew up the shade. As she did so she touched one of his hands. It felt cold.

She bent closer, laying her hand on his arm and calling him by name. He did not move. She spoke again more loudly; she grasped his shoulder and gently shook it. He lay motionless. She caught hold of his hand again: it slipped from her limply, like a dead thing. A dead thing? ... Her breath caught. She must see his face. She leaned forward, and hurriedly, shrinkingly, with a sickening reluctance of the flesh, laid her hands on his shoulders and turned him over. His head fell back; his face looked small and smooth; he gazed at her with steady eyes.

She remained motionless for a long time, holding him thus; and they looked at each other. Suddenly she shrank back: the longing to scream, to call out, to fly from him, had almost overpowered her. But a strong hand arrested her. Good God! If it were known that he was dead they would be put off the train at the next station—

In a terrifying flash of remembrance there arose before her a scene she had once witnessed in travelling, when a husband and wife, whose child had died in the train, had been thrust out at some chance station. She saw them standing on the platform with the child's body between them; she had never forgotten the dazed look with which they followed the receding train. And this was what would happen to her. Within the next hour she might find herself on the platform of some strange station, alone with her husband's body.... Anything but that! It was too horrible—She quivered like a creature at bay.

As she cowered there, she felt the train moving more slowly. It was coming then—they were approaching a station! She saw again the husband and wife standing on the lonely platform; and with a violent gesture she drew down the shade to hide her husband's face.

Feeling dizzy, she sank down on the edge of the berth, keeping away from his outstretched body, and pulling the curtains close, so that he and she were shut into a kind of sepulchral twilight. She tried to think. At all costs she must conceal the fact that he was dead. But how? Her mind refused to act: she could not plan, combine. She could think of no way but to sit there, clutching the curtains, all day long.

She heard the porter making up her bed; people were beginning to move about the car; the dressing-room door was being opened and shut. She tried to rouse herself. At length with a supreme effort she rose to her feet, stepping into the aisle of the car and drawing the curtains tight behind her. She noticed that they still parted slightly with the motion of the car, and finding a pin in her dress she fastened them together. Now she was safe. She looked round and saw the porter. She fancied he was watching her.

'Ain't he awake yet?' he enquired.

'No,' she faltered.

'I got his milk all ready when he wants it. You know you told me to have it for him by seven.'

She nodded silently and crept into her seat.

At half-past eight the train reached Buffalo. By this time the other passengers were dressed and the berths had been folded back for the day. The porter, moving to and fro under his burden of sheets and pillows, glanced at her as he passed. At length he said, 'Ain't he going to get up? You know we're ordered to make up the berths as early as we can.'

She turned cold with fear. They were just entering the station.

'Oh, not yet,' she stammered. 'Not till he's had his milk. Won't you get it, please?'

'All right. Soon as we start again.'

When the train moved on he reappeared with the milk. She took it from him and sat vaguely looking at it: her brain moved slowly from one idea to another, as though they were stepping-stones set far apart across a whirling flood. At length she became aware that the porter still hovered expectantly.

'Will I give it to him?' he suggested.

'Oh, no,' she cried, rising. 'He—he's asleep yet, I think—'

She waited till the porter had passed on; then she unpinned the curtains and slipped behind them. In the semi-obscurity her husband's face stared up at her like a marble mask with agate eyes. The eyes were dreadful. She put out her hand and drew down the lids. Then she remembered the glass of milk in her other hand: what was she to do with it? She thought of raising the window and throwing it out; but to do so she would have to lean across his body and bring her face close to his. She decided to drink the milk.

She returned to her seat with the empty glass and after a while the porter came back to get it.

'When'll I fold up his bed?' he asked.

'Oh, not now—not yet; he's ill—he's very ill. Can't you let him stay as he is? The doctor wants him to lie down as much as possible.'

He scratched his head. 'Well, if he's really sick—'

He took the empty glass and walked away, explaining to the passengers that the party behind the curtains was too sick to get up just yet.

She found herself the centre of sympathetic eyes. A motherly woman with an intimate smile sat down beside her.

'I'm real sorry to hear your husband's sick. I've had a remarkable amount of sickness in my family and maybe I could assist you. Can I take a look at him?'

'Oh, no—no, please! He mustn't be disturbed.'

The lady accepted the rebuff indulgently.

'Well, it's just as you say, of course, but you don't look to me as if you'd had much experience in sickness and I'd have been glad to assist you. What do you generally do when your husband's taken this way?'

'I—I let him sleep.'

'Too much sleep ain't any too healthful either. Don't you give him any medicine?'

'Y—yes.'

'Don't you wake him to take it?'

'Yes.'

'When does he take the next dose?'

'Not for—two hours—'

The lady looked disappointed. 'Well, if I was you I'd try giving it oftener. That's what I do with my folks.'

After that many faces seemed to press upon her. The passengers were on their way to the dining-car, and she was conscious that as they passed down the aisle they glanced curiously at the closed curtains. One lantern-jawed man with prominent eyes stood still and tried to shoot his projecting glance through the division between the folds. The freckled child, returning from breakfast, waylaid the passers with a buttery clutch, saying in a loud whisper, 'He's sick'; and once the conductor came by, asking for tickets. She shrank into her corner and looked out of the window at the flying trees and houses, meaningless hieroglyphs of an endlessly unrolled papyrus.

Now and then the train stopped, and the newcomers on entering the car stared in turn at the closed curtains. More and more people seemed to pass—their faces began to blend fantastically with the images surging in her brain....

Later in the day a fat man detached himself from the mist of faces. He had a creased stomach and soft pale lips. As he pressed himself into the seat facing her she noticed that he was dressed in black broadcloth, with a soiled white tie.

'Husband's pretty bad this morning, is he?'

'Yes.'

'Dear, dear! Now that's terribly distressing, ain't it?' An apostolic smile revealed his gold-filled teeth.

'Of course you know there's no sech thing as sickness. Ain't that a lovely thought? Death itself is but a deloosion of our grosser senses.

On'y lay yourself open to the influx of the sperrit, submit yourself passively to the action of the divine force, and disease and dissolution will cease to exist for you. If you could indooce your husband to read this little pamphlet—'

The faces about her again grew indistinct. She had a vague recollection of hearing the motherly lady and the parent of the freckled child ardently disputing the relative advantages of trying several medicines at once, or of taking each in turn; the motherly lady maintaining that the competitive system saved time; the other objecting that you couldn't tell which remedy had effected the cure; their voices went on and on, like bell-buoys droning through a fog.... The porter came up now and then with questions that she did not understand, but that somehow she must have answered since he went away again without repeating them; every two hours the motherly lady reminded her that her husband ought to have his drops; people left the car and others replaced them...

Her head was spinning and she tried to steady herself by clutching at her thoughts as they swept by, but they slipped away from her like bushes on the side of a sheer precipice down which she seemed to be falling. Suddenly her mind grew clear again and she found herself vividly picturing what would happen when the train reached New York. She shuddered as it occurred to her that he would be quite cold and that someone might perceive he had been dead since morning.

She thought hurriedly:—'If they see I am not surprised they will suspect something. They will ask questions, and if I tell them the truth they won't believe me—no one would believe me! It will be terrible'—and she kept repeating to herself:—'I must pretend I don't know. I must pretend I don't know. When they open the curtains I must go up to him quite naturally—and then I must scream.' ... She had an idea that the scream would be very hard to do.

Gradually new thoughts crowded upon her, vivid and urgent: she tried to separate and restrain them, but they beset her clamorously, like her school-children at the end of a hot day, when she was too tired to silence them. Her head grew confused, and she felt a sick fear of forgetting her part, of betraying herself by some unguarded word or look.

'I must pretend I don't know,' she went on murmuring. The words had lost their significance, but she repeated them mechanically, as though they had been a magic formula, until suddenly she heard herself saying: 'I can't remember, I can't remember!'

Her voice sounded very loud, and she looked about her in terror; but no one seemed to notice that she had spoken.

As she glanced down the car her eye caught the curtains of her husband's berth, and she began to examine the monotonous arabesques woven through their heavy folds. The pattern was intricate and difficult to trace; she gazed fixedly at the curtains and as she did so the thick stuff grew transparent and through it she saw her husband's face—his dead face. She struggled to avert her look, but her eyes refused to move and her head seemed to be held in a vice. At last, with an effort that left her weak and shaking, she turned away; but it was of no use; close in front of her, small and smooth, was her husband's face. It seemed to be suspended in the air between her and the false braids of the woman who sat in front of her. With an uncontrollable gesture she stretched out her hand to push the face away, and suddenly she felt the touch of his smooth skin. She repressed a cry and half started from her seat. The woman with the false braids looked around, and feeling that she must justify her movement in some way she rose and lifted her travelling-bag from the opposite seat. She unlocked the bag and looked into it; but the first object her hand met was a small flask of her husband's, thrust there at the last moment, in the haste of departure. She locked the bag and closed her eyes ... his face was there again, hanging between her eye-balls and lids like a waxen mask against a red curtain....

She roused herself with a shiver. Had she fainted or slept? Hours seemed to have elapsed; but it was still broad day, and the people about her were sitting in the same attitudes as before.

A sudden sense of hunger made her aware that she had eaten nothing since morning. The thought of food filled her with disgust, but she dreaded a return of faintness, and remembering that she had some biscuits in her bag she took one out and ate it. The dry crumbs choked her, and she hastily swallowed a little brandy from her husband's flask. The burning sensation in her throat acted as a counter-irritant, momentarily relieving the dull ache of her nerves.

Then she felt a gently-stealing warmth, as though a soft air fanned her, and the swarming fears relaxed their clutch, receding through the stillness that enclosed her, a stillness soothing as the spacious quietude of a summer day. She slept.

Through her sleep she felt the impetuous rush of the train. It seemed to be life itself that was sweeping her on with headlong inexorable force—sweeping her into darkness and terror, and the awe of unknown days.—Now all at once everything was still—not a sound, not a pulsation... She was dead in her turn, and lay beside him with smooth upstaring face. How quiet it was!—and yet she heard feet coming, the feet of the men who were to carry them away... She could feel too—she felt a sudden prolonged vibration, a series of hard shocks, and then another plunge into darkness: the darkness of death this time—a black whirlwind on which they were both spinning like leaves, in wild uncoiling spirals, with millions and millions of the dead....

❧

She sprang up in terror. Her sleep must have lasted a long time, for the winter day had paled and the lights had been lit. The car was in confusion, and as she regained her self-possession she saw that the passengers were gathering up their wraps and bags. The woman with the false braids had brought from the dressing-room a sickly ivy-plant in a bottle, and the Christian Scientist was reversing his cuffs. The porter passed down the aisle with his impartial brush. An impersonal figure with a gold-banded cap asked for her husband's ticket. A voice shouted 'Baig-gage express!' and she heard the clicking of metal as the passengers handed over their checks.

Presently her window was blocked by an expanse of sooty wall, and the train passed into the Harlem tunnel. The journey was over; in a few minutes she would see her family pushing their joyous way through the throng at the station. Her heart dilated. The worst terror was past....

'We'd better get him up now, hadn't we?' asked the porter, touching her arm.

He had her husband's hat in his hand and was meditatively revolving it under his brush.

She looked at the hat and tried to speak; but suddenly the car grew dark. She flung up her arms, struggling to catch at something, and fell face downward, striking her head against the dead man's berth.

A NEW ENGLAND NUN

Mary E. Wilkins Freeman

It was late in the afternoon, and the light was waning. There was a difference in the look of the tree shadows out in the yard. Somewhere in the distance cows were lowing and a little bell was tinkling; now and then a farm-wagon tilted by, and the dust flew; some blue-shirted labourers with shovels over their shoulders plodded past; little swarms of flies were dancing up and down before the peoples' faces in the soft air. There seemed to be a gentle stir arising over everything for the mere sake of subsidence—a very premonition of rest and hush and night.

This soft diurnal commotion was over Louisa Ellis also. She had been peacefully sewing at her sitting-room window all the afternoon. Now she quilted her needle carefully into her work, which she folded precisely, and laid in a basket with her thimble and thread and scissors. Louisa Ellis could not remember that ever in her life she had mislaid one of these little feminine appurtenances, which had become, from long use and constant association, a very part of her personality.

Louisa tied a green apron round her waist, and got out a flat straw hat with a green ribbon. Then she went into the garden with a little blue crockery bowl, to pick some currants for her tea. After the currants were picked she sat on the back door-step and stemmed them, collecting the stems carefully in her apron, and afterwards throwing them into the hen-coop. She looked sharply at the grass beside the step to see if any had fallen there.

Louisa was slow and still in her movements; it took her a long time to prepare her tea; but when ready it was set forth with as much grace as if she had been a veritable guest to her own self. The little square table stood exactly in the centre of the kitchen, and was covered with a starched linen cloth whose border pattern of flowers glistened. Louisa had a damask napkin on her tea-tray, where were arranged a cut-glass tumbler full of teaspoons, a silver cream-pitcher, a china sugar-bowl, and one pink china cup and saucer. Louisa used china every day—something which none of her neighbours did. They whispered about it among themselves. Their daily tables were laid with common crockery, their sets of best china stayed in the Parlor closet, and Louisa Ellis was no richer nor better bred than they. Still she would use the china. She had for her supper a glass dish full of sugared currants, a plate of little cakes, and one of light white biscuits. Also a leaf or two of lettuce, which she cut up daintily. Louisa was very fond of lettuce, which she raised to perfection in her little garden. She ate quite heartily, though in a delicate, pecking way; it seemed almost surprising that any considerable bulk of the food should vanish.

After tea she filled a plate with nicely baked thin corn-cakes, and carried them out into the back-yard.

'Ceasar!' she called. 'Ceasar! Ceasar!'

There was a little rush, and the clank of a chain, and a large yellow-and-white dog appeared at the door of his tiny hut, which was half hidden among the tall grasses and flowers. Louisa patted him and gave him the corn-cakes. Then she returned to the house and washed the tea-things, polishing the china carefully. The twilight had deepened; the chorus of the frogs floated in at the open window wonderfully loud and shrill, and once in a while a long sharp drone from a tree-toad pierced it. Louisa took off her green gingham apron, disclosing a shorter one of pink and white print. She lighted her lamp, and sat down again with her sewing.

In about half an hour Joe Dagget came. She heard his heavy step on the walk, and rose and took off her pink-and-white apron. Under that was still another—white linen with a little cambric edging on the bottom; that was Louisa's company apron. She never wore it without her calico sewing apron over it unless she had a guest. She had barely folded the pink and white one with methodical haste and laid it in a table-drawer when the door opened and Joe Dagget entered.

He seemed to fill up the whole room. A little yellow canary that had been asleep in his green cage at the south window woke up and fluttered wildly, beating his little yellow wings against the wires. He always did so when Joe Dagget came into the room.

'Good-evening,' said Louisa. She extended her hand with a kind of solemn cordiality.

'Good-evening, Louisa,' returned the man, in a loud voice.

She placed a chair for him, and they sat facing each other, with the table between them. He sat bolt-upright, toeing out his heavy feet squarely, glancing with a good-humoured uneasiness around the room. She sat gently erect, folding her slender hands in her white-linen lap.

'Been a pleasant day,' remarked Dagget.

'Real pleasant,' Louisa assented, softly. 'Have you been haying?' she asked, after a little while.

'Yes, I've been haying all day, down in the ten-acre lot. Pretty hot work.'

'It must be.'

'Yes, it's pretty hot work in the sun.'

'Is your mother well to-day?'

'Yes, mother's pretty well.'

'I suppose Lily Dyer's with her now?'

Dagget coloured. 'Yes, she's with her,' he answered, slowly.

He was not very young, but there was a boyish look about his large face. Louisa was not quite as old as he, her face was fairer and smoother, but she gave people the impression of being older.

'I suppose she's a good deal of help to your mother,' she said, further.

'I guess she is; I don't know how mother'd get along without her,' said Dagget, with a sort of embarrassed warmth.

'She looks like a real capable girl. She's pretty-looking too,' remarked Louisa.

'Yes, she is pretty fair looking.'

Presently Dagget began fingering the books on the table. There was a square red autograph album, and a Young Lady's Gift-Book which had belonged to Louisa's mother. He took them up one after the other and opened them; then laid them down again, the album on the Gift-Book.

Louisa kept eying them with mild uneasiness. Finally she rose and changed the position of the books, putting the album underneath. That was the way they had been arranged in the first place.

Dagget gave an awkward little laugh. 'Now what difference did it make which book was on top?' said he.

Louisa looked at him with a deprecating smile. 'I always keep them that way,' murmured she.

'You do beat everything,' said Dagget, trying to laugh again. His large face was flushed.

He remained about an hour longer, then rose to take leave. Going out, he stumbled over a rug, and trying to recover himself, hit Louisa's work-basket on the table, and knocked it on the floor.

He looked at Louisa, then at the rolling spools; he ducked himself awkwardly toward them, but she stopped him. 'Never mind,' said she; 'I'll pick them up after you're gone.'

She spoke with a mild stiffness. Either she was a little disturbed, or his nervousness affected her, and made her seem constrained in her effort to reassure him.

When Joe Dagget was outside he drew in the sweet evening air with a sigh, and felt much as an innocent and perfectly well-intentioned bear might after his exit from a china shop.

Louisa, on her part, felt much as the kind-hearted, long-suffering owner of the china shop might have done after the exit of the bear.

She tied on the pink, then the green apron, picked up all the scattered treasures and replaced them in her work-basket, and straightened the rug. Then she set the lamp on the floor, and began sharply examining the carpet. She even rubbed her fingers over it, and looked at them.

'He's tracked in a good deal of dust,' she murmured. 'I thought he must have.'

Louisa got a dust-pan and brush, and swept Joe Dagget's track carefully.

If he could have known it, it would have increased his perplexity and uneasiness, although it would not have disturbed his loyalty in the least. He came twice a week to see Louisa Ellis, and every time, sitting there in her delicately sweet room, he felt as if surrounded by a hedge of lace. He was afraid to stir lest he should put a clumsy foot or hand through the fairy web, and he had always the consciousness that Louisa was watching fearfully lest he should.

Still the lace and Louisa commanded perforce his perfect respect and patience and loyalty. They were to be married in a month, after a singular courtship which had lasted for a matter of fifteen years. For fourteen out of the fifteen years the two had not once seen each other, and they had seldom exchanged letters. Joe had been all those years in Australia, where he had gone to make his fortune, and where he had stayed until he made it. He would have stayed fifty years if it had taken so long, and come home feeble and tottering, or never come home at all, to marry Louisa.

But the fortune had been made in the fourteen years, and he had come home now to marry the woman who had been patiently and unquestioningly waiting for him all that time.

Shortly after they were engaged he had announced to Louisa his determination to strike out into new fields, and secure a competency before they should be married. She had listened and assented with the sweet serenity which never failed her, not even when her lover set forth on that long and uncertain journey. Joe, buoyed up as he was by his sturdy determination, broke down a little at the last, but Louisa kissed him with a mild blush, and said good-by.

'It won't be for long,' poor Joe had said, huskily; but it was for fourteen years.

In that length of time much had happened. Louisa's mother and brother had died, and she was all alone in the world. But greatest happening of all—a subtle happening which both were too simple to understand—Louisa's feet had turned into a path, smooth maybe under a calm, serene sky, but so straight and unswerving that it could only meet a check at her grave, and so narrow that there was no room for any one at her side.

Louisa's first emotion when Joe Dagget came home (he had not apprised her of his coming) was consternation, although she would not admit it to herself, and he never dreamed of it. Fifteen years ago she had been in love with him—at least she considered herself to be. Just at that time, gently acquiescing with and falling into the natural drift of girlhood, she had seen marriage ahead as a reasonable feature and a probable desirability of life. She had listened with calm docility to her mother's views upon the subject. Her mother was remarkable for her cool sense and sweet, even temperament. She talked wisely to her daughter when Joe Dagget presented himself, and Louisa accepted him with no hesitation. He was the first lover she had ever had.

She had been faithful to him all these years. She had never dreamed of the possibility of marrying anyone else. Her life, especially for the last seven years, had been full of a pleasant peace, she had never felt discontented nor impatient over her lover's absence; still she had always looked forward to his return and their marriage as the inevitable conclusion of things. However, she had fallen into a way of placing it so far in the future that it was almost equal to placing it over the boundaries of another life.

When Joe came she had been expecting him, and expecting to be married for fourteen years, but she was as much surprised and taken aback as if she had never thought of it.

Joe's consternation came later. He eyed Louisa with an instant confirmation of his old admiration. She had changed but little. She still kept her pretty manner and soft grace, and was, he considered, every whit as attractive as ever. As for himself, his stent was done; he had turned his face away from fortune-seeking, and the old winds of romance whistled as loud and sweet as ever through his ears. All the song which he had been wont to hear in them was Louisa; he had for a long time a loyal belief that he heard it still, but finally it seemed to him that although the winds sang always that one song, it had another name. But for Louisa the wind had never more than murmured; now it had gone down, and everything was still. She listened for a little while with half-wistful attention; then she turned quietly away and went to work on her wedding clothes.

Joe had made some extensive and quite magnificent alterations in his house. It was the old homestead; the newly-married couple would live there, for Joe could not desert his mother, who refused to leave her old home. So Louisa must leave hers. Every morning, rising and going about among her neat maidenly possessions, she felt as one looking her last upon the faces of dear friends. It was true that in a measure she could take them with her, but, robbed of their old environments, they would appear in such new guises that they would almost cease to be themselves. Then there were some peculiar features of her happy solitary life which she would probably be obliged to relinquish altogether. Sterner tasks than these graceful but half-needless ones would probably devolve upon her. There would be a large house to care for; there would be company to entertain; there would be Joe's rigorous and feeble old mother to wait upon; and it would be contrary to all thrifty village traditions for her to keep more than one servant. Louisa had a little still, and she used to occupy herself pleasantly in summer weather with distilling the sweet and aromatic essences from roses and peppermint and spearmint. By-and-by her still must be laid away. Her store of essences was already considerable, and there would be no time for her to distil for the mere pleasure of it. Then Joe's mother would think it foolishness; she had already hinted her opinion in the matter. Louisa dearly loved to sew a linen seam, not always for use, but for the simple, mild pleasure which she took in it. She would have been loath to confess how more than once she had ripped a seam for the mere delight of sewing it together again. Sitting at her window during long sweet afternoons, drawing her needle gently through the dainty fabric, she was peace itself. But there was small chance of such foolish comfort in the future. Joe's mother, domineering, shrewd old matron that she was even in her old age, and very likely even Joe himself, with his honest masculine rudeness, would laugh and frown down all these pretty but senseless old maiden ways.

Louisa had almost the enthusiasm of an artist over the mere order and cleanliness of her solitary home. She had throbs of genuine triumph at the sight of the window-panes which she had polished until they shone like jewels. She gloated gently over her orderly bureau-drawers, with their exquisitely folded contents redolent with lavender and sweet clover and very purity. Could she be sure of the endurance of even this? She had visions, so startling that she half repudiated them as indelicate, of coarse masculine belongings strewn about in endless litter; of dust and disorder arising necessarily from a coarse masculine presence in the midst of all this delicate harmony.

Among her forebodings of disturbance, not the least was with regard to Ceasar. Ceasar was a veritable hermit of a dog. For the greater part of his life he had dwelt in his secluded hut, shut out from the society of his kind and all innocent canine joys. Never had Ceasar since his early youth watched at a woodchuck's hole; never had he known the delights of a stray bone at a neighbour's kitchen door. And it was all on account of a sin committed when hardly out of his puppyhood. No one knew the possible depth of remorse of which this mild-visaged, altogether innocent-looking old dog might be capable; but whether or not he had encountered remorse, he had encountered a full measure of righteous retribution. Old Ceasar seldom lifted up his voice in a growl or a bark; he was fat and sleepy; there were yellow rings which looked like spectacles around his dim old eyes; but there was a neighbour who bore on his hand the imprint of several of Ceasar's sharp white youthful teeth, and for that he had lived at the end of a chain, all alone in a little hut, for fourteen years. The neighbour, who was choleric and smarting with the pain of his wound, had demanded either Ceasar's death or complete ostracism. So Louisa's brother, to whom the dog had belonged, had built him his little kennel and tied him up. It was now fourteen years since, in a flood of youthful spirits, he had inflicted that memorable bite, and with the exception of short excursions, always at the end of the chain, under the strict guardianship of his master or Louisa, the old dog had remained a close prisoner. It is doubtful if, with his limited ambition, he took much pride in the fact, but it is certain that he was possessed of considerable cheap fame. He was regarded by all the children in the village and by many adults as a very monster of ferocity. St George's dragon could hardly have surpassed in evil repute Louisa Ellis's old yellow dog. Mothers charged their children with solemn emphasis not to go too near to him, and the children listened and believed greedily, with a fascinated appetite for terror, and ran by Louisa's house stealthily, with many sidelong and backward glances at the terrible dog. If perchance he sounded a hoarse bark, there was a panic. Wayfarers chancing into Louisa's yard eyed him with respect, and inquired if the chain were stout. Ceasar at large might have seemed a very ordinary dog, and excited no comment whatever; chained, his reputation overshadowed him, so that he lost his own proper outlines and looked darkly vague and enormous. Joe Dagget, however, with his good-humoured sense and shrewdness, saw him as he was. He strode valiantly up to him and patted him on the head, in spite of Louisa's soft clamour of warning, and even attempted to set him loose. Louisa grew so alarmed that he desisted, but kept announcing his opinion in the matter quite forcibly at intervals. 'There ain't a better-natured dog in town,' he would say, 'and it's down-right cruel to keep him tied up there. Someday I'm going to take him out.'

Louisa had very little hope that he would not, one of these days, when their interests and possessions should be more completely fused in one. She pictured to herself Ceasar on the rampage through the quiet and unguarded village. She saw innocent children bleeding in his path. She was herself very fond of the old dog, because he had belonged to her dead brother, and he was always very gentle with her; still she had great faith in his ferocity. She always warned people not to go too near him. She fed him on ascetic fare of corn-mush and cakes, and never fired his dangerous temper with heating and sanguinary diet of flesh and bones. Louisa looked at the old dog munching his simple fare, and thought of her approaching marriage and trembled. Still no anticipation of disorder and confusion in lieu of sweet peace and harmony, no forebodings of Ceasar on the rampage, no wild fluttering of her little yellow canary, were sufficient to turn her a hair's-breadth. Joe Dagget had been fond of her and working for her all these years. It was not for her, whatever came to pass, to prove untrue and break his heart. She put the exquisite little stitches into her wedding-garments, and the time went on until it was only a week before her wedding-day. It was a Tuesday evening, and the wedding was to be a week from Wednesday.

There was a full moon that night. About nine o'clock Louisa strolled down the road a little way. There were harvest-fields on either hand, bordered by low stone walls. Luxuriant clumps of bushes grew beside the wall, and trees—wild cherry and old apple-trees—at intervals. Presently Louisa sat down on the wall and looked about her with mildly sorrowful reflectiveness. Tall shrubs of blueberry and meadow-sweet, all woven together and tangled with blackberry vines and horse briers, shut her in on either side. She had a little clear space between them. Opposite her, on the other side of the road, was a spreading tree; the moon shone between its boughs, and the leaves twinkled like silver. The road was bespread with a beautiful shifting dapple of silver and shadow; the air was full of a mysterious sweetness. 'I wonder if it's wild grapes?' murmured Louisa. She sat there some time. She was just thinking of rising, when she heard footsteps and low voices, and remained quiet. It was a lonely place, and she felt a little timid. She thought she would keep still in the shadow and let the persons, whoever they might be, pass her.

But just before they reached her the voices ceased, and the footsteps. She understood that their owners had also found seats upon the stone wall. She was wondering if she could not steal away unobserved, when the voice broke the stillness. It was Joe Dagget's. She sat still and listened.

The voice was announced by a loud sigh, which was as familiar as itself. 'Well,' said Dagget, 'you've made up your mind, then, I suppose?'

'Yes,' returned another voice; 'I'm going day after to-morrow.'

'That's Lily Dyer,' thought Louisa to herself. The voice embodied itself in her mind. She saw a girl tall and full-figured, with a firm, fair face, looking fairer and firmer in the moonlight, her strong yellow hair braided in a close knot. A girl full of a calm rustic strength and bloom, with a masterful way which might have beseemed a princess. Lily Dyer was a favourite with the village folk; she had just the qualities to arouse the admiration. She was good and handsome and smart. Louisa had often heard her praises sounded.

'Well,' said Joe Dagget, 'I ain't got a word to say.'

'I don't know what you could say,' returned Lily Dyer.

'Not a word to say,' repeated Joe, drawing out the words heavily. Then there was a silence. 'I ain't sorry,' he began at last, 'that that happened yesterday—that we kind of let on how we felt to each other. I guess it's just as well we knew. Of course I can't do anything any different. I'm going right on an' get married next week. I ain't going back on a woman that's waited for me fourteen years, an' break her heart.'

'If you should jilt her to-morrow, I wouldn't have you,' spoke up the girl, with sudden vehemence.

'Well, I ain't going to give you the chance,' said he; 'but I don't believe you would, either.'

'You'd see I wouldn't. Honour's honour, an' right's right. An' I'd never think anything of any man that went against 'em for me or any other girl; you'd find that out, Joe Dagget.'

'Well, you'll find out fast enough that I ain't going against 'em for you or any other girl,' returned he. Their voices sounded almost as if they were angry with each other. Louisa was listening eagerly.

'I'm sorry you feel as if you must go away,' said Joe, 'but I don't know but it's best.'

'Of course it's best. I hope you and I have got common-sense.'

'Well, I suppose you're right.' Suddenly Joe's voice got an undertone of tenderness. 'Say, Lily,' said he, 'I'll get along well enough myself, but I can't bear to think—You don't suppose you're going to fret much over it?'

'I guess you'll find out I sha'n't fret much over a married man.'

'Well, I hope you won't—I hope you won't, Lily. God knows I do. And—I hope—one of these days—you'll—come across somebody else—'

'I don't see any reason why I shouldn't.' Suddenly her tone changed. She spoke in a sweet, clear voice, so loud that she could have been heard across the street. 'No, Joe Dagget,' said she, 'I'll never marry any other man as long as I live. I've got good sense, an' I ain't going to break my heart nor make a fool of myself; but I'm never going to be married, you can be sure of that. I ain't that sort of a girl to feel this way twice.'

Louisa heard an exclamation and a soft commotion behind the bushes; then Lily spoke again—the voice sounded as if she had risen. 'This must be put a stop to,' said she. 'We've stayed here long enough. I'm going home.'

Louisa sat there in a daze, listening to their retreating steps. After a while she got up and slunk softly home herself. The next day she did her housework methodically; that was as much a matter of course as breathing; but she did not sew on her wedding-clothes. She sat at her window and meditated. In the evening Joe came. Louisa Ellis had never known that she had any diplomacy in her, but when she came to look for it that night she found it, although meek of its kind, among her little feminine weapons. Even now she could hardly believe that she had heard aright, and that she would not do Joe a terrible injury should she break her troth-plight. She wanted to sound him without betraying too soon her own inclinations in the matter. She did it successfully, and they finally came to an understanding; but it was a difficult thing, for he was as afraid of betraying himself as she.

She never mentioned Lily Dyer. She simply said that while she had no cause of complaint against him, she had lived so long in one way that she shrank from making a change.

'Well, I never shrank, Louisa,' said Dagget. 'I'm going to be honest enough to say that I think maybe it's better this way; but if you'd wanted to keep on, I'd have stuck to you till my dying day. I hope you know that.'

'Yes, I do,' said she.

That night she and Joe parted more tenderly than they had done for a long time. Standing in the door, holding each other's hands, a last great wave of regretful memory swept over them.

'Well, this ain't the way we've thought it was all going to end, is it, Louisa?' said Joe.

She shook her head. There was a little quiver on her placid face.

'You let me know if there's ever anything I can do for you,' said he. 'I ain't ever going to forget you, Louisa.' Then he kissed her, and went down the path.

Louisa, all alone by herself that night, wept a little, she hardly knew why; but the next morning, on waking, she felt like a queen who, after fearing lest her domain be wrested away from her, sees it firmly insured in her possession.

Now the tall weeds and grasses might cluster around Ceasar's little hermit hut, the snow might fall on its roof year in and year out, but he never would go on a rampage through the unguarded village. Now the little canary might turn itself into a peaceful yellow ball night after night, and have no need to wake and flutter with wild terror against its bars. Louisa could sew linen seams, and distil roses, and dust and polish and fold away in lavender, as long as she listed. That afternoon she sat with her needle-work at the window, and felt fairly steeped in peace. Lily Dyer, tall and erect and blooming, went past; but she felt no qualm. If Louisa Ellis had sold her birth right she did not know it, the taste of the pottage was so delicious, and had been her sole satisfaction for so long. Serenity and placid narrowness had become to her as the birth right itself. She gazed ahead through a long reach of future days strung together like pearls in a rosary, every one like the others, and all smooth and flawless and innocent, and her heart went up in thankfulness. Outside was the fervid summer afternoon; the air was filled with the sounds of the busy harvest of men and birds and bees; there were halloos, metallic clatterings, sweet calls, and long hummings. Louisa sat, prayerfully numbering her days, like an uncloistered nun.

THE PIT AND THE PENDULUM

Edgar Allan Poe

'Here an unholy mob of torturers with an insatiable thirst for innocent blood, once fed their long frenzy. Now our homeland is safe, the funereal cave destroyed, and life and health appear where dreadful death once was.'

I was sick, sick unto death, with that long agony, and when they at length unbound me, and I was permitted to sit, I felt that my senses were leaving me. The sentence, the dread sentence of death, was the last of distinct accentuation which reached my ears. After that, the sound of the inquisitorial voices seemed merged in one dreamy indeterminate hum. It conveyed to my soul the idea of REVOLUTION, perhaps from its association in fancy with the burr of a mill-wheel. This only for a brief period, for presently I heard no more. Yet, for a while, I saw, but with how terrible an exaggeration! I saw the lips of the black-robed judges. They appeared to me white—whiter than the sheet upon which I trace these words—and thin even to grotesqueness; thin with the intensity of their expression of firmness, of immovable resolution, of stern contempt of human torture. I saw that the decrees of what to me was fate were still issuing from those lips. I saw them writhe with a deadly locution. I saw them fashion the syllables of my name, and I shuddered, because no sound succeeded. I saw, too, for a few moments of delirious horror, the soft and nearly imperceptible waving of the sable draperies which enwrapped the walls of the apartment; and then my vision fell upon the seven tall candles upon the table. At first they wore the aspect of charity, and seemed white slender angels who would save me: but then all at once there came a most deadly nausea over my spirit, and I felt every fibre in my frame thrill, as if I had touched the wire of a galvanic battery, while the angel forms became meaningless spectres, with heads of flame, and I saw that from them there would be no help. And then there stole into my fancy, like a rich musical note, the thought of what sweet rest there must be in the grave. The thought came gently and stealthily, and it seemed long before it attained full appreciation; but just as my spirit came at length properly to feel and entertain it, the figures of the judges vanished, as if magically, from before me; the tall candles sank into nothingness; their flames went out utterly; the blackness of darkness superened; all sensations appeared swallowed up in a mad rushing descent as of the soul into Hades. Then silence, and stillness, and night were the universe.

I had swooned; but still will not say that all of consciousness was lost. What of it there remained I will not attempt to define, or even to describe; yet all was not lost. In the deepest slumber—no! In delirium—no! In a swoon—no! In death—no! Even in the grave all was not lost. Else there is no immortality for man. Arousing from the most profound of slumbers, we break the gossamer web of some dream. Yet in a second afterwards (so frail may that web have been) we remember not that we have dreamed. In the return to life from the swoon there are two stages; first, that of the sense of mental or spiritual; secondly, that of the sense of physical existence. It seems probable that if, upon reaching the second stage, we could recall the impressions of the first, we should find these impressions eloquent in memories of the gulf beyond. And that gulf is, what? How at least shall we distinguish its shadows from those of the tomb? But if the impressions of what I have termed the first stage are not at will recalled, yet, after long interval, do they not come unbidden, while we marvel whence they come? He who has never swooned is not he who finds strange palaces and wildly familiar faces in coals that glow; is not he who beholds floating in mid-air the sad visions that the many may not view; is not he who ponders over the perfume of some novel flower; is not he whose brain grows bewildered with the meaning of some musical cadence which has never before arrested his attention.

Amid frequent and thoughtful endeavours to remember, amid earnest struggles to regather some token of the state of seeming nothingness into which my soul had lapsed, there have been moments when I have dreamed of success; there have been brief, very brief periods when I have conjured up remembrances which the lucid reason of a later epoch assures me could have had reference only to that condition of seeming unconsciousness. These shadows of memory tell indistinctly of tall figures that lifted and bore me in silence down—down—still down—till a hideous dizziness oppressed me at the mere idea of the interminableness of the descent. They tell also of a vague horror at my heart on account of that heart's unnatural stillness. Then comes a sense of sudden motionlessness throughout all things; as if those who bore me (a ghastly train!) had outrun, in their descent, the limits of the limitless, and paused from the wearisomeness of their toil. After this I call to mind flatness and dampness; and then all is MADNESS—the madness of a memory which busies itself among forbidden things.

Very suddenly there came back to my soul motion and sound—the tumultuous motion of the heart, and in my ears the sound of its beating. Then a pause in which all is blank. Then again sound, and motion, and touch, a tingling sensation pervading my frame. Then the mere consciousness of existence, without thought, a condition which lasted long. Then, very suddenly, THOUGHT, and shuddering terror, and earnest endeavour to comprehend my true state. Then a strong desire to lapse into insensibility. Then a rushing revival of soul and a successful effort to move. And now a full memory of the trial, of the judges, of the sable draperies, of the sentence, of the sickness, of the swoon. Then entire forgetfulness of all that followed; of all that a later day and much earnestness of endeavour have enabled me vaguely to recall.

So far I had not opened my eyes. I felt that I lay upon my back unbound. I reached out my hand, and it fell heavily upon something damp and hard. There I suffered it to remain for many minutes, while I strove to imagine where and what I could be. I longed, yet dared not, to employ my vision. I dreaded the first glance at objects around me. It was not that I feared to look upon things horrible, but that I grew aghast lest there should be NOTHING to see. At length, with a wild desperation at heart, I quickly unclosed my eyes. My worst thoughts, then, were confirmed. The blackness of eternal night encompassed me. I struggled for breath. The intensity of the darkness seemed to oppress and stifle me. The atmosphere was intolerably close. I still lay quietly, and made effort to exercise my reason. I brought to mind the inquisitorial proceedings, and attempted from that point to deduce my real condition. The sentence had passed, and it appeared to me that a very long interval of time had since elapsed. Yet not for a moment did I suppose myself actually dead. Such a supposition, notwithstanding what we read in fiction, is altogether inconsistent with real existence;—but where and in what state was I? The condemned to death, I knew, perished usually at the auto-da-fes, and one of these had been held on the very night of the day of my trial. Had I been remanded to my dungeon, to await the next sacrifice, which would not take place for many months? This I at once saw could not be. Victims had been in immediate demand. Moreover my dungeon, as well as all the condemned cells at Toledo, had stone floors, and light was not altogether excluded.

A fearful idea now suddenly drove the blood in torrents upon my heart, and for a brief period I once more relapsed into insensibility. Upon recovering, I at once started to my feet, trembling convulsively in every fibre. I thrust my arms wildly above and around me in all directions. I felt nothing; yet dreaded to move a step, lest I should be impeded by the walls of a TOMB. Perspiration burst from every pore, and stood in cold big beads upon my forehead. The agony of suspense grew at length intolerable, and I cautiously moved forward, with my arms extended, and my eyes straining from their sockets, in the hope of catching some faint ray of light. I proceeded for many paces, but still all was blackness and vacancy. I breathed more freely. It seemed evident that mine was not, at least, the most hideous of fates.

And now, as I still continued to step cautiously onward, there came thronging upon my recollection a thousand vague rumours of the horrors of Toledo. Of the dungeons there had been strange things narrated—fables I had always deemed them—but yet strange, and too ghastly to repeat, save in a whisper. Was I left to perish of starvation in this subterranean world of darkness; or what fate perhaps even more fearful awaited me? That the result would be death, and a death of more than customary bitterness, I knew too well the character of my judges to doubt. The mode and the hour were all that occupied or distracted me.

My outstretched hands at length encountered some solid obstruction. It was a wall, seemingly of stone masonry—very smooth, slimy, and cold. I followed it up; stepping with all the careful distrust with which certain antique narratives had inspired me. This process, however, afforded me no means of ascertaining the dimensions of my dungeon; as I might make its circuit, and return to the point whence I set out, without being aware of the fact, so perfectly uniform seemed the wall. I therefore sought the knife which had been in my pocket when led into the inquisitorial chamber, but it was gone; my clothes had been exchanged for a wrapper of coarse serge. I had thought of forcing the blade in some minute crevice of the masonry, so as to identify my point of departure. The difficulty, nevertheless, was but trivial, although, in the disorder of my fancy, it seemed at first insuperable. I tore a part of the hem from the robe, and placed the fragment at full length, and at right angles to the wall. In groping my way around the prison, I could not fail to encounter this rag upon completing the circuit. So, at least, I thought, but I had not counted upon the extent of the dungeon, or upon my own weakness. The ground was moist and slippery. I staggered onward for some time, when I stumbled and fell. My excessive fatigue induced me to remain prostrate, and sleep soon overtook me as I lay.

Upon awaking, and stretching forth an arm, I found beside me a loaf and a pitcher with water. I was too much exhausted to reflect upon this circumstance, but ate and drank with avidity. Shortly afterwards I resumed my tour around the prison, and with much toil came at last upon the fragment of the serge. Up to the period when I fell I had counted fifty-two paces, and upon resuming my walk I had counted forty-eight more, when I arrived at the rag. There were in all, then, a hundred paces; and, admitting two paces to the yard, I presumed the dungeon to be fifty yards in circuit. I had met, however, with many angles in the wall, and thus I could form no guess at the shape of the vault, for vault I could not help supposing it to be.

I had little object—certainly no hope—in these researches, but a vague curiosity prompted me to continue them. Quitting the wall, I resolved to cross the area of the enclosure. At first I proceeded with extreme caution, for the floor although seemingly of solid material was treacherous with slime. At length, however, I took courage and did not hesitate to step firmly—endeavouring to cross in as direct a line as possible. I had advanced some ten or twelve paces in this manner, when the remnant of the torn hem of my robe became entangled between my legs. I stepped on it, and fell violently on my face.

In the confusion attending my fall, I did not immediately apprehend a somewhat startling circumstance, which yet, in a few seconds afterward, and while I still lay prostrate, arrested my attention. It was this: my chin rested upon the floor of the prison, but my lips, and the upper portion of my head, although seemingly at a less elevation than the chin, touched nothing. At the same time, my forehead seemed bathed in a clammy vapour, and the peculiar smell of decayed fungus arose to my nostrils. I put forward my arm, and shuddered to find that I had fallen at the very brink of a circular pit, whose extent of course I had no means of ascertaining at the moment. Groping about the masonry just below the margin, I succeeded in dislodging a small fragment, and let it fall into the abyss. For many seconds I hearkened to its reverberations as it dashed against the sides of the chasm in its descent; at length there was a sullen plunge into water, succeeded by loud echoes. At the same moment there came a sound resembling the quick opening, and as rapid closing of a door overhead, while a faint gleam of light flashed suddenly through the gloom, and as suddenly faded away.

I saw clearly the doom which had been prepared for me, and congratulated myself upon the timely accident by which I had escaped. Another step before my fall, and the world had seen me no more and the death just avoided was of that very character which I had regarded as fabulous and frivolous in the tales respecting the Inquisition. To the victims of its tyranny, there was the choice of death with its direst physical agonies, or death with its most hideous moral horrors. I had been reserved for the latter. By long suffering my nerves had been unstrung, until I trembled at the sound of my own voice, and had become in every respect a fitting subject for the species of torture which awaited me.

Shaking in every limb, I groped my way back to the wall—resolving there to perish rather than risk the terrors of the wells, of which my imagination now pictured many in various positions about the dungeon. In other conditions of mind I might have had courage to end my misery at once by a plunge into one of these abysses; but now I was the veriest of cowards. Neither could I forget what I had read of these pits—that the SUDDEN extinction of life formed no part of their most horrible plan.

Agitation of spirit kept me awake for many long hours; but at length I again slumbered. Upon arousing, I found by my side, as before, a loaf and a pitcher of water. A burning thirst consumed me, and I emptied the vessel at a draught. It must have been drugged, for scarcely had I drunk before I became irresistibly drowsy. A deep sleep fell upon me—a sleep like that of death. How long it lasted of course I know not; but when once again I unclosed my eyes the objects around me were visible. By a wild sulphurous lustre, the origin of which I could not at first determine, I was enabled to see the extent and aspect of the prison.

In its size I had been greatly mistaken. The whole circuit of its walls did not exceed twenty-five yards. For some minutes this fact occasioned me a world of vain trouble; vain indeed—for what could be of less importance, under the terrible circumstances which environed me than the mere dimensions of my dungeon? But my soul took a wild interest in trifles, and I busied myself in endeavours to account for the error I had committed in my measurement. The truth at length flashed upon me. In my first attempt at exploration I had counted fifty-two paces up to the period when I fell; I must then have been within a pace or two of the fragment of serge; in fact I had nearly performed the circuit of the vault. I then slept, and upon awaking, I must have returned upon my steps, thus supposing the circuit nearly double what it actually was. My confusion of mind prevented me from observing that I began my tour with the wall to the left, and ended it with the wall to the right.

I had been deceived too in respect to the shape of the enclosure. In feeling my way I had found many angles, and thus deduced an idea of great irregularity, so potent is the effect of total darkness upon one arousing from lethargy or sleep! The angles were simply those of a few slight depressions or niches at odd intervals. The general shape of the prison was square. What I had taken for masonry seemed now to be iron, or some other metal in huge plates, whose sutures or joints occasioned the depression. The entire surface of this metallic enclosure was rudely daubed in all the hideous and repulsive devices to which the charnel superstition of the monks has given rise. The figures of fiends in aspects of menace, with skeleton forms and other more really fearful images, overspread and disfigured the walls. I observed that the outlines of these monstrosities were sufficiently distinct, but that the colours seemed faded and blurred, as if from the effects of a damp atmosphere. I now noticed the floor, too, which was of stone. In the centre yawned the circular pit from whose jaws I had escaped; but it was the only one in the dungeon.

All this I saw indistinctly and by much effort, for my personal condition had been greatly changed during slumber. I now lay upon my back, and at full length, on a species of low framework of wood. To this I was securely bound by a long strap resembling a surcingle. It passed in many convolutions about my limbs and body, leaving at liberty only my head, and my left arm to such extent that I could by dint of much exertion supply myself with food from an earthen dish which lay by my side on the floor. I saw to my horror that the pitcher had been removed. I say to my horror, for I was consumed with intolerable thirst. This thirst it appeared to be the design of my persecutors to stimulate, for the food in the dish was meat pungently seasoned.

Looking upward, I surveyed the ceiling of my prison. It was some thirty or forty feet overhead, and constructed much as the side walls. In one of its panels a very singular figure riveted my whole attention. It was the painted figure of Time as he is commonly represented, save that in lieu of a scythe he held what at a casual glance I supposed to be the pictured image of a huge pendulum, such as we see on antique clocks. There was something, however, in the appearance of this machine which caused me to regard it more attentively. While I gazed directly upward at it (for its position was immediately over my own), I fancied that I saw it in motion. In an instant afterward the fancy was confirmed. Its sweep was brief, and of course slow. I watched it for some minutes, somewhat in fear but more in wonder. Wearied at length with observing its dull movement, I turned my eyes upon the other objects in the cell.

A slight noise attracted my notice, and looking to the floor, I saw several enormous rats traversing it. They had issued from the well which lay just within view to my right. Even then while I gazed, they came up in troops hurriedly, with ravenous eyes, allured by the scent of the meat. From this it required much effort and attention to scare them away.

It might have been half-an-hour, perhaps even an hour (for I could take but imperfect note of time) before I again cast my eyes upward. What I then saw confounded and amazed me. The sweep of the pendulum had increased in extent by nearly a yard. As a natural consequence, its velocity was also much greater. But what mainly disturbed me was the idea that it had perceptibly DESCENDED. I now observed, with what horror it is needless to say, that its nether extremity was formed of a crescent of glittering steel, about a foot in length from horn to horn; the horns upward, and the under edge evidently as keen as that of a razor. Like a razor also it seemed massy and heavy, tapering from the edge into a solid and broad structure above. It was appended to a weighty rod of brass, and the whole HISSED as it swung through the air.

I could no longer doubt the doom prepared for me by monkish ingenuity in torture. My cognisance of the pit had become known to the inquisitorial agents—THE PIT, whose horrors had been destined for so bold a recusant as myself, THE PIT, typical of hell, and regarded by rumour as the Ultima Thule of all their punishments. The plunge into this pit I had avoided by the merest of accidents, and I knew that surprise or entrapment into torment formed an important portion of all the grotesquerie of these dungeon deaths. Having failed to fall, it was no part of the demon plan to hurl me into the abyss, and thus (there being no alternative) a different and a milder destruction awaited me. Milder! I half smiled in my agony as I thought of such application of such a term.

What boots it to tell of the long, long hours of horror more than mortal, during which I counted the rushing oscillations of the steel! Inch by inch—line by line—with a descent only appreciable at intervals that seemed ages—down and still down it came! Days passed—it might have been that many days passed—ere it swept so closely over me as to fan me with its acrid breath. The odour of the sharp steel forced itself into my nostrils. I prayed—I wearied heaven with my prayer for its more speedy descent. I grew frantically mad, and struggled to force myself upward against the sweep of the fearful scimitar. And then I fell suddenly calm and lay smiling at the glittering death as a child at some rare bauble.

There was another interval of utter insensibility; it was brief, for upon again lapsing into life there had been no perceptible descent in the pendulum. But it might have been long—for I knew there were demons who took note of my swoon, and who could have arrested the vibration at pleasure. Upon my recovery, too, I felt very—oh! inexpressibly—sick and weak, as if through long inanition. Even amid the agonies of that period the human nature craved food. With painful effort I outstretched my left arm as far as my bonds permitted, and took possession of the small remnant which had been spared me by the rats. As I put a portion of it within my lips there rushed to my mind a half-formed thought of joy—of hope. Yet what business had I with hope? It was, as I say, a half-formed thought—man has many such, which are never completed. I felt that it was of joy—of hope; but I felt also that it had perished in its formation. In vain I struggled to perfect—to regain it. Long suffering had nearly annihilated all my ordinary powers of mind. I was an imbecile—an idiot.

The vibration of the pendulum was at right angles to my length. I saw that the crescent was designed to cross the region of the heart. It would fray the serge of my robe; it would return and repeat its operations—again—and again. Notwithstanding its terrifically wide sweep (some thirty feet or more) and the hissing vigour of its descent, sufficient to sunder these very walls of iron, still the fraying of my robe would be all that, for several minutes, it would accomplish; and at this thought I paused. I dared not go farther than this reflection. I dwelt upon it with a pertinacity of attention—as if, in so dwelling, I could arrest HERE the descent of the steel. I forced myself to ponder upon the sound of the crescent as it should pass across the garment—upon the peculiar thrilling sensation which the friction of cloth produces on the nerves. I pondered upon all this frivolity until my teeth were on edge.

Down—steadily down it crept. I took a frenzied pleasure in contrasting its downward with its lateral velocity. To the right—to the left—far and wide—with the shriek of a damned spirit! to my heart with the stealthy pace of the tiger! I alternately laughed and howled, as the one or the other idea grew predominant.

Down—certainly, relentlessly down! It vibrated within three inches of my bosom! I struggled violently—furiously—to free my left arm. This was free only from the elbow to the hand. I could reach the latter, from the platter beside me to my mouth with great effort, but no farther. Could I have broken the fastenings above the elbow, I would have seized and attempted to arrest the pendulum. I might as well have attempted to arrest an avalanche!

Down—still unceasingly—still inevitably down! I gasped and struggled at each vibration. I shrunk convulsively at its very sweep. My eyes followed its outward or upward whirls with the eagerness of the most unmeaning despair; they closed themselves spasmodically at the descent, although death would have been a relief, O, how unspeakable! Still I quivered in every nerve to think how slight a sinking of the machinery would precipitate that keen glistening axe upon my bosom. It was hope that prompted the nerve to quiver—the frame to shrink. It was HOPE—the hope that triumphs on the rack—that whispers to the death-condemned even in the dungeons of the Inquisition.

I saw that some ten or twelve vibrations would bring the steel in actual contact with my robe, and with this observation there suddenly came over my spirit all the keen, collected calmness of despair. For the first time during many hours, or perhaps days, I THOUGHT. It now occurred to me that the bandage or surcingle which enveloped me was UNIQUE. I was tied by no separate cord. The first stroke of the razor-like crescent athwart any portion of the band would so detach it that it might be unwound from my person by means of my left hand. But how fearful, in that case, the proximity of the steel! The result of the slightest struggle, how deadly! Was it likely, moreover, that the minions of the torturer had not foreseen and provided for this possibility! Was it probable that the bandage crossed my bosom in the track of the pendulum? Dreading to find my faint, and, as it seemed, my last hope frustrated, I so far elevated my head as to obtain a distinct view of my breast. The surcingle enveloped my limbs and body close in all directions—save in the path of the destroying crescent.

Scarcely had I dropped my head back into its original position when there flashed upon my mind what I cannot better describe than as the unformed half of that idea of deliverance to which I have previously alluded, and of which a moiety only floated indeterminately through my brain when I raised food to my burning lips. The whole thought was now present—feeble, scarcely sane, scarcely definite, but still entire. I proceeded at once, with the nervous energy of despair, to attempt its execution.

For many hours the immediate vicinity of the low framework upon which I lay had been literally swarming with rats. They were wild, bold, ravenous, their red eyes glaring upon me as if they waited but for motionlessness on my part to make me their prey. 'To what food,' I thought, 'have they been accustomed in the well?'

They had devoured, in spite of all my efforts to prevent them, all but a small remnant of the contents of the dish. I had fallen into an habitual see-saw or wave of the hand about the platter; and at length the unconscious uniformity of the movement deprived it of effect. In their voracity the vermin frequently fastened their sharp fangs in my fingers. With the particles of the oily and spicy viand which now remained, I thoroughly rubbed the bandage wherever I could reach it; then, raising my hand from the floor, I lay breathlessly still.

At first the ravenous animals were startled and terrified at the change—at the cessation of movement. They shrank alarmedly back; many sought the well. But this was only for a moment. I had not counted in vain upon their voracity. Observing that I remained without motion, one or two of the boldest leaped upon the frame-work and smelt at the surcingle. This seemed the signal for a general rush. Forth from the well they hurried in fresh troops. They clung to the wood, they overran it, and leaped in hundreds upon my person. The measured movement of the pendulum disturbed them not at all. Avoiding its strokes, they busied themselves with the anointed bandage. They pressed, they swarmed upon me in ever accumulating heaps. They writhed upon my throat; their cold lips sought my own; I was half stifled by their thronging pressure; disgust, for which the world has no name, swelled my bosom, and chilled with heavy clamminess my heart. Yet one minute and I felt that the struggle would be over. Plainly I perceived the loosening of the bandage. I knew that in more than one place it must be already severed. With a more than human resolution I lay STILL.

Nor had I erred in my calculations, nor had I endured in vain. I at length felt that I was FREE. The surcingle hung in ribands from my body. But the stroke of the pendulum already pressed upon my bosom. It had divided the serge of the robe. It had cut through the linen beneath. Twice again it swung, and a sharp sense of pain shot through every nerve. But the moment of escape had arrived. At a wave of my hand my deliverers hurried tumultuously away. With a steady movement, cautious, sidelong, shrinking, and slow, I slid from the embrace of the bandage and beyond the reach of the scimitar. For the moment, at least I WAS FREE.

Free! and in the grasp of the Inquisition! I had scarcely stepped from my wooden bed of horror upon the stone floor of the prison, when the motion of the hellish machine ceased and I beheld it drawn up by some invisible force through the ceiling. This was a lesson which I took desperately to heart. My every motion was undoubtedly watched. Free! I had but escaped death in one form of agony to be delivered unto worse than death in some other. With that thought I rolled my eyes nervously around on the barriers of iron that hemmed me in. Something unusual—some change which at first I could not appreciate distinctly—it was obvious had taken place in the apartment. For many minutes of a dreamy and trembling abstraction I busied myself in vain, unconnected conjecture. During this period I became aware, for the first time, of the origin of the sulphurous light which illumined the cell. It proceeded from a fissure about half-an-inch in width extending entirely around the prison at the base of the walls which thus appeared, and were completely separated from the floor. I endeavoured, but of course in vain, to look through the aperture. As I arose from the attempt, the mystery of the alteration in the chamber broke at once upon my understanding. I have observed that although the outlines of the figures upon the walls were sufficiently distinct, yet the colours seemed blurred and indefinite. These colours had now assumed, and were momentarily assuming, a startling and most intense brilliancy, that give to the spectral and fiendish portraitures an aspect that might have thrilled even firmer nerves than my own. Demon eyes, of a wild and ghastly vivacity, glared upon me in a thousand directions where none had been visible before, and gleamed with the lurid lustre of a fire that I could not force my imagination to regard as unreal.

UNREAL!—Even while I breathed there came to my nostrils the breath of the vapour of heated iron! A suffocating odour pervaded the prison! A deeper glow settled each moment in the eyes that glared at my agonies! A richer tint of crimson diffused itself over the pictured horrors of blood. I panted ' I gasped for breath! There could be no doubt of the design of my tormentors—oh most unrelenting! oh, most demoniac of men! I shrank from the glowing metal to the centre of the cell. Amid the thought of the fiery destruction that impended, the idea of the coolness of the well came over my soul like balm. I rushed to its deadly brink. I threw my straining vision below. The glare from the enkindled roof illumined its inmost recesses. Yet, for a wild moment, did my spirit refuse to comprehend the meaning of what I saw. At length it forced—it wrestled its way into my soul—it burned itself in upon my shuddering reason. O for a voice to speak!—oh, horror!—oh, any horror but this! With a shriek I rushed from the margin and buried my face in my hands—weeping bitterly.

The heat rapidly increased, and once again I looked up, shuddering as if with a fit of the ague. There had been a second change in the cell—and now the change was obviously in the FORM. As before, it was in vain that I at first endeavoured to appreciate or understand what was taking place. But not long was I left in doubt. The inquisitorial vengeance had been hurried by my two-fold escape, and there was to be no more dallying with the King of Terrors. The room had been square. I saw that two of its iron angles were now acute—two consequently, obtuse. The fearful difference quickly increased with a low rumbling or moaning sound. In an instant the apartment had shifted its form into that of a lozenge. But the alteration stopped not here—I neither hoped nor desired it to stop. I could have clasped the red walls to my bosom as a garment of eternal peace. 'Death,' I said 'any death but that of the pit!' Fool! might I not have known that INTO THE PIT it was the object of the burning iron to urge me? Could I resist its glow? or if even that, could I withstand its pressure? And now, flatter and flatter grew the lozenge, with a rapidity that left me no time for contemplation. Its centre, and of course, its greatest width, came just over the yawning gulf. I shrank back—but the closing walls pressed me resistlessly onward. At length for my seared and writhing body there was no longer an inch of foothold on the firm floor of the prison. I struggled no more, but the agony of my soul found vent in one loud, long, and final scream of despair. I felt that I tottered upon the brink—I averted my eyes—

There was a discordant hum of human voices! There was a loud blast as of many trumpets! There was a harsh grating as of a thousand thunders! The fiery walls rushed back! An outstretched arm caught my own as I fell fainting into the abyss. It was that of General Lasalle. The French army had entered Toledo. The Inquisition was in the hands of its enemies.

AN IDEAL FAMILY

Katherine Mansfield

That evening for the first time in his life, as he pressed through the swing door and descended the three broad steps to the pavement, old Mr Neave felt he was too old for the spring. Spring—warm, eager, restless—was there, waiting for him in the golden light, ready in front of everybody to run up, to blow in his white beard, to drag sweetly on his arm. And he couldn't meet her, no; he couldn't square up once more and stride off, jaunty as a young man. He was tired and, although the late sun was still shining, curiously cold, with a numbed feeling all over. Quite suddenly he hadn't the energy, he hadn't the heart to stand this gaiety and bright movement any longer; it confused him. He wanted to stand still, to wave it away with his stick, to say, 'Be off with you!' Suddenly it was a terrible effort to greet as usual—tipping his wide-awake with his stick—all the people whom he knew, the friends, acquaintances, shopkeepers, postmen, drivers. But the gay glance that went with the gesture, the kindly twinkle that seemed to say, 'I'm a match and more for any of you'—that old Mr Neave could not manage at all. He stumped along, lifting his knees high as if he were walking through air that had somehow grown heavy and solid like water. And the homeward-looking crowd hurried by, the trams clanked, the light carts clattered, the big swinging cabs bowled along with that reckless, defiant indifference that one knows only in dreams.

It had been a day like other days at the office. Nothing special had happened. Harold hadn't come back from lunch until close on four. Where had he been? What had he been up to? He wasn't going to let his father know. Old Mr Neave had happened to be in the vestibule, saying good-bye to a caller, when Harold sauntered in, perfectly turned out as usual, cool, suave, smiling that peculiar little half-smile that women found so fascinating.

Ah, Harold was too handsome, too handsome by far; that had been the trouble all along. No man had a right to such eyes, such lashes, and such lips; it was uncanny. As for his mother, his sisters, and the servants, it was not too much to say they made a young god of him; they worshipped Harold, they forgave him everything; and he had needed some forgiving ever since the time when he was thirteen and he had stolen his mother's purse, taken the money, and hidden the purse in the cook's bedroom. Old Mr Neave struck sharply with his stick upon the pavement edge. But it wasn't only his family who spoiled Harold, he reflected, it was everybody; he had only to look and to smile, and down they went before him. So perhaps it wasn't to be wondered at that he expected the office to carry on the tradition. H'm, h'm! But it couldn't be done. No business—not even a successful, established, big paying concern—could be played with. A man had either to put his whole heart and soul into it, or it went all to pieces before his eyes.

And then Charlotte and the girls were always at him to make the whole thing over to Harold, to retire, and to spend his time enjoying himself. Enjoying himself! Old Mr Neave stopped dead under a group of ancient cabbage palms outside the Government buildings! Enjoying himself! The wind of evening shook the dark leaves to a thin airy cackle. Sitting at home, twiddling his thumbs, conscious all the while that his life's work was slipping away, dissolving, disappearing through Harold's fine fingers, while Harold smiled.

'Why will you be so unreasonable, father? There's absolutely no need for you to go to the office. It only makes it very awkward for us when people persist in saying how tired you're looking. Here's this huge house and garden. Surely you could be happy in—in—appreciating it for a change. Or you could take up some hobby.'

And Lola the baby had chimed in loftily, 'All men ought to have hobbies. It makes life impossible if they haven't.'

Well, well! He couldn't help a grim smile as painfully he began to climb the hill that led into Harcourt Avenue. Where would Lola and her sisters and Charlotte be if he'd gone in for hobbies, he'd like to know? Hobbies couldn't pay for the town house and the seaside bungalow, and their horses, and their golf, and the sixty-guinea gramophone in the music-room for them to dance to. Not that he grudged them these things. No, they were smart, good-looking girls, and Charlotte was a remarkable woman; it was natural for them to be in the swim. As a matter of fact, no other house in the town was as popular as theirs; no other family entertained so much. And how many times old Mr Neave, pushing the cigar box across the smoking-room table, had listened to praises of his wife, his girls, of himself even.

'You're an ideal family, sir, an ideal family. It's like something one reads about or sees on the stage.'

'That's all right, my boy,' old Mr Neave would reply. 'Try one of those; I think you'll like them. And if you care to smoke in the garden, you'll find the girls on the lawn, I dare say.'

That was why the girls had never married, so people said. They could have married anybody. But they had too good a time at home. They were too happy together, the girls and Charlotte. H'm, h'm! Well, well. Perhaps so ...

By this time he had walked the length of fashionable Harcourt Avenue; he had reached the corner house, their house. The carriage gates were pushed back; there were fresh marks of wheels on the drive. And then he faced the big white-painted house, with its wide-open windows, its tulle curtains floating outwards, its blue jars of hyacinths on the broad sills. On either side of the carriage porch their hydrangeas—famous in the town—were coming into flower; the pinkish, bluish masses of flower lay like light among the spreading leaves. And somehow, it seemed to old Mr Neave that the house and the flowers, and even the fresh marks on the drive, were saying, 'There is young life here. There are girls—'

The hall, as always, was dusky with wraps, parasols, gloves, piled on the oak chests. From the music-room sounded the piano, quick, loud and impatient. Through the drawing-room door that was ajar voices floated.

'And were there ices?' came from Charlotte. Then the creak, creak of her rocker.

'Ices!' cried Ethel. 'My dear mother, you never saw such ices. Only two kinds. And one a common little strawberry shop ice, in a sopping wet frill.'

'The food altogether was too appalling,' came from Marion.

'Still, it's rather early for ices,' said Charlotte easily.

'But why, if one has them at all ... ' began Ethel.

'Oh, quite so, darling,' crooned Charlotte.

Suddenly the music-room door opened and Lola dashed out. She started, she nearly screamed, at the sight of old Mr Neave.

'Gracious, father! What a fright you gave me! Have you just come home? Why isn't Charles here to help you off with your coat?'

Her cheeks were crimson from playing, her eyes glittered, the hair fell over her forehead. And she breathed as though she had come running through the dark and was frightened. Old Mr Neave stared at his youngest daughter; he felt he had never seen her before. So that was Lola, was it? But she seemed to have forgotten her father; it was not for him that she was waiting there. Now she put the tip of her crumpled handkerchief between her teeth and tugged at it angrily. The telephone rang. A-ah! Lola gave a cry like a sob and dashed past him. The door of the telephone-room slammed, and at the same moment Charlotte called, 'Is that you, father?'

'You're tired again,' said Charlotte reproachfully, and she stopped the rocker and offered her warm plum-like cheek. Bright-haired Ethel pecked his beard, Marion's lips brushed his ear.

'Did you walk back, father?' asked Charlotte.

'Yes, I walked home,' said old Mr Neave, and he sank into one of the immense drawing-room chairs.

'But why didn't you take a cab?' said Ethel. 'There are hundred of cabs about at that time.'

'My dear Ethel,' cried Marion, 'if father prefers to tire himself out, I really don't see what business of ours it is to interfere.'

'Children, children?' coaxed Charlotte.

But Marion wouldn't be stopped. 'No, mother, you spoil father, and it's not right. You ought to be stricter with him. He's very naughty.' She laughed her hard, bright laugh and patted her hair in a mirror. Strange! When she was a little girl she had such a soft, hesitating voice; she had even stuttered, and now, whatever she said—even if it was only 'Jam, please, father'—it rang out as though she were on the stage.

'Did Harold leave the office before you, dear?' asked Charlotte, beginning to rock again.

'I'm not sure,' said Old Mr Neave. 'I'm not sure. I didn't see him after four o'clock.'

'He said—' began Charlotte.

But at that moment Ethel, who was twitching over the leaves of some paper or other, ran to her mother and sank down beside her chair.

'There, you see,' she cried. 'That's what I mean, mummy. Yellow, with touches of silver. Don't you agree?'

'Give it to me, love,' said Charlotte. She fumbled for her tortoise-shell spectacles and put them on, gave the page a little dab with her plump small fingers, and pursed up her lips. 'Very sweet!' she crooned vaguely; she looked at Ethel over her spectacles. 'But I shouldn't have the train.'

'Not the train!' wailed Ethel tragically. 'But the train's the whole point.'

'Here, mother, let me decide.' Marion snatched the paper playfully from Charlotte. 'I agree with mother,' she cried triumphantly. 'The train overweights it.'

Old Mr Neave, forgotten, sank into the broad lap of his chair, and, dozing, heard them as though he dreamed. There was no doubt about it, he was tired out; he had lost his hold. Even Charlotte and the girls were too much for him to-night. They were too ... too ... But all his drowsing brain could think of was—too rich for him. And somewhere at the back of everything he was watching a little withered ancient man climbing up endless flights of stairs. Who was he?

'I shan't dress to-night,' he muttered.

'What do you say, father?'

'Eh, what, what?' Old Mr Neave woke with a start and stared across at them. 'I shan't dress to-night,' he repeated.

'But, father, we've got Lucile coming, and Henry Davenport, and Mrs Teddie Walker.'

'It will look so very out of the picture.'

'Don't you feel well, dear?'

'You needn't make any effort. What is Charles for?'

'But if you're really not up to it,' Charlotte wavered.

'Very well! Very well!' Old Mr Neave got up and went to join that little old climbing fellow just as far as his dressing-room ...

There young Charles was waiting for him. Carefully, as though everything depended on it, he was tucking a towel round the hot-water can. Young Charles had been a favourite of his ever since as a little red-faced boy he had come into the house to look after the fires. Old Mr Neave lowered himself into the cane lounge by the window, stretched out his legs, and made his little evening joke, 'Dress him up, Charles!' And Charles, breathing intensely and frowning, bent forward to take the pin out of his tie.

H'm, h'm! Well, well! It was pleasant by the open window, very pleasant—a fine mild evening. They were cutting the grass on the tennis court below; he heard the soft chirr of the mower. Soon the girls would begin their tennis parties again. And at the thought he seemed to hear Marion's voice ring out, 'Good for you, partner ... Oh, played, partner ... Oh, very nice indeed.' Then Charlotte calling from the veranda, 'Where is Harold?' And Ethel, 'He's certainly not here, mother.' And Charlotte's vague, 'He said—'

Old Mr Neave sighed, got up, and putting one hand under his beard, he took the comb from young Charles, and carefully combed the white beard over. Charles gave him a folded handkerchief, his watch and seals, and spectacle case.

'That will do, my lad.' The door shut, he sank back, he was alone ...

And now that little ancient fellow was climbing down endless flights that led to a glittering, gay dining-room. What legs he had! They were like a spider's—thin, withered.

'You're an ideal family, sir, an ideal family.'

But if that were true, why didn't Charlotte or the girls stop him? Why was he all alone, climbing up and down? Where was Harold? Ah, it was no good expecting anything from Harold. Down, down went the little old spider, and then, to his horror, old Mr Neave saw him slip past the dining-room and make for the porch, the dark drive, the carriage gates, the office. Stop him, stop him, somebody!

Old Mr Neave started up. It was dark in his dressing-room; the window shone pale. How long had he been asleep? He listened, and through the big, airy, darkened house there floated far-away voices, far-away sounds. Perhaps, he thought vaguely, he had been asleep for a long time. He'd been forgotten. What had all this to do with him—this house and Charlotte, the girls and Harold—what did he know about them? They were strangers to him. Life had passed him by. Charlotte was not his wife. His wife!

A dark porch, half hidden by a passion-vine, that drooped sorrowful, mournful, as though it understood. Small, warm arms were round his neck. A face, little and pale, lifted to his, and a voice breathed, 'Good-bye, my treasure.'

My treasure! 'Good-bye, my treasure!' Which of them had spoken? Why had they said good-bye? There had been some terrible mistake. She was his wife, that little pale girl, and all the rest of his life had been a dream.

Then the door opened, and young Charles, standing in the light, put his hands by his side and shouted like a young soldier, 'Dinner is on the table, sir!'

'I'm coming, I'm coming,' said old Mr Neave.

A HAUNTED HOUSE*

Virginia Woolf

Whatever hour you woke there was a door shutting. From room to room they went, hand in hand, lifting here, opening there, making sure—a ghostly couple.

'Here we left it,' she said. And he added, 'Oh, but here too!' 'It's upstairs,' she murmured. 'And in the garden,' he whispered. 'Quietly,' they said, 'or we shall wake them.'

But it wasn't that you woke us. Oh, no. 'They're looking for it; they're drawing the curtain,' one might say, and so read on a page or two. 'Now they've found it,' one would be certain, stopping the pencil on the margin. And then, tired of reading, one might rise and see for oneself, the house all empty, the doors standing open, only the wood pigeons bubbling with content and the hum of the threshing machine sounding from the farm. 'What did I come in here for? What did I want to find?' My hands were empty. 'Perhaps its upstairs then?' The apples were in the loft. And so down again, the garden still as ever, only the book had slipped into the grass.

But they had found it in the drawing room. Not that one could ever see them. The windowpanes reflected apples, reflected roses; all the leaves were green in the glass. If they moved in the drawing room, the apple only turned its yellow side. Yet, the moment after, if the door was opened, spread about the floor, hung upon the walls, pendant from the ceiling—what? My hands were empty. The shadow of a thrush crossed the carpet; from the deepest wells of silence the wood pigeon drew its bubble of sound. 'Safe, safe, safe' the pulse of the house beat softly. 'The treasure buried; the room…' the pulse stopped short. Oh, was that the buried treasure?

A moment later the light had faded. Out in the garden then? But

---

* Published in 1921, 'A Haunted House' was one of eight short stories in her collection, *Monday or Tuesday*.

the trees spun darkness for a wandering beam of sun. So fine, so rare, coolly sunk beneath the surface the beam I sought always burned behind the glass. Death was the glass; death was between us, coming to the woman first, hundreds of years ago, leaving the house, sealing all the windows; the rooms were darkened. He left it, left her, went North, went East, saw the stars turned in the Southern sky; sought the house, found it dropped beneath the Downs. 'Safe, safe, safe,' the pulse of the house beat gladly. 'The Treasure yours.'

The wind roars up the avenue. Trees stoop and bend this way and that. Moonbeams splash and spill wildly in the rain. But the beam of the lamp falls straight from the window. The candle burns stiff and still. Wandering through the house, opening the windows, whispering not to wake us, the ghostly couple seek their joy.

'Here we slept,' she says. And he adds, 'Kisses without number.' 'Waking in the morning—' 'Silver between the trees—' 'Upstairs—' 'In the garden—' 'When summer came—' 'In winter snowtime—' 'The doors go shutting far in the distance, gently knocking like the pulse of a heart.

Nearer they come, cease at the doorway. The wind falls, the rain slides silver down the glass. Our eyes darken, we hear no steps beside us; we see no lady spread her ghostly cloak. His hands shield the lantern. 'Look,' he breathes. 'Sound asleep. Love upon their lips.'

Stooping, holding their silver lamp above us, long they look and deeply. Long they pause. The wind drives straightly; the flame stoops slightly. Wild beams of moonlight cross both floor and wall, and, meeting, stain the faces bent; the faces pondering; the faces that search the sleepers and seek their hidden joy.

'Safe, safe, safe,' the heart of the house beats proudly. 'Long years—' he sighs. 'Again you found me.' 'Here,' she murmurs, 'sleeping; in the garden reading; laughing, rolling apples in the loft. Here we left our treasure—' Stooping, their light lifts the lids upon my eyes. 'Safe! safe! safe!' the pulse of the house beats wildly. Waking, I cry 'Oh, is this your buried treasure? The light in the heart.'

A CHARMING WOMAN

Jerome K. Jerome

'Not the Mr—, really?'

In her deep brown eyes there lurked pleased surprise, struggling with wonder. She looked from myself to the friend who introduced us with a bewitching smile of incredulity, tempered by hope.

He assured her, adding laughingly, 'The only genuine and original,' and left us.

'I've always thought of you as a staid, middle-aged man,' she said, with a delicious little laugh, then added in low soft tones, 'I'm so very pleased to meet you, really.'

The words were conventional, but her voice crept round one like a warm caress.

'Come and talk to me,' she said, seating herself upon a small settee, and making room for me.

I sat down awkwardly beside her, my head buzzing just a little, as with one glass too many of champagne. I was in my literary childhood. One small book and a few essays and criticisms, scattered through various obscure periodicals had been as yet my only contributions to current literature. The sudden discovery that I was the Mr Anybody, and that charming women thought of me, and were delighted to meet me, was a brain-disturbing thought.

'And it was really you who wrote that clever book?' she continued, 'and all those brilliant things, in the magazines and journals. Oh, it must be delightful to be clever.'

She gave breath to a little sigh of vain regret that went to my heart. To console her I commenced a laboured compliment, but she stopped me with her fan. On after reflection I was glad she had—it would have been one of those things better expressed otherwise.

'I know what you are going to say,' she laughed, 'but don't. Besides, from you I should not know quite how to take it. You can be so satirical.'

I tried to look as though I could be, but in her case would not.

She let her ungloved hand rest for an instant upon mine. Had she left it there for two, I should have gone down on my knees before her, or have stood on my head at her feet—have made a fool of myself in some way or another before the whole room full. She timed it to a nicety.

'I don't want you to pay me compliments,' she said, 'I want us to be friends. Of course, in years, I'm old enough to be your mother.' (By the register I should say she might have been thirty-two, but looked twenty-six. I was twenty-three, and I fear foolish for my age.) 'But you know the world, and you're so different to the other people one meets. Society is so hollow and artificial; don't you find it so? You don't know how I long sometimes to get away from it, to know someone to whom I could show my real self, who would understand me. You'll come and see me sometimes—I'm always at home on Wednesdays—and let me talk to you, won't you, and you must tell me all your clever thoughts.'

It occurred to me that, maybe, she would like to hear a few of them there and then, but before I had got well started a hollow Society man came up and suggested supper, and she was compelled to leave me. As she disappeared, however, in the throng, she looked back over her shoulder with a glance half pathetic, half comic, that I understood. It said, 'Pity me, I've got to be bored by this vapid, shallow creature,' and I did.

I sought her through all the rooms before I went. I wished to assure her of my sympathy and support. I learned, however, from the butler that she had left early, in company with the hollow Society man.

A fortnight later I ran against a young literary friend in Regent Street, and we lunched together at the Monico.

'I met such a charming woman last night,' he said, 'a Mrs Clifton Courtenay, a delightful woman.'

'Oh, do you know her?' I exclaimed. 'Oh, we're very old friends. She's always wanting me to go and see her. I really must.'

'Oh, I didn't know you knew her,' he answered. Somehow, the fact of my knowing her seemed to lessen her importance in his eyes. But soon he recovered his enthusiasm for her.

'A wonderfully clever woman,' he continued. 'I'm afraid I disappointed her a little though.' He said this, however, with a laugh that contradicted his words. 'She would not believe I was the Mr Smith. She imagined from my book that I was quite an old man.'

I could see nothing in my friend's book myself to suggest that the author was, of necessity, anything over eighteen. The mistake appeared to me to display want of acumen, but it had evidently pleased him greatly.

'I felt quite sorry for her,' he went on, 'chained to that bloodless, artificial society in which she lives. 'You can't tell,' she said to me, 'how I long to meet someone to whom I could show my real self—who would understand me.' I'm going to see her on Wednesday.'

I went with him. My conversation with her was not as confidential as I had anticipated, owing to there being some eighty other people present in a room intended for the accommodation of eight; but after surging round for an hour in hot and aimless misery—as very young men at such gatherings do, knowing as a rule only the man who has brought them, and being unable to find him—I contrived to get a few words with her.

She greeted me with a smile, in the light of which I at once forgot my past discomfort, and let her fingers rest, with delicious pressure, for a moment upon mine.

'How good of you to keep your promise,' she said. 'These people have been tiring me so. Sit here, and tell me all you have been doing.'

She listened for about ten seconds, and then interrupted me with—

'And that clever friend of yours that you came with. I met him at dear Lady Lennon's last week. Has he written anything?'

I explained to her that he had.

'Tell me about it?' she said. 'I get so little time for reading, and then I only care to read the books that help me,' and she gave me a grateful look more eloquent than words.

I described the work to her, and wishing to do my friend justice I even recited a few of the passages upon which, as I knew, he especially prided himself.

One sentence in particular seemed to lay hold of her. 'A good woman's arms round a man's neck is a lifebelt thrown out to him from heaven.'

'How beautiful!' she murmured. 'Say it again.'

I said it again, and she repeated it after me.

Then a noisy old lady swooped down upon her, and I drifted away into a corner, where I tried to look as if I were enjoying myself, and failed.

Later on, feeling it time to go, I sought my friend, and found him talking to her in a corner. I approached and waited. They were discussing the latest east-end murder. A drunken woman had been killed by her husband, a hard-working artisan, who had been maddened by the ruin of his home.

'Ah,' she was saying, 'what power a woman has to drag a man down or lift him up. I never read a case in which a woman is concerned without thinking of those beautiful lines of yours: "A good woman's arms round a man's neck is a lifebelt thrown out to him from heaven."'

❧

Opinions differed concerning her religion and politics. Said the Low Church parson: 'An earnest Christian woman, sir, of that unostentatious type that has always been the bulwark of our Church. I am proud to know that woman, and I am proud to think that poor words of mine have been the humble instrument to wean that true woman's heart from the frivolities of fashion, and to fix her thoughts upon higher things. A good Churchwoman, sir, a good Churchwoman, in the best sense of the word.'

Said the pale aristocratic-looking young Abbé to the Comtesse, the light of old-world enthusiasm shining from his deep-set eyes: 'I have great hopes for our dear friend. She finds it hard to sever the ties of time and love. We are all weak, but her heart turns towards our mother Church as a child, though suckled among strangers, yearns after many years for the bosom that has borne it. We have spoken, and I, even I, may be the voice in the wilderness leading the lost sheep back to the fold.'

Said Sir Harry Bennett, the great Theosophist lecturer, writing to a friend: 'A singularly gifted woman, and a woman evidently thirsting for the truth. A woman capable of willing her own life. A woman not afraid of thought and reason, a lover of wisdom. I have talked much with her at one time or another, and I have found her grasp my meaning with a quickness of perception quite unusual in my experience; and the arguments I have let fall, I am convinced, have borne excellent fruit. I look forward to her becoming, at no very distant date, a valued member of our little band. Indeed, without betraying confidence, I may almost say I regard her conversion as an accomplished fact.'

Colonel Maxim always spoke of her as 'a fair pillar of the State.'

'With the enemy in our midst,' said the florid old soldier, 'it behoves every true man—aye, and every true woman—to rally to the defence of the country; and all honour, say I, to noble ladies such as Mrs Clifton Courtenay, who, laying aside their natural shrinking from publicity, come forward in such a crisis as the present to combat the forces of disorder and disloyalty now rampant in the land.'

'But,' some listener would suggest, 'I gathered from young Jocelyn that Mrs Clifton Courtenay held somewhat advanced views on social and political questions.'

'Jocelyn,' the Colonel would reply with scorn; 'Pah! There may have been a short space of time during which the fellow's long hair and windy rhetoric impressed her. But I flatter myself I've put my spoke in Mr Jocelyn's wheel. Why, damme, sir, she's consented to stand for Grand Dame of the Bermondsey Branch of the Primrose League next year. What's Jocelyn to say to that, the scoundrel!'

What Jocelyn said was:—

'I know the woman is weak. But I do not blame her; I pity her. When the time comes, as soon it will, when woman is no longer a puppet, dancing to the threads held by some brainless man—when a woman is not threatened with social ostracism for daring to follow her own conscience instead of that of her nearest male relative—then will be the time to judge her. It is not for me to betray the confidence reposed in me by a suffering woman, but you can tell that interesting old fossil, Colonel Maxim, that he and the other old women of the Bermondsey Branch of the Primrose League may elect Mrs Clifton Courtenay for their President, and make the most of it; they have only got the outside of the woman. Her heart is beating time to the tramp of an onward-marching people; her soul's eyes are straining for the glory of a coming dawn.'

But they all agreed she was a charming woman.

BENEDICTION

F. Scott Fitzgerald

I

The Baltimore Station was hot and crowded, so Lois was forced to stand by the telegraph desk for interminable, sticky seconds while a clerk with big front teeth counted and recounted a large lady's day message, to determine whether it contained the innocuous forty-nine words or the fatal fifty-one.

Lois, waiting, decided she wasn't quite sure of the address, so she took the letter out of her bag and ran over it again.

'Darling,' IT BEGAN—'I understand and I'm happier than life ever meant me to be. If I could give you the things you've always been in tune with—but I can't Lois; we can't marry and we can't lose each other and let all this glorious love end in nothing.

'Until your letter came, dear, I'd been sitting here in the half dark and thinking where I could go and ever forget you; abroad, perhaps, to drift through Italy or Spain and dream away the pain of having lost you where the crumbling ruins of older, mellower civilizations would mirror only the desolation of my heart—and then your letter came.

'Sweetest, bravest girl, if you'll wire me I'll meet you in Wilmington—till then I'll be here just waiting and hoping for every long dream of you to come true. 'Howard.'

She had read the letter so many times that she knew it word by word, yet it still startled her. In it she found many faint reflections of the man who wrote it—the mingled sweetness and sadness in his dark eyes, the furtive, restless excitement she felt sometimes when he talked to her, his dreamy sensuousness that lulled her mind to sleep. Lois was nineteen and very romantic and curious and courageous.

The large lady and the clerk having compromised on fifty words, Lois took a blank and wrote her telegram. And there were no overtones to the finality of her decision.

It's just destiny—she thought—it's just the way things work out in this damn world. If cowardice is all that's been holding me back there won't be any more holding back. So we'll just let things take their course and never be sorry.

The clerk scanned her telegram:

'Arrived Baltimore today spend day with my brother meet me Wilmington three P.M. Wednesday Love

'Lois.'

'Fifty-four cents,' said the clerk admiringly.

And never be sorry—thought Lois—and never be sorry—

II

Trees filtering light onto dapple grass. Trees like tall, languid ladies with feather fans coquetting airily with the ugly roof of the monastery. Trees like butlers, bending courteously over placid walks and paths. Trees, trees over the hills on either side and scattering out in clumps and lines and woods all through eastern Maryland, delicate lace on the hems of many yellow fields, dark opaque backgrounds for flowered bushes or wild climbing garden.

Some of the trees were very gay and young, but the monastery trees were older than the monastery which, by true monastic standards, wasn't very old at all. And, as a matter of fact, it wasn't technically called a monastery, but only a seminary; nevertheless it shall be a monastery here despite its Victorian architecture or its Edward VII additions, or even its Woodrow Wilsonian, patented, last-a-century roofing.

Out behind was the farm where half a dozen lay brothers were sweating lustily as they moved with deadly efficiency around the vegetable-gardens. To the left, behind a row of elms, was an informal baseball diamond where three novices were being batted out by a fourth, amid great chasings and puffings and blowings. And in front as a great mellow bell boomed the half-hour a swarm of black, human leaves were blown over the checker-board of paths under the courteous trees.

Some of these black leaves were very old with cheeks furrowed like the first ripples of a splashed pool. Then there was a scattering of middle-aged leaves whose forms when viewed in profile in their revealing gowns were beginning to be faintly unsymmetrical. These carried thick volumes of Thomas Aquinas and Henry James and Cardinal Mercier and Immanuel Kant and many bulging note-books filled with lecture data.

But most numerous were the young leaves; blond boys of nineteen with very stern, conscientious expressions; men in the late twenties with a keen self-assurance from having taught out in the world for five years—several hundreds of them, from city and town and country in Maryland and Pennsylvania and Virginia and West Virginia and Delaware.

There were many Americans and some Irish and some tough Irish and a few French, and several Italians and Poles, and they walked informally arm in arm with each other in twos and threes or in long rows, almost universally distinguished by the straight mouth and the considerable chin—for this was the Society of Jesus, founded in Spain five hundred years before by a tough-minded soldier who trained men to hold a breach or a salon, preach a sermon or write a treaty, and do it and not argue.

Lois got out of a bus into the sunshine down by the outer gate. She was nineteen with yellow hair and eyes that people were tactful enough not to call green. When men of talent saw her in a street-car they often furtively produced little stub-pencils and backs of envelopes and tried to sum up that profile or the thing that the eyebrows did to her eyes. Later they looked at their results and usually tore them up with wondering sighs.

Though Lois was very jauntily attired in an expensively appropriate travelling affair, she did not linger to pat out the dust which covered her clothes, but started up the central walk with curious glances at either side. Her face was very eager and expectant, yet she hadn't at all that glorified expression that girls wear when they arrive for a Senior Prom at Princeton or New Haven; still, as there were no senior proms here, perhaps it didn't matter.

She was wondering what he would look like, whether she'd possibly know him from his picture. In the picture, which hung over her mother's bureau at home, he seemed very young and hollow-cheeked and rather pitiful, with only a well-developed mouth and all ill-fitting probationer's gown to show that he had already made a momentous decision about his life. Of course he had been only nineteen then and now he was thirty-six—didn't look like that at all; in recent snap-shots he was much broader and his hair had grown a little thin—but the impression of her brother she had always retained was that of the big picture. And so she had always been a little sorry for him. What a life for a man! Seventeen years of preparation and he was even a priest yet—wouldn't be for another year.

Lois had an idea that this was all going to be rather solemn if she let it be. But she was going to give her very best imitation of undiluted sunshine, the imitation she could give even when her head was splitting or when her mother had a nervous breakdown or when she was particularly romantic and curious and courageous. This brother of hers undoubtedly needed cheering up, and he was going to be cheered up, whether he liked it or not.

As she drew near the great, homely front door she saw a man break suddenly away from a group and, pulling up the skirts of his gown, run toward her. He was smiling, she noticed, and he looked very big and—and reliable. She stopped and waited, knew that her heart was beating unusually fast.

'Lois!' he cried, and in a second she was in his arms. She was suddenly trembling.

'Lois!' he cried again, 'why, this is wonderful! I can't tell you, Lois, how MUCH I've looked forward to this. Why, Lois, you're beautiful!'

Lois gasped.

His voice, though restrained, was vibrant with energy and that odd sort of enveloping personality she had thought that she only of the family possessed.

'I'm mighty glad, too—Kieth.'

She flushed, but not unhappily, at this first use of his name.

'Lois—Lois—Lois,' he repeated in wonder. 'Child, we'll go in here a minute, because I want you to meet the rector, and then we'll walk around. I have a thousand things to talk to you about.'

His voice became graver. 'How's mother?'

She looked at him for a moment and then said something that she had not intended to say at all, the very sort of thing she had resolved to avoid.

'Oh, Kieth—she's—she's getting worse all the time, every way.'

He nodded slowly as if he understood.

'Nervous, well—you can tell me about that later. Now—'

She was in a small study with a large desk, saying something to a little, jovial, white-haired priest who retained her hand for some seconds.

'So this is Lois!'

He said it as if he had heard of her for years.

He entreated her to sit down.

Two other priests arrived enthusiastically and shook hands with her and addressed her as 'Kieth's little sister,' which she found she didn't mind a bit.

How assured they seemed; she had expected a certain shyness, reserve at least. There were several jokes unintelligible to her, which seemed to delight every one, and the little Father Rector referred to the trio of them as 'dim old monks,' which she appreciated, because of course they weren't monks at all. She had a lightning impression that they were especially fond of Kieth—the Father Rector had called him 'Kieth' and one of the others had kept a hand on his shoulder all through the conversation. Then she was shaking hands again and promising to come back a little later for some ice-cream, and smiling and smiling and being rather absurdly happy...she told herself that it was because Kieth was so delighted in showing her off.

Then she and Kieth were strolling along a path, arm in arm, and he was informing her what an absolute jewel the Father Rector was.

'Lois,' he broken off suddenly, 'I want to tell you before we go any farther how much it means to me to have you come up here. I think it was—mighty sweet of you. I know what a gay time you've been having.'

Lois gasped. She was not prepared for this. At first when she had conceived the plan of taking the hot journey down to Baltimore staying the night with a friend and then coming out to see her brother, she had felt rather consciously virtuous, hoped he wouldn't be priggish or resentful about her not having come before—but walking here with him under the trees seemed such a little thing, and surprisingly a happy thing.

'Why, Kieth,' she said quickly, 'you know I couldn't have waited a day longer. I saw you when I was five, but of course I didn't remember, and how could I have gone on without practically ever having seen my only brother?'

'It was mighty sweet of you, Lois,' he repeated.

Lois blushed—he DID have personality.

'I want you to tell me all about yourself,' he said after a pause. 'Of course I have a general idea what you and mother did in Europe those fourteen years, and then we were all so worried, Lois, when you had pneumonia and couldn't come down with mother—let's see that was two years ago—and then, well, I've seen your name in the papers, but it's all been so unsatisfactory. I haven't known you, Lois.'

She found herself analysing his personality as she analysed the personality of every man she met. She wondered if the effect of—of intimacy that he gave was bred by his constant repetition of her name. He said it as if he loved the word, as if it had an inherent meaning to him.

'Then you were at school,' he continued.

'Yes, at Farmington. Mother wanted me to go to a convent—but I didn't want to.'

She cast a side glance at him to see if he would resent this.

But he only nodded slowly.

'Had enough convents abroad, eh?'

'Yes—and Kieth, convents are different there anyway. Here even in the nicest ones there are so many COMMON girls.'

He nodded again.

'Yes,' he agreed, 'I suppose there are, and I know how you feel about it. It grated on me here, at first, Lois, though I wouldn't say that to anyone but you; we're rather sensitive, you and I, to things like this.'

'You mean the men here?'

'Yes, some of them of course were fine, the sort of men I'd always been thrown with, but there were others; a man named Regan, for instance—I hated the fellow, and now he's about the best friend I have. A wonderful character, Lois; you'll meet him later. Sort of man you'd like to have with you in a fight.'

Lois was thinking that Kieth was the sort of man she'd like to have with HER in a fight.

'How did you—how did you first happen to do it?' she asked, rather shyly, 'to come here, I mean. Of course mother told me the story about the Pullman car.'

'Oh, that—' He looked rather annoyed.

'Tell me that. I'd like to hear you tell it.'

'Oh, it's nothing except what you probably know. It was evening and I'd been riding all day and thinking about—about a hundred things, Lois, and then suddenly I had a sense that someone was sitting across from me, felt that he'd been there for some time, and had a vague idea that he was another traveller. All at once he leaned over toward me and I heard a voice say: 'I want you to be a priest, that's what I want.' Well I jumped up and cried out, 'Oh, my God, not that!'—made an idiot of myself before about twenty people; you see there wasn't any one sitting there at all. A week after that I went to the Jesuit College in Philadelphia and crawled up the last flight of stairs to the rector's office on my hands and knees.'

There was another silence and Lois saw that her brother's eyes wore a far-away look, that he was staring unseeingly out over the sunny fields. She was stirred by the modulations of his voice and the sudden silence that seemed to flow about him when he finished speaking.

She noticed now that his eyes were of the same fibre as hers, with the green left out, and that his mouth was much gentler, really, than in the picture—or was it that the face had grown up to it lately? He was getting a little bald just on top of his head. She wondered if that was from wearing a hat so much. It seemed awful for a man to grow bald and no one to care about it.

'Were you—pious when you were young, Kieth?' she asked. 'You know what I mean. Were you religious? If you don't mind these personal questions.'

'Yes,' he said with his eyes still far away—and she felt that his intense abstraction was as much a part of his personality as his attention. 'Yes, I suppose I was, when I was—sober.'

Lois thrilled slightly.

'Did you drink?'

He nodded.

'I was on the way to making a bad hash of things.' He smiled and, turning his grey eyes on her, changed the subject.

'Child, tell me about mother. I know it's been awfully hard for you there, lately. I know you've had to sacrifice a lot and put up with a great deal and I want you to know how fine of you I think it is. I feel, Lois, that you're sort of taking the place of both of us there.'

Lois thought quickly how little she had sacrificed; how lately she had constantly avoided her nervous, half-invalid mother.

'Youth shouldn't be sacrificed to age, Kieth,' she said steadily.

'I know,' he sighed, 'and you oughtn't to have the weight on your shoulders, child. I wish I were there to help you.'

She saw how quickly he had turned her remark and instantly she knew what this quality was that he gave off. He was SWEET. Her thoughts went off on a side-track and then she broke the silence with an odd remark.

'Sweetness is hard,' she said suddenly.

'What?'

'Nothing,' she denied in confusion. 'I didn't mean to speak aloud. I was thinking of something—of a conversation with a man named Freddy Kebble.'

'Maury Kebble's brother?'

'Yes,' she said rather surprised to think of him having known Maury Kebble. Still there was nothing strange about it. 'Well, he and I were talking about sweetness a few weeks ago. Oh, I don't know—I said that a man named Howard—that a man I knew was sweet, and he didn't agree with me, and we began talking about what sweetness in a man was: He kept telling me I meant a sort of soppy softness, but I knew I didn't—yet I didn't know exactly how to put it. I see now. I meant just the opposite. I suppose real sweetness is a sort of hardness—and strength.'

Kieth nodded.

'I see what you mean. I've known old priests who had it.'

'I'm talking about young men,' she said rather defiantly.

They had reached the now deserted baseball diamond and, pointing her to a wooden bench, he sprawled full length on the grass.

'Are these YOUNG men happy here, Kieth?'

'Don't they look happy, Lois?'

'I suppose so, but those YOUNG ones, those two we just passed—have they—are they—?

'Are they signed up?' he laughed. 'No, but they will be next month.'

'Permanently?'

'Yes—unless they break down mentally or physically. Of course in a discipline like ours a lot drop out.'

'But those BOYS. Are they giving up fine chances outside—like you did?'

He nodded.

'Some of them.'

'But Kieth, they don't know what they're doing. They haven't had any experience of what they're missing.'

'No, I suppose not.'

'It doesn't seem fair. Life has just sort of scared them at first. Do they all come in so YOUNG?'

'No, some of them have knocked around, led pretty wild lives—Regan, for instance.'

'I should think that sort would be better,' she said meditatively, 'men that had SEEN life.'

'No,' said Kieth earnestly, 'I'm not sure that knocking about gives a man the sort of experience he can communicate to others. Some of the broadest men I've known have been absolutely rigid about themselves. And reformed libertines are a notoriously intolerant class. Don't you think so, Lois?'

She nodded, still meditative, and he continued:

'It seems to me that when one weak reason goes to another, it isn't help they want; it's a sort of companionship in guilt, Lois. After you were born, when mother began to get nervous she used to go and weep with a certain Mrs Comstock. Lord, it used to make me shiver. She said it comforted her, poor old mother. No, I don't think that to help others you've got to show yourself at all. Real help comes from a stronger person whom you respect. And their sympathy is all the bigger because it's impersonal.'

'But people want human sympathy,' objected Lois. 'They want to feel the other person's been tempted.'

'Lois, in their hearts they want to feel that the other person's been weak. That's what they mean by human.

'Here in this old monkery, Lois,' he continued with a smile, 'they try to get all that self-pity and pride in our own wills out of us right at the first. They put us to scrubbing floors—and other things. It's like that idea of saving your life by losing it. You see we sort of feel that the less human a man is, in your sense of human, the better servant he can be to humanity. We carry it out to the end, too. When one of us dies his family can't even have him then. He's buried here under plain wooden cross with a thousand others.'

His tone changed suddenly and he looked at her with a great brightness in his grey eyes.

'But way back in a man's heart there are some things he can't get rid of—an one of them is that I'm awfully in love with my little sister.'

With a sudden impulse she knelt beside him in the grass and, Leaning over, kissed his forehead.

'You're hard, Kieth,' she said, 'and I love you for it—and you're sweet.'

III

Back in the reception-room Lois met a half-dozen more of Kieth's particular friends; there was a young man named Jarvis, rather pale and delicate-looking, who, she knew, must be a grandson of old Mrs Jarvis at home, and she mentally compared this ascetic with a brace of his riotous uncles.

And there was Regan with a scarred face and piercing intent eyes that followed her about the room and often rested on Kieth with something very like worship. She knew then what Kieth had meant about 'a good man to have with you in a fight.'

He's the missionary type—she thought vaguely—China or something.

'I want Kieth's sister to show us what the shimmy is,' demanded one young man with a broad grin.

Lois laughed.

'I'm afraid the Father Rector would send me shimmying out the gate. Besides, I'm not an expert.'

'I'm sure it wouldn't be best for Jimmy's soul anyway,' said Kieth solemnly. 'He's inclined to brood about things like shimmys. They were just starting to do the—maxixe, wasn't it, Jimmy?—when he became a monk, and it haunted him his whole first year. You'd see him when he was peeling potatoes, putting his arm around the bucket and making irreligious motions with his feet.'

There was a general laugh in which Lois joined.

'An old lady who comes here to Mass sent Kieth this ice-cream,' whispered Jarvis under cover of the laugh, 'because she'd heard you were coming. It's pretty good, isn't it?'

There were tears trembling in Lois' eyes.

IV

Then half an hour later over in the chapel things suddenly went all wrong. It was several years since Lois had been at Benediction and at first she was thrilled by the gleaming monstrance with its central spot of white, the air rich and heavy with incense, and the sun shining through the stained-glass window of St Francis Xavier overhead and falling in warm red tracery on the cassock of the man in front of her, but at the first notes of the 'O SALUTARIS HOSTIA' a heavy weight seemed to descend upon her soul. Kieth was on her right and young Jarvis on her left, and she stole uneasy glance at both of them.

What's the matter with me? she thought impatiently.

She looked again. Was there a certain coldness in both their profiles, that she had not noticed before—a pallor about the mouth and a curious set expression in their eyes? She shivered slightly: they were like dead men.

She felt her soul recede suddenly from Kieth's. This was her brother—this, this unnatural person. She caught herself in the act of a little laugh.

'What is the matter with me?'

She passed her hand over her eyes and the weight increased. The incense sickened her and a stray, ragged note from one of the tenors in the choir grated on her ear like the shriek of a slate-pencil. She fidgeted, and raising her hand to her hair touched her forehead, found moisture on it.

'It's hot in here, hot as the deuce.'

Again she repressed a faint laugh and, then in an instant the weight on her heart suddenly diffused into cold fear…It was that candle on the altar. It was all wrong—wrong. Why didn't somebody see it? There was something IN it. There was something coming out of it, taking form and shape above it.

She tried to fight down her rising panic, told herself it was the wick. If the wick wasn't straight, candles did something—but they didn't do this! With incalculable rapidity a force was gathering within her, a tremendous, assimilative force, drawing from every sense, every corner of her brain, and as it surged up inside her she felt an enormous terrified repulsion. She drew her arms in close to her side away from Kieth and Jarvis.

Something in that candle…she was leaning forward—in another moment she felt she would go forward toward it—didn't any one see it?… Anyone?

'Ugh!'

She felt a space beside her and something told her that Jarvis had gasped and sat down very suddenly…then she was kneeling and as the flaming monstrance slowly left the altar in the hands of the priest, she heard a great rushing noise in her ears—the crash of the bells was like hammer-blows…and then in a moment that seemed eternal a great torrent rolled over her heart—there was a shouting there and a lashing as of waves…

She was calling, felt herself calling for Kieth, her lips mouthing the words that would not come:

'Kieth! Oh, my God! KIETH!'

Suddenly she became aware of a new presence, something external, in front of her, consummated and expressed in warm red tracery. Then she knew. It was the window of St Francis Xavier. Her mind gripped at it, clung to it finally, and she felt herself calling again endlessly, impotently—Kieth—Kieth!

Then out of a great stillness came a voice:

'BLESSED BE GOD.'

With a gradual rumble sounded the response rolling heavily through the chapel:

'Blessed be God.'

The words sang instantly in her heart; the incense lay mystically and sweetly peaceful upon the air, and THE CANDLE ON THE ALTAR WENT OUT.

'Blessed be His Holy Name.'

'Blessed be His Holy Name.'

Everything blurred into a swinging mist. With a sound half-gasp, half-cry she rocked on her feet and reeled backward into Kieth's suddenly outstretched arms.

V

'Lie still, child.'

She closed her eyes again. She was on the grass outside, pillowed on Kieth's arm, and Regan was dabbing her head with a cold towel.

'I'm all right,' she said quietly.

'I know, but just lie still a minute longer. It was too hot in there. Jarvis felt it, too.'

She laughed as Regan again touched her gingerly with the towel.

'I'm all right,' she repeated.

But though a warm peace was falling her mind and heart she felt oddly broken and chastened, as if someone had held her stripped soul up and laughed.

VI

Half an hour later she walked leaning on Kieth's arm down the long central path toward the gate.

'It's been such a short afternoon,' he sighed, 'and I'm so sorry you were sick, Lois.'

'Kieth, I'm feeling fine now, really; I wish you wouldn't worry.'

'Poor old child. I didn't realize that Benediction'd be a long service for you after your hot trip out here and all.'

She laughed cheerfully.

'I guess the truth is I'm not much used to Benediction. Mass is the limit of my religious exertions.'

She paused and then continued quickly:

'I don't want to shock you, Kieth, but I can't tell you how—how INCONVENIENT being a Catholic is. It really doesn't seem to apply any more. As far as morals go, some of the wildest boys I know are Catholics. And the brightest boys—I mean the ones who think and read a lot, don't seem to believe in much of anything anymore.'

'Tell me about it. The bus won't be here for another half-hour.'

They sat down on a bench by the path.

'For instance, Gerald Carter, he's published a novel. He absolutely roars when people mention immortality. And then Howa—well, another man I've known well, lately, who was Phi Beta Kappa at Harvard says that no intelligent person can believe in Supernatural Christianity. He says Christ was a great socialist, though. Am I shocking you?'

She broke off suddenly.

Kieth smiled.

'You can't shock a monk. He's a professional shock-absorber.'

'Well,' she continued, 'that's about all. It seems so—so NARROW. Church schools, for instance. There's more freedom about things that Catholic people can't see—like birth control.'

Kieth winced, almost imperceptibly, but Lois saw it.

'Oh,' she said quickly, 'everybody talks about everything now.'

'It's probably better that way.'

'Oh, yes, much better. Well, that's all, Kieth. I just wanted to tell you why I'm a little—luke-warm, at present.'

'I'm not shocked, Lois. I understand better than you think. We all go through those times. But I know it'll come out all right, child. There's that gift of faith that we have, you and I, that'll carry us past the bad spots.'

He rose as he spoke and they started again down the path.

'I want you to pray for me sometimes, Lois. I think your prayers would be about what I need. Because we've come very close in these few hours, I think.'

Her eyes were suddenly shining.

'Oh we have, we have!' she cried. 'I feel closer to you now than to any one in the world.'

He stopped suddenly and indicated the side of the path.

'We might—just a minute—'

It was a pieta, a life-size statue of the Blessed Virgin set within a semicircle of rocks.

Feeling a little self-conscious she dropped on her knees beside him and made an unsuccessful attempt at prayer.

She was only half through when he rose. He took her arm again.

'I wanted to thank Her for letting as have this day together,' he said simply.

Lois felt a sudden lump in her throat and she wanted to say something that would tell him how much it had meant to her, too. But she found no words.

'I'll always remember this,' he continued, his voice trembling a little—'this summer day with you. It's been just what I expected. You're just what I expected, Lois.'

'I'm awfully glad, Keith.'

'You see, when you were little they kept sending me snap-shots of you, first as a baby and then as a child in socks playing on the beach with a pail and shovel, and then suddenly as a wistful little girl with wondering, pure eyes—and I used to build dreams about you. A man has to have something living to cling to. I think, Lois, it was your little white soul I tried to keep near me—even when life was at its loudest and every intellectual idea of God seemed the sheerest mockery, and desire and love and a million things came up to me and said, 'Look here at me! See, I'm Life. You're turning your back on it!' All the way through that shadow, Lois, I could always see your baby soul flitting on ahead of me, very frail and clear and wonderful.'

Lois was crying softly. They had reached the gate and she rested her elbow on it and dabbed furiously at her eyes.

'And then later, child, when you were sick I knelt all one night and asked God to spare you for me—for I knew then that I wanted more; He had taught me to want more. I wanted to know you moved and breathed in the same world with me. I saw you growing up, that white innocence of yours changing to a flame and burning to give light to other weaker souls. And then I wanted some day to take your children on my knee and hear them call the crabbed old monk Uncle Kieth.'

He seemed to be laughing now as he talked.

'Oh, Lois, Lois, I was asking God for more then. I wanted the letters you'd write me and the place I'd have at your table. I wanted an awful lot, Lois, dear.'

'You've got me, Kieth,' she sobbed 'you know it, say you know it. Oh, I'm acting like a baby but I didn't think you'd be this way, and I—oh, Kieth—Kieth—'

He took her hand and patted it softly.

'Here's the bus. You'll come again won't you?'

She put her hands on his cheeks, add drawing his head down, pressed her tear-wet face against his.

'Oh, Kieth, brother, someday I'll tell you something.'

He helped her in, saw her take down her handkerchief and smile bravely at him, as the driver kicked his whip and the bus rolled off. Then a thick cloud of dust rose around it and she was gone.

For a few minutes he stood there on the road his hand on the gate-post, his lips half parted in a smile.

'Lois,' he said aloud in a sort of wonder, 'Lois, Lois.'

Later, some probationers passing noticed him kneeling before the pieta, and coming back after a time found him still there. And he was there until twilight came down and the courteous trees grew garrulous overhead and the crickets took up their burden of song in the dusky grass.

VII

The first clerk in the telegraph booth in the Baltimore Station whistled through his buck teeth at the second clerk:

'S'matter?'

'See that girl—no, the pretty one with the big black dots on her veil. Too late—she's gone. You missed somep'n.'

'What about her?'

'Nothing. 'Cept she's damn good-looking. Came in here yesterday and sent a wire to some guy to meet her somewhere. Then a minute ago she came in with a telegram all written out and was standin' there goin' to give it to me when she changed her mind or somep'n and all of a sudden tore it up.'

'Hm.'

The first clerk came around tile counter and picking up the two pieces of paper from the floor put them together idly. The second clerk read them over his shoulder and subconsciously counted the words as he read. There were just thirteen.

'This is in the way of a permanent goodbye. I should suggest Italy. 'Lois.'

'Tore it up, eh?' said the second clerk.

THE IDIOTS

Joseph Conrad

We were driving along the road from Treguier to Kervanda. We passed at a smart trot between the hedges topping an earth wall on each side of the road; then at the foot of the steep ascent before Ploumar the horse dropped into a walk, and the driver jumped down heavily from the box. He flicked his whip and climbed the incline, stepping clumsily uphill by the side of the carriage, one hand on the footboard, his eyes on the ground. After a while he lifted his head, pointed up the road with the end of the whip, and said—

'The idiot!'

The sun was shining violently upon the undulating surface of the land. The rises were topped by clumps of meagre trees, with their branches showing high on the sky as if they had been perched upon stilts. The small fields, cut up by hedges and stone walls that zig-zagged over the slopes, lay in rectangular patches of vivid greens and yellows, resembling the unskilful daubs of a naive picture. And the landscape was divided in two by the white streak of a road stretching in long loops far away, like a river of dust crawling out of the hills on its way to the sea.

'Here he is,' said the driver, again.

In the long grass bordering the road a face glided past the carriage at the level of the wheels as we drove slowly by. The imbecile face was red, and the bullet head with close-cropped hair seemed to lie alone, its chin in the dust. The body was lost in the bushes growing thick along the bottom of the deep ditch.

It was a boy's face. He might have been sixteen, judging from the size—perhaps less, perhaps more. Such creatures are forgotten by time, and live untouched by years till death gathers them up into its compassionate bosom; the faithful death that never forgets in the press of work the most insignificant of its children.

'Ah! there's another,' said the man, with a certain satisfaction in his tone, as if he had caught sight of something expected.

There was another. That one stood nearly in the middle of the road in the blaze of sunshine at the end of his own short shadow. And he stood with hands pushed into the opposite sleeves of his long coat, his head sunk between the shoulders, all hunched up in the flood of heat. From a distance he had the aspect of one suffering from intense cold.

'Those are twins,' explained the driver.

The idiot shuffled two paces out of the way and looked at us over his shoulder when we brushed past him. The glance was unseeing and staring, a fascinated glance; but he did not turn to look after us. Probably the image passed before the eyes without leaving any trace on the misshapen brain of the creature. When we had topped the ascent I looked over the hood. He stood in the road just where we had left him.

The driver clambered into his seat, clicked his tongue, and we went downhill. The brake squeaked horribly from time to time. At the foot he eased off the noisy mechanism and said, turning half round on his box—

'We shall see some more of them by-and-by.'

'More idiots? How many of them are there, then?' I asked.

'There's four of them—children of a farmer near Ploumar here… The parents are dead now,' he added, after a while. 'The grandmother lives on the farm. In the daytime they knock about on this road, and they come home at dusk along with the cattle… It's a good farm.'

We saw the other two: a boy and a girl, as the driver said. They were dressed exactly alike, in shapeless garments with petticoat-like skirts. The imperfect thing that lived within them moved those beings to howl at us from the top of the bank, where they sprawled amongst the tough stalks of furze. Their cropped black heads stuck out from the bright yellow wall of countless small blossoms. The faces were purple with the strain of yelling; the voices sounded blank and cracked like a mechanical imitation of old people's voices; and suddenly ceased when we turned into a lane.

I saw them many times in my wandering about the country. They lived on that road, drifting along its length here and there, according to the inexplicable impulses of their monstrous darkness. They were an offence to the sunshine, a reproach to empty heaven, a blight on the concentrated and purposeful vigour of the wild landscape. In time the story of their parents shaped itself before me out of the listless answers to my questions, out of the indifferent words heard in wayside inns or on the very road those idiots haunted. Some of it was told by an emaciated and sceptical old fellow with a tremendous whip, while we trudged together over the sands by the side of a two-wheeled cart loaded with dripping seaweed. Then at other times other people confirmed and completed the story: till it stood at last before me, a tale formidable and simple, as they always are, those disclosures of obscure trials endured by ignorant hearts.

When he returned from his military service Jean-Pierre Bacadou found the old people very much aged. He remarked with pain that the work of the farm was not satisfactorily done. The father had not the energy of old days. The hands did not feel over them the eye of the master. Jean-Pierre noted with sorrow that the heap of manure in the courtyard before the only entrance to the house was not so large as it should have been. The fences were out of repair, and the cattle suffered from neglect. At home the mother was practically bedridden, and the girls chattered loudly in the big kitchen, unrebuked, from morning to night. He said to himself: 'We must change all this.' He talked the matter over with his father one evening when the rays of the setting sun entering the yard between the outhouses ruled the heavy shadows with luminous streaks. Over the manure heap floated a mist, opal-tinted and odorous, and the marauding hens would stop in their scratching to examine with a sudden glance of their round eye the two men, both lean and tall, talking in hoarse tones. The old man, all twisted with rheumatism and bowed with years of work, the younger bony and straight, spoke without gestures in the indifferent manner of peasants, grave and slow. But before the sun had set the father had submitted to the sensible arguments of the son. 'It is not for me that I am speaking,' insisted Jean-Pierre. 'It is for the land. It's a pity to see it badly used. I am not impatient for myself.' The old fellow nodded over his stick. 'I dare say; I dare say,' he muttered. 'You may be right. Do what you like. It's the mother that will be pleased.'

The mother was pleased with her daughter-in-law. Jean-Pierre brought the two-wheeled spring-cart with a rush into the yard. The grey horse galloped clumsily, and the bride and bridegroom, sitting side by side, were jerked backwards and forwards by the up and down motion of the shafts, in a manner regular and brusque. On the road the distanced wedding guests straggled in pairs and groups. The men advanced with heavy steps, swinging their idle arms. They were clad in town clothes; jackets cut with clumsy smartness, hard black hats, immense boots, polished highly. Their women all in simple black, with white caps and shawls of faded tints folded triangularly on the back, strolled lightly by their side. In front the violin sang a strident tune, and the biniou snored and hummed, while the player capered solemnly, lifting high his heavy clogs. The sombre procession drifted in and out of the narrow lanes, through sunshine and through shade, between fields and hedgerows, scaring the little birds that darted away in troops right and left. In the yard of Bacadou's farm the dark ribbon wound itself up into a mass of men and women pushing at the door with cries and greetings. The wedding dinner was remembered for months. It was a splendid feast in the orchard. Farmers of considerable means and excellent repute were to be found sleeping in ditches, all along the road to Treguier, even as late as the afternoon of the next day. All the countryside participated in the happiness of Jean-Pierre. He remained sober, and, together with his quiet wife, kept out of the way, letting father and mother reap their due of honour and thanks. But the next day he took hold strongly, and the old folks felt a shadow—precursor of the grave—fall upon them finally. The world is to the young.

When the twins were born there was plenty of room in the house, for the mother of Jean-Pierre had gone away to dwell under a heavy stone in the cemetery of Ploumar. On that day, for the first time since his son's marriage, the elder Bacadou, neglected by the cackling lot of strange women who thronged the kitchen, left in the morning his seat under the mantel of the fireplace, and went into the empty cow-house, shaking his white locks dismally. Grandsons were all very well, but he wanted his soup at midday. When shown the babies, he stared at them with a fixed gaze, and muttered something like: 'It's too much.' Whether he meant too much happiness, or simply commented upon the number of his descendants, it is impossible to say. He looked offended—as far as his old wooden face could express anything; and for days afterwards could be seen, almost any time of the day, sitting at the gate, with his nose over his knees, a pipe between his gums, and gathered up into a kind of raging concentrated sulkiness. Once he spoke to his son, alluding to the newcomers with a groan: 'They will quarrel over the land.' 'Don't bother about that, father,' answered Jean-Pierre, stolidly, and passed, bent double, towing a recalcitrant cow over his shoulder.

He was happy, and so was Susan, his wife. It was not an ethereal joy welcoming new souls to struggle, perchance to victory. In fourteen years both boys would be a help; and, later on, Jean-Pierre pictured two big sons striding over the land from patch to patch, wringing tribute from the earth beloved and fruitful. Susan was happy too, for she did not want to be spoken of as the unfortunate woman, and now she had children no one could call her that. Both herself and her husband had seen something of the larger world—he during the time of his service; while she had spent a year or so in Paris with a Breton family; but had been too home-sick to remain longer away from the hilly and green country, set in a barren circle of rocks and sands, where she had been born. She thought that one of the boys ought perhaps to be a priest, but said nothing to her husband, who was a republican, and hated the 'crows,' as he called the ministers of religion. The christening was a splendid affair. All the commune came to it, for the Bacadous were rich and influential, and, now and then, did not mind the expense. The grandfather had a new coat.

Some months afterwards, one evening when the kitchen had been swept, and the door locked, Jean-Pierre, looking at the cot, asked his wife: 'What's the matter with those children?' And, as if these words, spoken calmly, had been the portent of misfortune, she answered with a loud wail that must have been heard across the yard in the pig-sty; for the pigs (the Bacadous had the finest pigs in the country) stirred and grunted complainingly in the night. The husband went on grinding his bread and butter slowly, gazing at the wall, the soup-plate smoking under his chin. He had returned late from the market, where he had overheard (not for the first time) whispers behind his back. He revolved the words in his mind as he drove back. 'Simple! Both of them… Never any use! … Well! May be, may be. One must see. Would ask his wife.' This was her answer. He felt like a blow on his chest, but said only: 'Go, draw me some cider. I am thirsty!'

She went out moaning, an empty jug in her hand. Then he arose, took up the light, and moved slowly towards the cradle. They slept. He looked at them sideways, finished his mouthful there, went back heavily, and sat down before his plate. When his wife returned he never looked up, but swallowed a couple of spoonfuls noisily, and remarked, in a dull manner—

'When they sleep they are like other people's children.'

She sat down suddenly on a stool nearby, and shook with a silent tempest of sobs, unable to speak. He finished his meal, and remained idly thrown back in his chair, his eyes lost amongst the black rafters of the ceiling. Before him the tallow candle flared red and straight, sending up a slender thread of smoke. The light lay on the rough, sunburnt skin of his throat; the sunk cheeks were like patches of darkness, and his aspect was mournfully stolid, as if he had ruminated with difficulty endless ideas. Then he said, deliberately—

'We must see…consult people. Don't cry… They won't all be like that…surely! We must sleep now.'

After the third child, also a boy, was born, Jean-Pierre went about his work with tense hopefulness. His lips seemed more narrow, more tightly compressed than before; as if for fear of letting the earth he tilled hear the voice of hope that murmured within his breast. He watched the child, stepping up to the cot with a heavy clang of sabots on the stone floor, and glanced in, along his shoulder, with that indifference which is like a deformity of peasant humanity. Like the earth they master and serve, those men, slow of eye and speech, do not show the inner fire; so that, at last, it becomes a question with them as with the earth, what there is in the core: heat, violence, a force mysterious and terrible—or nothing but a clod, a mass fertile and inert, cold and unfeeling, ready to bear a crop of plants that sustain life or give death.

The mother watched with other eyes; listened with otherwise expectant ears. Under the high hanging shelves supporting great sides of bacon overhead, her body was busy by the great fireplace, attentive to the pot swinging on iron gallows, scrubbing the long table where the field hands would sit down directly to their evening meal. Her mind remained by the cradle, night and day on the watch, to hope and suffer. That child, like the other two, never smiled, never stretched its hands to her, never spoke; never had a glance of recognition for her in its big black eyes, which could only stare fixedly at any glitter, but failed hopelessly to follow the brilliance of a sun-ray slipping slowly along the floor. When the men were at work she spent long days between her three idiot children and the childish grandfather, who sat grim, angular, and immovable, with his feet near the warm ashes of the fire. The feeble old fellow seemed to suspect that there was something wrong with his grandsons. Only once, moved either by affection or by the sense of proprieties, he attempted to nurse the youngest. He took the boy up from the floor, clicked his tongue at him, and essayed a shaky gallop of his bony knees. Then he looked closely with his misty eyes at the child's face and deposited him down gently on the floor again. And he sat, his lean shanks crossed, nodding at the steam escaping from the cooking-pot with a gaze senile and worried.

Then mute affliction dwelt in Bacadou's farmhouse, sharing the breath and the bread of its inhabitants; and the priest of the Ploumar parish had great cause for congratulation. He called upon the rich landowner, the Marquis de Chavanes, on purpose to deliver himself with joyful unction of solemn platitudes about the inscrutable ways of Providence. In the vast dimness of the curtained drawing-room, the little man, resembling a black bolster, leaned towards a couch, his hat on his knees, and gesticulated with a fat hand at the elongated, gracefully-flowing lines of the clear Parisian toilette from which the half-amused, half-bored marquise listened with gracious languor. He was exulting and humble, proud and awed. The impossible had come to pass. Jean-Pierre Bacadou, the enraged republican farmer, had been to mass last Sunday—had proposed to entertain the visiting priests at the next festival of Ploumar! It was a triumph for the Church and for the good cause. 'I thought I would come at once to tell Monsieur le Marquis. I know how anxious he is for the welfare of our country,' declared the priest, wiping his face. He was asked to stay to dinner.

The Chavanes returning that evening, after seeing their guest to the main gate of the park, discussed the matter while they strolled in the moonlight, trailing their long shadows up the straight avenue of chestnuts. The marquise, a royalist of course, had been mayor of the commune which includes Ploumar, the scattered hamlets of the coast, and the stony islands that fringe the yellow flatness of the sands. He had felt his position insecure, for there was a strong republican element in that part of the country; but now the conversion of Jean-Pierre made him safe. He was very pleased. 'You have no idea how influential those people are,' he explained to his wife. 'Now, I am sure, the next communal election will go all right. I shall be re-elected.' 'Your ambition is perfectly insatiable, Charles,' exclaimed the marquise, gaily. 'But, ma chere amie,' argued the husband, seriously, 'it's most important that the right man should be mayor this year, because of the elections to the Chamber. If you think it amuses me…'

Jean-Pierre had surrendered to his wife's mother. Madame Levaille was a woman of business, known and respected within a radius of at least fifteen miles. Thick-set and stout, she was seen about the country, on foot or in an acquaintance's cart, perpetually moving, in spite of her fifty-eight years, in steady pursuit of business. She had houses in all the hamlets, she worked quarries of granite, she freighted coasters with stone—even traded with the Channel Islands. She was broad-cheeked, wide-eyed, persuasive in speech: carrying her point with the placid and invincible obstinacy of an old woman who knows her own mind. She very seldom slept for two nights together in the same house; and the wayside inns were the best places to inquire in as to her whereabouts. She had either passed, or was expected to pass there at six; or somebody, coming in, had seen her in the morning, or expected to meet her that evening. After the inns that command the roads, the churches were the buildings she frequented most. Men of liberal opinions would induce small children to run into sacred edifices to see whether Madame Levaille was there, and to tell her that so-and-so was in the road waiting to speak to her about potatoes, or flour, or stones, or houses; and she would curtail her devotions, come out blinking and crossing herself into the sunshine; ready to discuss business matters in a calm, sensible way across a table in the kitchen of the inn opposite. Latterly she had stayed for a few days several times with her son-in-law, arguing against sorrow and misfortune with composed face and gentle tones. Jean-Pierre felt the convictions imbibed in the regiment torn out of his breast—not by arguments but by facts. Striding over his fields he thought it over. There were three of them. Three! All alike! Why? Such things did not happen to everybody—to nobody he ever heard of. One—might pass. But three! All three. Forever useless, to be fed while he lived and... What would become of the land when he died? This must be seen to. He would sacrifice his convictions. One day he told his wife—

'See what your God will do for us. Pay for some masses.'

Susan embraced her man. He stood unbending, then turned on his heels and went out. But afterwards, when a black soutane darkened his doorway, he did not object; even offered some cider himself to the priest. He listened to the talk meekly; went to mass between the two women; accomplished what the priest called 'his religious duties' at Easter. That morning he felt like a man who had sold his soul. In the afternoon he fought ferociously with an old friend and neighbour who had remarked that the priests had the best of it and were now going to eat the priest-eater. He came home dishevelled and bleeding, and happening to catch sight of his children (they were kept generally out of the way), cursed and swore incoherently, banging the table. Susan wept. Madame Levaille sat serenely unmoved. She assured her daughter that 'It will pass'; and taking up her thick umbrella, departed in haste to see after a schooner she was going to load with granite from her quarry.

A year or so afterwards the girl was born. A girl. Jean-Pierre heard of it in the fields, and was so upset by the news that he sat down on the boundary wall and remained there till the evening, instead of going home as he was urged to do. A girl! He felt half cheated. However, when he got home he was partly reconciled to his fate. One could marry her to a good fellow—not to a good for nothing, but to a fellow with some understanding and a good pair of arms. Besides, the next may be a boy, he thought. Of course they would be all right. His new credulity knew of no doubt. The ill luck was broken. He spoke cheerily to his wife. She was also hopeful. Three priests came to that christening, and

Madame Levaille was godmother. The child turned out an idiot too.

Then on market days Jean-Pierre was seen bargaining bitterly, quarrelsome and greedy; then getting drunk with taciturn earnestness; then driving home in the dusk at a rate fit for a wedding, but with a face gloomy enough for a funeral. Sometimes he would insist on his wife coming with him; and they would drive in the early morning, shaking side by side on the narrow seat above the helpless pig, that, with tied legs, grunted a melancholy sigh at every rut. The morning drives were silent; but in the evening, coming home, Jean-Pierre, tipsy, was viciously muttering, and growled at the confounded woman who could not rear children that were like anybody else's. Susan, holding on against the erratic swayings of the cart, pretended not to hear. Once, as they were driving through Ploumar, some obscure and drunken impulse caused him to pull up sharply opposite the church. The moon swam amongst light white clouds. The tombstones gleamed pale under the fretted shadows of the trees in the churchyard. Even the village dogs slept. Only the nightingales, awake, spun out the thrill of their song above the silence of graves. Jean-Pierre said thickly to his wife—

'What do you think is there?'

He pointed his whip at the tower—in which the big dial of the clock appeared high in the moonlight like a pallid face without eyes—and getting out carefully, fell down at once by the wheel. He picked himself up and climbed one by one the few steps to the iron gate of the churchyard. He put his face to the bars and called out indistinctly—

'Hey there! Come out!'

'Jean! Return! Return!' entreated his wife in low tones.

He took no notice, and seemed to wait there. The song of nightingales beat on all sides against the high walls of the church, and flowed back between stone crosses and flat grey slabs, engraved with words of hope and sorrow.

'Hey! Come out!' shouted Jean-Pierre, loudly.

The nightingales ceased to sing.

'Nobody?' went on Jean-Pierre. 'Nobody there. A swindle of the crows. That's what this is. Nobody anywhere. I despise it. Allez! Houp!'

He shook the gate with all his strength, and the iron bars rattled with a frightful clanging, like a chain dragged over stone steps. A dog nearby barked hurriedly. Jean-Pierre staggered back, and after three successive dashes got into his cart. Susan sat very quiet and still. He said to her with drunken severity—

'See? Nobody. I've been made a fool! Malheur! Somebody will pay for it. The next one I see near the house I will lay my whip on…on the black spine…I will. I don't want him in there…he only helps the carrion crows to rob poor folk. I am a man… We will see if I can't have children like anybody else…now you mind… They won't be all… all…we see…'

She burst out through the fingers that hid her face—

'Don't say that, Jean; don't say that, my man!'

He struck her a swinging blow on the head with the back of his hand and knocked her into the bottom of the cart, where she crouched, thrown about lamentably by every jolt. He drove furiously, standing up, brandishing his whip, shaking the reins over the grey horse that galloped ponderously, making the heavy harness leap upon his broad quarters. The country rang clamorous in the night with the irritated barking of farm dogs, that followed the rattle of wheels all along the road. A couple of belated wayfarers had only just time to step into the ditch. At his own gate he caught the post and was shot out of the cart head first. The horse went on slowly to the door. At Susan's piercing cries the farm hands rushed out. She thought him dead, but he was only sleeping where he fell, and cursed his men, who hastened to him, for disturbing his slumbers.

Autumn came. The clouded sky descended low upon the black contours of the hills; and the dead leaves danced in spiral whirls under naked trees, till the wind, sighing profoundly, laid them to rest in the hollows of bare valleys. And from morning till night one could see all over the land black denuded boughs, the boughs gnarled and twisted, as if contorted with pain, swaying sadly between the wet clouds and the soaked earth. The clear and gentle streams of summer days rushed discoloured and raging at the stones that barred the way to the sea, with the fury of madness bent upon suicide. From horizon to horizon the great road to the sands lay between the hills in a dull glitter of empty curves, resembling an unnavigable river of mud.

Jean-Pierre went from field to field, moving blurred and tall in the drizzle, or striding on the crests of rises, lonely and high upon the grey curtain of drifting clouds, as if he had been pacing along the very edge of the universe. He looked at the black earth, at the earth mute and promising, at the mysterious earth doing its work of life in death-like stillness under the veiled sorrow of the sky. And it seemed to him that to a man worse than childless there was no promise in the fertility of fields, that from him the earth escaped, defied him, frowned at him like the clouds, sombre and hurried above his head. Having to face alone his own fields, he felt the inferiority of man who passes away before the clod that remains. Must he give up the hope of having by his side a son who would look at the turned-up sods with a master's eye? A man that would think as he thought, that would feel as he felt; a man who would be part of himself, and yet remain to trample masterfully on that earth when he was gone? He thought of some distant relations, and felt savage enough to curse them aloud. They! Never! He turned homewards, going straight at the roof of his dwelling, visible between the enlaced skeletons of trees. As he swung his legs over the stile a cawing flock of birds settled slowly on the field; dropped down behind his back, noiseless and fluttering, like flakes of soot.

That day Madame Levaille had gone early in the afternoon to the house she had near Kervanion. She had to pay some of the men who worked in her granite quarry there, and she went in good time because her little house contained a shop where the workmen could spend their wages without the trouble of going to town. The house stood alone amongst rocks. A lane of mud and stones ended at the door. The sea-winds coming ashore on Stonecutter's point, fresh from the fierce turmoil of the waves, howled violently at the unmoved heaps of black boulders holding up steadily short-armed, high crosses against the tremendous rush of the invisible. In the sweep of gales the sheltered dwelling stood in a calm resonant and disquieting, like the calm in the centre of a hurricane. On stormy nights, when the tide was out, the bay of Fougere, fifty feet below the house, resembled an immense black pit, from which ascended mutterings and sighs as if the sands down there had been alive and complaining. At high tide the returning water assaulted the ledges of rock in short rushes, ending in bursts of livid light and columns of spray, that flew inland, stinging to death the grass of pastures.

The darkness came from the hills, flowed over the coast, put out the red fires of sunset, and went on to seaward pursuing the retiring tide. The wind dropped with the sun, leaving a maddened sea and a devastated sky. The heavens above the house seemed to be draped in black rags, held up here and there by pins of fire. Madame Levaille, for this evening the servant of her own workmen, tried to induce them to depart. 'An old woman like me ought to be in bed at this late hour,' she good-humouredly repeated. The quarrymen drank, asked for more. They shouted over the table as if they had been talking across a field. At one end four of them played cards, banging the wood with their hard knuckles, and swearing at every lead. One sat with a lost gaze, humming a bar of some song, which he repeated endlessly. Two others, in a corner, were quarrelling confidentially and fiercely over some woman, looking close into one another's eyes as if they had wanted to tear them out, but speaking in whispers that promised violence and murder discreetly, in a venomous sibillation of subdued words. The atmosphere in there was thick enough to slice with a knife. Three candles burning about the long room glowed red and dull like sparks expiring in ashes.

The slight click of the iron latch was at that late hour as unexpected and startling as a thunder-clap. Madame Levaille put down a bottle she held above a liqueur glass; the players turned their heads; the whispered quarrel ceased; only the singer, after darting a glance at the door, went on humming with a stolid face. Susan appeared in the doorway, stepped in, flung the door to, and put her back against it, saying, half aloud—

'Mother!'

Madame Levaille, taking up the bottle again, said calmly: 'Here you are, my girl. What a state you are in!' The neck of the bottle rang on the rim of the glass, for the old woman was startled, and the idea that the farm had caught fire had entered her head. She could think of no other cause for her daughter's appearance.

Susan, soaked and muddy, stared the whole length of the room towards the men at the far end. Her mother asked—

'What has happened? God guard us from misfortune!'

Susan moved her lips. No sound came. Madame Levaille stepped up to her daughter, took her by the arm, looked into her face.

'In God's name,' she said, shakily, 'what's the matter? You have been rolling in mud… Why did you come? … Where's Jean?'

The men had all got up and approached slowly, staring with dull surprise. Madame Levaille jerked her daughter away from the door, swung her round upon a seat close to the wall. Then she turned fiercely to the men—

'Enough of this! Out you go—you others! I close.'

One of them observed, looking down at Susan collapsed on the seat: 'She is—one may say—half dead.'

Madame Levaille flung the door open.

'Get out! March!' she cried, shaking nervously.

They dropped out into the night, laughing stupidly. Outside, the two Lotharios broke out into loud shouts. The others tried to soothe them, all talking at once. The noise went away up the lane with the men, who staggered together in a tight knot, remonstrating with one another foolishly.

'Speak, Susan. What is it? Speak!' entreated Madame Levaille, as soon as the door was shut.

Susan pronounced some incomprehensible words, glaring at the table. The old woman clapped her hands above her head, let them drop, and stood looking at her daughter with disconsolate eyes. Her husband had been 'deranged in his head' for a few years before he died, and now she began to suspect her daughter was going mad. She asked, pressingly—

'Does Jean know where you are? Where is Jean?'

'He knows…he is dead.'

'What!' cried the old woman. She came up near, and peering at her daughter, repeated three times: 'What do you say? What do you say? What do you say?'

Susan sat dry-eyed and stony before Madame Levaille, who contemplated her, feeling a strange sense of inexplicable horror creep into the silence of the house. She had hardly realized the news, further than to understand that she had been brought in one short moment face to face with something unexpected and final. It did not even occur to her to ask for any explanation. She thought: accident—terrible accident—blood to the head—fell down a trap door in the loft… She remained there, distracted and mute, blinking her old eyes.

Suddenly, Susan said—

'I have killed him.'

For a moment the mother stood still, almost unbreathing, but with composed face. The next second she burst out into a shout—

'You miserable madwoman…they will cut your neck…'

She fancied the gendarmes entering the house, saying to her: 'We want your daughter; give her up:' the gendarmes with the severe, hard faces of men on duty. She knew the brigadier well—an old friend, familiar and respectful, saying heartily, 'To your good health, Madame!' before lifting to his lips the small glass of cognac—out of the special bottle she kept for friends. And now! … She was losing her head. She rushed here and there, as if looking for something urgently needed—gave that up, stood stock still in the middle of the room, and screamed at her daughter—

'Why? Say! Say! Why?'

The other seemed to leap out of her strange apathy.

'Do you think I am made of stone?' she shouted back, striding towards her mother.

'No! It's impossible…' said Madame Levaille, in a convinced tone.

'You go and see, mother,' retorted Susan, looking at her with blazing eyes. 'There's no money in heaven—no justice. No! … I did not know… Do you think I have no heart? Do you think I have never heard people jeering at me, pitying me, wondering at me? Do you know how some of them were calling me? The mother of idiots—that was my nickname! And my children never would know me, never speak to me. They would know nothing; neither men—nor God. Haven't I prayed! But the Mother of God herself would not hear me. A mother! … Who is accursed—I, or the man who is dead? Eh? Tell me. I took care of myself. Do you think I would defy the anger of God and have my house full of those things—that are worse than animals who know the hand that feeds them? Who blasphemed in the night at the very church door? Was it I? … I only wept and prayed for mercy…and I feel the curse at every moment of the day—I see it round me from morning to night…I've got to keep them alive—to take care of my misfortune and shame. And he would come. I begged him and Heaven for mercy… No! … Then we shall see… He came this evening. I thought to myself: 'Ah! again!' … I had my long scissors. I heard him shouting… I saw him near… I must—must I? … Then take! … And I struck him in the throat above the breastbone… I never heard him even sigh… I left him standing… It was a minute ago. How did I come here?'

Madame Levaille shivered. A wave of cold ran down her back, down her fat arms under her tight sleeves, made her stamp gently where she stood. Quivers ran over the broad cheeks, across the thin lips, ran amongst the wrinkles at the corners of her steady old eyes. She stammered—

'You wicked woman—you disgrace me. But there! You always resembled your father. What do you think will become of you…in the other world? In this… Oh misery!'

She was very hot now. She felt burning inside. She wrung her perspiring hands—and suddenly, starting in great haste, began to look for her big shawl and umbrella, feverishly, never once glancing at her daughter, who stood in the middle of the room following her with a gaze distracted and cold.

'Nothing worse than in this,' said Susan.

Her mother, umbrella in hand and trailing the shawl over the floor, groaned profoundly.

'I must go to the priest,' she burst out passionately. 'I do not know whether you even speak the truth! You are a horrible woman. They will find you anywhere. You may stay here—or go. There is no room for you in this world.'

Ready now to depart, she yet wandered aimlessly about the room, putting the bottles on the shelf, trying to fit with trembling hands the covers on cardboard boxes. Whenever the real sense of what she had heard emerged for a second from the haze of her thoughts she would fancy that something had exploded in her brain without, unfortunately, bursting her head to pieces—which would have been a relief. She blew the candles out one by one without knowing it, and was horribly startled by the darkness. She fell on a bench and began to whimper. After a while she ceased, and sat listening to the breathing of her daughter, whom she could hardly see, still and upright, giving no other sign of life. She was becoming old rapidly at last, during those minutes. She spoke in tones unsteady, cut about by the rattle of teeth, like one shaken by a deadly cold fit of ague.

'I wish you had died little. I will never dare to show my old head in the sunshine again. There are worse misfortunes than idiot children. I wish you had been born to me simple—like your own…'

She saw the figure of her daughter pass before the faint and livid clearness of a window. Then it appeared in the doorway for a second, and the door swung to with a clang. Madame Levaille, as if awakened by the noise from a long nightmare, rushed out.

'Susan!' she shouted from the doorstep.

She heard a stone roll a long time down the declivity of the rocky beach above the sands. She stepped forward cautiously, one hand on the wall of the house, and peered down into the smooth darkness of the empty bay. Once again she cried—

'Susan! You will kill yourself there.'

The stone had taken its last leap in the dark, and she heard nothing now. A sudden thought seemed to strangle her, and she called no more. She turned her back upon the black silence of the pit and went up the lane towards Ploumar, stumbling along with sombre determination, as if she had started on a desperate journey that would last, perhaps, to the end of her life. A sullen and periodic clamour of waves rolling over reefs followed her far inland between the high hedges sheltering the gloomy solitude of the fields.

Susan had run out, swerving sharp to the left at the door, and on the edge of the slope crouched down behind a boulder. A dislodged stone went on downwards, rattling as it leaped. When Madame Levaille called out, Susan could have, by stretching her hand, touched her mother's skirt, had she had the courage to move a limb. She saw the old woman go away, and she remained still, closing her eyes and pressing her side to the hard and rugged surface of the rock. After a while a familiar face with fixed eyes and an open mouth became visible in the intense obscurity amongst the boulders. She uttered a low cry and stood up. The face vanished, leaving her to gasp and shiver alone in the wilderness of stone heaps. But as soon as she had crouched down again to rest, with her head against the rock, the face returned, came very near, appeared eager to finish the speech that had been cut short by death, only a moment ago. She scrambled quickly to her feet and said, 'Go away, or I will do it again.' The thing wavered, swung to the right, to the left. She moved this way and that, stepped back, fancied herself screaming at it, and was appalled by the unbroken stillness of the night. She tottered on the brink, felt the steep declivity under her feet, and rushed down blindly to save herself from a headlong fall. The shingle seemed to wake up; the pebbles began to roll before her, pursued her from above, raced down with her on both sides, rolling past with an increasing clatter. In the peace of the night the noise grew, deepening to a rumour, continuous and violent, as if the whole semicircle of the stony beach had started to tumble down into the bay. Susan's feet hardly touched the slope that seemed to run down with her. At the bottom she stumbled, shot forward, throwing her arms out, and fell heavily. She jumped up at once and turned swiftly to look back, her clenched hands full of sand she had clutched in her fall. The face was there, keeping its distance, visible in its own sheen that made a pale stain in the night. She shouted, 'Go away!'—she shouted at it with pain, with fear, with all the rage of that useless stab that could not keep him quiet, keep him out of her sight. What did he want now? He was dead. Dead men have no children. Would he never leave her alone? She shrieked at it—waved her outstretched hands. She seemed to feel the breath of parted lips, and, with a long cry of discouragement, fled across the level bottom of the bay.

She ran lightly, unaware of any effort of her body. High sharp rocks that, when the bay is full, show above the glittering plain of blue water like pointed towers of submerged churches, glided past her, rushing to the land at a tremendous pace. To the left, in the distance, she could see something shining: a broad disc of light in which narrow shadows pivoted round the centre like the spokes of a wheel. She heard a voice calling, 'Hey! There!' and answered with a wild scream. So, he could call yet! He was calling after her to stop. Never! … She tore through the night, past the startled group of seaweed-gatherers who stood round their lantern paralysed with fear at the unearthly screech coming from that fleeing shadow. The men leaned on their pitchforks staring fearfully. A woman fell on her knees, and, crossing herself, began to pray aloud. A little girl with her ragged skirt full of slimy seaweed began to sob despairingly, lugging her soaked burden close to the man who carried the light. Somebody said, 'The thing ran out towards the sea.' Another voice exclaimed: 'And the sea is coming back! Look at the spreading puddles. Do you hear—you woman—there! Get up!' Several voices cried together. 'Yes, let us be off! Let the accursed thing go to the sea!' They moved on, keeping close round the light. Suddenly a man swore loudly. He would go and see what was the matter. It had been a woman's voice. He would go. There were shrill protests from women—but his high form detached itself from the group and went off running. They sent an unanimous call of scared voices after him. A word, insulting and mocking, came back, thrown at them through the darkness. A woman moaned. An old man said gravely: 'Such things ought to be left alone.' They went on slower, shuffling in the yielding sand and whispering to one another that Millot feared nothing, having no religion, but that it would end badly someday.

Susan met the incoming tide by the Raven islet and stopped, panting, with her feet in the water. She heard the murmur and felt the cold caress of the sea, and, calmer now, could see the sombre and confused mass of the Raven on one side and on the other the long white streak of Molene sands that are left high above the dry bottom of Fougere Bay at every ebb. She turned round and saw far away, along the starred background of the sky, the ragged outline of the coast. Above it, nearly facing her, appeared the tower of Ploumar Church; a slender and tall pyramid shooting up dark and pointed into the clustered glitter of the stars. She felt strangely calm. She knew where she was, and began to remember how she came there—and why. She peered into the smooth obscurity near her. She was alone. There was nothing there; nothing near her, either living or dead.

The tide was creeping in quietly, putting out long impatient arms of strange rivulets that ran towards the land between ridges of sand. Under the night the pools grew bigger with mysterious rapidity, while the great sea, yet far off, thundered in a regular rhythm along the indistinct line of the horizon. Susan splashed her way back for a few yards without being able to get clear of the water that murmured tenderly all around and, suddenly, with a spiteful gurgle, nearly took her off her feet. Her heart thumped with fear. This place was too big and too empty to die in. To-morrow they would do with her what they liked. But before she died she must tell them—tell the gentlemen in black clothes that there are things no woman can bear. She must explain how it happened… She splashed through a pool, getting wet to the waist, too preoccupied to care… She must explain. 'He came in the same way as ever and said, just so: 'Do you think I am going to leave the land to those people from Morbihan that I do not know? Do you? We shall see! Come along, you creature of mischance!' And he put his arms out. Then, Messieurs, I said, 'Before God—never!' And he said, striding at me with open palms: 'There is no God to hold me! Do you understand, you useless carcase. I will do what I like.' And he took me by the shoulders. Then I, Messieurs, called to God for help, and next minute, while he was shaking me, I felt my long scissors in my hand. His shirt was unbuttoned, and, by the candlelight, I saw the hollow of his throat. I cried: 'Let go!' He was crushing my shoulders. He was strong, my man was! Then I thought: No! … Must I? … Then take!—and I struck in the hollow place. I never saw him fall… The old father never turned his head. He is deaf and childish, gentlemen… Nobody saw him fall. I ran out… Nobody saw…'

She had been scrambling amongst the boulders of the Raven and now found herself, all out of breath, standing amongst the heavy shadows of the rocky islet. The Raven is connected with the main land by a natural pier of immense and slippery stones. She intended to return home that way. Was he still standing there? At home. Home! Four idiots and a corpse. She must go back and explain. Anybody would understand…

Below her the night or the sea seemed to pronounce distinctly—

'Aha! I see you at last!'

She started, slipped, fell; and without attempting to rise, listened, terrified. She heard heavy breathing, a clatter of wooden clogs. It stopped.

'Where the devil did you pass?' said an invisible man, hoarsely.

She held her breath. She recognized the voice. She had not seen him fall. Was he pursuing her there dead, or perhaps…alive?

She lost her head. She cried from the crevice where she lay huddled, 'Never, never!'

'Ah! You are still there. You led me a fine dance. Wait, my beauty, I must see how you look after all this. You wait… '

Millot was stumbling, laughing, swearing meaninglessly out of pure satisfaction, pleased with himself for having run down that fly-by-night. 'As if there were such things as ghosts! Bah! It took an old African soldier to show those clodhoppers… But it was curious. Who the devil was she?'

Susan listened, crouching. He was coming for her, this dead man. There was no escape. What a noise he made amongst the stones… She saw his head rise up, then the shoulders. He was tall—her own man! His long arms waved about, and it was his own voice sounding a little strange…because of the scissors. She scrambled out quickly, rushed to the edge of the causeway, and turned round. The man stood still on a high stone, detaching himself in dead black on the glitter of the sky.

'Where are you going to?' he called, roughly.

She answered, 'Home!' and watched him intensely. He made a striding, clumsy leap on to another boulder, and stopped again, balancing himself, then said—

'Ha! ha! Well, I am going with you. It's the least I can do. Ha! ha! ha!'

She stared at him till her eyes seemed to become glowing coals that burned deep into her brain, and yet she was in mortal fear of making out the well-known features. Below her the sea lapped softly against the rock with a splash continuous and gentle.

The man said, advancing another step—

'I am coming for you. What do you think?'

She trembled. Coming for her! There was no escape, no peace, no hope. She looked round despairingly. Suddenly the whole shadowy coast, the blurred islets, the heaven itself, swayed about twice, then came to a rest. She closed her eyes and shouted—

'Can't you wait till I am dead!'

She was shaken by a furious hate for that shade that pursued her in this world, unappeased even by death in its longing for an heir that would be like other people's children.

'Hey! What?' said Millot, keeping his distance prudently. He was saying to himself: 'Look out! Some lunatic. An accident happens soon.'

She went on, wildly—

'I want to live. To live alone—for a week—for a day. I must explain to them… I would tear you to pieces, I would kill you twenty times over rather than let you touch me while I live. How many times must I kill you—you blasphemer! Satan sends you here. I am damned too!'

'Come,' said Millot, alarmed and conciliating. 'I am perfectly alive! … Oh, my God!'

She had screamed, 'Alive!' and at once vanished before his eyes, as if the islet itself had swerved aside from under her feet. Millot rushed forward, and fell flat with his chin over the edge. Far below he saw the water whitened by her struggles, and heard one shrill cry for help that seemed to dart upwards along the perpendicular face of the rock, and soar past, straight into the high and impassive heaven.

Madame Levaille sat, dry-eyed, on the short grass of the hill side, with her thick legs stretched out, and her old feet turned up in their black cloth shoes. Her clogs stood nearby, and further off the umbrella lay on the withered sward like a weapon dropped from the grasp of a vanquished warrior. The Marquis of Chavanes, on horseback, one gloved hand on thigh, looked down at her as she got up laboriously, with groans. On the narrow track of the seaweed-carts four men were carrying inland Susan's body on a hand-barrow, while several others straggled listlessly behind. Madame Levaille looked after the procession. 'Yes, Monsieur le Marquis,' she said dispassionately, in her usual calm tone of a reasonable old woman. 'There are unfortunate people on this earth. I had only one child. Only one! And they won't bury her in consecrated ground!'

Her eyes filled suddenly, and a short shower of tears rolled down the broad cheeks. She pulled the shawl close about her. The Marquis leaned slightly over in his saddle, and said—

'It is very sad. You have all my sympathy. I shall speak to the Cure. She was unquestionably insane, and the fall was accidental. Millot says so distinctly. Good-day, Madame.'

And he trotted off, thinking to himself: 'I must get this old woman appointed guardian of those idiots, and administrator of the farm. It would be much better than having here one of those other Bacadous, probably a red republican, corrupting my commune.'

CW01432767

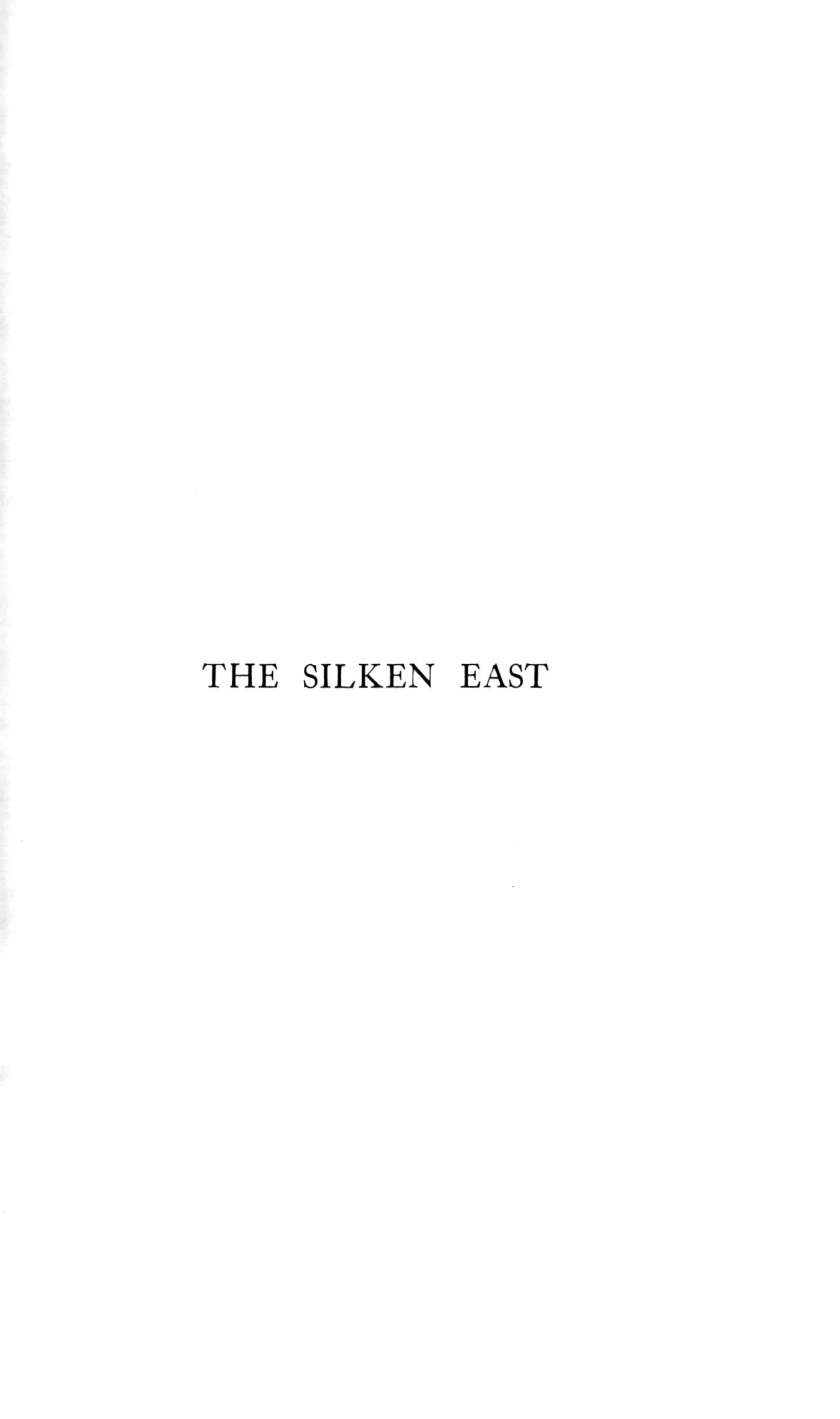

THE SILKEN EAST

MR. SCOTT O'CONNOR has also written the following books:

MANDALAY AND OTHER OLD CITIES OF BURMA..

TRAVELS IN THE PYRENEES.

THE SCENE OF WAR: Personal impressions of the Great War in France, Italy, Greece, Macedonia, Egypt, the Sinai Desert and the Mediterranean.

THE CHARM OF KASHMIR. Illustrated by A. N. Tagore.

AN EASTERN LIBRARY. With illuminated pages.

A VISION OF MOROCCO: The Far-West of Islam.

THE EMPIRE CRUISE. A story of the Royal Navy and the Empire.

AEGEAN ISLES. (*In preparation.*)

From a painting by J. Raeburn Middleton

STAIRCASE OF THE SHWE DAGÔN PAGODA

THE SILKEN EAST

A RECORD OF LIFE & TRAVEL IN BURMA

BY

V. C. SCOTT O'CONNOR

INTRODUCED BY

SIR HARCOURT BUTLER, G.C.S.I., G.C.I.E.

TWICE GOVERNOR OF BURMA

WITH 200 ILLUSTRATIONS
INCLUDING 8 COLOURED PLATES
BY J. R. MIDDLETON AND SAYA CHONE

Paul Strachan
KISCADALE

FIRST PUBLISHED IN 1904

THIS THIRD EDITION IS REPRODUCED FROM
THE 1928 EDITION AND PUBLISHED IN 1993 BY
PAUL STRACHAN - KISCADALE (LTD)
GARTMORE, STIRLING FK8 3RJ

ISBN 1 870838 21 1

Printed in Hong Kong
by Colorcraft

TO

MY DEAR MOTHER

INTRODUCTION

MY old friend Mr. Scott O'Connor has asked me to write a few words in introduction to the new edition of *The Silken East*. Of the book itself I need say little. It has been a favourite with the public for a quarter of a century: it has been quoted in guide-books and by writers on Burma: it has been much thumbed in the libraries: in fact it may be said to have attained the position of a standard work. It gives with beautiful illustrations a picture of a lovely land and a delightful people.

Few countries are so romantic as Burma or appeal so strongly to the imagination. Its long sea-board of about a thousand miles, its archipelago of about a thousand islands at its southern end, its great rivers, its forest-clad hills, its rich rice-fields laughing and swaying in the sunlight, its myriad pagodas, are a joy to remember. The first view of the great golden Shwe-Dagôn Pagoda as one comes up the Rangoon River, the glorious prospect from the Ridge at Moulmein, the great sweep of the plains of the Shweli and Irrawaddy valleys as seen from the hills above Bernardmyo, the mighty forest trees, leave an impression that time cannot efface or weaken. The smiling people in their delicately blended silks enjoying life and the sunshine and the rain, the graceful and daintily clad women, the monks in their yellow robes, have won the hearts as they have fascinated the eyes of many generations of foreign people who have seen them.

To beat the bounds of Burma one has to touch Siam on the south, French Indo-China and China on the east, and in the far north Assam and Tibet, and from all these distant countries people come to Burma in small bands, singly or in caravans. Hence the great variety of life and language in different parts of the province. Chinese and Indian labour supplement its sparse population; over three hundred and fifty thousand Indian labourers come over every year to reap the rice crop and help in the development of the country. For Burma, the largest province in area of all the provinces of India, had a population of only thirteen millions at the last census, of whom a million were Indians. British enterprise, largely Scottish, has sunk vast sums in the country and created employment and prosperity for numbers of men and women. The timber, the rice, the oil, the silver, tin, lead and spelter of Burma are known throughout the markets of the world. Rubies sapphires and other precious stones, amber and jade, are found within its borders and many people believe that the resources of Burma are still to a large extent unexplored.

The Government is pushing forward communications as fast as funds permit. An active policy of railway extension and road construction is being pursued. Education is being spread. The generous public, including the British firms, have subscribed some fifty lakhs for the endowment of the new Rangoon University. The great Burma Oil Company has given £100,000 for the construction of an up-to-date college of mining and engineering. Attention is being devoted to agricultural improvement. All the sources of wealth and prosperity are being investigated. The public services have been reorganised and salaries have been increased. A period of great activity in all departments has been inaugurated.

For the ethnologist linguist and naturalist Burma offers a wide field of enquiry. Quite recently slavery has been abolished, some eight thousand slaves having been given freedom, and the last traces of human sacrifice have, it is believed, now been removed. Civilisation is slowly but surely spreading among the wild tribes of the frontier and the process will continue. The motor-car is now rushing along the roads, bringing mechanisation in its train, teaching the value and importance of time. As said the prophet Daniel, many shall run to and fro and knowledge shall be increased. Conditions are changing. Under the pressure of economic growth Burma and Burmans will doubtless change. Something will be gained and something will be lost. Let us pray that the gain will be much and the loss little. For myself I have little doubt. For me, as I said in parting, Burma will always be the land of the lotus and the rainbow—the land that bids one linger, the land that bids one hope.

Those who want knowledge of Burma, one of the most interesting undeveloped and fascinating provinces of the empire, will find it in this most attractive and informing volume.

Harcourt Butler.

June, 1928.

PREFACE

MANY years have elapsed since I first went to Burma, yet the memory of that time remains fresh and vivid in my mind and as I read these pages I forget that I am in England. The tasselled limes outside my window fade from sight, the gurgle of wood-pigeons ceases, the Irrawaddy swings below my keel. I hear the lascars droning "*Ek bam mila Nahin*"; the tinkle of Pagoda bells; the rustle of palm leaves in the wind; the laughter of people at a Pwè; the murmur of Buddhist litanies. I see the anchored rice-boats turning with the tide in Rangoon river, *laungzats* flying before the monsoon wind, and golden spires bright in the Eastern sun;—and much more.

For those were happy days. Drop a young man of say twenty-three into a land more extensive than France, double his pay, and give him license to travel through it from China to Malay; tell him you trust him to play the game; assume that he has some love of beauty and sufficient health, and if he is not going to be thoroughly happy he never will be.

Looking back on Burma I have nothing to reproach myself with, nothing to regret; and if I could start afresh and were given the same chance I should take it. Of course I know that Burma is not all beer and skittles. It has its hardships, and I encountered some of these during my first two years in Rangoon before this glorious Odyssey began. Perhaps if I had left then I might not have thought so much of it. A Judge who was thirty years in Burma told me he had never been to Mandalay and did not wish to see it; and the general view in those days was that if one could choose between Burma and India one should choose the latter. For those who had an option it was considered rather a misfortune to make even a short stay in Burma. I gratefully admit that I was fortunate, and I am glad that I showed my gratitude by returning there later when I had a better job offered me elsewhere. Also, I can recall many less fortunate cases; of those who fell by the wayside, or married wives who hated Burma, or suffered ill-health, or came in other ways to a disgruntled or untimely end. But that is life. If a beautiful country, a happy and good-tempered people, an admirable religion, and a climate that seldom goes to extremes, can help to keep a man cheerful and contented, then Burma should ensure that.

When I first saw the Shwe Dagôn, the last Burmese war, which gave us Burma, had not long been concluded. In fact it had run to ground and was still cropping up in the form of "Dacoity," a cheerful variety of insurgence peculiar to Burma; while upon the frontiers, in the Chin Hills where Burma and Assam meet, and in the Unadministered Tracts where slave-owning head-hunting Nagas acknowledged no dominion; in Kachin-land about the head waters of the Irrawaddy; and in the vast territory known as the Shan States, where the rivalries of France and England and the Celestial Empire came to a focus, there was even open and constant war; and each winter saw the advance of British punitive columns into country that we claimed, was nominally at least, within our Empire.

These incidents were reflected in the society of that time and they gave Burma a peculiar flavour of its own. Lord Roberts visited it on military tours. Sir George White was G.O.C. nearly all through the pacification; and at the Clubs one used to meet men swaggering about, gay and light-hearted enough, only to hear of them perhaps a little later as having been killed at Myitkyna or Haka or Kyeng Tung or other exotic spot in that vague half-administered borderland. Others fresh from these adventures used to come down to Rangoon for what they called "Blood-money," in other words a wound-gratuity or pension. There were casualties of another sort due to too much poker, and stories worthy of Bret Harte were told of polite Italian Counts who rode into some lonely outpost for a night's hospitality and left it equipped with everything it had to offer in the way of portable property; and of others who played too high in the throne-room of Thibaw's palace, and simply dropped out and vanished from the society of that time.

There were other queer fish on the banks of the Irrawaddy in those lively days. There was one who by his exploits earned the title of The White Dacoit; others who though useful members of society had antecedents a little unusual in the sober classifications of the Civil Service. One of these who proved an invaluable officer on the frontier, was said to have begun life as a cook; a reputation he may have earned from the excellent dinners he gave his friends. Another known throughout Burma as "The Signor" possessed books of photographs with their corresponding negatives which he had taken in the trenches at Sebastopol, and acquired wealth by the sale of Burmese antiques to American and other travellers. But he was kind to us who stayed. "From my friends," he would say, "I ask but five per cent; from the friends of my friends, ten; from Globe-trotters *as much as I can get.*" And as globe-trotters are not popular amongst people who have to "stick it," we were content that it should be so. There was a keen-witted Frenchman who lashed our national failings with his satirical tongue, kept his deceased wife in a glass case, and had come to King Mindon, it was said, direct from the Tuileries.

Apart from these attractive adventurers, the peculiar conditions of Burmese life developed in members of the Civil Services qualities and characteristics Elizabethan rather than Victorian; so that men who a few years earlier had been undergraduates or schoolboys, by their prowess or their virtues came to be known as "Tigers," and "Great White Chiefs." One was almost worshipped in his district as an incarnation of the Buddha so greatly did his magnanimity appeal to the people. These splendid opportunities compensated many for the "amenities," the lack of which was considered a drawback to life in Burma. English women too were still in a minority; and the "Companionate marriage" of Judge Lindsay, was for good or ill, but quite in keeping with Burmese sentiment, almost an established institution. It was officially disapproved of, and a good many admirable injunctions on the subject were issued from Rangoon; but *Quis custodiet ipsos custodes?*

There were other picturesque people. Flotilla Captains who had been through the War carrying troops up and down the river, and could spin a good yarn when their ships came to at anchor each night and the wine went round. Some had had narrow escapes when war was declared, for it came suddenly and they were trapped in the upper reaches. There were Missionaries of several persuasions who had travelled over Burma in the King's days, one of whom had been tutor to King Thibaw; but one whom I like to remember above all others was the aged Bishop Bigandet of the French Foreign Mission who translated the Burmese legend of Buddha into English, and told me that he had been nearly sixty years in Burma with less than one year in his own country. "When we were leaving Paris," he said, "we heard the sound of guns and were told it was in honour of the accession of Queen Victoria." He was the authentic saint and scholar.

Besides all these of our own people, there were the old Burmese folk—simple old Abbots of Buddhist monasteries who knew little of the world, Ministers of the King, and Princesses and Maids of Honour who could tell of palace life in the last days of the Alaungpaya Kings. So that the life of a traveller up and down the great river had much to recommend it; and always there was kindness and hospitality, from a bed in the spare room, to the loan of a polo-pony or even a steam-launch for a Christmas vacation.

In those relatively early days also there was not much railway communication. There were few roads. One rode on ponies or travelled by water; and travelling by water was inexhaustible in its pleasure and its variety. The Irrawaddy was navigable for nine hundred miles by the splendid craft of the Irrawaddy Flotilla ; there were sea-going ships along the coast to Arakan and Tenasserim ; steamers of the Royal Indian Marine, and Government launches ; rafts and country-boats wherever a foot or two of water offered passage. Each one of these means of locomotion brought its own contentment, but perhaps the most enticing of all were the country-boats. It was the custom to travel by night. The boats were long and narrow with a roof at one end, and under its shelter a bed was laid for the traveller. The steersman sat behind ; the crew sat for'ard at their oars. But the great river did most of the work. As the night grew, the boatmen fell asleep, the steersman nodded ; the embers in the hearth fire faded, the stars or the moon came out, and the sky was bright and clear overhead. Slowly the boat drifted, making no sound, finding its own way down the unresisting stream ; the mighty Irrawaddy, whose shores were often invisible beyond the vast expanse of waters. These were incomparable experiences. But they were not always so easily come by. The river had its seasons of flood when the dangerous current moved swiftly, and the Irrawaddy lashed by a sudden storm, plunged in great waves, tumultuous as Benacus though an inland water ; and all the efforts of the crew barely sufficed to keep a small and heavy-laden craft afloat. Upon one such occasion at the end of an hour's struggle we found ourselves blown three miles up-stream from the place whence we had started. In the Great Defiles journeys by boat in the monsoon were a furious adventure for those compelled to make them. Yet the mails travelled up them to Myitkyina.

The most placid and interesting of these journeys by boat was one I made in the low amphibious country between the sea and the Arakan Hills. That is a territory designed by Nature for pirates, and in the days of the Portuguese and doubtless for centuries earlier, their favourite harrying ground. One of the most famous of them, Sebastian Gonsalves Tibaõ, was a renegade who had turned against both his King and his religion and set up for himself. In after years I came upon his tracks at Lisbon, in letters that passed between the King and his Viceroy at Goa, which offer so delicate an example of State cynicism that I am tempted to relate it. The King after recapitulating all that his Viceroy had told him, directed that so infamous a scoundrel should be hanged the instant possession could be got of his person ; but in the meanwhile, as he was a man of authority and influence in those parts, he was to be informed that His Majesty had been graciously pleased to bestow upon him the Third Class of the Order of the Habit of Christ. It was in these waters that Philip de Brito y Nicote, who married the Viceroy's daughter and became King of Pegu, first learnt his trade.

This country that is half land and half water follows the coast from

Chittagong to Sandoway. I navigated it for several days in the course of a journey from the Sea of Arakan to the Valley of the Irrawaddy, by a recognised though little frequented route. After a while I lost my bearings in that network of creeks and mangrove swamps and islands, but the boatmen knew their way, and each evening took care to anchor by the open sea; for a deadly malaria prevails in all this tract. As we came in sight of it at sunset they would rise in the boat and in sonorous voices cry out "*Pinle-Gyi!*"—the Burmese Thalassa. It was there I think that I first came to realise the latent energy of the Burmese race. The *Cha-bathas* as they sang to their oars could always be inspired to an enthusiastic effort.

The road over the mountains was constructed after the Second Burmese War, when our frontier was extended to Prome. It never fulfilled its promise. It carries a telegraph wire, but few people. From the water-shed of the Arakan Hills, where oak-trees and violets grow, we looked out upon one of the great views of Burma. On one side the sea with its thousand ramifications five thousand feet below, passing in the gleam of the sunset into the Indian Ocean; the silver ribbon of the Irrawaddy on the other.

* * *

In these following pages I have made as few changes as possible. Changes there have been in Burma, but these concern politics with which I am not concerned, and such things as the oil-wells of Yenan-Gyaung and the Ruby Mines of Mogôk. The former have brought untold wealth to many and have become, with the oil-wells of Persia, an Imperial asset; the latter have disappointed the hopes of their owners and have fallen back into the failure from which it was hoped at one time that they could be rescued. For the rest, I am indebted to Sir Harcourt Butler, who has generously spared some part of his valuable time in writing for me an introduction to this volume, telling of the evolution of the country during his own tenure of office. Others, like Sir Herbert Thirkell White who filled the same high office, Sir George Scott (Shway Yoe), the most distinguished of all the Frontier officers of Burma, Major Énriquéz, and Fielding Hall, the author of "The Soul of a People," have told their tale in volumes of their own, of much greater importance than anything I can have to write about Burma. The photographs of Max and Bertha Ferrars remain unsurpassed.

One word in conclusion. Sir Walter Lawrence in his recent book about the India he served, has remarked that "there is nothing in the whole world more admirable than the manners of Indians high or low." If that be true, one may claim that it is even more so of Burma, where to the grave courtesy of Eastern manners there is added an unfailing sense of humour that is peculiarly pleasant to ourselves. For my own part and it was only a small one—I always felt that it was the good manners and innate breeding of this youthful people which made life amongst them so agreeable for me ; in addition, their absence of reserve, their generous tolerant and kindly ways. It has been with some regret therefore, that I have heard from travellers unconnected with the government of Burma, of a change in sentiment that is making them less kindly and hospitable to the stranger in their midst. I have said a great deal of the Shwe Dagôn and of the joy and happiness it gave me to visit it ; and it is disconcerting therefore for me to learn that it is now practically closed to Europeans who do not care to walk barefooted up its stairs. Few, quite naturally, are willing to comply with this condition. Those who do—like an American lady of refinement who told me that from her love of Buddhism and great desire to see the sacred fane she had given way—feel that they have been subjected to an unnecessary and insanitary obligation. Yet the Shwe Dagôn is a masterpiece of the world, and the religion that inspires it is one of the most gentle and beautiful in its charity and kindness to others. It should not be impossible to find a means of satisfying their desire that reverence should be paid to the shrine, while making a fair and reasonable concession to the habits of Western people. No such restrictions are placed upon Eastern people who desire to enter our places of worship. Yet I would like to add that a Military officer, writing to me from Burma, says, "Though the country is not quite so happy as of yore ; yet the heart of the people is *true*, and they are really as delightful and fascinating as ever. I have travelled through most parts of Burma, and I must say I have been received with hospitality everywhere. Every lover of the country hopes that the present unrest is only a passing ripple, and that things will soon become more settled."

The new wine, it may be, has proved too heady for the old bottle ; and the failure of the monastic schools to rise to the needs of our modern secular education has deprived the people of the training they received in them ; for there was no school of manners like that of the old *Pôngyi-Kyaung*, with its gradations of rank and its measured respect, from the old and often saintly Abbot at its head, to the small but eager lad entering it as a little English boy enters his Preparatory school. The absence of a Court, too, has helped in the process of social disintegration, and few have been left to set the example of those "delightful, and even divine manners" which Sir Walter Lawrence attributes to Indian Rajas.

CONTENTS

Book VI

THE DELTA

Book VII

THE SOUTHERN COAST

Book VIII

THE SALWIN

Book IX

THE YUNZALIN

Book X

OVER THE PAUNG-LAUNG HILLS

Book XI

THE SITTANG

Book XII

RUBIES

LIST OF ILLUSTRATIONS

My renewed acknowledgements are due to Messrs. Benny and R. Grant Brown, I.C.S., and to Messrs. Beato, Klier, Francis, and Bourne and Shepherd for the use of some of these photographs.

COLOURED PLATES

BY J. RAEBURN MIDDLETON

BY SAYA CHONE

Book I

INTRODUCTORY

Book II

THE CAPITAL

Book III

THE NORTHERN IRRAWADDY

Book IV

THE SOUTHERN IRRAWADDY

Book V

THE CHINDWIN

Book VI

THE DELTA

Book VII

THE SOUTHERN COAST

Book VIII

THE SALWIN

Book IX

THE YUNZALIN

Book X

OVER THE PAUNG-LAUNG HILLS

Book XI

THE SITTANG

Book XII

RUBIES

THE SILKEN EAST

Book I

INTRODUCTORY

The Country—The Peoples

CHAPTER I

THE COUNTRY

BURMA, the country described in this book, occupies a remote corner of South-eastern Asia. Hidden away there in the folds of mountains which reach down like the fingers of a hand from the heights of Asia to the sea, it has had leisure to develop a character and a personality of its own. Its best friends in this sense have

MOUNT VICTORIA

been these mountains, which have protected it on the one hand from the aggression of Indian invaders, on the other from the enormous absorbing power of China. Yet placed as it were between these vast millstones, it would be surprising had it escaped all traces of their contact. From India it has received the religion, which more than any other factor has moulded the Burmese people; from India there came to it the earliest impulse of civilisation. The influence of China is less patent. On successive occasions Burma has been called upon to resist with all its power the military aggression of the Chinese races; on one notable occasion it received through them a blow from which its civilisation has never recovered; and from time to time it has gone some way towards accepting the suzerainty of China. But the influence of China has been social rather than political. The instinct of race has taught the two people their essential kinship, and if the Burman is proud of his quite mythical descent from the princes of India he is

EXPLORER'S CAMP, MOUNT VICTORIA

much more in his daily life in sympathy with the Chinaman, in whom he recognises an "elder brother."

But the mountains which have hitherto preserved the nationality of this people are no longer a protection. The sea has opened the flood-gates of invasion, and under the political supremacy of England, the economic competition of inferior and cheaper races from India whose standard of comfort is definitely lower, and of the superior Chinese now crowding up from the Straits, the Burmese personality runs in some peril of extinction. There is no longer a Court to form the heart of any national feeling; there is no longer, it would seem, any motive in keeping the race supreme in its own country; and there is lacking in the people that sternness which might alone, in the absence of such fostering influences, help to maintain their idiosyncrasy intact. It will be seen then, that I am concerned with an interesting people at a very interesting period in their history.

Of these mountains which reach down like the fingers of a hand from the great arm of the Himalaya to make the country of Burma, the first are the Arakan Yoma, known to the main stock of the Burmese race as the Mountains of the West. On one side of them there lies the sea (the Bay of Bengal)—on the other the river Irrawaddy. The habitable land along their sea-swept threshold is known as Arakan—the home of a great branch of the Burmese race. The mountains themselves

MOVING THE FELLED LOGS

are inhabited by a kindred people known as the Chin ; more numerous, more warlike, more organised in the north, where the width of the mountains is greater, than in the south. East of them lies the valley of the Irrawaddy, the true Burma, the spacious cradle of the race. This valley is shut in still further on the east by the Shan highlands, which spread away in waves to the Salwin river. They provide a home for the Shan, a race that long struggled with the Burmese for the possession of the valley, but has ended by holding the lesser heritage of the Shan plateau under the suzerainty of Burma. Beyond the Salwin lie Siam and the Far Eastern territories of France.

The valley of the Irrawaddy narrow and confined in the north, opens out at Mandalay the capital of the race, and widens as it reaches the sea. It culminates in one of the finest of deltas. South of Mandalay the parallel valley of the Sittang has its being, the outcome of the low range of Pegu hills which separate it from the Irrawaddy, and of the Shan hills which in the south fall away somewhat to the east. The Salwin, for the greater part of its course a river essentially foreign, enters the limits of Burma in its last hundred miles, and pours its waters into the Burmese seas under the golden spires of Moulmein. The mountains reach down in a narrowing peninsula to Victoria Point, the

TEAK LOGS READY FOR THE TORRENT

southernmost limit of Burma. This last strip of coast is known as Tenasserim. It is thinly populated and it has never played any substantial part in the development of the race. An archipelago of singular interest and beauty lies off its western face, and a thousand islands own its supremacy.

One great river, the Chindwin, remains to be mentioned. Coming down from the mountains that lie about the upper reaches of the Irrawaddy it flows through the Hukong valley and under the Chin territories through scenery of great beauty, till it enters the valley of the Irrawaddy and adds its quota to the volume of that great river.

The capitals of this country are Mandalay and Rangoon ; the former located in the centre of Burma, where the widening valley leaves space for the growth of a nation ; the latter at the mouth of the Irrawaddy, facing the sea. Mandalay still stands for the old régime as the city of Shah Jahan in India stands for the glory of the Moguls. Rangoon, like Calcutta, is the outcome of British rule. All the wealth and the power are there.

The nature of the country, of its landscape and its climate, may be gathered from its conformation. It is a long country reaching from the tenth to the twenty-sixth degree of north latitude. In its extreme south the sensation of cold is unknown. Save that there is more rain at one

JAMMED TIMBER

season than at another, there is little to choose at Mergui between June and December. In the far north, on the borders of China, the cold is bitter of winter nights and men go clad in fur-lined satins. In the middle country a great dryness prevails and the rainfall, excessive at either end, is reduced there to twelve inches a year.

The great river Irrawaddy marshalled by hills and mountains makes scenery that is as stately as it is beautiful, as passionate as it is serene. The mountains visited by tropical rains sustain forests of primeval growth, in which herds of elephants and rhinoceroses, of wild cattle and deer, wander in comparative peace ; and at their summits, reaching in Mount Victoria a height of eight thousand and in Saramati a height of twelve thousand feet, there grow the trees and flowers of temperate

ON THE RIVER

climates—the oak, the pine, and the violet. The gleam of snow upon Saramati and the more distant mountains of the northern *hinterland* remind the traveller in Burma that he has put the tropics behind him. In the flat lands of the Delta the largest surplus rice crop of the world is produced ; from the Mogôk valley there have come the finest of

ASHORE

rubies. And lastly there is the sea with its infinite variety. All along the coast it runs in a million ramifications into the land, and the traveller for whom such travel has any fascination is borne, as in Arakan, for days through an amphibious world, a bewildering network of creeks, in which all comprehension of geography is lost. And in the far south there are those islands of which a particular account is given in this book.

CHAPTER II

THE PEOPLES

VARIED as is this country it is surpassed in variety by the number of races that occupy it. I can only mention the principal of them here : viz. the Burmese, the Shan, the Mun or Talaing, the Karen, the Chin, the Kachin, and the Salôn.

Of these the Burmese are beyond comparison the most numerous. It is the Burmese idiosyncrasy that gives to Burma its fascination and its charm ; that makes of it, with its colour, its luxury, its beauty, and its

KAREN MAN AND WIFE

ease, a Silken East. Of the other races the smallest and most backward are the Salôn, a fast-dying people of some few hundred souls who inhabit the islands of the southern coast. They are probably the oldest inhabitants of the land. Since their day Burma has been peopled by three great waves of immigration from the north. Of these the earliest is represented by the Mun or Talaing; the second and third by the Burmese (including the Chin) and the Shan. The Karen, who are of kin, stand in a category somewhat apart. The Kachin are of the same stock as the Burmese, but their descent into Burma is of recent date.

PALAUNG WOMAN AT SHWEGU FAIR

THE MUN

A hundred and seventy-five years ago the Mun were still a people, and Englishmen and Frenchmen, rivals here as throughout the world, leaned now towards the one now towards the other of these conflicting races. But to-day the Mun are all but absorbed in the Burmese race and three hundred thousand people alone represent in Burma a race whose civilisation once extended from the Assam hills to Annam. Broadly speaking they are now indistinguishable except as to language from the Burmese. People who know them well can however distinguish between them; and on the whole the Mun is apt to be fairer and stouter than the true Burman. Of kin with the Mun, but separated from them by a wide space of country, are the Palaung, of whom numbers frequent the bazaars of the Ruby Mines. The Palaung run to sixty thousand souls. The men wear the Shan dress, the women a picturesque costume of their own, which comprises a hood, coat, and skirt, with leggings of cloth. Upon the English mind the Palaung does not leave an altogether favourable impression. He is described as peaceful and industrious, but at heart a coward and in his money transactions a Hebrew of pronounced proclivities; in business ability and wit superior to his Kachin neighbour, but in the sterner qualities his inferior. The Palaung in fact are a little and an oppressed people who must have been swallowed up in the Kachin advance had we not come to shelter them under the cloak of Imperial rule.

THE KAREN

The Karen, far more numerous and more powerful than the Palaung, are also a people who owe their regeneration to British protection. Borne down by the dominant Burmese, they must have been gradually annihilated, or at best reduced to the least hospitable portions of the country. The Pax Britannica has given them political freedom, and Christianity, which they have adopted *en masse*, has given them self-respect and an impetus towards civilisation. In the modern history of Christianity there is no more interesting episode than the conversion of the Karen. Prepared by prophecies current among them and by curious traditions of a biblical flavour, they embraced with fervour the new creed brought to them by the missionaries, and there are to-day upwards of a hundred thousand Christian Karen in Burma. The Karen occupy a long strip of country on the east of Burma and a considerable portion of the Delta of the Irrawaddy. By temperament the Karen differ radically from their Burmese neighbours. They are singularly devoid of humour, they are stolid and cautious, and they lack altogether the light gaiety and fascination of the Burmese. Yet it is not suggested that in some qualities they do not surpass them. If their origin is still obscure, it is at least certain that they are not the aborigines of the land. All their traditions point the other way. "In my early travels," wrote Mason, their picturesque apostle, "the

GIRLS AT A KAREN MISSIONARY SCHOOL

From a painting by J. Raeburn Middleton

A GIRL PAINTING HER EYEBROWS

Karen pointed out to me the precise spots where they took refuge in the days of Alompra, and where they had come down and avenged themselves on their enemies; but when I asked them who built this city, as we stood together on the forest-clad battlements of a dilapidated fortification they replied: 'These cities of our jungles were in ruins when we came here. This country is not our own. We came from the north, where we were independent of the Burmese and the Siamese and the Talaing who now rule over us. Then we had a city and a country of our own near Ava, called Toungoo. All the Karen of Siam, Burma, and Pegu came originally from that region.' When I asked for the time of their dispersion they were silent. The fact was clearly before them; but the retrospect was too obscure to determine the distance. Yet they saw far beyond Toungoo. On the edge of the misty horizon was the river of running sand which their ancestors had crossed before coming. That was a fearful trackless region, where the sands rolled before the winds like the waves of the sea. They were led through it by a chieftain who had more than human power to guide them." The river of running sand was boldly identified by Mason with the Gobi desert, of which Fa Hian, the Chinese pilgrim, has left this description: "There are evil spirits in this river of sand and such scorching winds that whosoever encountereth them dies, and none escape. Neither birds are seen in the air, nor quadrupeds on the ground. On every side as far as the eye can reach, if you seek for the proper place to cross, there is no other mark to distinguish it than the skeletons of those who have perished there; these alone seem to indicate

SHAN GIRL, BHAMO

the route." But the identity of the traditional desert of the Karen with the desert of Gobi has yet to be established.

THE SHAN

The Karen in Burma has to be looked for; the Shan with his wide trousers and flapping hat, his instinct for trade, his princes and feudatory states, and his considerable civilisation is a much more notable person.

The race began to spread into Burma from South-western China about two thousand years ago. Its migration was hastened by the pressure of the Chinese races behind, and as this pressure increased it

Thibaw Taung-Baing Theinni Son of Thibaw Nyaung-Ywe

SHAN PRINCES

spread from the valley of the Shweli river, its first home in Burma, southwards to the Siamese seas, eastward to Tongking, and north and west till it reached the Brahmaputra and founded the Ahom kingdom of Assam. The Shan are now found in Burma, in the Shan States and far down the eastern peninsula to Mergui. In the north they spread over the whole of the upper territories of the Irrawaddy from Myitkyina to the Third Defile; and along the Chindwin, where traces of their former supremacy survive in the principalities of Singkaling—Hkamti and Thaungdut. They have ruled at Ava, and have come near to the mastery of Burma. They owe their failure to their inability to combine on any national scale. In economic qualities they surpass the Burmese, adding yet another to the list of competing peoples destined, unless the latent vigour of the Burman awakes, to divide up his heritage.

CHIN AND KACHIN

The Chin and Kachin have bulked largely in the recent history of Burma. Long after Thibaw the last of her kings had been carried away to a sordid exile, and the British peace had been established over the land, the Chin and the Kachin continued to make war upon the Empire. The plains of Burma had long been their plundering grounds, where men and cattle lay at the mercy of their raids. They were more

SHAN OF THE YUNZALIN

habituated to individual war than the more civilised Burmese, and their protection lay in the rough hills which they inhabit and in the poverty of their country, which is of small attraction to people better furnished with the good things of this world. The Chin, if anything, made a more vigorous resistance because they realised that the final conquest of their country was at issue ; the Kachin had an extensive *hinterland* to which they knew that they could retreat. But of the two the Kachin is the sterner man, with a greater future before him than the Chin. And this is illustrated by the relationship to Burma in which we found them. The Chin lived in his hills, making raids only at intervals on the plain country at his feet. But the Kachin was steadily advancing, dominating the peoples before him and establishing his colonies. He had already instilled at the Court of Thibaw a substantial fear.

Of the Chin who lie upon the mountains which separate the true Burma from Arakan and Assam there are two great divisions—the Northern and the Southern. Of these the Southern Chin, living as they do upon the narrowest portion of their country, are of the least consequence. They have yielded most to the pressure of the Burmese races on each side of them and they are a sparse and disorganised people. Their tribes lap over into the subsidiary valleys which lie between the Irrawaddy and the main spine of the Arakan Yoma. The Northern

A VILLAGE BALLET IN BURMA

Chin have a wider territory, known administratively as "The Chin Hills." It consists of a much broken and contorted mass of mountains intersected by deep valleys and it is utterly devoid of plains and tablelands. The Northern Chin have a strong tribal organisation and time has developed in each of their tribes a separate idiosyncrasy. The Chin is of interest because he reveals the material out of which Buddhism and civilisation between them have evolved the Burmese people ; the Chin in short is the rough wood out of which the Burman has been carved.

THE BURMESE

Of the Burmese as a whole I do not propose to give here any formal account.

I seek only to describe the life of the people as I have come upon it in the course of many years of travel in their country, and for the most part what I have to say will be found interspersed in the narrative of travel. But of the man himself I should like here to say a few words.

Physically the Burman is for his size a fine fellow; short, well made, broad-chested, stout-limbed, and muscular. A "weedy" Burman outside the small percentage of the large towns and the sedentary occupations is rare. The boatman, the cartman, the peasant, the artificer, is nearly always a strong man, capable when put to it of great effort. Living as he does in a tropical climate, abjuring meat from religious scruples, branded as incorrigibly lazy by all his critics, he is yet as a rule a man in fine training, full of momentum and vivacity. The criticism to which he is subjected on the score of laziness is overdone. For there are kinds of laziness. There is the laziness for instance of the man

CHINS OF MOUNT VICTORIA

who shirks work, who slouches about, with thin legs, a stooping back, and an effete mind; to whom strenuous labour is no joy, yet a man who works on day after day, putting in his tale, driven by the necessity for a wage by his own prolific pauperism and the low standard of life to which he has reached; a man without reserve force, without latent enthusiasms; a slave—such a man for instance as the Chittagonian, one of the economic superiors of the Burman. There is also the laziness of the man with a fine physique, with a sporting nature that exults in athletic expression, in racing, swimming, boxing, and rowing; of the man whose mind is full of lively fancy, of wit, even of creative power; of the man who enjoys life and finds in it infinite possibilities of amusement, of love, of good fellowship; a man who has fashioned for himself a goodly standard of life and lives well with little toil; above all, of a man whose being is permeated with a philosophic contempt for the accumulation of material things, with a generous desire to bestow in charity and in good works all that is over and above his own needs. Much of the laziness of the Burman is of this type. It is reflected in his life.

Put him on the river he loves, with a swift and angry current against him and he is capable of superb effort. Turn his beautiful craft, enriched with exquisite carvings, down stream, with wind and tide in his favour, and he will lie all day in the sun and exult in the Nirvana of complete idleness. And this is not because he is "a lazy hound," but because there is something in him of the philosopher and the artist; because there is a blue sky above him which he can look at, a river before him rippling with colour and light; because he lives in a beautiful land; because the earning of pence is a small thing to him in comparison with the joy of life, and material things themselves but an illusion of the temporary flesh.

SIYIN CHIN

But the world, some will say, is not a world of philosophers and artists but an economic world of manufacturers, of creators and distributors of wealth; and since that is the case there is no room in it for people of this kind unless by extraordinary efficiency in their own pursuits they are able to compete with the rest of mankind. And in any case the demand for such goods is limited. The Burman must go unless he is willing to work like the aboriginal Coringhi, from early dawn to night; unless he is willing to accept in the long run a wage like that of the Indian proletariat, of whom many millions live all their lives upon the verge of starvation; unless he is willing to wear grey cotton instead of tartaned silk; to forego his hospitalities to his friends, his donations to his church, his liberality to the stranger within his gates; unless he is willing to abandon his gaiety, his light-heartedness, his love of sport and amusements, his leisure and happiness, and turn to the cheap, inferior, squalid life of his poor "untouchable" Indian neighbour.

But are we quite sure that we want all these things to happen either to him or to anyone else? The drift of our time is in the direction of shorter hours, higher wages, greater scope for the cultivation of life and

A BURMESE LADY

THE MOTHER

its possibilities. We are coming to see that these things are not incompatible with prosperity. The Burmese came as a youthful conquering race into a bountiful land, and they took full possession of it. They have contrived to remain one of the happiest of the peoples of the earth; and even the religion they adopted from India, marked as it is by the sentiment of sorrow and illusion, has had no power to crush their buoyancy. Leisure and independence, equality, a near approach to an even distribution of wealth; a happy temper cheerful in adversity; which of us does not desire these ideals to prevail? And many gravely concerned with the problems of our ancient society, of pauperism and congestion in the slums of great cities; with social hatreds and the deep antagonisms of class, would gladly arrive at a little more of what this people already possess. The competition of life will develop in its own time the toughness of the race, increase its power of resistance, and enable it to maintain its own ascendancy—it is doing so now—and I doubt if there are many Englishmen who do not love the Burman for his qualities of breeding and courtesy, his adaptability, and generous impulses. The empire of which he is now a member is nothing if it

FROM THE YAWDWIN

is not a great trust in which he has his rightful share and part. Upon these convictions it rests, and it is in this spirit that the evolution of Burma is most likely to be happily accomplished.

Let us not then find fault too much with the happy Burman's love of life and laughter. He will grow up soon enough, and if he holds firmly to the instincts of his race will not fail to add his quota to the common stock.

To pass him over without mentioning his wife and daughter would be

CHINESE-SHAN LADIES

uncivil, and also in this case dull ; for the sex contributes greatly to the liveliness and charm of the country. Burma, as in many other things, is in advance of more reputedly civilised countries in the status it accords to its women. The infant marriages and shutting up in walled houses, the polygamy, the harems, the social punishment of widows, the denial of spiritual rights, which prevail in the neighbouring continent of India, and whose terrible penalties cannot be denied, are unknown in Burma. Here women marry when they are of age and after they have seen

TAUNGTHU WOMEN

"FULL OF LAUGHTER AND FUN"

somewhat of the world; they marry, for the most part, whomsoever they will, and from love. They are not, save in exceptional cases, handed over as chattels to a man whom they know not; but are courted and won. The Married Woman's Property Act, a recent flower of our own civilisation and still unknown in France, has in effect been established for centuries in Burma. In this country, where the women earn so much, the woman's earnings are her own. Divorce is easily obtained but seldom asked for. The lightness of the marriage laws, the readiness of the Burmese woman to enter into an easy alliance, shock the

TAKING HIS EASE

virtue of the strenuous foreigner; but within her ideals she is a perfectly proper, modest, and well-mannered woman. She is of the world to her finger tips, and at theatres and elsewhere her appreciation of the sallies of the actors is of an Elizabethan frankness; yet her conduct there is beyond reproach. Amorous vulgarities in public are unknown in Burma. When she is young the Burmese woman is, after her own type, fair and attractive, full of laughter and fun and the enjoyment of life; witty and self-possessed; seldom if ever brazen-faced; frank to a degree. It is one of the wayside amusements of travel in Burma to see her at her toilette before the world, to see her calmly unwind the false tresses in her hair (itself generally luxurious and ample); to see her enamel her face with ingenuous *thanaka*, to follow her frequent contented glances at her mirror. And later in life she is capable, when circumstances are in her favour, of great dignity and exquisite manners. She dresses, when not reduced to the poverty which some might seem to desire for

THE DANCER

her, in a very charming way; in a delicately coloured silken skirt, a white muslin jacket, with a silk scarf thrown over her shoulders, and flowers in her hair. And while she dresses well, she is free of the tyranny of fashion, the unending longing after something that is new. She has failings; who has not? Her practice of chewing betel is inelegant and destructive to her teeth; her voice is apt under the pressure of adversity to be shrill; her keen business faculties detract a trifle from the romance in which, as in a halo, all women should be enveloped ; in old age she is very ugly ; and even in youth her nose is stumpy, her lips a little thick, her cheek-bones high and heavy—but these are Caucasian objections ! In the eyes of the young men of the land, the Burmese girl is a peerless creature ; and her influence over their hearts and their passions is immense. What is more, few men in Burma ever undertake anything of magnitude without first seeking the able counsel of their wives.

THE DAUGHTER

I cannot leave even this slight account of the men and women of Burma without saying a separate word about its old men and its little children. Vain, bumptious, arrogant as the Burman is apt to be in his youth, old age brings with it for him a wonderful change. His manners become gentle and reserved, his face catches a spiritual expression. His costume is adapted to his years. The flaming tartans of his youth are put aside for silks of a paler hue ; the gorgeous *gaungbaung* is replaced on his head by a slender fillet of white book-muslin. But the change is not merely superficial. It is the reflection of an inner development, of the growth within him of the spiritual desire. If, unlike most of his countrymen, he has accumulated a store of wealth, his aim now is to distribute it in good works. If any worldly desire survives in his heart it is to win the title of Phaya-Taga, " Builder of a Pagoda," or Kyaung-Taga, " Builder of a Monastery " ; titles bestowed upon him by his fellows as an expression of their respect and dearer to him, as implying a spiritual attainment, than any magnificence, such as " Bearer of a Golden Sword," that the State may bestow upon him. This vanity is the last infirmity of his mind ; and to the end of his days

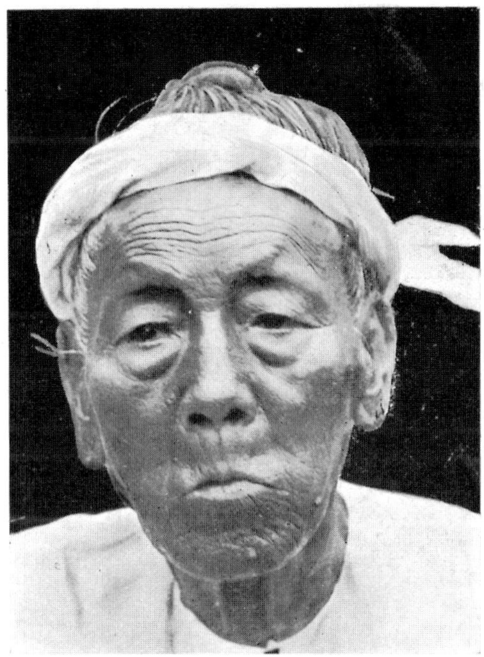

THE OLD MAN

he is particular that his wife shall address him by his full title of " Builder of a Monastery." The good lady is more than willing, for the glory of her husband is reflected upon herself, and it is with her willing consent that the distribution of his wealth proceeds. He also in calling to her in the presence of strangers will be particular to address her as Kyaung-Taga-mah, or " O Wife of the Builder of a Monastery." Religious duties at this season of his life greatly occupy his attention. A rosary is constantly in his hand, and upon his lips there move all the day long, when he is alone, the phrases of his faith. He is much at the pagoda, to which he climbs in spite of his failing powers each day with an offering of flowers; and his constant haunt is the local monastery, his own if he be a Kyaung-Taga, where he sits reverently at the feet of the abbot listening to pious homilies and in moments of weakness retailing the day's news. I know of no country in the world in which old age comes so serenely upon its men as Burma, no country in which the movement towards better things at this season is so universal; and it has long been a pleasure to me to see these old men going to and fro upon the closing

BEGINNING LIFE

business of their lives, to come upon them at the monasteries, and to talk with them. For the manners of even the humblest of them are grave and fine.

At the other end of life to the old men are the small children. In them the liveliness and happiness of the race are crossed by no flaw. The sheer joy of life abides in them, and they seem to live perpetually at play; in the village street, where they play a game of ninepins with the great seeds of a jungle creeper; in the monastery, where they lie

A BURMESE MAIDEN

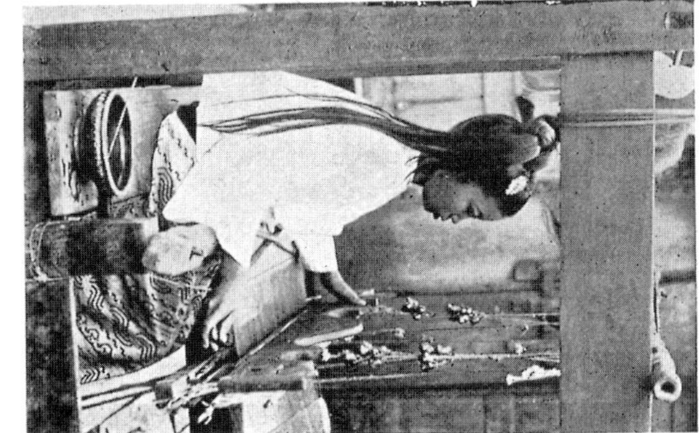

AT THE LOOM

upon the floor and scream out their lessons with lusty delight ; in the river, in which they splash and plunge before they can walk ; at the play, where they crawl about amongst the feet of the prima donna and the posing kings ; and at the pagoda, where they hold flowers before them with faces screwed up to gravity, with laughter pent up behind it. And if there be any dispute about the good looks of their elders, there can be none as to the prettiness of Burmese children. A little Burmese girl or boy is the most doll-like creature in the world. Children's clothes, as such, are unknown in the simple economy of Burma, and every little girl is dressed like her mother, from her sandals to the flowers in her hair ; and every little boy like his father, in a tartan kilt of silk, a white muslin jacket, and a flaming *gaungbaung* on his head—that is, when he is dressed at all. In the country, and within the precincts of his own home, he is apt to go about with nothing on at all.

KATHÉ BRAHMIN

Book II

THE CAPITAL

Its Beginnings—The Modern City—The City at Night—The Puzun-Daung Creek—The Shwe Dagôn

CHAPTER III

ITS BEGINNINGS

A CITY which faces the ocean whence world-travellers come, and is served by a river navigable for nine hundred miles, the main artery through which the life-blood of a nation pulses, is a city clearly destined to be great. Yet it is only in the last half-century or so of the many during which these conditions necessary to the birth of a great city have in some measure prevailed, that Rangoon has responded to them. Why not sooner, it would be difficult to say. The causes which make great cities and great nations seem as palpable on the surface as in reality they are mysterious and obscure. One may infer that some psychologic moment is necessary, some sudden and subtle coming together, in order that from causes long known to exist the new and splendid offspring should be born. Yet there are circumstances which partly explain the long delay before Rangoon definitely stepped out upon the highway of its present prosperity. There was a time when the sea ran into the coast of Burma much farther than it does to-day; when ships cast anchor at Thatôn, the earliest capital of the south; when Pegu, in later days the gorgeous and magnificent city of Branginoco, was almost itself a seaport. There was a time also when the ocean brought less to the gates of Burma and took less away than it does in its iron ships to-day; when the absence of a strong hand and a settled peace within the country frightened away Trade, as timid as she is daring; when war slew a million of men in a single generation; when civilisation in fact had not yet come to marshal the resources of the nation and to stay.

Moreover, there was already across the water a city which is now forgotten, whose history is the true history of the beginnings of Rangoon. It was at Syriam that Rangoon, the city facing the sea and served by a lordly river, the main artery of a nation, first came into being. It was the fame of Syriam which brought men trafficking to the mouth of the river on which Rangoon is built, and it is the tale of Syriam, broken by adversity, that the newer city has taken up with fresh vitality.

RANGOON A GENERATION AGO

Viewed from this standpoint, Rangoon is no longer the *nouveau riche* loudly proclaiming his possessions, but a city that has been growing for many generations, a city which has known the flavour of great days in the past.

Syriam, according to the Burmese tale, began its career as a king's city five hundred and eighty-seven years before the birth of Christ. But cities which depend on kings are prone to lapse into insignificance, and there is practically nothing known of Syriam till the discoveries of Vasco da Gama, that great pioneer, opened the gates of the East to Western adventurers, and half the galleons of Europe trimmed their sails for the new El Dorado. The known history of Syriam is the history of their efforts to capture one of its great prizes; and it is a strange circumstance that all, until within the last century, should have failed. But Burma, in spite of her charms, is apt from her situation to be overlooked by travellers with the lust of India in their eyes; and to this circumstance she probably owed her immunity. Men straining every nerve for the conquest of India had little attention to bestow upon her smaller and less sumptuous neighbour.

Yet the Portuguese, heroic in all their early enterprises, made a great bid for sovereignty in Burma ; and it was at Syriam that the drama was played out. The tale is connected with the career of one Philip de Brito y Nicote, who began as a cabin boy, grew as a palace menial in Arakan, rose to be King of Pegu, and ended writhing on a stake in the sun, where he lingered for three days in mortal agony, overlooking the city which for the space of thirteen years had been the centre of his power. But the story of De Brito is not for these pages.

The site of Rangoon itself is immemorial, and the chronicles of the people talk with customary liberality in thousands of years. Five hundred and eighty-five years before Christ, they say, two pious merchants who trafficked to Bengal with Peguan rice came at a time of famine upon the Buddha meditating under the trees of Gaya. Asked whether they sought the goods of this world or the next, they replied with becoming piety that they were in search of " heavenly treasure." They then made their obeisances before the Buddha, and received four hairs of his head and were told to bury them in the Thein-Got-Tara Hill, where his three predecessors had left respectively a staff, a water-filter, and a robe. They were to know the locality from a *takoon*, a felled wood-oil tree lying athwart, and touching the ground neither with its root nor its branches. On their return, after a somewhat distracting search, they found the place indicated, and they buried in it, in a golden casket, the relics they had brought. Over them was built the first nucleus of the Shwe Dagôn Pagoda. The town of Takoon or Dagôn grew up around this sacred spot, and from time to time there is mention in Burmese history of visits to it from kings and princes, and of the gradual growth of the pagoda. Stone inscriptions in its courts date back to the year 1485, and it is well known that Shinsawbu, Queen of Pegu early in the sixteenth century, visited the town and greatly enlarged the pagoda.

The first account of it that we have from any European observer is that in 1579 of Gasparo Balbi, jeweller of Venice. Balbi entered Burma at Negrais, and having made " a very commodious and pleasant voyage " across the Delta to Pegu, came to Dagôn.

" After we were landed," he says, " we began to go on the right hand in a large street about fifty paces broad, in which we saw wooden houses gilded and adorned with delicate gardens after their custom, wherein their *talapoins*, which are their friers, dwell and look to the pagod, or varella, of Dagôn. The left side is furnished with portals and shops, and by this street they go to the varella for a good mile straight forward, either unc' paint-houses or in the open street, which is free to walk in." The town was in fact an appanage of the Shwe Dagôn Pagoda, and it continued to preserve this character with varying fortunes till the growth across the water of Syriam, thronged with the ships of European adventurers, brought it political importance. The final phase in the struggle of the Burmese and the Mun or Talaing races was now approaching. At last in A.D. 1763 Alompra, having annihilated Pegu, signalised his conquest by raising the Shwe Dagôn to a height greater than that of the rival Mun fane at Pegu, and bestowed upon the city at its foot the name of Yan-koon, the City of Victory. It was made the seat of a viceroy and considerable traffic passed through its gates; yet it had not really made any beginning towards greatness. The accounts of travellers at this period vary concerning it. Some, like Colonel Symes, the British Ambassador who visited Burma a hundred and twenty-five years ago, give it a character of importance; others, like the officers who accompanied the British Army to Burma in 1825, find little to say in its favour. In Symes' day it lay upon the river shore and was a mile long and a third of a mile wide. The inner citadel was surrounded by an indifferent stockade, the streets were well paved, but inferior to those of Pegu. All the officers of Government, the most opulent merchants, and persons of consideration lived within the stockade. It had three wharves, and close to one of these there were "two commodious wooden houses, used by the merchants as an exchange,

THE LEGEND OF THE SHWE DAGÔN IN WOOD

where they usually meet in the cool of the morning and evening to converse and transact business."

"We had been so accustomed," wrote Major Snodgrass some thirty years later, "to hear Rangoon spoken of as a place of great trade and commercial importance, that we could not fail to feel disappointed at its mean and poor appearance. We had talked of its Custom House, its dockyards, and its harbour, until our imaginations led us to anticipate, if not splendour, at least some visible sign of a flourishing commercial city; but however humble our expectations might have been, they must still have fallen short of the miserable and desolate picture which the place presented when first occupied by the British troops. The town, if a vast assemblage of wooden huts may be dignified with that name, is surrounded by a wooden stockade, from sixteen to eighteen feet in height, which effectually shuts out all view of the fine river which runs past it and gives it a confined and insalubrious appearance. There are a few brick houses, chiefly belonging to Europeans, within the stockade, upon which a heavy tax is levied; and they are only permitted to be built by special authority from the Government, which is but seldom granted. The Custom House, the principal building in the place, seemed fast tottering into ruins. One solitary hull upon the stocks marked the dockyard and a few coasting vessels and country

THE LEGEND OF THE SHWE DAGÔN IN WOOD

canoes were the only craft found in this great commercial mart of India beyond the Ganges." Thus the indignant soldier. Greatness had evidently not yet come to Rangoon. From contemporary accounts of the town some eighty years ago the following particulars are taken.

The stockade covered an area of seventy-five acres, and lay roughly between the Sulé Pagoda and the Strand on one side, and Mogul Street and Ezekiel Street on the other. The Custom House lay on the river's edge outside the stockade. Within, there were two principal thoroughfares, one named the Kaladan, along which Armenians, Moguls, Parsis, Hindus, Jews, a few Chinamen, and other foreigners lived; and the other, the main street of the city, running east and west, past the "palace" of the viceroy, upon the site of which *The Rangoon Times* is now published. The European community consisted of ten persons, two of whom, Messrs. Crisp & Trill, had their place of business near where Balthazar's Buildings now stand, upon some of the most valuable land in Rangoon. Where 36th and Merchant Streets now meet, stood the British Residency, once occupied by Colonel Burney. Outside the stockade stood the house of Manook Sarkies, an Armenian resident; and in its neighbourhood, opposite the present site of the Irrawaddy Flotilla Company's office, was the yard in which he built a three-hundred-ton ship. The stockade was surrounded by a ditch, and a tidal stream ran up Latter Street. Shafraz Road remained till much later a canal. Buffaloes wallowed in the marshes beyond Ezekiel Street; gardens spread east of the S lé Pagoda; Puzun-Daung was a small village of boatmen; and jack and pineapple orchards like those of Kemendine spread where now the jail, the lunatic asylum, and St. John's College discharge their several functions.

On worship days the Viceroy usually went to the pagoda, leaving the stockade to be ruled by his lieutenant. All fires had to be put out while he was absent, and failure to comply with this regulation brought upon the offenders the *paquets* or executioners, an outlawed tribe of police, who had a circle tattooed on each cheek and were known as "Spotted Faces." These people found a vocation in perambulating the streets with hens' feathers in their ears, which they thrust into the ashes, "and if a feather was curled up by the heat, it meant blackmail upon the spot." Any effort to resist such exactions only led to worse ones at the hands of the town *wuns*. Each officer of note kept stocks in his yard, into which people were incontinently thrust on the most frivolous grounds; and the Rev. C. Bennet, to whose notes I am indebted, paints a quaint picture of stern parents and surly husbands suddenly put into the stocks at the private instigation of their frivolous wives and unfilial children. To revenge one's self upon a friend it was only necessary, it seems, to speak a word into the covetous ear of one of the town *wuns*.

In 1841 the stockade was removed a mile or more inland from the river. Eleven years later it was carried at the point of the bayonet by the British troops. Traces of its earthworks may still be seen crossing the Prome road, where the Rangoon golfer pursues his dusty vocation. Rangoon was now incorporated in the British Empire and definitely launched upon that career of prosperity which, in half a century, has lifted it to a city of a quarter of a million people and the position of third seaport in the Indian Empire. Life moves in its streets and waterways; prosperity, unbroken yet by any adverse fortune, smiles upon it; high hopes are entertained by all its citizens of a near future of still greater and almost boundless fortune; hopes that are being steadily realised. Every time that one who knows it returns to it, after a lapse of even a year or two, he is struck with its growth in the interval, with its new buildings, its new streets, its new institutions and its new pride. Yet its new buildings at least should teach it humility. For a wave of terrible architecture has for some years been passing over the devoted city, and cathedrals, town halls, and public offices have been growing up which are a torment to the eye.

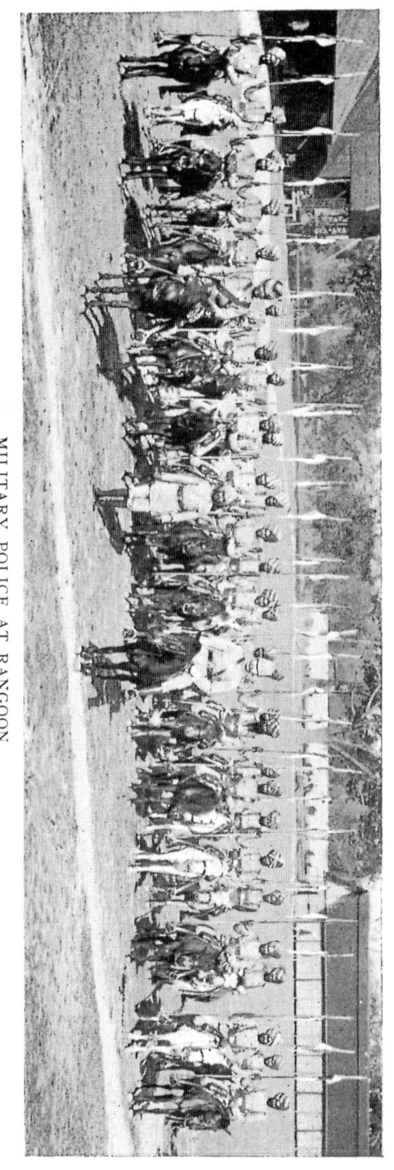

MILITARY POLICE AT RANGOON

Happily it is not all new. It is served by an immemorial river upon whose bosom a great life pulses; it is dominated by an edifice whose stateliness and beauty are unsurpassed in Burma, one might almost say in the world; and in its streets fifty races gather to give it picturesque-

THE SULÉ PAGODA
Under this pagoda Alompra buried alive a Talaing Prince to keep watch and ward over his new city of Rangoon

ness. Unlike most Eastern cities, it is devoid of mystery. Its streets lie open to the eye, its life moves much upon the surface. Superficial visitors are apt to pass it by as of little interest. Yet there is much in it that will "repay investigation."

CHAPTER IV

THE MODERN CITY

RANGOON'S most cosmopolitan thoroughfare is Mogul Street, which begins with the funnel of an ocean steamer, rises to the white minarets of a Musulman mosque, and ends under the wooden eaves of a Native Christian chapel. A Chettis' hall, with wooden columns of a design that was probably invented in Southern India twenty centuries ago, faces the white temple of Islam, and the voice of the green-turbaned muezzin as he calls the Faithful to prayer, is overborne by the clatter and chink of money and the guttural brawlings of that loudest of vulgarians, the Chetti. Over the way, in an adjoining street, the Hindu clangs his bell and blows his conch before the altars of Shiv, in defiance of his Musulman neighbour. His Musulman neighbour retorts by sacrificing the sacred cow and spilling her blood before the very eyes of those who worship her as a god. Gentle amenities of this kind, fomented by turbulent Afghans and by Hindu millionaires, whose care it is to establish an *alibi* by retreating at the crisis to a safe distance of fifteen hundred miles, are apt occasionally to end in conflicts of a serious character. In 1893 they ended in a riot which was only quelled after thirty persons had been shot down, some two hundred, mostly mounted policemen, had been wounded, and a regiment of English soldiers had been summoned to over-awe the populace. Often, as I drive down this crowded thoroughfare, past the archways of the mosque, I am reminded of the appearance it presented on that occasion when its steps were slippery with the blood of mullahs and muezzins and chulias pouring out of ragged wounds made by the sniders of the military police. I am reminded of the latent forces of an ancient hate under the new cosmopolitan unity of Rangoon.

For Mogul Street is a living bit of India. Except as a wayfarer no Burman occupies it. Parallel to it, on the left as one faces the town, are Latter Street and Tsikai Moung Khine Street, with their tributaries, in which the Chinese community musters in force. It is a community of exclusive people, with an atmosphere and an architecture of its own ; a community of rich merchants with broad views and the feelings and manners of gentlemen. Britishers, mostly Scotch, who stand at the top of the commercial ladder, readily admit that they would rather do business with the Chinaman than with any other Oriental in Rangoon. And this is as true of the carpenter who makes goods of mediæval solidity as it is of the leading Chinamen whose houses tower above the wide thoroughfares, an ornament to the city. Several here, as in the Straits Settlements and wherever the British flag is flown, have attained to fortune and honour. Yet the Chinaman of Rangoon is not quite an angel in disguise ; he is a man of many secret vices and one or two pronounced weaknesses. His leading clubs, modelled ostensibly on the lines of British institutions, cover a good deal of hard gambling ; his secret societies are credited by rumour with some of the attributes of the Camorra ; and most of his gains are made from liquor and opium, for which he takes out a licence from the State.

The Burman, whose capital this is, is retreating more and more into the suburbs. With his philosophic habits, his indolent ways, his love of good things, and his spiritual yearnings, he is no rival to the thrifty Surati, the aboriginal Coringhi, and the strenuous Chinaman. To see him thoroughly at home one must now go as far as Kemendine. There, under the shade of the great trees, the sculptor of alabaster Gautamas plies his chisel, the umbrella-maker displays the delicate feeling of the race for beautiful things in the manufacture of yellow and green transparencies of perfect design, the weaver weaves tape for binding palm-leaf manuscripts into texts from the sacred books, the lacquer artist paints and gilds his cabinets for the monastery libraries. There in short one who would see the Burman at work in his own way, and upon objects meant for Burmese use, must go. There are silver-workers and wood-carvers in Godwin Road and other thoroughfares of the city, but they cater almost solely for European tastes.

MOGUL STREET

In the Surati Bazaar there is the most "Oriental" part of Rangoon. In its half-lit passages, its avenues bordered by stalls, in which the mixed populace of traders transact their business, there is somewhat that recalls the flavour of Smyrna and Stamboul; but it is a little flavour only, a thing in its beginnings. Here and there a silk-stall is kept by a daughter of the soil, but the majority of those who wait for the custom of the visitor are underbred Suratis with the mannerless manners that come to Orientals under British rule. The bazaar is owned by a company of Suratis whose enterprise forestalled that of the City Fathers. The shares of the Surati Bazaar Company are unpurchasable, and their dividends reach fabulous dimensions.

It is upon the south of Rangoon that the energy of the Municipality has long been concentrated. Enormous areas of land which were little better than buffalo pools half a century ago, and portions of which survived in that capacity to within a year or two ago, have been reclaimed at great expense, to provide for the growth of the city. A resolute belief in its future is one of the best characteristics of Rangoon, and its confidence is likely to be justified. New blocks are being occupied, new streets are being made, new centres of life are being opened out—parks and gardens and offices—at this southern end of Rangoon, between the Puzun-Daung and the Hlaing. There is a fascination in the evident process of growth. Every year there is somewhat added, and in ten years there is an absolute transformation. Every time that I come back to Rangoon I walk out to look at the new town, the new houses, the newly metalled roads, running between the wide unoccupied spaces of newly reclaimed land. Thinking of Rangoon I feel that the interest of it lies much more in the future than in the present or the past. If it were not already very proud of its achievements it might adopt as its civic motto the phrase that Cicero applied to youth—" *Non res sed spes est.*" It has no history to speak of ; no buried past. Here is no " rose-red city, half as old as time " ; but it is full of life and colour, a kaleidoscope of races, with a growing character of its own and the joyous atmosphere of youth.

East of Rangoon lie the Royal lakes, and Dalhousie Park which owes its inception to the great Viceroy. There is no city in the East with a finer playground, and in time, when the Victoria lakes which provide Rangoon with its drinking-water are added to the total of finished beauty, they will become famous. Some of the turf is as fine already as the turf of an English park. Amongst the trees are many of the sumptuous kind, which break into one dazzling mass of bloom, such as the pagoda-tree, the *padouk*, the *pinma*, and the laburnum acacia. These trees are already a feature of Rangoon, but their wealth is too widely scattered to make its full impression. If they were collected as at Honolulu in long avenues of several miles of each species—the labour of a single generation—they would make Rangoon in the spring-time a spectacle of the most striking beauty. The roads of the Municipality run into a hundred and twenty miles. I sometimes picture a hundred and twenty miles of trees in the most dazzling, riotous, bloom, each marshalled under its own kind.

The neighbourhood of the lakes is becoming more and more the resort of the wealthier classes. Villas, many of them of considerable beauty, have sprung up of recent years in large numbers ; and the descendants of those merchants who met a century ago on the main wharf of Rangoon to converse and transact business now pass the cool of the morning and evening in their country houses at Kokine.

CHINESE JOSS-HOUSE

Such is Rangoon the prosperous, the rising city. To catch some of the flavour of its romance one must leave its villadom and enter its crowded heart, and preferably at night. For the night is the time to judge of an Eastern city.

CHAPTER V

THE CITY AT NIGHT

THE sea-breeze blowing up with the tide freshens the night, and the streets swarm with a populace bent on relaxation. All men, and most women, come out at this hour. The pavements are crowded with those who minister to the public pleasure—the pineapple man, with his tray of fruit ; the Burmese girl, with her petty stall of cigars ; the Hindu seller of betel, with his little mirror, to tempt the glance of the passing *beaux ;* the lemonade man, with his moving barrow ; the seller of ice-creams ; the Chinaman under his swaying burden of cooked meats and strange luxuries ; the vermicelli man ; the Indian confectioner, with his silver-coated pyramids of sugar and cream. It is of all crowds one of the most cosmopolitan. Here the long-coated Persian, with his air of breeding and dignity, is jostled by the naked Coringhi with rings in his nose ; the easy beauty from Japan dashes by in her rickshaw, drawn by a Chinese coolie ; the exclusive Brahmin finds himself shoulder to shoulder with a laughing daughter of the soil who has never heard of caste and would make merry over it if the notion was presented to her mind ; the

CHINESE GAMBLING AT A FAIR

Chetti rolls his obese person beside the straight-stepping soldier fresh from England ; the Italian organ-man collects his coppers with humility, a white man in decay ; a gentleman going out to dinner drives rapidly through the crowd, his dress-front flashing against the dark.

But the life is not all out of doors, and as the night grows it becomes concentrated within. Here is the new Burmese theatre, which is taking the place of the open-air entertainments of thirty years ago. A celebrated company is performing and the most popular prima-donna in Burma is on view. The audience is seated on the floor, with the exception of a number of small boys who hang over the footlights and crawl on the stage amongst the legs of the actors. Sonorous declamation is the leading feature of the entertainment, varied by witty sallies which are much enjoyed by the spectators. It is some old story of a king and his court, which has little of definite interest in itself; but the sententious wisdom of the councillors, the immense dignity of the king, the atmosphere of royalty, are of great attraction, and every flash of wit is caught up in one instantaneous ripple of laughter. A large proportion of the audience is made up of women, many of whom have brought their babes. Little girls, fascinated at first by the spectacle, soon fall asleep, and slumber peacefully till their parents are ready to go home in the morning. The audience, indeed, is more interesting than the play. The women laugh in the discreetest way at the doubtful

THE RISING GENERATION OF CELESTIALS

sallies of the actors. Their quick perception is only equalled by the innate modesty of their manners and the perfect reserve that marks their relationship with their men. Although they are people of warm passions and much affection, they contrive to restrict the exhibition of these emotions to their own homes.

The play moves on to the strident voices of the actors, the vigorous music of the orchestra, and part of the audience is comfortably asleep, when there is a sudden movement in the back seats near the entrance, and the whole body of men in the house rush to their feet as a party of sailors breaks in at the wicket. A free fight, the crashing of chair legs, the thud of fists, a stream of hard words in two languages, a rush for the door; and the dramatic interlude is over. But outside there are broken heads and faces streaming with blood, and mariners who wish they had kept out of a hornets' nest. Episodes of this kind, whether brought about by an invasion from without or a quarrel within, are not infrequent at the play in Burma. But they are episodes with little power to stay the declamations of royal councillors and the posturings of tireless prima-donna.

As the night wears on men move away from the play to other haunts. Outside the little houses that flank the more secluded streets there sit the painted *demi-monde*, the women of half the world, from Paris to Japan ; and they drift here by successive stages of decline, raking up here the very lees of life. There are other places too, associated with the midnight life of the city : the haunts of the opium smoker, where men lie as in a shambles, forgetful of time ; the inner parlour of the Ah-Sin club, where is heavy gambling, and little cards are heaped with money on the tables. But the life of a city at night is an oft-told tale, and if it is undoubtedly interesting, it is somewhat unsavoury to chronicle. The river is not open to the same objection.

THE RIVER

On the dark road that winds between the Strand and the river's edge all life seems stilled, save that of the overshadowing palms which rustle in every breeze. Behind me lies the city, with its brick avenues, its multitude of lights, and its swarming populace. A few yards ahead of the silence in which I am engulfed lies the river. Under the laterite shore there gleam the white flanks of a forest of stakes, lean and vague against the dark. Lashed to them there ride upon the waters a fleet of sampans, and as the waves lap their sides the scene, the grouping, recall to mind a wind-driven night when high tides are in at the Piazetta of St. Marc.

I sit by the iron stanchions of a floating jetty and look out across the dark, while the river slowly reveals its mystery. In its mid-stream there lies a great liner anchored for the night. Her dark bulk surges up out of the faint level of the water, and the smoke from her funnels floats back across the clouds. I can hear the roar of her steam-cranes and trace the sweep of their shadowy arms as they work ceaselessly through the long night, under the concentrated flame of a hundred electric arcs. The light is stark and dazzling when one is under it, and it blinds the eyes to all the surrounding world ; but from these distant stanchions it is a flash only in the vastness of the dark. Faint waves stream from it over the river in zones of light ; and across these, recalling old Viking similes of life, the dark shapes of sampans glide. One can trace for an instant the swift curve of the prow, the bent and shadowy form of the oarsman. A faint huddled figure suggests his fare. They pass like shadows on a screen, simulacra of sentient life. . . . One wonders idly, vainly, who they are.

As I look closer yet, new aspects of the river unfold before my vision. The dark I perceive is really ablaze with a myriad lights ; far up to the reaches of Kemendine, down away to the meeting of the waters by Puzun-Daung, and all across to the murky Dalla shore, the lights twinkle, a great host. Out of the distance come twin lights threading their way through the motionless crowd, and out of the gloom there grows a slight outline, and there comes a flash like the undergleam of a shark, as a launch, with a quiet policeman seated within her, throbs past. Here all, or nearly all, is peace and silence ; but down-stream the night wind bears the burden of the dock labourers' song, as they sweat and labour into the dawn under the flare of the furious Lubigen.

THE SAMPAN IN ACTION

The great elemental forces work in silence, their stupendous drama is accomplished almost invisibly. But the mute trail of the liner's smoke tells of the changing wind, the swing of the anchored ships of the outgoing tide, and overhead the stars as they pass one by one into darkness speak of yet greater mysteries.

At the jetty stairs, under the shadow of the iron bridge, the sampan-men wait for the chance passenger. I hail one and pass swiftly into mid-stream, where the liner, blazing with lights from prow to stern, flings her ribbons of flame across the water. Overhead the young moon now shines, at play with the drifting clouds. My boatman steers in her silver track up the river, and the scene that lies before me is one that Venice herself cannot surpass. The myriad lights on the water rival the twinkling firmament overhead ; the river heaves with the billows of passing ships ; great cargo boats spread their black sails against the sky and bear down upon my frail craft like raiders of the night ; *laung-zats*, long and low in the water, sweep down with stately sterns and the measured fall of oars, the bending forms of the rowers outlined against the gloom ; the masts and rigging of sailing-ships trace their old-world fretwork against the crescent of the moon ; through all my small bark speeds on her way, gliding now between the prows of her sister craft, now, with swift daring, circling the sterns and anchor chains of the iron ships. One slip, a second's hesitation, the snapping of an oar, would suffice to throw my boatman and me upon the mercy of the waters ; and the waters of the Rangoon river know no mercy.

On the Dalla shore, where the steamers of the Old Flotilla lie in dock, the painters and the caulkers are at work, and their fires flame and quiver on the face of the river. And beyond, where creeks lead up into the heart of the Twanté plain, rice-mills groan and vibrate, and Chinese iron-smiths mould their red-hot cauldrons. Strange worlds these of midnight life, into which for the curious there is entry. I put my hand into the water, and feel the derelicts of the mills, the paddy-husks drifting in millions out to sea, and they run and circle up my arm, and I know them though they are invisible to my eyes. The feel of the water is warm to my fingers ; the air ambrosial and laden with the scent of the sea. Above the harbour lights and the mizzen-lanterns, strung high against the violent night, is a chaplet of flame, the diadem of the city. It is held aloft by the Shwe Dagôn, invisible itself in the night.

CHAPTER VI

THE PUZUN-DAUNG CREEK

THE little river of this name, where it enters the Hlaing under the guns of Monkey Point, is at the heart of the rice trade of Rangoon, which runs into several million tons a year. Its mouth during the rice season is crowded with the carved boats of the peasantry, freighted with the harvest of three million acres ; and here more energy and wealth are concentrated than in any other equal area in the city. Between January and May this back-water palpitates with life ; and day after day and through the night the rice is husked here in the giant mills which stand upon its banks. Here launches rush up and down with frantic energy, cargo boats lie thick as flies upon the water, and sampans sweep up in an unbroken stream. The passing of the rice season brings the creek some measure of repose, and of a misty evening at such times it has often recalled to me, from its character of isolation rather than from any similarity in detail, the Canale di San Pietro, as one comes upon it fresh from the Public Gardens. It is dominated at its far end by the superb beauty of the Shwe Dagôn. The creek curves round the foot of the hill on which the golden pagoda is built, and as one ascends it the whole view gradually swings round. It is an engrossing transition from the pride of action, the modern pulsing of life, the symbols of wealth and civilisation that crowd the estuary of

NATIVE CRAFT AT PUZUN-DAUNG

the stream, to the stark slime of the tide-uncovered banks, the loneliness and the primitiveness of the upper reaches; it is a swift passing from the twentieth to the first century. A thatched hamlet lifts its roofs above the plain; on the edge of the low water a fisherman toils at his nets; a canoe with two occupants goes by; a party of naked lads wallow in the slime of the foreshore, taking the mud baths to which the twentieth century is returning. Such are the symptoms of life along its upper courses; but loneliness is the character of the Puzun-Daung above the territory of the mills, and the land, washed and left soaking by the daily tide, seems scarcely yet to have emerged from its subaqueous infancy.

CHAPTER VII

THE SHWE DAGÔN

"*Take it all in all, it is the fabric in India in all that I have visited most worth seeing, the Taj alone excepted.*"—MARQUESS OF DALHOUSIE.

OF the origin of the Shwe Dagôn I have already spoken in connection with the origin of Rangoon. The life that animates it to-day is of more interest, and it is true that if all else in Burma were destroyed and only the Shwe Dagôn with its life were preserved, there would remain enough to tell the world of all that is best in the idiosyncrasy of the Burmese race. There is no other centre in Burma that can compare with it for the display of colour, for the physical pageantry and the spiritual expression of life, for the grand movement of many peoples on a stage as splendid as any in the world.

Rising to a height of three hundred and sixty-eight feet, it is loftier than St. Paul's, and its size is greatly enhanced by the fact that it stands on an eminence that is itself one hundred and sixty-six feet above the level of the city. This circumstance gives it an air of great dignity and makes it conspicuous over a wide horizon. Its spire of gold, touched by the flaming sun, is the first object upon which the eyes of the world-traveller rest as he approaches Rangoon, and it is the last of the city he looks upon when his steamer is bearing him away; and the memory of it never fades from the eyes of one who has once looked upon it.

It is covered with pure gold from base to summit, and once in every generation this gold is completely renewed by public subscription. Yet throughout the interval the process of regilding goes on perpetually. Pious people who seek in this way to express their veneration and to add to their store of spiritual merit, climb up daily with little fluttering packets of gold leaf, which they fasten on some fraction of its great surface; and one may see them there, these silken worshippers, outlined high against its gold, in the act of contributing their small quota to its splendour. It is in such episodes as these that the fundamental democracy of Eastern life is happily revealed. For the East, and especially this East about which this book is written, is above all things tolerant. Time has taught it the faculty of leaving the individual alone. To live and to let live is its philosophy, and it is the keynote of the life that daily throngs the platform of the Shwe Dagôn.

This platform, with a perimeter of nearly fourteen hundred feet, is the place of worship. *The pagoda itself has no interior.* It is a solid stupa of brick raised over a relic chamber. A cutting made into its

COMING AWAY

centre has revealed the fact that the original pagoda had seven casings added to it before it attained its present proportions. The shape of the pagoda is that of an elongated cone. It is divided by Burmese convention into twelve parts:[1] first, the base surrounded by a great number of small pagodas; then the three terraces, called Pichayas; next the Bell; the inverted Thabeik, or begging bowl; the Baungyit, or twisted turban; the Kyalan, or ornamental lotus flower; the Plantain Bud; the brass plate for the Hti, or umbrella; the Hti; the Sein bwin, or artificial flowers; the Vane; and last of all, the Seinbu, or bud of diamonds.

Of these the *hti* with its accessories is of exceptional interest. It was presented to the pagoda by Mindon Min, King of Burma, and its transmission from Mandalay to Rangoon was almost a political event. The placing of *htis* on the chief pagodas of the country has always been an expression of sovereignty in Burma, and few indeed of a more striking description can well be imagined. The king strove hard, therefore, to

[1] For some of these particulars I am indebted to a little book on The Pagoda, compiled by my old chief, the late Thomas Hesketh Biggs, Comptroller of Burma, to whose memory, and that of Maung Hla Oung of the same service, who helped him, I pay this tribute.

secure the consent of the British Government then established in Rangoon, to the placing of his gift by his own representatives upon the summit of the Shwe Dagôn; but, for political reasons, without success. The gorgeous object, valued at £60,000, was brought down by a deputation of the Royal officers as far as the border, where it was taken over by a British subject. The king was thus gratified in his spiritual desire; his political yearning had to remain unappeased. The *hti*, which to the eye of the spectator standing at the foot of the pagoda,

THE JEWELLED VANE

seems but a very small object, is in reality a canopy of iron and gold thirteen and a half feet in diameter, and forty-seven feet in height. It is hung with nearly fifteen hundred bells, of which more than a hundred are of gold and the rest of solid silver. Large as many of these bells are they cannot be seen with the naked eye from the pagoda base; but their music can be heard in the night watches, when the wind blows amongst their silver and golden tongues. The vane and the *seinbu* are practically invisible. Certainly no gleam of their jewels[1] ever reaches the human eye. Let us recognise the nobility of sentiment that underlies this matter. In a like spirit one sees placed at the climbing pinnacles of

[1] 3,664 rubies, 541 emeralds, and 433 diamonds.

a grey cathedral in Europe the fine work of the artist lavished on hidden gargoyles and saintly figures far out of reach of the thronging world below; and one admires the restraint, the humility, and the fine purpose. But it is only in Burma, so often accused of superficiality, that men put a great ransom in jewels where no eye can testify to their splendour.

The platform upon which the pagoda stands is approached by four great flights of stairs at the cardinal points. Of these, the southern stairs are the most frequented, facing as they do the immemorial road which leads up from the banks of the river, straight through the heart of the town to the pagoda. The eastern and the northern stairs are used by the smaller communities of people who reside in their neighbourhood. The western stairs have been closed to worshippers at the pagoda since the irony of events converted it into a British fortress. Each of these stairs has an individuality of its own.

THE SOUTHERN APPROACH

Here the first steps on the roadside are flanked by a pair of colossal gryphons, at whose feet there are strange contrasts of lepers in the toils of death and children unconsciously at play. Beyond the gryphons there is a modern arch of masonry, unworthy of its place in the forefront of the great fane. Beyond it again there reach away in deep gloom the first stairs of the covered passage to more open spaces where the light falls in golden bars upon the silk of the ascending and descending worshippers. On both sides of the passage sit the vendors of gold leaf and waxen tapers for the pious, and coloured beads and mirrors for the vain, and books for the learned, and toys and supple-jacks for the young. Pretty women dart out from behind the gay stalls and twang their little triangular gongs in the faces of the passers-by, and children run to the stranger with offerings of flowers and requests for pence. Here in these half-lit corridors is gathered a singular epitome of life. Women sit nursing their babes, girls throw amorous glances and quick words at the passing youth, nuns beg gently in the open spaces, and loud-voiced beggars call upon the charity of the world: "*Amado, Amaungdo. Thanahma sayaba myi khinbya; tabya lauk thanadaw moogai-gyaba khinbya*" ("Good Folk—Ladies, gentlemen, by your pity alone can I eat; a copper, a copper, I pray you").

Ascending still. one comes upon the first moat of the citadel, spanned by a drawbridge and defended by an iron gate whose chains and loop-holes are rusty from want of use. On the east the long moat reaches away to the corner bastions; on the west to the barred door of the arsenal guard-house. Here in this gate made for purposes alien to the Buddhist faith there is a mist of sunlight through which the figures

THE PILGRIM'S REST

of the ascending crowd pass into the shadow of the upper stairs. The outer porch is of grey wood and mosaic gold and dark intricate carving, and the Chinese letters testify to the race of the donor. The slant red sunlight streams in unexpected bars amongst the shadows of the stairs, falling here upon a woman's face, transfiguring it, there upon a mass of lambent gold on a white pillar ; or it flames in the heart of the amber beads which fall in curtains before the stalls. And thus, climbing on up the stairs, polished by the bare feet of the worshipping millions, one comes with a swift transition upon the great court of the pagoda, and all that it has to show of wonder and splendour and moving life. There is no spectacle in the world more fit to dazzle the eyes.

There is a quieter scene at the south-east corner, where, under the shelter of great trees, and remote from the world that throngs about the inner aisles, there are wooden platforms built up to the level of the high containing wall. So skilfully is the place chosen that one can visit the pagoda a dozen times without coming upon it. Here pilgrims rest ; finding shelter from the noontide heat, a resting-place at night, and at all hours that there is light, from the first coming of the morning to the passing of the sunset beyond the Dalla plains, a view of surpassing interest and beauty. Tufted palms rise up here dark and stately in the forefront ; the grass-covered bastions of the fort lie below ; and beyond, reaching away to the horizon, spreads the fair site of the city of Rangoon. The Pegu river and the Hlaing meet there under the guns of Monkey Point, and the loops of the smaller river reach away through the heart of the level plain to the misty land of the dawn. The spire of Syriam pierces the distant sky ; the dark smoke-clouds of factories trail in the wake of the invisible winds. Where the Puzun-Daung creek opens out like an estuary into the wide space of waters, the pent roofs of the mills, and the masts of the cargo boats, cluster together, and in the sapphire mist there are traced in outline the lineaments of a great and populous city. Much nearer and under the eastern slopes the Royal lakes lie like a chance mirror, and every phase of the passing day is caught upon their surface.

Here, true to his instinct of piety, his love of the beautiful, the Burman pilgrim who has paid his devotions at the great shrine retires for silent meditation. Maybe it is an old man who sits here alone as the evening draws in, his eyes turned towards the world of palm-trees and distant rivers, of red roofs and the paling hues of the sunset ; while a rosary moves in his fingers, responsive to the prayer falling from his lips, his face rapt in an ecstasy of holiness. There is some quality in the Burman which lifts him up at such times and in such places to a great dignity. I can only suggest in explanation his absolute sincerity, the transparent humility of his piety, his unconsciousness of self and

FROM THE WEST

of the world in his effort to reach the heart of the spiritual life ; and his artistic instinct, never in his personal actions at fault.

A little way from this secluded corner of the pagoda, in a privacy still greater, there lie the graves of our dead who fell in an assault on the shrine.

On the eastern face of the pagoda there is another flight of long stairs that is often crowded with worshippers, but there are no stalls here, and for great portions of the day the silent corridors are void. Their loneliness was long enhanced by the presence of a single tenant, an old leper, nearly blind and in a terrible state of dissolution. He was a singular creature who never asked an alms. Of nights he sat by the flame of a smoky lamp whose wick flickered in every passing gust. I could never learn his history, but he has long since attained peace, and no successor has come to fill his place or prolong his awful vigil. The stairs lead down through vermilion aisles to the outer moat and drawbridge, and beyond them by a paved causeway to Bahan, the village of the pagoda slaves. Here of an evening the faint blue smoke hangs in a cloud above the little houses ; and of a morning on feast days the causeway in the sunlight is thronged with silken worshippers on their way from the eastern country-side to the great shrine.

The northern entrance is quiet ; yet even after the concentrated splendour of these two other approaches, possibly on that account it makes it own appeal. Here the golden mass of the pagoda is seen in unbroken unity through an avenue of dark Palmyra palms. The steps that climb up to it are seldom trodden. Quiet is their charm ; and on many a day when the heart is heavy and little able to face the pageantry of life—of the life that ever streams up the pathway from the white dragons to the southern *tazoungs*—people are glad to come up this way and rest in silence in the comforting beauty and stateliness of the great temple.

On the west there is nothing but a dead wall, the limit of arsenals and barracks.

THE ARCHITECTURE OF THE PAGODA

I do not propose here to give any complete account of the architecture of the pagoda. Not only is there a wealth of minute detail, the description of which would involve something like a dissertation on Buddhism and Burmese mythology, but there is the fact that the buildings at the base and on the platform of the pagoda are for ever changing. A description of the pagoda as it was when this book was written would be incomplete to-day. This is due as much to the ephemeral nature of the wooden buildings as to the progressive character of Burmese art. For Burmese art is essentially alive. It is full of vitality and is ever receptive

CHAPELS IN GLASS MOSAIC

of new ideas. The spirit of the people is buoyant and full of *élan*, and the rapidity with which new developments begin and advance towards fruition is amazing. Thus of late years a great advance has been made in the art of glass mosaic, and where a decade ago a few pillars wrought into simple designs alone represented it, there are now scores of elegant columns worked in the most daring colours into patterns of great beauty and intricacy. Unhappily the advance is not always in the right direction and much that has been done marks a falling away, both in simplicity and in taste. If the Burmese mind be, as I believe it to be, thoroughly alive, it is also prone to extravagance and excess, and this failing is nowhere so marked as it is in Burmese art. There is a fascination in the mere multiplication of things which it is unable to resist, and objects beautiful in themselves become an occasion of fatigue to the eye by their incessant repetition. One notable example of this is furnished in the base of the pagoda. Originally of a design remarkable for its antique simplicity and dignity, it has of late been almost entirely concealed by the accumulation of an enormous number of petty shrines. Some of these indeed are wrought with delicacy and skill. Yet they serve no true purpose of art, since they are wholly unnecessary ; and they are worse than unnecessary, since they obscure what was already beautiful and adapted to its purpose. To protests made by lovers of the great shrine the invariable answer is that the new chapels will look very fine when they are finished. The trustees to whose care the building is committed urge on the other hand, that it is not in accordance with Buddhist feeling that the right of any man to earn spiritual merit by adding something to the national pagoda should be denied, and that the sum now paid for permission to erect one of these little shrines is a valuable addition to the resources of the pagoda. Without even this justification is the introduction of tin and iron in place of the wooden roofs and pinnacles of the old *tazoungs*.

As one walks round the face of the edifice one is struck by the variety of strange creatures that ornament it. Here there are sphinxes and leogryphs, which hark back in their origin to Nineveh ; dragons with large eyeballs and pointed tongues ; and elephants that kneel in adoration. There are trees of gold with crystal fruit, begging bowls of glass mosaic, stone umbrellas of great antiquity, and altars upon which the floral offerings of the pious exhale strange perfumes into the air. Astronomical lore is manifested in the tall vermilion posts inscribed in gold with the names and symbols of the sun, the moon, and the planets ; and at intervals there are square tanks of masonry, into which the drainage of the pagoda charged with golden dust is borne. Hundreds of pounds' worth of gold are recovered from the residue of mire that remains in them each year when the waters have run off.

From a painting by J. Raeburn Middleton

COMING DOWN FROM THE PAGODA AFTER WORSHIP

At each of the cardinal points, with their backs to the pagoda and their faces set towards the four approaches to the shrine, there stand, open to the visits of the devout, *tazoungs* or chapels, with multiple tapering roofs supported on lofty pillars of mosaic and gold. Within there are seated images of the Buddha, some of them so charged with gold that all trace of features has been obliterated. Within the gloom of these chapels countless tapers flicker, lighting up the marble, the brass, and the gold of which the images are made. Here the devotion of the pious culminates, and the voices of the worshippers vibrate in loud unison through the golden aisles. Two of these *tazoungs* are the outcome of recent zeal, and if they lack the simple dignity of the earlier buildings which they have displaced, they certainly surpass them in their lavish use of gold. There is gold everywhere, from the pediment of the stately pillars to the topmost pinnacle of the ascending roofs. Each of them has cost the donors, prosperous brokers in the paddy trade, a sum of £10,000, and the details of the expenditure are recorded in golden letters upon marble stones which compel the attention of the visitor. The fancy of hiding his spiritual light under a bushel is unknown to the Burman Buddhist. The acquisition of merit—of the merit that helps souls to rise in the scale of perfection, which eventually floats the perfect into the infinite peace of Nirvana—is the laudable ambition of every earnest man and woman in Burma. It is the action that counts, and its efficacy is little affected by the manner in which it is performed. Moreover the Burmese mind is too direct and simple to entertain the idea of ceremonial modesty on the one hand, or of

FIGURES AT THE FOOT OF A "TAGÔN-DAING"

hypocrisy on the other. All men when they have prayed at the pagoda and bestowed their alms strike with a deer horn one of the great tongueless bells on the platform to rouse the attention of the Recording Angel.

These new buildings illustrate at once the vigour and the element of decline in Burmese art. Between the golden pillars there are screens of fine wood-carving most delicately and skilfully wrought. The artist has not followed any model but his own fancy. He has had the courage to break away from the traditional boldness of design and execution which characterise the national carving ; but his efforts, great in themselves, have led him into a style of work that is too delicate for open-air effect, for which this carving is pre-eminently intended. If Burmese carving proceeds too far along this line it can only end in extinguishing itself.

The colouring of these buildings is superb. Outside they are vermilion and gold—within they are green and gold and purple. They are carved to their summits and laden with numberless figures, each of which is alive with action.

Between these *tazoungs*, fixed at one end in the mass of the pagoda itself, and a vast outer circle of lesser pagodas and shrines, there is an open space, narrowing unhappily every year, which is flagged with rich flesh-coloured stone. It is upon these stones that the worshippers kneel in paying their devotions. Of the outer group of buildings there are many of great interest and charm ; amongst them stand the *htis* of a bygone day, and upon the edge of the platform the *tagôn-daings* which are perhaps the most graceful objects ever invented by Burmese art. Their lofty columns, inlaid with rich mosaic, are supported at the foot by striking figures of *nats*, and they are surmounted at their summits by effigies of the *galon* bird and the sacred Hansa of Pegu. Streamers of coloured gauze flutter from them upheld by the passing winds. They are the Burmese equivalent of the splendid flag-staffs that once carried the banners of the Republic before the front of St. Marc's.

Of such is the architecture of the pagoda. Great as it is it is surpassed in interest by the life that animates it. Year after year for more than ten years I who write this visited the Shwe Dagôn Pagoda. Upon countless occasions I have climbed up its dark stairs ; I have walked in wonder and delight upon its platform ; I have mingled with its silken throngs ; I have seen the men and the women and the little children at prayer ; I have looked upon the great drama of worship as it has unfolded itself before my eyes. I have walked there in the first freshness of the dawn, in the company of its earliest visitors ; I have spent the noontide in the shelter of its great trees ; I have followed the glory of the setting

THE NEW "TAZOUNG"

sun, as it has thrown its magic upon all that is splendid in the great shrine; I have walked alone in the company of the night and heard the music of its clear-voiced bells tinkling far overhead in the passing breeze; and I have seen the dawn come upon it again, and moonlight and sunlight for one supreme moment compete upon its golden face. I have gone to it in all times of joy and sorrow, and in every mood, for I have found it comforting and beautiful, and I suppose that I can claim to know it and to love it as well as any one in the world; yet, when I come to describe it, its fascination, its beauty, the life that moves upon it, the emotion it embodies, I realise that I am undertaking a task that is beyond my power of performance. Many who live within the sweep of its shadow, but seldom visit it, will not understand my estimate of it; but the Shwe Dagôn remains. This much may at least be said of it; it is the greatest cathedral of the Buddhist faith; it can be compared only with the great shrines of the earth. And if in many obvious respects they surpass it, in one it surpasses them all; for every one of them, for all its beauty, is covered in some form with a roof, whereas in the Shwe Dagôn there is architecture which has learnt how to keep for its dome the dazzling firmament above it. That is the great fact about this pagoda, which it takes some time to find out. Once it is realised the mighty fabric falls into its true perspective. It is no longer the main edifice, a mass of dead brickwork; but the great shaft of a temple of which the blue sky and the stars by night are the vaulted roof. Let the reader when he goes there remember this and he will find his delight, his admiration, his understanding of the great fane much enhanced.

THE PAGODA ON A FEAST DAY

To the occasional visitor there must always seem a plenitude of worshippers at the pagoda; but in truth its life ebbs and flows from day to day and season to season. It reaches its height at the full moon of Taboung, when pilgrims drawn from the farthest corners of South-eastern Asia assemble at it for the great annual festival. From the confines of China; from the highland principalities of the Shan; from the fastnesses of the Karen, though in numbers diminishing each year with the spread of Christianity amongst them; from Bangkok and Annam; the people come to pay their devotions at the Shwe Dagôn. But pre-eminently they come from the land itself in which the pagoda stands, and it is as a Burmese spectacle that the feast demands the notice of the world.

Lanterns making a circle of fire against the night are hung upon its circumference a hundred feet above the base of the pagoda. A million waxen tapers flame before the effigies of the Buddha, and upon the purple

MONKS AND MOSAICS

and the gold and the mosaic and the carved wood. The clang of bells, the refrain of the worshipping populace, the silken tread of unnumbered feet upon the polished stones, daze the ear with their multitudinous music. Vast as is the platform of the pagoda, there is at times scarcely room to move upon it for the press of pilgrims. White muslins and delicate silks, and flaming turbans, bangles of red gold, and pyramids of diamonds, and flowers placed in the uncovered coils of the women; monks in swaying yellow robes, Shans in flapping hats and wide trousers, pig-tailed Chinamen, and peasants clad in the rough homespun of the jungle, make up the varied scene.

THE BASE OF A "TAGÔN-DAING"

Before the dawn, "When the red star appears," the worshippers rise and prepare their offerings of fruit and flowers and sweetmeats, and one by one they converge upon the temple. A few, still earlier in their devotions, climb while it is yet dark, with the aid of lanterns, up the dark polished stairs. The morning finds a great company assembled. Here and there men pray in companies, representing some religious association; parties of villagers frightened by tales of town dangers keep together; but for the most part the worship is individual. The worshipper kneeling before the pagoda lights the tapers he has brought, and holding his offering of flowers in his joined hands, prays, repeating in adoration the excellences of the Buddha. Strange prayers, as to a being who hears and can help, for the things that are dear to men, go up from these unbelievers in a personal god. The man and his wife kneeling together pray that they may see the Buddha Arimaddeya when he comes again as the saviour of mankind, and that thus they may attain *neikban*. Till then they beg that they may live again as husband and wife. Others solicit with great earnestness at the feet of Thakiamuni the favour of becoming at some time a Buddha like himself, and

NEW "TAZOUNGS"

wish, like King Laukatara, " that they may be born in the same country of the same parents ; that they may ride the same horses and be attended by the same companions " as of old. Lovers come here and pray that their love may continue, and that if fate should separate them it may survive into a future existence ; that it may last for ever till *neikban* is attained. Aged men and young women, mothers, and children scarce able to lisp, all unite in the one great universal prayer : " May we attain by the merit of the three precious things—the Buddha, the Law, and the Assembly—to *neikban !* "

And this *neikban*—what is it ? Eternal extinction or eternal and conscious peace ? The everyday Buddhist in Burma at least is in no doubt upon the subject ; and for an exalted idea of Paradise, is there anything more reassuring than this ? " Where the believer expects to find a sure shelter against all errors, doubts, and fears ; and a resting-place where his spirit may securely enjoy the undisturbed possession of Truth."

A visit to the Shwe Dagôn Pagoda at the time of the annual feast is the goal of the pious Burman's ambition. The popular refrain at the festival sung by all classes and by people of all ages, runs thus :

> Ahpogyi-o Kongon, matheba hnin-on ;
> Naung hnitkha tazaung bon pwe kyizo on.

(" O old man, do not die yet ; live to see next year's tazaung bon pwe.") And old people full of gratitude at having seen it go to and fro in an ecstasy, chanting their " Nunc Dimittis " : " Lo, if I die now, I care not, for I have lived to look upon the great ' Phaya.' "

Yet devout as are the assembled people, profound as is their reverence for the shrine, it is not for purposes of worship alone that they come together here. The Burmese are a catholic people, with an instinctive appreciation of the good things of life. They extend their patronage as liberally to the white man's shops as they do to their own, and country visitors by their unaffected admiration and artless mistakes provide much delight to the town-bred citizen. They stand before the big windows of the English drapers and indulge in wonder at the fine things it contains. " A-mai-lai, what a paradise ! " At the Italian confectioner's —" He, Ko Saw. This is *nat awza*, the food of the gods. Nothing like this in the jungle." Familiar *contretemps* occur, such as an intemperate assault on the mustard-pot ; and old ladies who should know better nearly choke themselves by too rapid a consumption of *glace à la vanille*. And if Rangoon, to the annual pilgrim, bulks in this way as a kind of material paradise, it is also associated in his mind with dangers he must guard against ; such as the trite Shway-lain, the Shan-lain, and the Pyanpe. The Pyanpe involves the temporary abduction of a child or of one of the waggon bullocks, and the payment of a price by the distracted owner for its recovery. Young ladies who have come to worship at the pagoda remind themselves that Rangoon is a wicked city, and the knowledge that some dashing young fellow may carry them off in a fast cab adds a thrill of excitement to their simple pleasures. Every smart young fellow who throws an eye at a pretty girl looms up in her timid imagination as the abductor of tradition.

Yet these are but episodes. The great body of the pilgrims moves through the ceremony of devotion and pleasure with little anxiety or mishap. Perhaps the greatest pleasure of all is found in the plays that

OPEN-AIR PLAY

are performed in the thoroughfares of the town and on the outer slopes of the pagoda, where there is room for a vast encampment. The play, which is performed in the open, under the starry sky, is nearly always a tale of kings and queens and princes and princesses, to which the people listen with an interest as great and unabated as that of a child listening for the hundredth time to the same old fairy tale. These royalties who move upon the Burmese stage are very real people to the Burmese imagination, and their lofty ways and sad fortunes wring many a heart. Yet there is always a new element in the play imported by the topical allusions and jokes, the material for which is collected by the actors by listening with attention to the *voces populi* and noting the misadventures of the day. Jokes of this kind are received with exuberant delight by the assembled people. The plays near the pagoda are organised and paid for by the trustees; many of those in the town by notabilities of a generous habit. The audience assembles without invitation.

Thus, one by one, the days of the great festival are accomplished; the ox-waggons in which the nearest multitude has come are harnessed again, and the clanging bells of the cattle, the merriment of the occupants, prolong the festivity far into the country-side. Steamers and trains now bear away more distant dwellers. Yet even now many a pilgrim walks a month's journey to his home.

The festival passes; but the life remains. Every day has its harmony of colour, its passion of praise and worship, its unending change. Every day that one goes to the pagoda it has something new to offer and only the stranger comes quickly to the end of its mystery.

There is such melody there, the music of a thousand chimes, and great variety of beauty. In the west its tall palms outlined against the red sunset awaken memories of the desert; below, the city of Rangoon looks like a fleet of ships at sea, its mizzen lights high above the dusk water; the great *pipul* with its shrines—the *ficus religiosa*—carries with it a suggestion of oldest India. As the sun sets behind the Dalla plains the long shadow of the pagoda falls with an increasing reach upon the world, and the gold on its swelling curves flames into startling beauty, and every inch of gorgeous mosaic has its moment of supremacy. The tapers on the altars grow into life as darkness comes, the stars overhead break out in dazzling galaxies against the violet night, and the voices of the evening worshippers peal and vibrate through the pillared spaces. The white dragons and elephants at the foot of the pagoda become of an insistent supernatural whiteness; the mystery of night descends upon all that moves or flames upon its surface. Cressets of flame on the backs of the kneeling beasts rescue patches from the general obscurity as they flash on red and gold dragons, on the mirrored interiors of chapels, on the new delicate foliage of the overspreading trees, and throw long shadows from the kneeling women at prayer. A small child walks about before the rows of tapers at the feet of the polished gleaming Buddhas; a girl prattles on a mat of her little secular joys; a sad woman sits alone at a late flower stall; a little old man kneels in a remote corner at prayer; a devout society in a neighbouring *tazoung* chant their litanies together; men go to and fro with flowers in their clasped hands, *shekoing* before each shrine and repeating their praises of the Three Precious Things; monks, a long way off, murmur their prayers in attitudes of reverent humility. A handsome girl, alone at the pagoda at this late hour, prays with a strange earnestness and sadness for one so young. She has come here to pray for her father, a trustee of the pagoda, who is ill and like to die. Many sad people come for solace to the great shrine.

But even these leave, and the late moon, as she rises over the feathery masses of the trees, throwing her silver over the golden bulk of the pagoda, finds its courts untenanted. This is its hour of mystery, the supreme period in the daily life of the great sanctuary. The people have gone, but their tapers still flicker in lonely recesses where shelter from the winds prolongs their hour ; flowers exhale their perfume and glint in the pale moonlight ; blood-red hibiscus and orange canna, pink and white roses, yellow-hearted *tayouksaga ;* the idle wind as she passes

FIGURE OF GAUTAMA

rustles the broad leaves of the palms and makes a shimmer on the white gold-edged umbrellas. *Tagondaing* banners float with listless grace, and the tremulous *pipul* throws her young leaves like a shower of fire-flies against the sky. The palms are cut in silver. Overhead stray wisps of cloud hide for a passing moment the glory of Orion. The melody of bells peals out from far and near as the wind freshens, and underlying their tinkling music there comes to the ear of the careful listener the deep vibration of the whole mass of the building like the refrain of some distant elemental organ. Is there any cathedral in the world like this, so happy in its site, so splendid with its gold, so open to the universal life ?

Book III

THE NORTHERN IRRAWADDY

The Defiles—Bhamo—The Road to China

CHAPTER VIII

THE DEFILES

THE Irrawaddy is of all the great rivers of Indo-China the greatest. Through Burma it flows for a thousand miles, in a broad navigable stream, from the " confluence " in the far north, where, emerging from its mysterious birthplace, it unites with its first great tributary, to the sea into which it pours through a hundred mouths. The mountains in which it is born, an offshoot of the Himalaya, follow its destiny seaward, and when they sweep down to its water's edge, or tower mistily on its wide horizon, lend it an incommunicable charm and beauty. Lessening radually from altitudes of eternal snow, they sink with the river into the ocean, their last bluff crowned by the golden pagoda of Moodain, " Gleaming far to seaward, a Burmese Sunium."

It is no light undertaking to describe this majestic creature. Its length and volume, its importance as an artery of the world, its rise and fall—these are easily recorded facts. The beauty of its waters that mirror a sky of varied loveliness, of its hills and forests and precipitous heights, of its vast spaces that bring a calm to the most fretful spirit, of the sunsets that wrap it in mysteries of colour—these are things for which words are greatly inadequate. A great painter might attempt the picture, but he would do so with the knowledge that he must leave it incomplete, for he could paint only a phase of that which is infinite in its variety. He could tell but little of the human interest with which it is fraught ; of the long historic procession that fills the mind's eye, the migration of prehistoric races, the movement of peoples under the impulse of immutable laws, the advance of invading armies, the flight and agony of the vanquished, the triumph of exultant victors ; of kings and nobles and warriors ; of saints and ascetics ; of the life of the common people, with its passing joys and sorrows, in all of which the silent immortal

IN THE NORTHERN REACHES

river has played its continuous part. One cannot entrap the glory of that which lives and moves, and is yet in its entity and suggestiveness eternal.

The peoples of Burma came from the Highlands to the north of their present home many centuries ago, at a time of which no memory is preserved in local legend or tradition ; though nature, less forgetful, has written upon each man's face the evidence of his origin. Following the streams which rise in that elevated country, they gradually spread southward, reaching in the fulness of time the sea. In primitive ages, when the clan or tribe was the only political unit and there was no more obvious line of separation than the watershed between the streams that they encountered in their southern migration, it was natural that each tribe should separate itself from the rest. It was a separation however, which while it secured to each tribe its immediate liberty, carried in it the germ of ultimate reunion ; and read in the light of this physical fact the racial history of Burma becomes clear in its wide outline. The dominant Burmese represent the tribes that wandered down the tributary sources of the Upper Irrawaddy finally to coalesce in the valley of the great river. Their kindred with a lesser heritage are found in the many tribes on their borders. The Mun or Talaing, the people of the south, were amongst the first of those who came. The Burmese drove them before them, as they would probably have been driven themselves in time by the newer Kachin. But the Kachin has recoiled before the might of England, and the tide is now setting back to the first home of all these peoples.

The Irrawaddy, then, as it flows oceanward, ever accompanied by its hills, is symbolic in a profound sense of the history of the land. On its banks these rude Mongol wanderers grew up to civilisation under the influence of Hindu exiles from India ; a civilisation to which the ruins of ancient cities bear testimony to this day. About its northern reaches there was fought out the long battle of Burmese supremacy over the rival Shan race ; a struggle of many centuries and varying fortunes in which the prize was the great river itself. Shan kingdoms once powerful in the north, and as early as the first century of the Christian era in political relation with China, fell in the struggle, and save in tattered chronicles of small value, their memory has gone out from among their people. Down the valley of the Irrawaddy, too, there swept the all-but-engulfing tide of the Chinese invasions, in one of the earliest of which there perished PAGAN, the greatest of all Burmese capitals. And it has been up the Irrawaddy from the sea, reversing as in India the immemorial tradition of conquest, that the British power has advanced. The great conflict between East and West, more universal now than at any previous period in the history of the world, has once more been fought out along its banks. The people of Burma have become a subject people; its kings have passed for ever out of the category of sovereign princes. Once more the West has triumphed to the satisfaction of the West, and if there be 'a far-off divine event' to the ultimate benefit of the East. Yet no satisfaction can divest such changes of their tragic character. The most callous cannot regard the fall of a nation without some sorrow, or the final extinction of a picturesque Court and of ancient institutions without regret. "Burma," in the words of the royal chronicler of China, "Burma, from the Han dynasty until our day, has existed for over seventeen hundred years, and now alas! by reason of a few years of tyranny and indiscretion on the part of its monarch, the country has been obliterated in the twinkling of an eye."

KACHIN WOMEN

Not the least of its many fascinations is the mystery which has shrouded the river's birthplace. Soon after entering Burma it presents the appearance of a pellucid stream eight hundred yards in width. That is the farthest knowledge of it possessed by the ordinary traveller. The men who live up there, the Englishmen who rule and fight in the wild border country, know it a little farther, as far up as and beyond the confluence where the N'Maikha and N'Mlekha, its two main sources, unite. Beyond this point the Irrawaddy is unnavigable, and it has not yet been given to any man to say from the sight of his own eyes whence it comes. The secret of its birth is still in the wilderness of mountains which spreads away beyond the confluence to north and west. Yet it is being slowly wrested from its keepers. One by one the conjectures hazarded by investigators since the dawn of the nineteenth century have been disposed of; one by one the wild frontier tribes are being reduced to subjection, as the growing peace of Burma frees the Government for exploration and extension towards the north. Its mystery is scarcely any more a mystery.

Thirty miles below the confluence the new settlement of Myitkyina is laid out on the high right bank of the river. No change can be more

KACHIN

significant than the change which the last few years have wrought in the character of Myitkyina. It was once upon a time the *ultima thule* of Burma, a military outpost in the heart of the enemy's country. For six months each year it was cut off from nearly all communication. The only approach to it lay by the river, and the river is no highway at that season. The outpost of Myitkyina had to look out for itself, feed itself, and fight upon occasion for its life. One winter it was attacked and burnt down by the caterans of the hills over the heads of its garrison of a thousand men. Myitkyina is still the frontier town, it is still liable to have to fight for its life ; but it is no longer cut off from succour. It is easily reached by railway at all seasons of the year, and it is becoming a popular stopping-place for the tourist hurrying round the globe. It has all the freshness and charm of a new settlement, and though on the borders of savagery, it is full of life and action and hope.

From Myitkyina to near its junction with the Mogaung, the river flows in a broad clear stream over a pebbled bed. Steaming down-stream in the last days of December one can see the coarse sand churned up from amid the pebbles by the eddying current and glistening like gold in the sunlit waters. The simile is not altogether fanciful, for the gold-washers are at work on the river slopes below Myitkyina. Nearer the shallows which the steamers skirt in their course distinct glimpses can be had into the life of the river, and great fish may be seen scuttling away in agitation. The river, though broad and majestic to the eye, is comparatively shallow in its northern reaches, and the navigable channel is narrow. This is made obvious when a bank of yellow pebbles tilts its back half-way across the stream, or a reef of grey rocks stretches in sawlike outline across the ship's course, narrowing the channel to a stream of deep water under the shelter of the opposite bank. Behind Myitkyina, now fading into the blue distance, there tower

A SHAN PRINCESS

up like "Breasts of Sheba" the twin peaks of Loi Lem and Loi Law, and behind these again there fade away into the empyrean the unexplored mountains of the north, upon which there is a gleam of snow. It is one of the most beautiful and most satisfying voyages in the world, this swift descent down the upper waters of the Irrawaddy. The keen ozone of a perfect air, the broad winter sunlight flooding a landscape of romantic beauty, the sense of encompassing infinity, fill the blood with a supreme vitality, and lift the soul into regions of exquisite peace. The great river, free for the present to go where it lists, flows on in serene untroubled beauty, the central chord in a grand harmony of nature. Overhead there is a flawless sky, and on every hand the mountains stretch away to the uttermost horizon in shades of colour; from tints so faint that they are scarcely to be known from the ether beyond, to the rich purples of near peaks and the deep blue-greens of heavily wooded spurs which reach down to the water's edge, laving their uncovered foundations in the stream. At points like these in its course, where the dense shadows fall on the seemingly motionless waters, the river presents its most characteristic and beautiful aspects, resembling some still mountain lake.

Sixty-five miles below Myitkyina, the Mogaung, emerging from between low flat banks, clothed in giant grass, pours its tributary waters into the Irrawaddy. It flows through a district fruitful in serpentine and amber and indiarubber, inhabited by a medley of hill tribes of kindred origin, whose truculence and savagery long prevented its being opened up. The town of Mogaung has earned an unenviable notoriety as a penal settlement. Banishment to Mogaung was almost the greatest misfortune that could overtake a Burman official in disgrace under the old regime. Near it is the Indawgyi Lake, from which the Mogaung derives a portion of its waters, and a legend of the country tells the old tale of an ancient city at its bottom, suddenly engulfed. Soon after the union of the Mogaung and the Irrawaddy a new range comes prominently into view, broadening out into a beautiful amphitheatre of blue hills, at the foot of which the united stream must seemingly come to eternal pause. But the river makes a grand south-westerly sweep, and there presently becomes visible in the vicinity of the Shan-Talok village of Senbo, the great gorge through which it must pass, known in the nomenclature of the river as

THE FIRST DEFILE

Here in the shadow of the hills spreads a vast receiving-basin in which its waters must perforce stay their course, since the narrow and circuitous defile is all too small for the broad stream demanding imperious admission. At this, the winter season, the river threads its way far down amid the sands which in flood-time form the bottom of an immense lake. There can, indeed, be few more magnificent episodes in the life of a river than this. For when, swollen with melting snow and heavy rain, it rushes turbulently seaward in obedience to the first law of its being, it is here suddenly checked in its course by the iron hand of the mountains. Signs of its terrible recoil are evident on every side. The spectator standing under the barbed frieze of the military outpost near Senbo and looking down, first on the now quiet river and then across a yawning interval to the opposite heights, realises something of its greater life. Far above the present limit of its waters, to a height of eighty feet, marking the woods with an even line in testimony to its dominion, the river climbs in its session of wrath. In a single night it rises fifty feet, as though it would sweep the mountains before it, and at such times the defile within is a mad inferno of waters in which no boat can live.

For thirty-five miles the river flows through the mountains of the First Defile, whose rocky sides, torn and lacerated, lie bare in winter, the embodiment of savagery. This is more especially the case at one point, the most dangerous in the entire defile, where the black rocks rise sheer out of the river's bed, threatening destruction. Through them there has been cut a passage, now high above water-level, for the slow country boats, which formerly performed the perilous duty of carrying the mails in the flood season. From May to October the defile is entirely closed to steamers, and even for country boats the service is one of danger. The journey up-stream is then sometimes of three weeks' duration; the descent is a matter of six hectic hours, so fierce is the current. Strettell, who made both journeys at a comparatively quiet season, left of the journey up-stream the following account:

"The scenery throughout this defile is sublimely grand and picturesque, but in places awful to contemplate, as one stands watching the trackers, encouraging one another by fiendish yells that echo through the woods and straining every muscle to gain ground as the boat sluggishly quivers through the fierce rapids now running flush with the boat's gunwale. All now depends on the trueness of the towing-line: that gone and we are lost, for the best and strongest swimmer could not live in such places." Returning in March, three months later, the journey was even more fruitful of excitement: "The danger of the defile had in no way been exaggerated. Indeed, as we shot down the impetuous stream every moment seemed to be our last. It was with difficulty the helmsmen kept the boats from being carried round by the violent eddies and whirlpools, and the boatmen rowed their strongest against stream to reduce the terrific pace at which we were being borne by the fierce rapids. Our position was too critical to admit of accurate observation."

IN THE FIRST DEFILE

These are fearful joys to which the present-day traveller is not subjected ; yet, for the seeker after it, the swift delirium of a race down the river in its turbulent season is an attainable joy any time between May and October. The river, restricted in this portion of its course to a narrow rocky channel, assumes again, though in a less transparent degree, the pure green tint which characterises it at Myitkyina. On each hand the nobly wooded hills run down in *échelon* to the river's edge, and there is at all times that play of colour characteristic of hills piled behind one another in receding distances.

At frequent intervals the hills send down their tribute to the river in streamlets that babble over great polished boulders and gleam and sparkle in the sunlight. This is their season of security and charm. In the rain season their music swells to a deafening roar as they rush down in cataracts, bringing with them, in helpless chaos, boulders and trees and sand. Near the lower end of the defile the river, winding a narrow and sinuous course through the rocks known as the Elephant, Cow, and Granary, enters on one of its most exquisite passages. The rocks fancifully so named stretch across in a broken line from shore to shore. For half the year they are covered, but in winter they lie exposed, glistening in the sun and revealing the true width of the channel, here scarcely more than eighty yards across, but of unfathomed depth. Their sheer bare sides, of a polished grey-green hue, afford no footing for life ; but on their rugged summits the receding river leaves a thin deposit of rich silt, in which tussocks of vivid grass find a home, their lively beauty enhanced by their grim setting. In the days soon after the war, when the channel was less known, a small steamer came to a violent end amid these dangerous reefs, which in the flawless calm of a winter afternoon present an aspect of placid beauty.

Below the Elephant and Cow the little hamlet of Tamangyi shows out from the leafy hillside, and the river, freed from its iron fetters, lengthens out into a long dreamy reach in which the varied hills and woods and the opalescent clouds that trail like the pinions of another world overhead, attain redoubled beauty. A moment, and the dream sweeps by, the great curtain of the hills folds swiftly back, revealing a distant glimpse of the Shan mountains ; and the waters, sparkling in

THE ELEPHANT

the broad sunlight, seem visibly to rejoice at the termination of their long and arduous passage through the territories of the First Defile.

Few signs of life greet the traveller between Senbo and Tamangyi. An occasional boat or dugout, a thatched hut high up on the steep declivities, at the lower end some blue-coated Chinese Shan quarrying for stone, a rare pagoda ; such are the faint symptoms of man's dominion. For the rest, a startled otter on the rocks ; a white-headed fish-eagle

GREAT CLIFF IN THE SECOND DEFILE

with keen gaze intent on his prey ; a cormorant poised on a stake and drying his dripping wings with obtrusive philosophy ; a panther swimming hurriedly for life across the fast-flowing river ; the short, quick call of barking deer, or the sullen roar of a tiger making off, up one of the leafy watercourses. All else is loneliness and solitude.

Leaving the hills, the river spreads out to ambitious dimensions, and flowing past the site of ancient Sampenago, receives before it reaches Bhamo the tributary waters of the Taping.

THE SECOND DEFILE

A few miles below Bhamo the Irrawaddy, leaving behind it a great mass of mountains, the loftiest peaks of which are the possession of China, gildes into the gorge known as the Second Defile. There are no signs here of a vast accumulation of waters similar to that at the mouth of the defile above. The channel, broader and less obstructed, offers a more adequate highway, and the river is less turbulent in its entry. Yet on all sides there is grim testimony to its power in the pedestals of the surrounding hills, torn, contorted into the most fantastic patterns, and swept bare of every vestige of life to a height of thirty feet. It is this sense of conflict between elemental forces which, felt intensely here, makes the Second Defile a great spectacle of the world. Near the northern entrance a mighty cliff which turns its worn face to the river speaks with eloquence of the conflict. It rises sheer into the sky from the water's edge, eight hundred feet from its massive foundations made smooth by the constant friction of the speeding river, to the delicate clustering bamboos on its summit. Round its base graceful creepers climb and hang in festoons amid the branches of noble trees. A pagoda in miniature, one of the smallest of the myriads which taper heavenward in this land of religion, crowns the top of a small rock at its foot. Its diminutive size throws into relief the great rock seared with the stress of centuries, which towers majestically above it. An instinctive hush settles down on the ship as we race under its shadow, and there is deep silence in the gorge, broken only by the steady paddle-throbs which echo through it like mysterious heart-beats. In this battle-chamber of nature, stamped with the records of a long unceasing strife, the soul of the spectator shrinks into itself, finding no vent in the commonplace.

There is a legend attached to the great rock that is not unworthy of its tragic grandeur and beauty. It is a tale of the first king and queen of Sampenago, who were driven in a far-away day from their kingdom by Kuttha, the king's brother. The king, with true Buddhist philosophy, when he heard of his brother's advance forbade any resistance. To take life would be wrong and the issue must turn on the extent of his accumulated merit through all past existences. If this were great the threatened evil could not befall him ; were it small it could not be averted. So while the king turned to prayer and good works, his princes and generals stayed their measures for defence, until the usurper swept in on the tide of destiny and seized the kingdom. The king fled, but was pursued overtaken and cast into prison. The queen escaped to the enchanted mountain Wela, where a son was born to her in her sorrow.

When the little Prince Welatha (" son of Wela ") was six years old he saw his mother in tears and by questioning her learnt that he was a prince and his father a captive. When he was seven his mother yielded to his importunity and sent him with her royal ornaments to visit his father. On approaching Sampenago he met his father being led out to execution. The brave boy stopped the procession and revealed himself, offering to die instead of his father. The king Kuttha thereupon ordered him to be thrown into the Irrawaddy. *But the river rose in tremendous waves, the earth shook*, and the executioners could not for terror obey the royal order. This being reported to Kuttha, he ordered that the prince should be trodden to death by wild elephants; but the beasts could not be goaded to attack him. A deep pit was then dug and filled with burning fuel, into which the prince was cast: but the flames came on him like cool water, and the burning faggots became lilies. When Kuttha heard this he grew furious in his rage and had the young prince taken down to the spirit-haunted mountain and cast from the great precipice into the river, but he was caught up by a Naga and carried away to the Naga country. *The earth quaked, many thunderbolts fell, the Irrawaddy rolled up its waves and broke down its banks.* Kuttha was seized with terror, and as he fled forth from the city gate the earth opened and swallowed him up.

It is an interesting feature of many old legends that they enshrine the traditional knowledge of some ancient historical or natural fact, and there is perhaps in this pretty tale the record of some great convulsion, an episode of more than usual moment in the ceaseless conflict between the great river and its encompassing hills.

This, the place of the Great Cliff, is the finest portion of the Second Defile. Soon after leaving it the river sweeps round in more than a semicircle, to emerge once more in untrammelled splendour at the foot of a rounded hill tinted with reddening grass and not unlike an English down.

Below the defile lie the island and village of Shwegu, through the treetops of which gleam the golden spires of many pagodas, the centre of a great annual festival attended by many thousands of pilgrims. An island of green and gold set in the folds of a sunlit river fading away to steel-blue mist at the threshold of the mountains, on the summits of which an army of opal clouds is enthroned, Shwegu is thrice lovely.

Henceforth, till it reaches the Third Defile, the river's course is uneventful, save where, encircling many islands, it receives from China the many-mouthed homage of the Shweli. Yet it never ceases to be beautiful. At evening the sun sinks behind the clear-cut amethyst hills in a blaze of gold, and the hues of sunset pervade the still reaches, slowly changing like chords of some divine music till they pass imperceptibly away into the dusk of twilight. Later the stars shine out in the clear winter sky and their light, like quivering spear-points, plays on the face of the waters, hastening on to their union with the sea. The Great Bear climbing the heavens, points coldly northward, where imagination pictures the snows of æons lying on the summits of mountains on which man has left no footprint. Near by the lights of a small village die out one by one, and a great and brooding silence falls upon hillside and plain. It is midnight on the Irrawaddy.

THE THIRD DEFILE

Below the picturesque village of Malé, enclosed in a red-thorn stockade, the river for the third time in its course between the Confluence and the sea forces a right of way through hilly country. Malé was once the resting-place of a fugitive queen and for a short time served as a royal capital. In later days it was the Burmese customs-station on the upper river, and in the last days of 1885, when the kingdom of Burma was hastening to its end, a fleet of the king's warboats and steamers lay at anchor at Malé, in wild hopes of a French advent across the frontiers of Tonquin. But the French never came, and the last of the house of Alompra was already on his way into exile, followed by his weeping wife and a stricken court, before His Majesty's itinerant ambassadors in Europe had concluded their wanderings in search of an alliance. Leaving Malé, the river, confined between low hills, flows in tranquil splendour under the shadow of the Shwé-u-daung, whose bare peak and sharp declivities rise majestically into the sky like the Spanish sierras beyond Gibraltar. The Shwé-u-daung, nine thousand feet in height, is the outer citadel of that fortress of magnificent mountains in the chambers of which are treasured the finest rubies of the world. Sixty miles inland, in the beautiful Mogôk valley, are the famous ruby mines of Burma. The road was rough and steep in my days and for five months each year impracticable for wheeled traffic. At best it was hard going for the long trains of bullock-carts, which creaked and toiled along its ruts, laden with machinery for the mines and all the requirements of a colony of Englishmen planted in a secluded valley sixty miles from a highway of communication. But the traveller on horseback, lightly equipped, made the journey in two days.

Mogôk itself, surrounded by magnificent peaks like the Pingubaung, seven thousand feet in height and apt to be transfigured at sunset in a glow of red fire suggestive of their priceless contents, is unique in its seclusion and its world-known fame.

Below the village of Thabeit-kyin—the port of Mogôk, on the Irrawaddy—there is a charming island pagoda and monastery. Once, and it is not many years ago, the monastery was tenanted by an abbot and his monks and acolytes. Every year at a great annual festival the countryside came over in long boats and dugouts, and the pagoda platform was gay with the brilliance of a Burmese festival. Monastery spires and columns, the chapels of the Buddha, and the slopes of the island pagoda, were renovated and gilded with the lavish gold of Burmese Buddhism. In the still waters of the river between the island and the near shore, dogfish, tame and gentle from years of immunity, came each day to be fed by the monks, and at the year's festival to be decorated with leaves of gold by the followers of a religion the highest attribute of which is its tenderness for all created life. For the traveller the pagoda of Thihadaw, with its singular appanage, was one of the most interesting spectacles to be met with on the upper river. But a few years have wrought a change which is not without its symbolism. The island pagoda set in the heart of the Third Defile is still beautiful; but the fingers of decay are busy with its monastery roofs and spires. Its halls and closets lie empty and deserted. The waters of the river are slowly but certainly eating into the fence of wood and stone, built in an earlier decade to protect the island, and time must bring destruction, The monastery fish, no longer fed by its tenants, no longer protected by their presence from secular attack, have grown wild and timid, and no artifice will now induce them to come when summoned by the familiar call. It is believed that the island, consecrated to religion, can never be flooded, however high the river may rise. The pagoda is still firm on its base, its buildings are still habitable; and yet it is silent and untenanted. No one will say why. The old monks at Thabeit-kyin shake their heads and mutter impossible reasons; the fishermen of Thihadaw village say it is because their village has become small. An evil tale of war, which broods sadly over the deserted place, attributes it to another and a harsher cause. But whatsoever the cause the result is there, and in a sense it is symbolic of an inevitable decline. Fewer monasteries are built now than in years gone by; fewer scholars chant their lessons in the monastic schools; everywhere there is a loosening of the bonds of the great religious organisation which has ministered so long to the spiritual life of Burma.

THIHADAW PAGODA, THIRD DEFILE

At Thihadaw the defile grows to greater beauty. The single line of hills which has confined the river on each bank rises in height and breaks up into a greater variety of groups, through which the river wanders in long reaches and curves as placid and calm as untroubled slumber. At Kabwet village, where an enterprising German used to work the coal mines of the neighbourhood, the river emerges in a great curve from the midst of the higher hills and widens out, though still restrained for many a mile by low undulating country, beautiful in December with warm autumn hues, till, at Kyaukmyaung, the Third Defile quietly ends. The view, hitherto confined, now broadens out and far ahead on the river's horizon loom successive spurs of the Shan mountains towering in stately beauty above the distant city of Mandalay.

Here the great defiles of the Irrawaddy end. The river, leaving its infancy and hot strenuous youth behind it, settles down to maturer life, till at the delta still many hundred miles distant, its power is broken and lost in the ocean.

The present-day traveller in Burma is borne along the great highway under very pleasant conditions. For nine hundred miles the Irrawaddy is navigated by the steamers of the Irrawaddy Flotilla Company, most of which are well equipped with the comforts of civilisation. For purposes of rapid travel the fast mail-steamers are the more suitable; but for interest and local colour and for the insight they offer into the life of the people, the great cargo boats of the flotilla are to be preferred. To the gay light-hearted Burman, whose philosophy is perfect indolence, and to whom time is infinite in its opportunities for doing nothing, the speed of the express steamer is of no attraction. A Burmese village which treats the arrival of the mail-packet with calm indifference is plunged into excitement when the hoarse whistle of its slower fellow is borne up the river. On such occasions Sleepy Hollows where no one appears to have anything to do but doze in a comfortable corner or bathe in the cool river, attain to a ridiculous energy. For to every little village secluded from the great world beyond it, save in so far as it rests on the shores of the noblest of highways, the cargo-boats with huge flats in tow mean the advent of news, of gossip, and of trade, things especially dear to the Burman woman's heart. Each week they leave Mandalay, the centre of all things to the Upper Burman mind, for the long voyage up the river to Bhamo, and they bring with them all that a Burman heart can desire, all that a Burman village cannot furnish, from tinned Swiss milk and potted salmon to silk and pearls.

AFLOAT

The process is eminently simple. The cargo-boat and at least one of her flats are partitioned out into stalls which are let for the entire voyage, a matter of a fortnight, from Mandalay to Bhamo and back. But the stall-holders are wisely conservative and retain their stalls for years. In this way they build up a business connection and are well known in all the towns and villages along the river. Thus if the Headman, Moung Bah, of Moda village, wishes for a new silk *putsoe* of the fashionable dog-tooth pattern, or his wife a *tamein* of the new apple-green and pink tartan, or Ma-Hla, the village belle, a necklace of Birmingham pearls, they go down to the steamer landing, and with much detail describe their requirements to Ah Tun the Chinaman, or Sheik Ibrahim the Mohammedan trader, whose long grey beard contrasts strikingly with the hairless faces about him ; and in the fulness of time the " fire-boat," trumpeting its advent, brings to each of them his heart's desire.

The transaction, gratifying in itself, is made more so by time. Moung Bah's wish for a fashionable garment was probably inspired by an eloquent hint from the silk dealer, or a glimpse of a Mandalay dandy when the last boat passed through. A week's reflection eked out with clouds of green tobacco smoke and the enthusiastic advice of his neighbours, a calculation of ways and means, have brought him to a pleasant decision before the boat's return down-stream ; and then, the order given, there follows a period of blissful anticipation. If you are travelling up in the boat next voyage you will see Moung Bah sitting on his haunches on the high foreshore of Moda village, chewing betel-nut with apparent calm ; and when the boat is run alongside and the lascars plunge overboard into the river with a rope to make her fast, and the gangway planks are laid, Moung Bah will walk up gravely to the upper deck and enter into possession of his long-expected purchase. A period of further excitement will follow on his return home, when the fashionable garment will run the fire of domestic criticism and the loud praise of the village cronies. Business transacted under such conditions is laden with subtle charms for the Oriental. Time, the mere element of hours and minutes, is a thing of no account in a bountiful land where there are no paupers and no poor law ; in a smiling land where it is always afternoon.

The deck of a cargo-boat is itself a microcosm of Burmese life. Down the centre there is the long double line of stalls, back to back, each stall separated from its neighbour by a row of bales or boxes; and in the small square spaces between, the stallholders have their habitation. Here at all hours you see them seated on gay carpets, reclining on soft quilts, slumbering under silken tartans, flirting, gossiping, smoking contentedly, or playing animated chess. A Burmese game of chess is an unique entertainment. Everything pertaining to it is of massive proportions. The chessboard is of solid wood nearly two feet square ; the squares look gigantic ; the pieces, rudely carved, are made to stand hard usage, for the Burman throws a curious vigour into his play, each piece being brought down on the board with a sounding thwack. In addition to the players there is always a group of friends and self-constituted advisers round the chessboard. Each of these takes a keen interest in the game and pours forth his advice with great eagerness. The player, with an amiable superior smile, plays his own game, and when this is at variance with proffered advice each move is followed by long-drawn sounds of pessimistic regret and resolute head-shaking. One or two spectators who do not understand the game look on in silence, smoking their long green cheroots in a manner suggestive of deep and concentrated thought. The game, in short, is interesting, because there is so much human interest in it.

The flats in tow of a cargo-steamer are occupied as a rule by a poorer class of stallholders than those in the steamer itself. Silks, cotton goods, fur coats, socks, linen, china, pottery, ironware, and the gewgaws of vanity here give way to the necessities of life—to salt and onions, piles of imported flour, molasses in little rhomboids like toffy, sugar in crystalline heaps, baskets of potatoes, red and yellow chillies, and raw produce of the most bewildering variety. Most of the stallholders here are women. The atmosphere is wholly different from that in the adjoining steamer. The curtains are let down and a soft half-light pervades the flat. In the dim vista, broken here and there by bars of light in which the myriad motes riot, women lie asleep resting against soft flour-bags, or sit chatting in undertones in small groups. In this way the hours and weeks pass by, till they grow to years, and in some cases a lifetime.

CHAPTER IX

BHAMO

BHAMO, like the river on which it is built, lives a double life. In the rains its low grounds and pasture-lands lie flooded by the encroaching waters. Its tenements on the river's edge exist on sufferance, in imminent danger of being flooded and swept away. Its streets are moribund and squalid. One looks in vain for the famous trading-town on the border, the southern gateway of China, the traditional meeting-place of Chino-Burmese commerce. One looks in vain because the road to China, on which so many embassies have travelled, is impassable for caravans in the rains and Bhamo has perforce relapsed into a small and unimportant Burmese town.

But the approach of winter heralds a great change. Over the wild border-land through which winds the Ambassador's road, roughest of international highways, come the long caravans from China—thousands of hardy mules, hundreds of blue-clad labourers, and many portly merchants, filled out to abnormal size by dint of satin coats and furs, upon small ponies which amble hardily along. From the Shan States, north and east, come picturesque crowds of varied nationality, a permutation of Chinese Burmese and many-tribed Shan. And from the border highlands descend the cateran Kachin, to whom the Government now pays a fixed toll in lieu of the income they formerly derived by robbery murder and blackmail, from the traders who made their way

COOLIE LADS

along this dubious highway. Bhamo now breaks out into new life and colour, exchanging its moribund isolation for the concourse of many visitors, like any tourist resort in the season.

The centre of its life in one sense is the Court-house, where the administrative Power resides. Here, when he is not tramping over the hills with dynamite cartridges in his pockets, blasting roads, pursuing malefactors, and generally bringing home to the people in his charge the personality of rule, sits the Head of the District. Like most Englishmen in the East he is a man who plays many parts, and during the long hours of each day that he sits in the red-roofed Court-house he transacts a curious variety of business. Vendettas of many generations are healed here; thieves are sent to prison; murderers to death; frontiers are delimited; gun-licences are issued; tribute is brought to the coffers of the State; campaigns are planned; all indeed that concerns the administration of a frontier tract, from high politics to the parochialism of a petty municipality, is centred here in his person. Outside a miscellaneous life, the reflex of what is transacted within, has its being. A Sikh sentry, with bayonet gleaming in the sun, walks to and fro before the treasury; in the litigants' shed the witnesses are assembled; on the grass of the court-yard the harnessed mare of the Deputy Commissioner feeds complacently, aware of her privileges.

Burmans in silken kilts and flaming headgear, Shan in loose trousers and big straw hats, Kachin with naked swords, real Chinamen in felt boots and black satin caps, hybrid Chinamen in English hats, come and go in an incessant leisurely stream. And out on the white high-road a British soldier swings by, his shoulders square, his boots creaking, the silver head of his regimental cane glinting in the light.

About the Court-house lies the town. Here is the street of the Indians, a thoroughfare of tailors, industrious to the click of sewing

LANDING THE PASSENGERS

machines; of tinkers surrounded by their flashing wares; of small-store men; of dealers in cloth and haberdashers. At its corner there is a billiard saloon kept by a Jew. Beyond it is the market-place, the rendezvous of all strangers to Bhamo. There of a morning the country folk bring the produce of their gardens for sale. Laughter and high voices fill the air and the life of the many peoples is afoot. Along the stony highway the trader from Yunnan rides by in a fast amble on his shaggy steed. An almond-eyed porter, a man of thews and sinews, struggles slowly behind with a heavy load upon his back. One has seen his counterpart upon many a Chinese vase.

Outside the market one looks across to the white and grey walls and distinctive roofs of Chinese houses. In the space between, in hollows into which the river at its rising rushes in, Chinese market gardeners

BHAMO AT HIGH WATER

are toiling over rows of cabbages and beans. They go to and fro in their blue clothes and large sun-hats, with cans of water slung from poles across their shoulders. An ingenious bamboo spout in each can makes the water splash in large silvery jets. In all that a Chinaman does, and has, there is something distinctive, from the decoration of his house to the pattern of his pipe and the spray of his water-can. To understand him one must clear one's mind of all prepossession.

From the market-place it is an easy transition to China Street, the most important thoroughfare in Bhamo. A loud clatter of hoofs upon

DEPUTY COMMISSIONER'S HOUSE AT BHAMO

the stone pavement marks the approach of a party of traders, one of whom dismounts before a shop. A small lad running out leads off his stout nag with its tasselled trappings swaying about it, through a dark passage, to a stable hidden away in some presumptive backyard, while the man of trade, stretching his legs cramped by the short high stirrups of his people, yields himself up to the attentions of his wife, upon whose round celestial face there is spread a gratified smile. Crowds of his friends gather round him to hear the news, and there, seated on the floor of his counting-house, we may leave him in peace.

A more accessible person to-day is a leading member of the community, a plump figure of a man, whom I am just in time to stop as he is dashing off on his new bicycle to a meeting of the Town Council. He is dressed in a loose coat, trousers which are bound tightly about his ankles, a black silk cap, and white felt shoes; and he is portly, affable, and clean. He walks some way with me up the street to the handsome doorway of his house, with its carved front and fantastic eaves, and begs me to enter. In the narrow front-verandah, open to the street, bales of cotton are piled high against the wall, and a tired and dusty traveller from China is taking his ease. Passing in through the first room I enter a court open to the sky and arched over at intervals with roses. To come in here is to step into another and more delightful world, from the blazing thoroughfare without. Beyond it is the reception-room, with its lacquered furniture and its pictures hung upon the walls. One of these is a portrait done by a Rangoon photographer; another is a screen painted in water-colours, an exquisite study of pink flowers drooping over water. It was done by some far-away artist in civilised China. Tea is served in delicate porcelain cups; and cigarettes, the handiwork of my host's Burmese wife, are produced from an inner room by the lady herself. We sit in the lacquered chairs ranged stiffly against the wall with the formality of a French salon. Two of the more taciturn members of the party remain silent, smoking their long silver pipes; but my host is cheery and sociable and quite ready to talk. He explains that he and his two brothers are in partnership, and that the arrangement between them is that each shall spend three years, after an absence of six, in his

YUNANNESE

native town of Momein, in Southern China. They have houses at Momein, Bhamo and Rangoon. They deal in raw cotton and piece-goods, and import a variety of Chinese goods, including silk and felt. As to railways, they are very well and those that the Government has made are likely to do Bhamo no harm so long as they stop short at Myitkyina. Certainly there is no lack of brisk business in Bhamo to-day, and even as I sit here in the cool shelter of the inner court men go to and fro through the business premises, packing bales and studying invoices, and a stream of traffic passes down the sunlit street.

But city fathers have their duties, so bidding my host adieu I join the moving throng and glance as I go at the strange shops of chemists and of the dealers in felt rugs, and at crowded eating-houses, and the Chinese Secret Societies' Club, till I reach the entrance to the joss-house, a gateway in the roadside, opening into a long sunlit corridor paved with brick which ends at the door of the first court of the temple. Through its circle there is a full view of the joss-house, rising up from the shady court, all gilt and colour and winged roof. On each side of the porch there is a caparisoned horse, led by a splendid figure of a man, with a great waist, and Tartar eyebrows and a tremendous air. Horse and man are screened behind a circular window, richly carved in a pattern of rosettes. Overhead there is a theatre, where entertainments are given to the company assembled below.

THE JANITOR

There follows the second court, bounded at its far end by a temple in which strange figures are depicted, and incense burns perpetually. Through a narrow doorway behind the shrine there is a passage into the third court

UNDER THE CLIFFS OF BHAMO

and so on to the ultimate shrine, where on high there is raised a white marble figure of the Buddha. Extraordinary beings surround this central image, making of the place more a chamber of horrors than the shrine of a pure faith.

The joss-house is used as a club, and under the shelter of its trees in the open courts men with time upon their hands pass many hours of the day sipping tea and smoking their elegant silver pipes. Here, too, the opium smoker finds seclusion, and as I go by, where a young peach-tree is breaking into bloom, the very harbinger of spring, I find him lying stretched upon a sofa of polished vermilion lacquer, his glazed unconscious eyes half shut, dreaming the strange dreams for which he lives.

Outside of Bhamo lies Sampenago, the dead city which was great for a thousand years before Bhamo—the potters' village—came into existence. Pathways lead to it through the heart of the river-jungle, where the purple Taping, laden with the waters of Momein, steals through waving grasses to its union with the Irrawaddy. Aisles of old pagodas bring me to the Shwe-Kyina with its golden spire. Here the highland Shan encamp, and the smoke of their cooking fires climbs up into the placid sky. Beyond the red-gold and grey spires another path leads down through a wide tract of dog-roses in bloom to the edge of the Irrawaddy. The foreshore under the heights of the village is crowded with rose bushes which lie buried for half the year under the waters of the river, but in spring they become the home of thousands of little birds, whose melody fills the air with joy.

But it is the river that claims attention, for it lies here below the lofty bank, broad and beautiful, a highway of the world. The sun, nearing the horizon, is partially hidden by broken masses of cloud, through which his flame breaks in long ribbons and searchlights of fire. All the river, north of a clear straight line across it, lies in purple shadow; all to the south, in a blaze of light. I stand and watch the river porpoises

STRANGE GODS

plunging like steel in the oily water, the swallows wheeling in swift circles of flight; and the voices of men are borne up to me, dim at first, then swelling louder as they come by in boats, invisible under the cliffs, and so till they drift past into the silence. And I experience that strange and rare emotion of looking on at a world of which I form no part; a new world of blue mountains and wide river and placid calm and unknown peoples, into which I have dropped by some mysterious chance.

A SHAN

From Sampenago a sheltered way leads through the village of Wethali, where lives a colony of Assamese, the descendants of five hundred men-at-arms who came over in the reign of Bodaw-phaya with the brother of the King of Assam.

Among the races who throng during the winter months the streets of Bhamo town the Kachin, with his embroidered bag slung under one arm, his broad half-naked *dah* thrown across his back, is not the least conspicuous. He comes down from the hills with vegetables and fruits, and such sundries as a tiger-skin, some gold-dust, or a spinel picked up in a watercourse, and barters these in Bhamo for the civilised commodities he desires.

On the outskirts of the town, facing the highway, stands the Kachin Waing or caravanserai. It is not the kind of place in which Haroun-al-Raschid might have sojourned, for it consists of little more than an open shed in a yard enclosed by a bamboo fence. Yet it is possessed of a primitive interest. The Kachin, who carries his few necessaries with him, is content with such shelter as a bare roof may afford, and it is here in the Waing that he sleeps and feeds during his brief visits to the town. Sometimes I go out there in the early morning while the night mists still brood over the low pasture-lands of Bhamo, to see him making ready his breakfast. A small earthen pot is hung like a gypsy kettle over a fire of slender twigs, and seated before it, surrounded by the baskets of fruit and vegetables he has brought down to sell, he leisurely peels a pile of onions, dropping them one by one into the simmering pot in which a handful of small fry are already stewing. His fellow near him pares small faggots with dexterous *dah* strokes for the fire. From a basket of miscellaneous articles he draws forth neat cylinders of bamboo containing salt and condiments, and finally a short cylinder cut from the giant *wabo*, and containing drinking-water filled the previous day at a mountain stream. The sooty pot is then removed from the fire and the company settle down to their meal, with a savage, phlegmatic,indifference to observation. The same process is going on throughout the Waing, and I pass out by a small mat cottage at the gate (where a small clerk sits compiling trade statistics) with the feeling of having emerged from a bygone and primitive existence.

Far away at the other end of the town is the Shan Waing, even more primitive in the hospitality it offers ; for here the Shan and the Panthay who frequent it are all encamped out on the open plain. Yellow masses of straw lying scattered about contrast with the blue clothes of the muleteers at work, packing sacks with dried fish and salt. I see them there seated in the open, chatting and laughing hoarsely far into the night, in groups collected round blazing fires. Out of the dusk loom pack-saddles piled in heaps to make a shelter, and pack-animals herding close together from instinct. Overhead the stars gleam bright in the clear winter sky, and a few paces away the river flows darkly past, with a hurtling murmur against the high mud cliffs.

CHAPTER X

THE ROAD TO CHINA

PAST the Kachin Waing, and Bhamo Fort, where of nights the bugles blow and the King's health is drunk in regimental messes, the road to China takes its dusty way through a great forest of noble trees and dense underwoods, the blue mountains ever beyond. Here the long caravans defile, and strange people take their way—the tall Yunnanese on his saddle mule, the Panthay with his string of beasts led by the *gaung* with his clanging bell, the Shan with his red salt-laden cattle, the Kachin driving harnessed pigs to market, the trooper with his rifle at his saddle-bow and chain-armour on his shoulders, the Head of the District on his blood Arab, the little clerk with his pen behind his ear. Before some of those who travel to-day there lies a long rough journey into China. My own way is a shorter one—to Sinlum-kaba.

This place, with its long name, is the summer retreat from Bhamo.

THE ROAD TO CHINA

It stands upon a crest of the Kachin hills six thousand feet above the sea, and it is good to go out to, for it is a place with the atmosphere of a new world—a place of beginnings. Its wooded knolls are being cleared to-day, for the first time it would seem since time began ; an orchard of fruit trees—the pear, the cherry, and the peach—is growing up from plants brought from England, and this is their first season of flower. A garden of daisies, primroses, heart's-ease, and other gracious things is beginning to bloom. The little rivulets are being spanned by rustic bridges, the sound of saws and hammers floats across the valley, breaking the slumberous stillness with the music of man, the dwelling-maker ; nameless places are for the first time coming into possession of a name. The little men of the hills, who wear blue clothes and carry *dahs*, sword and axe in one, and distend their ears with amber tubes as wide as the barrel of an 8-bore, go to and fro, digging and blasting ; unspoilt children ready to take a lesson from the right man. And the right man seems to have come here to teach them the necessary lesson. "The Kachin," he says eloquently, "is of all road coolies that I have seen the best, for hill-roads at all events. Working on daily labour he will willingly do eight or ten hours' hard work a day, attacking a piece of rockwork or jungle-cutting with a furious energy, and signalising his success over obstacles with shouts of delight. He requires, however, to be handled carefully, sympathetically, and with perfect justice, or he is absolutely intractable."

On a knoll above a streamlet there is the military post, and a sentry walks to and fro before it through the hours. One can see the gleam of his bayonet a long way off in the noon sunlight. The silver flash of a heliograph on the hill links the settlement with the outer world. The air on a spring day is cool and mellow, the sun a friendly neighbour. But the nights are chilly, and towards dawn a great cold clutches the earth and quickens the air. The view from here stretches away in the west to the plain country, where the Irrawaddy winds in great loops and folds of silver and gold. One can see from this height how, coming from the north, it sweeps north again through the Second Defile, as if it never meant to reach the sea. And east and south and north there is a billowy sea of mountains half veiled in mist. The peaks of China climb up on the distant horizon, the border states of Hotha-Lahsa lie between, and here and there, alone on the wide sea, stand the British outposts.

Of the nature of life in these hill-tracts on the edge of China some curious particulars are recorded in the diaries of the British officers who travel over them every winter. Vendetta is the keynote of Kachin politics, and nowhere in the world is it carried to a more subtle point. One of the aims of the British administration is to stop such feuds and teach the hill-men the meaning of a central power. Yet year after year the vendetta goes on, and strange cases are chronicled in the Government annals. "On the 9th," I read, "the Civil Officer moved on to Sadasup. He had asked the Walawpum Duwa to meet him, but the latter regretted his inability to come, as he had lately raided 'Nong village and was expecting retaliation. This raid was in unadministered territory, but the history of it is worth recording. The Walawpum Duwa's younger

KACHIN POLICEMEN: FULL DRESS

KACHIN POLICEMEN: UNDRESS

brother had at the close of the last rains put up during a journey at the house of one 'Nlon-Lein 'Nong. On leaving, he had given offence to two women by mounting his pony in the porch. He dismounted, but again mounted at the *nat* stools; the women then cursed him and foretold his death for flouting their *nats*. On his return home he fell ill with fever, and it was evident to the Kachin mind that the curse of the 'Nong women was at work. Then the Duwa's general set off with sixty followers armed with thirty guns, attacked the 'Nong, burnt N'long-La's house to the ground, and killed two of his women. The spell, however, was not lifted and the Duwa's younger brother died."

Again: "Two sepoys deserted in 1892 and found their way into the Sana tract. They were promptly murdered, the reason given being revenge for the death of two relations of the murderers after they had been arrested at the instigation of the British authorities for the murder of Margary. It was admitted that the Chinese officials were directed to release these Kachins upon a representation by the English officer, to whom they were shown for identification, that they were not the persons wanted; but their death was due to their arrest and therefore indirectly to the energy of our representatives in pressing the Chinese for reparation."

The Kachin's contempt for life is only a little less acute than that of a Chinese officer for the life of any Kachin or similar barbarian.

KACHIN WOMAN WEAVING

The following is a refreshing example: "A Kachin named Saw Taw had lent four annas (four pence) to a Burman called Me Dain. Some time afterwards Me Dain went up into the Kachin hills, where he met Saw Taw, who asked him to repay the four annas. Me Dain told the Kachin not to bother him, and called him a dog. The Kachin went away, and coming back about an hour afterwards, speared Me Dain, who was sitting in a house with several others. Saw Taw was sentenced to death and executed."

Of the curious medley of duties discharged by the British officers who rule these tracts, some impression may be gathered from the following illustrations: "On November 13th, some twenty Kachins from Mutu came to Saingkin, eight miles from Bhamo on the Taping, murdered the headman's wife and carried off two of his daughters. The Deputy Commissioner went after the raiders with seven military policemen and the Myo-ôk, but owing to delay in information he started eight or nine hours behind them. He actually passed them, but it was then dark, and they got up and did not halt till they were over the border." (I well remember his hurried departure in pursuit, for I was in Bhamo that night.)

"A dispute between the Marus and Asis, which had long been threatening to come to open conflict, had to be finally disposed of. Some time back Mr. Rae and Mr. Todd-Naylor had ordered the Asis to remove the small village of Laban out of the territory of Mungkung

KACHIN BURYING-PLACE IN THE FOREST

village of the Marus; they had not done so, and encouraged by immunity and the presence of the Chinese, had been increasing the number of houses from other Asi villages. Mr. Hertz visited the place, had the village completely pulled down and removed and fixed the boundary beyond further dispute. He then returned to Pansibum and proceeded with the construction of the post. The establishment of the post at Pansibum is of high importance to the peace of the frontier tribes, the Asis, and it enables us to get behind nearly the whole of the Kachins, both present and future, north and south of the Namsiri valley.

"On January 16th, Mr. Rae started again from Bhamo with a reduced escort of twenty-five men to Sinlum-kaba. Mr. Rae, who had been interviewing the neighbouring Kawri chiefs, devoted his attention to the constant cattle thefts for which these Kachins are responsible. The northern Kawris, owing to their proximity both to the Chinese frontier and to the plains about Bhamo, had become increasingly daring cattle thieves, and fining and punishment had proved ineffective. Great assistance was received in the work from the Duwas of Sima, Hoton, Sinlum-gale, Lawmun, and Mantan, especially by the first named, an influential and loyal man. The result was that thirty-four cattle and ponies were recovered and twenty-eight persons convicted and punished for cattle theft, and it is hoped that the traffic will have received a crippling blow."

And of the *raison d'être* of Sinlum-kaba, this place where the daisies and heart's-ease are growing to-day through the generosity of its founder, and the peach and the cherry from English stock are coming into bloom, there is this account in the official annals : " It is evident now that the Kachins in Bhamo have realised that they have found their masters, and are prepared to settle down into law-respecting, if not law-abiding subjects. Government by column has now died a natural death ; the time for that has passed, and what we now require is to impose a form of yoke which will be found to press lightly, but firmly, and above all continuously. To bring this about it is desirable to make the hill tribes conscious of a presence constantly in their midst, instead of the bright meteoric passage of a column, leaving increased darkness behind it. We require to establish a permanent centre for enlightenment and domination, to which Kachins will be able to come without obstruction from all parts and at all times. Instead of having to undergo, whenever they have a complaint to make, the expense and discomfort of a visit to Bhamo, where heat and dust and alien surroundings make the Kachin wretched, and he wastes day after day at the court, fleeced by petition writers, and worried by Burman underlings, he wants to have a court held by a sympathetic official, who knows his language well, and to which he can go without ever leaving the shelter of his hills."[1]

[1] These words are taken from a report by N. G. Cholmeley of the Indian Civil Service, who founded Sinlum-Kaba. Since his day the administrative border has advanced, and the Pax Britannica established throughout the hills ; the tribesmen recognising in the Englishman a strong but a just master whom he can respect.

Book IV

THE SOUTHERN IRRAWADDY

The Lower Courses—Prome—To Thayetmyo—A Side Issue—To Minbu—The River in Action—Mud Volcanoes—To Yenan-Gyaung—The Road to Pagan—Tangyi-Sway-Daw—Above Pagan—In Mandalay

CHAPTER XI

THE LOWER COURSES

"*It was impossible not to ask oneself when looking on that splendid stream: Can it fail to become, before many years are past, one of the great highways of the world, though so lately unlocked for the real entrance of Commerce, and still but imperfectly set free? Of what trade may it not become the channel? To what nations may it not open the way, along whose coasts we are now vainly seeking an entrance that is denied us? What new power, arts, knowledge, and religious truth may not crowd upwards within a few years along this magnificent avenue?*"

Marquess of Dalhousie.

THERE is a break in the rains: it is mid-August, and we are steaming serenely up the narrowing waters of the Hlaing, that branch of the Irrawaddy on which Rangoon is built. The capital already seems far away and the true Burma is unfolding before my vision. The air blows free here over the wide fields, green with the young rice; the little villages deploy on the water's edge; the beautiful long boats of the people lie at anchor like ships of vikings, or drawn up ashore—*siccas machinæ carinas*—mingling in the landscape with the gardens and the palms and the brown house-tops.

Here the spires of lonely monasteries cleave the air, the monks go by in small canoes, under a nimbus of yellow glory shed by their parasols; the nets of the fishers spread their toils on the face of the river or loom up like inky shrouds over the verdant fields. Here the sailing-boats speed by and the white gleams of their sails flash over the country-side as they sweep along their secret highways invisible to the eye. They look very beautiful, and a little mysterious, for the creeks lie low below the level of the fields, and the great sails only pattern the air. One can follow in this way the winding of a creek, although one cannot see it, and for my part I am never tired of tracing the white flash of their wings as they speed over these hidden inland waters. The river banks are gay at intervals with vast plantations of the Dhanni palm, whose green and orange blades curve and shimmer under every breath of the passing wind. But a full hour is accomplished before the ship gets clear of the suburbs of Rangoon, and into the heart of the country.

Near Rangoon itself there is a different picture, scarcely less attractive; for the river pulses there with the life of a great maritime city. Tugs with the heart of Leviathan throb gallantly on their way; cargo-boats heavily laden, move slowly; sampans creak for ever up and down the channel, bobbing on the waves like gulls; rice mills, immense and stately, with the old-fashioned air of Dutch houses, tower

FULL SAIL

up like amphibians from the edge of the water, their pent and gabled roofs glistening with yellow dust. Clouds of dark smoke trail away from their lofty chimneys, dun cataracts of husk pour incessantly from their waste-pipes, and all the river crinkles with laughter to see the stuff floating helplessly away to sea. Long before the outlines of the first great chimney become visible one can tell that one is nearing the city from the husks that go drifting by. Some day a man will find out a way of turning these husks to gold, and then he will grow rich and return to his own country, and the river will be carpeted no more.

From the mills the river banks slope down to where the *peingaws* and the *hnaws* ride buoyantly at anchor, and a living stream of men flows to and fro between. Very swiftly the rice is borne away from their holds

ALL SAILS DOWN

and cast into the agony of the mills, thence to emerge only for its long voyage to the West. And these men at work look from the ship as she sweeps by like some colony of ants industrious on a sunlit morning.

Over all this world of detail, over all the throbbing fretful life of the river there gleams the golden bell-top of the Shwe Dagôn, serene, majestic, almost divine, and it is the last object upon which the eyes rest before the ship, swinging out of the main river, enters the narrower channel of the Panhlang.

As we move on, the minor incidents of travel unfold themselves, each with its inner significance. I note the superiority of the iron-roofed monasteries over the humble tenements of the peasantry; and the prominent house of the Chinaman, pushing his way to fortune. The Burman folk plough through the slush to the river's edge, the Chinaman makes for himself a wooden causeway. I note the signboard of the public-house, here in the rural part of the country, with its symbols, a scarlet tumbler and a black bottle; the police stations of yellow, loop-holed masonry, and the villages, each like a little ruddy-purple island in a vast wind-ruffled sea of green. Creek after creek leads inland to other centres of life, and vistas of shining palms and winding water-courses flash before my eyes.

Gradually the face of the landscape changes, the river passing slowly from a tidal creek to an inland water. No longer does my vision range over vast deltaic spaces. The mightiest trees, dark, cumulose, and splendid, clothe both banks of the river, marshalling its progress. Miles of glistening plantains follow its curves, and hedges of tall river-grass wave over the lips of the water. There is, in spite of tropic exuberance, a regularity and order in the scenery which give it a park-like character. Red villages appear at intervals between the river and the lines of trees, and as the ship goes by little children bare as Adam in his better days, dance and clap their hands and mimic the droning chant of the leadsman as he calls the deeps of the channel. The more curious of the village folk come out of their houses to look at the passing show and make remarks about the white man on the steamer. These are nearly always women.

Returning rice-boats, high out of the water, lie at anchor, waiting for the tide to take them home, while others with bellying sails and holds full to the brim with rice, go gallantly down to their traffic with the world. A stray launch sends her shrill whistle down the lane of waters, bringing a bevy of laden boats in her wake. Flags and streamers flutter in the air, and slow grey rafts of timber, the produce of primeval forests, float down the yellow stream. It is yellow and thick with loam, and far away on the fringes of the ocean it is building up a new world as in bygone days it built up all that the eye now rests upon here.

Through the gaps in the endless avenues which line the river's banks I get a glimpse of the world of tropic splendour that lies beyond. Heart-shaped creepers cluster up the giant trunks of trees, parrots shriek, and kingfishers tremble in the air. An added richness of colour comes with the afternoon. The trees in shadow gather new depths of green, and look as if they were cut in velvet ; the slant sunlight falls with a new glory on the opposite shores, and the face of the river grows beautiful with a lustrous calm.

I cease to ask the names of villages as they pass by, to take account of the passing hours, to count the miles. Nothing seems here of much account beside the dreamy endless river ; nothing of any consequence at all in this El Dorado of peace.

A climax comes with the setting of the sun. At this season of the year, when the sky is not overcast with rain, this last hour of the day is inexpressibly beautiful. The river turns to a flood of gold, and the marble clouds become transfigured in mysteries of light. It would be useless to attempt the description of so much glory in words, the "shadows of a shadow world."

Lastly there comes the night, and the crickets cheep from the thickets and the frogs croak from the marshy fringes of the river. And here it may be noted that this paradise breeds the largest and most virulent mosquitoes in Burma. "At this place," wrote an ambassador of England a hundred years ago, "we spent a very comfortless night ; it is a part of the river remarkable for being infested by mosquitoes of an unusual size, and venomous beyond what I ever felt in any other country ; two pair of thick stockings were insufficient to defend my legs from their attacks." As long as the steamers run at full speed the draft made by their movement keeps the enemy at bay ; but the grinding of the anchor chains is a signal for attack, and he invades in hordes. The slow-moving boats of the country fare worst, but a night in the Panhlang creek is an experience that all travellers willingly avoid.

YANDOON TO PROME

Some time in the dawn we pass up by Yandoon (rendezvous of all the boats that bear the Irrawaddy trade and chief depôt for the sale of stinking fish) into the main eastern branch of the great river. It is wide enough here and splendid enough to rank by itself as a river of the world. No longer is it possible to shout across it from bank to bank. It loses much of its winding beauty, its hedges of giant grass, its avenues of stately forest. Its sweep is too wide to be compassed at a glance, or measured by the eye. Immensity is now its chief characteristic. It trails away from one end of the misty horizon to the other ; it dominates the entire landscape, and conveys the impression of a world of waters.

As we near Donabyu there is a village on our right protected by embankments against the flood. All along here these embankments exist, and the bed of the river is being slowly lifted above the level of the surrounding lands. Some day the river will burst its bonds and produce great catastrophes.

The little village is graced with a small pagoda covered with new gold. On the foreshore the village boys play at "Association" football with such a degree of vivacity and animation as only the laziest people in the world are capable of. Sometimes the football falls into the river, where it bobs helplessly to and fro till it is rescued and sent back ashore with a

CROSSING THE CREEK

kick from a naked toe. The village cattle and the village dogs reflect in their appearance the general prosperity. Wealth is stamped upon every feature of the landscape, and there is room for many millions more than there are at present to share it.

On the farther shore lies Donabyu, its importance marked by its golden pagoda and its long lines of iron roofs. Facing it is one of the many low-lying islands engulfed by the river in its flood season. It is covered with a dense forest of river-grass, which bends under the breeze, and is blown about like the tresses of a girl. Here as all along the river the *peingaws*, drawn ashore and loftier than the houses, or propelled by twenty rowers, or flying like great birds up the river with the gale behind them, are the feature of every landscape and objects of perpetual interest. Burmese craftsmanship has produced nothing to surpass them.

REAPERS AT DONABYU

Donabyu (White-Peacock Town) has played its part in history, and one cannot pass it by without thinking of the brave Bandoola, who tried all in vain to stem the tide of British invasion. Rangoon had already fallen and the hopes of the country were centred in the little town with its fortress and its garrison of fifteen thousand men.

"The main work," as the historian tells, "was a stockaded parallelogram of one thousand yards by seven hundred, which was on the bank well above the level of the river. On the river face were fifty cannon of carious calibre, whilst the approach on the land side was defended by two outworks. General Cotton's force carried the first stockade at the point of the bayonet, but was repulsed from the main work, Captains Cannon and Rose being killed and the greater number of the men killed or wounded. General Cotton then retreated down the river waiting for reinforcements. Sir Archibald Campbell, the Commander-in-Chief, who was advancing north up the valley of the Hlaing, fell back, established his headquarters at Henzada and proceeded down the river. On arrival before Donabyu he constructed batteries of heavy artillery, the enemy making numerous sorties with a view of interrupting the work. When the batteries were completed they opened a fire of shot, shell, and rockets, and next day the Burmans were discovered to be in full retreat. This was subsequently found to be due to the death of Bandoola, who had been killed by the bursting of a shell."

Again, a little later, a Dacoit chief held for a little while a British force at bay at Donabyu. But the tale is an old one fading swiftly into the past. The rice-fields in their season wave yellow in the midst of Bandoola's entrenchments, and a grave or two and lines of grass-covered ramparts are all that survive of that episode.

Two hours north of Donabyu there become visible for the first time the blue outlines of those hills which henceforth to the uttermost northern frontier are never absent from the landscape. At noon the river spreads over immense areas, encircling islands and flooding the low-lying tracts. At two o'clock it still continues immense, but is less scattered. Numerous villages deploy on its banks, many of them large and flourishing. But a village here makes in truth but a small feature in the landscape, little more than a line between vast spaces of cloud-emblazoned sky and dun water. Palmyras mark its presence and the tapering spires of pagodas and monasteries lift it up to some little dignity. Women clad in the one garment that does not detract from their natural beauty, come down with their pitchers to the water, and the children clad in nothing, plunge into it and swim, as happy and as much at home in the bountiful river as they are on land.

The colours at this season (August) vary with the rain, which comes down in purple sheets, blotting out whole tracts of the horizon, while

From a painting by J. Raeburn Middleton

A LADY OF QUALITY

the sunlight pours and flames on the rest of the circle. The only monotony is that of space.

As we near Henzada, the apex of the Delta, the river makes a splendid curve and the waste of waters looks like the opening of a sea.

At Henzada the people are busy at prayer and the chant of the worshippers is borne in measured cadence over the dark face of the river. Within, the raised highways are lined with the trays of Burmese maidens, whose clear brains were meant for the business of life, as their eyes, dark and lustrous, were assuredly meant for love. Near at hand the rollicking Chinaman does a roaring trade at the eating-houses and liquor-shops. Small boys play at marbles on the highway in the thick of the traffic. The wind blows where it lists, amongst the stately palms and the tinkling summits of monasteries and fanes.

The late evening brings us to Myanoung. And this is what Myanoung looks like at evening, on a day in the rainy season.

Lofty embankments protect it from the river floods. Tall palms rise up in procession about these highways, and cluster in stately groups beside the water. The embankment highway escaping from the tenements, cleaves its way through the country-side parallel to the river. Marshy hollows, the relics of some inundation, flank it on the one side, a muddy cattle-track scored with the hoof-prints of the driven beasts runs below it on the other. Vast spaces, emerald-green with rice, stretch away to the foot of the blue mountains which shut out the western sea from the home of the Burman. Up there in their fastnesses elephants in herds roam unmolested through the primeval forest, the sambhar bellows in the dense thickets, the tiger and the panther stalk their prey, and the stray Chin alone stands for the supremacy of man.

The scene that is thus unfolded before the eyes is one of distinct beauty ; a feast of colour in its way. The sky, laden with heavy rain-clouds, runs the whole gamut of the spectrum. But when the sun goes down and the clouds chance to gather in an unbroken canopy overhead they become a burden upon the spirit. The world grows small, the motionless air lies heavy on the lids of earth, the soul of the spectator is prisoned within the universal gloom. It is at such times that the white man, whose destiny has brought him here, feels himself an alien and alone. The merry people, the blue hills, the shining river, are phases only of his exile. Pestiferous insects fall in hecatombs into his food and leave their malodorous trail in his hair. Vicious ones inflame the tender places on his skin. The dank air creeps into his blood, the loneliness sours his heart and breaks his nerve. Tinkle of pagoda bells, rustling breezes in the palms, the murmur of the river ; what are these but aspects of an endless monotony ? He would give them all for the sound of an Englishwoman's voice, the sight of an English pasture-land in spring.

Myanoung, like most of the towns along this portion of the river's course, stands on the right bank; for it is this right bank which is most protected against the river floods. At Myanoung the present Delta is strictly at an end, but it may be said to extend to the cliff of Akouk-taung, which juts out into the river like the ram of a man-of-war some miles farther north.

The cliff of Akouk-taung has an interest that corresponds to its striking appearance. The name implies the "Customs Hill," and it is the universal tradition in Burma that in bygone, but still historic days, it marked the limit of the sea and the point at which the Customs dues were levied. It stands three hundred feet out of the water, and its scarped face is riddled with caves, containing images of Gautama, the

SOLID-WHEELED COUNTRY CART IN THE DELTA

Buddha, and the members of the Sacred Order. Twice during the second war it was held in force by a grandson of Bandoola, and was carried by storm by the British troops. Here under the massive ledges the stream of the river runs very swiftly, and as we pass under it the throbbing steamer makes slow progress. Buffaloes swimming across the swiftest part of the current are borne away like matchwood. Above Akouk-taung the river is flanked by hills on both its banks, and in the vista between lies Prome, a dark headland protruding into the waters.

The city upon nearer approach presents an attractive appearance. Its green banks are shaded by an avenue of trees, each of which is a beautiful object in itself. A broad road with white railings runs parallel with the water—the King's highway from Rangoon to Prome. Behind it, through masses of green foliage, peep out the dark red roofs of European houses. The river, with no licence to spread its waters, flows here in one broad deep stream, full up from shore to shore. All along the west the sky-line is broken by a range of hills whose slopes are laid out with custard-apple orchards ranged with the regularity of the vine. As the sun comes out from under the grey clouds, and shines on the ripples of the river, on the grassy slopes and spreading foliage, there is created an impression of indescribable cheeriness, and all that one looks upon promises well of the city.

CHAPTER XII

PROME

BETWEEN the river and the road is the little club of Prome, with its white tennis court outside and its tables within, spread with pictures and papers from England. Once a week to this serene little island of European life there is brought the news of a greater world than is contained within the seas of Burma. Beyond it, on the ram that juts into the river, is the house of the District Magistrate. It is flanked by a lofty court-house, where all day long the business of empire is transacted ; the punishment of one, the lifting up of another, the assessment of revenue, the weighing of money in the treasury scales, the writing of those letters, reports, and tabulated papers, whose turgid volume is slowly swallowing up the instinct of Imperial rule ; for the East loves a Man.

Overlooking the pleasant roadway stand, almost beyond recognition, the tree-clad remains of two gryphons that once marked the water-gate of the city. Beyond these the river spreads out to a vast circular sheet of water, restrained only by the embankment, along which the highway runs. A few paces bring one to the bazaar, that centre of life in every Eastern town. Outside, under the green boughs of the gold *mohur* and the *padouk*, there is a colony of large yellow umbrellas fixed in the soil under which there sit the fruit and vegetable dealers driving a brisk trade.

They love, these delightful souls, to sit out here in the fresh morning, and willingly take their chance of sun and rain. Laughter and joy are in the air, cheeriness is writ on the faces of the passers-by, there is colour in every detail. The scene is interesting by the hour. How different to its Indian fellow of the same name, in the happy laughter-loving note that brightens its life !

The great iron building which spreads its wings above the *al fresco* shops is more favoured by the dealers in silks and shawls, in Birmingham trinkets and the embroidered trappings of horses. For an iron building in the British style, it is not wholly bad ; two quadrangles lie open to the sky and they are full of shrubs and grasses ; and under the iron the long aisles of stalls are tenanted by the prettiest girls of Prome. They come here in the early mornings one by one and open their stalls, shaking their silks to the light, till the whole rich interior is filled with the shimmer of the beautiful fabric ; with the glint of pink and green *pawas*, of gorgeous *gaungbaungs*, of layers of many-hued *putsoes* ranged in order on the shelves, and coils of the soft raw silk, vivid and beautiful.

In the midst of this fairy-land of colour the daughters of the city pass the day ; here they sit and slumber, make ingenuous toilets before the

"PEINGAW" SAILING UP-STREAM

world, gossip and play and flirt, and learn more of life and human nature than many more important people. They are gifted with the clearest vision ; and there is no shrewder trader, no keener judge of character, no wittier person of her age and sex than the girl who sits here in a silken glamour, with *thanaka* on her face and a flower in her hair. And yet a stall here is seldom taken up as a purely business speculation. Its attraction lies in this, that all men come sooner or later to the silk bazaar.

Outside the roads are lined with rich avenues of trees and houses, most of which are neat and attractive. Flowers are grown in front of the doorways ; here a cluster of roses, there a line of pink and yellow balsams. In front of one house, making a cool green screen between it and the road, is a trellis work of posts covered with the betel-vine. It is the house of Saya Pah, maker of the gold lacquer-ware for which his town is famed. It is lifted high on posts and he meets me at the foot of his stairs *shekoing* on his knees. I cannot discover any servility in the attitude or in the action as he performs it. It seems to me suggestive only of good manners. The old man, whose face is that of an artist, is clad only in a waist-cloth and is unashamed. Why should he be ashamed?

PROME

His daughter, a pretty girl of sixteen, laughingly shakes hands—English fashion. Timidity and self-possession make a little battle in her face, but she is a woman to her finger-tips, and her father's kneeling attitude throws no shadow on her self-respect. Upstairs, in the large living-room, with its bedsteads and mosquito curtains, Mah Soo, the wife of the Saya, meets us, a picture of what pretty girls in Burma come to; fat and round of face, with a calm eye and no illusions; dowager-like. There is no mystery in a Burmese house, and the Saya welcoming me within, takes me beyond this room into another narrower, but more cheerful, in which he works at his art. A Burmese harp, worked in with a graceful pattern in black and gold, is on the stocks, and beyond it there is a *karaweik* bird glinting with fresh mosaic. The old man, stooping to show respect, explains that the body of the harp is cut from the *padouk* tree, and the curving bow of it from the *acacia catechu*. The sounding board is of varnished deer-skin, and the strings are of twisted silk. Tea-tables for European customers, and manuscript boxes illuminated with stories from the Zats, for use in the monasteries, are amongst the objects upon which the Saya lavishes his skill.

Beyond this simple *atelier* there is a balcony decked with roses and

JACK FRUIT

open to the sky. High above it cluster the broad leaves of palm-trees, between whose dark boles there is framed a beautiful picture—the red roofs and climbing spires and great gold bulb of the Shwe San Daw Pagoda. It is here that the Saya when he is resting from his labours pays his devotions. It is a serene and beautiful oratory in which any man might pray.

The Saya is growing to be an old man now and the things of the spirit are increasingly with him. One can see the change in his eyes, in the gentle inflexion of his voice, and in the subdued tones of the silken skirt he wears when he goes abroad. Fame has come to him in her devious way. She has brought him framed diplomas from exhibitions in Calcutta and Rangoon, which he hangs upon his walls. He is ready, he says, to take any orders the *thakin* may be pleased to give him. His wife, a practical soul, is more direct.

"What," she inquires, the betel trickling at her lips, "has His Worship come to buy?"

But there is no pressure, no solicitation; least of all any trace of that covert discourtesy with which some shopmen frighten sensitive people into purchasing goods they do not desire. These good people are well bred in their way; there is a Viennese politeness about them: the Graben could do no better.

A DAUGHTER OF THE SOIL

Some little way from Saya Pah's in another quarter of the town, I enter the house of a Kathé weaver, where, in the squalid gloom, rich patterns grow into beauty on the silken looms. It is not easy to distinguish between a Kathé and a Burman, but close observation reveals a difference, some elusive hint of race, rather than any marked difference of feature. Many generations ago the ancestors of the Kathé were brought here, prisoners of war, to Burma, and they are now of the soil. But they still talk the Manipur tongue, the language of their forefathers, and they employ a teacher of their own to teach their children how to write it. The old weaver who speaks is a taciturn and gloomy man, and the burden of his talk is of a decaying and unprofitable industry.

"Twenty years ago," he says, looking in the dust—"twenty years ago I sold a hundred *putsoes* where now I sell ten."

He will vouchsafe no explanation; but he knows it is due to the competition of cheaper Western fabrics, and the passing away of the Royal court.

It is a poor-looking quarter, this famous quarter of the silk-weavers of Prome, and there is a whole street of Kathés. Seeing that they are of the Hindu persuasion, it is no long way from them to the house of a Brahmin. The master is away at Rangoon; but his wife, a comely woman, receives me. She laughs, and says that if I am going to photograph her, she must go in and change her dress. Her husband keeps the school for the Manipuri children. She looks like a Burman, but states that she and her people keep to rules of caste, and only marry within the proper limits. Buddhism has at least taught her to come out from darkened chambers into the sunlight of life.

I go from her to the house of a painter and find him busy with his assistants over a large canvas destined for a theatre. He does a considerable business in portraits, which he achieves by painting splendid backgrounds and fine clothes and putting in for the face a photograph. This compromise is eminently satisfying to his customers, and it is certain that an air of reality is imparted to the photographs by their curious setting.

Burmese art is still in its infancy ; but it has this of merit at least, that it is alive. A Burmese painter is quite prepared to grapple with any subject, from a sunset to a buffalo fight. Crude as his efforts are, it has always given me pleasure to come into contact with the Burmese painter. For he has the true spirit of the artist. He will come when you send for him to your house, clad in his best silk *putsoe* and whitest muslin coat (his manners being the fine manners of his race), and he will *sheko* and crouch down on the floor and carry himself as if he had been brought up at court. His air will be one of the gravity that befits ceremonial occasions, and he will say *phaya* (" my lord ") at the proper intervals. But gradually as the plan you put before him unfolds before his vision, a light will come into his eyes, a new pose into his stooping figure. He will enter enthusiastically into your proposals, and vow to accomplish a picture that will please you. He is always quite sure that he can do what is wanted and that he can do it better than any of his contemporaries. And sometimes he will do it, and sometimes he will not (for the ardour cools) ; and nearly always you will have to wait a long time and send him delicate reminders before he will bring it to completion.

Perhaps the best painter in Burma is Saya Chone of Mandalay. He has painted several pictures for me, and upon all of them he has inscribed in gold the cryptic symbol " No. 1." I believe that he means it to refer to the excellence of his work. But the last time I saw my friend in Mandalay he was gloomy and dejected. His ardour did not equal mine for the production of a picture of the Let-dwin-Mingala, that beautiful festival of the Kings of Burma which took place once a year, when they went out in the spring-time with a pair of white oxen in harness of gold to plough a furrow outside the Royal capital.

" You are not yourself, my friend," I said. " Is it not well with you ? "

" It is ill with me," he answered. " Art does not pay. I will become a trader in rice."

THE BURMESE HARP

And then he talked of the disinclination of people to buy pictures and pay for them, of the decline in Phôngyi-Byans (the monk-burnings), at which of old his pictures found a market.

" Now, rice, sir," he said, " is a much more profitable business ; but the Let-dwin-Mingala is a good subject, and I will paint it for your honour."

This he eventually accomplished.

Passing on by a neighbouring silversmith's, where dragons and elephants are shaping into form on the bulging sides of bowls and betel-boxes, I enter the Chinese quarter. Shoemakers are numerous here, and the produce of their toil is exported a long way from Prome. There

BURMESE PAINTING
An abduction. Policeman to the rescue. The groom offers a bribe

is no creature on earth more industrious than the Chinese cobbler, and you will see him all over Burma, from dawn to midnight, in the gloom of his shop, a stooping yellow figure with awl and needle in hand, surrounded by a host of shoes. There are two joss-houses in Prome, representing the two sections of the Chinese community, those Long-coats and Short-coats who live apart and do not love each other. In one of these a number of Chinese lads are at school, painting alphabets with laborious care and astonishing skill. No pen can compare for suppleness with the Chinese brush. A grey monolith within the walls records in letters of gold the names and contributions of the builders of the temple. Its roofs and eaves are richly ornamented with figures of men and animals. The other joss-house is in a different style ; double-storied, like a private house, and it opens on the street. Within two men are lying on tables, lost in opium dreams; huddled figures unconscious of the world. A third, who is cheerily at work, plaiting a basket, makes me welcome. Upstairs there is an altar, and there are some fine paper lanterns large enough to hide a man in. Adjoining this temple is a lofty building, the dwelling-house and place of business of the opium farmer.

WOOD-CARVING

A pleasanter spectacle awaits me at the house of a cigar-maker. A number of laughing girls stand outside, very daintily dressed, and the whole front of the house is scarlet with the tasselled hibiscus. Within lie the materials for the day's work, the raw tobacco and the broad leaves in which it is to be wrapped. All the work is done by hand and nearly every girl in Burma can roll a cigar. The indigenous article is a monster eight inches long, consisting of chopped wood, tobacco, molasses, and various herbs, wrapped in the silver-white skin of a bamboo; and so wide in diameter that it completely fills up the mouth of any young damsel who tries to smoke it. For presentation purposes this long cheroot is often wrapped at one end in a coat of purple or gold paper. It accumulates a formidable mass of fire at the lighted end and requires some skill in the smoking. But the Burman infant acquires this skill before he can walk, and while he is still at the breast. No one thinks of smoking such a cigar through. Two or three long puffs, the lips of the smoker thrust out to meet the circle of the cigar, and it is put down or passed on to some good fellow sitting by. This old-fashioned cheroot is gradually giving way to the cigar of rolled tobacco and the trifling cigarette.

Leaving now the thoroughfares of the town, I climb by red stairs and narrow lanes, under the shelter of yellow-hearted *champaks* to the summit of the hill that dominates the city. Here half a century ago the British battalions were quartered ; but traces of their occupation have all but passed away. Here on the camping grounds the red cattle now graze, the partridge calls, and the hare finds a shelter for her young. The roadways are choked with tropical thickets. A great view spreads away over the heads of the dark palmyras and dense woods to the cloud-embattled horizon. The river, very broad, lies at one's feet, trailing away in the south to the spurs of the Pegu hills and the ram of Akouk-

A PICTURE SHOW

taung. One can look over the crest of the opposite hills, patterned with orchards to the distant blue of the Arakan Yoma. A fresh air, of which there is no hint down among the tenements, blows about the summits, and one realises that here, if anywhere in Prome, is the place to live. The prospect is so cheerful that every one who comes to Prome should climb up here to look upon it. The traveller along the river levels, beautiful as they are, can form no idea of the world that expands from every one of the peaks that crown the valley of the Irrawaddy.

Half-way down the hill on the further side, under the spreading boughs of a bombax, there is an open *zayat* which affords exquisite little glimpses of blue water and mountains. Here pious elders come to meditate, turning their rosaries by the hour. The Burman's love of nature is not to be learnt from his writings or his words, but from his choice of beautiful places like this in which to pray and ponder on the transitoriness of life. On a neighbouring hill stands the most beautiful object in Prome, the Shwe San Daw Pagoda.

There are four approaches to it, on the north, south, east, and west ; and each of these is of a hundred steps ; but the most frequented of all is the northern approach. Here a pair of white gryphons tower above the road and a stream of worshippers flows between them. Children, running naked, dive and splash in the open culvert, and thrust their heads from below through the open spaces between the planks, over which the good-humoured crowd passes on. Every one carries his shoes in his hands, and a notice over the archway requests " all but Europeans and Asiatic Englishmen " to remove the covering from their feet.

THE REALISM OF THE BURMESE ARTIST
Blind Beggar and Carved Figure

The long flight of pillars, in vermilion and gold, leads from the crouching gryphons to the last step and flagged pavement of the temple, making a vista of striking beauty ; and up and down this avenue, lit with the slant rays of the sun, the worshippers pass with flowers in their hands, cheroots at their lips, and piety on their faces. Two lads with a clanging bell hung from a pole ; children who can scarcely compass the width of the stairs ; groups of laughing girls ; old folk with trembling limbs—of such is the ascending and descending throng. Under the vermilion columns sit the beggars and lepers of Prome. Here is one, a woman hideously disfigured, with a child on her knees, whose face is yet unscarred by the fell disease. And there are others, upon whose faces there is the look of men to whom life has nothing left to offer. Intellect, will, hope, all have gone, and only the sad mortal disfigured husk remains. These poor creatures sit here, a piece of rag or a broken bowl spread before them, too weary of life to make any other appeal than that which is involved in their presence, to the passers-by.

On the platform all is beautiful. Under the *tazoung* at the summit of the stairs, a party of women is kneeling, their figures cut in dark outline against the blaze of gold beyond. All round the central fane, which towers eighty feet into the air, the worshippers are assembled: little children with flowers in their hands and faces solemn as they can make them; women in silken skirts bowing low before the object of their adoration; men silently turning their beads or praying with loud voices. And up the long flight of eastern stairs there come, emerging suddenly into this world of sunlit splendour, growing girls with trays of pink balsams heaped high upon their heads; and aged men in black and purple tartans, with white muslin fillets bound about their brows. To these last the long ascent is a work of real merit, for they are nearing the limits of life.

All here is gracious and beautiful, such a harmony of genuine piety and exterior beauty as makes one's heart glad. There is no set worship, no shutting up within doors; neither gloom nor affectation. The men, the women, and the little children are genuinely happy in their devotions, and they worship here under the blue sky and in the golden sunlight, nearer in this than the rest of the praying world to heaven. In other lands where the fibre is strong and prone to excess they would convert it all into priestcraft, or some mere secular cult of the beautiful; into some gloomy mystery or indecorous amusement. Here the simplicity, the natural piety, some gentle quality of equilibrium in the blood of this people, combined with an instinct that is profoundly artistic, enable them to effect a great compromise.

From the lofty platform of the pagoda, raised far above the neighbouring country, there expands one of those views which are the glory of Burma. The central chord of all is the great river, flowing in copper-coloured shade and silver light below the western bulwark of hills. Northwards it spreads out into a wide lake with the flush of evening on it, and beyond it the soft green hills are lit by the sunshine, free to roam over them; and the colouring is as tender as that of the hills beyond Florence as Turner saw them on a spring day from Fiesole. Eastwards, in the direction of the ancient city of Thare-Kettaya—long dead—spreads a lowland country rich with groves of tamarind and drooping palms, and rice-fields flooded with the rain.

The pagoda is a mass of gold, and the four-square platform, with an area of 12,000 feet, is set about with chapels richly carved, in which are countless figures of the Buddha in the three attitudes in which the great teacher is depicted. His features run the gamut of a face in contemplation, from sensual lips and the coarse profile that come from

ON THE PLATFORM OF THE SHWE SAN DAW PAGODA

FIGURES OF THE BUDDHA

India, to the idealised being conceived by the soul of this people. There are rows of bells, slung from wooden crossbeams and inscribed with pious texts and the names of those who gave them ; there are masses of gold mosaic which coruscate in the sun, trees of red-gold bearing green and purple fruit, and at the eight points of the compass the symbols of the planets, depicted in gold on scarlet pillars.

MANIPURI DANCERS

An old blind beggar, crouching on the flagstones of the platform, looks up at the pagoda, and asks an alms with astonishing fervour and energy. You would not know that he was doing so, for he appears to be addressing the golden bulb before him. Protruding mobile lips, concentrated air, furrowed brow, stentorious voice—surely a very singular figure.

Worshippers passing by clang the bells with deer-horns ; in a remote side-chapel a woman and her pretty daughter, holding flowers in their hands, pray alone before a company of colossal Buddhas. The last rays of the setting sun fall on the red-gold fabric, wrapping it in a haze of glory ; the fresh rain-clear air blows amongst the little bells ; trays of delicate pink flowers on altars exhale faint odours ; all is serene and strangely beautiful, here on this noble summit under the spaces of heaven.

It is little wonder they come up here to worship. Little wonder that they do not wish to change their faith, and all it means to them, for any other on earth.

As the stars come out and the dusk of evening overtakes me, I pass a procession on the way. A small lad swings manfully in front under a double burden of flowers slung in baskets from a pole, which fall in masses and sprays of pink and blue and yellow and white, and an old man follows behind in white muslin robes, beating a little triangular brass bell, and calling upon people by the way to contribute their quota of flowers for the service of the pagoda. What could be more beautiful?

CHAPTER XIII

TO THAYETMYO

THE barrier of the hills facing Prome, which seem strung in a single line, opens out on a nearer view, and the main ridge is seen to recede a half-mile into the background. The interspace is made up of green glades and small streams, of fields of Indian corn, solitary palmyras, and splendid mango and teak. Red hamlets cluster about the edges of the river, and a monastery spire cleaves the air. In the background the hilly slopes are covered with a maze of custard-apple orchards. The natural features are of marked beauty, and one reflects that in a civilised country this favoured spot might bear a famous name.

After Po U Daung, the opposite hills on the east take up the tale of beauty, and looking up-stream I can see the river in a narrow gap between blue headlands. Passing through this defile, we come to Kama, with its white gryphons staring across the water. Later, the spectacle presented on the eastern shore is one of hill-slopes and grassy knolls of the liveliest green, splendid trees in bloom, falling curtains of creepers, river-grasses silver-tufted, and feathery bushes of the wild plum. Through this tempting world the highway runs, its black railings in a line along the river, the telegraph wires overhead. Scattered palms and the roofs of a monastery proclaim the approach to the station of Palaw. Up north, a mountain spur comes down to the river's edge, and beyond this lies Thayetmyo, the old-time frontier-town of British Burma. Its wide roofs glisten in the sun, and behind it a blue hill, twin to the nearer one, stretches away in a north-westerly direction.

I am now on the threshold of the "Dry Zone," and the picture is already changing from rain curtains and drifting squalls to opal clouds and the features of a laughing summer. The grassy glades that mark the river between Prome and Thayetmyo are a new feature in the landscape, and they afford a welcome relief to eyes weary of the wealth of unbroken forest. The grass covers the high red cliffs with a mantle like velvet, and falls in showers down the little gullies to the water's edge. At Thayetmyo I pass from all the gracious circumstances of Burmese life to a town born of half a century of foreign military tenure. The main street along the banks of the river is a low-type reproduction of an Indian bazaar; brick houses, built in execrable taste, flank it on either hand; natives of India flock in it, and the Burman here looks like a stranger in his own land. Stray pagodas elbowed by court-houses and sentry-boxes, reflect in their derelict appearance the change that has come over the settlement. It is in many ways a disagreeable metamorphosis; most of all perhaps, in the warning it conveys of a future,

THE KAMA "NATS"

that to the pessimistic seems inevitable, when all the gaiety and the charm and the ease and plenty of Burmese life will be overlaid, if not annihilated, by the squalor and the indigent prose of an Indian proletariat.

Yet to do this new town of our creation justice, one must come away from the bazaar, from the company of the squalid Madrasi, the Hindu sweet-seller and the Musulman pedlar, to the military cantonment of which all these are the parasites.[1]

Here there are fair wide roads and splendid avenues, a fortress, a church, a racecourse, and a polo-ground. White men in uniform, with little canes, come swinging down the roads; men from Essex, from Yorkshire, and from Enniskillen; bearded Sikhs from the Punjab, and ruddy Afridis from the Afghan border. Here of an afternoon the thunder of hoofs is heard on the polo-ground, the clang of the time-keeper's

[1] Thayetmyo has since ceased to be a military cantonment; the legions have gone further north.

gong, the swish and click of stick and ball ; and strong men lie panting on the grass in the intervals between the *chukkers*. In the evening the bugles of England peal out in the alien air and junior subalterns proclaim the health of " The King." " The King—God bless him."

To this extent, at least, there is compensation for the change that has come over the Burmese settlement.

There is compensation and there is the price. Look at it. A stream flows through it, its flood having left the long grass stooping on its borders. Two black bridges cross it at each end. The place is more like some gloomy park in Hades, than the acre we call God's. It is far from the haunts of living men. There is no church here to bear the lone graves fellowship, no ivy-covered walls, no English flowers. It is the resting-place, you understand, of men who have died in an alien land. The price of empire.

Even here they lie, as they lived, with wide spaces round them. An acre or two is of little account in a waste of jungle. In one corner rest the mortal remains of the man who made the Arakan mountain-road, " worn out by exertions too great for his physical frame," in another is the tomb of one whose life closed early, an ensign of twenty-three. Not far from him lies a young Englishwoman. . . .

All is solitude, save where from a remote corner of the wide desolate place there comes a scent of incense. A party of Tamils, with lighted tapers placed on the tomb before them, is going through some strange litany. Here alone, amidst all these graves, is there one that is linked in any way with the living world about it. As to the rest—they lie for the most part forgotten ; the generation to which they belonged has passed away.

There is an irony in the one and only symptom of living remembrance, for it savours more of some half-savage rite than of a Christian ceremony. The flickering tapers, the burden of incense, the uncouth litany, only deepen the isolation of those other dead. What have they in common, but their common mortality ?

CHAPTER XIV

A SIDE ISSUE

SIRIUS and Aldebaran and chivalrous Orion glisten in the rain-washed sky. Venus hangs like a splendid jewel over the gateways of the dawn. At four o'clock all is dark save the twinkling firmament overhead. At five the dawn, blushing and beautiful, comes forth and the stars pale and the river quickens with swirling life.

THE MINDON ROAD

By this time I am well on the Mindon road ; the grass a-twinkle with the dew, the thickets, far as my ear can reach, melodious with the matin-song of doves. It seems to me as if I have come upon the Spring and caught her unawares ; Spring laughing and astray in the territories of Summer. Pale mists lie in the valley of the river and along the skirts of the mountains, adding by their ethereal lightness to the spiritual beauty of the morning. Then the sun rises, making an arch of red-gold on the horizon, and in a little while, wide shafts of light are abroad in the green glades and on the barred highway. It is a beautiful road, laid out on the swelling uplands that gradually climb, broken by little valleys and rivers, to the threshold and so to the summits of the Arakan Yoma. The outlines of the Yoma are visible from here, of that clarity

SUNSET ON THE ARAKAN HILLS

combined with softness, that is only attained in a country of distant horizons after days of rain. Splendid trees and delicate grasses border the highway on either side: the great teak with her clustering flowers ruddy against the blue sky ; the feathery palm, the versatile acacia.

At Nathé there is a rest-house on a hill and a police post with a trifling stockade round it. But the guard-house of solid teak is interesting. The basement is a prison for malefactors on their way to be tried by a magistrate. It is constructed on the principle of a tiger's cage—two compartments, only one of which is open at the same time. This makes a rush impossible. The upper story is reached by a ladder and a drawbridge. It is loop-holed, and furnished with handcuffs and leg-irons and rows of *dahs*. It is built on a knoll, half-surrounded by a stream which is crossed by a wooden bridge. A little way off, outside these entrenchments, is the palisade of huts in which live the wives and children of the guard. Across the road is their patch of Indian corn.

From here we go on over hill and dale till we come to Kyaukgyi. Behind me rides a Sikh trooper.

"The Sikh," he complacently observes, "do great work for the Raj. They are brave men, ready to die; but they are quiet, orderly, obedient, and quarrel with no one. The Pathan also is a fine man, but turbulent and passionate; reckless in moments of anger."

Here are the two fundamental types of men. They have bravery in common; in all else they differ as the ardent Celt from the sober Teuton. Both have found a foreign master, and here, three thousand miles away from their native homes in the plain-lands of the Manjha, the highlands of Tirah, they fight side by side for the glory of the empire, and help to keep its peace. Splendid material—half-savage at the core—here they have become docile instruments of civilisation, panthers treading out the corn.

ON THE ROAD

The Sikh is exclusive and mingles little with the people of the soil. Only a bad five per cent marry the women here and are outcasted accordingly. The Mohammedans universally take wives. Many are settling down, mainly as cattle owners. Every Sikh of the garrison at Mindon keeps a cow, and the milk, he will tell you, keeps him well. The instinct of the pastoral Aryan is strong in the man from the Punjab. Butter and milk, these are the good things he craves after.

"In time, Presence," observes the trooper, "all Burma will become like the Punjab." *Absit omen.*

At Kyaukgyi there is a rest-house on a hill-top, overlooking the fields of rice and the thatched roofs of the hamlet. A swift red stream flows past it, animated by rain that fell three days ago in the distant mountains. The country all around is broken, undulating, richly wooded; an amphitheatre surrounded by hills. It is a splendid summer day. Butterflies twinkle in the sunlight, wind-waves sweep over the young rice-fields, orioles flash golden wings as they speed from shade to shade; and the blue heaven is patterned with white clouds of restless beauty. The full tide of summer is here, yet the air is cool and the tropics manifest only in the vivid sunlight and the rich trappings of the world.

It is true also that all the eye rests upon from here is fever-haunted ; tainted with a subtle poison that enters in and destroys the blood, even as one is exulting in its beauty. The people are grateful for presents of quinine.

We leave Kyaukgyi at three in the afternoon, and two miles of travel bring us to the banks of the Pani river. I am making a dash for Mindon, a matter of some sixty miles, during a break in the rains. There are mountain streams to be crossed, there are no bridges. Six hours' rain can make them impassable, and three weeks can pass without any break in the barrier of waters. So I come to the Pani with some qualms.

There is a monastery in a tamarind grove overlooking the river, and monks and scholars come out to the carved railings to see us ride by. The Pani, red and heavy with silt, is flowing swiftly on its way. Although not in full flood it is too deep to be forded, and there is no passage for carts which would merely be swept away. So we cross over in a small flat-bottomed boat, with the saddles, rifles and trappings, while the horses are led a little way higher up the river. Man and horse plunge in and are instantly carried off their feet. The stream bears them rapidly down till they succeed in landing on the farther shore, some distance from where they started. Immediately the horses are ashore they fall to cropping the soft grass, having apparently enjoyed the plunge into the water.

ON THE ROAD

As we go on the road grows worse, and so grows admiration for the little beasts that carry us. They plunge bravely through the heaviest slush, often to their knees in its grip, and my feet dip in the thick liquor and become coated with it. In the dark they pick their way with equal skill and resolution. It is here amidst the difficulties of his own country that one comes to love and appreciate the Burmese pony. Little more than twelve hands in height, he will carry a strong man fifty miles in a day ; put into a four-wheeled cab, he will dash off with it regardless of its burden of half a dozen occupants ; turned out to grass after a long day's march he will cheerfully find himself his food and accept with lively approval the handful of bamboo leaves you may give him ; of grooming he takes little ; and for sheer pluck, intelligence, vivacity and an iron mouth he is hard to beat.

Presently we come upon the cart containing the advance baggage stuck deep in the mire and unable to proceed. It is not for any lack of spirit in the little beasts that are harnessed to it, for small though they are, scarcely bigger than big dogs, the cattle in this district are extremely well-bred, very handsome, and full of pluck and endurance. One of the little cattle is half buried in the slush, and his legs are entirely hidden. The yoke presses heavily upon his neck, and he is in sore straits. The cart is slowly unladen of all its burden, the driver stands up and calls to his cattle by name. They make a splendid frantic effort, go down on their knees, recover, and so come panting out of the slough in which they

LOOKING DOWN ON THE VALLEY OF THE MAHTOON

have been all but entombed. Such is the Burman unmetalled highway at this season after three days of fine weather.

After tea partaken of under the shelter of a village stockade I set out again, leaving the cart to follow. The darkness comes very swiftly after the sun has set. Happily the moon is nearly full.

Ye-gyan-zin lies high on a ridge of hills, the water-shed between the valleys of the Mahtoon and the Pani, and to Ye-gyan-zin we climb. The road is bad in places, running into and along the beds of streams ; but much of it lies through waving grasses and rich forest, bathed in the moonlight.

From the rest-house at Ye-gyan-zin one gets a glimpse into the true life of these wild and sparsely inhabited countries. There is scarcely a breath of air stirring, but the night is resonant with the cheep of crickets, and there is a wide view over hilly tracts to the blue outline of the Yoma and the white moonlit clouds beyond. A pony tethered here was carried off by a tiger a few days ago ; a Chin was killed in the early dawn as he went out to his fields. Night after night there is the same stillness ; the pageantry of the hours unfolds itself ; dawn and noon and evening follow incessant in each other's footsteps ; as they have done all through the incalculable years. Here is something of the romance of the primeval country ; wide spaces are visible from here which no human being has yet brought under dominion. Nature, romantic and terrible, confronts one ; and the civilised man sojourning here for a night feels himself an alien of the moment, standing upon the brink of vast and awful arcana.

Half an hour before the dawn I wake to find all the mists of the night gathered in like a white sea in the valley of the Mahtoon. The clear

LONG-BOAT ON THE MAHTOON RIVER

blue hills rise up about them as if to protect them in their secluded home. The full moon, gathering splendour from the growing dawn, hangs above the crest of the western hills. The first waves of light come streaming over the world as we start, and for a long while we ride in silence in the company of the morning.

Even in an old world, in the midst of prosaic and commonplace surroundings the spirit of youth is seldom absent from this first hour of the day ; but here in the heart of a country of primeval forests, secret streams, and sunlit glades, in a world still all but virgin to man, it thrills with extraordinary joy.

Even the stolid Sikh behind me, the man of milk and butter, is moved by it. " Lo ! " he says, thrusting forth his hands, " lo ! how the morning spreads herself abroad."

The road, like the old Pilgrim-road the Canterbury Pilgrims took along the North Downs, follows the spine of the hill ; and such roads in a mountain country never fail to attract the traveller upon them. This one is no exception to the rule. It winds through grass-lands bordered by dense forest, and it looks as though a giant's plough had passed over it, making this single furrow over the mountains. Every blade of the tangled myriads is sown with dewdrops. Noble vistas

CLOUDS ON THE MAHTOON RIVER

unfold on either hand ; wide hillsides bathed in sunlight ; patterned aisles of teak, and swooning avenues of cane ; and last of all, most beautiful to a human eye, the silver loops of the Mahtoon river, in the far populous valley below.

Leaving the crest at last, the road plunges into pools and rivulets, and gloomy halls of forest blind to the sun, and so comes to the red roofs and palm-clusters of a Burmese hamlet. The spires of Mindon gleam across the river, which we cross in a ferry-boat.

It is the river that accounts here for the presence of man. Its valley levels yield him food, its waters are a link for him with the outer world. But for the Mahtoon, the burden-bearer, all that the eye looks upon now from the hill-tops of Ye-gyan-zin, finding it good because it is human, might still have remained a pathless wilderness. Upon a day in the misty past, a man, one can fancy, stricken with a new desire, and tired of the Great River along which his progenitors had come, took the turning up the mouth of the Mahtoon until he came with his people after many vicissitudes to anchor at Mindon under the shadow of the western hills. And so the townlet came into being. But Mindon has not increased under British rule. A Burmese under-magistrate presides over the township, and a small guard of military police, constantly changed because of the malaria, protects it against aggression from the mountain Chins. But in former times it was the seat of government of a *wun* or Provincial Governor, and it gave to King Mindon Min his territorial title.

It is a long day's journey by boat down-river to the Irrawaddy. The scenery along the route is of great beauty. Large quantities of the produce of the fertile valley of the Mahtoon are sent down to Kama upon rafts of bamboo. The current after rain is very swift, and where it enters the Irrawaddy there is a violent impact, fraught with grave danger to boats. At Natmauk, where a great cliff abuts upon its waters, the spirit of King Mindon—the good king—is believed by the people to have taken up his abode.

CHAPTER XV

TO MINBU

ACROSS the river, and facing Thayetmyo, is the small town of Allanmyo. It owes its name to Major Grant Allan, who demarcated the old frontier between Upper and Lower Burma in 1853. Frontiers have a tendency to follow the natural features of the land; but this one—it has ceased now to be of any importance—runs with an uncompromising directness across Burma from east to west. And the tale is that when the imperious Dalhousie saw no prospect of getting the Court of Burma to recognise the British occupation of Pegu, he ruled a line across the map, and ordered the frontier to be delimited accordingly. White pillars half buried in jungle still survive in memory of his fiat. Allanmyo, like its name, is a product of British rule. In the king's days Meaday, facing it on the Thayetmyo side of the river, was the centre of life. "At noon," wrote Symes, in the narrative of his Embassy to Ava in 1795—"at noon we reached Meaday, the personal estate of the Maywoon of Pegue, who is oftener called from this place Meaday Praw or Lord of Meaday, than by the viceroyal titles. Here in compliance with the wishes of the Maywoon, we proposed staying some days. During our stay I made short excursions to different parts of the country, and found little variation in its appearance ; it was very beautiful, though but half-cultivated, and I was everywhere treated with respect."

At Sinbaung-we there is a large island mentioned both by Symes and Yule. A short distance above it is Longyi-ua, and the people relate that a king's boat was once caught in the whirlpool near this island, and that it had to be pulled ashore by the villagers with a rope made of their *longyis* or silken kilts.

THE LAUNCH AT ANCHOR

Just before coming to Sinbaung-we, there is a cluster of white pagodas on the west bank, and a little village on the low undulating ground between the river and the hills. Opposite this village there is a beautiful wooded tributary, which comes winding its way from the remote heart of the country. Plantain orchards and palmyra groves ; park-like trees ; armies of silver-headed river-grass, pink when ruffled by the wind (sign of a falling river) ; dark ruins of old pagodas ; wild plum hedges ; banners of *tagôn-daings ;* the gold of new *htis* on white pagodas ; red-striped cliffs rising sheer from the water, with gaps at intervals, showing in perspective, wooded hollows and grassy knolls which tempt the river traveller to step ashore and make a nearer acquaintance—of such is the world compact at this portion of the river's course.

At Mijaung-yé (Crocodile Water) there are white pagodas and red houses in a line, and a road from here leads over the rolling uplands to the old walled city of Taung-dwin-gyi, under the flanks of the Pegu Yoma. Sudden squalls overtake us at this season of mid-September ; first a purple bank coming up from the south, then a yellow mist, and the driving swish of rain. The river turbulent one moment, is quiet again the next. The sun shines in splendid patches on the green hills, while the purple storm is still on its way.

At Malun, an eminence crowned with white stairs and pagodas, there is a cenotaph in memory of the famous Bandoola. Here in its neighbourhood, at Minhla, the Burmese army made its only attempt to stay the final British advance in 1885.

The fort at Minhla stands above the edge of the water, and if ever there was a frail defence for a nation to rest its hopes upon it is this. Four-square and of plastered brick, it can boast neither of ditch nor bastion, nor of any of the other devices that help a fortress to defend itself. Its walls slope inwards, so that its area at the top is smaller than at its base. It has double walls with earth between, and low-arched gateways. A series of vaulted rooms lines the inner courtyard, and a double flight of stairs leads up north and south to the level of the ramparts. If ever there was a rat-hole it is this, and it proved true to its character when our troops carried it and slew the defenders cooped up within. " The Madras scouts," I read in a narrative of the war, " fell back on their supports, by a movement which was unfairly attributed to want of steadiness ; the European officers raced for the stockades, on the further side of which they saw the Victoria Cross. They rushed up the high and narrow ramp, which was defended by a cannon. The piece was fired off over their heads, and in an instant they and some thirty or forty men entered the fort and shot down the Burmese. Panic-stricken, most of these fell on their knees and asked for mercy. The *woon* ran out at the further gate and escaped. Eighty Burmese were slain in the fort, and several officers were severely wounded."

This place, once a shambles, is now become a bazaar crowded with the stalls of those who trade in beans and pumpkins. It holds also a few stalls in which silk and cotton goods are sold.

On the far side of the river there is another and a stronger fort, built upon a lofty cliff, but so well concealed that one might pass up and down the river a hundred times without suspecting its existence. It is approached through the little village of Gwe-Gyaung—in at one creeper-covered gate of its stockade and out at the other—and by way of a lane bordered by hedges of *kanakho* and the *say-galon*, which has a blossom of pink and carmine petals with speckled interior and one long streak of rich yellow down its back. Practically the whole of the fortress is under ground. It was constructed by the Italian engineers of the king who declared it to be impregnable, but it made no resistance. The river below it makes a great bow from north to south, and lofty hills make a chain across the west. Under the eastern cliffs the river runs into little wooded coves and sheltered bays, which are like a miniature Riviera. Volcanic Popa looms up faintly on the northern horizon; an extinct Vesuvius.

The Headman of Gwe-Gyaung, an old gentleman of frank and perfect manners, discourses on the war. "When the English were as far away as that little boat," he says, pointing to a canoe on the water half a mile away, "the shot from our guns fell short of their steamers, but *their* shot when they fired lodged upon yon distant hillock," pointing to a spot some two miles inland. "What, *thakin*, could the Burmese do in the circumstances? Ka-maw-hta the Italian, meant to fight the English Min, but U-Gaung the Kinwun Mingyi, sent word to the soldiers not to fight, because the two princes, the Nyaung-Oke and the Nyaung-Yan, who were with the British Government, were coming up and we were to have one of them for king. As to Minhla, they fought there because the Bo Cha was there, a brave man in command; a brave man, your honour."

Below the fort by the side of the pathway there is a *nat*-house sacred to Thagya-Thamee, a little lady like a doll who lives within. The house is like a dovecot, and a shed is built over it to give protection from the weather. She is a benevolent creature, and people come here to worship because, as the Headman observes, it has been the custom for generations to do so. Orchards of mangoes, limes, and custard-apples surround the village, and a few small boats are tethered by the river's edge. The receding waters leave rich meadows under the cliffs, and upon these and on the grassy slopes under the fort the red cattle find ample pasturage. It is a serene and beautiful spot, not meant for war.

CHAPTER XVI

THE RIVER IN ACTION

IN its flood season the river is subject to sudden gusts of passion. The current above Minhla runs with great violence, and when the river is up, the traveller in a country boat or a small launch is like to have strange experiences.

After leaving Minhla in a small launch I came to anchor one night under the village of Myingun. Overhead a few pale stars were faintly visible ; a wind on the lee shore made a lapping like that of the sea ; the dark river swirled by, laden with driftwood brought by the heavy rain ; and the passing derelicts ground against the sides of the launch with sinister music. All night long the river swept down with its derelicts, its level rising with each hour ; and every time I looked out into the dark I could see them coming like raiders of the night. At last there came a ship from the vastness upon us. A lascar in a startled voice cried out :

" Allah ! A ship goes by. Whose can it be ? "

The Serang sleepily murmured : " No ship, but a tree let loose."

" Tree ? " said the other, awe in his voice ; " look at it."

We crowded under the white awnings to see a great *hnau* floating swiftly down, shadowy, unhelmed, no lights upon her, a ship of the dead. We were still wondering when a great crash shook the air. The pity of it came upon us, for a great *hnau* with her rich carved stern, her vast rigging and shapely bows, makes a noble spectacle upon the water. She passed within a fathom's sweep and must have rammed us, had we not anchored for the night in the shelter of a rocky ledge, protruding a few feet into the river. We crept a foot nearer in to the bank and put a fresh rope out. The anchor offered no security, and had we held by it the current must have lifted it and swept us away. So it lay with a slack chain at the bottom, where it collected large quantities of drift during the night.

All through the night the rain fell and the river rose, and the dawn broke grey and wet. Hills in the mist, seemed scarcely real, and within the full sweep of the eye all was grey and boundless flood ; every boat and figure on its surface stood out black against the grey, like a paper silhouette.

We had some trouble in getting away, for both screw and anchor were encumbered with the *débris* of the flood, and the instant we let go, the current began to sweep the launch down. For a few exciting moments full steam ahead made no progress. She was slowly but certainly drifting down to the rocky headland on which the *hnau* had broken. It was a struggle between steam and tide, and the betting was in favour of the tide. Happily the launch at last made way, slowly she mastered the current and steamed out of danger into mid-stream. It was a singular spectacle that now met my eyes ; for that same river, which can at will simulate an immortal calm, or break into passionate wrath ; which can look like a molten sea under the full blaze of the noon, or become like some rapturous instrument upon which, after the sun has set, every emotion of colour throbs ; can in the grey dawn of such a morning veil itself in inscrutable mystery. Every feature of it takes on a new and strange complexion. In the vague light, distant islands and promontories become transfigured. Trees loom up above the belt of waters as though they had no roots. The flat sands disappear, and headlands shoot out into the air, 'twixt sky and water. Sailing-boats, fickle as any mob, sweep down with their banner sails in the van of the northern winds. Seen against the pale sky of the morning their outlines make startling patterns, as of some mystic procession trailing away to a mute and shadowy world. In such company one comes in mid-September to Minbu.

CHAPTER XVII

MUD VOLCANOES

MINBU is notable for its mud volcanoes. They own a small territory between the Sabwetchaung and the metalled road behind Minbu, and for the most part they adhere to these limits. But they have been known after heavy rain, which excites them, to flow in a great sluggish deluge over the road, and a portion of their overflow streams into the Sabwetchaung. They consist of one lofty central cone, rugged and broken in outline ; several, either closed or on the point of becoming so ; and two open baths of liquid mud. A light is said to ignite the gases that escape and the oil that may be skimmed from their pools. There are in addition many miniatures of these three types.

The volcano begins as a little bubble of liquid mud, and gradually builds for itself a cone, on the completion of which its existence appears to terminate. In the case of the large central member of the group, however, the uprising fluid has burst its way through the walls of the crater, reproducing as nearly as possible the features of a true volcano. There is about them all a mean and clammy character, which makes the resemblance *bizarre*, as though they were of kin, but the product of another and an inferior world. The stuff they exude is slate-coloured, cold, and malodorous. When it dries, it turns a yellow-brown, and the mud-volcano in decay is more like an ant-heap than any other thing on earth. If you climb up to the top of the central peak you will find a circular pool of this ill-looking mixture, contained within jagged walls which are broken through at one point. This pool is for an instant still. It then quickens with a sudden impulse, and the whole mass shivers as though some life engulfed in it were seeking for a means of escape. An instant later a dome of grey matter is created from the surface. There is an upward push and a rupture. Air escapes, and the upheaved liquid flops back in a large circle. This process is repeated in various forms, sometimes as a small quick upheaval in a double circle, which makes a soft squelch, without ever getting to the point of rupture, as though the motive power within were exhausted ; at others in a great dome which flings up the grey matter into the air with a violent effort, and sends a large overspill into the trough which lies in the gap of the crater.

This trough widens as it follows the downward slope, from a few inches to several feet, and it is curiously fascinating to trace the progress of the sluggish stream, slimy and glistening in the sunlight, till it ceases to move, or is lost in one of the deep gullies that bear away to the river. The tendency of this stream is to raise its bed until it is several inches higher than the surrounding soil. After some time the crater breaks at some other point in its circumference and the original stream, no longer reinforced, quickly dries and cracks in the sun, making a series of transverse lines, like those of a ladder, down its length. A number of these defunct streams clothe the slopes of the volcano, dividing them into a pattern of tortuous ribbons. An unbroken volcano is not less interesting. Its shape is that of an elongated and rounded cone, and a small stream ejected from an orifice at its top spreads a fresh glaze from moment to moment on its surface.

The depth of these pools is greater than at first sight seems probable. Into one of them—a little bubbling circle less than four inches in diameter—a long thick sapling will find its way to a depth of six feet. The principal crater probably has a depth of fifty feet, and it provides a very dingy and terrible *oubliette* into which to fall. Stories are current of people who have fallen in from losing their balance. One realises for the first time, with something of a shock, that a small pool scarcely bigger on its surface than a watch is deep enough to hold a man, and it might be supposed that there would be danger in the case of the larger pools of the outer husk tumbling in under pressure ; but no accidents appear to have been ever due to this cause. Sightseers constantly climb to the very lips of the craters, and herds of cattle drift across the volcanoes, wandering over their slopes, without suffering any greater harm than a sudden immersion up to their knees in one of the moving streams of grey matter.

The people of the country-side attach a mysterious character to the volcanoes. A fabulous snake is said to be imprisoned within, and a house has been built in the vicinity for the tutelary *nat*. Nervous people do not willingly pass by his territories at night. And it must be admitted that they have a disagreeable character. No more secret grave for a murdered man could well be found. No blade of grass grows anywhere within their sinister neighbourhood. All power of reproducing life seems to have been crushed out of this grey clay, and even at the height of the tropical year, when life strains upwards from the soil and all things that come within the compass of the eye are clothed in verdure, it spreads, devoid of every symptom of life, broken and furrowed only by the rain, like a cold blister on the smiling face of the world. The volcanoes owe their existence, it seems, to petroleum springs below the surface.

CHAPTER XVIII

TO YENAN-GYAUNG

ON the way to Yenan-Gyaung the river races and swirls under the high cliffs so furiously that often a launch at her greatest speed can make no progress. The cliffs are of a worn and romantic beauty, the home of sand-martins which fly and circle unceasingly in the light ; of secret orioles ; of a gracious and tender-hued acacia ; of pink and crimson convolvuli, which trail like a rich carpet from the window of a rejoicing citizen ; and of groups of trees with twisted white trunks and wind-driven foliage, like Roman pines, where they cluster on the cliff-tops. There is no note of the tropics in this scene. The full bounty of the season does no more than to keep it green ; and in the dry weather all is parched and arid as the desert.

I come upon the village of Gya, built upon the green slope of a hill, a smiling interlude in the great procession of the cliffs. It overlooks a sheltered cove, which is made by the arrival here of a freshet ; a brawling and turbulent creature for brief moments of its life, but commonly moribund or dry. Like all of its kind, it has marked out for itself a territory far greater than it can fill.

The cliffs of soft sandy formation show in an interesting manner how the action of rain supplements that of the great river in widening its borders. The action of miniature falls is here well marked, the cliff sides being cut into pinnacles which look like stalactites. The whole surface is scoured with the prints of water. In places the cliffs look as if they had been sliced with a razor, in others as if the whole front of them had been brutally torn away, as a bear tears away the flesh from a man's face, exposing the grinning bones. One talks of human interest, but the war of nature is of terrible fascination when the eye has once learnt to look for it.

This is the order of the landscape here where it overlooks the swirling river—cliff, watercourse, cliff, watercourse, cliff, large watercourse, a village ; and so again. It is only where the large streams come down that there is space for a settlement. There are no villages in Burma more charmingly placed than these that lie transverse to the river, between Minbu and Yenan-Gyaung. And many of the patches of swelling down and trees in cluster on the eastern bank are English in their suggestion. One might suppose as one goes by that some skilled gardener had been at work here, preparing a park for an English gentleman. I speak of them at this season after the monsoon rains.

Yenan-Gyaung as I approach it is like every other village here in its natural site, but on a greater scale ; and distinguished, since it is a town, by white and gold pinnacles of pagodas and dark monastery spires ; and

CLIFFS

by serried lines of long-boats and white flats under the cliffs, where the oil steamers call. The river is mightily spread out here, and looks at sunset like a purple sea.

EARTH-OIL

Yenan-Gyaung, " the river of stinking water," seems to have lost its odour. None at any rate assails me when we anchor for the night in the company of a number of Burmese *peingaws*, under the village. The last sound I hear is that of an old man's voice, chanting from a religious work, inculcating the practice of many virtues. In the early morning I ride on to the oil-fields. The road after crossing the dry sandy bed of the creek, pitted with water-holes dug by the people, climbs up to a plateau along which it winds for a couple of miles. The soil is meagre and barren, though at the right season happily clothed with green grasses and small acacias. A wide expanse of rolling country, scarred and broken up by deep ravines, spreads away on every hand, save on the west, where the Irrawaddy lies in a long silver trough bounded by wide plains and distant mountains. It is a country that in the midsummer heats, before the rain has fallen, is wholly devoid of beauty.

The most prominent feature in the landscape, as I approach the wells, are the lofty spider-like derricks which crown the knolls and make strange patterns against the sky as if they were the skeletons of some extinct settlement. Under these, and scarcely visible above the soil, are the primitive works of the Burmans. Each well is marked by a splash of dark stained earth made by the refuse and wastage of the oil. These, and the patches of the purple croton, give the hill-slopes a singular blistered look, that is in harmony with their arid character. Red drums of oil like gas tanks, clusters of thatched huts in which the work-people live, the wider roofs of the European houses, the dark tapering spires of a monastery, and the cupola of a white pagoda complete the picture. In the fenced yard of the superintendent there is a flower garden, gorgeous with scarlet and yellow canna and purple convolvuli; the only patch of lively colour on the brown slopes.

The superintendent, an American, with clear blue eyes, a soft lazy drawl, and a loud, frank, explosive laugh, shows me round.

"Wal," he says, "thar ain't much to see around here; but I guess you're welcome to see what thar is."

We begin at the forge, where a motor pants in a side room, and blacksmiths are at work on bars of red-hot iron; and from here pass on to a derrick where another American, in a large mushroom hat that helps to keep off the oil-drippings, is at work on the boring of a well.

The boring implement is a gigantic crow-bar, which bores its way down by force of its own weight as it falls. A steel cylinder with a simple valve scoops into itself the slush and clay in the tube made by the drill and disgorges these outside the well. A big windlass wound with rope works the drill, lifting it up and letting it fall, and it is itself worked by an engine in a neighbouring shed. The oil spouts up from time to time in a jet which reaches high above the mouth of the well, and covers the derrick with an evil-smelling filthy coat, which drips long after the jet has ceased, turning all the surrounding area into a puddle of mud and oil. In this environment the coolies work, and the overseer stands, an elfish man, covered with dripping oil. The coolies wear small basket hats, and little besides.

This process continues till the full depth of the well, some seventeen hundred feet, is reached.

The oil is pumped out by steam engines, or it comes up of itself driven by the pressure of gas below. In the latter case, when the stop-cock at the well's mouth is turned on, the gas rushes out with a roaring,

YENAN-GYAUNG

grinding sound and is quickly followed by a stream of yellow brown oil, which foams out of the pipe into an iron tank, where it lies covered with iridescent bubbles and gradually thickens as it cools. Part of it is burnt as fuel in the engines, where it makes a raging flame like a sword of fire.

The Burmese system is yet simpler. A well is dug to a depth of from two to three hundred feet, and lined with wood to keep the sides from falling in. Looking down into its deeps, I can see the oil glinting at the bottom, and quivering with the secret action of the springs ; overhead, at a height of four or five feet, a tree trunk to which pulleys are attached

THE BURMESE SYSTEM

is placed horizontally on supports. A rope is passed over the pulleys and hauled by girls and men, down a long slope, till the bucket of oil reaches the surface. Human labour from start to finish. The contents of each bucket are poured into large Ali Baba jars, which lie half-embedded in the dark slush at the well's mouth. These girls get four-pence a day for their toil, and they prefer the hard labour of it to more lucrative employment, " because they can flirt here all day long." " Only girls in search of husbands go to Yenan-Gyaung," is the envious comment of the women along the river, to whom such opportunities are denied.

The Burmese process is literally the same to-day as it has been for generations, with one single exception. They have found an air-pump and a diver's helmet useful for the digger, and these may be seen here and there in use.

The diggers are better paid than any one else in Yenan-Gyaung.

They get one rupee (1s. 4d.) a day for their toil, and would prosper accordingly if they could be persuaded to work when they had some earnings in hand. Diggers are no longer brought up *in articulo mortis*, their tongues lolling out of their mouths; but their calling still claims an occasional victim. Only the other day a digger on his way up from the pit lost his hold of the rope and was killed; and the party of rope-pullers found themselves on their backs on the towing path. The Burmese well is by preference always on a slope, where a good towing path can be found, leading away at times down to the very bed of the ravine. One can measure the depth of a well from the length of the towing path, for they are exactly equal. From the heaving centre of the wire suspension bridge which spans the biggest of the ravines, there is a curious view of these wells, on little ledges protruding from the slopes, each with its dark circle of oily refuse and its winding path beaten white by the feet of the towers.

But it is at the receiving station, where the Burmese output of oil is measured and taken over by the company's agents, that the *bizarre* character of Yenan-Gyaung becomes intense. The inner space, where these operations are gone through, is surrounded by a wide circle of black greasy pitch, an amalgam of oil and mud, stamped with the foot-prints and the hoof-marks of men and cattle, and crowded with carts full of glistening jars of oil. Beside them are the great Ali Baba-like vats, agape and half-buried in the mire. The suggestion is one of an infernal kraal.

Making my way through this outer barrier, whose oily filth is far from inviting, I find myself within the inner circle, set round with lofty sheds which face inwards, like the seats of an amphitheatre. The platforms of the sheds are crowded with the strenuous naked figures of men employed in pouring oil from jars into iron reservoirs. The oil pours in a green glutinous stream; the sun glints on the polished muscles of the toilers; above in long rows on the topmost tiers sit the Indian supervisors and tally-clerks, in white robes, silent and taciturn. The stairs of the platforms are slippery with oil, and all the arena is alive with the moving figures of the oil-bearers, hastening up with their quota. They look like demons from some under-world, rather than human beings; they look least of all like the happy people of the soil who elsewhere go to and fro in silken skirts to worship at some golden pagoda, lifted high above a world of beauty. Some strange metamorphosis has overtaken them here. And as I look I am reminded of the pictures that would-be prophets draw of the Industrial Future.

For there are the debased workers, inhuman in appearance; supervisors over them of another race, silent but ready to intervene should a scuffle or riot take place among them; and over all the shadow of a Colossus, into whose maw the toil of the under-workers runs. They are made to sell here to the company all they produce, at the rate of 2 rupees 8 annas a hundred viss, and the company's selling price is 6 rupees for the same quantity. Capital and cool intellect have been busy these years amongst the ancient owners of the wells; judicious loans have swept nearly all of them into the Capitalists' grip, and the Twin-sa, the hereditary "Well-Eater," trembles under his little finger, because he knows that his mortgages are overdue and foreclosure must crush him. He is glad enough to get the company's price for his oil.

"Wal," comes a lazy humorous voice, "seems to me you have seen pretty near all thar is to see here in this God-forsaken place. Come away home now and have a drink. I guess there is some champagne going still of the stuff the old man sent along to drink success to our new four-hundred-bar'l well."

THE LEGEND OF YENAN-GYAUNG

"Once upon a time," according to the story-teller, "the stinking water of Yenan-Gyaung was sweet, and of such fragrant odour that all the world voyaged there to take away a little of it. For centuries the people came and went, the waters retained their magic property, and Kyaukka-Myo, as the old city was called, prospered by the influx of the strangers. Till one day, there came up the river a great king in a golden raft, with his queens and his courtiers and an army of eighty thousand men. And when they got near the city, seven of the queens, very weary of their golden raft, asked the king's leave to step on shore and take a stroll. The king consented, but said that they must be sure not to stay away very long. And no doubt they would have returned in good time had they not come upon the pool of fragrant water for which Kyaukka-Myo was famous.

"But its odour stole upon their senses and they forgot all about their promise to the king. When the night came and the king found they had not yet returned, he set out in search of them, and when towards the morning he found them by the scented waters of Yenathasi, he fell into a great passion and commanded them instantly to be killed. After a time the king's anger passed away, and then he blamed the Yenathasi for prompting him to commit this crime. He therefore resolved that the water should be sweet-scented no more, and by the aid of the miraculous powers which he possessed, changed the perfume to the stench of earth-oil. From that day forth the place has been known as Ye-nan-kyaung—the river of stinking water."

This legend, with variations, is played to audiences at Yenan-Gyaung by the amateur players of the town. It has a practical moral in the testimony it bears to the oil-rights of the local families which as the play runs, had to be defined by the great king before his golden raft could be induced to resume its journey. These rights, now fading away under the pressure of modern causes, present a somewhat curious illustration of the tendency common in all lands and amongst all people to keep wealth "in the family."

THE CLIFFS

At Yenan-Gyaung one may make a nearer acquaintance with those cliffs which are so striking a feature of the river in the dry region. Wholly distinct as they are from the mountains, which by their fellowship with the Irrawaddy give it much of its romantic character, they are

FROM THE CLIFFS OF YENAN-GYAUNG

not lacking in beauty of their own; and indeed they offer a welcome relief from the tropical exuberance which so perpetually assails the eye throughout other portions of the river's course. They are austere and beautiful in their idiosyncrasy, and they add much to the variety of Burma.

There is a pathway that winds up to them on the south of Yenan-Gyaung, which is like a pathway over sea-cliffs in England, and along this pathway there are many vantage points, which tempt one to stay and look upon all the world that spreads away below them, from Yenan-Gyaung, on the river where the boats lie, to the last derrick on the hills. The river runs some way into the dry bed of the Yenan-Gyaung, making a sheltered harbour which is the nucleus of the settlement. In the hollows there are brown thatched houses, dark tamarinds, and slender palms. A large house with white gables and a big vermilion drum of iron that is full of oil, proclaim the presence of the white man. Every little knoll and every commanding eminence has its pagoda, white or gold, or weather-beaten grey. Several of these rise up in their new grace from the red crumbling ruins of much older buildings. For a full mile under the cliffs, the *peingaws* and *laungzats* lie waiting for their burden of oil. The native sounds, the clang of the monastery bells, the laughter of women bathing by the river, the shrill voices of lads at school, calling their Kah-gyi-Kha-gwe, the incessant crooning of doves, have here a bass accompaniment like the beating of a loud fretful heart that would bid them all be still. This is the new power at work, the voice of the engine which, from dawn to dark, labours and toils in the service of its masters. Up here on the downland the grass is tender and green, and diversified with dew diamonds and a world of minute beauty. The morning air blows cool and fresh, and in early September in the shadow of a white pagoda, or the shelter of a carved *piasath*, one attains here an exquisite climate. A summer morning on a cliff overlooking the sea, when balmy breezes are afoot, has no greater power to lull or to charm the spirit.

And if morning on the cliff-tops has her secret of fresh delights, evening comes with revelations of surpassing beauty. The picture she paints is so tender and so majestic, that it must be difficult to overstate its charm. First there are the great cliffs with white faces overlooking the river. Beyond them there spread the waters, over spaces so vast that the eye cannot compass them. The river embraces in its folds a succession of islands, so numerous and varied that all sense of a single stream is lost. They are covered with meadows of silver-pink *kaing*, in the midst of which lie purple lakes and rosy pathways of waters ; but where the islands cease, the river spreads in a single expanse from the foot of the white cliffs to the low misty western shore. The opal gleams of the sunset, breaking through grey cloud masses, fall in long reflections on its surface. To the eye ranging swiftly over it, the wide world of waters seems motionless—a mystic sea of infinite depth. A water-fowl skims its surface, bird and shadow, and the air is so clear, the waters are so mirror-like, the environment so still and lone, that for a long while its wings flapping lazily over the water convey the only hint of motion in a spectacle of arrested beauty. In the far west the gleam of fires and the smoke ascending from villages and hamlets greet the eye with the wistful suggestion inseparable from signs of human life, in a world of infinite and inanimate calm.

THITTA-BWÊ

Over the cliffs it is a Sabbath-day's journey to Thitta-bwé. Two miles of cliff divide it from the derricks and engines of Yenan-Gyaung, giving it seclusion and peace ; and a little bay runs up from the lordly Irrawaddy to help to make it beautiful. Like all the villages along this coast, it lies at the mouth of a freshet, which holds water only after heavy rain. But the freshet makes a little valley, and a fan of alluvial sand along which the great boats of the Irrawaddy and the dugouts of the village lie at anchor. The village lies snugly within a stockade of purple thorn and giant cactus, interspersed with flowers. Some noble trees shelter it from the excessive sun, each as beautiful as an English oak ; and the green swelling downs rise up on every hand, broken here and there into patterns by the hedgerows. In the soft haze of evening the little settlement looks the very picture of rural peace.

There is a house at Thitta-bwé built for the European traveller. Airiness is its chief characteristic. Its front room is made up entirely of windows. These are covered by slight awnings of plaited mat that can be thrust open or let down by means of wooden props. It is with reluctance that one closes them for an hour or two each day, when the sun-blaze on the waters is too dazzling to the eyes ; for the picture they frame is of a vast mirror-world of waters, dreamy islands of cloud, and a wave of rolling mountains so etherealised by the pouring sun, that they seem to guard no material world beyond, but to stand for the very frontiers of space. And all beyond them is indeed vague and unreal to the dwellers in the valley of the great river. They are " The Mountains of the West," a barrier that not one man in ten thousand ever dreams of crossing.

From Thitta-bwé the pathway runs on over the cliffs to Nyaunglay, another little village hidden in a similar little valley. It has a colony of Musulman river pilots, who have settled down in it and have married the catholic daughters of the soil. They have a small mosque of their own, and a muezzin who calls them to prayer. I wonder, in a generation or two, how much of the Indian Musulman will survive.

At Thitta-bwé the night comes with the gentlest of transitions. The dark river twinkles back the message of the stars ; the great boats make shadowy forms along its banks ; from the village comes the litany of pious elders at prayer. Clear and quick across the still waters peal the notes of a distant flute, the player rapt in the ecstasy of his art. There is no music in the world so mellow and artless, no music so instinct, as the music of the flute, with the primitive spirit of man. As I sit here in the dark and listen to the mellow notes floating over the spaces of the river, it seems that I have bridged ten thousand years of life ; the trappings of civilisation fall insignificantly away from me ; I forget who I am and remember only that I must have heard this flute-player and his music on some such river-edge, long long ago in the past. I sit on long after he has ceased, while the waters flow on into the dawn, rapt in the mystery of life.

CHAPTER XIX

THE ROAD TO PAGAN

A GREAT sandbank has been forming for years before the town of Yenan-Gyaung, and the present channel in consequence lies far to the west; so far is it, that the cliffs of Yenan-Gyaung are almost lost to sight as I slowly travel on. The western shore is low, and villages, almost treeless, cluster on the edge of the alluvial plain. Popa with his cloud-cap, like an embodied

COTTON-RAFT

memory of his past, is lifted high above the rolling uplands. White-sapphire clouds have taken the place of his smoke, as though the ages had purified him, bringing peace to his fierce heart.

Presently the channel swings back under the eastern cliffs and we come upon the village of Kyanye, hidden in dark woods, its long-boats drawn up by the water's edge. The river like an hour-glass, compresses into a single stream, then spreads out again, encircling islands of *kaing* meadows. Later, in the west, there are wide green plains, with herds of cattle grazing on them, dark blue masses of oak-like woods, villages with monastery roofs and pagoda spires. Electric clouds swoon in the sky above the blue mountains of Arakan, and the river spreads unbroken from shore to shore.

Pagan-galay and Sinbyu-gyun (White Elephant Island) face each other

THE ANANDA PAGODA AT PAGAN

across the water. I have left my little launch, with all her struggles to breast the tide, and am embarked upon one of the great ships of the Flotilla with two flats in tow. One hundred and fifty feet of pathway is the right we claim, and the roar of our thundering paddles, the deep throbbing of the hidden engines, mark the unequal conflict between the immemorial river and this new factor driving ruthlessly ahead, and caring nothing for its protest. Brute force driven by pitiless mind is the burden of the iron paddles as they tear through the heart of the water ; of the engines as they swing to the wrath of the driven flame. The waters plunge in great billows between the flats and the steamer's side, and the rudder cleaves a line between. Long after the ship has passed, her course is marked upon the river's surface, and every inch of the shore and every boat drawn up along it, or abroad upon the waters, knows by the strange paroxysm of the portent that has passed.

Salé, at which we anchor for the night, is a place of ancient ruined pagodas, giant gryphons, and carved monasteries. There are two new white and gold pagodas here in the Pagan style. The Phaya-taga, the builder of one of these, a fine old man who has made his money in trade, is cheerily superintending the completion of the details : the painting of the four *tagòn-daings* of vermilion and gold with the galon-bird at their summits, and the gilding of the Recording Angels over the great bell. There is a very beautiful view, from where he stands, of the wide river ; so still that it would look asleep, but for the long canoes almost racing down its tide. This old man has amassed a fortune and has lived the strenuous life. Now that the evening of his days has come upon him he turns with the fine instinct of his people to better things. He is giving up the pomps and vanities of colour, of rich raiment, of secular pride. Trade is less and less with him ; the lust of possession is passing away from his heart. Yet, as I look at him, I see clearly that he is a man of the world, with the strong air of one who has fought for his place, and such manners as come only to one who is conscious of power and success.

Beyond Salé lies Singu, a village very successfully concealed from view by a low curtain of hills. Some white pagodas alone mark its presence, but the village is growing in prosperity, and the oil company at Yenan-Gyaung will shortly begin operations here. Passing on, we meet low cliffs in the west growing into blue mountainous spurs, and in the east there are the broken Tharrawaddy hills and Popa, the old volcano, showing four points. Between there is a low country slowly sloping up, and conveying what is not uncommon here, an impression of a long hollow, into which it would seem the river might easily tumble over. There is scarcely an island here to break the vast mirror of the river, spread from shore to shore. While we wait to repair some damage to the engines, the lesser life on its surface deploys before us. Rafts of glazed Ali Baba jars bear down upon us, and barely escape disaster. The largest pots sustain the raft, which is laden with the rest, their backs a-glisten, and their small mouths gaping at the sky. Four idle men make the crew of each raft, and seeing disaster imminent, they suddenly develop a furious energy and pull the raft out of the main current in which we are detained; but for the most part they lie on their backs and dream, trusting to the bounty of the great stream. Rafts also bring large quantities of paddy and stone grinding-slabs for sharpening *dahs*.

Boats bring cattle, and one passes us full of buffaloes. These come from the dry country about Mingyan, and are sold in the prosperous Delta. In seasons of drought in the upper country, the river is laden with such cattle-rafts and boats on their way to Maubin. But this life does not begin to move on the river till the last expected rise has taken place, and the bare sandbanks leave the channel more defined. Raft-owners profit also by the buoys of the Flotilla Company, which begin to appear by the first of November. At that time an officer of the company who spends each summer in England returns to his work on the river, and day by day and foot by foot, marks out with a hundred thousand buoys the navigable channel. The company is in fact supreme on the Irrawaddy. Its steamers bear its trade, and every hamlet and town along the river's course for nine hundred miles is conscious of its presence. But a hundred years ago it would have done more; it would have won for itself the sovereign power in Burma.

As we near Yenan-gyat there become visible for the first time the countless pyramids and spires of Pagan, the most stately capital Burma has ever known. The nearer ones are cut in dark outlines against the sky; the most distant are so faint that they seem like the unreal fabrics of a city of dreams. Yet there is nothing in this superb picture, in all these hosts of pinnacles and domes and spires, to hint that before one there lies a city of the dead. Instead, it looks, hung here between the drowsy clouds and the mirror-like calm of the mighty river, like some new Venice of the East, destined to play an immortal part in the history of the world. There is no one who would judge, from here, that seven hundred years have passed since its day was closed—for ever.[1]

[1] The story of Pagan and of its magnificent architecture is told in my book supplementary to this volume, entitled *Mandalay and other old Cities of Burma*; which I believe the finest collection of photographs of the dead city ever published.

M

CHAPTER XX

A THOUSAND FEET ABOVE THE IRRAWADDY

YENAN-GYAT is the lesser brother of Yenan-Gyaung, and like it a place of oil-wells and commercial adventure. A certain interest is imparted to it by the little war that wages here between the two companies who are exploiting it; but I am concerned to-day with the great white building which gleams on the summit of the Tangyi hills, a thousand feet above the world. From its platform there is a view of Pagan that is unsurpassed in Burma, and a legend of the people tells that in a bygone day the Buddha stood upon this peak, and prophesied the coming greatness of the city.

Above Yenan-gyat is the village of Ayadaw, to which the river runs up in a side channel. From here the road to the pagoda marches along the fore hore under white cliffs. The strewn wreckage of timber, the sandy shore, the fragrant water, have that about them that recalls the fringes of the sea. Half a mile more brings me to the village of Sekwa, lying at the mouth of a valley. The road turns up at a right angle through the fenced homesteads of the village, over wooden bridges and under the spires of a monastery, till it is well on its way up the valley, where steam-engines thump and fill the air with vibrant energy, and derricks make patterns against the wild hill-slopes. Fields of millet bear me company for a space, but soon I am alone in the solitude of the gorge.

Euphorbias and cactus rise up in fantastic forms, and tamarisks cluster in the bed of the valley, where a parched streamlet lies in pools in the midst of boulders crusted with white salts. Aridity and desolation are the characteristics of the place, and even in September the heat palpitates fiercely on its barren red slopes.

Leaving the roadway, which has been made by the oil-adventurers, a pathway of the people climbs up the steep ascent to the Tangyi-Sway-Daw Pagoda, now in steps cut in the stone, now along a level way bordered by grasses, and fields of yellow and pink wildflowers. Trees are dwarfed and few and far between. The first steep climb brings its reward in a sudden and superb view of the city of Pagan, its white spires twinkling in the distance, framed in a wave of the mountains. And looking back from here I can see the whole of the little valley up which the road has lain, from the white powdered boulders in its bed to the houses of the village at its mouth. Distance and the growing shadows of afternoon soften the arid ferocity of the scene, and the derrick spires speak a word of civilisation and of man's courage. The view over the hills gradually expands, and bold crests rise up between the sky and the Irrawaddy plain. The pathway, proceeding along the eastern face of precipitous cliffs, brings me at last within sight of the pagoda, poised on the utmost summit of the hills.

The pagoda, build by Anawrata the Great, King of Pagan, is worthy of its builder and of its site. Its rounded outline a lustrous white, culminates in a golden spire, and the dark winged roofs of monasteries cluster about its base. Its size is enhanced by knowledge of the task involved in its construction here, far from all human resources. The long climb to it is extravagantly repaid by the noble view that expands from its platform.

In the east, below it, there are the crumpled spurs of the mountain, with villages cheerily embowered amongst trees, and green fields in the valley openings; then a blue ribbon of water, followed by alluvial flats left bare by the falling river. They are green now, with red patches where fields are being sown. Here and there on their vast surface a hamlet, lifted a fraction above the water-level, maintains its insignificant existence. Beyond lies the main volume of the river under the mighty plain of Pagan. Its dark and white pagodas rise up, each one clearly visible; and from here, if anywhere, one may form a just estimate of the greatness of the ancient city. The Tawni hills beyond make a red ruffled line across the plain, and above them, in the extreme east, there towers volcanic Popa, whose great size can only be justly gauged from a neighbour such as this. The hills of Mingyan and Monywa appear on the northern horizon, where the river in loops reaches away into misty space.

As the sun sets the pagoda-crowned peak sends its mighty shadow over the plain, and the spires of the dead city flame for the last time in the fading light. In the west, the crumpled hills reach away over low undulating lands to the meridian chains of the Yoma Daung, and the still loftier summit of Mount Victoria, ten thousand feet above the sea. The Yaw river makes its way through the landscape, a river of gold in the flooding sunset.

Stone umbrellas fixed upon the backs of elephants ornament the platform of the pagoda, bells hang there from carved posts, flamboyant roofs surmount the southern stairs; under the dark *tazoungs* there are colossal monk's bowls of grey marble; a stone python protrudes from the earth near the base of the pagoda; steps on the west lead down to the monastery courts where pilgrims assemble, to the dwelling-place of the abbot and his monks, to a white-walled hall of ordination overlooking the panorama of the hills, to a water reservoir in a sheltered hollow, dug, they say, by Anawrata the king, and last of all to stone caves and temples of great antiquity, frescoed with legends of the Buddha.

There is one remaining spectacle. A wall runs round the platform of the pagoda on three sides, but on the fourth the flagstones impend directly over the depths. Whether this be by chance or from the ruin of time, it is certain that instinct in architecture could devise nothing more superb. Here within a child's reach of the edge, there kneels an aged woman at prayer, the one solitary occupant of the pagoda. The fading sunlight envelops her in its golden mist. Her hands are clasped before her, her visionary eyes are turned towards the distant city, her face is transfigured with sincerest piety. High above her tower the white corner dragons, the tapering spires, and the golden bulb of the pagoda. She has climbed here by a miracle of effort from some little hamlet in the plain below, because she believes that in a bygone day the Buddha, the founder of her faith her Lord, stood here upon this sacred spot.

CHAPTER XXI

ABOVE PAGAN

PAGAN TO MINGYAN

AFTER the chambered cliffs of Pagan and the last outposts of the once mighty city there is a flat shore slowly ascending on the east, dotted with villages and palms and small clustering trees. On the west the land, more level, reaches away in a plain to the Tangyi hills. The falling river releases from its embrace the island villages, which here, near Pakoku, almost float upon the water at high flood.

Pakoku itself has grown into importance since the caprice of the sovereign river left Konywa high and dry. Half the town, aristocratic with its court-house, its polo-ground, its club and its tennis-courts, and the houses of the European community of officials, stands on a promontory, which is separated from the other half by a thirsty freshet bed which is heavy sand for three parts of the year, and flooded channel for the remaining fourth. Elephants bathe here and cart-wheels creak and drone across it, from its cliffs in the east, to the yards of the timber-sawmen on the west under the lee of the native town. On this further side live the Wesleyan missionary and the skippers of the Chindwin. The town, whose marked prosperity has come to it only since the British annexation, can boast of a number of straight metalled roads ; a bazaar where silks gleam and the Burma girl rules ; groups of airy pagodas, graceful in form, after the manner of Pagan, though poor in detail ; carved monasteries, worth going some way to see ; and the little houses of the people, some of which are very neat and smart, while many are made beautiful by the presence of feathery tamarinds, masses of pink creepers, and yellow-blossomed gourds. Of a morning its lanes fill with processional monks, whose yellow robes gleam in the vistas.

A MASTER-BUILDER AT PAKOKU

But the keynote to the character of Pakoku, and that which distinguishes it from its fellows, is struck where the shipwrights labour under leafy tamarinds for two miles along the river shore. Here the great boats of the Irrawaddy may be seen in every stage of their evolution, from round timber to stately craft. Steel saws scream and crash in the heart of the prisoned logs ; carvers with skilled fingers trace their rich patterns on steering chairs and sterns, and delicate chisels transform the dead wood into figures alive with action, and flowers of intricate beauty ; planks with red ashes smoking over them take the curves which will lift them into grace ; and here, last of all, having passed through every phase of their gestation, the finished craft are launched upon the bosom of the great river, there to accomplish their destiny.

Behind Pakoku there is a low ridge of sand-hills running east and west, and the popular tradition is that of old these were the right bank of the river, and that the prosperous modern town is built upon its ancient bed. Konywa, whose decline has contributed to the prosperity of

Pakoku, was less than fifty years ago the principal town at the mouth of the Chindwin. "Striking across towards the western shore," wrote Yule, "we approach the large village of Koonyuwa, marked by conspicuous temples and two gigantic griffin-lions. The shore was lined with magnificent trees, their large boles surrounded by the risen stream which now washed almost the floors of the cottages. The stooping branches laden with thick foliage, the numerous cottages buried in the trees, and the small pagoda-spires here and there visible, rising through the further groves, presented a succession of beautiful pictures. We anchored almost among the lofty stems of a palmyra-grove, which the waters had inundated." Mingyan, higher up, which he describes as lying "very low, just above the water-level at its greatest height, and without an inch to spare," is now three miles away from the river's edge.

Approaching Mingyan I come upon the full moon rising as the sun dips over the world. "*Vos O clarissima mundi lumina, labentem cælo quæ ducitis annum*"; I murmur the Virgilian invocation. Flocks of wild duck flying swiftly overhead; slow-winged peewits floating parallel with the face of the river; troops of egrets wheeling in wide circles and showing their white under-wings to the silver moon; desert palms sable against the red-lit west; dark figures of boatmen on the river; and over all the growing beauty of the moon's trail on the purple spaces—of such is the spectacle that meets my eye. And long after the sun has set the steamer throbs on, favoured by the radiant clouds and the white splendour of the moon.

Towards midnight new lights appear on the northern horizon, and gradually grow into the transports *Freebooter* and *Rob Roy*, with flats in tow, and three hundred men with racked muskets on board. The placid calm of the moonlit night is broken by these new-comers. All moves as in a play. The panting steamers race past me down the river, till they find an open space at which to touch; then in a flash they swing to, and move slowly up into place. The river, lashed into fury by the paddles, plunges in great waves and breaks vehemently against the shore. The smaller craft, catching the infection, strain madly at their moorings. Lascars shout, and Captains roar their orders above the din. The placing of the gangway planks is a signal to the hungry troops on board and sixty seconds see as many men ashore with cooking pots that glitter in the moonlight, foraging for firewood and seeking out places in which to cook their food. Spectators talk in bated whispers of war in the Chin hills, and there is some quality in the spectacle that makes the blood run and the heart beat faster. Up there in those distant highlands, so far away that for all their ten thousand feet they are invisible from here, the rude tribesmen are unaware of the power they have evoked, of the destiny that is already in train. The British Administrator up there turns from his day's toil with a feeling of irritation, to the tale of tribal raids and the necessity for meting out punishment; the soldier in command of the frontier battalion looks with small pleasure at the prospect of a trifling expedition; these men, now going up there to fight, are all thinking only of their empty stomachs, and the supreme need of staying their hunger; but the spectator, called up in the stilly night, perceives that Life—and Death—are afoot. For him the veil of the commonplace is lifted, the beating heart of the empire sounds in the night watches. "War," say the sailors on the ships and the idlers on the shore, and the word is a moving one. Stray men who have seen the passing spectacle go home with a new-found reverence in their hearts for the mysterious entity under whose shadow they live.

As the night wears on, the fires of the bivouac die down; the bearded men fall into deep sleep; and the late moon, as she moved from mid-heaven to the shadowy west, looks down upon rows of white sleepers, who might be dead men, stretched here upon the shore of the immortal river.

CHAPTER XXII

IN MANDALAY

THE ARAKAN PAGODA

IN 82, Cathedral Street, as I pass down it on my way to the Arakan Pagoda in Mandalay, there is life afoot which tempts me often to linger.

It is the early morning hour when monks go forth to beg, and the street and all the little alleys leading from it are full of the men in yellow. In the wayside shops the sandal-makers are busy, the *hti*-smiths are hammering, and cabinet-makers are plying their minute vocation. From the lay-schools come the voices of children, like the voices of hedge-sparrows cheeping together; bullock-carts creak along the road; ponies, rich with embroidered trappings, amble swiftly by; here and there a nun in faded yellow steps gently in the dust.

Cathedral Street, thus bravely started, ends abruptly, as many things in Mandalay used to, in a ditch. At its bottom women wash clothes, pigs rout for food, and the blue hills of Sagaing and the Shan highlands flank the vista east and west. A crazy bridge a little way off takes me to the other side, where the shops are nearer to each other, and tinmen, and the makers of gold and silver umbrellas display their wares. All along the way the painted acacias make vivid patches of green, most vivid in Mandalay, when all else is dry and withered in the sun. White and gold pagodas line the road; there is a clanging of great bells, the tinkle of little ones on lofty spires. Chinese eating houses tempt the passers-by, silken skirts flash in the sunlight, and dustwhirls drive along the beaten track.

And here, as a matter of fact, I have come upon the threshold of the Arakan Pagoda, where all Mandalay gathers for worship. Tailors labour here, sewing pink and yellow silk coats for children; shoemakers sit

IN 82, CATHEDRAL STREET

surrounded by green and crimson broadcloth shoes; the shops jostle each other, growing more numerous, till I reach where the great masonry cats are scarcely visible for the press of their multitude.

From here to the latticed doors, behind which the profile of the Buddha is faintly visible in the interior gloom, there is a long aisle, half-lit, and filled with yet other stalls.

Some of the pillars of the hall are of plain unpainted wood, others are rich with mirror mosaic and gold. The scene is so attractive, so charged with incident and multiplicity of beauty, that I come insensibly to a standstill. The long vista ahead tempts my feet forward; the shops, the bars of diffused light streaming through the corridors behind, tempt me to stay and look back. One who came here for the first time would need to be callous indeed, if he hoped to go straight through from end to end without a pause. Four corridors with gold-beamed roofs make the square of the edifice under which the Buddha is enthroned.

From a painting by Saya Chone

IN THE PALACE GARDENS, MANDALAY

The exterior of it, now of masonry carved as intricately as wood, rises in diminishing stages to a spire, and the whole fabric is overlaid with gold. False as the workmanship may be, meretricious as you would say it is to work in brick and mortar as if they were wood, hybrid as is the architecture, nothing can detract from the splendour of this gold. Outside, where the unimpeded sun flames on the roof of the temple all is dazzling almost blinding light ; within, in the long corridors, there is a cloistral gloom, and in the innermost sanctuary there would be darkness, were it not for the tapers that flicker on its threshold, and the stray beams which enter in at the great doors, and flame on the new-laid gold of the image.

The pagoda is approached by four corridors at the cardinal points, and each of these ends in a wall of the central shrine. At the north, east, and south, there are pointed arches filled with latticed doors, two of which are seldom opened. The western wall, which stands at the back of the image, has no opening. It is towards the east that the Buddha faces, and here the devotion of his people culminates.

The scene as I look upon it from the eastern corridor is one of extraordinary interest. Over my head is a frescoed porch, gorgeous with the colouring and the imagery of the East. Palaces, crenelated walls, and lotus-covered waters ; ascending spires ; kings and princes in cloth of gold and jewelled vestments, nobles and monks, fabulous beings, elephants and horses, myriads of soldiery, demons of the grossest ugliness, and all the pains of hell, the transitoriness and the suffering of life, are here depicted with singular if primitive realism. To stand here and look up to this painted roof, is to be carried away into the crowded thoroughfares of a strange and grotesque world, from which the transition back to the life surging about one is more than bewildering.

Here under this painted roof sits a blind leper, his hands held forward in mute appeal to the passing world ; and in his stark face there is written the terrible history of his life. Look at it, for here is something that is inexpressibly sad, inexpressibly patient and resigned. Pride, fire, vivacity, hope, all have left it. Yet this man lives on.

Here, before a stall of twists of silk, a blaze of the richest colours, lies a comely girl, full-hipped, asleep. Here, a flower-stall distils its fragrance, the gloom of the passage lit with the pink and purple glory of its lotuses, the wax-white sprays of its tuberoses, and the starry masses of its jasmines, plucked in some garden in the early dawn. A blind fiddler plays in a sunlit alcove, supported by his wife on the mellow *puttala*. A great crowd for ever surges by ; a crowd of monks and nuns, little children and white-filleted old men, wrinkled hags like skeletons at a feast, the prettiest women and the prettiest silks of Mandalay ; wide-hatted Shans, Paloungs from the tea-country, women from distant highlands, in plush and velvet ; the aged slow of foot, the young impetuous ; faces stamped with the sadness and the weariness of life, faces of laughter and lovelit eyes ; voices mumbling the never-ending litany of sorrow—Aneitsa, Dookha, Anata—Change, Sorrow, Unreality ; voices like the tinkle of pagoda bells with an added human thrill. All pass on under the shadow of the painted arch, to the wide corridor beyond, where the light streams in through the lofty Roman archways.

There they come, one and all, to a pause, kneeling on the spread mats and carpets in rear of the lines of worshippers already assembled ; the men in front, the women behind. Beyond the bowed heads is a long trough of flowers and paper pennons, then the rows of flickering lights, and last of all, shrouded in the tremulous gloom, the figure of the Lord Buddha.

Shadowy forms move within, climbing to his knees, and reaching fingers charged with fluttering gold, to every part of his body ; and the effect of the fresh gold as it cleaves in the gloom is that of a flame playing over the image.

For hours one can stand here and look with unrelaxed intensity on this spectacle, which is so vivid, so imposing, so genuine, and so spontaneous. Here there are no attendant priests, there is no liturgy, there is no marshalling of the worshippers. The spectacle remains ; its units for ever change. Men and women come and go, passing right across the scene ; some rise to leave, while others stoop to pray ; each, unconscious of the rest, plays his part in the moving drama. Near me there is a woman with a tray laden with small flowers, which she holds up towards the shrine as she kneels. Her child of two, barely able to stand, clutches at her slender arms, and as the tray goes up, pours into it a cup-full of white petals—her share ; and it is such a picture of artless devotion as no country in the world can rival.

The child is an exquisite being, pretty as all Burmese children are ; the mother has not yet lost the freshness of her youth. Her dark hair, coiled with infinite care and finish on her small head is decorated with a spray of tuberoses ; her short coat of muslin is immaculately white ; a pink *pawa*, light as gossamer, blows about her shoulders ; there is a shimmer of silk about her knees ; her bare feet turned up have a subtle feminine attraction. There is no trace in her soft face of that straining after concentration while at prayer which is characteristic of the strenuous peoples. All that she does seems to come to her without thought. A little Pagan if you will, worshipping without any more effort than some field-flower when it opens to the sky above it.

There is a party of nuns behind her, wrinkled and small and old. They tell their beads, and wag their toothless jaws, and come and go with the large red-lacquered trays and water-bottles which are as much

IN THE EASTERN CORRIDOR

a part of them as the begging-bowls and palmyra fans are of the male fraternity.

A group of Chinese Shans, in strange head-dress and long coats, cling together here, as do all provincials on a visit to the capital. A mother sits nursing her babe; small urchins lie about,with no idea of worship; monks in flowing robes pick their way through the prostrate crowd; young fellows in silks swagger about; stall-holders take their ease under sign-boards of fantastic design, unconscious of any impropriety, and keen spectators of the moving drama that unfolds before them from dawn to dark. Few occupations can rival theirs, for an indolent sociable man, with an eye to the pageantry of life. Foreigners stalk about unmolested, Sikhs and Mohammedans from the barracks at Mandalay, and "Globe-trotters" from the capitals of the world. And all this while the worship at the great shrine goes forward. All that one has seen of Roman Catholic churches in Europe, all that one has pictured of the synagogue, where money-changers and the sellers of doves were used to congregate, is here epitomised.

Outside the eastern entrance there are two large and handsome masonry pools in which the sacred turtle live. Here in the still green water the golden pinnacle of the pagoda is mirrored; and the turtles come up to the surface to be fed by crowds of pretty women who sit waiting on the sun-flooded stairs.

At the gateways there are cages full of small birds, which the simple and the pious buy to free them from captivity. But the birds are little slaves at heart, and they are only too glad to return to their cages.

In the outer courtyard, north of the shrine, and propped against the wall are the bronze giants and three-headed elephants brought from Arakan with the Image in the days of the great King Bodaw Phaya, who made war upon his neighbour for its possession. Hard by is a small shrine with a wishing-stone before it; and within its bars there are the gilded figures of *nats*, who receive no small share of the devotion of passing visitors. But here people are conscious of observation and are ashamed.

THE KUTHO-DAW

There are other things to be seen in Mandalay, the last capital of the Burmese kings. There is the Royal palace, the Burmese Alhambra, enclosed within its red embattled walls, and surrounded by a moat of clear water on which the lotus blooms; there is the seven-roofed spire known as the Centre of the Universe under which the King sat in state and received the homage of foreign ambassadors and of his own people; there is the richly carved and gilded monastery built by Supyalat, the last Queen who sat beside her lord upon the throne of Burma; there are many other things which people go to Burma to see, but nearly all of these are concerned with the history of Burma, which is not for these pages. I have tried to tell that story in another place. But there is one building in Mandalay that can fitly find mention here with the Arakan Pagoda ; which is indeed one of the wonders of the world. It is the Kutho-Daw or Lawka Marazein Pagoda ; a Bible bigger than our own, carved in stone. Every one of its pages, seven hundred and twenty-nine in number, has a temple to itself. The white temples stretch away in long avenues like an army of soldiers, and if you get them in a line and

A STALL

look down it, the great stones recede like colossal mile-posts, till they are lost in the distance. There are rows upon rows of them facing east and west and south and north ; and set in their midst is a lofty white pagoda with a golden spire. It has four grand gateways at the cardinal points ; and trees aligned along the temple avenues. But unlike the Arakan Pagoda it is a place of stillness, like a library, whose solemnity is broken only by the chant of some scholar lying prone upon the floor of a temple —before a leaf of the great book—correcting his copy of the life-giving text. Outside kneeling at the far end of the white stone aisles a small group of worshippers is assembled ; old women with white hair, children with shut eyes and folded hands, and wrinkled elders whose race is nearly run. They kneel here in humility, outside its precincts, because they are a people of fine instincts, and because they think much of this place which enshrines in imperishable stone the message of their Lord ; the wisdom they believe will guide their footsteps into the pathway of eternal peace.

Of these two great shrines, it need only be said that the Arakan Pagoda divides with the Shwe Dagôn the homage of the Buddhist world, because it believes that there is here contained the only contemporary likeness of the Great Teacher; and of the Kutho-Daw, that its text was revised, and the accuracy of its carving was certified to by the most learned monks and officials of the royal city. This labour extended over five years, and it was shared in by all the Ministers of State, as well as by King Mindon himself. No circumstance in the whole of his worthy peaceful life brought him greater contentment than the title of "Convenor of the Fifth Great Synod" which accrued to him as a devout patron of the Buddhist Church, the spiritual successor of Asoka. And maybe he judged wisely.

Book V

THE CHINDWIN

CHAPTER XXIII

THE CHINDWIN

THE Chindwin is the greatest tributary of the Irrawaddy, and it is worthy, alike by reason of its volume, its beauty, and its own strong individual personality of the part it plays in the life of Burma. Its sources lie in the midst of snow-touched peaks and unexplored mountains in the far north. It is not till with its tributaries it enters the Hu Kawng valley in the 27th degree of North Latitude, that it becomes known to civilisation, and even thence it flows for a long way through country to which a traveller can only commit himself at considerable peril. For the Pax Britannica has not yet settled upon the wild tracts that border its northern waters. Nor is any continuous navigation of it possible till after it has emerged from the defiles which bar its progress between the 26th and 27th degrees of North Latitude. Thereafter, before the depletion of winter lessens the volume of its waters, shallow stern-wheeled steamers can traverse it without hindrance to its junction with the Irrawaddy. It enters the greater river in two streams, with a space twenty-two miles in extent between. One of these streams, the present highway, is an old royal canal cut by a bygone kind of Pagan. It silted up and foı centuries it remained unused, till in 1824 a great flood came and cut a new passage through it.

This arm of the Chindwin now enters the Irrawaddy at an acute angle, and the land between is low. Hence, for some distance from the apex the two rivers look as if they ran parallel to each other. From the bridge of a Chindwin boat the funnels of the great steamers on the Irrawaddy can be seen racing over the level of the fields; the town of Mingyan gleams on the far eastern shore ten miles away, and the farthest bank of the great river can be traced from the mid-current of its feudatory. At high floods the narrow peninsula between them is submerged, and tree-tops and hamlet roofs alone mark the division between.

Leaving the Irrawaddy in the early dawn of an October morning, I am well into the Chindwin, whose scenery comes with a sudden transition upon me, accustomed since I left the wide spaces of the Delta, to meridian mountain-chains, to lines of broken irregular hills, high cliffs, and a rolling undulating country. For here at the mouth of the Chindwin, the Delta, it would seem, begins again. Blue hills are still happily visible; but the main impression is of flat lands, and groves of tufted palms and umbrageous sheltering trees; and a narrow river unbroken from one low shore to the other. Villages are numerous along the banks;

COMING ON BOARD

monastery spires, thatched cottages, and here and there a pagoda in the Pagan style lend diversity to the landscape. White-winged boats, laden with the produce of the valley, speed down-stream under stress of a northerly wind, to the mightier traffic of the Irrawaddy. Haystacks on piles, like great bee-hives, built high to protect them from the floods, strike a new and individual note. Sandy spaces left bare by the shrinking river are strewn with logs and derelict trees. Here the people are busy with dragging chains and cattle; and trunk after trunk, the harvest of the flood, is borne away into the mist.

The navigation of the river in its lower courses is hazardous and difficult. All the way since dawn I have listened to the leadsman's song. For it is the turn of the year, new channels have been forming all the flood season, and all is yet new and unknown. I am travelling in the first stern-wheeler of the season, the skipper on the bridge has a reputation to lose and the company is intolerant of mistakes. But for me, who am but an idle traveller below, there is much entertainment. The almost noiseless paddles, the summer day, the white processional clouds, the drowsy blue of the nearer hills, make serene travelling for any one not freighted with responsibility.

The trees, undone by the floods, lie like Goliaths on the sandy banks. The walls of the islands in our course are striped with strange patterns

EARLY TRIBUTARIES

where the blowing wind makes furrows in the unresisting sand. Fragments of them fall all through the day into the river, as though to reverse the very process which called them into existence. Ceaseless change, ceaseless unrest, is the character of these Eastern rivers, notwithstanding that they attain to heights of superficial calm.

As we go a quartet of peaks like Pyramids in Egypt rise up on the river's horizon. Dark blue masses of foliage, and intense yellow-green strips of rice line the rich foreshore; overhead there is a blue cloud-puffed sky. In the fields the people toil, and yellow-robed monks pass in procession amongst the palms. The country is slightly more broken and undulating in the west, ending on the river in high mud cliffs. The quartet loom bigger and nearer and a long wave of low hills comes down to the river. The village of Hnaw-Kado greets us, facing an unbroken line of palms.

At sunset, in the short half-hour before the dark, there is a beautiful climax to the day, in wide spaces of pink sky, shadowy purple hills, and a great reach of waters blending these two colours and spreading unbroken from shore to shore. It is no longer the Chindwin or any definite tract ; but a rich and splendid page in the book of the world's beauty. The dark tufted palms cut against the sunset blaze, the wide reach of waters, the blue pyramidal isolated hills recall, if anything, the Nile.

We anchor for the night in mid-river, and as the stars begin to shine, the skipper comes down red-eyed and tense-featured from his day's toil. He has been up on the bridge since early dawn, his eyes straining through the hours over the river spaces. This is the most anxious season in the year for him. Thirty seconds of carelessness might ruin his career. Hence the chant,

> Ek bam mila nahin,
> Hath kum do bum,

I have listened to all day.

As we ascend at dawn the quartet lose their character, and develop into a blue-green hill on the west bank of the river, and Monywa, with its long lines of waiting boats, its dark trees and white pagodas comes into view. Once the plaything of the floods, a settlement in which the court-house frequently became an island accessible only by boat, Monywa is now protected by an embankment behind which it lies like a fortress behind its walls. It is a pleasing little town of seven thousand inhabitants, commanding views of no little beauty. A military air pervades it ; bugles peal above the voices of its people ; and the twinkling lance-heads of men-at-arms gleam of an afternoon through its deep-fringed foliage. It can boast of a little social club at which the small colony of English folk meet of an evening. Like all such colonies *in partibus*, it is hospitable and willing to be friendly to the stranger. The hills that face it are tenanted by austere anchorite monks of another faith, who live their lives in complete seclusion from the world

We stay a long while under the high shore at Monywa, to take the mails brought hither from Mandalay by train. All that lies beyond Monywa is accessible only by water. While we wait the river edge is lively with bathers of all ages. They leap and make somersaults into the water, swim under it, and feel their way with the help of slim bamboos and laugh and shout through the hours. A pleasant sight and a pleasant life all but sealed to our very serious selves at the club.

EARLY TRIBUTARIES

We come away past timber-rafts and palm-encircled villages to Alôn, a place of dark old pagodas and fine trees. In the days of the kings of Burma, Alôn was the seat of a governor and a place of consequence, but the tide of destiny has passed it by.

Dust-winds and clouds of flying sand diversify the uneventful landscape till we come to Kyauk-hmaw and its tapering spires; beyond which there is a glimpse of mountains in the west soaring between translucent layers of cloud.

At Ayaungthamya Natdaung, which means a great deal to the tutored ear, a wooded and very picturesque promontory crowned by a white pagoda, ends abruptly in the river in sheer cliffs. Here the river parts finally with its deltaic character, and the transition from the Dry Zone is complete. At Shwezayé the river runs through a narrow defile, two hundred yards in width. On the left bank the village rises above a rocky base, and ends at a considerable height in a large well-shaped pagoda. On the right the scenery is of the grand order. The precipices overlooking the river are worn into fantastic forms by the river's action at their base, and above, where they soften into rounded hill-tops, they are clothed with exuberant tropic vegetation. A small pagoda, and a *tagôn-daing* that glitters in the sun, crown a prominent cliff where the river makes its curve. Shwezayé (the Golden Whirlpool) is a truculent water, and more than one steamer and innumerable small craft have come to grief in its toils. The villagers make a living, like Cataract sheikhs, by navigating rafts through it at its turbulent season. On such occasions all the raft people land and leave their craft entirely to these pilots of the whirlpool. Three miles from Shwezayé there is the crater of a dead volcano, with a lake and a village at its bottom. Strange superstitions cling to this water which is believed to be of immeasurable depth. Its level is said to rise when the river is low, and to fall when it is in flood.

Beyond the defile the river is wider, and the waters held back by its presence stretch unbroken from bank to bank. At Maukko the channel narrows and here we sleep for the night. The dropping of the anchor is the signal for a general exodus from the ship. The nearest village is two miles away; but an ample sandbank offers its hospitality to all. The men light their cooking fires, the women take to washing clothes on the gangway planks, the children make sand-castles and roll on the grateful earth. All through the night these good people camp out under the stars, singing, laughing and telling tales, till a sudden blast of rain towards dawn drives them in confusion to the refuge of the steamer.

As we move on past Natgyi low wooded banks contain the river on either hand. Gaunt trees that have survived the year hold on by their roots with something like desperation; but they are doomed to go with

MINGIN: CHIN HILLS ON THE HORIZON

next year's flood. The river's path, as I strain up its vistas, is traceable through a gap in the line of forest, beyond which ranges of hills rise up in successive folds. Each mountain wave varies in colour from its neighbour ; each moment sun and cloud ring the changes from blue to green, the colours of the peacock; and the river moving on its way bestows upon the scene the continuity of sentient life. It is scenery of a restful order, content-bringing, and pleasant to the eyes. The gap as we approach it becomes the gateway of Kani and Kané ; the former a lofty cliff surmounted by a pagoda, with a charming village of palms and betel-vines below it, and wooden stairs reaching up from the water. Here the steamer waits, and the passengers for Kani make their way up the slippery cliff-side and up the narrow stairs to their own and every one else's entertainment. Amongst them there is one, a pretty girl, with pink *pawa* blowing over her shoulders and a bale of blue cloth poised on her head, a plump and rather lively caryatid ; beside her there is a lad with a heavy cargo, with which he climbs up, every muscle on his fine limbs quivering from the strain of the slippery cliff ; next an old dame, withered and lean, in the one scant garment that age here unhappily affects. As the steam from the ship's side puffs out with a sudden roar, enveloping the climbers, the girl laughs and affects to be frightened, hiding her face in her hands. She has for an audience all the village idlers—that is to say, the entire population—and each one of them is vastly interested in the spectacle provided for his entertainment. Every slip in the puddle is greeted with joy, and every passenger on the steamer is discussed with penetrating candour. This is the biweekly treat of the village.

The pagoda-crowned spur of Kani is the outwork of an almost concontinuous line of hills, with a precipitous front overlooking the river. It is known as the Shwé-myinbyu-Taung—or Golden Hill of the White Horse—from a legend which connects it with the fate of a bygone governor of Kani. The governor was viceroy of Anawrata King of Pagan, in the year A.D. 1040, and he rebelled against his august master. He was utterly defeated and met his death, as the tale runs, by riding his white pony at full gallop over the cliff into the river beneath. He became in due time a *nat*, and his memory was kept green by the people at an annual festival till the war of 1885 swept the custom away. A more pleasing tale attributes the name of Kani to the happy fortune of a wild boar, who, being pursued by a prince of the U dynasty and hard pressed, escaped with his life on the site of the present village.

The remains of a fort built by King Anawrata's rebellious viceroy, can still be traced on the summit of the cliff. The hills beyond Kani continue in *échelon*. Near the village of Yin-yein, with its pagoda spire glittering like a jewel in the sun, lies the island of Pho-su-ua, clothed

THE JUNCTION OF THE CHINDWIN AND THE MYITTHA UNDER KALEWA

with meadows of *kaing* and splendid trees; the first wooded island since we left the Irrawaddy. New and loftier ranges of mountains stretch across the river's horizon; and the great colonies of palms have disappeared. Tributary streams come down at intervals, mainly from the west, the level of their great beds many feet above that of the river. When in flood they pour down immense volumes of water with great impetuosity, and the places of their union are dreaded by all who navigate the Chindwin. The current here runs strong, and the deep rustling sound of the steamer contending with it fills the air. Making curve after curve of great range and beauty, and travelling past silvery islands and lofty wooded cliffs, we come to anchor once more at the village of Yindaw.

At Maukka-daw, in the dawn, there is a great concourse of people assembled to greet the steamer. Bold cliffs with white faces front the river abruptly as if they had been cut with a knife. They are pitted with the nesting holes of sand-martins, who wheel and flutter like butterflies before them. Exuberant creepers hang in festoons over the cliff-sides, engulfing whole trees. Up-stream there is a vista of long blue mountain and unruffled water, half-veiled at this hour and season in lifting fog. Higher up, the cliffs are found on the west, the width of the river is unbroken and its windings conceal its path, so that it looks like a lake, till each curve is accomplished and a new scene challenges the eye.

At Pindin there is a swift transition. The river banks, parting like doors, yield a view of wooded islands, pagoda-crowned promontories, and a lofty range of mountains, whose summits are only partially visible under the clouds. The Patolan here rushes down from the west, pouring in its flood of red waters. The two arms of the Chindwin sweeping round the island of Chundaw, meet in fierce union, and the strength of their current is a powerful obstacle to progress. The western arm curves round under the heights of Mingin, happily placed between wide spaces of cloud and water, in the forefront of the mountains. Peaks, ten thousand feet in height, are visible from here.

Mingin is a prosperous and cheerful place, the residence of many timber merchants and of people well-to-do. It has a reputation for piety, and contributes *htis* to pagodas and manuscripts to monasteries lower down the river. "If you want work, go to Kindat; fun, go to Mingin; if you want to die go," the wise people say, "to Maukka-daw."

The island that divides the river below it becomes at flood time the scene of a curious *battue*. The wild pigs that live there, driven by the encroaching waters, seek shelter in the highest part of the island. Then the villagers go forth with clubs and slay them. It is a beautiful island of dark trees and plantain-groves and waving grasses set in the wide encircling folds of the river, and the blue Chin mountains tower greatly above it.

After Mingin the river sweeps round under lofty cliffs on the west, separated from its edge by a line of woods. No islands break its continuity. Near Mindin we steer straight in the face of the sun, and the river—steeped in calm, a mirror for the dazzling clouds, the dense thronging forest and the peaks of the mountains; and diversified with light and shadow and misty curtains of rain—reaches a climax of beauty. At Chaungua, half hidden by an outer wall of cliffs, there are low hills on the west, grassy and lightly wooded, which rise in successive peaks like the teeth of a saw. Reefs stretch across the water from the eastern shore and the river pours over them in angry disorder. The village of Phayanga suns itself in the east under a line of palms, and wide spaces of rice-land spread out, putting all other green things to shame. As the sun descends the cliffs by the river flame pink and so go with us into the dusk.

BALUSTRADE OF MONASTERY AT MINGIN

The character of the river grows wilder and more turbulent as we gradually approach its junction with the Myittha at Kalewa. This is a very notable point in its course and the approach to it loses nothing by its protracted grandeur. Sheer cliffs and rocky islands worn into complex forms ; seething whirlpools, the dread of all who must pass through them ; forests of primeval richness—these are the main features of the river's course below Kalewa. There are few signs of cultivation. The people are mainly timber-cutters and raftsmen and salvors, whose labour is witnessed by the rescued logs on the banks.

At Kongua there is a hamlet very charmingly placed on a little tongue of land at the junction of a small tributary with the river. Its line of brown huts and feathery palms is invisible to the eye till one is very near it. Then a gap discloses itself in the continuous wall of cliffs, and one by one the features of the village deploy. The cliffs facing the river are scarred with white gashes, where a part of the weather-worn surface has been rent away. As the river recedes from its high flood level, it leaves bare the pedestals of the hills which confine it. These are worn into water-holes by the swirling current. Ferns and grasses grow up between the receding water-line and the woods, making a vivid belt all the way up the curving river. The Péwé whirlpool waits for the unwary just below Kalewa. It is the most dangerous spot on the Chindwin, and steamers have often to wait for days at Kalewa before attempting it. Shut in here amongst the mountains the river attains a depth of sixty-five fathoms.

Kalewa, famous in the annals of British pacification in Upper Burma, owes its importance to the fact that it stands where the Myittha pours its waters into the Chindwin ; and the Myittha is the key tò Chinland, that vast sub-Alpine tract of savagery, which reaches away, a barrier since the beginning of things, between Burma and India. From Kalewa as a base, the wild highlands of Chinland were conquered, and for years this village, hidden in remote places, resounded to the tread of armed battalions on their way to the scene of war. Heroes like Sir George White and Sir Power Palmer have stepped ashore at Kalewa. In the Chin Hills Sir Bertram Cary won to fame.* Its main street is built on the blade-edge of a narrow promontory, between the swift Myittha and the Chindwin. An amphitheatre of hills surrounds it. From the river it looks like a dilapidated collection of hovels, but the street itself runs through a double line of shops, in which many English goods are exhibited for sale, and it gains picturesqueness from its over-hanging palms its betel-vines and scarlet-tasselled hibiscus. The slopes of the promnotory overlooking the Myittha are sheer, and in spite of piles, appear to be giving way to the river's attack. On the summit of the ridge are placed the barracks of the military police, and the houses of the European officers who live here to maintain this outpost of an empire their hands have helped to build. On the hill-slope, facing the Chindwin, and often flooded by its rising waters, are the graves of those

*The story of those exploits was told in a 'Gazetteer,' written by him and H. N. Tuck.

THE ENTERING MYITTHA

who have died in the same cause. Under the foreshore lie the flat boats of the country, shallow of draught and incapable of turning over, but rough in workmanship and outline, and not to be compared for beauty with the great Hnaus of the Irrawaddy builders. One can tell a Chindwin boat anywhere in Burma. The Myittha is navigable by boats as far as Kan, and steamers have ascended it a hundred and twenty miles. But the numerous rapids which mark its course make its navigation hazardous and difficult.

Kalewa, "the mouth of Kalé," stands at the entrance to the Kalé valley. Kalemyo, "the town of Kalé," which is approached by way of the Myittha through scenery of extraordinary beauty, was for long the capital town of the valley and its walls and ramparts can still be traced. The valley is rich and fruitful, but cursed with malaria; and before the British arms overcame the Chin highlanders, it lay at their mercy and was frequently harassed by raids.

CHAPTER XXIV

THE CHINDWIN—Continued

ABOVE Kalewa, the sandstone cliffs that are a peculiar feature of Chindwin scenery increase in height and continuity, and between these mighty walls there lies in a gap the village of Balet. To this remote settlement were deported many of those prisoners, French and Portuguese, who fell into the hands of the King of Ava after the fall of Syriam, three hundred years ago; and here their descendants, completely Orientalised, may still be traced. Not far from Balet there is the site of an ancient walled city of whose origin little is known. It is believed by some to mark the track of those who first came from India to civilise the Burmese races. The story of the origin of Balet itself is too characteristic of the Burmese idiosyncrasy to be omitted. In the year 990 of the Burmese era, the King of Ava resolved to invade Pegu. He consulted his astrologers with a view to victory, and was told that his Commanding-general must be a man with black hands. Search was made for such a person and he was found fishing near the river bank at Letmetaung. He was appointed by the king the commander of his armies and led them to victory. To reward him the king bestowed upon him land two square miles in extent; the revenue of which (*petlet*) he might enjoy (*eiksa*), and he was left free to choose it where he would. Accordingly he set out with a cock placed in the prow of his canoe and resolved to settle where the cock might crow. At Sin-Kaung Seik his cock crowed while he was eating and there he took his land of the king and settled down, naming the place Petlet-samyo, subsequently whittled down to Balet.

Above Balet, there appears one of those gateways which are characteristic of the Chindwin. The river narrows between hills, through which it has forced a passage, and beyond, and transverse to the river's course, a line of mountains runs like a great barrier across the horizon. The river widens to a large circular lake above the gates, enclosing an island, and the two streams rush together in tumult as they come through. The western current is swift, and flows under the lofty precipices which rise from its edge, and raftsmen say their prayers when they reach this corner. Steamers coming down in the high floods descend tail first, ready to steam away from collision with the rocks. Polesmen, with long poles thrust out, wait by the ship's side to break the impact. Above Masein the Government steamer *Pagan* came to an end. Finding that there was not room enough for her to turn in she took her chance of cutting the corner and smashed into it.

A TRIBUTARY

Masein displays a grassy foreshore to the falling river, a white pagoda, a telegraph office, and many palms. The telegraph-wire spans the whole width of the river. Masein bore an evil reputation in the first days after the war, and from its cliffs the outlaws who haunted it kept a sharp lookout for the coming of the troops. These cliffs indeed are like the walls of a mighty natural fortress.

For a long distance above Masein the river curves majestically under the blue wooded mountains. Their crests are cut like the sharp overreaching teeth of a saw, and the effect of this succession of curved teeth all curving up-stream, is a singular one, for they make the mountains look as if they were pursuing the river. For miles there is no sign of human habitation, till we come upon the hamlet of "Nancy Lee," a collection of huts and plantain-groves, a small pagoda, and a chapel built to appease the evil spirit of the place. It is built on the bank of a creek which flows through a deep gorge, from whose far gloomy interior the trunks of trees are floated down by the timber-contractors. In the flood season the timber, rushing together down the narrow waters, is stayed in its progress, and the chaos of logs plunging and crashing in the fury of the river, piles up incessantly as each new log is added to the mass. The loneliness, the savage isolation of such a spot, is heightened for a white man by the knowledge that far away behind the gorge, and in the remotest places of the hills, there are Englishmen who spend their lives in the timber trade. It is one thing to pass swiftly by in a steamer equipped with the comforts of civilisation and another to live a dog's life in the jungle.

The timber-salvor himself, a half-clad son of the forest is oppressed with the isolation of his life. Festivals and gaiety are little in his way, and at all times he is surrounded by the spirits of nature, nearly all malevolent, all to be appeased with sedulous care. For one lives in his house, another in the whirlpool before his door, a third in the tree he is cutting down, a thousand in the dark mountains that shut his country away from the traffic of the world. A decade ago, to the malevolence of spirits was added the lust and fury of his fellow man. The head-hunter came raiding for his head ; the cateran of the hills for his wife, his cattle, for himself. From Ningin, inland, there is a road of the Shan which climbs up to the crest of a hill, its ascent or descent on the far side being accomplished by ladders ranged along the sheer face of the cliffs. By this road the harassed people were used to retreat before a Chin raid, lifting their ladders after them. Here, as we steam on our way to the upper waters of the Chindwin, we are well within the limits of the empire, but very near for all that to the core of unrestricted savagery. And I remind myself that, if to-morrow the empire were to withdraw its legions, the curtain of savagery would instantly be let down again.

Continuing from " Nancy Lee " the river runs on under the open glades of the forest, its course broken by sandbanks and grassy islands, till near Maulaikgyi it presents again the spectacle noticed at Mingin. The banks of the river disclose between them an island, green with noble trees, and silvery with the plumes of *kaing*, round which, and under the broad barrier of blue peaks and mountains, the divided stream circles. Not very far from here there is a lake where the rhinoceros is shot. It is a fever-stricken place, a haunt of the Chin, but carefully avoided by the Burman.

Kindat, the winter limit of the company's steamers, is the last British settlement on the Chindwin. Above this point Englishmen go as travellers, to inspect a military outpost, to supervise the construction of a road, to control the work of a native magistrate. But no Englishman lives north of Kindat. The vaguely defined frontier is still several hundred miles away ; but all that lies between is ruled by a native officer, or a feudatory prince, or it is not ruled at all. To the British official in

THE HAMLET OF SITTAUNG

Burma, accustomed to life in remote settlements, Kindat is the *ultima Thule* of official employment, and if he goes there, it is either because he is young and must begin somewhere, or because he has offended and must be punished, or because it is cheap living there and he is in debt. And Kindat is hated for these things, and because it is built on a low slip of fever-haunted land, between a marsh and a river. Yet all things have their relative value, and to the timber-cutter, fresh from the solitude of the jungle, Kindat is a little capital; for it is a place in which there is more than one white man.

From Kindat to Homalin, a distance of 147 miles, there is little regular traffic, save by means of the Government launches which ply to and fro with military stores and rations and bodies of armed men. Yet it is above Kindat that the fascination of remote travel finds its full expression

Past Tatkon, where peewits wing their flight, and glossy ferns and foliage rising in tiers grace the steep banks of the river, the traveller bound for Homalin comes to Pantha and its clusters of white pagodas. Thereafter, the river sweeps round under two thousand feet of hills, and receives the tribute of the Yu from the valley of Kalé. Manipur is not far distant, and troops have marched this way to the relief of beleaguered garrisons. The telegraph wire, earliest pioneer of British civilisation, here crosses the Chindwin to Tammu, as far as which outpost the Yu is navigable. At Kadugyabaung, the river flowing through a picturesque defile, makes a curve from the apex of which its course can be traced through three-quarters of a circle. The curve completes itself under a magnificent cliff that is crowned with pagodas and is sacred to a *nat*. It is known as the Shwé Palin Daung, and it is typical of the hills along this portion of the river's course, which slope easily on their eastern faces and end in sudden precipices on the west. The blue mountains, the precipitous cliff, the great curve, make here between them, an episode of beauty and power. Thirty-one miles of travel from the junction of the Yu bring us to the hamlet of Sittaung, a place of ten houses, which exists because it is on the road to Manipur. It is very unhealthy, but serene of a morning, with its monastery at one end, surrounded by betel-palms, its Government rest-house at the other, and its one narrow street of thatched houses overlooked by *papayas* in full fruit, by plantains and betel-vines. Although remote and isolated it has nearly all the most beautiful things in nature to look at if it will.

Leaving it, and past a big island and splendid avenues of forest, we come to Paungbyin, a place of some note on the river. A long line of new houses stretches along the high flat shore; a court-house, reached by a bridge and a pathway through the jungle, stands on an adjoining hill; a monastery lies in the seclusion of a grove of palms and other trees. Paddy-flats and snipe grounds spread away beyond. Paungbyin does a considerable trade in buying and rafting down the rice grown in the interior, and in supplying the inland villages with European goods. Every house in the village is a shop, and every inhabitant, by virtue of locality, a trader. Some little time ago the village was burnt down, and now it has arisen again with new splendour. Flower-pots grace the front doors of most of the cottages, and every one is taking a hand in levelling the open strip of land between the village and the river. House property is cheap at Paungbyin, and the best house in the village, a large and pleasant-looking habitation, is tenanted by a man whose income is only £12 a year. But the habitable space is limited by the lowlands and swamps that surround the village; and there is consequently a large

SUNSET AT PAUNGBYIN

colony of water-dwellers under the river bank whose houses are built on rafts. On the farther shore is the neat village of Pasagon, and beyond it flats and marshes stretch away to the foot of successive ranges of blue hills, which divide the Kubo valley, once in dispute between the kings of Burma and Manipur, from the Chindwin. Of an evening, the view from the court-house, which stands on the fringe of the impenetrable jungle, is one of superb beauty; for the Chindwin may be seen from there winding away in great loops, yet still as if life had never moved upon it; a water of infinite calm, painted with every glory of mountain shadow and cloud aflame. But Paungbyin is unwholesome, lonely and fever-stricken; a place of bitter memory to Englishmen who have spent a year or two of their lives there. It has been supplanted now by

Homalin, at the junction of the two principal rivers of the district, and the task of ruling the wild country that spreads away to an indefinite border beyond it has been confided to a Burmese officer. It is not the least interesting feature of Paungbyin to-day, that its headman is a woman—a pleasant-looking girl, who has succeeded her father in that office.

After leaving the hilly crests of Paungbyin, the river runs a long straight course like some noble canal, between grassy banks and forest, till at Minya there appears a great island in mid-stream, and the approach to Mingin is repeated. Above the island, the river, very wide to the eye, curves slowly through a dark forest, whose summits helped by the natural elevation of the banks, rise to stately heights. On a little rock at Letpantha, the golden spires of a cluster of small pagodas gleam in the forefront of the forest masses.

Thaungdut, capital of a principality, lies on the mid-curve of the river, where it makes a great sweep a short way above Letpantha. It is a clean little village, with one long wide street facing the river, under avenues of palms and horse-radishes. The palace is a collection of mat huts within an enclosure of high mat walls, the posts of which are decorated with orchids. But the Saw-bwa is careful to explain that he occupies it only as a temporary measure, that his predecessor's widow, a lady of strong character, is in possession of the ancestral site ; and he comes down with his retainers, with a gift of spears and peacocks, to lay this matter before the English ruler of the district, as we let go our anchor under the foreshore of his capital. And after he has gone, comes the lady with her daughter, to state *her* view of the matter. The Saw-bwa hates her because she has allowed her daughter to contract a *mésalliance* with the son of a goldsmith, and the goldsmith's son, who was turned out of the state by the Saw-bwa, has come up with us to claim his right to live in his native village with the wife of his choice. Such are the matters of state that bring us in the Government yacht to Thaungdut, and while we smile at the comedy, we remember that life is cheap in these localities.

The Saw-bwa is a person of some consequence in his own country. He claims that the history of his state began twenty-eight centuries ago, and that its first capital was a walled city in the days of Gautama the Buddha. The blood of Anawratta the Great flows in his veins, and the right of his ancestors to a palace and a throne was admitted by that monarch, and in more recent times confirmed by Mindon, King of Burma. A sumptuary law of that monarch lays down that the front pavilion of the Saw-bwa's *haw* or palace shall have nine mainposts, and the main room five stories, a gold *hti* on the spire of the court-room, a vane with a flowered shaft, a white umbrella, and a throne with twelve

THE SAW-BWA OF THAUNGDUT

chambers. These concessions were made by the King in return for the Saw-bwa's gift of a white elephant, happily found within the limits of his state. The Saw-bwa is now a feudatory of the empire, and the area of his state is five hundred and fifty square miles. He leaves behind him, after a visit, the impression of being a gentleman; and he plays polo in the Manipurian manner when his polo-ground is not flooded by the river.

Above Thaungdut the river encircles a large island, then runs on in a straight path facing a mountain barrier, and attains in the full noontide an exquisite beauty, where it curves by Hwemadai Laungmin, with rich forests on either bank, and a range of blue-green mountains curving in fellowship with it on the west. It loses nothing of its apparent size here being broad and full from one bank to the other, and unbroken by sands or islands. From moment to moment as the wind blows, or as it dies away, the face of the river changes from crinkling ripples to a crystal calm; and the clouds in rhythm fling their shadows lazily on the mountain slopes.

Beyond these passages of varied beauty the double-mouthed Nampanga pours her quota into the sovereign river, and all the land between is of alluvial flats and winding broken channels, overlooked by great mountains. Then, as the river circles to the west, the Uyu comes down to it, flowing between low mudbanks.

Above the junction an island, laden with silver-green *kaing*, cuts the broad purple spaces of the river with its sharp outline, and beyond lies Homalin, a line of lowly houses at the foot of the giant mountains. The village is in fact a long way from them, for the river making an unsuspected curve to the north, sweeps in between them and Homalin. But the illusion remains of a village in a mountain country, Swiss or Tyrolese, with great masses towering above it. The mountains here run into nine thousand feet, and their nearer slopes are marked with patches of rough cultivation. Their summits are constantly veiled in clouds which impart to them an air of grandeur and mystery; and white wisps of cloud lie in the lofty valleys, deepening the perspective, and causing the nearer peaks and ridges to stand out sharp and blue against their quiet curtains. Rain-mists gather in the far interior, lit with the last rays of the fading sun; distant peaks seen through this diaphanous veil become transfigured; and the great material barrier of the mountains, frowning over the dark river and the little street of houses, seems only the threshold of a far-withdrawn land of spiritual and unearthly beauty

Little is known of many of these mountain tracts. In the language of the State they are "unadministered," and there is little desire on any one's part to break through the immemorial seclusion in which they live.

Down by the river all is peace. Spread abroad here over vast spaces it is almost motionless. It is shallow and the winter waits to expose its shallowness. Yet the purple shadows of the mountains lend it the suggestion of unfathomed depths. Little if any life moves upon its surface. A derelict log floats by with scarcely perceptible motion; sand-bubbles break and spread their concentric rings in silence. From the cover of the silver *kaing* a buffalo waddles slowly down to the river's edge, mammoth-like—a counterpart of the slow quiet world about him. In the fading light he makes a clear black spot on the landscape—a lictor of the night. On the distant eastern horizon, clouds, like white puffs from a furnace stayed in the full tide of their life, become a palette for the last light of the sun, and their lustrous reflections make all the river looking down a mirror of pink and opal loveliness, that is in supreme antithesis to the dark mystery, the deep unfathomable purple of it, under the mountains.

Mountains and river are here in close fellowship, yet those blue-green patches on the slopes, and the line of little houses by the river, are a whole world apart. To the mountaineer all below is a forbidden tract of civilisation, once in the great days gone by his prey. To the plainsman all that is of the mountains savours of a savagery greater than his own, and a hate that is never asleep. The one from his valley hamlets, the other from his eyrie on the cliffs, regard each other and pass by. There is no communion between them.

Homalin is in the keeping of an Arakanese officer, one of the ablest of his countrymen. He rules here over a country more than 2,500 square miles in extent; the finest of all the fine shooting-grounds of Burma.

Early dawn, and I am afloat once more on the Chindwin, making the great curve above Homalin under forest-clad cliffs; while the mountain masses deploy in the west in peaks and waves and precipices. Faint clouds hover near their summits, but this morning not *on* them, and the first efforts of the sun only make shadows fall on their broad expanse. These are no hills, but mountains of a grand order, and the spectacle of them, their rocky peaks and wooded valleys so near that one can recognise all the familiar features, stirs up a great longing to be up amongst them. Ah! what views must expand from there over the fair river valley, and the waves upon waves of mountains that roll away to the far plains of the west. What under-worlds of fern and bracken and violets dew-besprinkled. What beakers of divine air! And for the rest, elephants crashing through the forest, rhinoceroses in the secret woods, panthers in lair, wandering herds of bison, and visionary pheasants dropping from heights into the gloom of the sheltered valleys.

But I am bound to-day to the river and may not neglect its beauty at this hour of soft lights and long shadows. An island with its familiar chisel-like apex, bears down upon us in mid-stream. The river enfolds it in two sweeping curves and it looks like a mighty ship afloat. It is of a new order, for all the islands we have hitherto met have borne the family feature of rustling wind-blown savannahs set with noble trees, park-like, and of a light emerald green. Here we come to dark forest and white stems; forest to the outer bulwarks, overhanging the very lips of the river. All that I can fancy of American rivers in the north is here depicted. There is no whisper of the East. The change is opportune, for it reminds me that we have passed out of the tropics and are now within the Temperate-zone—a comforting reflection when one lives very near the Equator.

Sein Kan, with its orange orchards and the red spires of its monastery, waits at the turning of the river, and its next curve, a quick short loop, brings us up to Kawya. For a long while past, the wooded banks of the river have talked of pines, and here the likeness may be recorded. Straight grey trunks of the silver hue and the nude beauty of the longifolia, gnarled and twisted arms, and light summit foliage, make these trees look like twin brethren of the pines, and one is grateful for the suggestion. Also, when the red light of evening flames on their bare trunks and arms, and the sky is cut into patterns by their fantasies, it is difficult to resist the illusion.

SARAMATI IN THE DISTANCE

Kawya is a pleasing little village of the Shan. Lanes wind through it piloted by rustic fences. Flowers add to its charm. The houses stand in little enclosures of their own and it is not their way here to face the street. They are roofed with rough palm thatch which projects far over the front of each house in a semicircle. Under its open shelter, weaving and winnowing and many other household avocations are performed. Tea grows at Kawya but the bushes are allowed to grow up untrimmed. Behind the village, amongst the tea-plants, one is rather in a rough orchard, half jungle, than in a trim tea-garden. The leaves are boiled and sold to trading Burmans who raft them down the river. Seeds have been sold to " men from the west "; but no purchasers have appeared for the past three years. The last comers were emissaries from the white Planters of Assam. The seed trade is not it would seem a prospering one ; but a large business is done in boiled tea for export to Lower Burma.

At Kawya there is a colony of dark pagodas overlooking the river, *tagôn-daings* of glittering mosaic, and a thousand-Buddha stupa overlaid with gold. The river bank recalls Bhamo. The people dress like Burmese. Yet the village is not Burmese in its suggestion. I have long since left Burma behind me and am here amongst the Shan.

Kawya has for its neighbour an island cleaving south. Above it the river runs on unbroken, between rich woods to Maung-Kan where oranges grow.

Tazon follows, also a place of tea. From Maing Taung to Shwelaung there is a straight way marked out for the river, between near woods in the east and great forests in the west, reaching away over flat and rolling country to the foot of the mountains, whence they climb in unbroken splendour to heights of eight thousand feet. The Nan-Kaung here comes down with its tribute, and the place of its union with its over-lord is green and tempting. One would willingly stay to trace its secret course of which there is but a glimpse from the passing ship. Later the Namwe enters. A waterfall of great size is visible on the face of the distant cliffs, and at Maingwe the further course of the river is concealed from the eye, so sharp is the curve it makes there. A passage of marked beauty follows, the river winding in and out through " zones of light and shadow," its waters gaining clarity with every mile, till it reaches the climax of a horseshoe curve where the Nayayin enters at Yet Pa. Both arms of the river here reach away like lakes, through avenues of forest to the stately mountains, whose king is Saramati snow-crowned like Soracte in winter. The winds that blow here at this season are laden with the scent of forest flowers—a rich heavy scent as from a distillery. There are miles upon miles of it here.

After the horseshoe turn at Yet Pa—noblest passage of the Chindwin —the river breaks away to the east, and the mountains pass out of sight ; but the woods line it with continuous beauty, and in the waning afternoon every white trunk on the eastern shore meets its image in the clear water.

At Tamanthé the river returns again to its mountains, which loom up blue and majestic in bold outline against the sky ; waves upon waves of them, ramparts and peaks and shadowy valleys. The sun passing on to the portals of night, sends his last splendour abroad from behind the clouds that marshal his retreat. Wide shafts of light flame in fans over the spaces of heaven. From cloud to cloud the fires race, until through infinite gradations, the day runs out to its close.

Tamanthé is the last British outpost on the Chindwin. It is garrisoned by half a hundred fighting men under the command of a Sikh officer. The steamer has scarcely done screaming, the gangway planks are not yet slippery with the wet footprints of the crew, when he comes hurrying along under the stress of a tight uniform, his long sword dangling by his side, to pay his respects. White man to him is synonymous with ruler, and three Englishmen do not come this way in the year. His men are hastily forming up on the parade ground and he is disappointed that they are not to be inspected. No one ever comes to Tamanthé except for some such purpose. The Subahdar practically rules here alone.

Two miles beyond Tamanthé is the village of Htwatwa, on the further shore of the Nam Talei, which comes down a broad swift stream fresh from the Naga strongholds. There is a pathway to Htwatwa from Tamanthé through the dense forest, and midway in its stillness one can hear the booming of the village drums, falling clear and seemingly close at hand like the hammered notes of a woodpecker.

And now the last day of my voyage has come. The actualities of rule have almost ceased, and wide *incognita*, unvisited by any European, surround me on every hand. For another day or two I might prolong the journey to where the cataract of Taro forbids all progress; but, for all practical purposes, I am at the end of civilised means of travel. Leaving Tamanthé at grey dawn, I am now ascending through loops and curves and under cliffs buried deep in forest. Miles of wild plantains line the more level banks, and bamboos reach over with a million fingers to the river's edge. Toucans and hornbills flutter purple through the spaces; peacocks throw their splendid plumage to the sun; the narrow turnings blaze with the jewels of the morning. Here and there at long intervals a village shelters, poignant in its suggestion of human loneliness. At Tonma Hlut the river turns westward; the mountains deploy. In the foreground there are green hills, and at the turn-again north—the whirlpool of Tonlon lies in wait. Duck wing in flights up the river courses. Tributaries steal through the woods, charged with the secrets of their hidden birthplace. The air pulses with the spirit of the unknown. That is the charm of these lonely reaches.

I continue north. Saramati and the great peaks rise above me in a great wall to the west. Every mile the ship steams on takes me nearer to blessed centres of the Temperate-zone; and here, and at this season (October), the climate attains to something that is very near perfection. The sky is a clear and limpid blue. The clouds that are never wholly absent through the hours add to it only gracious things—light and action and infinite variety. At the close and at the dawn of each day they are palettes for every colour that can rejoice the eyes of man. All through the long hours of the day they swoon on the mirror face of the river and every peak has their benediction. High noon has no power in it to overcome the coolness of the air. Midnight has not yet learnt her secret of chilling cold. There is no rawness yet in the dawn. At this turning season Nature seems to suspend her life in some subtle state of equilibrium. Summer and winter mingle in full harmony; and the coming panoplies of autumn give no note of their approach in the heart of the green forests, where ferns drip and flowers breathe as if the spring were young.

IN THE TEA ORCHARDS AT KAWYA

Fresh curves and avenues bring me to Malin, and the river still runs on in its pride, as though it derived its life from secret springs and cared nothing for its tributaries—the Myittha, and the Uyu and the Nam Talei—left far in the fading south.

I pass into the territories of Singkaling Hkamti, three hundred miles due west of Tali Fu, and in a line with the confluence of the Irrawaddy. The state, almost extinct when the British power advanced up the waters of the Chindwin, was revived in favour of a scion of the old royal house. Would that this could oftener have been done in Burma! It has an area of two thousand square miles, extending northwards as far as the waterfall which finally forbids the navigation of the Chindwin, and it is one of the last surviving relics of the ancient Shan kingdoms which long disputed the supremacy of the Burmese race in the valley of the Upper Irrawaddy. From Minsin in the east, the river curves to Naukpè, and looking back from here, there is a fine view of the troubled outline and citadel-like forms of the hills that rise between the river and the mountain wall of the wild Chins in the west.

Ledges of cliff and rock abut on the river, deep in hanging fern and velvet moss. At these points the river swirls and foams, impeded in its straight course ; and the line of the high floods on its rocky walls tells eloquently of a greatly fallen river. Foot by foot, and inch by inch, till the melting of winter snows again replenishes its flood, the river gives back to the land the territories it has won. But the marks of its supremacy, like blast-holes and chisel-cuts, bespatter the rocky banks all the way from Monywa to Hkamti.

Pink and black buffaloes all along the river, stare through the reeds out of wild eyes at the passing steamer. Here and there a party of men with *dahs* slung over their naked shoulders, and women in scarlet wrappings which drop in a fall over their ample breasts, march along the banks, stopping to gaze like their cattle at the portent on the river.

Past Yan-ywa the river gains a sudden access of beauty. A cliff runs down to it on the east. Low hills rise on the western bank. Through this gateway the river stretches away to the great mountains. Their slopes are so close now that I can count on Saramati the trees in flower, which make a yellow pattern on the pervading blue ; and the deep gorge ten thousand feet above the sea, mist-clad and shadowy in the sunlight that whispers of Himalaya.

Here also the navigation is dangerous. Under the cliff the river runs hard. Sands lie across it near the further bank. The channel is narrow, the current rapid, the bend acute. To turn it, coming down-stream, is something of a feat. A little farther on the same episode is reproduced on the opposite bank ; but complicated by a reef which stretches like a paw from the hills into the river. There is a great curve above it, and the waters, sweeping round in its fold, hurl themselves upon the reef, and surmount it in waves that leap with life, and in eddies that bubble and scatter with the rapidity of lightning. A golden galon-bird high up on a grey post marks this spot of sinister character.

Traces of cultivation are visible at long intervals along the banks ; the cultivation of the migrating peasant, whose system is so rude that the finest soil cannot pay his drafts upon it for more than a few seasons. There is no mistaking the symptoms of the *taung-gya* cultivator ; the white skeletons of burnt trees standing gaunt and bare in the rough rakish-looking fields. It is a bad wasteful system, and it can never be made the basis of any racial progress ; yet it must be difficult for men to break from this restless life ; for it has its joys, its recurring excitement, its novelty, its sense of freedom, its little toil. It is the antithesis of the life of an English villager, living upon his immemorial site.

At Auk Taung my journey ends. It is a small village newly come into existence. There are blade-marks on a *ficus elastica* of great age and size and many columns; the only relic of a former settlement. The people here are Shan, with the figures of mountaineers, short, broad, and immensely muscular.

As I wait here under the high mud-cliffs, the sunlight passes, and the night comes dark and still. The village falls into deep slumber. A cricket beats his kettledrums from a neighbouring tree. The plaint of the nightjar is borne across the dark.

Even these pass.

A great silence falls upon the world.

But the river knowing no pause, moves on, and the stars in their courses come and go. These two alone stand for life.

Late, towards dawn, the fading crescent of the moon climbs up like a tired pedlar over the low eastern hills, followed by the morning star.

Book VI

THE DELTA

Mosquitos—The Pomp of Travel

CHAPTER XXV

MOSQUITOS

MAUBIN, if you descend upon it from Upper Burma in the dust-choked days of early April, will smile upon you with its air of perpetual summer ; and you will wonder at its clarity and freshness and its undying verdure. But Maubin, like most of the Delta from which it has sprung into being, conceals much that is vile under a smiling exterior. From its immense riches nothing can detract, but it lacks one or two of the constituents of civilised happiness. It has been ironically named the Garden of Eden, after the Governor who founded it, and in scorn of its less inviting characteristics. Perhaps its chief claim to the notice and the execration of mankind resides in its populace of mosquitos. These, in number, size, and virulent activity, are unsurpassed in the world. One's first visit to Maubin in the mosquito season is unforgettable, and to see them under the flare of an electric searchlight coming over the ship's side in hordes, and occupying like an irresistible army every fraction of its surface ; to see them hanging in festoons from the white canvas awnings, the mosquito nets, the table-linen, and the *punkha* flaps, and from every object on which they can secure a footing, including notably the *corpus vile* of the white man for whom Providence made the universe, is to have lived indeed. How to continue to live after the novelty of the spectacle has worn off is the definite problem that occupies every one's mind in Maubin. It is achieved in the main by entrenching one's self within an iron fortress of fine mesh.

A European house in Maubin is thus a curiosity. Every window—and in the tropics there is an infinity of windows—is protected by sliding curtains of iron gauze ; every ventilator under the eaves, every open space between the room partitions and the roof (and for the sake of air, such spaces are large and frequent), is barred against invasion by sheets of gauze. In some houses there is a special room, a kind of inner citadel and last refuge, which is wholly of iron gauze, and within it the master of the house sits like a vanquished lion in a cage.

To enter this fortress in advance of the enemy calls for the exercise of no mean agility. The doors have swing-backs and are made to close the instant they are released. Outside them, the light cavalry of the enemy hover in clouds. The man within, this Englishman in his strange castle, observes your approach with furtive and anxious eyes, and if you be a newcomer, he begs of you to be careful in entering. Immediately you enter he falls with an astonishing onslaught upon such of the

FISHING IN THE DELTA

enemy as have come in on your back, in your hair, in the creases of your clothes, and in an aurora of cloud about your brows.

At one end of the Chief Magistrate's house there used to be when I was last at Maubin, a long room thus defended, in which he sat daily to dispense justice; and great activity in entering was expected of the prisoner under trial, the assembled witnesses, and the counsel employed in each case. Many a sentence, it is whispered, has fallen with enhanced severity from judicial lips; many a prisoner has come away with a lighter punishment as the consequence of his manner of entering the court. And the same circumstance has played, it is hinted, no little part in the rise and fall of advocates; in the lifting of one man to some giddy pinnacle of honour, in the degradation of another to depths of official displeasure.

It is not to be expected that a career at Maubin should leave no trace upon the habits of one who has been there; that the faculty and practice of entering and leaving a room by a narrow door in the shortest possible time should not betray itself in the style and poise of his figure. And in fact, long after your Chief Magistrate—he is sometimes sent here for his sins—has left Maubin behind him on his way to the stars of the official firmament, or to leisured retirement in England, he is to be known by his looks, by his gait, above all by his slick manner of entering a half-closed door. There is a man now living at the Bhanchuds, in the opulent ease of the fabled Anglo-Indian. His chair is placed in view of the doors that open when members enter. And he sits here and waits. His head, once auburn, is now bald ; his skin, once fresh, is yellow now and tough ; his eyes are fishy and lack lustre. He is not a conversational man. But at long intervals the doors upon which his eyes are fixed open to a newcomer, who, entering with a sudden dart, slams them to and looks anxiously about him as if pursued by an enemy. It is the signal for a strange metamorphosis in the figure of the expectant sitter. His limbs quicken with electric suddenness ; pleasure beams in his fishy eyes, and rising, he welcomes the newcomer with voluble delight. For once upon a time he also was Chief Magistrate of Maubin. 'Tis an exclusive caste.

There is a tale also of an old tragedy which is told by the Delta skippers in their cups. It is one of those awful histories which men tell with reluctance, and never to a stranger. It relates how a young magistrate who came to Maubin loved a fair daughter of the soil. She was soft and gentle,—they often are—and her eyes were of the large, dark, and lustrous kind that are crucibles for the very hearts of men. Grey-headed captains are still moved to emotion when they describe this beautiful creature—The Lily of Maubin. She wore the yellow-hearted *champak* in her glossy hair, red-gold on her wrists, and shimmered in rich silks amongst the sunflowers of her native land. For a year or more they lived happily together, heedless of Circulars, of the Bishop, of the passing world ; and they might have lived happily to the end, had not Miss Mary Smith arrived at Maubin. She was the sister of the Commandant ; a good girl, fresh, rosy, unspoilt ; an English maiden, who brought with her memories of half-forgotten things, of country lanes and buttercups and blackberries ; of rural joys and of grey churches hidden under immemorial trees. Yet dear and innocent as she was, tragedy chose to follow in her train.

As the days passed the dark lustrous eyes of the girl amongst the sunflowers widened with dismay and pain, for she saw her world, all her world of love and wonder, riches and honour, falling about her in ruins. And one day the end came. "Mah May," said her Magistrate, "you are a good girl—I am sorry to say good-bye. In this bag you will find a hundred and fifty rupees. My clerk Maung So is a rising man. Good-bye, little one ; I am going—to be married."

Mah May broke her heart of despair ; but before she died, she bored

THE LANDING-PLACE AT WAKEMA

a small hole with her dagger in the gauze. In his chair within the magistrate dreaming of happiness lay asleep. It is surmised by some that Mah May put him to sleep. That has never been proved. But the stark fact remains that the next morning when his servants darted in through the swing-backed doors, they found their master had vanished. All they came upon was a peculiar-looking object shrivelled and dry, in a suit of European clothes made by a tailor in the Strand. The frame-work of bone and withered flesh, the crinkled sheet of skin which enclosed it, pointed to the conclusion that this was once a man. *But every drop of blood had been sucked out of his body.*

There are other tales, certified to by gentlemen of veracity and honour; tales which are among the commonplaces of life, in this beautiful country of great rivers, and bellying sails, and tropic luxury; and yet I am reluctant to repeat them lest in other lands they should meet with a foolish incredulity.

Apart from mosquitos, Maubin, built on the edge of a winding river and immersed in the metallic beauty of the south, has qualities that make for attraction. Here there is no sense of isolation, for the river is the highway of the Delta. All through the dry season, from the ceasing of the rains in November to their coming again in June, big steamers pass down it and up it, to the number of a score a week.

And when they come at night, they fling their searchlights up the winding avenues, and transform the world of dark cumulose trees, of swaying forests of cane, of red-roofed houses, and spired pagodas glittering with gold, into a stage-land of extraordinary picturesqueness. The trees look as if they were cut in stiff velvet, the people as if they were actors in a play. Movement is personified as the coolies swarm up the gangways and lascars plunge into the flame-lit water and strain at the hauling-ropes as they race along the grass-covered banks.

Some of the steamers that come this way are of the largest size; mailers on their way from Mandalay; cargo-boats with flats in tow, laden with the produce of the land; and when they come round the bend of the river into view of Maubin, the great stream shrinks and looks strangely small, as if it were being overcome by a monster from another world. Three hundred feet they are in length, these steamers, and with flats in tow, half as wide, and they forge imperiously ahead as if all space belonged to them and swing round and roar out their anchor chains, while the lascars leap and the skipper's white face gleams in the heavy shadows by the wheel—the face of a man in command.

And when you see this wonderful spectacle for the first time, and step on board the great boat, you expect to find an imperious man, with eyes alight with power, and the consciousness of power, and the knowledge that he is playing a great part. But you are like to be disappointed, for

BASSEIN RIVER

you find a plain man, very simple in his habits and ways, with weariness written about the corners of his red eyes. Ah ! they know their work, these men, if any one does ; and they do it, as the good sailor always does, thoroughly and without talk, and they race these ships of theirs big as ocean steamers, round corners and over shallows, with less than a foot of water between them and a blasted reputation, with a skill and daring of which they seem unconscious. And I say nothing of the Clydesmen who rule the throbbing engines, and sweat in the fierce tropic heat, and say even less than the skipper.

Besides the big steamers there are numerous little launches which puff with importance, and there are the boats of the people ; the great *hnaw* with her bellying sails, gliding like a beautiful phantom up-stream, or trailing down to the measured fall of twenty oars ; the cargo-tub with her red canvas, full-bosomed to the wind; the sampan flying under stress of sail ; the ferry dugout paddled by a woman and a boy. All these come and go, and they are to be seen from any one of the many windows of Maubin that overlook the river.

The town is built on the lip of a large island, which a few years ago was like an atoll or soup-plate, sunk in the centre ; and in this centre lay malaria-haunted marshes and trackless forest. Then there came along that Government which, according to the gospel of the new revilers, is the cause of all famines, and it built a great embankment, the object of which was to reclaim this wilderness by shutting out the flood waters that every year came in at its gates. Emigrants poured in thereafter and populated tracts that were totally uninhabited ; places " where a man would be afraid to meet his own brother in the dark." Dedaye, Wakema, Maubin, all flourishing centres are of recent birth. The State in this enterprise was in advance of the people, and at first they were afraid to come in and be drowned, as they said ; but a start was made, the first crops yielded a hundred and twenty baskets to the acre (eighty being a full crop), and the horde came in. The Delta of the Irrawaddy is thus for all its limitations, a land of romance. The element of growth in it alone is sufficient to seize upon the imagination. For it is growing every year, and new land, the building-up of ages, is lifting its head above the level of the waters. New rivers and waterways are being created ; old ones, swept within easy memory by the passing ships, are now sealed and ready almost for the plough. From an amphibious savagery there is growing up a country that ranks amongst the most prosperous, the most densely peopled, in the world.

CHAPTER XXVI

THE POMP OF TRAVEL

THE steamer to Bassein is due at Maubin at half-past one o'clock in the morning. At two, I walk down to the wharf, a cloudy moon overhead. In the porch a crowd of people lies asleep. A little farther, on the open planking of the wharf, my baggage is piled. Beyond, there spreads the silent river. For half an hour I wait here, my eyes fixed on the dark bend of the river, looking every moment for the flare of the coming searchlight. But I look in vain. It is now three hours after midnight and all the world lies in the shadow of sleep. As I pass my hand over the railings of the wharf it grows wet with the fallen dew. Sleep cries out in my bones. At four, and at last, the steamer comes. The wharf becomes alive with the awakened people; but the silence of night broods insistently upon all things.

The steamer comes slowly alongside, gliding and sidling up to the wharf, and the voice of her muffled engines is like the low bubbling purr of a hungry panther. You have heard it in the jungle? As she touches, the tired Skipper under the glare of his electric lights turns away with a movement of great weariness, stumbles over the threshold of his cabin, and throws himself on his couch for thirty minutes of oblivion. The Mate stands by the gangway-planks and sees the people come on board. Up and down by the engines, like a caged beast, the Glasgow engineer walks, his face livid under the white insistent glare. There are still two hours to dawn when the captain wakes, the hawsers are flung on board, and the steamer takes her way, relentless, into the night.

All next day we thread the winding ways of the Delta, the waters laden with the tide, now level with the plains. For scores of miles neither ridge nor hillock breaks the level monotony. The rice-fields stretch beyond the fringe of the river to the horizon. But towards evening there comes a great change. The water-ways are lined with avenues of drooping forest, the tropical wildness spreads far into the distance. We pass from the broad highway into narrow sinuous creeks; sluggish, like gorged pythons. The steamer with her flats in tow, fills all the available water space, and the tarred flanks of her flats hustle and rasp against the drooping branches of the trees. Ahead, the sun flares in red gold, and the dark tracery of the forest is cut against it. Then night falls swiftly, stars come forth in myriads, and the searchlight sends her flame before the ship. Once again all the world becomes unreal.

Every shadow deepens, every reflection is intensified. The face of the waters is like a mirror, a creature without a soul; yet it reflects the infinite deeps of heaven; and the ship floats as though she lay over a bottomless pool of waters. Millions of fire-flies flash in the trees, lighting up their dark forms against the darker sky.

And here there is room for nothing else but the ship. All other craft lie for safety at the creeks' mouth till she has passed and we suddenly come upon them all drawn up under the banks of Myaungmya, where the homing steamer is waiting, monstrous and flame-clad, her funnel amongst the palms, for right of way.

At Myaungmya there is now a large population. Boats, carved and gilded and lofty of stern, rise up like shadows along its banks; open-air plays are in full progress ashore; raftsmen lie on the water, and at one point where there is narrow passage, an incautious raft is rent asunder as the iron prow of our starboard flat crashes through. We move slowly and carefully, but with the momentum of a thousand tons and more. The searchlight flames on the banks, making vivid the swaying palms, the crowded alleys, and the wharves where Chinamen wait beside the black Coringhi, and Sikhs in *khaki* stand for order. As the steamer runs out her gangways, the crowd surges on board, and coolies chanting a wild refrain roll the cargo down the pontoon to the flats. The homing ship, with a clear passage before her, passes swiftly away into the dark world of the forest, and in half an hour we too leave all animated spectacles behind us and plunge into the silent creeks.

BOOK VII

THE SOUTHERN COAST

LEAVING THE CITY—THE PEARLING TOWN—THE ARCHIPELAGO—MOULMEIN

CHAPTER XXVII

LEAVING THE CITY

HIGH noon and a turning tide. The yellow river, laden with its burden of land-creating loam, rushes by, and there is a turmoil in the narrow ways between ship's side and wooden pier. Spread abroad over the great stream the ocean-going steamers and the sailing-ships lie at anchor, their prows swinging northward in obedience to the tide. The foreshore-slime glistens in the light. A multitude of small craft ply or are at rest in its neighbourhood. Up near the concrete river wall there are rows of idle sampans lashed to a forest of stakes. Their brethren on the water are busy, and boat after boat swings by, laden with passengers for the other shore. Here are the panting launches, full of a swift vitality ; the heavy barges ; the red-funnelled river-streamers of the Flotilla ; the Burmese country-boats with half-moon roofs of matting in red and yellow and dark vandyke ; and a long perpetual stream of passengers which flows from the shore to the river, along the sloping pontoons that rise with the rising tide and float or bridge the intervals of slime. Burmese families in silks of colour and under the shelter of yellow translucent parasols, draw the eye away from the traffic of life to its beauty, and small craft with sails bellying to the breeze, speed across the turbid waters. All that is here is new, deriving but little of its charm from history or old association. Its interest is vital, of the present. Thus as the pageant discloses itself, and calicoed Chinamen, cottoned Coringhi, and silken Burman play their parts upon the sunlit stage, we slip our anchor at Rangoon and make with the tide for the ocean.

THE NIRVANA OF NIGHT

Night comes, and with her a sea of snow under the trail of a flaming moon. A warm-lipped wind from the south, sensuous and caressing, the very breath of some mystic ardour of Nature, plays over the restless face of the sea. On the white awnings of the ship, the dark stamped outline of the cordage makes fantastic patterns; so clear that the pattern seems an inalienable part of the fabric, yet in each line is there the tremor of separate life. Time and space loom infinite on a borderless horizon, the ship moves over the trackless seas as if impelled by some secret universal spirit of life. The dark man at the wheel, yellow ovals of light from the compass playing on his face ; the lonely officer on the bridge ; the droning voice of the watchman ; the clang of the ship's bells ; seem like simulacra of some hidden reality, phantoms of something else that is.

DAY UPON THE THRESHOLD

Dawn breaks off the Tavoy coast, a symphony in purple. The sea, the Moscos islands, the mountains of the coast, the violet sky still lit by the full orb of the moon, prolong the royal note of colour. Heavy purple clouds, children born of the night, lie upon the peaks and in the valleys. As Day grows they gather together and sweep away to sea, playthings of the red-lipped dawn ; or sink in soft mists into the valleys where they were born. The ship steers east, as the risen-sun shelters for a moment behind a shield of cloud, his glory effulgent behind it, and manifest in the downpour of gold and in the cloud's rim of fire. Then very swiftly he emerges and the colours change ; soft niagaras of cloud pervade the secluded places of the hills ; pale mountains, scarcely more real than the sky above them, rise up on distant horizons ; and the ship, swinging round, enters upon a long canal of sea, between the mainland and a cathedral island on our right. Flights of pagodas glitter in the sun, and rich woods climb the opposing shores. Fishing boats with square sails on a point trail over a complacent sea.

And it is thus within the space of a night and half a day that I come from the thoroughfares of a crowded, an aggressive, a commercial city, to the threshold of a strange country of nameless islands, of so many fascinations that to escape from one is only to fall into the happy toils of another. In its wooded and unexplored island interiors, in its secluded bays and silent backwaters, in its little valleys of nameless rivers, in its company of unascended peaks, there lies a perpetual feast for the imagination. And Fame has not yet come with her train to stale their infinite variety.

MERGUI

Mergui, as I see it from the *Ramapoora*, is a narrow strait, with a double-peaked island on one side, and a low palm-clad shore rising to a hilly eminence on the other. On this shore is built the town, a line of thatched huts on piles along the water's edge. The summit of the hill is crowned with a white pagoda of golden rings and a glittering spire, with monasteries of many roofs, with a great court-house, and the houses of the British officers. A long stone jetty protrudes across the foreshore into the water. Two launches lie at anchor, four cutters, and a multitude of native craft. While I am yet engaged upon the scene before me, there enters up the ladder a yellow mariner with a sea-tanned face, a grizzled beard, a straw hat in a white cloth cover and black ribbon, seedy clothes held together by large iridescent mother-of-pearl buttons. His name, he states with a flourish, is Captain Le Fevre, and he launches forthwith into the true adventure.

ON THE SOUTHERN COAST

"This," he remarks, embracing the settlement in a wave, contemptuous, of his hand, "this is a gone-before kind of place; the pearlers made it, and now it is done with, same as Thursday Island, where the Jap is supplanting the white man. You see," he explains fraternally, "they will work for a wage that you and I would turn up our noses at. And now," he adds inconsequentially, "I am a Wrecker. Who knows what the next turn in the varied kaleidoscope of life will bring me?"

I suggest good luck and drink a health to it; on the basis of which he gives me a narrative of his adventures with Thursday Island blacks, and of many things which he declares happen in remote latitudes but never become known; of the men he has killed and of the men who have tried to kill him; of "Admirality" charts and the ways of men upon the seas. He is a good liar, and I am fain to listen to him here on the edge of the pearling lands and the country of numberless islands. About noon the rakish-looking craft under his command takes herself off to the salvage of the *Amboyna*, and so, for the moment, exit Captain Le Fevre.

CHAPTER XXVIII

THE PEARLING TOWN

THERE is a house at Mergui on the hill, built half a hundred years ago for the comfort of the European traveller; with a row of convex windows facing the sea, and in all Burma there is no resting-place more attractice than this. It is high enough to command a view of great extent and beauty, but not so high as to cut one off from the sense of human fellowship. The spectacle it offers changes with every hour of the day, and as the tide ebbs and flows, as sunlight and shadow change from east to west, and storm and calm succeed each other on the mutable face of the sea, I, who am its tenant, know that chance has made me a spectator from a royal box of a great play. I awake of a morning to its splendour, and the spectacle that greets my half-conscious vision is one of a pale sapphire sea, of brown housetops and fishing-boats and tufted palms, suffused in a blue mist of hanging smoke; and I see these through a lace-like tracery of green boughs and opulent scarlet bloom. My eyes follow the first gleams of sunshine as they come racing along the under-surface of the leaves, reddening the dappled wood. From every window there is a view of sea and sky and island, and far down by the foreshore there is the first cluster of human beings, and a flight of wheeling gulls about the fishing-boats that have come in with the dawn.

Just now, in spite of the pessimism of Captain Le Fevre, the town is agog with excitement; if such an emotion can be said to assail a settlement wrapped in Lydian airs, and far from the highways of the world. Pearls of great price have been found, and every dweller in Mergui believes that he is destined to find others like them. So the populace is going to and fro, borrowing or begging the wherewithal to start in pearling adventure. Olpherts, the little town-clerk, talks of throwing up his place. As it brings him in a hundred a year I am surprised to hear this, and suggest that he has some offer of a greater post.

"No, sir," he replies, "but I am thinking of turning pearler."

I wonder at him, looking upon his slim clerkly figure and pale little face.

AMHERST : ON THE SOUTHERN COAST

"In fact," he adds with a jerk, "I have already entered the business. Last season I bought a boat and a pump—it was second-hand, but a good pump, Sir—and my wife went out and looked after the shells. We found two pearls worth 2,200 rupees, and after paying all expenses made a profit of four hundred. But two months ago my wife died and the boat is now upon my hands. I cannot work it if I remain here. Last week I sent it out in the charge of the tender, and, Sir" (his eyes grow moist and his voice husky with emotion), "he brought me back only eight shells, but in one of them there was a pearl worth 10,000 rupees."

The statement clothes the little man in a sudden nimbus of glory. So small is my spirit that a moment before I was thinking only of his rashness in wishing to surrender a certain income for the doubtful chance of pearling, and now I am smitten with the sense of his self-restraint. Imagine a man sticking to his desk and posting figures all the long day into a futile horde of books, while thousand-pounder pearls are lying under the clear water, in a country of sea-breezes and tropic islands only a day's journey away!

"I have here, sir," continues the little clerk, "two pearls, which I did not like leaving at home, as there is now no one there to look after them," and thereupon he thrusts his hand into the pocket of his grey coat and pulls out—a match-box.

"Heavens!" I think, "he is going to display me his thousand-pounder!" But he denies me that emotion, and produces two pearls of lesser price, and they lie upon the table for an hour, gleaming among his folios till I beg him to put them out of danger. He informs me that he is not the only lucky person in Mergui; that there are six men who have found pearls of price, and that one of these is worth no less than 18,000 rupees. Lindsay, the Australian, he says, found one before he left Mergui which he sold for 17,000. Very quickly after that it was sold for 23,000, and three times after that in Bombay, and each time at a higher price.

"U Shway E, Sir, the Salôn trader, has two quart bottles full of pearls, and they say that in the old days before people knew their value, he bought them from the Salôn at one rupee each!"

These pearling grounds have in fact a very recent history. In the 'eighties they were almost unknown. In the early 'nineties they were worked by Australian adventurers, most of whom have now departed. The pearling grounds are leased in blocks to a syndicate of Chinamen, who grant sub-leases to individual adventurers at the rate of twenty-five pounds a pump for the pearling year. The main harvest is of mother-pearl, and it is this harvest that pays the working expenses. The pearls are a speculative asset; a glorious and limitless possibility that sheds the lustre of romance over a difficult means of livelihood.

Over and beyond the lottery of the pearl, there is the gamble and excitement of the blister. You dive and you bring up a shell. Good. You open it and you find a blister. Splendid possibility! Many hopes assail you. Does your blister contain a pearl? Is the said pearl matchless in colour and form? Of great size? Almost priceless? Or——? You see, there is always the fatal alternative. To add a new thrill to your excitement you must now face the matter of its disposal. Will you part with it unopened to some other speculator, pocketing a substantial but very moderate price, or will you follow your fortune? The town is

THE DIVER EMERGING

aware of your dilemma, and deeply interested in your decision. Meanwhile if you are a *gourmet* of the emotions you will gaze at your blister by day and dream of it by night. You will receive visitors, you will listen to their comments, and you will laugh disdainfully at the offers they make you. If you are wise you will prolong this golden period, and bask for a season in the warm sunshine of fame.

But let us say that some day before it is too late, you sell it. Away goes the speculator, his heart in his mouth, the beautiful iridescence in his hand. The blister is cut open, and there emerges the pearl of the season, or there emerges—nothing!

Thus the flavour of romance lingers on in the air of this pearling town. It is a little paradise of the Celestial, for no Chinaman could desire more than the opportunity it offers of making an ample income by the steady pursuit of business, and of losing it in a sudden gamble.

The European here, with his many pumps and schooners, accumulates much shell and little pearl. For the seas are wide and schooners drift with wind and tide. He cannot be everywhere at once. When he visits one of his boats at work the diver becomes delicate, develops a racking headache, and lies down. The weary pearler sails away to another boat. Then the diver recovers and his boat drifts out of sight and reach of interruption. When it is found again and the pearler comes on board, he finds laid out for him a neat row of rifled shells. The jaws of oysters gape quickly in the sun, and it takes no long time to slip a finger sensitive to pearls, along the lip of the open bivalve.

The small capitalist, with a pump or two in his own charge or in that of his wife, reaps a smaller harvest of shells, *but he gets his pearls.* And so the white man goes and the yellow man and the brown man stay and work at a profit.

But let us enter the town while the morning is still fresh, and call upon its inhabitants.

Here is the house of the latest celebrity—the man who has found the pearl worth 18,000 rupees—a Burman. Ascending the stairs at the side of his house we enter a large square room with many windows facing the street. In the centre there is a round table, with the open shell of the oyster in which this thing of price was found displayed upon it. The walls are hung with oleographs of the German Emperor, of a Franco-Prussian battle, of an old man in a frock coat being kissed by a ballet-girl. Mats are spread upon the floor, and curtains conceal the inner rooms.

The entire family appears, consisting of the old father a retired goldsmith, the old mother, the son who found the pearl, and the son's wife. They are in the main humble people, but no Burman is ever at a loss for good manners, and the possession of this great pearl imparts to all of them a new air of dignity. The treasure is produced from a small ointment bottle filled with pink cotton, and is deposited on the table. It is a large gem, the size of my thumb-nail, almost flat-bottomed, but spherical above, displaying a faint series of concentric rings—a bauble of price. It is not yet sold, but the owner has received an offer of 17,000 rupees. From whom? Ah! he does not know! But it is rumoured abroad in the town that he may command that price. Bargaining is a delicate affair, and if you seek a wife or a pearl of price, you begin thus tenderly, floating a rumour upon the air through the mouth of a friend.

Some more talk, and we move on past the bazaar where large-eyed girls sell silk, to the house of U Shway E, the Chinaman with the quart bottles full of pearls. His father, he tells me, piloted the English to Rangoon in the year 1825; and when the English left Rangoon, having

" allee fixee " with the Burmese, he, feeling his life might be a troubled one if he stayed, took the opportunity to embark for Calcutta. But long before this, when his father was a young man, he had visited London and learnt the ways of the English.

U Shway E's intimacy with the Salôn of the archipelago began when he accompanied Captain Shore to these islands. Since then he has ever been their friend. Every Englishman who has sought to know anything

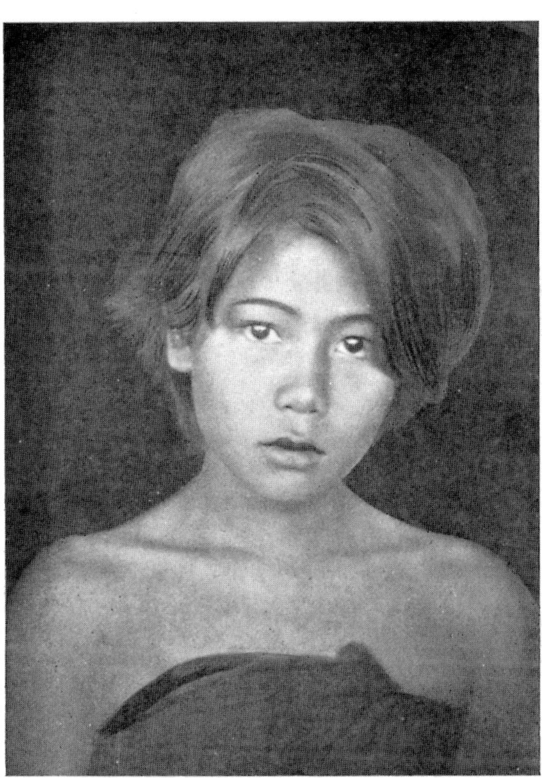

A GIRL OF MERGUI

of these strange people has come to him. He supplied Dr. Anderson with his facts and made a census of the gypsies for Master Eales, the Census Commissioner.

This old man of the silvery pigtail and courteous manner, who has made a fortune out of the simple Salôn, poses as their friend and benefactor. Recently, he says, he asked the Government for a grant of the islands, with a view to reclaiming them to civilisation : but the Deputy Commissioner said : " Do you want the Salôn then to be your subjects for ever ? " He claims that he has always been kind to them and has never sold them liquor. It is very true that they have been harshly treated by Chinese and Malay traders, who have forcibly taken their possessions and given them little if anything in return.

U Shway E's house fronts the street, under the bamboo-clad hillside on which the Roman Mission is established; and the back of it opens on the sea. It is a dark pile of wooden buildings, sloping away with the foreshore from the level of the street. There are many rooms, and in one of these a small Burmese handmaiden is swinging a child to sleep. While we sit by at a table on which fresh roses are set, and take stock of the neat writing-table at which a Chinese clerk who talks fluent English is at work; of the letters and invoices in slips of bamboo, which line the wooden walls; of the water-pots in an alcove kept cool by draughts of air; of the Burmese women of the household, wives and daughters of U Shway E and his sons; the old man, from an inner chamber, brings out to gratify us the " quart bottles " we wish to see. They are full of pearls of all shapes and sizes and represent only a fraction of his real possessions. He brings out also a strange collection of the sea-commodities in which he deals, *bêche de mer*, and the shells of green sea-snails.

A boat from the islands is in, and he sends for some Salôn to see us, and three fine young fellows, soft of tread and shy of face, enter and huddle together on the floor. They have broad shoulders, fine limbs, and attractive features. They are dark of skin, and wear brief loin-cloths, and red and yellow bandanas about their heads; bamboo earrings of great size in their ears. There is an irony in the contrast between their physique and youth, and their timid cowering manner, and their eyes that drop instantly they encounter ours. The moment we turn to some other matter they silently and swiftly disappear. U Shway E leads us after them down some stairs and across a backyard of rough tree-trunks raised high on piles, to the edge of the scaffolding looking out to sea, and there we come upon the entire party at anchor.

There are several boats lashed to the wooden piles, and in each boat there is a group of three or four Salôn, heartily busy with an ample and varied breakfast. They eat as men to whom food is the supreme luxury, and a square meal at the house of the old Chinaman, when they come to Mergui, is one of the links in the system of barter which binds them together. For the Salôn has come a very little way on the road of life. He can grow nothing for himself, and for all but the natural products of the islands and the sea, he is dependent on some one else. His only home is his boat, in which he lives throughout the north-east monsoon. During the south-west monsoon he builds himself a little hut on piles; but this is the most temporary of erections and forms no part of his real belongings. The Salôn boat, a dugout at bottom, is well finished and admirably designed for buoyancy and speed. Its accommodation is increased by side walls of cork and cane which begin where the wooden base ends. The oars are shapely, and end in a blade like that of a broad-sword. The boats before us here this morning are laden with green shells and bags of *bêche de mer*. One of the occupants hands up a spear which is partly of his own manufacture, a rude and primitive weapon of

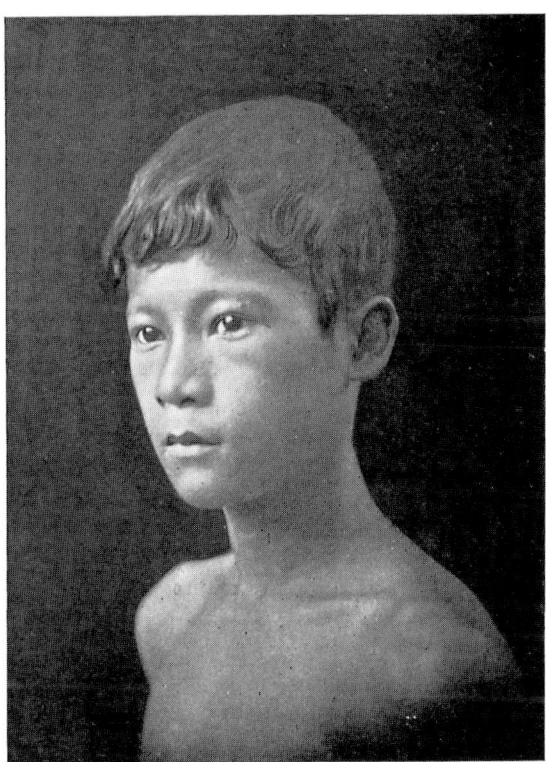

A LAD OF MERGUI

slender bamboo, with a three-pronged head. With this spear he plunges into the water after fish, following the weapon home.

As we stand here on the windy sea-edge of his house overlooking the gypsy boats, the old Chinaman tells us something of what he knows about them. According to him they are believers in *nats*. As to death, they say it comes from the malignancy of a spirit, and accordingly no sooner is a man dead, than they cut a boat in two and place him between the two parts, and depart hastily, leaving him to the carrion lizard and the wild hog. They all now wear clothes, but very little more than a narrow loin-cloth. Their country is divided by the Government, for pearling purposes, into blocks, and he speaks of them as "No I man," "No. 3," and so forth.

The Salôn here to-day have come from St. Matthew's Island, four days' journey from Mergui. As to their language, it is, he says, throughout the same. They all understand each other. The only difference is like the difference between English and what Captain Leed talkee——Ah, yes, Sclotch!

"I buy," he says, as we come away to his counting-house, "many more pearls than I sell; but very few now from the Salôn, for the shallow waters in which alone they can dive have been cleared of all their pearls by the pearlers."

For this habit of buying many more pearls than he can sell, and of storing them up in quart bottles, U Shway E is regarded by his fellow-townsmen as a mysterious character—"a very curious man!" He has also a great store of blisters which he keeps unopened. For one of these which he shows us, he has been offered 2,000 rupees, but he has no desire to part with it. He offers me two small black pearls as a gift; but we do not take gifts in the East.

From the Chinaman's we go to the house of a painter in a less delectable quarter of the town, but find the good man is away at a *kyaung* gilding and carving. Amongst the wooden piles under the floor of his house is his workshop, littered with samples of his craft: gilt wooden figures of mythological beings; paintings of the *zats* being made for an approaching *Phongyi byan;* and pencil drawings of arabesque. Rude as are the details, there is about this workshop amongst the piles the indefinable air of an *atelier;* somewhat that distinguishes it from a place of purely material preoccupations. The artist is humble, but he desires to create.

From here to the monastery on the hill, whose gilded spire is conspicuous in any panorama of the town, there is a steep ascent up a long flight of stairs. A colossus of Buddha under a temporary shelter in the open air, is approaching completion. His body is of brass, his head of gold and silver. The workmen standing on the soles of the Buddha's feet, or seated behind him filing and polishing his brazen limbs, look very small beside him. Some brass shavings are being molten over a green fire with the aid of a pair of ingenious bellows. They consist of two cylinders of bamboo, which stand upright from the earth and two more, scarcely an inch wide, connected with these, but leading along the surface of the ground to the lip of the furnace. Two light pistons of bamboo, garnished with red cocks' feathers, move in the upright cylinders with the least pressure of the hand, and as they move, drive a fierce current of air through the long cylinders.

The Abbot is busy with his breakfast in a corner of the new *kyaung*

From a painting by J. Raeburn Middleton

EVENING OF A PAGODA FESTIVAL

where the glass and gold mosaic flames in many colours in the morning sun. His food, which presents an appearance of luxurious variety, has just been brought to him by two lads, in a red basket slung from a gilded pole. A pale woman of saintly mien, sits reverently in the doorway, glad to think that she is earning merit for the hereafter by ministering to his wants, while the carnal old man, fat with ease and good living, sits on his dais by the window and moves slowly through his meal.

From the windows of a neighbouring structure, where the gilt catafalque containing the bones of his predecessor awaiting cremation, towers up to the roof, there is a view of tropical richness and beauty. The monastery is built on an eminence, whose eastern slope is laid out in terraced gardens and orchards crowded with palms and jack-trees, *durians*, *mangosteens*, Liberian coffee, and many flowers. Through the interspaces of the lustrous foliage, there are glimpses of blue hills and monastery spires; a picture of intricate beauty. Adjoining the catafalque, there is a chapel with golden doors, through whose bars there is visible an interior of barbaric splendour. In the centre a colossal figure of the Buddha sits under glittering umbrellas, and three sides along the walls there are rows of golden figures. The light, pouring in through stained-glass windows, gleams on these figures, and fills the spacious room with a haze of gold. Outside in the open ante-room, the white walls are frescoed with pictures of "heaven and hell"; the former insipid and restricted to winged cars and means of swift locomotion, the latter truculent and awful to behold. Here is the chemist guilty of selling poisonous drugs, writhing on a heated stake; the maker of implements of war with a hot spear thrust through his mouth; the monk taken in adultery being sawn in two and very bloody, the woman undergoing torture with outstretched hands which clutch for support at red-hot iron balls; evil-doers of all descriptions are being flung into cauldrons and kept in place by giants with three-pronted forks, while the virtuous man, with a look that is happily compounded of horror fear piety, and conscious worth, looks on from his winged chariot under the guidance of a *nat*. It is comforting to find that the wicked men are always black, and the good invariably white.

From this sermon in colours we move on to where the Chinese joss-house with its winged roof, its dragons and lobsters cut in profile against the sky, testifies to the importance of the Celestial community. We enter, to find a dozen lads at school under the tutelage of an old priest. They are seated at a long table, under a frescoed wall which depicts the adventures of a traveller with a turbulent white mule—some Celestial Stevenson afoot. Along the wall, in picturesque covers, there are hung letters and cards of invitation, sent it would seem to the joss-house priest. The scholars under the stimulus of our presence rise to perfervid heights of zeal, intoning their lessons in shrill voices that make the incense-laden air vibrate with learning. They are pleasant almond-eyed lads with boyish faces, till they begin to declaim, and then their faces, with uplifted eyebrows and airs of immense concentration suddenly become like those of the strange people you see on a Chinese vase. The old priest brings in cups of tea and every one is very obliging and civil. It is a little world in itself, with its own subtle atmosphere of distinction, its touch of an old civilisation, and it is a whole nation away from the sunlit street into which we step directly from it. For the Chinaman ever carries a fragment of his country with him, and in his temples, at least, never perpetrates the monstrous architecture to which the Englishman abroad too often succumbs. We have the reputation of aloofness in foreign countries, but there is no one so aloof as the Chinaman. All foreigners in his eyes are Barbaroi.

CHAPTER XXIX

THE ARCHIPELAGO

A PAGE FROM THE PAST

IT is a natural transition from the pearling town with its notable past, to the island country that spreads away beyond it, far into the territories of the sea. Of all that has happened amongst these islands since men first came to live and move amongst them, there is no record, and there never will be any now. Here and there only the curtain of the unknown is lifted for a passing moment. Their main, and it would seem their earliest, human interest centres in the fast-dying colony of the Salôn, which has made of these islands its last refuge. When or whence they came, one can only guess ; and whether they had any human predecessors it is difficult even to conjecture. But it is probable that they are an extremely ancient people, kindred of that aboriginal stock which peopled the mainland before the advent of the Htai. The main body of these aborigines drifted away under the pressure of the Htai to the south, there to develop into the Malay race. A fragment of them retreated to the shelter of the islands ; and there, cut off from civilising influences, they have made no progress, and too weak to face their adversaries, they have developed the nomadic life, the habit of few possessions, of flight at the sight of a stranger. The attrition of time and the cruelty of man have worn away the race to its present proportions. It has too long bowed down its head, too long ceased to make any effort after greater things to have any future before it. The Malay who is of kin will acknowledge no relationship, and in times that are past he has been its most cruel oppressor. The fire of Islam, which has molten the Malay into a people, has never warmed the aboriginal Salôn. A great gulf of time must therefore separate them and these islands must have known the Salôn for far more than a thousand years.

THE VISIT OF CÆSAR FREDERICK

Almost the first account of the archipelago, written by a European traveller, is that of Cæsar Frederick the Venetian. It has all the charm and interest of early travel; and is best told in the language of his time.

A GLIMPSE FROM ASHORE

" From ye port of Pechineo," he says, " I went to Cochim, and from Cochim to Malaca, whence I departed from Pegu eight hundred miles distant, that voyage was wõt to be made in twentie five or thirtie dayes, but wee were fowre moneths, and at the end of three moneths our Shippe was without victualles. The Pilot told us that wee were by his altitude from a citie called Tenassiry, a citie in the Kingdome of Pegu, and these his wordes were not true, but we were (as it were) in ye middle of manie Islands, and manie uninhabited rocks, and there were also some Portugals that affirmed that they knew the land. I say being amongst these rockes, and from the land which is over against Tenassary, with great scarsitie of victualles, and that by the saying of the pylate and two Portugalles holding them firme that we were in front of the aforesaide harbour, we determined to goe thither with our boat and fetch victualles, and that the shippe shoulde stay for us in a place assigned; we were twenty and eight persons in the boat that went for victualles, and on a day about twelve of the clocke we went from the Ship, assuring ourselves to be in the harbour before night in the afore saide port; wee rowed all that day, and a great part of the next night, and all the next day without finding harbour, or any signe of good landing, and this came to passe through the evil counsel of the two Portugalles that were with us.

MERGUI ARCHIPELAGO: A DENIZEN OF THE ISLANDS

"For we had overshot the harbour and left it behind us, in such wise that we had loste the lande, enhabited with the ship, and we twentie eight men had no manner of victuall with us in the boate, but it was the Lordes will that one of the Mariners had brought a little Ryce with him in the boat to barter away for some other thing, and it was not so much but three or forwe men would have eaten it at a meal: I tooke the government of this Ryce promising by the helpe of God that Ryce should be nourishment for us untill it plesed God to send us to some place that was enhabited, and when I slept I put the ryce into my bosome because they shoulde not rob it from me: We were nine dayes rowing alongst the coast, without finding anything but Countries uninhabited, and deserts Iland, where if we had found but grasse it woulde have seemed Sugar unto us, but wee coulde not finde any, yet wee founde a fewe leaves of a tree, and they were so hard that we could not chew them ; we had water and wood sufficient, and as we rowed, we could goe but by flowing water, for when it was ebbing water, we made fast our boat to the bancke of one of these Ilands, and in these nine dayes that we rowed, wee found a cave or nest of Tortugals egges, wherein was a hundred and fortie fowre egges, the which was a great helpe unto us : these egges are as big as a hennes egge, and have no shell about them but a tender skinne, everie day wee sodde a kettle full of them egges with an handfull of ryce in the broth thereof : it pleased God that at the ende of nine dayes, wee discovered certaine fishermen, a fishing with small barkes, and wee rowed towards them, with a good cheere for I thinke there were never men more glad than we were, for we were so sore afflicted with penurie that we could skarce stand on our legs. The first village that we came too, was in the Gulfe of Tavay, under the King of Pegu."

For the subsequent experience of the travellers, and the fortune of the ship left behind without a boat to help her, reference may be made to the original of Messer Frederick.

THE PORTUGUESE TRACE

His adventures occurred about the year 1567, and it is certain that at that time the islands were well known to the Portuguese. For it is on record that a fleet of Portuguese ships sent by the Viceroy of Goa about the year 1545, to search for an island of gold in the Bay of Bengal found it in a manner, by taking to piracy and preying on passing vessels from the shelter offered by the archipelago. " For eight months and more," says Ferdinand Mendez Pinto, " our hundred Portugals had scoured up and down this coast in four well-rigged Foists, wherewith they had taken three and twenty rich ships, and many other lesser vessels, so that they which used to sail in those parts were so terrified with the sole name of the Portugals, as they quitted their Commerce, without use of their shipping ; By this increase of trade the Custom houses of the Ports of Tanancarim, Junçalan, Merguim, Vagarun, and Tavay fell much in their Revenue, in so much that those people were constrained to give notice of it to the Emperor of Sornan, King of Siam, and Sovereign Lord of all that Country, beseeching him to give a remedy to this mischief, whereof every one complained."

The king despatched against the pirates a fleet of " five Foists, four Galliots, and one Gally Royal," under the command of a Turkish adventurer, named Heredrin Mahomet ; and " Within these vessels he inbarqued eight hundred Mahometans, men of combat (besides the Mariners) amongst the which were three hundred Janizaries, as for the rest they were Turks, Greeks, Malabars, Achems, and Mogores, all choyce men, and so disciplined that their captain held the victory already for most assured"

The Portuguese were nevertheless victorious. "The dog Heredrin Mahomet was slain amongst the rest, and in this great action God was so gracious to our men, and gave them their victory at so cheap a rate that they had but one young man killed, and nine Portugals hurt."

Piracy has in short ever found the archipelago a happy resort.

In later days Ilha Grande, now known as King's Island, was bestowed on the French by the King of Siam, and might have become, with its ample bay, an important settlement. But it was never used, except in later days by French ships of war, during the wars between England and France, as a place from which to attack and capture British merchant vessels; and as a place of refuge, when British ships of war were abroad.

THE *ESTHER* BRIG

Almost the first English attempt to navigate the islands and prepare a chart of the archipelago was made by Captain Forrest, whose *Journal of the* Esther *brig, from Bengal to Quedah*, narrates how, in 1783, he was driven amongst the islands by the monsoon winds, and gave to many of them names (which they still bear) "in remembrance of Friends whom I Honour and Respect," and others "according to striking appearances and figures."

The ardent Helfer spent a whole winter here in 1838–9, shortly before his death from an Andamanese arrow. Since then many persons have visited the islands, and more than one effort has been made to reclaim the Salôn to Christianity and civilisation. But little has been done towards the complete exploration of the archipelago. Its islands range from bare rocks to rich territories like those of Kisseraing and King's susceptible of the finest cultivation. Their fauna include elephants, rhinoceroses, and tigers, and the whale may often be seen plunging amidst the calm of their interior seas.

ON OUR WAY

The launch, with loud heart beating, drives a pathway through the narrow strait. Turning our backs upon Mergui, now hidden behind Patit, we reach a space of green sun-touched water, with low mangrove swamps upon our larboard bows. Upon our starboard the mountains of King's Island, cloven to a third of their height by dark lines of swamp forest, reach into the heart of the swooning clouds. We are steering south by west for the island country, and the most notable object in

DENIZENS OF THE ARCHIPELAGO

view is the pyramid of Merghi Island, sixteen hundred feet above the sea. Nearer, several others lie in our way, outlined in solid forms against the misty blue of their lofty companion. Away under the opal sky, there is a narrow mirror-like calm, which makes the islands in its compass seem unreal; mere phantoms of the vision suspended between earth and heaven. In striking contrast, the sailing-boats of the coastfishers are cut in black patterns against the clouds.

No two consecutive moments present the same spectacle. The clouds melt from one ecstasy of beauty into another; the sea, played upon by the wind, is one instant billowy and placid as oil, another crimped with laughter, a third a meadow of diamonds in the sudden sun; and the brave launch, leaping forward, overcomes space, so that the dreamiest island becomes a reality, the most palpable one of woods and precipices a dream. The sailing-junks, with their double diamonds of black sail suspended above their small hulls, fill the eye with the spectacle of their grace; saying that man has never invented anything more in harmony with nature than a sail.

And presently we fall into company. The junks driven by the wind, come up in a great flight, with the swell of a bevy of portly matrons, all ribbons and bosom; the wrecker, very surly and dirty, overtakes us to starboard, flinging silver from his bows; and in the offing there is the first Salôn boat moving to the impulse of a small white sail. The wrecker looks evil enough for any trade, and as he leaves us behind him in spite of all our pace, is like a big cur in a run after Jack, outpacing some gallant little panting fox-terrier, all heart and pluck, but too short dear fellow, in his legs to keep ahead. No matter; we will come in yet.

The Salôn here is eloquent of the irony which relegates this country of beautiful islands to an abject and dying race. Their rich luxuriance is beyond belief. They look as if they were forests sprung from the bottom of the sea. There is scarcely an inch of them that does not teem with life. There are islands of such length and altitude that they might be portions of a continent, and others, happily, that are palpable islands, with the sea in a ring all round them, waiting for you or me to go along and give them a name. And out of the misty void each moment, new islands are born like stars on a summer night.

As the afternoon grows we steer for a silver strait, all molten and a-fire, between blue island portals. And passing through them we come up a wide sea, Ross and Elphinstone in long mountains on the west, Burnett behind us, and Merghi Islands hard on our left; dark blue, with a lane of sea between and faint purple ridges beyond. It is a lane that invites one to enter. On Cantor, a brief way ahead, with single palms in outline on its crest, there is a settlement of Salôn, learning, or trying to learn, the hard alphabet of civilisation.

As the afternoon wanes and earth moves up against the sun, islands that have been every colour all day, from tropic green to misty northern blue, turn to their proper purple. In the east a curtain of velvet rain blots out the main of bay and peak and cove; but elsewhere each island stands out distinct and clear in its own serene personality. Nearest to us now and happily appropriate to the season of our voyage are the Christmas Islands. The sea is billowy, undulating, tumultuous almost. In a bigger ship it's swell would pass unnoticed, but our *Marguerite* is a small craft. We are steering for the Criddles in twenty fathoms of water, but the gunner has his eyes on a sunken rock. Soon we shall turn away to the south to anchor for the night in the bay of the *Amboyna* disaster. The white clouds above the rain purple of Morrison's Bay catch the lessening light and fling it down upon the sea, which straightway becomes all silver as though the moon were up. Between Court and Criddles there is nothing but the monsoon sea.

And so we come upon the glory of the closing day. The sun's golden light, stealing out from under clouds, sends a long stream of fire down the sea, fills with lightning a diadem of cloud that sits upon the brows of the Mew Stone, and swiftly turns that island, purple a moment earlier, into such a haze of supernatural flame as our eyes dare not look upon. It is flame cut in flame, and no more an island.

In a little while the pageant is over. The great world swings up like a porpoise in the sea; the sun's last arc of fire is swallowed in the void, and the Mew Stone, in the instant of its passing, becomes the darkest purple under the firmament. For a rose haze still lingers upon the fringes of the sea, and clouds in a great circle catch up and reflect the fragments of prismatic colour into which the pure sunlight is now broken. The sky becomes a palette, the sea a pool of pink. And as the grey closes in, the patch last touched by the sun grows iridescent as a pearl, in waves upon waves of transient blending colour.

Beautiful as is the day, there is a subtle and deeper fascination in the dark.

The world closes in and leaves us the centre of a new universe. I seem by some miracle to have been brought here into the midst of these lonely islands, and the panting dauntless engine that has brought me is like another carpet of Solomon magically put at my service. For, a month ago, I was afoot in the greatest of cities, a straw on the driving tide of its life; this morning I was ashore, near a court-house, a prison, and a town; and now, in the company of nameless shadowy islands, I am being swiftly borne away upon the bosom of the dark. A star shines out on the horizon like a beacon or a lighthouse, larger than any star I have ever seen; grey clouds drift like phantoms in the wake of the departed sun, and each moment the constellations grow in multitude and splendour.

Steering by instinct through the pitchy night, we cast anchor at last in the wake of the wrecked *Amboyna ;* and the speculative salvage-man in blue garments, his feet naked, comes on board to tell me how he has fought with Chinese and Malay, been prisoner and escaped ; how he has lived for three and thirty years in the East, and has a wife and children in Scotland, but finds folk at home cold and indifferent to one who has spent his life abroad. The cry of all old wanderers.

I pass the night on the floor of the launch with nothing between my vision and the stars. The sea is but a yard below, the roof shelters me without shutting out the sky. All my world for the time is about me ; the gunner, the sea-cunny, the engineer, and the crew. And here on the trackless seas, the sentiment of our common humanity surpasses all lesser considerations. The same conditions affect us all alike.

Some time in the night I wake, and my eyes are dazzled by the lustrous moon hung up in the firmament above me. I sleep again, and wake to find the messengers of day abroad ; lictors with their fasces, who fling themselves upon the world and bid it prepare in beauty for the coming of their lord. Strung along the east there is a chain of islands each link a mountain pyramid, the pale sea between crinkling with the first breeze of the dawn.

The first familiar object that greets me is the *Marguerite's* gig in the wake of the golden dawn ; the crew in her fishing with lines. Far away in the distance a ship is passing silently, a phantom amidst the islands.

A MORNING WITH THE SALVAGE-MAN

Turning to look about me I find that we are at anchor in a small bay, which lies but half awake in an arm of Bentinck Island. As the sun climbs, the island turns a rich and golden green, its beauty reflected in the olive water. But for a wisp of yellow sand along the sea-edge, its entire face is covered with woods of the noblest character. Little valleys run down it to the sea, a thousand birds are singing their unfamiliar matins to the day, and trees with long white trunks shining in the light, break up the mass of foliage into aisles, and make the island seem like some Gothic cathedral wrought in an Oriental texture. A few paces off lies the dishevelled *Amboyna*, her funnel once black, now rust-red in the sea air.

I make my way on board, climbing with some effort through the trenchant air to the upper deck. Mr. McPhairson in blue clothes cut all of a piece like the garments in which infancy is wont to pass its nights, is on board, tanned and ruddy, grizzled, large and weighty of hand and foot, smoked glasses veiling his small blue dogged eyes.

THE ONLY INHABITANT

" You don't notice a smell ? " he asks—" a kind of effluvium ? "

Candour and courtesy conflict in my mind.

I admit at last that I do.

" Ah," he replies, a little troubled upon the matter, " I was just wondering if it was away, or that I was growing accustomed to it a bit."

Half of her is under water. The fore-end of her is out of the wet, and a Chinese carpenter is at work drilling holes in a plank. On the hurricane-deck—the Captain's walk—the pumps are busy, and the glass face of the indicator, like a ship's clock, shows the pressure under which a man is working twenty feet below the level of the sea. A long tube of gutta-percha leads away across a hoarding built of planks, over the sunken middle of the ship. At the edge a strange man in blue with a Chinese hat is standing acting as a human pulley for the tube. Another sits holding a rope connected with the diver's helmet. Yet another holds the tube of air—*the life-line*—and lets it slowly slip through his half-closed hand. With head bowed down and hands outstretched, he is, I can see, absorbed in the delicate work that is his. There is something electric in the slow rustle of the rope through his nervous hands. And he has in his keeping the life of the man below in the blind water.

To my unaccustomed eyes there is nothing visible but a hoarding below the surface, and a tube let into the water, but the silent men clustered in the daylight above know well what is afoot below. Old McPhairson, the speculator, interjects occasional remarks. " He is walking now, along the lower deck," as the line suddenly runs out.

" Eh, but he is in the hold away below now, lifting the cargo," as a few bubbles rise to the surface.

" He would be about there now," pointing to a white stanchion out of the water; and then quickly, " here she comes," as a sudden turbulence in the water and a rush of air bubbles herald the approach of a sack of cargo.

" Chillies," he observes sententiously, as a party of red skirmishers rise up and spread out in a fan upon the water, to be followed by a black and rotten sack, which a waiting man with a large pole thrusts away to sea. In this way rice, chillies, prawns, and tobacco come up and float away, the bay becoming alive with them.

McPhairson, who goes down frequently himself, says the prawns cut his skin, and he points to his red scarred feet.

Silently a diver comes up, has his iron helmet lifted off his collar-bones, and sits dazed and dull in the sunlight, shivering in the gills. Another takes his place.

" They get mortal cold down there," says McPhairson.

" It's a warm day," I remark.

" And may it continue so," he replies ; " for the water takes all the heat out of you down below, and the wind cuts you when you come up.

The other day now, when it was a bit cold, every time I came up I had to get them to wrap me in a blanket."

All this time there is an anxious manner about the man. *His launch, the wrecker, and Captain Le Fevre has not yet come in.*

"And the Lord," he says, "knows what has become of her. Oh! but, if she is wrecked, there will be a shindy at home when her owners come to hear of it."

At last the laggard comes in sight.

"There she is."

"Time she was," he cries out. "I have passed but a poor night because of her. If I am so fortunate as to get this job through successfully, I will never again undertake another like it. I am fifty-five the day," he adds, mopping his strong face, "and not the man I was." Yet he looks a man of iron.

The wrecker comes up; the captain with unkempt hair, and blue shirt flapping outside his trousers, blowing his last anxious instruction through a speaking tube to the engine-room below. The mate, with a big hand which he uses with emotion, and bare feet in white canvas shoes, out at toes and heels, steps on the hurricane deck of the *Amboyna*. He speaks, encouraged by McPhairson, with anger and contempt of his captain. Clearly in this triumvirate Le Fevre is in a minority of one.

"Hect," says McPhairson, "he is that sort of man who can neither lead nor follow. A coward, Sirr, always on the look-out for what he don't want to see; a-dreamin' of rocks ten miles inside his course. Phew!" he adds, sweeping his ruddy face with a blue bandana, "and to think of the night I've spent."

McPhairson by his venture stood to lose two thousand pounds, or win a competency. Long after, I heard with regret that he had lost.

THE PEARLER

Steaming along by South Passage Island we come suddenly upon a Salôn camp. There is a fan of white sand with some boats and huts upon it, and I can see a few men and women moving. By the time I can step ashore—and it takes no more than five minutes over the transparent water—they have all effaced themselves in the primitive woodland, and only one man remains looking ill at ease. The sea-cunny goes with him, shouting to the woods, in the hope of inducing the others to return. The encampment consists of three boats and three huts; but to call them huts is to misname them, for they are of all human habitations the slightest. They consist of a few thin sticks—I can count six upright and three laid horizontally, in one—and a frail pleated mat laid over the top. A mat of bamboo strips is spread on the white sand within. Some of their few possessions are scattered around; bags, baskets, and bedding of mat, and other articles showing some contact with civilisation; large Pegu jars, Chinese bowls and plates, a knife or two, an old beer bottle full of wild honey, a couple of wooden boxes—that is all. The spectacle that spreads beyond is of a purple lake, studded on its circumference with blue islands. The sunlight dances on the water, the sea hurtles very gently against the white sand, bees hum in the motionless air, and a bird pipes in the brake. From the deep recesses of the woods comes faintly the voice of the sea-cunny, calling to the trembling hidden people without avail. It is a dreamy soft and beautiful corner of the world, oceans away from this morning's bay and the Scotchman with his divers at work. The *Marguerite* lying at anchor in the offing, and puffing clouds of white steam against the purple seascape, looks like the denizen of another world. The shimmering heat plays a fugue before my drowsy eyes. . . . I turn with an effort to the realities about me.

The white sand is marked with the footprints of the colony. Its only representative stands half-cowed with fear, a deep, dull, suspicion lingering in his eyes. He is a short, strong, black-skinned man, with a sparse moustache and no beard, a loin-cloth and a bandana, both red. He tells the sea-cunny that they came here yesterday, and that they will leave as soon as they have collected enough of a palm with which to renew the upper portions of their boats. It is fiercely hot, and the sea-cunny says the heads of the Salôn infants grow red in the sun. They live rough lives, and die hard.

Leaving Bentinck Island and the Perforated rock, we steer directly for the Sisters. Islands bare as Sark lie upon our right, of fantastic form. One is like a Japanese eagle, another like a palace, a third is like a cathedral in the distance.

For the first time now we come upon a pearler, sweeping slowly with long oars along a line of shadow, under the precipitous flanks of Maria, most northerly of the Sisters. These islands nearly all stand clean out of the water, and look as if they had no interiors but only summits to be climbed with difficulty. The first of the boats I see is the property of Olpherts the little clerk; the second of the German Hertzog. The sea is placid as blue marble swaying with the first beat of life. Black rocks show their fangs in the sun, and deep pacific harbours lie between the islands. Between Maria and Elizabeth, where the rocks are strung in a line across the strait, there is a wonderful blaze of sea.

The pearlers, more numerous now, are scattered like islands on the sun-steeped ocean, and with the aid of a telescope I can tell if they are at work, from the dark figure of the life-line man erect at the stern.

As we gradually approach I find that four men are working at the pump wheel, two with their hands and two with their feet. A man at

THE DIVER BELOW

the oar is slowly propelling the boat in sympathy with the buried diver below, and two men stand silhouetted against the sky, one at the life, the other at the head-line ; the latter the tender and leader of the boat.

For a little space of time we wait, listening to the monotonous screeching of the wheel ; then the rope tightens, the tender hauls, a burst of bubbles is borne up in tumult to the surface, the tenders run swiftly together, and the diver, like a strange beast hooked up from the sea-deeps, emerges and clings to the ladder over the side of the boat. And there he lies, bent over, the type of exhaustion. The crew hasten to raise his helmet, and lightened of its burden, he steps on deck, his startled Japanese head showing out of his monstrous clothes, his eyes blinking with the change from the deep sea floor to its sunlit surface. In a small brown net, like those which old ladies use in England when they go a-shopping, lie the shells he has found. Anything from sixpence each to a thousand pounds.

We move on and I find Allingham in the midst of his boats, a pile of shells about him. He uses a big flat blade and peers as he opens the shells into their lustrous depths ; flinging the meat with its food of live red prawns into a bucket of water, which he afterwards searches with fingers skilled with usage. When he has gone tragically through the entire pile finding nothing, I descend with him into his cabin, garnished with bottles of sauce, a rusty tin containing a few pearls, an iron safe, an open shell with the mark on it of a rifled pearl, a pipe or two, a tin of "Navy Cut." Enters the German Hertzog, brusque, keen, intelligent, curiosity written large in his eyes. For the coming of the *Marguerite* is a riddle to be solved. Meanwhile we lie at ease on the cabin roof, and get the launch to tow us to the *Bertha* at anchor in the shelter of an island. They talk of a Salôn camp assembled in the neighbourhood, and as we go, I see their fleet of boats making away across the water, in the wake of a double-sailed Chinaman, who has come to trade and barter.

It is evening, the closing hour, and there is a general movement on the seas. The pearling-boats are coming in to their rendezvous beside an island, the home of the edible-nest builder, which from its strange picturesque outline is a landmark to them all. It is nearly bare rock, but at its corners trees droop over the sides, like parasols, and it is so much like a Japanese picture, that I give it, in emulation of the worthy Captain Forrest, the name of O Mimosa San. The last pink of the sunset turns the space between the islands into sea-ways of exquisite colour. Cliffs and precipices rise up about us, and in their shelter we anchor for the night.

I spend an hour in the *Bertha* listening to the pleasant German talk of the pearler's wife.

"Ach," she says, speaking of the islands, "when I camen heere, I did think I could never wonder enough. Nicht Mark? Oh, but they are so beautifully."

While we talk the pearler cleans and searches his shells by the lantern-light; in all he does a man of character. It was he who wrecked the *Amboyna;* he has a master's certificate; but he sits here undaunted in spirit, and he holds on while the Englishmen go, one by one, because he knows how to make an income in many ways. He takes photographs of the islanders, and sells their skulls and skeletons to anthropological institutes in Berlin. He took home a pair of ourang-outangs for which he asked 20,000 francs. One died on the way, and the other, as his wife says, "did sigh with his head in his hands; oh! so sad, for one of his own nation." A year ago they found a pair of dwarfs, and took them away to Germany, where they are now famous and a source of unascertained income to the pearler and his wife. He has sent for whaling tackle; and is, in short, a man of ability. His wife is a plump, bright-eyed, brown-faced girl, with some English which she has learnt since she came to these seas, and many pretty Germanisms. She talks well, and is full of appreciation of every kind of beauty, and what she calls "the Nat-ure." "Ach Gott!" she says, speaking of the archipelago, "but it is so beautifully. It do make such a théma for the letters home."

Allingham, a red man, sad and bashful, sits on a stool offering a word only now and then.

They talk of ambergris, and whales, and divers' risks; of two recent deaths from the snapping of the tube (the life-tender hauled hand-over-hand, but not quick enough to save his man, who came up dead and black in the face); of divers half-paralysed and scarce able to walk, who still dive; of one who tired of life as a cripple, shot himself; of the man whose helmet being unadjusted let in the water (he signalled, but was kept down, being supposed nervous, and ultimately came up, dead); of one whose head swelled up, so that they could scarcely remove the helmet. The diver's life in these seas is risky, short, riotous, lucrative, and there is no lack of apprentices to the trade. And so as we talk, the German finishing his work, falls back into a long armchair; the poultry in the hen-coop cackle and fill the air with the scent of feathers; the schooler's dog still wet with the sea, dozes under the lantern's light; a kettle boils on the hob in the cabin below, and oars splash in the darkness, as boats go to and fro. From the distance there are borne upon the swaying sea the voices of the assembled crews, in song, in laughter, in the telling of strange tales before they sleep.

"Well," says Allingham mournfully, "I haven't given up hope yet. From now till April there are still four months to run, and who knows what we may find."

She.—" Oh, but England is already—what you say ?—internatsio ; but in Shermanie they do think much of a tiger-claw necklace. Nicht Mark ? " and at intervals she says soothingly : " So—o " . . . " So—o."

WITH THE SALÔN

During the night the launch and the schooner *Bertha* developed an intimacy, and the dawn as it came stealing over the seas, found them linked in an embrace of their anchor chains. When at length we got away, day had broken, and we steered into the lake of water between Jane and Charlotte, and thence across the sea to Bushby in the track of the departed gypsies. In the far distance I could trace the smoke of their moving fires, and the gleam of an oar blade as it caught the sun. Skate were flapping about in the sea, and a shoal of small fish leaped and plunged, pursuing and pursued ; the war of nature incessant under the smiling surface of life. The Sisters, all blue and green now, lay strung in a line upon the western sea, and O Mimosa San was fading out of sight. Father and Son, a solemn couple, greeted us on the south. I hailed the Chinaman as we came up to him, and he sent off a present of green-snail shells, and a polite message to say that the Salôn would rendezvous in his neighbourhood in the evening after the day's work.

The green-snail shell is a beautiful object, deep sea-green without, white and iridescent within. All the beauty of the sunset is by some miracle of nature caught and imprisoned in the mould of this deep-sea dweller. And so as we went on, I came upon the Salôn in the clear green water, under a rocky coast. There were several boats, and from one a man with a Burman air about him, a very merry fellow, signalled to us to come up that he might look upon us. In the boats before me there were men and women, children and boys, but the young unmarried girls must have hidden themselves away, for I could see none. The children were of a fairer complexion than their parents, and all but the very youngest were at work with oar or punting pole. The most attractive child of all was a girl almost grown up, bedecked with beads, and swathed in a single garment of blue cloth. She had brown eyes and dark ringlets, and was so frightened at being photographed, that she broke into tears, and was with difficulty reassured. As it was, the tears lay in a rim about her eyes long after she had ceased to cry ; and she could not be persuaded to resume the pole, which she used at the prow of her father's boat with an admirable grace. Behind her in the recesses of the boat crouched her grandmother, a midnight hag—type of the terrible old age of the Salôn woman. I do not suppose that there is anywhere in the world any one more ugly than an old woman of the Salôn.

A SALÔN BOAT

HARPOONING

Some of the men plunged with harpoons to show me how they did it, and the exhibition was greeted with peals of laughter from the assembled boats. The harpooner before plunging strains forward, every muscle taut, the whole weight of his body resting on the ball of his foot—a missile incarnate. Then he flings his harpoon with a whirr through the sunlight, and leaps after it into the water. Spear and man are lost to sight. A moment later up he comes with dripping hair, clutches the cut in the shapely gunwale, and climbs with a swift action into the boat. When engaged in the serious business of fishing, the Salôn spear a large fish, like a skate, which lies upon its back in the water and paddles with its wide fins. When the agitation reaches the surface and is caught in the straining vision of the fisher, his boat flies forward, and the harpoon-man, poised on its prow, plunges swiftly on seeing the white stomach of the fish, and drives home his weapon with the weight of his body. This done, he loosens the spear-head from the shaft and climbs back into his boat, now speeding over the water in the wake of the maddened fish. Gradually its strength fails it, its speed slackens, it can go no farther. Then it is hauled on board, cut into strips, and dried in the sun.

The Salôn also dive for pearls, but only in shallow water, now rifled for the most part by the regular pearler.

" But Lord ! there was a time," as the old sea-captains say, " when good pearls could be had for a pouch of tobacco." That was when the Salôn had his island seas to himself, and knew nothing of the value of pearls. But the coming of the pearler has brought enlightenment, and with it scarcity, and the Salôn when he does find a pearl, sells it to advantage. The *bêche-de-mer* is caught by him in baskets of rattan, trailed slowly over the muddy shallows. It is dried in the sun and looks unappetising enough ; but when soaked in water it becomes like a clean white jelly, and makes a soup that is esteemed good and delicate by the Chinese *gourmet*.

When you think of the Salôn's place on the ladder of human life, of his limitations, his approaching extinction, you pity him ; but he has his compensations. His toil is to his liking. He is ever plunging in the warm transparent water, or chasing the wild hog with his dogs. Save that he must live, he is burdened with few cares ; and all said he lives a free, wild, and unfettered existence. That must be dearer to him than the sordid drudgery of his brother, learning here and there the slow lesson of the primitive tiller of the soil. As to schools and so forth, who on earth would willingly exchange the sunlit water, the white sands, and the wandering life, for the finest school in the world?

And religion? his immortal soul? It is true the poor Salôn is limited in his religious notions. He is much concerned with the devil, whom he finds active in many uncomfortable forms; he has glimmerings of a good spirit, whose power is unhappily, he finds, usurped by the devil. But the world that might teach him is itself oppressed with such burdens.

THE HARPOONER

Asked where the spirits of evil reside, my cheerful friend to-day, stretching forth his hands, replied: "Everywhere; in the sea, in the air, in the forests, in the mountains; sometimes behind one island," pointing vaguely to Eliza, "sometimes behind another," pointing to Jane. He spoke with conspicuous gaiety at the moment, but a mental weariness crept over his eyes as he answered my unfamiliar questions. He grew bored, and his fellow at the prow of their boat began to unfasten the cane that bound it to the launch.

I hastily changed the subject, and with revived interest they came on board the launch, and looked into the engine-room and the cabin, making long-drawn clicking sounds expressive of a certain limited wonderment. The engine-room, they said, was hot, the sleeping-places very fine, and an inner room, only partially visible through a half-open door, filled them with a sense of mystery.

The ship, they said, moved with a screw; but they couldn't say what made it revolve. One man was full of cheeriness and curiosity now that he was released from the toils of theology, but the other was dull. Even in these early stages there are marked differences between man and man. When I suggested that now they were bound to the launch, I would take them away with me, they showed a fine alarm, and the dull fellow again began rapidly to unfasten the cane that bound us together. They were as quickly reassured, and laughed at their own timidity. They could hazard no opinion at all of what the white man's country might be like. Being gently led back to the way of cross-examination, they said that when any one died it was due to an evil spirit. They stayed with the dying man to the last, and then laid him out on a platform of canes on piles, after which they went away and never came back. All the people, they said, wept when any one died. Of time they had no conception beyond that involved in the succession of darkness and light, and the changing of the dry and wet seasons. They could tell nothing of any one's age. They live only in the present, looking neither forward nor back. Once a year they change their habitat, from the western or outer side of the islands, to the inner or eastern side. This is at the time the north-west monsoon begins to blow, lashing the unprotected sea into fury. In the turmoil of the long-drawn battle between wind and wave, which lasts from May to October, there is no place for the frail craft of the Salôn, and he lives with his boats drawn up ashore, in the sheltered inlets on the eastern face of the archipelago. Testimony to this double life is written on the face of the islands; and there is no contrast in nature more striking that that between the gothic calm, the tropic splendour, of the island woods which look towards the rising sun, and the torn storm-wrought landscape that faces the western sea and the fury of the winds. Thus, on a calm winter day when the sea is billowy as oil, one is confronted on turning the point of an island with a strange picture of an embodied gale. There is no ripple on the sea, the woods are still and silent, yet they seem shaken in the grasp of a pitiless and furious storm. It is as though a god had stilled for ever the blast in the climax of its wrath.

WITH THE DEVIL

Bidding our Salôn adieu, we steer across a blue oily sea for the Elephant, a monstrous group of rocks that rise in sheer cliffs out of the

PUNTING

sea. On our left other islands deploy in long lines, broken by deep and narrow straits, inter-island lakes, and sweeping bays, which recede to blue mountains in the distance against the opal of the sky. Every corner tempts one to go round it and look for some yet uncaptured beauty; and that is one secret of archipelagian charm. One is never at the end of its mystery. One feels that satisfaction cannot come till one has explored every strait and island; and when one has done this, one must of needs begin again, because of the infinite variety which comes of an ever-changing perspective, of the play of sun and wind and shadow and cloud.

Elephant Island as we approach it, surpasses all other objects in interest. It is the most wild and stern and romantic of all the islands I have yet seen. Its dark walls rise straight from the rim of the green motionless sea, and the lowest footing on it seems to be five hundred feet high. Its crest is like a sierra of sharp iron teeth. A few trees find, as if by miracle, a foothold on this forbidding exterior. Purple jelly-fish with streaming beards swarm in its neighbourhood, and small fry leap in terror out of the sea about it, like fireworks of silver. A low dark line at its pedestals marks the limit of high water. The passages between it and its satellites are like the fiords of some inferno, and the transition from its shadow into the sunlight is as quick and sudden as the transition of a solar eclipse. Its black sides stream with milky cataracts of lime; dark caves lead into its bowels near the sea-rim, and in them, reaching away into blind interiors of the rock the edible-nest makers build their homes. It is a terrible, picturesque place. An echo resides under its bastions, and the launch's heart beats near it with a muffled roar that borders on the supernatural.

Such at least were some of the impressions made by a first circumnavigation of this island—and at some distance, for the launch approached it at her peril. To make a closer acquaintance with it I caused the launch to anchor, and made in the gig for a small strip of yellow sand, the only visible landing-place on the island. This brought me unexpectedly into a circular bay, of which a fraction only was open to the ocean. The water here was an opaque green, the colour of *vert-de-gris*. The harsh grey cliffs towered above its edge, their sheer sides wonderfully made a foothold by the sago palm and a few straggling shrubs. Skirting the curve of the bay I came upon a cave, black and yawning, with huge bulbous stalactites depending from its roof. Some thongs of a creeper, hanging downwards, showed that the place was used by the Salôn for tying up their boats. In this dark and lonely place the swallows were building those nests that furnish a soup for the *gourmets* of China.

The air within was hot and close, the stalagmites and projecting

A BOAT FAMILY

bastions of the cave were covered with a mosaic of shells and other marine life. The water lapped the cave with a hoarse long-drawn sigh. I don't suppose that I can communicate the horror of that sound, for the cave seemed to me, who had never heard of it or seen it before, like some evil monster on the outskirts of sentient life, dark, blind and awful, swallowing up its daily tribute from the sea. Big jelly-fish floated by into its recesses, and I discovered with a disagreeable sensation, that a strong current was making for the low-hung lips of the cave, along which the hapless fish were being borne. Looking back from the tense gloom of the cave, my eyes turned with relief to the open landscape of the world outside ; to its beautiful reaches of luminous water, to an island framed in a sky of small pink clouds, drifting slowly with the wind ; and I emerged from the cave with a feeling of sheer physical relief.

Outside, the strip of yellow shell-sand that had brought me so far, offered its smiling hospitality. I was soon at ease in the buoyant water. At such a temperature ! rich refreshing and cool. I had come it seemed upon a bathing-pool of the Gods. On such occasions one's spirit reverts by a natural cadence to its primitive youth ; the youth, not alone of the individual, but of the race. So it came that I swam about and lay on the yellow sand just covered by the lambent water, wondering at the new view of the world that comes to one who lies upon his back and looks out across the level face of the sea. I shouted to the world and laughed, and raced against my dog, who was scarcely less infected with delight than I was. And the sea-cunny who had come with me in the gig, ran to and fro flinging his casting-net for minnows.

But the sand, we found on subsequent inspection, had traces on it of a curious pattern. *The bathing-place of the gods was an alligator pool !*

" Wah," said the sea-cunny, staring at the prints on the narrowing sand, while from the cave there came the booming of the tide, " wah—it is a place of devils, a Shait-an-ka-jagah."

The sea-cunny, for it is time to introduce him, is the kind of elemental person one likes to travel with ; with sinews and a chest of iron, a square jaw, a deep harsh baying voice, and bloodshot eyes ; a splendid figure of a man, intended by nature for the piratic calling of his ancestors but yoked by fate to a civilised life, and now a desperate assistant in any cause that appeals to his sense of loyalty.

Taking to the gig, we made for the opening of the bay, and had nearly come out of this cauldron of devilry and beauty, when the conviction came upon me that the massive bastion of rock under which the cave lay was part of an outer defence, and not the main wall of the island fortress. " Allah—Khuda ! " said the sea-cunny, rising to his feet in the swaying boat, " there is surely something on the other side." Some trick of the slant fading sunlight revealed to us in a moment, what we had failed to see during the hours we had been looking upon the stony face of the island. Late as the hour was, we turned with a common instinct to the exposing of its mystery. Rowing slowly under the forbidding bastions of rock, which offered no foothold, we came upon a place up which a man might venture to climb. It was inhospitable, but the sea-cunny was not to be restrained. While he was away and lost in the growing darkness I rowed into the cave, and flung into the blind water objects which I meant to go and look for on the other side of the island, in the view that there might be an exit for the flood now visibly being swallowed into the recesses of the cave. My plans were obliterated by the harsh roaring voice of the sea-cunny, which, coming from afar, filled the dark vault above me with its echoes. "God," I heard him calling; for the man was frequent in his appeals to heaven, "I have found it. There is water, water, a lake within." Leaving the boat to the lascar, I clambered up the face of the rock. It struck up on all sides in thin fluted pinnacles like the columns of an ant-hill. "*Churry-Ké-mafik*," said the sea-cunny, tapping one large pinnacle with his hand till it rang like steel.

"Allah," he said, "but they are sharp. If a man were to fall here—*Bus Khalas ho giya*" (There would be an end of him). Allowing for picturesque phraseology, there was in fact some risk in climbing at this dark hour, and the only means of ascent were offered by these sword-edges of rock that rose one above the other.

By these means, and before the night made seeing impossible, I caught a glimpse of what the sea-cunny had discovered; a lake of copper green water set in an inferno of cliffs and precipices. A stone flung by him as he hung on to a knife-edge of rock blobbed with a dull sound in the still water. We came down after this and reached our boat, the sea-cunny bleeding at his feet. We rowed, the sea-cunny loyal and contemptuous of protest from the less keen Chittagonian, all in the dark, half-way round the island, on the chance of finding the exit of the waters. The island towered above us into the starry sky, and each time the blade of an oar ploughed the inky sea it flung off a cloud of phosphorus, that floated away like a jelly-fish on fire. We were all by now fallen under the dominion of the dæmon of the place. The sea-cunny had no longer any word to say. We rowed in silence. The truculence of nature obsessed us. And even now, as I sit and look out on the stars and the heaving sea, I cannot shake off the pervading horror of this place. We seem, and I am sure my companions think, that we have lighted upon the secret home of the Spirit of Evil. They call it Elephant Island, but that is a name bestowed by a stranger from afar. There is nothing of the elephant about this place at close quarters. It is purely diabolical, and the whole is a palace of the devil—a cathedral of wickedness. Every time I look into the night and see its sinister pinnacles and revetments outlined against the stars, I am assailed by their awful suggestion. Even the wash of the sea, so pleasant at other times and in other places, is here of a sinister purport, like that within the cave, of some blind gross being of another world, into whose jaws life is drawn unresistingly without hope or power of escape.

It comes, no doubt, of the eccentric action of water on limestone; but the explanation counts for less than nothing here. Are not all impressions of nature illusions?

And now think of this infernal interior of the sea-lake we have found, of this dark cave under its colossal propylon, hidden away in the heart of this smiling archipelago. Who would suspect its existence if he were not told of it? And if there be such things in one island of these seas, what may there not be hidden away amongst its thousand fellows? Such are the speculations that are filling our minds.

THE HIDDEN LAKE

Last night the sea-cunny, untiring in adventure, sailed away through the night in search of a Salôn camp, whose fires shone like pinpoints in the dark. For it seemed probable that the Salôn could pilot us by an easier route to the lake whose existence we had discovered. The first light of dawn showed me a Salôn boat lashed under the bows of the launch, the sea-cunny in possession; and I am sorry to say, its owner lying on its bottom trussed like a fowl. He made no protest. Taking him with us we climbed once again up the sharp pinnacles, and looked down upon the hidden waters; but descent to them from there was impossible. We turned back, somewhat torn as to our hands and feet, and rowed away to the cave, as interesting as it was the night before, but less tragic now in the light of day. The hoarse lapping of the sea still echoed there, but the sun, stealing in under the stalagmites, counteracted these dark suggestions. The water was now a translucent green, and its roof was lit with dancing water-gleams. The Salôn informed me that through this cave at low water I could enter the hidden lake. In the direction of the passage, still invisible, there was silence; a roar came only from the blind walls where the sea could find no entry. Through this passage the sea enters and retreats, and the evil genius of the lake gorges and disgorges daily. At spring tides the mouth of the cave is filled to the roof, and there is no passage.

Coming away, till the ebbing of the tide should serve our purpose, I made a tour of the island, and entered another cave called Gwa Chee Boh. It lies outside the perimeter of the island on its eastern face, and is overhung by sheer and tragic cliffs from which great stalactites depend, threatening to fall upon an intruder. Long ropes of rattan, leading up into secret places, and now rotting with half a year's disuse, show that the cave is visited. The Salôn on being questioned disclaimed, with a sort of awe, their ever exploiting these cliffs for nests. They were too ignorant, he said, to find the nests, and too fearful of falling down from the great heights to attempt to do so. But the Malay come twice a year from Pulo-Penang and climb up. They bring dammer torches with them and remain within the inner cave ten days, getting shut in there by the sea ; and they collect six gunny bags of nests. It is a fearful place, where men fall and are killed. Formerly it was worked by Burmans, and the cave is named after one who fell and broke his back here.

The sea-cunny, who extracted this information by slow degrees,

AT VICTORIA POINT: THE SOUTHERNMOST LIMIT OF BURMA

for all primitive folk hate being cross-examined, sent forth volumes of amazement at hearing that for ten days the Malay went in and came not out. I imagined the wild scene within when these men are at work ; the roaring echoes that fill and resound in the dark vaulted cave finding no outlet, the glimmer of the dammer torches, the daring climbers far up in the pitchy recesses, the whirring of a thousand wings, the sea beating hoarsely against the blind walls of the cave.

As we went on grey egrets skimmed the water like phantoms before us, streamers of colour, reflected from the cliffs, painted its lustrous surface, and silver showers of fish, driven up to the light for their lives, flashed in the sun. The Salôn tried with his spear, under the shadow of the walls where larger game lay concealed, and the sea-cunny toiled up steep places after delicate orchids, plunging back into the sea, and spluttering and laughing like a child.

We lay for hours outside the island until at noon there became visible to us in the launch a faint pinprick of light in the cave, and we knew the way was open to us at last. It was dead low water, and the bay, as we rowed across it to the cave's mouth was lean from the depletion of the tide. The cave from the same cause had quadrupled in size, and its roof under which I had stooped to enter, now rose far out of reach above my head. Water still dripped from it as we advanced, and green and scarlet weeds and berries flung a colour over the interior. The sinister murmur of the lapping sea was stilled, but every sound we uttered gathered a monstrous intonation from the vaulting of the cave. A cool wind blew through the narrow tortuous aperture, as lying flat upon our backs in the boat, we propelled it forward with our hands against the roof. Beyond its darkness there lay a sheet of pale green water and a world of sunlight. Steering slowly through the passage we emerged at last upon the lake. Its walls rose up, sheer and steep in a million pinnacles of rock, to a height of a thousand feet. But for the low-browed passage by which we had come, there was apparent neither inlet nor exit. The waters lay calm, unruffled, and still. The blue sky gleamed overhead. It was hard to believe that here we were in the midst of the ocean.

The Salôn who accompanied me led us to a cave that lies at the south-east corner of the lake. The approach to it was heavy with slime and the strange débris of the departed tide. From the deep gloom of the inner hall the swallows flew out in swarms, and high up from invisible recesses came the million-fold " *chuck-chuck* " of the nesting birds. A strange creature, with prawn-like lip, beady eyes, and twitching antennæ, the whole pose of his body indicative of vigilant dread, advanced with his shell on his back across the slime. The place was fitly peopled with creatures such as he. As I climbed back into the boat, a young python in the water stole away swiftly in the effort to escape unseen. The lascar at the boat's prow struck him with an oar, and pinned him down to the muddy bottom. He broke away with a wound in his back and made a dash for the rock, but meeting a wall which he essayed with impotent fury, he came by his death.

The lascar moralised on fate. It is the Musulman's favourite text. " See," he said, as the vivid coils lay broken in the bottom of the boat, " his hour had come, and we came here this day that his destiny might be accomplished." The Salôn, with expressive action, stated that great pythons lived in the cave and on the island. The Malay who come here every year for the swallows' nests and hold a feast on the rocks at the cave's mouth, never kill the python, he said, considering him in some way associated with the spirit of this inferno. The Salôn come here to spear the devil fish, and slay a giant lizard that frequents the island.

The tide was now running in, and the waters of the lake were beginning to rise. Having no taste for an enforced detention within its walls, we made for the passage, and shortly after emerged on the open sea where the launch lay waiting for us, and the crew stood wondering where we had been. The lascar and the sea-cunny each had his tale to tell; for no one on board the launch had ever in their long experience of these seas, heard of the hidden lake.

* * *

Leaving the shadowy battlements of the island behind us, we steam up Celerity Passage, wooded Domel the isle of honey, on our left, and a low country of brown sandy flats and pale swamps on our right.

Towards evening we attain once more the full island country, and the sun sets in a blaze of salmon-pink between Money and Trotter, touching with his light the crest of Rosy, far away in the purple distance. The anchor drops, and there follows the peace of the long evening. The launch ceases from her hard throbbing, the fires are put out, and the embers pale. The tired crew, one by one, drop asleep. Almost the last sound that breaks the stillness of the night comes from the sea-cunny's voice, as he retails his adventures, and goes over in bold picturesque terms the incidents of the morning.

A single lantern burns at the stern. A world of dark sea, and starry sky, and the shadowy immense forms of islands brooding on the horizon lies about me. I am glad that there is no one here to break in upon my solitude. For in the dusk and the silence strange thoughts move through one's mind; thoughts luminous one instant, faint and dark the next; revelations of the firmament, and sudden lights into the dark places of the human spirit; hints of a world plan, faint uncertain tremors of a Creator's will, fading convictions of the destiny of life.

It is not at such seasons of loneliness, nay, of fellowship with elemental life, that the heart feels its isolation. The true home of loneliness is the great city. *Magna civitas, magna solitudo.*

CHAPTER XXX

MOULMEIN

MOULMEIN is the most beautiful town in Burma. It is one of the oldest of British settlements in the country, for it passed into our hands a century ago; and for twenty-five years it bade fair to be the capital. But the conquest of Pegu made Rangoon a British possession; the fitness of its site for a great city surpassed that of Moulmein, and in a little while, Moulmein, unable to keep pace with its powerful rival, fell back. It stands at the mouth of the Salwin river, and commands the timber trade of the interior; but Rangoon is supported by the Irrawaddy, which bears nearly the whole of the traffic of Burma. Between the two cities there never can be any serious competition. Yet, although the hopes of Moulmein were long since broken, and although its atmosphere is one of decline, Moulmein has seen its worst days. As time advances it must share in the general movement towards prosperity that is taking place throughout the country.

It has practically no past. It is a product of British rule, and is less a centre of Burmese life than any other town of its size in the country. And yet, no one who has lived in Burma would willingly forget it; for its old-world air, for this very sentiment of failure that clings to its atmosphere. It is a place to which old clerkly pensioners retire when their life's work is done. Rangoon, they will tell you, is too great for them. Lesser towns are too small. Moulmein with its colony of resident Europeans, its friendly and unpretentious ways, its temperate climate, its cheap living, makes a special appeal to quiet people.

When it came into British hands a century ago, it was scarcely more than unreclaimed jungle. Yet was it not unknown in the great days when Pegu dazzled the imaginations of men, and Martaban across the water, was a vice-regal city. "Some of the Peguans," wrote the Jesuit Pimenta, early in the seventeenth century, "in this time had with the Siamites' help brought the Castle of Murmulan into their possession, whom the king besieged a year together. And the Siamites coming on them unexpected, overthrew his armie, killed his Horses and Elephants, slew and drowned many, took others, and so became Lords of all that Countrie. And many Peguan Peeres fled together, whose wives, children and families, the King after his manner destroyed utterly, with fire sword and water. And thus the whole tract from Pegu to Martaban and Murmulan was brought to a wildernesse." Such incidents were common enough in Burmese history, before we came.

When the southern coast became a part of the British Empire, there was some question as to whether its capital should be placed at Amherst or at Moulmein. Military reasons decided in favour of Moulmein, because of its neighbourhood to the Burmese fortress at Martaban, and the power it gave the British garrison of defending the left bank of the Salwin from aggression. But military reasons have long ceased to have any weight in the councils of Moulmein; the British frontier has advanced seven hundred miles since it was founded, from Martaban to the gates of China, and the last soldier has been withdrawn from its garrison.

WHERE THE GYAING AND THE ATTARAN MEET

The town is built at the foot of a ridge of hills, in an arm of the Salwin river. The large island of Bilu-Gyun faces it in the west. At its northern end the Gyaing and the Attaran meet the Salwin, and by their presence add to the beauty of its environment. The actual town of houses strung along its main switchback street and for several miles along the shore, is not delectable. It is a hybrid of foreign races, many of whom are inferior and lack the natural charm of the people of the soil. Not till one approaches the great stairs, which climb up the hillside to the pagodas and monastic buildings on its summit, is the sentiment of Burmese life revived ; a precious thing not easily replaced.

On the pagoda-platform, where golden pinnacles flame in the sun, and light and shadow lie in bars upon the paved courts, one is liable of a morning to come upon such spectacles as this. Under the lofty multiple roofs of a *tazoung* with golden pillars, a company of the silken people is gathered for purposes of devotion. In the centre under a glass dome, there is exposed for the edification of the pious a relic case of gold and jewels, offered by some ardent seeker after merit as a gift for the Buddhist fraternity of Ceylon. Above it in the shadowy recesses, sits a figure of the Buddha on a golden throne. Along the walls in its neighbourhood the members of the Sacred Order are ranged in a double line, their faces passionless, or bowed in prayer. Before the relic case, a group of aged men in white muslin, with the saintly faces that Burmans develop in old age, sit in an inner circle, their silver hair and white fillets of muslin conspicuous in the midst of the crowd that fills the rest of the hall. What a crowd it is ! First the men in white coats and silken tartans and *gaungbaungs*, never worn before, lustrous in their freshness in colours of the dawn. Then behind them, filling the wide outer circles, women with coils of glossy black hair lit with fresh flowers ; soft silks and velvet thrown over their shoulders, pyramids of diamonds on their fingers, their small bare feet turned up to the light behind.

A low resonant voice the while repeats the holy text, and at intervals the whole company, with folded hands, and fluttering paper pennons, and bowed heads, join in audible devotion.

And outside, across the open court, small boys race and laugh, and no one is worried by their laughter. The old are here to pray and to ponder on the sadness, the transitoriness, and the illusion of life ; the young to play and laugh in the sunlight. Of them (as of all created things and in all their human relationships) these people are tolerant. For every one, it would seem, there is room. A few paces away, and under the very gleam of the pagoda, large cauldrons are set over a fire, and rice for the assembled company of the religious is being cooked. Overhead the bells tinkle and palm-leaves rustle and murmur together in the wind. The pagoda is built upon the summit of a hill, and the world that expands

CARVED FIGURES AT THE PAGODA

from it is of rare and great beauty. From where these people are seated at prayer, there is unfolded between each of the golden pillars and the carved eaves of the *tazoung* a picture of wide plains yellow with the ripening harvest ; of green villages under the shelter of great trees, of winding rivers and straight highways, and mountains flung in fantastic forms upon the level spaces. From the town below a stream of worshippers flows up and down the steep winding stairs ; old men who laugh at each other for getting blown ; pretty women in silks of delicate hues ;

THE SOUTH-WESTERN ANGLE OF THE PAGODA

and flower-like children who climb, holding their sandals in their hands out of reverence for the sacred place.

The view from Moulmein Hill is famous in Burma, and its praises are for ever on the lips of its people.

From the south-west angle of the southernmost pagoda, where a double sphinx looks out across the spaces, there is unfolded a picture of a wide river making its last progress in loops and curves to the sea. Enthusiastic people say that it is as fine as the harbour of Sydney. Since these words were written I have seen Sydney and I think it is finer. Some distance from the river a long low line of hills runs down on the east, and another, the nucleus of Bilu-Gyun, runs along the west, a rampart for the retreating sun. The river enfolds in its course several large low-lying islands, and at one point, at Mopun, it makes a beautiful curve ending in a headland, where rice and timber mills send their smoke into the air and ships in the harvest season wait for their cargoes to a distant world.

BOAZ

Looking more directly now to the west, there is the river again in a straight bar of gold under the long town of Moulmein. More ships lie here, and they look to me as if they had dropped mysteriously from the great world outside, into this land-locked anchorage under the swooning palms. For as I look, the conviction is borne in upon me of a drowsy land of extraordinary beauty, but not of a modern city ; and the ships that lie here for a season form no part of it.

Looking a little more towards the north, my eyes are greeted by the Zingyaik hills, whose loftiest peak three thousand feet in height, dominates the wide embroidered scene. Between these hills and Bilu-Gyun the right branch of the Salwin makes its way to sea. In times gone by—in the days of the Castle of Murmulan, when Portuguese artillerymen manned the guns of Martaban, and hungry adventurers from the West swept by in their galleons up the gulf—and even in more recent times, *this* was the main channel of the river. It is not the channel now. It has ceased for more than a generation to be navigable by steamers, and the time is approaching when it will cease to be navigable at all. Even now the aspect it wears is of a low country slowly rising from the sea ; a new world shaping into being. The claim of this western channel to be the main stream of the Salwin was, however, curiously established a hundred years ago. The Salwin had been fixed as the boundary between British and Burmese territory after the first war, and it became a question as to which branch of it was the real Salwin. The island of Bilu-Gyun with an area of one hundred and seven square miles, was the stake at issue. The rival diplomatists resorted to the simple device of

THE LIMESTONE CAVES AT MOULMEIN

tying two cocoanuts together and sending them adrift upon the main river. At Martaban, where the river divides, these cocoanuts for an instant remained stationary; then they were caught by an eddy and swept to sea down the western channel, and Bilu-Gyun became British.

Turning away now from all that lies to the west, I see from my splendid vantage-point how this process of transition from water to land has been already accomplished. For here, where chequered rice-fields now turn up their patterns to the sky like some tesselated pavement; where monasteries now shelter under clusters of drooping palms, where villages and hamlets smile, and rivers, the Gyaing and the Attaran, wind across the landscape in ribbons of silver and blue, there once moved, if one may believe the testimony of the earth, the implacable sea. One feature of that bygone day still survives, a landmark of the past, as it is of the present. For the fantastic isolated hills that rise up abruptly from the level plain, were once in reality islands, and the sea swept round them, and the blind waves roared in their caves. Elephant island is one of these.

Book VIII

THE SALWIN

En Voyage—Pha-an—The Caves of Pha-gat—To Shwegun—Shwegun—Primitive Travel—The Last Stage

CHAPTER XXXI

EN VOYAGE

NINE o'clock of a January morning, and I am abroad upon the great expanse of the Salwin. The river, of a grey-green colour, winds away through vast savannahs, flanked in the distant west by the Zingyaik range, and on the east by the Zway-kabyin peaks, and the far faint outline of loftier mountains. As we progress, fresh hills rise up like the phantasms of a dream ; strange, shadowy, and tragic in form.

But the near banks are clothed with rare beauty, with waving grasses, and forests of wild cotton trees in bloom. At this season they break into a splendour of cardinal blossom, devoid of foliage. The rich tracery of their boughs is cut with the clarity of a cameo against the blue mountains and the momentary glory of the sunset.

We stop at little villages by the way to pick up passengers ; and the village girls come down to the ship's edge with trays of green papayas and red plums, bosom deep in the river ; and they laugh as they sink yet deeper in their efforts to reach the passengers on board. Each of these, leaning forward over the rails, takes what he needs, and puts the price into a little cup in the middle of the tray.

Laung-gos sail swiftly down the river, their cordage taut, their white sails full blown to the wind. Anon a man rises up in a small canoe and shakes his silken *gaungbaung* to the air. The steamer whistles, the engines slacken, the single passenger is taken in. There is already assembled on board an interesting company ; for besides our Burman travellers, there are the caravan Shan, with their pack-baskets ranged in line upon the upper deck, and blazing turbans on their heads, and great hats delicate as Venetian lace within. There are groups also of Panthays in blue, and

THE SALWIN

Yunnanese in satin caps ; and at one end of the deck, a party of Christian Karen who sing hymns in a strange tongue, to the familiar tunes of an English parish church. An Elder expounds a text as the steamer throbs upon her way, and the company about him follow him with quiet zeal. Strange as is the spectacle, it is of the East eastern. There is no trace

WAITING FOR THE STEAMER

of self-consciousness in any of their faces, no idea of posing as pious people. No pious gloom surrounds them; they sing and worship, apparently because it gives them genuine pleasure to do so. Their fellow-passengers, when not preoccupied with their own affairs, look on with profound interest, as they would at a steam-engine, or any other novelty. Certainly no one of them would ever dream of objecting to the singing. Nor is it customary in the East to scoff at the display of religion. And to the only Englishman on board, as he sits alone in the foreways of the ship, there is a subtle attraction in these foreign voices singing some old familiar hymn, the first music of his youth.

As we approach Pha-an the limestone hills come nearer to the river. The Kaw-gun caves lie at the end of a narrow water on our left, and at Pha-gat, a little higher up, the width of the river contracts. Through these gateways there is entry into a dreamy world of wide calm waters, of wooded islands, and distant peaks: and the splendid Titanic form of Zway-kabyin. Here we are very near the turning point of the range, and its form changes completely within a few hundred yards of our ascent up the river.

CHAPTER XXXII

PHA-AN

AT Pha-an one may well come to a pause, for there are few more beautiful places in Burma than this small village struggling to be a town, on a cliff-top above the Salwin. There is a house here for the European traveller, built upon a promontory that juts like a great ram into the river; and every vista from it is one of beauty. Looking up-stream, there is the wide splendour of the Salwin, a great island in its arms; behind it the ruddy peak of Pha-oo, whose shadow at dawn and evening lies mirrored in the stately water. On the western shore is the pyramid of Pha-boo, with a little white and gold pagoda on a hillock at its feet. The river runs by it under high banks, rich with grasses and plantain-groves, to the gateways of Pha-gat. Below the house in the east, and first lit by the day, is a sheltered harbour in which the cargo dinghies lie, and the white masts of sailing vessels rise straight from the water. Here at all hours there is life: bullock-carts wait to ship and unship their burden, while the red cattle browse under the trees; women and girls come down to laugh and bathe; Burmans squat on the sloping bank and smoke with philosophic calm; the lying Chittagonian sleeps and prays.

Turning away from here to the village, my eyes are drawn by the

WILD PLUMS AT PHA-AN

white wide highway, past hayricks and plantain-groves and a monastery on a hill, to the lofty summit of Zway-kabyin and its one pagoda like a lighthouse on its crest. At night at this season, the hill Karen set fire to the jungle near its top, and then there is a wonderful circle of fire hung up against the starry sky, a thousand feet above the world. Zway-kabyin—" The Mooring of the Ship "—is the local Ararat ; for it is said that when the whole world was covered with water, and the only survivors of the human race were in a ship afloat upon the deeps, they found a haven here at the summit of the great peak. Its majestic outline, its enormous form towering over the spaces at its foot, well fit it for the office that tradition with poetic right has assigned to it. " A stream that is clear as crystal, and cold in the hottest weather, gushes out of a purple grot at its base. It has been the theatre of more agonising scenes than the muddiest and hottest stream in the provinces, scenes that have won for it the name of Teegaung—' The Brook of Weeping.' For it has not been only in time of deluge that Zway-kabyin has been chosen as a refuge." In the days of the conqueror Alompra, a large number of Karen were besieged here by the Siamese, and nearly all of them perished for want of food and water. Whence the place is known as Dongyang—" The Weeping City."

Once a year at the harvest season when all the Burmese world goes on pilgrimage, the pagoda on the summit of the range is visited by all in its neighbourhood who can manage the arduous climb. The view it offers is one of extraordinary variety and beauty, and it may fittingly be described in the words of the great missionary to the Karen who first climbed up it : " At the base of the western mountains the Salwin is seen plunging down its mighty waters to Martaban and Maulmain, where they are joined by the Gyaing that bounds the prospect on the south and east, while little islands of forest trees each concealing beneath its shade a quiet hamlet, dimple the whole plain, and babbling brooks thread their wandering ways like veins of silver, or mark the courses of their hidden waters by the emerald hue of their banks. On the inner side the spectator is astonished to find himself on the edge of a large basin, like the crater of an extinct volcano. Around and beyond, on the opposite side of the gulf, for miles in extent, dark precipitous gaps, of every imaginable and unimaginable form, fling down their tall shadows a thousand feet about the place of entrance, enclosing an area of several square miles." Maybe the sea was once there.

Pha-an itself is one of the chief centres of trade with the Shan States, and here, unexpectedly to the traveller fresh from the far-distant northern frontier of Bhamo, are reproduced within thirty miles of a seaport the picturesque elements of frontier life and trade—Panthay caravans and merchandise from China, traders and mulemen, and the

A TAUNGTHU GIRL OF PHA-AN

thronging of many races. Of nights when the river is silent, one can hear from the high mud-cliffs the baying of the Panthay dogs, and the laughter of muleteers ; one can see in the darkness the glow of their camp-fires amongst the feathery plum-trees. Cattle, ponies, and silk, elephants and gold, are brought here for sale, and from here the fabrics of Manchester and Birmingham, brought so far by steam, start on their long journey over the highlands to the most distant markets of Shanland and Yunnan. The concourse of many strangers brings with it its customary penalty, and Pha-an, lifted above a world of extraordinary beauty, has long been known as the haunt of bad characters. Many of its people are Taungthus, now fast merging in appearance and dress into the Burmese type.

CHAPTER XXXIII

THE CAVES OF PHA-GAT

A BOLD promontory of rock with its crowning pagoda, reaching far over into the territories of the river, marks the western gateway of the Salwin at Pha-gat. I land here and make my way past monasteries where scholars are at play, down a footpath sheltered by great trees, to the entrance of the cave. The stark face of the overhanging cliff is decorated with little images of the Buddha, fixed very close together in successive lines, which look like an inscription on the stone. The interior of the cave is dark and chaotic. Its floor, with beams flung across its pitfalls, suggests an abandoned mine. In the half-lit middle of the cave there is a rough ladder, which leads to a hidden chamber in the roof. The first part of the roof over the long entrance-hall is clean and level, save where in places, half-spherical domes have been carved out by the departed sea. In these shadowy places, and in the deep gloom of the cave's interior, the bats hang like soot. As we enter with flaming torches, myriads of them disturbed, wheel in circles overhead, and the cave is filled with the humming of their wings. In rows down the long hall, and on the stalactite ledges, there is a great company of Buddhas, a fraction only of the multitude that was once here. Yet at a glance one can see that many types and ages are represented. The guano lies in black heaps on the floor, the odour is sickening. There are two exits, one above a great rock that bars the cave's mouth, chosen of the winged tenants in their daily flight to the sea ; the other below this rock, and as I stand in its shadow a moment before departing, there is a wonderful view from it, of the still face of the river, of shadowy hills beyond, and a flaming

THE CAVE'S INTERIOR

sunlit sky. I step from the cave into my boat, and slip down the river to the Kogun cave.

A narrow water of the Salwin curves below it, encircling an island rich with river-grasses, with fields of hemp, and rows of egg-plums. The bow-like vista of water ends in monasteries and trees at the foot of the hill in which the cave lies hidden. I land and make my way through fields of purple beans and ground creepers, past little huts under the drooping boughs of the wild plum, into the village. At its far end, the " street " tails off into a narrow avenue, which runs through the rice-fields up to the entrance of the cave. The cliffs rise up abruptly from the last furrow, as they once did from the sea. At one point they bend outwards in a concave curve, and here, sheltered from

PHA-GAT

rain and wind, the strange ornamentation of the Kogun cave begins. Masses of rock, running parallel to the cliff's face, make the outer wall of the first chamber; not strictly a cave, but a singular and striking spectacle. Ten thousand images of the Buddha lie within the first sweep of the eye, from yellow-robed figures which line the footpath, to terra-cotta plaques fixed high on the jutting face of the cliff; from golden giants, the height of Goliath, to miniature figures fit for a penwiper. A great stalagmite, rising up from the floor to near the brow of the overhanging cliff, is completely covered with small images of the Buddha enthroned, and its summit is crowned by a small pagoda.

Imposing as is this spectacle, it shrinks to insignificance when compared with the scene which opens before one on entering the cavern itself. In the words of a bygone traveller: " It is of vast size, chiefly in one apartment, which needs no human art to render it sublime. The eye is confused, and the heart appalled. . . . Everywhere, on the floor, overhead, on the jutting points, and on the stalactite festoons of the roof, are crowded together images of Gautama—the offerings of successive ages. Some are perfectly gilded ; others encrusted with calcareous matter ; some fallen, yet sound ; others mouldered ; others just erected. Some of these are of stupendous size ; some not larger than one's finger ; and some of all the intermediate sizes—marble, stone, wood, brick, and clay. Some, even of marble, are so timeworn, though sheltered from change of temperature, that the face and fingers are obliterated. Here and there are models of temples, *kyoungs*, etc., some not larger than half a bushel, and some ten or fifteen feet square, absolutely filled with small idols, heaped promiscuously one on the other. As we followed the path, which wound among the groups of figures and models, every new aspect of the cave presented new multitudes of images. A ship of five hundred tons could not carry away the half of them."

BUFFALOES

Here, in fact, are the accumulations of ages ; and the interest of this strange spectacle, to the student of Buddhism, lies in the key it offers to the history of the religion in Burma, of its origins, and of the way by which it entered the country.

The long day of my visit to the caves nears its close and in the quiet shelter of evening I make my way back to Pha-an. Yet, one more sensation remains to complete the *bizarre* suggestions of the day. For as I near the gateways of Pha-gat, I am startled by the sound of a great flight of birds, a sound as of grey geese on the wing, but of such volume as can come only from a great host. These are the bats of the Pha-gat cave. For more than twenty minutes they sweep out, in a long swift line that grows tortuous as it recedes ; and, far as I can see into the ruddy twilight the line extends. Swiftly as each creature in it is flying, it looks in the distance like a smoke spiral waiting for a wind to blow it away. They go every evening, say my boatmen, to drink the salt water of the sea ; and they cross in their flight the crests of the Zingyaik hills.

We move slowly along the dead water, a half-moon overhead White mists gather on the shadowy face of the river, the air grows chill.

CHAPTER XXXIV

TO SHWEGUN

FROM a faint shark streak, glinting white on the river's horizon, to a puffing monster of fire and iron; from faint paddle-throbs like the humming of distant bees on a summer's day, to a loud roar and shriek; the steamer comes to take all the travelling world of Pha-an on its way. It is in great solitudes that the poetry of swift motion makes its most eloquent appeal. Englishman, Shan, Panthay, Indian, Taungthu, and Karen—all who are waiting here—embark; and we are borne away on this new throbbing carpet of Solomon, with a sensation that delights us all. Past the shadow of Pha-boo, we enter the left channel of the river skirting an island in our

THE CALM OF THE SALWIN

course, and Pha-nwé is lost to sight behind us. The route we are following is in a sense historic, since the names of all these peaks and precipices are associated with the past tribulation of the Karen race. The story of their own struggles is told under the guise of a legend of the frog (*pha*).

The place of Pha-nwé is taken as we advance, by new masses of rock on our left, each duplicated in the satin calm of the river, until we come to a great cliff and are face to face with a majestic spectacle; for the sheer face of it rises from the river to stupendous heights, and boats on the water look like little flies under its shadow. Its magnetism is such, that one looks at all human objects in its neighbourhood in a new perspective. Three hours yet remain to sunset, and we are seventeen degrees from the equator, yet the eastern face of the cliff, and all the gardens at its feet, are already deprived of light.

In a little while this splendid passage is also of the past ; the ship takes her relentless course, and the great mass of cliff and mountain grows smaller and ever smaller in our wake. Other and mightier hills rise up in its place, changing in form with every moment of our advance as Gibraltar does before the ocean traveller ; and in the blinding sunlight all detail of delicate tracery is lost in the one supreme beauty of form.

After this we take a quiet way with something of a sense of physical rest, with somewhat of desire to prepare for the next great spectacle, until we come as evening falls, to the last great passage between Pha-an and Shwegun. Dark blue hills curve up to right and left on the western shore like the claws of a crab, holding between them a mountain of the palest blue, that towers to a high pyramid. Every detail of this mountain picture is reproduced with fidelity in the motionless calm of the river. Timber-craft lie under the near banks, and piles of rescued logs, and the huts of the timber-salvors. As we come nearer to Shwegun, the river faces the east again, and in the distance, fresh and more alarming peaks and battlements tower up against a misty sky.

And now as I write this, it is midnight, and the white moonlight is flooding a voiceless world. The swooning palms are still ; the river appears to have attained immortal calm. From the dense jungle behind the house of Shwegun, no sound proceeds. It is as though I had strayed upon the threshold of a physical Nirvana.

CHAPTER XXXV

SHWEGUN

A GLIMPSE OF VILLAGE LIFE

SHWEGUN is the end of civilisation on the Salwin. From here the steamers turn back to Moulmein, and he who would travel farther must embark in the slow-moving boats of the country, and face the primitive life. It is a place in which to wait a day, before taking the final plunge.

There is a house here for the traveller, built by the river bank, and the village street which is also the highway, runs past it. Life therefore is ever afoot under the windows of the house.

Here is the Myo-ôk of Hlaingbwé, on his way back from the burning of a monk at U-daung. The Myo-ôk is the greatest man in Shwegun. He is an officer of the empire, a link in that chain of office which begins with the village headman and ends in the august person of the Viceroy. And here in all the wide Hlaingbwé tract he is the personal embodiment of British rule. No Viceroy has ever come to Hlaingbwé ; no Governor ; no Chief Justice ; no Commander-in-Chief. The District Magistrate, the Ayé-Baing, who is greater than the Myo-ôk, seldom, if ever comes. All these are white men. The Myo-ôk is of the soil, and upon him here the burden of empire falls. It is he who comes into nearest touch with the people. There was a Burman who rose to high office elsewhere ; he

THE SALWIN

went to London and was presented to the King and Queen. When he returned to Burma his old friends said to him " You are a great man now, why do you not get them to make you a Myo-ôk ? " There are men who are born and live and die in Hlaingbwé, who know no other representative of British rule. As to the man, you see that he has self-respect, dignity, not to say *hauteur ;* his silken skirt is a thing of texture and beauty ; his muslin coat is fine and immaculately white. An attendant follows him, holding a long umbrella over his head ; another carries his silver betel-box. An ironical spectacle, if you will ; for the man is unconscious of the glory for which he stands ; he is in his own country, and yet in a measure an alien ; a judge, but of doubtful honour ; a pro-consul in his way, but a son of the jungle in his innermost heart.

PACING THROUGH THE FOREST

After him, slowly pacing through the forest, comes a man of both worlds, a *pothoodaw*. His nondescript garments are neither lay nor clerical; from their colour one might fancy them to be the cast-off garments of a monk, worn with usage, and soiled by the wayside dust. The pole he carries over his shoulders, with a basket slung at each end, is unmistakably lay; the yellow parasol, with the sunlight pouring through it on his shaven head, is of clerical suggestion. His carriage is grave and reverend; his manner is that of a saint; and his two companions address him in words suitable to these pretensions. He is in reality a simple-hearted and devout old man, upon whom the conviction of holiness has grown; he spends his life in pious works, and has put the world behind him; but he is not a monk. His companions are a pair of old and wrinkled Shan, with faces graven like the face of a sailor —originals both. One of them carries an English pipe, which he smokes with stoic calm, his fingers closing over the bowl with the solicitous grip of the smoker. Experience of many things is written large upon the faces of this couple; shrewd humour, the indefinable air of worldly wisdom; and over all there is a layer of recent respectability, in keeping with their new character as the companions of a saintly man.

Soon after they pass there comes, with a great creaking and droning of wheels through the chambered forest, a long line of carts, bearing back from a scene of piety the members of the Sacred Order. They recline, like true priests, on the soft hay spread for them within; they look about them with the innocent curiosity of their race and character. Here and there amongst them is one with the gentle face of an ascetic, of a philosopher trained in the sadness of life and deeply convinced of its illusion. One such lies back, an old man weary with the wayfaring, his life's history easy to read upon his saintly face.

Across the road, Burmese policemen, shorn of all the picturesqueness of their race, amble about in khaki garments, and forage caps set with an imitation of jauntiness on their shaven heads. The British effort to convert a nation of artistic philosophers into disciplined policemen is a comedy of fine flavour. In the village the people crowd at their doors and under the swaying palms, to see the procession go by; the clerkly postmaster beside his letter-box, scarlet with the imperial cypher blazoned upon it; the Chinaman before his liquor shop; the girl fresh from her silk-loom; the old man, too old now to totter more than a few feet from his door.

Past the house in the opposite direction, there runs a pathway to the river's edge. Down this way, as the afternoon wanes, the people pass to bathe. Madame comes along in a dark green skirt and breast cloth; only a single garment wrapped about her, and tucked in with a simple twist over her bosom. Her feet and ankles and her shoulders are free

From a painting by J. Raeburn Middleton

EVENING PRAYER

to the air ; and as she comes swaying along, with the peculiar gait of the Burmese woman, half waddle, half swagger, and wholly different from the statuesque poise of the nearer East, she looks comely and attractive enough. Holding one hand and tripping beside her, two steps to her one, is her little daughter, a pretty laughing child with the voice of a happy tom-tit. The sun, as they reach the pebbled edge of the river, is nearing the horizon, and the whole width of water is turning to red-gold, freighted with the shadows of distant trees. The child slips her one small garment swiftly to her feet, and tumbles into the water. Her

EVENTIDE

mother and her grown-up sisters are obliged to proceed with more discretion; but a woman is old indeed who does not presently behave like a child in the water. Here, in her native element, the most affected belle—though affectation is far from these people—speedily forgets herself. She splashes about and flops suddenly into the water, which fills the only garment like a balloon ; and by dint of this she contrives to swim a yard or two. The air exhausted, and its wearer being nearly out of her depth, she rises again to her feet with laughter, shakes the fresh water from her face and renews the joy. Then she reaches out an arm for her spare garment, lets it fall over her dark Japanese head and soft shoulders, rises, and in a trice is into it and out of the old one ; all *coram populo*, but achieved with infinite grace and discretion. After which, there is some washing to be done, and then mother and daughter return home ; contented and happy.

All the women of the village are at this hour by the river's edge ; some with babies barely able to walk, but receiving early initiation into the joys of the beautiful river that flows by their homes. There is a curious contrast to be found between the face of the unhappy urchin enduring the gaunt ministrations of a nurse, familiar to every purchaser of a certain English soap, and that of a little Burmese child, taking its first lessons by the river's side. It is in the river, where he plays and splashes for hours every day of his youth, that the Burman learns his gaiety of heart, and develops the fine muscles of his race.

CHAPTER XXXVI

PRIMITIVE TRAVEL

THE grey dawn calls us, sleepers on the pebbled shore; and we wake one by one, each after his own habit. We have been sleeping under the stars for the sake of the cool air and an early start. A pot of rice is put on the fire; the polers get ready for the long day's work. The sun is not yet risen as we get under weigh, the boat glides forward under the banks. It is a grey day heavy with clouds, and the sun when he comes, sends down broad ribs of light in a manner that makes the firmament overhead seem like a richly striped dome.

Very quickly the fascination of primitive travel steals over one's spirit, and all that spoke at the outset of discomfort is forgotten. The broad river lies about us and laps our bows ; familiar friend and stately companion. Its wide expanse reaches away to the horizon, its cool green stream runs laughing through the fingers of one who leans over the boat's edge. The water is as clear and limpid as that of a mountain rivulet, and as the boat glides on over its shallows, the rocks and pebbles of its bed lie discovered to the eye. Splendid giants of the forest marshal both its banks ; creepers, purple and azure, hang in masses from the boughs. Plantain-groves and sloping fields of beans and broad tobacco tell of man, the newcomer, his small and scattered beginnings. Wild and majestic as is the river here, after a course of more than a thousand miles from its infancy in unknown lands, its near banks along which we steer, are graced with many of the minor charms of an English river—grasses and ferns, and drooping willows and cool shady places under trees.

DEFILES OF THE SALWIN

The poling keeps us well in touch with these, and the rough bark of the willow-trees is scarred and pitted with the prints of the passing pole-heads. Year by year, the boats go up in a long procession and each boat as it passes leaves its trace.

The art of the poler is itself a thing of fascination. The men, of whom there are two, run down the centre of the boat along a single plank, and the poles of fifteen feet with pointed iron heads, glide through the fingers with a " slick " grace, till they ring on a rock under the water. Then they bend and quiver like reeds in the wind as the

PRIMITIVE TRAVEL

polers bear upon them and the boat leaps forward. At times they run out to the last rung and find no bottom; the boat swings nearer to the bank, and they shoot out to a tree-trunk, find a lodgment there, and the polers strain at their butts. As the boat moves, the poles fall with a splash into the water, and so on.

The process fills many an hour of travel with its fascination. For there is judgment in the selection of each vantage-point, dexterity in the swift slipping of the pole, fine balancing, precision ; and as the day grows proof of the arduous training which enables these slight men—they are Muslim Chittagonians—to labour up the river for twelve hours of each day.

The chief feature of the river between Shwegun and Kawkarit is the big island of Kawlon. Up the western arm, above Shwegun, there is a vista of blue water and rich grasses that ends in a peak three thousand feet in height. As we turn up the eastern branch this is lost to sight, and we steer a peaceful way under overhanging willows and the shelter of forest-clad banks. Again and again the river is bisected by islands in its course, and the way we follow narrows, gaining in homely beauty. Anon it widens out, and so till we enter once more the full river. At Kamamau, white rocks rise up in the river's bed and along its banks, narrowing and dividing its course; the murmur of rushing water fills our ears; where the river is narrowest, cables of twisted cane are strung across it to catch the derelict timber of distant forests; the huts of the salvors lie amphibious under the banks, and the logs gather in thousands in the bays and curves of the river. Up-stream a wooded island is mirrored in its calm; blue mountains rise up beyond, and in the east, gigantic cliffs and precipices of shadowy limestone. As the sun nears the horizon, we turn into the mouth of the Yunzalin and anchor for the night under the hamlet of Kawkarit.

THE POLER

And here it may be noted that the personality of the Salwin is distinct from that of the Irrawaddy and the Chindwin. Its distinguishing features are its fantastic and tremendous limestone hills; its rapids and rocky islands so near the sea; its mystic and half-tragic character; its undertone of homely beauty. No one knows it from source to sea.

Although at Kawkarit it is only some seventy miles from the sea, although for a hundred years it has been under the influence of British civilisation, it retains even here its character of a remote and savage river, flowing through half-known lands. Its people are mainly Karen, shy, sullen and difficult of access. The stillness of its forests is unbroken by the hum of the telegraph wire ; no engine has ever throbbed above Shwegun. There is only a weekly post, which achieves with difficulty twenty miles a day, and it takes longer to cover the distance from Shwegun to Pha-pun, the headquarters of the district, than it does to travel from Edinburgh to Moscow. Yet in this isolation there resides its particular charm ; for it takes the traveller into great solitudes, among almost silent highways, into a land of primitive people ; and the means of travel are such as men were used to when the world was young.

CHAPTER XXXVII

THE LAST STAGE

EARLY dawn again finds us moving on the face of the waters. Grey mists brood over them, and wisps of cloud lie in the valleys and athwart the hills. The faint sunlight of the morning adds to the ghostly character of the scene. Tremendous precipices tower up against the sky. A great stillness broods over all. The unreality of things lies insistent on one's spirit.

The channel of the main river is broken by great masses of white rock, half-hidden under willows. The current runs swiftly under the east bank, which is deeply and sumptuously wooded. Looking down from an eminence on to the river I obtain a full impression of its savage and desolate character. But all along the banks, and under the lee of the white rocks there are places of miniature beauty ; mirror-like pools and sheltered inlets, where the clear water glints green.

At Kamaulé there is a village, and the river is crossed by successive cables of twisted cane to hold the derelict logs as they come floating down. Each cable is the property of a separate owner, who takes his own timber and lets the rest go on. The cables are fastened to the high rocks on either bank, and they stretch across the river, like Himalayan rope bridges, except that they lie for the most part *on* the water. The trunks of gigantic trees fastened to them increase the weight of their resistance, and they make a boom across the river which looks as if it meant to bar all progress. But there are intervals of bare cane, and it is like working through a Chinese puzzle or a barrage of mines, to find one's way through them all. As the boat slips over the cane yields under the water and rubs along the keel with the sound of stage thunder. A ferry canoe plies across the river, and at the far end, beyond the last

A dug-out. A raft house. The boom. My boat. A travelling monk.

AT KAMAULÉ

cable, the house-raft of the Forest Ranger lies at anchor. Here for many months of the year this Englishman lives in solitude. The raft lies in a sheltered cove, protected by an array of rocky pinnacles against the driving flood. The jungle, all but impenetrable, rises behind him, and every movement of the river conveys its message to his floating home. It looks like a neat little Japanese house, with its thatched eaves and its hanging orchids, and it is built on mammoth logs of teak that bear the marks of a dozen owners. Seventy feet of limpid water lie below, and one can look down into it when one is there between the great logs of the floor, and into the sunlight quivering in its depths. The view as I turn

THE MYSTIC SALWIN

my face away to the south is of white scarred rocks, motionless timber, and water that seems asleep. Up-stream there are near mountains, lofty and precipitous, under whose pedestals the river curves in ample spaces, in which the whole world of sky and mountain is mirrored.

A few miles more and our limit is reached. At Yinbaung the mountains close in upon every hand; shadowy and fantastic masses deploy behind each other; the river is in the grip of its iron keepers. Yet its power is unabated, and traces of its scorn and fury are legible in the shattered rocks that have come into contact with it. Scarcely a vestige of their own individuality survives; in everything they betray their subjection to its caprice. Worn into fantastic forms, hollowed out into caverns, sliced like sawn timber, pitted like the target of a battery of guns, cut into pinnacles like ant-hills, they are graven with the image of water in its rise and fall and infinite succession of waves.

The face of the river itself is at this season calm and untroubled. One might take it, at a glance, for some land-locked water without exit or entrance. But a nearer look reveals a world of subdued life and passion, of which symptoms may be traced on its calm. Some of these are faint dimples, delicate as on a woman's face; others are as rich in their involute beauty as the rose windows of a cathedral; others, again, like wayward strings of pearls moving under a secret influence:

THE HOME OF THE FOREST RANGER

and some are like open-mouthed trumpets whirling round at incredible speed. They are very wonderful to look at, and they tell the whole tale, if one could read it, of the river's life. Each whirl and dimple has its immediate cause, in some hollow worn with years of strife, some sharp dagger of rock, some crag or boulder far out of sight. For the river here is of great depth and velocity; and but for its depth, it would be hard to believe as one stands and looks down upon it from the rocky heights, that it has come a journey of fifteen hundred miles or more. Its first discoverer as he found his way up its clear green waters, past rocky islands and narrowing ways, into the heart of the grim defiles and turbulent mountains that encompass it here, might well have believed that he had come to within a measurable distance of its source.

We turn back in the late evening, with slow and measured oars, and I sit, where it is my custom, alone at the boat's prow, the clear impenetrable water a yard below. It is a narrow perilous seat impending over great deeps and implacable whirlpools, and there is nothing ahead of it but the wonderful landscape of blue mountains and quiet waters ; for all the rest of my world in the boat is behind me and out of sight. The moon rises, a yellow orb patterned with her dead lands and imaginary seas against the lavender of the sky. Her light makes a silver pathway down the long river ; shadows of cliffs and crags lie motionless upon the surface of the river ; and as we sweep down by grace of the current, the boatmen rest on their oars, and all is still save the faint cheeping of crickets from the woods. One draws nearer, by some secret affinity, at this late hour, to the tremulous heart of Nature.

The lights of Kamaulé and the rafts by the river twinkle out as we draw near, and in a little while the day's toil is over, and we are at rest for the night.

The solitary white occupant of the house-raft is glad of company, and dinner over, we sit out on the little bamboo shelves under the sloping eaves of the house, talking in low tones ; while the moonlight streams over the still face of the river, the timber cables, the white rocks mirrored in it, and the mighty jungle about us. As we move to turn in for what remains of the night, the little house sways over the great logs that support it, upheld by seventy feet of living water. And when in the night I wake, to sleep again, I hear the murmur of the river flowing by.

These raft-houses are renewed each year, and the timber on which they are built is sent on its way at the beginning of the flood season. The cables across the river are twisted and strung at the beginning of the cold weather, when the rush of water is abated ; and they are swept away by the first floods in the rains when the felled logs that have lain insensate all the winter, come roaring down the river. Last season a great flood came, and for two days they swept down in furious procession, jamming, creaking, and dashing to pieces against the cliffs ; filling the small canoes with fear ; and forbidding any man to cross from shore to shore.

As the floods recede many a derelict log is left high and dry on the worn summit of some cliff or island, or in the fork of a tree ; and there it remains for years—till some new flood big enough to answer its call, heeds it lying there, and sweeps it on to its destiny. Thus a man may die and his heirs inherit his wealth, and some of it may still remain unrealised, into the days of his son's sons, or even for ever.

But this is of the Romance of the Timber-Cutter. There is no lonelier life for a white man than that of the forest assistant, whose duty it is to see that the timber is cut in accordance with the State

ABOVE YIN BAUNG

regulations, and sent upon its way to the seaport towns. The pictures given in the first chapter of this book illustrate better than many words the history of a log from the time it is cut to the time it reaches its destination. They were taken by an officer of the Bombay-Burma Company—that famous company to which the fall of the kings of Burma is attributed.

Book IX

THE YUNZALIN

CHAPTER XXXVIII

THE YUNZALIN

At Kawkarit the character of my journey suddenly changes. From a great and deep river, I pass into a shallow-hearted forest stream; the frowning crags and mystic battlements of the Salwin have no fellowship with the narrower Yunzalin; and the sense of space gradually passes away. A new world of travel opens before me, for here I have the jungle very near me, resonant with the music of many birds; swift waters racing over stony rapids; and a sultry air. The polesmen run up and down, and are hard put to it at places where the rapids tax their utmost skill.

At one of these as we pass on, a bamboo raft is wrecked and jammed, fragments of it floating aimlessly away, while its occupants labour to release what survives from the clutches of the rocks. Teak logs float past us, and where the press of timber obstructs the passage of the Yunzalin, elephants toil to relieve its congestion. Again and again I come upon the felled timber lying high and dry, wedged in among the rocks, or shattered into touchwood.

As the shadows lengthen, a cool air blows upon the river, the forest is pierced by shafts of light, peacocks sun their plumage on the sands, wildfowl come out to feed, and monkeys run along the shores. Still later crickets cheep, and the shrill call of the peacock is supplanted by the raucous barking of deer. The stars shine out, first one by one and then in a great company; musk odours fill the air.

There are no hamlets now in sight, we have come into the heart of the jungle. Its fascination is immense, but incommunicable. There is that cry of the peacock! If you have heard it only in an English park, how shall you judge of its wild melancholy note in the still truculent jungle? How it wails through the forest spaces! The very cry and embodiment of solitude.

An hour before dawn, my eyes open in obedience to some primitive instinct, and I find it good to lie abed and watch the jungle. Bamboos rise up in graceful forms, their stems making a pattern against the dense foliage. They are eloquent to me at this fanciful hour, of the realism of the Japanese artist. Overhead, above the crowding masses, the new growth shoots out for light and air. A wind comes by, filling the jungle with life; from a tall tree on the edge of the clearing, dying leaves loose their hold of life, and flutter noiselessly to earth. Ripe fruit falls with a soft thud on the mould. There is a strange stillness in this world that is teeming with life.

Faint washes of colour sweep at last over the face of the sky; slowly the dawn comes, and the jungle wakes. The wail of the peacock echoes

TIMBER AGROUND IN THE YUNZALIN

through its solitudes, the wild cock crows, and monkeys begin to chatter in the dusk trees. The sleeping polers awake and rout the live embers from the night's ashes. There is a simmering of rice in the pot. Down in a long trough of the forest lies the Yunzalin asleep—a creature of mystery, beautiful, inscrutable; so strong is this feeling that I wonder if we really understand at ordinary times the life about us. I leave the rest-house in its clearing in the jungle—a curious exotic. There is furniture within it, of the kind necessary to Western life. The house lies open and unprotected. I enter it in the still darkness and leave it in the grey dawn. There is no caretaker; no price to pay. What is it? has it a soul of its own?

MORNING ON THE YUNZALIN

Soon we are all on board and the long day's poling begins. For an hour or more there is the engrossing pageant of the morning ; then the river claims attention, for it is broken up and thwarted by sandy willow-hidden islands, round which the waters race with great velocity. The polers are put to their utmost exertion. For many consecutive moments, the boat remains motionless, in equilibrium between human muscle and the river's purpose. The polers can no longer work in couples for fear of losing, in the brief interval between their pole thrusts, the hard-won ground. Each man takes up the tale where the other leaves it, crying out : " *Bismilla*, in the name of God." Thus is the passage won and we climb into slacker water.

" Lal-la-lal-la-lal-la, there-is-but-one-God-and-Mahomet-is-the-prophet-of-God, lal-la-lal-la-lah."

Such at each rapid is this strange Arabian prelude.

The waters swish and murmur about us ; the drooping willows lave their tresses in the stream ; under its sunlit surface pebbles glisten like marble of many colours. Purple hornbills wing their resonant flight from tree-summit to tree-summit, across the river's width ; kingfishers with sapphire and turquoise wings, dart over the shallows ; king-crows sail overhead, and grey egrets like some slippered pantaloon, cross the boat's track.

The peacocks love best at this hour, and at evening, the sandy spaces where willows silver in the wind, and the near jungle provides a rapid and sure retreat. When stalked or convinced of pursuit, they emit a quick note of warning to all the denizens of the jungle. Monkeys look up from their clutched fruit ; the lusty crowing of cocks dwindles to a short responsive cluck ; tigers pause in their lordly progress to wonder, with such curiosity as befits a sovereign, what is astir.

There is a flash of something at play in the water, as I look, transformed into an otter making swiftly for the shelter of the bank. He is shot as he leaps across an open bit of sand, squeals and tumbles over, rises, and makes for the willows only to die at the river's lip. From the sunlit surface of the water, curious heads emerge, to look swiftly about them, and then to disappear, only to come up again for the sake of knowing what is afoot.

Follows the weary blazing noon, from which all seek shelter but the polers toiling inch by inch up the river. Here and there a canoe darts past us, the single poler bending to his work with classic grace ; girls with fair smooth limbs, and great piles upon their backs regard us open-eyed with wonder ; a field of tobacco on the sandy shore confirms the human note. And so once more, the sunset and the dark.

All through the night it is cold, and towards dawn so cold that sleep

EVENING ON THE YUNZALIN

becomes impossible. We go down shivering to the boat at six o'clock, just as the sun is coming up over the tree-tops, a pale orb hung suspended in the mist. The river is shrouded in dense fog, and the spectacle, as his faint rays shoot out in widening ribbons through its motionless curtains, is ghostly and unreal. But an hour later all trace of this is gone, sunbeams laugh on the water and in the glades and aisles of the forest there is light.

Four boats with sweeping oars come swiftly upon us ; in the last of them a white man, dignity upon his face and in the poise of his body. We measure at a glance ; a second, and it may be that we shall pass each other for ever. We raise our hats and pass on, and somewhere in the jungle there is lost the echo of two belated " Good mornings." But brisk dialogues have been exchanged between the crews, and a letter that has been waiting for some such chance has been sent on the first stage of its long journey home.

As day wears on, incident after incident contributes to the character of the world through which we are travelling Monkeys swim in long files across the river ; a snake writhes up the steep bank, only to be caught in the talons of a hawk ; a small red deer, picking her way leisurely amongst the dead trees of the foreshore, darts instantly to cover on seeing us approach.

After hard straining over rapids, we enter long passages of calm river, winding through forest avenues of the most stately character. Sheer walls of forest, two hundred feet in height, shut us in. Creepers hang over the water from lofty boughs ; masses of silver leaves adorn the trees like flowers ; palms that would grace the garden of a palace grow here in waste profusion. What a picture it is at once of crowded life and individual beauty !

Men glide down on bamboo rafts, strung lightly together for the day's journey ; pole in hand, muscles that quiver in the sun, a bag of meal at their feet. In a flash one's mind is carried back three thousand years by the Hellenic grace, the simplicity of it all. Nothing that we gain from ships and engines can ever take its place.

The white moon-like bloom of the wild gourd ; the secret gleam of water upon tree-trunks ; the flight of starlings across blue bays and estuaries of sky ; the rustle of wildfowl in the jungle ; the insistent *cule-cule* of water, where passing swiftly over a hidden stone, it breaks against itself in music ; in the clear dawn, peaks that show afar-off beyond the river hills, cutting the blue heaven like Alps ; wild-eyed buffaloes only a little less savage than the true denizens of the jungle ; white egrets that make a living on their backs as allies ; red and olive tints on the waters where sunlit shallows join with shady deeps ; fallen giants of the forest, stark wrecks in the pitiless noon, and blocking half

A PINEAPPLE ORCHARD AT MINTABYI

the river where they lie ; here and there, at long intervals, frail human beginnings ; girdled trees withering under the hand of man ; a hut ; a pathway marked with footprints in the jungle ; the spoor of a Karen elephant ; small fields of tobacco on the river's edge—of such is the day's journey.

The river becomes more arduous as we advance, and at places it is sheer ascent. Rapids grow more frequent, and at some of the swiftest it needs all our united efforts to surmount them. Gun-bearer and cook, valet and clerk, plunge breast high into the river with a rope, and the polers find in me a mate.

RIVER TRAVEL ON THE SALWIN

After these strenuous passages come long intervals of deep calm water. Blue hills appear in the river vistas, and patches of *taung-gya* cultivation—the reckless surface tillage of the wild man—lie bare in the sun upon their slopes.

At Mintabyi there is a Shan village immersed in trade. In the shops by the wayside, there are French sardines in oil, Dutch milk in tins, aërated lemonade, dried fish and groceries, Karen fabrics, red and white striped cloths and embroidered coats. The houses have gardens of pineapples and palms. As I enter the village from the river, a dove-catcher goes forth with a decoy-bird and nooses on a string.

PHA-PUN: THE WILD COTTON TREE IN BLOOM

THE BIVOUAC

Darkness overtakes us far from any habitation ; we anchor for the night under a nameless shore. A sand-bank that is clean and soft offers us its hospitality. Soon there is a great fire ablaze, a hut in construction. Food partaken of, we sit round the fire and smoke, wrapped in blankets, for the night is cold. The sky overhead is a cloudless violet, lit with the great northern stars that still, happily, bear me company. An hour later the moon comes up over the tree-tops and over the hills that part the Salwin from the Yunzalin. The shadowy jungle grows visible, one tree from another ; the light falls in rippling bars across the river. From the forest across the water there peals the shrill sex-call of a tigress seeking her mate.

For a little while longer we smoke on under the spell of the night and the bivouac. Then, one by one, each turns in under shelter ; voices die down ; the gurgle of *huquahs* ceases ; the embers of the untended fire pale amidst the ashes. The moon has not climbed three spears' lengths of her way across the heavens, when one and all of us lie in the deep sleep that comes after a long day of toil.

As we near Pha-pun, the valley of the river widens and yields more room for cultivation. Wild cotton trees reappear in great luxuriance, their rose-scarlet tracery of bloom cut into the blue sky, their branches peopled with monkeys and starlings ; and where they rise from the river's edge, whole navies of red blossom sweep along the surface of its waters. Towards sunset the colours become exquisitely soft and tender, and the wild primeval character of the jungle is no longer manifest.

PHA-PUN

Pha-pun is a little island of shadowy civilisation, amidst the wilds of the Salwin and the Yunzalin. It is the capital of the district, and the only settlement within its limits that can under any pretence be described as a town. Its claim to notice lies in this, that it stands here an embodied symbol of the British power.

At Pha-pun there resides the administrator of the vast territory known as the Salwin Hill Tracts. Here there is a court-house for the dispensation of justice—a building that is half jail, half fortress, built within a stockade on the hill—a hospital for the sick, and house accommodation for a forest officer, an engineer, a doctor, and a policeman. The settlement can lay claim besides to a few short roads, lined with avenues of planted trees, sure sign that it has been in British hands some years ; a few shops kept mainly by Chittagonians, in which Western luxuries are sold at prices that would sound extravagant to any one who had not been poled up the long journey from Moulmein ;

a wooden mosque for the use of the pious Chittagonian ; and a public ground that resounds of mornings to the tread of Shan and Karen yokels learning their drill and the English voice of command of the Afridi instructor, and of evenings to the laughter of the same people at play—minus the instructor—and the thud of an English football. The discipline at both ends is improving, and if the baggy-trousered recruit looks questionable as a soldier, let it be said that he looks, when stripped, the *beau ideal* of an athlete made for sport.

A few yards away from the official settlement stands the mission-house of the American mission to the Karen. The missionary has been absent for a year and the affairs of the little community are managed by its elders. They hold a service on Sundays, and the friendly airs of their hymns, coming across the little strip of jungle that divides them from the white community, make a pleasant interlude in the stillness

CHITTAGONIAN BOATMEN

of the day. The congregation is a small one, and the hill tracts of the Salwin appear to have been but partially absorbed into the missionary fold. The chief elder is a young man named Moung Lon Le, with a refined and clerkly face, and English which he talks with an American drawl. He seems to feel acutely the general backwardness of his race.

Apart from these exotic advantages, Pha-pun—the primitive site as the Creator made it—is a place of great natural beauty. Behind it there rise, in fold behind fold, a mass of exquisite hills tapestried with woods, and their colouring, where they reach away in faint waves to the north, is at this season, of such soft and delicate tones as go to the making of an English landscape after rain on a summer day. Facing these in the west there is another line of hills, beginners of the Paung-Laung range; and between them lies all there is of the valley of the Yunzalin.

The little river is spanned at the landing-place by a temporary bridge of bamboos, raised a few inches above its surface, and the waters pour clear and limpid under it. There are rapids just below, which for the last time strain the muscles of the polers ascending to Pha-pun, and all through the still hours of the night I can hear their murmur as they break over the stones. Sleeping, I dream of the Jarlot and the Queffleut where they mingle at Morlaix.

Above the bridge, there is a long stretch of silent water winding in easy curves, and almost flush with the low grassy banks. The mystic beauty of the Lower Salwin, the stately pomp of the Irrawaddy, the sad grey wastes of some Indian river toiling through spaces it cannot fill—there is no hint of these on the banks of the Yunzalin as I look upon it to-day at Pha-pun. There is little happily to detract from its homely English beauty. But the human note is Eastern. Women bare to the shoulder come to the river's edge to bathe and fill their waterpots ; small lads splash about on rafts of green bamboo ; groups of wayfaring Shan ford it at the shallows ; and elephant-men scrub their restless beasts, lying prone and immersed to the skull in the water. By the bridge a fleet of Chittagonian boats lies at anchor—the only link that binds Pha-pun with the outer world.

Book X

OVER THE PAUNG-LAUNG HILLS

CHAPTER XXXIX

OVER THE PAUNG-LAUNG HILLS

FROM Pha-pun, the traveller who would re-enter Burma without making the long return to Moulmein, can do so only by crossing the Paung-Laung hills, which are the watershed between the Sittang and the Yunzalin. But the road is rough and wild, the jungle dense, the people primitive. Shelter for the night is often unobtainable, food is scarce when it is to be had at all, and transport is not easily procured. Yet, until he makes such a journey as this, one who would taste the full flavour of Far Eastern life is likely to go away unappeased.

Having, through the good offices of the district magistrate, secured the services of two elephants with Karen drivers, to carry my baggage, it remained only to gather some idea of the route and the distances to be traversed. Many persons were called into consultation, and all claimed to have some knowledge of the facts, either from personal travel or from the talk of the country-side ; but no two of them could be prevailed upon to agree. However, the mission Elder sent word to the Karen villages in the hills ; and the police inspector furnished me with two constables, one of whom had once before made the journey. The other was a typical " fat boy," with a laughing face and a radical love of ease, which came to be sorely tried during our progress over the hills. For three days I had been detained at Pha-pun by fever, the penalty of the Yunzalin ; but on February 14th I was ready to start.

At this, if at any time of the year, I was entitled to hope for fine weather ; but heavy rain overtook me soon after I had topped the first line of hills, within six miles of Pha-pun. There is nothing more melancholy than tramping through a sodden jungle, with fever in one's bones, and no definite prospect of shelter for the night ; and it seemed to me, as I toiled painfully behind my party, that I had embarked upon a very foolish enterprise. Happily, as the day wore on, I found shelter in a wayside hut, and settled in it for the night.

I woke the following morning feeling ill and dull, as one does who wakes after a late night and broken sleep in a closed room ; but there had been no late night here, and the room was as clean and airy as any of nature's own sleeping-places. It was the fever that was still in my system, at war with the quinine I had taken during the past week, and morning and evening, during this journey I had to continue the struggle till the fever was finally vanquished.

The first sound that fell upon my ears as I lay abed came from a Shan caravan on its way from the farther Salwin. The pack-bullocks passed one by one in a long procession under my door, and it seemed to me as I dozed that the air was laden with the music of an endless host of bells. I spent all the forenoon in drying my things, and making preparations for rain during future marches, and I could not but admire the skill with which the Karens plied their heavy *dahs* on the bamboos, from great trunks which they felled with ease, to strips for thongs which they peeled off as thin as brown paper. There was neither pause nor hesitation ; every stroke of the sharp weapon, heavy enough to kill a man, reached its goal. Here were artists at work, unconscious of their own grace and skill, the product of centuries of usage. Like all perfect work it seemed so simple, till a native of India from a country where bamboos are unknown, tried his hand at cutting a few strips for the fire and failed completely.

At last the elephants were laden and started off on their journey to Na-Kaw-Khé, and I waited another hour to give them time, for Leviathan is a slow mover. Sunlight and shadow came and went, as I lay there at peace in the wayside hut. Travellers at long intervals passed by : Shan and Burman, Karen and Coringhi ; most curious of all a half-caste in a sombrero, the son of a British officer, a little man with a fluent manner, a dash of servility, more than a dash of covert pride, and the gift of tongues. From a neighbouring sawpit there came the steady " swish " of a steel saw at work.

The hut in which I had passed the night drew my closer attention. It was made entirely of bamboo, save the thatch which was of palm-leaves. There was not a nail in its composition. Its framework was of round bamboos of graduated size, and its walls and floor were of hammered bamboo. It was cheap, it was ephemeral, and it let in the sun and the cold ; but it was new and clean and in harmony with its surroundings. The tent is for the desert Arab ; a bamboo hut at every resting-place is its happy equivalent in Burma.

At two o'clock in the afternoon I set out for Na-Kaw-Khé, and the

THE KAREN MISSION AT PHA-PUN

track I followed ran along a level, through aisles of overarching bamboo. The country was similar to that I had traversed the previous day, but the sky showed blue overhead, the sun shone in the glades of the forest, and in the place of gloom there was rejoicing. At four I reached my destination, a hamlet of little bamboo houses strung along the wayside. There were signs of petty trade here, and green vegetables were exposed for sale in small packets done up in plantain-leaves, for passing travellers. At the farther end the Shan caravan of the morning was outspanned on a plain near the village monastery.

Passing on, I crossed a stream bridged by a single tree, and so came to the *sa-khan*, or travellers' "eating place." The three or four huts, neat, clean, and attractive as usual, were already occupied by parties of Shan and Burmese. My elephants had gone on, so while a messenger went to call them back I waited in the shelter of one of the huts.

It is an unfailing charm of travel in these countries that the traveller is left alone by the people he meets. The innate good-breeding of these races sweetens the atmosphere of the land they live in and one is often happier therefore amongst them in a wayside hut, than in the midst of more imposing surroundings where the strain is cheap. No one, as I sat here alone, came to pry, or to ask me questions, and no one was in a hurry to be abject or useful. My coming, though the passing of an Englishman must be of rare occurrence in these wilds, seemed to make no sensible difference to the occupants of the hut, or to my other neighbours. Each man pursued his vocation; one sang as he collected some bits of bamboo for a fire, another went gravely to and fro fetching water from the stream; a third cleaned rice for the evening meal—each had his laugh and his joke in season. Not that there was any question of ignoring the stranger, for a strip of Brussels carpet quietly found its way to where I sat, and an English folding chair, the pride of its possessor, was dusted and set up for my comfort. At a word they were willing to vacate any one of the houses which sheltered them, but they made no fuss in anticipation.

And for my part I was content to sit down quietly in their midst. One big fellow exercised a decoy-cock, another displayed a gorgeous pheasant bred by himself, a third was a crafty man at dove-noosing; and all were happily free from the squalid poverty of the nearer East.

Although these men were roughing it so to speak, in the jungle, as travellers away from home, they were possessed of flexible sleeping mats, coloured rugs, tumblers, and drinking mugs. They had time for leisurely meals and they ceased work at sunset. While waiting for the rice to boil they sipped tea from small Chinese cups, chewed betel, and smoked cheroots. Good-humour and consideration for each other prevailed among them. Each man seemed to do his share of such work

THE CARAVAN

as entailed co-operation without any pressure. They were all on the best of terms, and all the evening, though there was much hilarity and voices were raised in story-telling and laughter, there was no note of anger or quarrel. The Madrasi cook hectored the Karen within his radius and quarrelled with the Mohammedan peon. The European deemed it necessary to censure the dullness of the guide who had misled him the previous day. But bland good-humour was the atmosphere of the Shan-Burmese encampment. What a precious quality it is!

I do not suggest that these people are angelic or incapable of truculent rage; but many years of life and travel in Burma have convinced me, that in the minor self-control which sweetens human relationships, they far surpass the most of us who are here to set them an example. I shall not easily forget these pleasant hours in this little clearing in the jungle. How the slant sun sent his broad shafts of light through the shady places! How clear was the air and pure, after the previous day's tribulation of rain! How the quiet life of the place unfolded itself before me with the interest of a play!

As evening closed in, men who had been at work came back from their toil; carpenters with their tools over their shoulders, from the new bridge across a neighbouring stream; herdsmen with their droves of red cattle; labourers with their mattocks. A small world of travelling men drew up and gathered at the *sa-khan* for the night; the Shan, with his red wallet, his flapping hat, and his *dah* across his shoulders; a Burman party of traders from Kyaikto; a *pothoodaw* in semi-clerical guise, a rosary in his hand. The cooking fires were lit, the rice began to boil and simmer in the pot, and groups of men sat round the smoking food to eat it with their hands. Thereafter white cheroots, and story-telling, and ease; and so, as the night closed in, while bugles were blowing in far-away centres of life—sleep. The broad laugh, the bland voice, were stilled in slumber, and no sound prevailed save the cheeping of the crickets, the murmur of running water, the intermittent call of the night-jar, and the crash of the elephants feeding in the jungle.

* * *

Tinka-linka, tinka-linka, tink—tink—tink,
Tinka-linka, tinka-linka, tlink—tlink—tlink.

The melody of bells, now in unison, now in *échelon* as the speed of the cattle varied, for a long while filled the stillness of the dawn. There is some quality in this music, some suggestion in this early passing by of the caravan which steals with a subtle fascination over the senses. It stands in some sort for the romance of wayfaring, for the poetry of vagrant life. The bells and the red cattle, and the white-hatted Shan as they emerge from the stillness of the forest, come nearer and yet

THE HEAD OF THE CARAVAN

nearer in the grey dawn ; pass by with the added base of hoofs and are lost in the chambered stillness ; and this at that middle hour when the spirit of the listener still hovers in the borderland between the slumber of the night and the full awakening of a sun-clad morning. Only once before, and in another country, have I heard such music with its infinite appeal. But it came neither from bells nor caravans ; but from the shepherd's pipe of a lad from the Pyrenees who came away each year with his herd of goats, browsing as they wandered over France, till in the early days of spring he reached the small Breton town in which I lived. From door to door the lad piped, while the shaggy travellers stood still, and small householders came forth with cups and bowls for a little of the goat's milk. But to me, as to many others, it seemed that he came each year as the messenger of spring.

By six o'clock the elephants were laden for the day's journey, and I set out on my wayfaring. My fellow-travellers were already afoot, and of the hilarious camp of the previous night only the carpenters remained, leisurely peeling bamboo strips to mend the roof against the rain.

My way wound across rice-fields and embankments ; the dew lay heavy on the stubble and the grass, chanticleer crowed lustily from the edge of the jungle ; and the sunlight streamed in great waves across the valley through which I was passing. But in a very little while I broke away from human settlements and became immersed in the cloistered gloom and silence of the forest. Under my feet the dead leaves lay, moist and clammy from the recent rain ; overhead the bamboos met, leaving but faint glimpses of the sky. Jungle-fowl dashed away with astonishing agility at my approach ; great pied hornbills flew with whirring pinions across the upper world of the forest ; turtle-doves murmured from leafy recesses ; monkeys swept along their overhead pathways ; a wild cat, startled from its lair bounded into the undergrowth and was lost to sight.

The pathway was carpeted in places with the petals of tree-flowers, scarlet and pale heliotrope, and crinkled white and pink. From time to time a forest stream, clear, shallow and silver-tongued, crossed my path. Footprints of men and elephants graven on its crisp sands ; betel-vines growing up some stately tree ; a Karen tree-ladder, struck the human note in a tremulous minor key. As I progressed, the bamboos became supreme, and for miles I tramped in their company alone ; ascending hills, walking for awhile along their crests ; descending and again ascending with no sign of the outside world, but such as came from an occasional glimpse of some sun-clad hill-slope, blue in the distance. Hills in fact lay all about me and views of an extensive world, but forbidden to me in my bamboo tunnel.

In time I came out of it and into a fire-track, wide as a national highway, punctuated by cairns and cross-posts with the Government mark upon them. So I knew that I had come within the radius of the Forest Act and at a cross-road I came upon a *kyawnyasa* or public notice, printed in Burmese and signed by an Englishman, forbidding all travellers between January and June to smoke by the wayside, or otherwise bring about a jungle fire and so endanger His Majesty's teak plantations. Under this notice a party of Shan travellers sat taking a passing rest ; amongst them, a monk, a woman and an infant of two years of age. The rank and file of the party smoked placidly from English pipes, unashamed and unconscious of the terrors of the law detailed in the document over their heads.

About noon I came to the river of Maywine, my resting-place being just beyond it. The indigenous traveller is not for a moment stayed by such an obstacle. His loose trousers swing up with the facility of a stage-curtain and his tattooed limbs descend into the water. Even as I arrived a party in this guise, with packs across their shoulders and oiled-silk hats flapping in the sun, was fording the stream. It is another matter for the white man, equipped with boots and European garments.

It is well that this is recognised by the people of the country. A woman who sat at work on the farther shore, seeing me, ran off for some thongs of peeled bamboo, a couple of Shan came hurrying up from a plantain-grove, a raft was constructed in a trice and pushed across to where I stood. From there it was gently pushed back again, and so as it touched the pebbles of the west bank I stepped ashore at Maywine.

A few yards away on the river's bank was the rest-house, a little bamboo structure of two rooms and an open verandah, built by the villagers. The Kyi-dan-gyi, or headman, brought an offering of papayas, another fetched water for the kitchen, while a third filled a couple of goblets at the river. After which they all sat down in a friendly way on the floor and smoked their pipes and talked.

In the afternoon the rain, which came just as I had found this welcome shelter, ceased ; the sun shone out and I took a stroll in the village. I found it a Shan village, peopled from Pha-pun, Bilin and Toungoo some ten years before. It ran to forty houses, which clustered along narrow lanes, shady with jack and horse-radish trees, the papaya and the plantain. Betel-vines grew on trellises before the doors, and small gardens displayed beds of chillies beans and pineapples. The cottages were of thatch and bamboo, with plank floors and wooden posts and rails. Most of them were large and airy, with projecting roofs, under which the people sat cleaning rice and pursuing their household avocations. There were reception-rooms open to the street, and bedrooms on a higher level behind. Seclusion finds no place in the economy of the farther East.

Many of these front rooms were shops, in which broad-cloth, silk trousers, tinned stores and groceries were exhibited for sale. In all, there was a quiet corner garnished with shrubs in pots and flower vases, sacred to the house spirit. Even in the rest-houses along the road I noticed masonic signs which showed that the cult of the house spirit had not been neglected. Nearly every inhabitant was an agricultural labourer, the village being the centre of a wide circle of rice *kwins*, rough at this season with the harvest stubble. The garnered rice was stored in mat cylinders under the eaves of the houses.

The only artisan of the village, a blacksmith, was occupied in a leisurely artistic way in designing an iron *hti* or umbrella for the village monastery. This building, with its thatched palm roof and plain architecture, made no great claim to distinction. The collection of images of the Buddha within it was a curious one and purported to have come from Mandalay; but there was a total absence of the conventional Burmese type. Some were of wood, and most might well have come from some cave-collection, the hoarding of ages, like that at Kaw-gun.

The house of the Kyi-dan-gyi was no larger or finer than that of his neighbours and the man himself differed in no respect from them save in this, that he was the responsible head and obliged therefore, by the laws of hospitality and of the Government, to make himself useful and attentive.

The chief peculiarity of the village lay in its complete lack of young people over ten years of age. There were some old men and women, and a number of babes at the breast, and urchins at the monastery; the rest were grown men and women, neither girls growing into full womanhood nor boys within reach of manhood. This peculiarity was clearly due to the age of the village. The ten years that had passed since it had been founded (by an old man, at the time of my visit sixty years of age, and still living in the village), had been well spent. There was an air of homeliness about the little settlement; the jack-trees had grown taller than the houses; the *kwins* had multiplied; herds of buffaloes grazed in its precincts; and three miles away, the village, I was told, had thrown out a hamlet of five houses, which was itself extending.

Exploring in this way and talking to a villager as I went I returned at last to the rest-house, and passed away an hour or more beside the river. It was pleasant to sit there smoking and watch idly the flight of water-fowl high overhead; to trace the five-pointed foliage and the scarlet bloom of the cotton-trees, patterned against the blue sky; to follow the passing glory of the sunset and the ceaseless monotonous change on the face of the little river. For in truth there was some serene quality in this place which made it, for all its remoteness and its

AT THE RIVER OF MAYWINE

isolation, attractive, and as the evening faded it passed insensibly into the category of places in the world I would fain re-visit.

The next morning there was a dense fog in the valley of the river and the sun was long up before I could make certain of the sky. It had rained hard during the night ; but in a little while the sky showed blue and clear, the fog-curtain rolled away, and I no longer had any hesitation in setting out. But now there was unlooked-for trouble with the elephant-men, who had grown sullen and wished to return. They were persuaded however to proceed.

We made a long and tiring march that day, and though we got away by seven the elephants did not reach their destination until half-past two, and it was three before I got my breakfast. On my way I passed the new hamlet of which I had been told and there were symptoms of Karen villages evident in plantations of the betel-palm, in *taung-gya* clearings, and in rough bamboo fences with wickets across the road.

From one of these a slight footpath led away to a village, but neither this nor any other village throughout my route, although I was travelling through a Karen country, was visible to my eyes as I went. This Karen instinct of concealment furnishes in itself an epitome of the history of the race.

My road lay at first along the edge of the *kwins*, through patches of dripping forest and over the river levels buried in tall grass, in which the elephants became invisible. But for the most part I walked on the soft yellow leaves, through tunnels of bamboos many miles long. I crossed the Maywine river four times, and on each occasion the little fat policeman found a new vocation in carrying me over on his back. Happily he was as strong as he was lazy.

Once in the course of my journey, I met a Shan caravan on its way from Shwe-gyin to which I was proceeding, and as it went by me, it filled the forest with its music. The road was level on the whole, but there were short ascents and descents, at each of which, although I was shut in in the bamboo tunnels, I could tell that I was negotiating the minor hills that run across the valley levels between Pha-pun and Shwe-gyin. But, so far, except on the first day, I had had very little real climbing. My camp for the night was pitched near Maw-pu, a Karen village of twenty-three souls, all of whom had to be named before the headman could tell me the number of its inhabitants.

The village itself was invisible ; but half a dozen villagers, amongst whom I recognised a man who had been presented to me at Pha-pun by the mission elder, came to see me at the *sa-khan*, where the accommodation was rougher than any I had yet experienced. Yet the locality had its charm. A thousand betel-palms stood about it in erect beauty ; blue hills towered over the little valley, shutting it in ; a stream murmured incessantly a few yards away. The place was wild, with the desolation of primitive nature, and of a narrow valley shut in by lofty hills. It lacked the open charm of Maywine. Yet for an hour or more, when we were all rested, and the cooking fires were lit under the trees, and the blue smoke curled upwards, and the last rays of sunlight streamed through the encompassing forest, there was a smile upon its face.

All through the night I caused a watch to be kept upon the elephant-men, lest they should decamp and leave me derelict in the jungle; and more than once I was awakened by the crashing of the great beasts in the jungle, to find a solitary figure taking his turn beside the flickering lantern, which threw its circle of pale light over the other sleepers. Thus I knew that the watch was being kept.

We were all up by five o'clock the next morning; but it took us two hours to make a start, because of the loading of the baggage and the sullenness of the drivers. Part of the freight consisted of green cocoanuts, which had a particular attraction for the elephants, and it was amusing to see them reaching out their trunks for them while every one was busy with the baggage. Occasionally they succeeded in purloining one and crushed it open under their forefeet. There is an endless fascination in the ways of elephants and they beguile many an hour of tedious travel when they form part of one's company.

This day we had not gone a hundred yards when we struck a bad bit of ground along the slippery hill-side, and simultaneously came upon a Shan caravan moving towards us. The elephants trumpeted with fear and swung round in their tracks, the bullocks of the caravan dashed in scattered groups into the jungle, whence they surveyed us with eyes of fear; bells jangled, the caravan-men shouted in dismay, and the only progress we made was towards Maywine as the elephants shuffled along the hill-side like a pair of nervous pantaloons.

The caravan was at last got out of the way and the elephants were bullied and coaxed into facing the slippery fragment of road, which they did with immense circumspection, leaning heavily against the hill-side, using their trunks for support and making certain of the safe lodgment of three feet, before adventuring the fourth.

Once before I had been placed in a similar, but worse, predicament. I was making my way up the Shan plateau, from the railway at Pyinmana to the site of a projected sanatorium at Byingyi, six thousand feet above the sea. The path was barely five feet wide and in bad repair—a mere scratch on the hill-side, which climbed up in a steep slope on one side of it and descended in precipices on the other, to the bed of the valley. Twenty yards ahead my elephant, filling the entire road, was taking his ponderous and stately way; behind him I rode on my small Burmese pony. For two hours or more we had been marching in this fashion, climbing foot by foot to the summit of Byingyi; when, of a sudden, a mad trumpeting filled the air and in a flash the elephant swung round and came thundering down the narrow track. My pony turned and fled before him. For a mile or more this pursuit continued, the elephant screaming with fear, his driver clutching at the iron goad he had succeeded in inserting into his skull, and calling anathemas upon every relative of the great beast he could name. At last the pace slackened and the whole breathless party of us came to a stand. The elephant not yet reassured twitched all over with a nervous fear, distracted between the fiend upon his back and the fiend he had not dared to face.

I called upon the driver for an explanation.

"Huzur," he replied, "the accursed beast—may his mother be dishonoured and his sister put to shame—took fright at a wasp."

Three years previously it seemed they had travelled this way and the elephant had been stung by a wasp. The memory of this adventure assailed him as he approached the scene of it, and seeing at the same moment one of his ancient enemies, he turned incontinently and fled.

"Nothing, Presence," added the *mahout*, "will induce this bastard to face that corner of the road."

The evening was closing in, we had come too far to turn back with any hope of shelter for the night; our destination was still some miles ahead. A precipice lay on our right, a steep hill covered with dense bamboo forest and sodden with mould rose up on our left. I could see no escape from the dilemma. But the driver knew his beast.

"I will make the infamous one climb the hill," he said, "and descend again on the farther side of the wasps' nest."

"Son of a disreputable mother," he added, addressing the mammoth under him, "climb this hill," and thereupon there followed such an exhibition of sagacity and skill as one who has never seen an elephant in a difficulty might deem incredible.

The driver, it may be remarked, was an Indian. Burman and Karen are less searchingly personal in their abuse of an elephant's relations.

To return to my journey from Maw-pu. The country I met as I went, proved to be similar to that I had hitherto traversed; bamboo-hidden pathways, flat patches of rice *kwins*, streams and rivulets. But it was more mountainous and evidently I was traversing a loftier barrier than any I had hitherto encountered. Steep ascents and sharp descents followed each other; splendid masses of wooded hill and mountain towered above me, where openings in the forest offered a glimpse of the landscape. Grassy peaks and stony crags and precipices spoke of grandeur, and cool moist forests, with streams rushing and tumbling through them, provided a welcome variation from the monotonous beauty of the bamboo.

There were signs of human tenure on the charred hill-slopes where *taung-gya* cutters had been at work, and in the valley bottoms where forests of areca-palms grew luxuriantly along the stream's edge ; but as usual not a single village was to be seen.

About half-way to my destination I came upon a party of Karen, building a rest-house of green bamboos, by the brink of a charming rivulet. They toiled, but with the utmost indolence, and spent far more time in pounding areca-nut, which they chew with betel-leaf, and in smoking their queer little pipes, than in actual labour.

RAFTMAN AT MAYWINE

Betel-chewing, the fashionable vice of Burma, is carried by these people to the last extreme. The process with them is so continuous as to be perpetual. The last I saw of the assembled villagers of Maw-pu, as the dusk closed in on the night of my stay amongst them, was of a party of squalid men in *déshabille*—the Paung-Laung Karen always suggests *déshabille*—pounding and chewing betel, reaching prehensile fingers for betel-boxes, trickling as to their gums ; and in the grey dawn, as I opened my eyes, they rested upon the same components of the same spectacle. The sinner who lights one cigarette at the butt-end of its predecessor is an angel to the betel-chewing Karen.

Their type of face is peculiar. In the eyes of the younger generation there is the steady gaze of the primitive and squalid savage, dully curious as to the novel objects about him. In the eyes of the older men there is a note of melancholy, of invincible sadness that seems to reflect the hereditary experience of the race. The women reach a certain plump comeliness during the brief season that intervenes between childhood and motherhood. Children of both sexes have few pretensions to beauty. One seldom sees here the engaging prettiness of Burmese children. What there is of childish charm lies in their sloe-like eyes; their faces are invariably overlaid with dirt.

The married women soon grow slovenly careworn and wrinkled. It is little wonder; for besides enduring all the pains and cares of maternity, they seem to do most of the hard work. They pound rice by the hour, wielding the heavy wooden pounder, which is in harsh contrast with their slender arms. They carry water in large hollow bamboos long distances from the stream's edge; they cook and weave; and when met with on the highway travelling with their men, appear to do most of the porterage.

Their garments look less squalid than those of the men, possibly because they are darker in colour and therefore show the dirt less. No Puritan could desire a costume better calculated to conceal the human form than that of the Karen woman. There is a skirt which reaches to the ankles, there is a long, loose robe, reaching half-way down to the knees. The sleeves are cut short and the robe, which is open in a small V-shape fore and aft, has rather the effect of a gorgeous surplice when it is new. It is much less prone to slip over the shoulder than the corresponding male garment, which is for ever askew. The colours of the women's garments are red and blue, and when new they look neat and attractive. The skirt is crossed by a wide blue band, and it ends in a scarlet strip about four inches wide. The upper robe is embroidered in horizontal and vertical patterns. Both men and women wear beads, the necklaces of the women being larger and prettier than those of the men. Bracelets of silver, clasped to the forearm, are also worn.

A KAREN VILLAGE

I had meant to camp at Nyaung-tha-da; but it proved to be an open camping ground by the wayside, without shelter of any kind. There was a village in the neighbourhood, although as usual it was invisible to the eye, and this I now sought out along a narrow hidden pathway, which gave no sign of being the main approach.

Half a mile or more brought me to a mountain stream full of boulders and deep pools, across which there was no obvious passage; but I sighted a party of Karen higher up, employed in fishing, and two of them, considerably startled, led me across its devious stepping-stones to the village.

The next symptom of life I met with was a herd of buffaloes, who came plunging and snorting through the long grass to look at me; and

I was warned that there was a "wild" buffalo in the neighbourhood of whom even the Karen lived in terror. I was destined, as it happened, to make a closer acquaintance with this potentate.

Leaving the herd and the thicker jungle I came upon some *taung-gya* clearings, where the new leaves were just bursting out of the charred trunks. Then suddenly, and not till I was right into it, I came for the first time in sight of the village. The *taung-gya* wreckage extended right up to the posts of the houses; there was no attempt at either a clearing or an enclosure.

The appearance presented by the village itself was almost comic. It looked as if it was tottering under the effects of an earthquake, or as if the houses had suddenly taken to strong drink. There was not a straight line in their composition; bamboos of all descriptions and at all angles lay scattered about; some in mere piles resting against the walls, others thrown out as buttresses to the posts on which the houses were built. In the forefront of all there stood the dilapidated remnants of an abandoned house, to complete a picture of trumpery disorder. The houses stood to each other at a variety of angles, two being long barracks with accommodation for several families.

A violent creaking of bamboos set up within, as I approached, followed by a sudden silence. Then eyes began to peer at chinks in the bamboo walls and fingers fell surreptitiously to work to widen these apertures for a better view. Whenever my eyes crossed a pair of eyes behind the chinks they were immediately withdrawn.

The first sign I made of a nearer approach was followed by an agitation within and the tumultuous creaking of bamboo floors. But for these symptoms the village might have contained no human inhabitants.

The houses were, as a matter of fact, swarming with a population of men, women and children, all of whom were stricken, as wild beasts are, with simultaneous fear and curiosity. When I summoned them a little later through some of the leading men, to be photographed on the verandahs of their houses, there was a display of men, of small boys and children, and a few wrinkled and awful hags. The young and the presumably good-looking kept strictly within. The old story.

But as the evening grew and I was out of sight, the women of the village came out to fill water and pound rice for the evening meal. I passed a quiet hour on the balcony of my house, looking to where the blue hills rose up in outline beyond the jungle, and sunset tints were flashed on the scattered clouds. It was a beautiful view, of the kind the Karen has looked upon with little profit for unnumbered generations.

The village is built on rising ground under the shelter of a lofty mountain on the west. The near neighbourhood of this, with its dense forests, provides the necessary retreat, in the event of panic. Small low hills rise parallel to it on the east. In the narrow space between, a stream babbles on its way and hosts of areca-palms find sustenance along it. Such is the village.

My house was square in shape, with a roof of bamboos cut in two and laid like tiles, leaving open an air and smoke space of a yard between it and the top of the walls. There was a lower inner framework of roof, which served as a storing place for spare bamboos, and this made it impossible for me, who am more than five feet high, to stand erect within. The walls were of hammered bamboo of the giant *wabo* species, and there were no partitions ; but a place was set apart for a fire, and there was a little alcove at one end where waterpots were stored. The one doorway faced away from the village, and could not boast of a door. The floor was raised about ten feet on piles, and a bamboo ladder, narrowing as it reached the ground, was the means of climbing up to it. The furniture consisted of cooking-pots and paddy-bins. It was quite tolerably clean and open to the air and sunlight. Children, dogs, pigs, fowls, and ducks quacked, crowed, grunted, growled and prattled below. At night the starlit sky was visible at the openings of the roof.

My preparations for a start began at four o'clock the next morning, for a long march lay before us and we were all anxious now to reach Shwe-gyin. However interesting such journeys may be, there is a strain involved in them which quickly begins to tell, both on man and beast. Of my party, all were showing signs of fatigue, and my Burmese writer was on the verge of breaking down. For the Burman, although a fine man physically when brought up in the country, becomes a weakling when he resides in large towns and rapidly deteriorates when he takes to an office stool. Frequently, when I have been travelling in the remoter parts of Burma, my Burmese clerks have been the first to succumb to malarial fever, and have seldom been able to take any hand in the physical pursuits that men readily fall to when on the march ; such as the carrying of a gun, or the felling of log for firewood. And when Moung San Nyun, who accompanied me on this journey, tried to use a punting pole on the Yunzalin, he succeeded egregiously in falling into the water.

But it was not only the men of my party who now began to show traces of the strain of travel. Each day the elephants took longer to accomplish the twenty miles or so I aimed at ; each day they grew visibly thinner and the drivers complained that they were not given sufficient time in which to feed. There was some truth in their contention ; for the elephant who depends on the jungle for his sustenance has practically to feed all day to fill himself. In this and in many other respects elephant transport is unsatisfactory ; yet the fact remains that

MARCHING THROUGH THE ARECA PALMS

the elephant, huge as he is, and unwieldly as he looks, will travel where no other pack-animal can go at all.

Before leaving the village I paid a visit to one of the long barracks and found it to consist of a series of four rooms, similar to mine, and opening into each other. They were extremely dirty, and the floor, which was of the slightest character, shook at every step I took. Their denizens had fled before my approach, and they must have presented to an onlooker outside a very comic picture as they hastily crowded down the narrow ladders at one end, while I entered at the other. Two minutes was as much as I could endure, at that early hour, of the terrible amalgam of smells that greeted me on entering. My own cottage of the previous night had been happily free from offence in this respect. This I attributed to the fact that it was much newer, that it had no pigstye under it, and that it belonged to a young couple beginning life, and was therefore neater and less populated than the other houses.

Again, when on the point of departing, I noticed women's faces peering through chinks in the bamboo walls, each one being instantly withdrawn, like the head of a turtle, on discovery. I have given them a somewhat limited character for beauty, but I am obliged to say that many of them look very well in their marching costume, which leaves their arms and shoulders bare and shows them to be fair and plump. But on meeting a white man on the road they look startled, pause, and seem in two minds whether to stand their ground or fly. The smallest advance on his part would certainly scatter them like jungle-fowl, and at the best they generally make a détour and get out of reach as quickly as possible. I sometimes wonder in what monstrous character I may inadvertently have appeared to these timid creatures; and when I reflect on the natural gaiety of all the Indo-Chinese people and on the charm and curiosity of the sex, I am haunted with a suspicion that at least a portion of their disinclination to be seen is due to the tutelage of their men. I fear that I must have been painted by them in the most sombre colours.

Soon after we started, my elephants having preceded me by an hour, I came upon a scene of devastation. I found my baggage scattered in fragments over the jungle; my followers shouting wildly to each other, but invisible; and a single elephant, his ears flapping, his trunk waving to and fro, and his small eyes twinkling with excitement and fear. His fellow, it seemed, had been called upon to do battle by the wild buffalo whose fame had reached my ears the previous day, and he had promptly dashed off in abject flight through the jungle. The path he had taken was strewn for some little way with the débris of his harness, and presently I came upon the driver, who had, by some miracle, fallen off without breaking his neck.

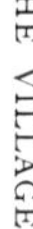

THE VILLAGE

From that day to this I have never seen or heard anything of the fugitive. Several of my cases containing wine and soda-water, were broken to pieces. Let me hope that the flowers that bloom there now, betoken some memory of that libation.

My great fear was for my negatives of the Yunzalin and others which now illustrate this narrative. These I had packed daily with my own hands and with the most scrupulous care, and they were happily preserved. But for the space of three weeks I lived in suspense, for I could not develop them sooner.

I had now had enough of elephants. The only beast that remained could not carry all my baggage, and I was of no mind to risk a further misadventure. I therefore despatched my two constables to the village to impress a number of porters, and with the aid of these people I continued my journey. The road climbed a steep hill that was densely wooded and very cool and moist. Scarcely any direct sunlight penetrated its gloom. I reached the crest of the pass an hour before noon and thereafter my way lay along bamboo-covered slopes and over valley-levels watered by numerous streams which I crossed and recrossed with tiresome frequency.

At half-past two in the afternoon I came to a halt at the *zayat* of Yeboo village. My servants did not arrive till five o'clock. They all looked thoroughly beaten and two of them went down with fever. They had been afoot since four o'clock in the morning, and on the march for nearly twelve hours. Below the *zayat* there was a pretty stream and across this, to fill up the interval between my arrival and theirs, I had myself carried, to shoot jungle-fowl in some *kwins* on the farther side. Beyond them rose a range of blue hills shutting in the valley.

On my return I found that a caravan of some mixed breed of Karen had come in. Both animals and pack-saddles were similar to those of the Shan. But the bells were of bamboo and I missed the fuller music of the Shan bells.

The pack-saddle used throughout these regions is a simple contrivance of two pillows tightly packed and placed on the animal's back at an angle of fifty degrees. Upon these the wooden frame holding a pannier at each end is deposited. A tailpiece, consisting of a rope strung out from a curved bamboo, helps in a measure to balance the panniers. No girths are employed and balance, if I am to judge from the manner in which the panniers oscillate, alone retains them in position. The panniers are tilted slightly forward and lie well over the animal's withers. The cattle, mainly of the ruddy colour that is common in Burma, are well trained, and stand motionless while the business of loading is in progress, but move off immediately the signal to start is given.

Tired as I was, it was long past midnight before I slept. The *zayat* was open to the night and sheltered me only from the dew, but I was grateful for the shelter it gave me. The stars shone brilliantly in the rich dome of the sky overhead; all my camp lay in deep slumber. The night was still but for the never-ceasing music of the stream; and it seemed to me, as I lay awake alone, as if my spirit, disembodied, had been caught up by some mystic influence into the very heart of life. It may have been mere fatigue, but I have never felt this sensation in a civilised environment.

KYAUNG-WA

The next morning I made another early start and saw the sun come up over the hills, throwing long shadows across the dew-laden *kwins*. There was one small climb and then steady marching along the Taung-salé, which gradually widened into a river as I went. I had to cross it many times, to my discomfort and to that of the little fat policeman who had to carry me over. It flows in a direction which is opposite to that of the Bilin, the Maywine, and most of the other streams along this road, and I knew from this that I had crossed the watershed. I met a caravan of elephants and Burmans going to Muang-Lem; men, women, children and a baby elephant. The Burmans *shekoed* and made obeisances of respect from their high wicker panniers and looked distinctly relieved at meeting an Englishman on the path of their exodus. It was not such a far-away land after all.

By two o'clock I came to the village of Kyaung-Wa and knew that I was back in Burma. The *zayat*, or rest-house, though plain, was of the substantial Burmese type, of timber and iron ; the women were placid and dignified and not at all disposed to run away ; the men were quiet and courteous, and appreciative of distinctions unknown to the untutored Karen. The headman proved himself to be a polite and sagacious gentleman ; a peasant, but a man of the world.

Rich orchards of guavas, papayas, palms, and other fruit trees confirmed in me the impression I had formed as I came, of a country that is rich in little valleys and wooded hill-slopes and running waters. It seemed to me that in the hands of a progressive community all this country, instead of being a sealed wilderness might become famous for its orchards, its populous villages and its beauty. I have met with few natural sites more charming in a minor key than that of Maywine, no country happier in its cool forests and innumerable streams.

The next day I pushed on to the village of Taung-salé-zeik, and leaving it behind me, emerged abruptly, about eleven of the clock, into open country. It was with a feeling of pleasure and relief that I looked again, after a detention of three weeks amongst mountains and forests, on open and wide-reaching plains. The slightly undulating landscape, spreading away in soft blue-green outlines to the horizon, seemed to me scarcely at all Eastern in character. Presently I reached the edge of the Shwe-gyin river, near its junction with the Sittang, and on the farther shore, in the peninsula between the two rivers, there spread in a long curving line the town of Shwe-gyin.

And here I must point out that it is only after a stay in the hill country, amongst backward races, that the traveller can really appreciate the nature and extent of Burmese civilisation. Here it was evident were a people capable of living together in large communities and in permanent homes. High up, where the curving Shwe-gyin seemed to melt away into the heart of the blue mountains, the golden bulb and spire of a large pagoda glittered in splendid outline over the dark tree-tops. The massive walls and tapering roofs of numerous monasteries spoke to the same purpose. And on crossing over and entering the town itself, laid out with wide and sheltered thoroughfares, and public buildings, such as court-houses, schools, a post and telegraph office, a jail, a church, I came into contact with the pioneer efforts of a still higher civilisation.

Thus it comes that a town which, to the newcomer from great centres of life, must seem small and insignificant, leaves on the mind of one emerging from the hill tracts, where civilisation still speaks only in faint whispers, an impression of dignity and importance ; and it is in this character that Shwe-gyin is regarded by its people.

Book XI

THE SITTANG

Shwe-Gyin—The Sittang—Sittang—The Canal to Pegu

CHAPTER XL

SHWE-GYIN

BUT, in fact, Shwe-gyin as a town has for many years been on the decline. At the outset, when Pegu was first incorporated in the empire by Lord Dalhousie, Shooay-gheen, as it was then spelt, was not only the chief town of the district, but also a military cantonment in which troops were quartered. Of that time, although it dates back less than half a century, there is now scarcely a trace. The barracks that were built on the laterite ridge which dominates the town have completely disappeared. Of those who occupied them the only surviving trace is in the cemetery—adjunct of every British settlement in the East. There you will find the graves of that period, with the customary legends inscribed upon them: "Major ——, to whose memory this monument is erected by his brother officers, in token of their regard and esteem;" "Captain ——, who combined high intellectual gifts with great sweetness and courtesy of disposition, to whose memory this stone is inscribed by his sorrowing mother;" "John, the infant son of —— and ——," who ran his brief course in an alien land, dying on the day he was born.

Like many others of its kind it is falling into decay. The wooden gate has fallen in on its hinges; the graves are black with stress of exposure to the weather; the inscriptions on the stones are half illegible; the interspaces are choked with weeds. The strong wall built about it still keeps the site inviolate, but desolation and abandonment are writ painfully upon all that is within.

There are some lines of Emile Souvestre in which he states the reluctance of the Breton peasantry to bury their dead in any but the immemorial churchyard of their fathers. "*Les restes de nos pères sont ici; pourquoi en séparer celui qui vient de mourir? Exilé, là bas au cimetière de la chapelle, il n'entendra ni les chants des offices, ni les prières qui rachètent les trépassés. C'est ici sa place; nous pouvons voir sa tombe de nos fenêtres ; nous pouvons y envoyer nos plus petits enfants prier chaque soir ; cette terre est la propriété des morts.*"

Often the memory of them has assailed me when I have come by chance upon these lonely derelict graves of my own far-scattered race.

Since 1895 Shwe-gyin has undergone a further contraction. It has ceased to be the headquarters of the district, till then administered from it. Thatôn, with its new lands rising from the sea has taken its place ; and the Sittang, to complete its abandonment, has for some years past been withdrawing its tortuous channel from the neighbourhood of Shwe-gyin. But although its importance has thus in some measure passed away, it must continue for long to be a town. Its position here at the foot of the hill country, some day to be exploited for its mineral wealth, secures its future. The fickle Sittang will perhaps one day return ; roads will connect it with the sealed wilderness of the Yunzalin, and as its population grows with the duration of the Imperial peace, it will continue its history far into the future. But it is sore and aggrieved just now at its abandonment, and the tale on the lips of its people is for ever one of their decaying fortunes.

Down by a dying backwater of the Sittang, the curious may still trace the site of the old Burmese stockade, precipitately abandoned when our troops first came up this way. That and all it stands for is fast fading into the misty tracts of the forgotten. It is a chapter that is never likely to be reopened.

A PROCESSION

CHAPTER XLI

THE SITTANG

THE Sittang, which rises at the foot of the Shan hills, in the Yamèthin plain, runs its course of three hundred and fifty miles to the sea, flanked on one side by the Pegu Yoma and on the other by the Paung-Laung hills. Tradition ascribes to it a mysterious subterranean connection with the Nyaung-ywé lake on the Shan plateau. Its stream, which in the rainy season flows with great velocity, is practically unnavigable by steamers beyond Shwe-gyin, up to which point the great tide of the Gulf of Martaban is felt. Its most striking feature is the Bore, of which I shall presently give an account.

At Shwe-gyin I first embarked upon its waters, and the wide sand spaces there between it and its tributary, the bare grey banks devoid of forest, gave it, to my eyes, the wonted character of an Indian river. Gradually, as I travelled down it the spaces narrowed, the river walls rose sheer, crested with giant grasses, and this impression wore away. Sand-martins twittered and made short flights before their nest-holes in the banks. Bronze-wings of exceptional size and brilliance skimmed the air after flies, and the pied kingfisher fluttered in the sunlight, poised high above the calm face of the river. Painted butterflies winged their lowlier flight, touching its ripples and heedless of the hungry fish that followed them, half out of water, in tense pursuit.

At Daung-sarit low hills rose above the river on the east bank, where long lines of village huts deployed. The black nets of fishermen hung like infernal shrouds from stakes in the sun, and each roof-top was conspicuous from the waterpots and fire-clappers laid on it, in tribute to the dryness of the season. The waters of the river were yellow and charged with silt, and at Daung-sarit it was perhaps two hundred yards across. But gradually it widened and trees and grasses increased.

The launch stopped at intervals to pick up and disembark passengers, who went to and fro in her sampan. I was in a country boat enjoying the novelty of being towed. The sensation of motion without effort is delightful; there was neither creak of oar nor throb of paddle, and it felt like floating over velvet. A faint oscillation alone conveyed a hint of movement. But whenever the launch forged ahead after a pause, the boat for an instant shot forward as the hawser pulled, only to lapse once more into its state of rest. Cotton trees with their candelabra tracery and scarlet bloom made rich patterns against the blue. The sky was charged with electric clouds; the landscape of mountains looked pale in the mists of advancing summer; the glare of noon was oppressive to the eyes; yet there was a breeze upon the river, and travel in this country boat proved far from unpleasant.

At Myit-kyo I reached the mouth of the Pegu-Sittang canal, constructed to circumvent the bore of the Sittang. Coringhi labourers abounded here, and natives of India generally. Lock-gates shut off the canal from the river, and an avenue of acacias followed the banks of the canal. There were a few shops by the wayside, and in the distance, emerging like an island from a sea of grass, stood a monastery, typical of the Delta. After a while the Pegu launch came in; we shipped some passengers and proceeded on our way. Villages lined the banks and the river ever widened as we went.

At Khayo low hills again descended to the stream's edge, and behind them rose the blue bulwarks of the Paung-Laung hills, an outcrop of white rocks near their summits giving an impression of snow. But as the sun paled they stood out clear and blue against the tinted sky. Cotton-trees and birds innumerable, plantain-groves and mangoes bursting into bloom, pagodas upon the river heights, met me as I took my way; and so I came in the late evening to Sittang.

CHAPTER XLII

SITTANG

SITTANG is built at the mouth of the Kha-wa streamlet and consists now of a few wide roads, a bazaar, and three hundred houses. It was built by the Talaing (Mun) under We-ma-la, the prince who founded Pegu, thirteen hundred years ago. Traces of the Talaing supremacy survive in the Kyaik-ka-lun-pun pagoda, and in the ruins of the town and palace of Kyaik-ka-tha, a few miles inland. The strange name of the pagoda is connected by the people with a legend of Buddha. A thousand giants, it is said, lived here in the days of the great teacher, and when he came to Sittang they grew hungry at the sight of him and resolved to eat him. But their efforts to catch him were in vain, for howsoever they pursued he was always out of their reach. At last, very weary and fatigued, they gave up the chase and asked him how he had succeeded in escaping them. To which he replied that he had never moved at all! Then he preached the law to them to their edification, and in their new-found zeal they built the pagoda whose name in the Talaing language is an epitome of the story.

The name Sittang, or Sit-taung, is associated by its people with the march of a general of Anawrata, King of Pagan, who paused here on his way to the conquest of Thatôn to ask the king for more troops. The story is trifling, but it shows that the historic march of the great king on the Talaing capital has never been forgotten.[1]

The lower base of the pagoda is of hewn laterite; its upper and newer portion is ascribed to a Burmese governor, and the flight of stairs that leads up its western face was cut by the British garrison, which appears to have used the summit as a signalling station. The view from it embraces the Sittang, or, as it is called by the people, the Paung-Laung river, and beyond it a level plain, slightly forested, which stretches away to the low hills near Pegu. In clear weather the golden spire of the Shway Hmaw Daw Pagoda can be seen, twinkling in the sun. In the west, wooded and slightly undulating country reaches away to the foot of the Kyaik-ti-yo hill, whose singular pagoda is visible from here. It is a day's journey from Sittang, or two days for slow travellers, old people, and women with small children. The pagoda festival lasts "from the full moon of Tabaung to the full moon of Tagoo," and it was to begin within four days of my visit to Sittang, on February 27th. This, in fact, is the festival season throughout Burma. It is a time of leisure and of plenty for the country-side; the harvest has been gathered in, and there is little work to be done till the setting in of the rains. It is a season therefore of sight-seeing and picnicking, which in a primitive society are closely intermingled with pilgrimages and religion. Most of the commanding heights in Burma have long since been crowned with pagodas, and a visit to any of these gratifies the innate piety and gaiety of the people, besides furnishing them with the change of scene that few of us are willing to go without. Changes have been at work at Sittang, as elsewhere, during the half-century that it has been a British possession. Troops were once quartered here, and in fact Sittang was not taken without the loss of many British lives. Relics of this period survive in a ditch that marks the site of the old barracks, and in a small whitewashed cemetery that overlooks the river.

The river too has been changing greatly. Thirty years ago the great bore of the Sittang was a familiar object to every inhabitant of the village. The village headman, aged sixty-three, has lively recollections of it, when in his youth it brought its spoil of dead fish and prawns to his door, and the old abbot of the monastery on the hill has often heard its incoming roar. But its voice is no longer heard in the village, and its wall of waters rushing in with tumult is no longer a familiar sight. Its limit now is the village of Khaya-soo.

The bore is caused by the union of two portions of the great tidal wave of the Indian Ocean, which here rushes up the funnel-shaped mouth of the Sittang at a speed of twelve miles an hour. Its contact

[1] *The story of Thatôn is told in "Mandalay and other Cities of Burma."*

with the descending waters of the river causes a deposit of silt, and the formation of the new lands which are so marked a feature of this coast. The bore rises at the mouth of the river to a height of twenty feet.

Cæsar Frederick, the Venetian, who visited Burma in 1567, has left an animated account of his journey from Martaban to Pegu, and of the bore of the Sittang.

" From Martaban," he says, " I departed to go to the chiefest Citie in the Kingdome of Pegu, which is also called after the name of the Kingdome, which voyage is made by sea in three or foure dayes. They may goe also by land, but hee that hath merchandize it is better for him to goe by sea and lesser charge, and in this voyage you shall have a Marcareo which is one of the marvellous things in the world ye Nature hath wrought, and I never sawe anie thing so hard to be beleeved as this. The great encreasing and deminishing that the water maketh there at one pushe or instant, and with the horrible earthquake and great noyse that it maketh where it cometh. Wee departed from Martaban in barks, which are like to our Pylot boates with the encrease of the Water, and they goe as swift as an arrowe out of a bowe, so long as the tide runneth with them, and when the water is at the highest, then they draw themselves out of the Chanel towards some bancke, and there they come to anker and when the water is diminished, then they rest a drye ; and when the barkes rest drie, they are as high from the bottome of the Chanell as any house toppe is high from the ground. They let their barks lie so high for this respect, that if there should any shippe rest or ride in the Chanell, with such force commeth in the water, that it would overthrowe ship or barke ; yet for all this, that the barkes bee so farre out of the Chanell, and though the water hath lost her greatest strength and furie before it come so high, yet they make fast their prowe to the strane, and often times it maketh them verie fearefull and if the Anker did not hold her prow up by strength she woulde bee overthrowne and lost with men and goods, when the water beginneth to encrease, it maketh such a noise and so great that you would think it an earthquake, and presently at the first it maketh three waves. So that the first washeth over the barke, from stem to stern, the second is not so furious as the first, and the third raiseth the anker, and then for the space of six houres yet the water encreaseth, they rowe with such swiftness than you woulde thinke they did flye in these tides there must be lost no jot of time, for if you arrive not at the stagions before the tide be spent, you must turne backe from whence you came.

" I coulde never," he gravely adds, " gather any reason of the noyse that this water maketh in the encrease of the tide, and in diminishing of the water."

As one travels of a quiet evening down the Sittang, one's fancy drifts

From a painting by J. Raeburn Middleton

THE BEGGING RECLUSE

back to these scenes of the past ; to the days of the pagoda builders, to the great march of Anawrata the king, to the coming of the Portuguese who fought upon all these sites, and so to the camp on the hill, and the Englishmen of a bygone generation. Many of them must often have found pleasure in drifting down the river as one is prone to do now after the day's work is done.

Save for the coming of the Coringhi fisherman on the river, the Coringhi coolie in the village, and the Chinaman, who trades in liquor and opium and European goods, our own presence here for half a century has made little apparent change. The people go about their avocations much as they do in Upper Burma, the village headman still wears silk, and has not forgotten his manners ; nor the village girl her native independence.

And yet, what change has come, is ominous for half a century's growth. The fish in the river a Coringhi perquisite, the steam launch that navigates its waters owned by a Surati, the sampans driven by Chittagonian Musulmans, the larger trade in the hands of the Chinaman —I wonder what it will come to in the end ! I hope that it will not finally oust the people of the soil ; for the world will be poorer for the passing of the Burmese race.

CHAPTER XLIII

THE CANAL TO PEGU

AT seven o'clock in the morning all at Sittang who mean to travel are awaiting the coming of the steamer, which sends its voice like that of a chapel harmonium up the river reaches, but itself keeps out of sight. The river is laden with white mists, which creep off its face and tend with the morning wind down-stream, rising as they go, till they grow into fog-banks and pass away. It is cold at this hour even in the last days of February, and the women cover themselves with shawls and the men with blankets. The smallest children face the chill air in nakedness, which either kills them off or fits them better for the struggle of life. The fittest only survive ; a circumstance which accounts in part for the fine physique of the race.

Every one waits with Eastern patience for the steamer's coming. A little way apart from the crowd two Chinamen in trade, squat by the water's edge, cheerful but exclusive. A monk in yellow robes, lit by the rising sun, waits a few paces off, accompanied by a layman who carries his begging bowl and stoops respectfully before him. A party of women, with coils of neat hair upon their heads, and pink *pawas* thrown round their necks, smoke placidly together discussing their neighbours. A native of Northern India plies a brisk trade amongst the assembled company. He is a seller of tea and hot cakes, which he carries slung at opposite ends of a swinging pole. It is a long call from his home on the shores of the Ganges to this little town on the Sittang.

At last, after an hour's trumpeting in the stillness of the morning, the steamer throbs up, passengers get under weigh, there is a bustle in the placid crowd, and the old Thugyi—the Headman of Sittang—bluff, hearty, and courteous to the last, *shekoes*, as my dugout takes the water.

We steam up the Sittang as far as Myit-kyo, where the acacia avenue along the canal banks makes as prominent a feature in the landscape as its kindred at Ismailia, and there I change into the launch that is to take me to Pegu. The banks of the canal are high at first and its waters stretch away between them laden with green scum and water cabbages, which drift helplessly to and fro, driven by the angry wash of the launch.

As we advance the avenue dies away, the banks dwindle and the canal becomes wider. A stream enters it on the north, and a village and boats at anchor mark the junction. But for some time the journey becomes uninteresting and the banks devoid of beauty. Nearer Pegu the interest grows. Villages and monasteries line the banks, passengers embark and disembark, cocoanut palms and groups of trees break the monotony of the level rice-lands ; signs of the harvest greet one upon every hand ; the yellow grain lies piled in great pyramids before the houses ; and boat after boat, with carved stern and bellying sail, sweeps by.

The telegraph wire hums by the banks, and at intervals there are houses built for the canal officers, which recall the little *gares* of the Suez Canal. It is with this on the whole that I compare the Pegu–Sittang Canal at this season ; yet the country through which it passes is one of the richest in the world, and its very monotony is due to its richness, since it has all been levelled for the cultivation of rice.

The company assembled on board provides material for entertainment, and this is as well since discomfort is the keynote of the only accommodation the steamer offers. Out of the crowd of Burmese and Indian faces, there is notably one that stands out in a kind of majestic supremacy. It is the face of a Bussorah Arab ; a face in which race and blood are written clear. Beside it, the flat mongoloid features of the Burmese look plebeian and unfinished ; those of the Madrasis, brutish ; of the Chittagonians and Suratis, weak and effeminate. The man looks like a king fallen upon evil times. He wears a saffron cloth over his head like a *burnous*, and it frames his clear grave features, his pointed grizzled beard, his straight-cut nose, and his forehead graven with lines. He can talk no language but his own and he sits here isolated, a world apart from the crowd about him, telling his beads as his lips murmur the name of the Prophet. What mission I wonder has brought him here?

As the poles to him, heavy of paunch, naked, the loud vulgarian, is the Chetti. The face of the man is carnal, half of it mouth and jaw. There are a number of Madrasis and Coringhis, black-skinned and

WAITING FOR THE STEAMER

aboriginal in type. One of them is a woman with much of the animal beauty of her race; but she is scarcely one degree removed from the savage, her nose pierced with jewellery and her ears distorted by its weight out of all human semblance. The steamer clerk is a Surati of anæmic appearance and rude hectoring manner; the *serang* and crew are sleek Chittagonians with oiled hair and beards. There are Chinamen in black calico and soft felt hats, who sit in a group by themselves and smoke cigarettes, and there is a crowd of Burmese passengers. These good people neither jabber gutturally like the Madrasis, nor hector like the steamer clerk, nor go naked like the Chetti. Most of them carry umbrellas and wear silk ; the old men are calm and dignified ; the young men humorous and genial ; the women are self-possessed and on this occasion preoccupied with babies, one of whom is a jovial character about half a year old, with black eyes intelligent but fathomless, and a skin that is almost white.

And thus, in the midst of this motley company, I come to the end of my water journey, at a village six miles distant from Pegu. At this season the launch can go no farther. From here a straight road cleaves its way through the level rice-fields and past a wide mere in which black buffaloes wallow and wild duck find a home. It brings me in the late evening to Pegu, boring its dusty way through the ruined walls of the ancient city. And here, where of old great armies went forth, and kings upon their litters, a few tired people enter now unquestioned.

Book XII

RUBIES

Thabeit-Kyin—On the Road—Capelan
Mogôk—L'envoi

CHAPTER XLIV

THABEIT-KYIN

THE grey mists of morning were slowly creeping off the face of the river where it lay in a fold of the hills, and the steamer was beginning to throb with angry life. The captain's voice, still husky with sleep, rose above the din of the anchor chains, and there was small space of time in which to step with my servants and baggage ashore. It was thus that I found myself at half-past six o'clock one morning, two days before Christmas, on the steep left bank of the Irrawaddy at Thabeit-kyin. On the slope of the hills, and farther south on the low foreshore, clustered the village houses, the post and telegraph office, the barracks of the military police, and the Government rest-house. Few of the inhabitants were yet astir.

In the white mist the forms of Panthay muleteers, the nozzling heads of mules, were faintly visible. On a pile of flour-sacks two policemen lay asleep; the one a Sikh from the Punjab, the other a Gurkha from Nepaul. They lay here guarding Her Majesty's stores, on a spot that in the flood season is buried under water deep enough to float a man-of-war. As I stood beside them and looked down on the silent and seemingly motionless river, the grey mists rolling away in successive folds gradually turned to cloud, and as they climbed skywards, touched by the early rays of the sun, passed into phantoms of the rarest beauty. Everywhere the morning was now breaking, and from my vantage-ground I could trace the climbing light on the face of the opposite hills. The steamer was fast disappearing at the end of a long grey reach of the river, and I turned with a feeling of some loneliness—for it is a lonely place—to the prospect of a stay at Thabeit-kyin.

To-day, after five years, I am here again under different conditions. It is the eve of the monsoon and the season is charged with the sense of great transformations. Luminous clouds climb in fantastic forms up

THABEIT-KYIN

the ladders of heaven, and all day long their pageantry fills the eye. Purple banks and curtains in lone corners of the horizon speak of the gathering rain, and at evening great shadowy drifting forms, grey, purple and ink-black, sweep over the world.

Summer is over. And yet, such is the strange medley of the seasons here, Spring laughing and youthful, is everywhere abroad; in the green delicate tracery of great trees; in the cherry-like bloom and laburnum gold of acacias; in the purple clusters of the *pinma*, soon to be shaken from their boughs by torrents of driving rain.

PANTHAY MULETEER

But on the hill-slopes all is withered and barren. Each shrub and tree stands clear of its neighbour, every leaf of the under-world is dead. If some forest creature, a deer or a panther, were to start from the river's edge, one could trace every movement of it against the hill-side, as it bore upwards through the skeleton maze of trunks. A month hence the jungle will be all but impenetrable. And there is colour in all this, and such variety as goes to the making of landscapes; green little valleys, ruddy brown hills, a river of purple silk; and cloud shadows alternating with the light on peaks and slopes and wooded lanes of water.

Thabeit-kyin is the port of Mogôk, capital of the Ruby-mines district, and this circumstance gives it its character. At this little village all the mining machinery, the electric plant, the batteries and engines of the company, have been landed. Through this little postern gate, the wealth of Capelan has passed for centuries on its way to the great world;

to the treasuries of kings, to the fingers of princes, to the necks of beautiful women ; to the making of one, the undoing of another. Yet of all this there is little trace in the sleepy lineaments of Thabeit-kyin. The red stream of wealth has left it a quiet village. Three or four times a week the steamers call here ; every morning at this season small caravans of pack-mules set out for the Ruby mines, and every day at noon, or evening, long lines of weary mules file in to this the last stage of their journey. Bullock carts and buffalo carriages creak and toil along the road. But there is no trace of any abounding life or vigour. No one hurries here but the new-comer ; and a day's delay in effecting a start for the mines, or the waste of a forenoon in adjusting the load of a single mule, are regarded with mild complacency by the idlers of the place. The village Headman in pink silk, sits on his hams in the shade and looks gravely on, the caretaker of the rest-house ambles to and fro in his loin-cloth, interjecting philosophic remarks, the caravan-man pulls a cord, mumbles in a strange Celestial *patois*, and makes prolonged journeys between the waiting baggage and his shed in the little hollow by the landing-place. Sixty miles from here there are rubies, *the finest rubies in the world ;* but at Thabeit-kyin there is indolence and peace.

Remote as the plaçe is, strange people drift here from far corners of the world. Beech-combers and other adventurers ; Australians, who have failed on Thursday Island ; discharged soldiers, who have fought over half the empire, or say they have ; voluble half-castes with restless eyes. They drift here drawn by the spell of the Ruby, and are undeterred by the company's type-written warnings in all the rest-houses on the way to the mines, that " by going to Mogôk, they are undertaking a tiresome journey to no purpose."

CHAPTER XLV

ON THE ROAD

SIXTY-ONE miles of cart-road cover the distance from the river to the mines. They say a motor-car is on its way from Europe, and that when it comes the favoured traveller will rush across in a day. I wonder what the placid cattle, the stout little ponies and the nervous mules as they come tinkling down the hill-side will think of their new competitor ; but for my part, I prefer the leisurely ride on horseback, up the cobbled bridle-paths, over the level rice-fields, and through the bamboo aisles of the forest. There are houses by the way, equipped for the European traveller ; villages and outposts ; and great company for one who cares for it. There are

Panthay mule-men, packmen from the Shan hills, bullock-carters and armed men in the service of the King. There are convoys of rationing mules and ponies, with the comfortable air that distinguishes all Government animals from the lean and ragged beasts of the Panthay caravans. There is a painted gig being carried up on a bullock-cart for a successful ruby-trader ; a smart led pony equipped with an English saddle, in the care of a Musulman groom ; there are carved and gilded poles and mosaic Buddhas, and other articles of monastic decoration ; the outcome of some one's success in the gamble of life at Mogôk.

It is a life fraught with vicissitude, and the pious builder of a gilded monastery, the late owner of a big house at Kyatpyin, is to-day the philosophic driver of a bullock-cart. Fortune has turned her back upon him ; but she cannot conceal the merit he has won by his piety, and cart-driver though he has become, he still remains Kyaung-taga U Saw, " Venerable-Builder-of-a-Monastery " Saw ; and herein dwells the wisdom of the innocent.

Wapyi-daung, ten and a half miles from the river, is a little village in a stockade, and its only street is the highway, which enters it at one gate and leaves it at the other. Kyauklebin, the next halting-place, is six miles farther on. It is a hamlet by the highway, where the latter descends to cross by a black bridge over a stream. Facing the rest-house is a military outpost, enclosed within a ditch and wall. At the gate a sentry, with bayonet fixed, walks to and fro through the twenty-four hours, and through it, over the narrow drawbridge, enter the long trains of rationing mules, the armed men afoot between Mogôk and the river, and the elephants laden with military stores. The great swaying beasts, as they enter, dwarf the little houses of the post, and I wonder in how many minutes they could trample down the whole interior of wood and thatch. In a little while the Sikh commandant calls, in his sword and sash, to pay his civilities and to say that all is well at the post. The day drifts slowly on to afternoon. The village cocks crow to each other ; a traveller passes down the road ; hard by in the little stream under the black bridge, ducks cackle and dive in the shallows, and the village girls laugh as they bathe and fill their waterpots for the day's use. Great trees fling their shadows over the stream, and through the foliage there are visible the spires of a monastery, the brown roofs of cottages. The picture is one of rustic beauty, that lingers in the recollection long after one has left the country.

The road from Kyauklebin ascends continually, till it attains the summit of a pass, from which there is visible the great outline of the Shwé-u-Daung, its precipices and ruddy downs fringed by dark woods. The country here is of a massive order and an impression of sombre grandeur pervades it at this season.

At Shwe-Nyaung-Bin there is another outpost, which stands on the crest of a conical hill, set in the midst of an amphitheatre of mountains. It is good in the heart of this wilderness, in the gathering dusk, to hear the quick enlivening peal of the bugles of England. There is no British soldier nearer than Shwebo, sixty miles away, but there is much in a great tradition. From Shwe-Nyaung-Bin, the road descends to the river of Kin. Dark peaks here rise up into the clouds as if from the bowels of the valley. One of these, darker and more rugged than the rest, is surmounted by a pagoda in ruins. In the valley bottom there are rice-fields, and by the edge of the little river, red with silt, slumbers the village of Kin. Under the jack-trees, on the river's fringe, sit through the noon the blue-coated muleteers, and all day long packmen cross and recross the little stream. Kin was of old notorious for its dacoits, and many a traveller bound for Mandalay with jewels for the court was waylaid and killed in its neighbourhood. Of a later period of lawlessness, there is record in a stone by the wayside raised to the " Memory of Jemadar-Adjutant Devi Sahai Misr and Sepoy Javala Singh, of the Ruby Mines Military Police Battalion, who fell in action with dacoits near this spot on December 18th, 1889."

From Hkabine on to Capelan is a matter of ten miles by the cart-road. The cobbled mule-track is shorter. The clouds gather in great masses overhead and thunder is abroad. Showers of rain fall; but under the sweeping curtains of cloud, views of the greatest calibre expand to a distant horizon. Reaching its summit, the road drops gently into the little valley which for four centuries was vaguely known to Europe as Capelan.

CHAPTER XLVI

CAPELAN

THE village of Kyatpyin, from which the name Capelan appears to have sprung, lies in the centre of the valley, at an elevation of 4400 feet above sea level. Although it never snows in these regions, the cold, even in the valley, is apt to be severe in winter. It is never very hot and the character of the climate is testified to by the rosy cheeks and fresh complexions of the children of the English at Kyatpyin. The village clusters about the roadside, and gathers much charm from the hollyhocks and roses which blossom about the houses and from the flights of white and dark pagodas which decorate the knolls and eminences about it. The valley is green and meadow-clad; and in the rains, when the waters accumulate, it recovers part of its old-time character of a lake. The Père Giuseppe d'Amato, the first European to visit the mines (about 1833), observes of it that "the soil is uneven and full of marshes, which form seventeen small lakes, each having a particular name. And it is this soil," he says, "which is so rich in mineral treasures."

But the chief glory of Kyatpyin resides in the beautiful mountains which encircle it. The most notable of these, the Chinthé Taung, or Lion Hill, is seven thousand feet in height. No effort of art could achieve a more exquisite tapestry of red heather and rounded slopes, defined by green woods along the water-courses, than is here presented to the eye. Its beauty is vivified by the constant play of light and shadow on it as the clouds travel overhead. Another conspicuous landmark is the Pingu-Taung, a conical hill, which holds aloft against the sky a small pagoda. This hill has long enjoyed the reputation of great riches, and baskets of earth have been taken from it of which the half have been rubies, so the people say. The Ruby-mines Company has been less fortunate; and it was here in the effort to wrest from the Pingu-Taung its store of rubies, that it wasted a great portion of its capital. Ten years ago Kyatpyin was the centre of the company's efforts; but the tide of enterprise has moved to the neighbouring valley of Mogôk, and Kyatpyin is now all but deserted.

CHAPTER XLVII

MOGÔK

THE TOWN

AS I look out of my window on the night of my arrival at Mogôk, I see before me, spread out in the valley bottom, the town of rubies, mist-clad, pricked with fire; and out of the mist, effulgent, the electric arcs of the company, in scattered *échelon*, blaze like sapphires. The Alpine forms of mountains rise up in vague outline above the valley. The rain-cleared sky is lit with a galaxy of stars. A silence as of death lies over the town, where every human emotion is afoot. The miner suddenly grown rich, the gambler poised between the strokes of fate, the sorter dreaming of his England, the tired digger, the easy beauty—all of them lie buried here in the mist. It is a curious spectacle, with nothing in it of the East; northern, rather, with its blue mists and its peaks strung like supernatural battlements against the stars.

In the morning when I wake and open my window to look again on the spectacle, I see a grey sky stamped with a settled melancholy; a sky that means, it would seem, neither to cry nor to smile; and down in the valley the town of rubies, clothed in and roofed over with grey iron, in a veil of mist. All about it are the peaked mountains, pale and unreal at their summits, green at their thresholds.

It is the day of the big bazaar and the market-place is astir and quick with traffic. Along the yellow road, all hammered matrix of rubies, sit the market-women with great hats on their heads, and the produce of their gardens spread before them. Fruits and vegetables abound. Here are small tomatoes done up in little cane cylinders, through the pattern of which the red fruit glints, baskets of scarlet raspberries, piles of flowers, and a variety of strange products from mushrooms to bamboo-roots. Down these lanes the crowd sways, laughing, talking, bargaining,

THE MARKET WOMEN

while the sun streams down upon the gay colours of their clothes. It is the East, the indubitable East; but clean, neat, and prosperous; the Silken East of the little-known peoples. Of those who come and go, some are clad in blue and red, in breast-cloth, coat, and stomacher and leggings; with crescent silver necklets, big again as the moon, about their throats. Some are of the Shan, flat of nose—'tis the failing of these people—fair of skin, with even a rosy flush in their cheeks; plump, waddling, comely, and comfortable. All are over-topped by the great hat, symbol of the Far East. Here and there in the crowd is a Burmese damsel, in silk, velvet, pearls and a yellow translucent parasol, the comforter of some ruby king or European adventurer.

Towering above the line of slight houses is the keep of a prosperous trader, all of stone, very high; and from its mid-storey protrudes the head of a retainer, pipe in mouth, his slit eyes restless, absorbing. At the window of a house in the main street, barred like a leopard's cage, sit groups of Chetti, naked and intent, sorting the rubies which lie in gleaming trays upon their knees. In a hut at a corner, where the stream of yellow tailings runs by, a tanner from Oudh sits at work on the leopard-skins of a miner. A countryman of his across the way rolls cigarettes by the hour, selling them to the passers-by. At intervals there are Chinese eating-houses, equipped with little tables and stools, and dressers fitted out with blue china, and chopsticks, and pewter spoons. The fare is varied and savoury, and pigs' trotters, plump fowls, cabbages and ducks, hang from strings like a curtain, behind which the cook, bland, indefatigable, plies his calling, a Ciro *in partibus*. Of a morning these houses fill with motley crowds of Burmans, Shan, Panthay, Meingtha, Paloung, and Lishaw, who crowd round the little tables and feed in groups, bowl to chin, their feet perched high up on the narrow stools. It is a replica, with the difference of place and people and ways, of the scenes that characterise any French or Italian town between the blessed hours of the midday meal. The company is jovial and loud hoarse laughter peals from the crowded interiors out into the sunlit road. Blue is the prevailing colour, from the pale hue of the Chinaman's much-washed coat to the dark indigo of the Meingtha woman's lofty turban.

It is a great tide of life that sweeps in here on these fifth days of the year. The people of the hills begin to come in on the previous evening and nearly all of those who have to come a long way sleep over-night at Mogôk, so that the day of prelude to the bigger day, has a name to itself —Zay-beit-nay—" The Eve of Market Day." The permanent shops are kept open throughout the week ; the shops of the haberdashers and the tinmen, of the sellers of Gautamas and *htis*, of gold leaf and parasols ; the booths of the little pedlars. At one end, in a quiet side-street, is a long range of tea-shops, where green and pickled tea is sold in their dusky interiors by Shan and Paloung. Lastly, there is the covered bazaar. The shimmer of a hundred delicate colours of silk, the coming and going of many races in the half-lit interior, while the sun blazes without, make of it a spectacle meet for the most fastidious eye.

THE STRANGE WORLD OF THE DIGGER

Following on by the roadside runs swiftly a stream, yellow as any Tiber. A few yards, and I step into the strange world of the digger. Picture a soil, yellow and scarred with pits, honeycombed like a burrow ; and at each pit's mouth, a rubbish heap. Overhead, an intricate array of bamboos, like the tracery of dahabeahs at the Kasr-el-nil, and in the background blue alpine mountains shimmering in the sun like steel. Set in this picture are the miners : people in blue clothes and yellow parasol-like hats ; people in loose trousers, showing legs tattoed with the figures of tigers and dragons ; a people lithe of limb, small of stature, with muscles of iron. The process of mining is stupefying in its simplicity.

There is a straight bamboo twenty feet high stuck like a mast in the yellow soil. Near its top, through a slit, works another horizontally; at one end of it a make-weight, a basket filled with mud or stones, at the other a long cane reaching down like the line of a fisherman ; last of all a bucket to hold water or mud, as the case may be. If it be water, your miner stands at the little pit's mouth, lowers the bucket, lets it fill and come up again, the cane slipping through his fingers ; and on its emerging, tilts the water from it into a channel, down which it runs yellow and turbid to swell the stream by the roadside. If mud, the digger in the pit fills it with a spade and lets it run up to the man overhead, who empties it with a jerk of his wrist on to an adjoining mud-heap. When this heap has grown big enough it is washed, and the rubies survive.

At a corner, in the dazzling sun, a small child stoops, scraping the yellow earth from a dry heap into a shallow basket. A child at play it would seem. But when the little basket is laden she carries it away to where a woman is at work—a comely woman, in a dark blue kilt, close to her figure as she sits, a pale yellow coat and pink silk bound about her coils of black hair. Her wide sleeves lift as she works, revealing her slender arms. And her business in life—so much at least as she transacts here—is to let the yellow stream run through each basket of earth, till all the concealing clay is washed away and pebbles alone survive ; from this remnant to pick out with precision rubies, which she slips under her tongue till her mouth is full. The occupation has its merits.

Under the bamboo houses and across the plain, making pools and puddles, run in bewildering variety the little streams of yellow mud.

Such is ruby-mining in its indigenous simplicity. A short way off the Company is at work, and the débris and offal of its energy are like the output of a mud volcano. But of the Company another time. Let us turn back and consider a part of the bazaar that is without a double in the world.

THE RUBY BAZAAR

In a very little space off the main street, and scarcely wider than a cottage kitchen-garden, there is gathered a dense throng of wide-hatted men. Their wide hats are clustered so close together, like minnows round a bait, that you are stricken with curiosity to know what they are about. You crush into the crowd and find yourself in the midst of the buyers and sellers of rubies.

In the centre of each group there is a shining brass tray on a stool, and it looks when you see it like a disc of beaten gold in the sun. By it sits the buyer, ringed by satellites, each of whom believes himself an expert. Then there is a swaying in the crowd, and a miner edges in, picturesque in his wide trousers and great flapping hat, and subsides by the tray on his haunches. There is a little cloth bag in his hands, tied very tightly round the neck with string. Slowly he unwinds the string and the masked eyes of the buyer glitter. No word is spoken. The seller is in no hurry. When at last the long string has been unwound and the hand clasping the little globe of cloth relaxes its amatory grip, the mouth of the bag is turned down, and from its interior there flows into the tray the red stream of stones.

Then the buyer moves. His long delicate nervous fingers reach out swiftly, and in an instant the little pyramid is spread over the shining

WASHING

disc, each stone blinking in the light. For the next few seconds, and still in silence, there is an eloquent pantomime of fingers. The good and the bad stones are unerringly separated from each other, and formed into two little piles ; the bad being pushed back to the seller's end of the tray, the good brought instinctively a little closer to the buyer. At this stage discussion supervenes. All the critics have their say ; the seller waxes eloquent, the buyer cold and deprecatory. Thus the duel proceeds.

There is a score of these trays, like suns in the close cluster of men. And that is nearly all there is to tell. Like all that is truly Eastern, the process is simple in its character, limitless in its fascination. One can describe in a minute what one can look upon with interest for hours.

Considering the men, it will be seen that of the buyers, many are foreigners. Here is one, scant of clothing, heavy of paunch, shaven as to his head—a Chetti. He is backed by a hundred thousand pounds of capital. A yard away is a little man who talks English mellifluously. He is the son of a local Crœsus, whose house, carved and wrought in stone, overlooks the market-place. Father and son are Hindus of Amritsar, small-headed, mean-looking, insignificant of figure, as you would think they were of brain. There is little in the circuit of their own small occupation you could teach them. While the son is hidden

THE CONNOISSEUR

here in the throng of miners his father, clad in an English shooting-coat, sits behind the iron-barred doorway of his house, a tray of purchased rubies on his knees. A few years ago he came here a poor man ; one of those people who follow humbly in the rear of advancing troops. Money adhered to his fingers. In a little while he began to lend it at usurious interest, on the security of gold and rubies. Then he took to the ruby trade ; and now he exports his rubies to London, to Paris, and to Delhi ; this fishy little man, with the face of a rat, and its fathomless eyes. His house reveàls his character. Its forefront bears ostentatious testimony to his wealth. Its dark interior, its bolted trap-doors and narrow tortuous stairs, exhibit the quality of his mind ; and the stone walls and the iron bars, strong as those of a tiger's cage, speak plainly of his caution, his cowardice, his rooted doubt in the stability of any power. For

U HMAT, THE RUBY KING

centuries his forebears have not known what it was to stand up in the open to any man. Yet withal a polite man with a manner that verges on the obsequious. He is one of the most regular and considerable of the company's local customers, and if you were to see his son walk into the agent's office to buy a thousand pounds' worth of rubies, you might take him for a lamplighter. But there is great store of insolence in his heart, and he can be pitiless on occasion.

Another great trader in Mogôk is U Hmat, "the ruby king." The title is a little fanciful perhaps, but U Hmat was great here in the days before any Englishman had come within sight of Mogôk. He is not a foreigner like the big Chetti and the little man from Amritsar; but a native of the soil. He lives some distance from the market-place, in a rambling wooden house on piles surrounded by limes and pomegranates. At one end he has built himself a strong-room of brick, in which lie hidden, according to popular tradition, rubies of extraordinary value. U Hmat is seldom seen abroad. He goes, it is said, in terror of his life; and his courtyard is thronged with retainers, who make for him a kind of personal bodyguard. But in bygone days he travelled every year to Mandalay with a present of rubies and was received in audience by the king. He is the builder of monasteries and pagodas; but is said to be less lavish in this respect than most of his compatriots in Burma. He is believed accordingly by his European neighbours to have "his head screwed on the right way." His character for economy is the topic of favourable discussion at the little dinner-tables of the settlement, and it is a commonplace of opinion that he is the only Burman at the mines who is not a fool. Let it be added that he is the father of a pretty daughter, whose jewels are the despair of every other woman in Mogôk, and that he keeps her in strict seclusion, lest some adventurous youth should steal away her heart, or her person, or both. He has been good enough however, to show me some of her most beautiful jewels.

All about the market-place in the little streets which ray out from it in the direction of the mines, the Ruby-cutters toil. Each man sits before a slab of grey stone, with a pile of little sticks a few inches long beside him. In the head of each of these a ruby is embedded in hard black paste, and the cutter, taking it up, rubs the face of the ruby slowly up and down on the surface of the grindstone, till the attrition wears away a facet. A wheel and pedal supplement the process in some of the larger shops; but the method is the same. Of these cutters there are at least fifty in the town.

Near the pits where the diggers are at work is the ruby-mart proper, which is open all the week. The long open sheds, with their low earthen floors and thatched roofs, stand in the midst of the turmoil of the mining. The yellow stream of tailings flows by the trays of the

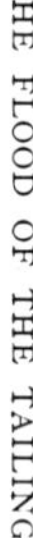

THE FLOOD OF THE TAILINGS

ruby-dealers, and the unceasing swing of the bamboo levers makes a restless rhythm against the sky. Here every morning of the year, a hundred brass trays clink to the musical fall of the precious stones, and the big-hatted men sit in long avenues under the pent thatch. There is scarcely any noise, for all the bargaining is made by the play of fingers under cloth. No self-respecting dealer will ever name the price of a ruby, and the Englishman's blunt question, " What is the price of this ? " brings stupefaction to the faces of all present. By each group there sits a *pwéza*, or broker, whose business it is to advise and negotiate a sale. He acts as a kind of arbitrator, and as a break on excessive demands. He knows a little about the quality and local value of stones, and is reasonably honest. I have said there is little noise, for few words are spoken. There is less haste. You would think these good people had a thousand years in which to buy and sell.

THE COMPANY

Little as the company may seem to shareholders in England, and to many who live in their sheltered parishes, in the shadow of old-world steeples, never having heard of this little fraction of their mighty empire, the company *in situ*, in the valley of Mogôk, is something of a power. It stands in a way for the supremacy of the white man ; for the colossus of capital ; for the State. The company's agent is a potentate in his own right. Elsewhere, in nearly every other district of the province there is only one great man, only one big house, only one repository of power. But at Mogôk there are two ; the head of the district and the company's agent. And there are some who would like to see an extension of the company's authority. One morning, as I rode over the mines with one of its engineers, an outspoken sort of man, he propounded to me a scheme for the rearrangement of matters at Mogôk. There should be, he said, a fence made about the company's territories, and within this fence the company should be supreme. No one else should have a word to say in the matter. " Do you think, now," he continued, " that Coolgardie, Kimberley, or Klondyke could be run on the lines of these ruby mines ? No, sir ! they manage their own affairs, with no Government of India to interfere with them."

A vision, as of a self-willed and imperious dame, drifted across my eyes and made me smile in the face of my downright companion. " My dear sir," I said, " there will never be a Coolgardie, or a Kimberley, or a Klondyke in the Indian Empire, and I am afraid you will not get that fence."

Nevertheless, the company to all the little people of the valley is a power ; and not the less so, because it is mysteriously linked with the State, which in all ages here has been the king, the fountain of all force.

The company began with immense expectations and great hopes. The rubies that for generations had shed a lustre over the court of Ava seized the imagination of investors in Mark Lane. The application of scientific methods to the working of mines that had for centuries been famous would, it was readily believed, increase their output enormously. The shrewd estimate of Tavernier might have occasioned some pause in these lively expectations; but Tavernier lived in the days of James I., and in the days of James I. there were neither steam-engines nor drills; and in short, a new era had dawned, and those who were early afoot would profit by their timeliness a hundred-fold. Accordingly the shares of the new company were boomed, and there was competition to possess them. The company was not less sanguine. It agreed to pay four hundred thousand rupees a year to the Government of India for the privilege of working the mines. The company's agent was granted a salary of £4,000 a year. An establishment of secretaries, engineers, clerks, sorters and miners was conceived on an ample scale, and thousands of pounds' worth of machinery was despatched to a far-distant scene of operations.

The most ambitious method of work was immediately adopted. The people of the soil who for generations had worked the mines, had come to recognise four methods of extraction: the method of pits sunk into the alluvium of the valleys; of open cutting in the hill-sides, over which water was led; of working in caves and fissures; of quarries by blasting in beds of calcspar in the limestone of the valley. Of these methods, that of alluvial digging offered a small but certain reward. Nature had here already performed the process of excavation, and in the bottom of the valley (once a lake) had put down a layer of ruby soil, washed from the sides of the surrounding hills. Here the hereditary diggers were at work, and in the fat alluvium the stored rubies of centuries were waiting for the company to come and take them. But the company's head was just a little in the clouds, and it would have little to say to any but the most ambitious of the methods at its disposal. This was the method "of working in caves and fissures." From such caves the finest rubies ever found have been obtained, and visions of extraordinary wealth opened up to those who claimed that the right course for the company to take was to drive its boring engines into the bowels of the mountains and wrest from there the perfect jewels in their keeping.

But it is one thing to know that there are rubies of price stored in the interior of a mountain in front of you; it is another to find them. The company was embarked upon a policy of adventure. Its slender capital was poured out like water. Here and there a ruby of price was found; here and there a pocket of unfractured stones rewarded the arduous labour of those who drilled into the darkness of the hills. And

2 A

meanwhile anxious shareholders waited for a dividend that never came; an anxious Government, prone to the prompt collection of its dues, waited for its rent; and hope, delusive, receded farther and farther away as the company's capital approached extinction. The value of its shares dropped down and soon touched the farcical limit of eighteenpence. When it was all but too late the company turned to the obvious remedy: it recalled its enterprising battalions, and began washing for rubies in the soft soil of the valley. It was soon apparent that the prosperity of the company was becoming a simple matter of arithmetic. It was found that in every truck of earth sent up from the alluvial pits there was on an average a certain proportion of rubies. The company's object became to produce each truck at a cost less than the value of the rubies it contained, and to produce as many trucks as possible. The history of the labours that followed has been a history of devotion to this idea. The cost of production has been steadily reduced. Salaries now are but a lean shadow of their opulent past. The Government rent has been lowered to two hundred thousand rupees a year; its demand for the payment of arrears has been withdrawn; and the substitution of electricity for steam and water-power for fuel, the multiplication of diggers and machinery, have completed the turn in the direction of prosperity. It is admitted that the company has now entered on a period of quiet but steady prosperity; and its shares that once went a-begging for eighteenpence have risen to a pound. Let us consider in more detail some of its methods of work.

The individual digger, who survives only under the paternal care of the State, takes out each year a licence from the company, for which he pays it a royalty of twenty rupees. Equipped with his licence he proceeds to dig a well in the manner already described and the excavated mud, quickly washed, is his harvest. When the well begins to tumble in, or to get flooded with water, he quits it and proceeds to dig another. The company excavates on a larger scale. It begins by taking a slice of several acres off the surface of the valley. It calls this "top-stripping," and the process means that it is taking off the layer of irrelevant matter that accumulated on the deposit of ruby alluvium after the lake had finally dried up. This upper layer is valueless, and for the most part it is thrown aside, unexamined. The ruby-bearing soil, known as *byon*, is then attacked by an army of diggers. Day by day the pit grows wider and deeper; and all this is no more than if navvies were at work digging earth for a railway embankment. There is nothing at the ruby mines more calculated to provoke astonishment in a spectator expecting to see advanced methods. For it is still sheer, primitive, human labour—the labour of the pick-axe, the crow-bar and the spade; the kind of thing that flourished soon after the Stone Age went out.

THE SPOIL OF THE JUNGLE

All day long, and far into the small hours of the night the blue-coated diggers toil incessantly. As the pit deepens, masses of hard white limestone, cleared of all surrounding earth, stand out like jagged islands. On the floor of the pit, rails are laid for the trucks to carry away the earth, and near the diggers these rails ray out like fans from a turn-table. Thus each digger has a truck at his elbow. From the pit to the washing engines on the hill a brace of endless wires moves on pulleys. The trucks are hitched on to these, and move as the wires move. But at a little distance the wires are invisible and then the trucks moving slowly in a perpetual double procession, as they go up and down, look a little mysterious. Each truck as it climbs the hill to the washing-machine is seized upon and emptied into a trough, and as its contents are poured out, coolies in savage-looking rain-coats bear down on them with swift jets of water. Under this vigorous solvent, clay and gravel immediately part company; the clay to descend with the water into a pool, whence it is hoisted away to the river.

The gravel is now classified by means of a moving cylinder of graduated mesh. Through the mesh it falls into the hands of the sorters waiting below. But to lessen their labours there is now in use an intermediate machine, the most interesting of those at work, and known as the pulsator. It offers a simple illustration of the application of fundamental laws to human use. Of all stones that enter the cylinder of mesh, the ruby is the heaviest, and all lighter stones can therefore be safely ignored. The pulsator separates the light stones from the heavy ones. It is an iron bucket, with a small aperture at the bottom, in which a piston moves up and down. Water pours into the bucket, and as the valve of the piston lifts, it rushes through this aperture, taking with it the heavier stones which by the constant churning of the piston and the sucking action of the water have sunk more quickly to the bottom. The piston is hidden from sight in the mass of gravel, and its movement makes the gravel pulse as if it were alive. The sucking of the water can be felt by placing one's open hand on the surface: it is slowly but irresistibly drawn down; and here, buried in the midst of the warm gravel, one feels as if it lay upon the pulsing heart of the machine.

I have spoken of the swift jet of water which is flung on the contents of each truck as it reaches the mouth of the washing machine, and of its object—viz. the freeing of the gravel from mud and clay. The process is completed by a mechanical separator before the gravel enters the pulsator. The separator consists of three revolving pans, which circle round iron combs let into their midst. Water pours in and the pans revolve from dawn till dark. At the close of each day the gravel is drawn; but all day long the water that has poured through them has borne away the yellow clay, not unmixed with a small percentage of rubies. This clay is distributed outside the works, and as it heaps up it makes a cone like that of a mud volcano, furrowed and built up, and furrowed again, by the water hastening on its way.

The motive power is electricity, and its action is communicated in the ordinary way by means of innumerable wheels and endless leather bands. The whole purpose of the machinery, which has been adapted from that in use at the diamond mines at Kimberley, is first to clear the gravel of clay, and then to classify it and make it ready for the finer work of the sorter. As the gravel pours out of the machines it is taken away in trays and flung in a heap upon a table. The sorter then, with a sweep of his arm, spreads out the dark red mass in a thin layer. With his iron blade he separates this layer still further and rapidly picks out the little pink stones, the palpable rubies, which lie gleaming in the mass. With another swift movement, he sends the surviving gravel flying into a truck by his side. When this is full it is taken away and its contents are subjected to a slower and more patient scrutiny by native assistants. Many rubies are picked out by them ; but there should be none in this second sorting of any size or value. There is yet a third stage. In the outer yard wait the *khanézimas*, women whose hereditary privilege it is to buy this refuse and search it for what it may contain. No man is permitted to share in this perquisite of the women of Mogôk. It is here—where the Gentlemen sorters sit, at the mouths of the grinding machines, swiftly reaping their precious harvest ; and their wild assistants pore over the refuse spread before them in the sun ; and *khanézimas* in strange attire scratch like hens amidst the débris—that the human interest again becomes paramount. Their place, at least, can never be taken by any machinery.

About sunset, and as the dark comes on, all the northern end of the valley where the company is at work, breaks out in discs of light, and as one looks down into the mist-clad valley lit with these electric fires, it presents a spectacle of unexpected beauty. All about the valley the great shadowy outlines of the mountains loom up against the sky ; and in the deep pits under the flare of the lights, the miners dig, and the trucks creep along the double rails, till the stars pale again with the coming of the dawn.

In the clay of the valleys, buried side by side with the rubies, there are found relics of a distant past—the fish-hooks and net-weights of the lake dwellers, the axe-heads and weapons of primitive man. It is a strange contrast that is here presented, and one's thoughts reach out with sympathy across the wide gulf of time, to the dead men of whom these are the few surviving relics. They are beautifully made, these first instruments.

But the primitive life is not quite dead yet. On the mountains which overshadow the valley, lifting their great heads up amongst the stars, there are dark evergreen forests perpetually wrapped in gloom. In these recesses herds of wild elephants still have room to wander, in their shelter the tiger still stalks his easy prey, and herds of deer, breaking from the coverts of the hills, look down with startled wonder on the strange scene being enacted in the valley. In the silence of the dark nights, they have many strange and unknown onlookers, these miners digging for the little stones under the blue electric flame.

THE GAMBLE OF LIFE

There are very fewe that are perfect in all pointes, specially being great, for they have always some faultes and spottes that are covered and hidden ; but right perfect there are none or very few, and not many men have any great knowledge therein.—LINSCHOTEN.

In the lives of those who traffic in precious stones there are many vicissitudes, and stories are not lacking of the great finds that are occasionally made. Even the *khanézimas* who pick the rejected gravel of the company, are credited with substantial rewards. Only the other day a woman declared she had found a ruby of price in this refuse, and she made a great clamour of joy on finding it. But there were witnesses to prove that the stone was found elsewhere by a man who was not in possession of a licence, and so the matter had to be settled in a court of law ; the company *versus* the owner of the stone. And not very long ago a Burman found a great ruby which was valued at £10,000. The company, at his request, sent it to England to be cut, and meanwhile lent him money on its security. But when it was cut, its value was found to have fallen to £2,000, and even for this price there is no one willing to buy it. Its owner has become too poor to redeem it. It is not improbable that great stones have been found of which the world at large never hears, and may never hear ; it is not impossible that once in a way the digger's pick unearths before his eyes a stone of price, and that he pockets it when no one is looking. The system of searching the miners is not very careful or very complete, and there are loopholes for evasion. But it is not easy to discover a little stone in a great block of yellow clay, and it seems probable that in the main the company gets its due. Once in a while the rubies in the valley bottom are found in a cluster, all together, and this is at once the chance of the company and of the digger. For rubies found in this way are usually rubies of purity and size. Down in the valley, in one of the pits, there rise up a pair of great boulders near which a miner found a fortune. Every grain of earth has been cleared away from about these monoliths, in the search after the precious stone.

The natural vicissitudes of mining are increased in the case of rubies by the difficulty of estimating the value of the uncut stone. A large ruby, of perfect colour and without flaw, is the most precious of all stones; and after it reaches a certain size it is almost impossible to put any limit to its value. Such stones, it is needless to say, seldom disturb the spirit of the local miner or the local dealer. But even in the case of smaller stones of fine colour, a just estimate of value can with difficulty be formed till they have passed through the ordeal of cutting. There is thus always a large margin for a gamble in the ruby trade.

And these natural vicissitudes are heightened by the character of the people. A Burman no sooner finds a stone of price than he embarks on a lavish expenditure. He must build a house, he must wear fine clothes, he must have a following of good fellows to share with him, while they enhance, his good fortune. But above all things he must accumulate merit, and lay up for himself great spiritual store to help him over his next incarnation. And to this end he must build a monastery, erect a pagoda, and bestow largesse upon the monks. When the sources of his wealth run dry he sheds these sudden glories one by one; all save the last and that is an inalienable investment.

When I came up to the ruby mines, I met on the way, where Yé-Wé village lies in a circle of the hills, a horseman on a quick-stepping little grey pony. For some time I had seen him making his way along the bridle path. He was the only other European within the circuit of a wide horizon, so I waited to greet him. He proved to be an Inspector of the ruby mines company, whose business it is to deal with illicit mining; and he told me as we rode forward many little tales of the illicit miner. Under the arrangement made with the company, it has the monopoly of the ruby tract. The interests of the people of the soil are protected in this, that any man can dig for himself so long as he buys at a fixed price a permit from the company, which it cannot refuse to give him.

Persons found mining without a licence are liable to be imprisoned for six months; and if more diggers are found at work than the licence provides for, the extra men are fined. But to satisfy a magistrate and secure a conviction, it is necessary to seize the illicit miner in the act. And it is to the accomplishment of this feat that my companion's energies are directed. The illicit miner is like the jungle-fowl of these hills in his talent for effecting an hairbreadth escape. Thus, when all the inspector's plans have been laid and success seems assured, he and his minions rush the mine; a ditch or obstacle intervenes, there is a second's pause; the surprised miner, leaving his tools, bounds out of his pit and plunges into the jungle. A pick-axe and a spade are the only harvest. But occasionally he is caught, pick in hand, his heap of ruby earth beside him, surprise upon his upturned face; and thereafter six months' enforced leisure await him in which to think of revenge. The spy—evil, if necessary, excrescence upon the society of honest men—is the pivot of the inspector's system; and the spy does not always get his information without betraying the confidence of a friend. When such confidences are lacking, he sets out for a likely country and wanders about in the guise of a woodcutter, or innocent collector of herbs. Then one day he comes upon the miner, and if he has the skill, escapes suspicion, and by lying in wait along the faint footpaths of the jungle, discovers the locality of the mine. After that it is hot-foot back to his master, and a swift return with success or not, as may be, in the sequel. The illicit miner has his own developed system of defence. He posts his sentries on some crag or vantage-ground, to give warning of his antagonist's approach. And occasionally he buys up the spy who is sent to discover him. But your inspector, in spite of his occupation, is a very human fellow. Very glad to see you, very hospitable and friendly. This one lives at Kyatpyin in a little house by the highway, overgrown with wild roses, and happy with its little garden of English flowers, in which his children play.

FACETS

It takes time to enter fully into the beauty of Mogôk and its great mountains, of its mining town in the little valley, its grassy spaces and its low swelling hills. There is nothing quite like it anywhere else in Burma. The climate, even in the middle of May, at the height of the Burmese summer, is cool all day long, and of an evening one is tempted to stroll away over the hills in the happy fashion of a better land ; all is so green, the landscape so attractive, the blessed air so cool and fresh. About most of the bigger houses English flowers bloom; lilies and roses, the honeysuckle, the heart's-ease and the daisy. And even the huts of the people are not without their flowers. Every day it rains a little, and the clouds gather in fantastic glory over the heads of the mountains, and make splendid cushions for the sun to rest on. When the hill-sides are not green, they are a deep red which glows in the evening sunshine, or purple when they are far away. The colours are superb.

The town itself teems as I have shown with curious life ; and a great many races congregate in this little valley hidden away amongst the hills. From the green recreation ground, soon to be mined by the company for rubies, there comes of an evening the thunder of the polo-players, and the changing fortunes of the game are followed with interest by a motley crowd pressing against the palings. In a little pavilion the European ladies of the settlement assemble. At the far end of the ground, *chinlone*, the graceful football of the Burman, is played simultaneously with cricket and polo. Down the white road beyond the farther palings, a Chinaman sprints on his bicycle, his pigtail flying in the wind ; while his wife, her small feet crushed into doll-like shoes, makes her way across the grass as if she walked on stilts. Even the polo-players are a medley of cavalry officers from India, of ruby-sorters and

THE CHIEF MULLAH, THE NEPHEW OF THE SULTAN, AND THE HAJI NUR-UD-DIN (KO-SHWE-TIN)

mining experts, of the doctor, the magistrate, and the policeman, with a Sikh trooper thrown in to make a team. So it comes about that the young man sent from a London office to be a sorter of rubies may end by becoming an expert player at the most fashionable game in the world.

Beyond the polo-ground, its triple roof rising high above the heads of the players, is the Panthay mosque. Texts from the Koran in sheets of Arabic letters are wrapped about its inner pillars, and from its tower the muezzin daily calls the faithful to prayer. Of the worshippers many are Chinamen of the obvious type ; but some have a Muslim strain in them, the strain of the Arab and the Turk. One man, in a long white robe and red fez, might have come from toll-collecting at the Golden Horn ; another in a blue *gelabieh*, would pass unnoticed in the bazaars of Cairo. But the most striking figure of all is that of the chief Mullah, a man of great height, with the beard of a prophet and the mien of a Hebrew patriarch. He came out with me into his garden of camelias, clothed in a *caftan* of dark green taffeta, a tablet of gold embroidery that lay like the Urim and Thummim of the High-priest on his breast, a turban, and a conical cap embroidered in dark and pale blue. He was accompanied by a nephew of Ibrahim, the last Sultan of Yunnan, and the Haji Nur-ud-Din (Ko-Shwe-Tin). They were well aware, through the medium of Chinese newspapers published at Hongkong, of the progress of events in the world, and took much interest in the Sultan of Turkey's mission to the Chinese Emperor on behalf of the Musulmans of China. The Sultan of Rúm, he called him, so pervading is the tradition of the everlasting city.

Ko-Shwe-Tin, otherwise the Haji Nur-ud-Din, is a ruby-merchant who has lived at Mogôk for twenty years. He is effusive in his loyalty to the British throne, and was, it appears, of some help to our columns when they first advanced to Mogôk after the fall of Mandalay. But he is now putting behind him the secular life ; he is become a pillar of the Church ; and having made the pilgrimage to Mecca, he is resolved to devote the remainder of his life to pious works. He lives, in pursuance of this ideal, next to the mosque, and the best chamber of his house is set apart for the entertainment of the Patriarch, who has come on a visit to him from Talifu.

CHAPTER XLVIII

L'ENVOI

I LEFT this morning for Kyatpyin, by the bridle road that climbs over the hills behind the European settlement. It was a morning of great beauty, half-cloud, half-sunshine and the noble form of the Chinthé-Taung overtopped everything with its splendour.

MUSULMANS OF YUNNAN

I do not think that there is anywhere in the world a hill more beautiful than this. In the winter it wears a wonderful garb of ruddy pink and green, and at this season it is coloured in hues of emerald and of purple. And this comes of the long grass that covers all its shoulders and of the deep woods that lie between in the furrows and little valleys made by the rain. Moreover it is seven thousand feet in height and very noble in outline.

Soon after leaving Mogôk my pony was picking his way along the cobbled lanes in the village of Yé-boo. It lies in the hollow of the little valley and a willow-bordered stream runs by it. Its hedges are of pink roses twined upon *espaliers* of bamboo, and every lane is a double line of flowers, overlooked by silky peaches, and orange-groves, and ripening plums. Beyond it there is a great expanse of mountain-side, diversified with yellow hamlets and dark monastery spires. Every moment as the narrow bridle path ascends, the landscape widens, gaining in clarity and beauty, and with each step the little valley of Mogôk falls farther behind. All that is human of it grows less and less, shrinking away to its own proportions ; and the discontent of one, the satiety of another, the little pride, and the little jealousies, and the little animosities, are withered in the splendour of the broadening world.

It is a little valley, shut in by lofty mountains, and cut off from the world ; and those who go to live in it grow very tired of each other, very weary of looking at the blue-green hills and the shadows of the restless clouds. They have an article of faith that the only fools in Mogôk are the Burmese, who, finding rubies, give them away again in pious works for the sake of a vague and far-away Nirvana ; and down there in the midst of the turmoil of the trucks and engines, in the heart of the pits where the diggers toil, in the crowded market-place where the rubies gleam on brazen trays, in the maelstrom of the little mining town where thousands, from the untutored Meingtha digger to the cultivated English gentleman, labour ; giving all their time and zeal and a great part of their lives to the digging, the buying, and the selling of the little red stones, it seems very foolish indeed to give them away again to so shadowy an end as the accumulation of merit.

Yet here is the truth : that almost the only note of the spiritual life in the midst of this Babel of materialism, is struck by the Burman fool. I cannot resist this conviction here on the mountain slopes, where the little villages slumber and dark spires of monasteries climb into the luminous heavens.

INDEX